THE BURNING CROWN

HUNTER'S REDOUBT

MICHELLE WEST

For Terry, who believed in these books when I was afraid

DRAMATIS PERSONAE

BREODANIR

MAUBRECHE

Stephen of Maubreche
Nenyane of Maubreche, his huntbrother
Cynthia, Lady Maubreche, mother of Stephen and Robart, wife to Corwin
Corwin, Lord Maubreche
Arlin, his huntbrother
Robart, son of Cynthia and Corwin
Mark, his huntbrother
Master Gardener of Maubreche

The Dogs

Steel
Patches
Sanfel
Brylle
Pearl
Corran
Senshal
Marrel

ELSETH

Alexander (Alex) of Elseth
Maxwell (Max) of Elseth
Gilliam, Lord Elseth, father of Alex, Max, William, Justine and Ingrid, husband of
    Espere
Espere, wife of Gilliam, mother to Alex, Max, William, Justine and Ingrid
Elsabet, Lady Elseth, mother of Gilliam
William of Elseth, Gilliam's heir
Lucas, his huntbrother
Stephen of Elseth, Gilliam's huntbrother; namesake of Stephen of Maubreche; dead 17
    years

MARGEN

Lord Margen
Edwin, huntbrother to Lord Margen
Lesagh, Lady Margen
Brandon, heir to Margen
Aelle, his huntbrother
Alfric, younger son to Lord Margen

BOWGREN

Lord Ansel, heir to Bowgren
Heiden, his huntbrother
Allise, Lady Bowgren
Anton, Lord Bowgren
Barrett, huntbrother to Anton; died in the Sacred Hunt of 429

THE KING'S PALACE

Breodan, Lord of the Covenant; the Hunter God
Iverssen, chief priest of Breodan
The King of Breodanir; also known as the Master of the Chamber
The Queen
Lord Declan, Keeper of the King's Keys; Huntsman of the Chamber
Lord Grayton, Huntsman of the Chamber
Weslin, huntbrother to Lord Grayton

ANNAGARIANS

Gervanno di'Sarrado, a caravan guard
Leial, Gervanno's dog
Devarro di'Sarrado, Gervanno's father
Evaro di'Pierro, husband of Sylvia, caravan leader
Sylvia di'Pierro, caravan cook, wife of Evaro
Silvo, a caravan guard

ESSALIEYANS (AVERALAAN)

Jewel ATerafin, the Sen of Averalaan, Lord of the East
Finch ATerafin
Teller ATerafin
Haval
Celleriant
Jarven ATerafin
Lucille, secretary to Finch and Jarven

Kallandras of Senniel College, Master Bard
Meralonne APhaniel, member of the Order of Knowledge
Sigurne Mellifas, Guildmaster of the Order of Knowledge
Moorelas, also called Morel of Aston
Hectore of Araven
Namaan/Andrei
Amarais ATerafin, previous Terafin

The Wilderness

Biluude
Fox, known as the Eldest
Steane

The Shining Court

Allasakar, Lord of the Hells, Lord of the Frozen Wastes
Cortano di'Alexes, Annagarian exile, former Sword's Edge
Ishavriel, member of the Lord's Fist
Anya a'Cooper, human mage
Rymark ATerafin, Essalieyan exile, mage
Vallarion

Arianni

The White Lady
Illaraphaniel, last survivor of the firstborn princes
Caralonne, Illaraphaniel's squire
Narianatalle, firstborn prince, Sleeper
Fanniallarant, firstborn prince, Sleeper
Taressarian, firstborn prince, Sleeper
Shandallarian

PROLOGUE

The winds howled.

Cortano di'Alexes had stood against the wind in the bitterest of his memories. The shadow of the desert loomed over life in the Dominion of Annagar: the bitter sun, the scouring sands, the howling, unpredictable storms. He had struggled against it, sand in his eyes, literally and figuratively; it was to the desert that he had often retreated, to the dismay of his serafs, in order to hone his art. Widan's art, magery, the power by which he had rendered his middling skill with a sword irrelevant.

He had nurtured that power, had grown it, had relied on it; he had taken the Sword's Edge for himself. He had ruled the fractious Widan and Widan-designates; he had killed many of them in their final test. What use a Widan who did not have the wit and the strength to survive a simple test?

None could rival him. Those that might had withered and perished.

Ah, the wind howled; it was a cold wind. The Northern Wastes were a desert, like unto the Sea of Sorrows; here, the wind howled constantly, a storm that carried not sand and heat but ice and chill.

Either was death for the unwary, but Cortano's knowledge of the latter had been theoretical until he had first been invited to the Shining Palace.

It was a structure unlike any Cortano had ever encountered, even in the youth that had carried him from the streets of the Dominion to the streets of the Empire; he had traveled the roads to the Western Kingdoms, but he had not chosen to study the North. Even had he, he would not have encountered the Shining Palace; he would never have learned of the Lord of the Frozen Wastes.

The Shining Palace was built of white, pale stone—stone that resembled ice. It was not cut stone such as was common in the edifices of the Empire's most august buildings. No, it was of a piece. The height of the greatest of the towers, the depths of the basements, the wide, gleaming halls—all of these were of a single piece: evidence of the power of a god. He had been told that it had been created in a single day, a single hour, and he believed it.

The Palace was occupied by both the mortal court and the demonic kin. The mortals could, on occasion, perish as befit the foolish and the unwary, but it happened seldom; no man or woman lacking power was offered quarters here.

Before his sojourn here, he had known of the demonic kin; had learned of their existence, and the possible reasons for their existence, in his studies in the shadows of the Imperial Order of Knowledge— forbidden arts, historical arts, arts long lost. A fiction, that. The North had always been meek; they had always veiled the acquisition of power, made it as pretty as possible, as if power itself was evil and men who claimed to have no interest in it, good.

Risible, yes. But there was a power in the Empire that was rooted in the very earth upon which it so arrogantly stood—*Averalaan Aramarelas*, the jewel of the Empire, a city situated within verdant farmland, as far from any desert as such a city could be. Widan oft considered the Empire's citizens soft, weak, even maudlin. This was true of many who dwelled within its borders.

But to consider them without power, to consider the whole of the Empire inconsequential was folly, given observed and undeniable fact. In the two wars that had occurred most recently, it had been the Empire who had carried the day, the Empire who had emerged victorious.

On the Dominion's side were the demons of the Shining Palace, the soldiers of the walking God. The Empire had no such allies save one: the treacherous daughter of the Lord of the Hells.

Ah, no. No. If the wind was nature's symphony, discordant and persistent in its howling rage, there was now a single voice that rose above it. A childish voice, a child's words, enwrapped in the strength of a woman long past the age in which such babble could be considered either charming or at least acceptable.

"I get to ring the bells! Me! I'm going to ring the bells!"

Anya a'Cooper was the one presence in the entirety of the Shining Palace that almost convinced Cortano di'Alexes that the Hells over which the Lord presided were a concrete reality. She lacked any hint of the dignity and self-control that the powerful were required to exert. Of the mortals clustered in this divine edifice, she was the only one who could traverse the halls in which the demonic kin resided with absolute impunity. She disliked demons—all save one—and when bored, when loudly, *petulantly* bored, would hunt them. Often they perished, although their bodies crumbled to dust; Cortano believed their essence was tied to the Hells of Northern legend, and to the Hells they returned.

Had Anya been one of those kin, he would have found her far less enraging.

She had power the like of which he had never seen; his decades of honing and refining his craft amounted to nothing—a flickering candle standing in the lee of a carelessly constructed bonfire. He had felt envy in his life—all men did at one time or another—but never like this: the bitterness, the rage, could climb almost to incandescence.

He was of the South; he could hide it all behind the perfect mask of his face. But he could not extinguish it. She had power such as he had never thought to desire, power that he knew, no matter how long he studied, how hard he worked, he would never even approach, and she was shrieking about *bells*, in a voice that easily sliced through the howl of the winds.

Power ruled.

Were it not for the power of the Lord of the Hells, Anya a'Cooper would be ruler in this benighted wasteland. He turned his thoughts away from her with difficulty. He had always understood that power did not guarantee rulership—some cunning, some ability to plan and organize, was also required. But in Anya he was confronted with the lie of that belief. A four-year-old child would have been far more cunning, far more organized, far more *competent*.

Far more easily controlled.

Her shrieking words penetrated his hidden rage. The bells. She had said she had been granted permission — in far more infantile fashion — to ring the bells.

Cortano was a man accustomed to masking his ignorance. Ignorance could be privately alleviated. In his time in the wastes, in his time in this icy desert, he had heard no bells, and very little music. Art existed in this palace, in this citadel, but it had not concerned him overmuch; just as the Palace had come into being, adornments had accompanied it. Or so he had been informed.

Art, grandeur — all were irrelevant, an afterthought, to the lord of these lands. To the being who would be lord of all lands in future.

It was a future Cortano wished to see. Time was not on his side. He was not in his dotage; he would not survive that fall in this place, or any other. But he could feel himself dwindling, year by year. Age was inevitable; he had once accepted that truth with seemly grace.

But a god walked these lands. A god. Should he serve that god well, he might attain eternity, an eternity in which age could not rob him of the power he had been at such pains to increase.

He rose slowly, as if age were indeed deeply rooted in his joints, his bones.

Artifice, yes. Still. But it would not remain so. Anya screeched in triumph again, but this time, Cortano was drawn from his rooms to the great hall. At the end of that hall was a balcony that dwarfed most buildings in size and grandeur; the doors, such as they were, had not been thrown wide. They had simply vanished in silence, the only such invitation the human court might receive.

He had no need to dress for the chill and the wind at these heights. He was Widan; weather did not affect him unless he desired its bracing touch. He desired privacy, but was not to have it: the balcony was crowded. Almost all of the human court, some heavily enrobed in fur, had come to watch. He wondered what they expected, for some of the court had been part of the Palace for far longer than Cortano.

In some familiar faces he saw unfamiliar anticipation. He had seen such gazes before, from those deprived of drink.

Cortano had not stood in the presence of the Lord of the Hells, except at the periphery of a large crowd; he had no desire to do so, had made no attempt to bathe in a god's radiance, and it was for this very reason. The men and women who yearned for the God were not fools; they were not uncanny. They were certainly not without will, ambition, power. But they had been diminished by exposure to a thing far, far beyond even the ambitions of the merely mortal. So, too, the demons, the *Kialli*.

It was his own will, his own desire, that had brought him this far; he had no desire to surrender any part of it. His compatriots were not mindless; they were not serafs. But in some ways, that made it worse, not better; they were so blinded by the full attention of the Lord they lost some part of their grasp on their faculties, their own will.

There was a difference between awe and obsession. The first, he desired; the second he abjured. Awe, he hoarded; he did not reveal it, did not show it. The whole of the Shining Palace might have been a mildly impressive architectural achievement, no more. The demons he treated as enemies — or rivals. But yes, he too had the desire, well buried, to experience things so monumental in scope, in existence, that only awe could remain in its wake.

The human court gathered in silence, their gazes skirting one another, their questions — if they had any — locked, as Cortano's were locked, behind closed lips lest they betray ignorance. Not even the oldest members of this court spoke — as they surely must if they wished to confirm superior knowledge.

Or perhaps it was not each other they feared, for the howling winds carried in their folds the winged demon-kin. They did not impress him, although the span of their wings could be a danger. No, it was the unwinged, those demon lords who most closely resembled humans, who did, for they, too, had taken to the skies and the damnable winds. Cortano could, with effort, mimic flight — but it was a costly effort now, in a place where power must be husbanded and carefully spent.

To the *Kialli*, flight was trivial.

He risked power to better see their faces, their expressions, as they rose and fell, their movement an aerial dance, an act of grace in this icy wasteland. A thing of beauty.

He almost regretted the use of that power, minor though it was, for he could see the Lord's Fist, chief among them Ishavriel, whose beauty was almost preternatural. In his years of contact with that lord, Cortano had seen brief flashes of irritation or anger, for Anya belonged to

Ishavriel. He had seen his natural condescension toward the lesser beings; it was his most common expression.

Never before had he seen any hint of grief or loss; indeed, Ishavriel and the demonic kin had always been above such things. Cortano thought it possible they might evince such emotions should their lord, the Lord of the Hells, perish—but perhaps not.

Today, in the folds of a wind so wild it could not be entirely natural, he saw a grief so deep it could not, could never, find voice in words that might explain the meaning behind it. Had Ishavriel attempted to wrap it in words, Cortano thought men might die of it, as if the grief of the ancient and endless were not a thing that the merely mortal could contain if they wished to survive.

FOR TWO DAYS, the Lord was silent; the bells, of which Anya had shrieked in distasteful glee, silent as well.

None of the *Kialli* were summoned, and none welcomed who dared to approach. They did not touch ground, did not speak. Even Anya fell silent. No one approached Anya, either, for she had begun to weep almost continuously—a waste of water, but she had never been practical.

If she slept, she slept in the short hours in which Cortano also slept; she took to the sky with the *Kialli* by the time he was awake and ready to engage the world. She did not shriek again, and he almost repented of his dismissive characterization of the sound. Although he could not hear what she heard, he no longer doubted that she did hear something, sense something; it was clear in the lines of her body, and clear, as well, in the flight of the Lord's Fist. They were not given to weakness of any kind, but there was something about their continual flight that spoke of grief.

For two days, the Lord of the Shining City cast the whole of his gaze outward, away from the seat of his power.

He summoned no one; allowed no one into his presence.

ON THE AFTERNOON of the third day, the bells began their sonorous toll.

From their cage of gravity and stone, the mortal court listened.

Cortano understood, when the bells began, why Anya a'Cooper had been chosen. Those bells required the terrible, unfair magery of Anya a'Cooper, for the voice of the bells was louder by far than the howling wind. These unseen bells pealed as if struck, and the note grew louder, larger before it dimmed into the silence of wind and grief.

He understood her infuriating glee. These were the chimes of God. Permission had been granted as a benison to the god's most powerful servant—foolish, feckless, willful though she might be. Even her disturbed mind could comprehend the honor she'd been granted.

The ripple of envy died, for he had continued to watch the Lord's Fist. This morn, he could not tear his gaze away from Lord Ishavriel. That lord was weeping, the tears frozen in air that would kill unwary mortals. They glittered across his cheeks before the wind tore them away, husbanding them in its ceaseless folds.

The bells were a gift. A benison of grief.

But it was not the only such gift, for into the wind as the bells at last fell silent, came a voice that dwarfed bells, and even the grief of the *Kialli*. Cortano watched as Lord Ishavriel opened his mouth—opened it, struggled with the movement of lips, as if, in harmony, he too might speak the words Allasakar now spoke.

The shape of the syllables did not come to the majestic, demonic creature, but the god's voice continued.

"Narianatalle. Fanniallarant. Taressarian."

II.

10TH DAY OF LATTAN, 428 A. A. MAUBRECHE ESTATES, KINGDOM OF BREODANIR

The wind carried three names. Howling, unseasonable in its ice, syllables could be heard in its wild cry, its fury of grief, of loss.

He heard, and he froze, his lips moving in a silent attempt to form syllables, although the attempt yielded nothing: he could not speak them.

The Master Gardener's work this day was slow but methodical; the habits of long, long years kept his hands from falling idle. He worked with shears, and at that, shears that had to be sharpened, oiled, honed. But such mundane labor had become oddly soothing, a habit of his years in exile.

That exile should have come to an end. It had not.

THE MASTER GARDENER of Maubreche remembered the first time he had opened his eyes. He remembered the first thing he had seen: the White Lady. Mortal children were oft told by adults not to stare at the sun or they might go blind. It was not so with the Gardener. She had filled the entirety of his vision and remained there for as long as she remained within his sight; he was struck dumb with the awe of her, with the sense of who she was and what she had made of him. There was no beauty the wilderness could offer that was her equal, and no comfort, either, if she was not in it.

"You are the last," she said, as she withdrew. He knew better than to follow, and far better than to cling. What he had of hers was all that he could hope for: his existence. His life.

"You will wonder why you are as you are; you will wonder why you are not as the heralds of other princes. The only person who can answer that question is Illaraphaniel. The firstborn princes, aware of war, asked for heralds who might strengthen their ability to fight it. Illaraphaniel alone did not.

"You will not have the gifts and abilities of the others who serve as herald, but you are the herald for which he asked. Absent those gifts, those abilities, you are nonetheless the shield he has chosen. You are the bearer of his standard while you live. You are *of* him, and should it be necessary, you will return to him, for you carry a part of the power with which he was born. I have borrowed it, and shaped it, and added some power of my own." She turned away; he could see her back, the length of her hair, the subtle texture of the blend of cloth and leaves and flowers. No hint of armor marred that vision, nor any hint of martial weapon.

"I name you Caralonne," she continued, although she did not look back. "While he lives, you will live; when he dies, you will die. Some small part of you will return to me, but it is a part that is larger in measure than that granted the other heralds.

"Go, serve Illaraphaniel. In serving him best, you serve me. Go," she said, when he failed to find the strength to move from her presence. "You carry both his hope and mine."

———

HE DID NOT KNOW, on that day, that the naming was significant. Did not know that the heralds of the princes shared the names of their lords. Names had not been necessary, their purpose was so pure, so focused, on the victory of those lords. What matter the name of a servant when the master was so significant? But they had chosen names by which others might approach or call them, and Caralonne had therefore offered his own, shorn of power, shorn of the intent of such an offering.

He wondered, now, if they had known or suspected.

He had felt an odd shame, a new shame, to be called a gardener. He had felt somehow out of place; he was not the equal of the only people who might be called his peers in matters of combat, of war. He was not his master's equal. He knew how to wield sword—of course he did. He knew how to ride, and how to tend to the mounts gifted the princes by the White Lady. He knew how to track, how to make use of the shadows in which he might hide his presence; he knew how to live as one of the White Lady's people.

Had he not been almost afraid of the answer, he might have demanded, in the newness and confusion of birth and childhood, to know why. Why was he the only one who was different? Why, when war covered the length and breadth of the wilderness, had his master chosen, of all things, a *gardener*?

A gardener, further, who had no garden to tend, to grow; a gardener, the whole of whose work would vanish in the disruption of the wild earth, the wild air. What use flowers, what use hedges, what use the cultivated, delicate plants that were housed in the court of the White Lady? They could not cut, could not kill, could not shield. Better, by far, that Illaraphaniel had asked the same gift his brothers had asked at the behest of the Lady.

And if, ah, if his lord were struck down in combat, if he lay injured, what hope had Caralonne of succoring him? What use would the power that returned to Illaraphaniel be?

But he had not asked. Not then. He had thought there would be time to ask if they survived, and if they did not, the question and answer would be rendered meaningless. The discomfort, the anxiety, of the questioning would help no one.

But after the end of the war, after the White Lady's enemy had escaped, there had been no time. All that existed was the Lady's rage, the Lady's judgment—and none of the White Lady's people could speak against it.

And yet, they had: three squires. Each had approached her, suppliant, fighting the very heart of their instincts; none could force themselves to lift face. They knew what had engendered her wrath. Four princes had failed her. Three had failed her utterly. They had chosen to disobey her.

Her enemy yet lived.

They understood that rage must be satiated. They understood that the princes they had been created to serve had broken the single law that governed the Arianni. Knew, as well, that the echoes of other betrayals tainted this one: the most significant of the people who served the god they would not name were *part of* the White Lady; they had been hers. Nothing would quench the fury, the hatred, the certainty of that loss, that betrayal: not even their deaths.

Perhaps it was good that his had been an unusual birth, an unusual creation, or perhaps he had become too much like the prince he served. He said nothing. Not to Illaraphaniel. Not to the White Lady. He had made no attempt to stop the squires.

How could he when he understood why they groveled so clearly? To them, the princes were the manifestation of the White Lady's grace, but larger in all ways; those fallen lords were the reason the White Lady had created them. It was to the princes that they owed allegiance, service, loyalty; it was for them that they had been told to lay down their lives if that became necessary.

They could not—and did not—argue with their masters when their masters made their choices. They could accept, they could support; they could change nothing. In mortal terms—and he had lived so long among mortals, that he could think this, be certain of it—those three squires, lesser in every way than the lords they followed, were innocent of any crime.

But they were not mortal, and the White Lady would never be a mortal lord. She was Winter, and mercy was beyond her.

While the three who had been granted the gift of the martial made their pleas to her, the lone gardener had stood a yard back from his master; he had said nothing. But he felt the ice of her rage and knew, then, it would pass over neither him nor his master.

"You wish to see your lords wake." Her words were cold. "You wish to serve them." She had risen from the throne she occupied. No, there was no mercy in her. Her lips curved in smile, a reminder of the cruelty of Winter. "Very well. You shall be by their side when the last horn is sounded; you will be by their side when they wake."

Not even the three could believe that there was no punishment in this; they knew. He wondered: had they felt relief at all?

"You came here, daring death, to face me on their behalf. Very well. You will not die. Not yet." She lifted her white, perfect arms, and into her hand came sword, and all the swords of the Arianni, be they the weapons of the most powerful of her princes, were pale, pale echoes.

He felt it then—just as Illaraphaniel did, as the squires did—the whole of her magic brought to bear in that moment.

The Firstborn, like the gods who had parented them, could *create*. Not even the most powerful of their many children could. Creation was a gift.

Creation was a curse. What she had birthed in the four—for his master was not exempt from the stain of failure—she remade in that moment.

Illaraphaniel was so pale and still, he resembled his sleeping brothers. The gardener who had served him remembered that moment clearly; it was one of the final few moments granted the two.

"You will serve your lords. You will wait for them, as I waited for the single chance to destroy my greatest enemy. You will find them, you will wake them, and until the moment that you do, they will sleep."

"But in the waking, you will perish. They will be returned the measure of the power I have taken from them in that moment, and you will cease to exist, you who were mere containers for all that they chose to do—or not to do."

He felt it. He felt it as he stood and bore witness. He could not turn away from the White Lady's incandescent face, for he had not once lowered his—as if on some level he had known, then, that this would be his last sight of her, his last contact. But he understood what must become of him, for he felt what the squires now felt: some part of Illaraphaniel bloomed within him, and it was a chain, a binding of thorns and pain, between the lord he had served and himself.

"Say your farewells," the White Lady said, as she lowered her sword. "If it is our fate to meet again on the field of battle, we will, for our enemy—due entirely to the treachery of your masters—has not yet perished."

Illaraphaniel did not sleep, as the other three did; he had not disobeyed her, had not betrayed her command. But he had failed her. Sleep was not his lot; exile was. And into exile he was sent.

He did not look back at Caralonne, offered no words of wisdom, no guidance, for the one who had existed to serve him as he could, within the confines of the ability for which he had asked. He had said nothing.

There was no return for him, and no forgiveness.

There was no return for Caralonne.

If they met again in the flesh, Caralonne would perish, becoming what he had been in the beginning: part of the power of the firstborn prince, with no will, no intellect, no individuality.

HE WORKED in a silence broken by moving shears. Birds came, as they often did, to sit on the branches of the hedges, hidden in part by leaves. Speckled breasts and flashes of red and blue could be seen within and beyond the stately green of the season. As if they understood the enormity of the change that had already begun, they were silent.

So, too, the Master Gardener of Maubreche. There would be no further tending of the hedge across which the future of Maubreche had been carefully sculpted, almost since its inception. The last of that work was done. The last of the line Maubreche, for whom the Master Gardener had toiled all these years to see to fruition, had been born. He could protect his workings from time, but not perfectly. Time would come for the hedge maze as it came for everything, and the glimpses of Maubreche's future—which had become history, old futures replaced by new—would, at last, be lost to the natural growth of branches, leaves, and seasons.

If he were to encounter his lord again after the long centuries of their personal exile, the question he had once dreaded to ask, no matter how intensely he had desired an answer—any answer—that made sense, he would not ask. He had been young, as all living things were young at the start of their life. He was no longer that youth.

He no longer served in the shadow of that prince of the White Lady's court. Like a fallen seedling, carried by wind to an unpredictable field, he had taken root and he had grown; he was not, now, what he had been so long ago.

But he had the desire of all Arianni to return to the White Lady's side, to stand in her presence, to feel, once again, that she was the center of the world.

He had a shadow of that same desire to once again return to his lord's side; it had persisted, in isolation, for centuries. He had become resigned to it, had accepted it; it was, or had been, as natural as breath, as breathing.

He knew the fate of the other heralds. He knew that they had, once again, rejoined the wakened Sleepers in the truest sense of the word. They had become part of what they had once been, and the three who had betrayed the White Lady's commands had, in the end, returned to her as well.

He was certain that that would be his fate.

———

THE MASTER GARDENER did not need to see the garden to know its shape; did not need to examine each hedge, each flower bed, each plant. He could see the way leaves drooped, the way flowers blossomed or wilted. Mortal seasons had turned, and would turn again, until all green was covered by winter colors: a blanket of white, beautiful as ivory untouched by paint or gems. But this time, when winter receded, the chaos of spring's growth would be handled by hands other than his.

It was one garden. One mortal garden, with of all the constraints mortality implied. He could not sing to the hedges, the flowers, could not quiet the growth of weeds by simple thought, could not will plants to grow in accordance with his desire. Not without work. Not without dirt, water, mud. Not without time, minutes becoming hours, dawn becoming dusk as he labored.

The greatest of the princes would not have noticed this garden had he passed through it—and he would have passed through, at the head of his host, traveling at speed from one point to the next. He would not have given a moment's thought to what had been crafted and curated and tended at the will of the Master Gardener for so long. If his passage had trampled the landscape, he would not have considered it destruction.

No more would any of the host, any of the Arianni. The Master

Gardener of Maubreche accepted as truth the things he could not change. The loss of this one small garden amounted to nothing.

A god walked the world.

And the three princes of the court that had once been chosen to stand against that very god had passed away; they would never take the field again, and the banners forbidden them would never be raised. The names, forbidden to the Arianni, could not be spoken; grief could not be shared, and by that sharing lessened.

Ah, he was old. But the wind had carried the names forbidden the White Lady's people; he recognized the voice that had uttered them. It was bitter to realize that their ancient enemy could voice a grief so profound, when the continued existence of that enemy had caused the downfall of those very princes.

All but one. All but one had slept. All but one had perished.

Illaraphaniel.

The one name the nameless god did not speak, did not scream. One prince, one remaining warrior. How, if four could not prevail, could one?

The Master Gardener stepped back from the hedge he had been sculpting, and froze—surprised by what he had unconsciously made of this section of the tallest hedge wall. He recognized the man, the mortal, that was in the process of stepping out of the wall of leaves.

Morel. Moorelas. The one mortal chosen to ride at the side of the four princes of that distant court. The mortal chosen to wield the godslayer—the only living being who could. The god they did not name would recognize him but would feel no grief at his passing, for Moorelas was, in all ways save one, insignificant. Not one of the wise understood why he had been allowed to wield the godslayer, but all understood that the sword itself had chosen.

It was the nature of the Arianni to offer respect to the choices of those powerful enough to kill gods, but even so, it took time. Undercurrents of resentment informed that acceptance, that respect. Moorelas had aged visibly from the moment he took the sword in hand until his death, although age was not, as it was with so many mortals, his killer. He, so slight, so mundane, had somehow been the sole hope of success.

He had not returned. He had not stepped out of the broken legends and stories that rose from his corpse, and spread in mortal streets high and low, mutating as they did. He, who was considered a mythic hero now had been nothing but a callow youth to start; had become nothing but a stronger man, informed in all ways by war, by death.

The legends that arose obscured the truth of the man.

The legends of the firstborn princes of the Arianni had not. Perhaps because the Arianni had no need of legends, of myth. History did not recede from their memories in the same fashion. But if time did not dim or tarnish memories, it did not gentle or comfort pain. Not for the White Lady. Not for her people. Not for the god they did not name.

He lifted a hand, touched the hedge, half expected in that moment that the man carved out of growing leaves and small branches might respond. But no, it was a passing fancy.

Stephen of Maubreche had been born: son of Bredan, son of Cynthia. And at his side, his huntbrother, truculent, obstructive, possessive. He had watched them grow.

He thought of Nenyane, and turned away from Moorelas.

The earth beneath his feet was humming; he could feel its voice, but beyond that voice, beneath it, an ancient song had entered its prelude. The lands would change. All lands, even this garden he had husbanded for so long.

But he could admit, in this place hallowed momentarily by grief and memory, that it was the garden's loss he would feel most strongly when the last of the walls between mortal lands and the hidden wilderness, high and low, crumbled.

III.

23RD DAY OF SERIL, 429 A.A. BORDER OF THE KINGDOM OF BREODANIR

It should have been night.

To think this was senseless, but it was the only thought that came to him, and it came to him as he huddled in the shameful space in the undergrowth at a remove from the road. Somewhere too small to contain a man. Too small to hide one.

Aiee, it should have been night. In the night, many sins could be forgiven. And in the night, many creatures might arise to bedevil the vision of men.

He knew. He had fought them, in the war that had brought tentative peace to his distant homeland. He had seen them come, in flickering torchlight and shadows that fire was too meager to cast—they were taller than he, broader, and oft armed with only claws, talons the length of blades, jaws the size of Northern shields.

In the South he had lifted the sword that now lay beneath his feet, housed in scabbard. In the South he had blooded it; he had taken his wounds above the fissures and cracks in the broken beds of the valleys of Averda. For his valor there, he had received the praise of his lord upon the field, and had been given a place of honor afterward.

But all valor was dust, now, and honor. The light of day was bright, the sky blue, the sun—the sun's inescapable face—shining in brilliance in the clarity of sky.

And beneath the sun, pinions spread like vast, glittering clouds, flew creatures that not even that Southern battlefield had disgorged. Their wings cast moving shadows as they roved the skies, their riders seated astride the vast stretch of their shoulders, their necks made slender by the artifice of distance, their jaws glittering like scales. Like the scales that adorned them, ebon and silver, sapphire, ruby, emerald—cold as cut gems, as things unearthed from the mountains before the bitter snows closed all passes.

They did not speak, but they were not silent; they roared with the voice of the storm. The desert storm.

In the open forests of the expanse of wilderness that only merchants traveled, it was wrong. Green leaves, wild grass, small white flowers, and blossoms a blue that hurt the eye stretched out beneath the trunks of old trees. He did not know their names.

Had not thought to know them, had not even wondered, when the day had first broken across an encampment some five miles to the east.

"HEY, GERVANNO."

He sat up, grabbing his sword as he lurched out of the comfort of sleep, such as it was. The tent that housed him was small and narrow—a poor man's tent. Or a guard's. Silvo, his companion in those cramped quarters, laughed loud and long as Gervanno hit his head on one of the small poles that kept the heavy tent fabric above the ground. He did this almost every time he was not allowed to wake naturally.

Silvo, great idiot, found it amusing no matter how many times he had seen it. Took delight, in fact, from causing it. Gervanno muttered something about blackened eyes as he rubbed his forehead.

"Not mine, old man," Silvo replied, his face losing none of the smile that laughter invoked. He had already made his way out of the hunched confines of the single exit, and only his face was framed by its waving grey flaps. "You're too slow. The North has made you complacent."

Gervanno growled, but his legs were caught in his sleeping silks, and his feet were bare; he could chase the young fool across the width of the encampment, but he would be seen as the bigger fool, in the end.

"Hurry up," Silvo said, retreating, "or you'll miss breakfast."

Aye, and it was probably true. Silvo was half his size, and ate three times as much as the next man whenever he could get away with it. As they had passed through the Free Towns some days past, they were well supplied.

Gervanno unrolled his socks, donned them, and shoved his feet into his boots. He didn't use a mirror—it was not a man's conceit—when he didn't bother to shave. This would also amuse Silvo, who was hairless as a child.

But in spite of being the fount of so much amusement, Gervanno was not unhappy. This was an easier life than any other life he had led, and perhaps Silvo was right in one respect: he was an older man.

Old enough to feel a night spent in cramped quarters in a damp environment. He grimaced; the Northern spring was cold, and the ache was in his joints. Not a warrior's complaint, and because it wasn't, he said nothing.

The merchant caravan was already in a frenzied state of motion when he at last chose to join the living. The fires were burning, and above their open flames, smoke billowed, twisting in the wind, man's version of cloud. The smell of eggs and meat wafted west in the morning breeze; his stomach growled. The women had been busy for some time.

"Gervanno," one of the women said, eyeing him with the critical appraisal usually reserved for sons or husbands. "You're putting on weight."

He laughed. "Sylvia, you could fatten even young Silvo with your cooking." His flat palms hit his belly, and chain links danced beneath his fingers.

Her smile was yellow with age, her hair grey with it, but she was strong yet, and her face, when she smiled, retained some of its hold on youth, suggesting a beauty that only barely lingered. She was the caravan master's wife, and her daughters, younger and still held fast by the promise of that youth, bustled around her stiff skirts as she worked.

"Well, to listen to my husband," she said tartly, "fattening the lot of you will bankrupt him."

He laughed. "Spitting in the wind on the wrong day will bankrupt Evaro, if his words are to be believed."

She rolled her dark eyes, eyes that were crinkled at the corners. This work, this mothering, half-nagging life, was a life she loved. Even here, in the wilderness between the Free Towns and the Western Kingdoms. Perhaps especially here. This was her domain.

And he was welcome in it. He had not thought to become so fond of it; it was a loose, graceless life, a rough thing. But although it was devoid of many of the elements that had defined his childhood, it reminded him of home.

"The wheels?" he asked her.

She shrugged. "You're late. They've tended them as they can."

"They'll hold?"

"Unless there's a storm, or the road is rocky, yes. They'll hold until we reach the outskirts of Breodanir, and in Breodanir, we can follow the King's Road. We'll find a real wheelwright."

He took a seat on the log beside her. She handed him his wide, flat bowl. He ate, as was his custom, with his fingers. She told him—as she did each day—that this was because he was too lazy to care for his own utensils. All the little rituals of life on the road, observed.

"So we'll make our fortune in the Western Kingdoms?" he asked.

"Evaro says we'll staunch the flow of our gold, at least."

"Evaro bleeds gold."

"And probably pisses it," his wife agreed genially. "But mind that you watch yourself. The Kingdom of Breodanir is a strange one."

He had never been this far north, or this far west, in his life. "Stranger than the Free Towns?"

"Aye. In Breodanir, they have houses for their dogs. Not small houses, mind—large houses, grand houses."

She had said it before, and he had paid little heed to the words; she was Evaro's wife, and as wives will, she had no doubt picked up some of his love of exaggeration.

And none of his apparent ignorance of being humored. She struck him sharply on the shoulder, and he laughed.

"I tell you, it's no lie. They have houses for their dogs, and it's said that they even speak."

"The men of Breodanir, or their dogs?"

She hit him again. He was as fond of this gentle attack as Silvo was of his morning wake-up. "The dogs."

He raised a brow.

"Well, it's said they speak to their masters."

"And you've seen this with your own eyes?"

"Not mine. I can't abide dogs."

"Or nobility?"

She shook her head. "The women are strange, there; they enforce the laws. And the men—stranger still. But we'll have none of your noise about nobles while we're there—the people seem to love them, and they take it ill."

He shook his head again.

"But they call themselves Hunters," she added.

"The people of Breodanir?"

She shook her head. "Their lords. Hunter Lords. And huntbrothers. It's why they love their dogs; it's said that nothing escapes them, when they're given leave to hunt. And," she added, lowering her voice, "it's said that they worship a strange, strange god. They call him the God of Hunters."

Gervanno laughed. She hit him again. "Well," he said, rubbing his shoulder as if her gnat's sting had wounded him, "it would make sense for Hunter Lords to worship a Hunter God, wouldn't it?"

Her expression soured. "Their Hunter God eats them," she said firmly.

"They sacrifice men to their god?" That disquieted him. His smile lost warmth a moment as she rolled her eyes.

"No, you great oaf. It's not a sacrifice."

"Then what is it?"

She shook her head, drawing the circle across her breast. It looked odd; he had seen the gesture so seldom outside of the South that it took him by surprise.

"He hunts them."

He might have asked more; he was still unsettled. But Sylvia was interrupted by perhaps the only person in the camp who could do so with impunity.

Evaro strode up to the campfire, his fingers tangled in his massive beard. "What?" he said, his brows rising, "Have you decided to use all of our meager stores on one meal?"

Sylvia handed him his bowl with about as much ceremony as she had handed Gervanno his—but she gave him Northern fork and knife as well, a concession to his role as the master of the caravan.

Evaro sat heavily, almost overbalancing on the rounded, rough curve of log. He righted himself with a mutter. "We'll be starving by the time we reach Breodanir," he said, around a mouthful of runny eggs. "And at the speed we're moving," he added, with a hint of familiar reproach, "we'll be stopping to bury the skeletons." He eyed Gervanno over breakfast. "You've been dallying with my wife again. She's being overly cheeky."

"Don't embarrass me in public," she replied, clipping his cheek affectionately.

"Aye. I know the rules. Has Gervanno been regaling you with war stories again?"

She shook her head. "And don't you start him, either. The only person who hasn't heard every one of those tales more than he can bear is young Silvo."

"They're good stories."

"Men," she snorted. "It's all demons and death—where's the good in that?"

"Well, Gervanno would consider it good that the death refers to the demons," Evaro said with a laugh.

Gervanno nodded, grinning. Thinking, as he tried to remove the stubborn smile from his face, that things were truly different on the wild, rough roads of this gentle Northern clime.

At home, no one laughed about demons.

And in the North, they would learn not to. Bitter lesson.

THE CARAVAN WAS MOVING in slow time to Evaro's cursing and Sylvia's quiet natter. The guards—with the exception of Silvo, old soldiers all—walked to the front and the rear of the moving convoy, bracketing it on either end. They had hands on swords, but they had not drawn them for weeks; not even in the Free Towns, where welcome was always an open question.

The caravan master had his crossbow, and some of the men who served as assistants also had theirs—but for the most part, they had come to trust the roads and the wilderness. Banditry, where it was to be found, would be found in the furthest of the Western Kingdoms, those bounded by harsher winters and leaner harvests. Or so they had been told.

Gervanno had been suspicious at first, but experience allayed suspicion, and in the end, as lax as the men with whom he served, he had relaxed into the hours of walking with a quiet confidence that he had grown to prize.

But his experience had been taken in different fields, and when the shadows began to grow against the flat, damp ground, when it had taken the pale green of new foliage, darkening its spread, he had rolled into the cover of trees. He could not later say that this instinct had served him well; it had, but the certainty of that knowledge was tainted in all ways by guilt.

He had found cover, found his hand upon his sword, found his knees upon the ground.

Only then, secure in some fashion, had he chosen to look up. He had not drawn horn; he had not called attention to the shadows of his past.

He had assumed that it, like waking, was a ghost left by the battle for the Southern Dominion. Haunted, as he would remain haunted while he lived, he had become accustomed to these reflexive actions that so amused young Silvo.

But he had little to laugh at.

No one to laugh with.

The skies were alive with more than the motion of tree branches and darting birds. In fact, there were no birds, and this should have served as warning; there were no insects, of a sudden, and no squirrels leaping from the heights of one branch to another in silence or angry chitter. Animals were prey to their own instincts.

Instead, there was fire.

Fire, from the heights; a brilliant, hot cloud that could be felt. Ashes fell like rain in its wake.

All men looked up; even Gervanno, girded by branches, by the slender shelter of undergrowth. The caravan had moved some yards from where he had taken shelter, and it moved again, the horses made suddenly wild, the wagons teetering as if driven by drunkards. The guards shouted in Torra and Weston, some reaching for reins, some drawing swords and looking up, and up again, to the skies.

To clear blue. To black.

Featherless, wings vast as Northern sails, creatures he had never before seen rode the winds. He started to count them. He stopped. Men did not pray, in his homeland. His God was a harsh god, a god who valued strength above all else—and prayer was an act of consummate weakness, a giving over of responsibility. An act of fear.

Gervanno was afraid.

Not at the sight of demons—and he called them nothing else—but at their timing; they rode in the clear of the day's height, in defiance of sun's light.

One of these creatures chose to land. Trees that were older than any of the caravan's men cracked and parted; the roads were narrow.

Move, he thought, but his legs would not obey him. To fight, he had to live. To live? To live, he must be still. Hidden.

Wings rose; fire spread before they at last folded. A long, long neck curved slowly; it was dark, but there was power in its elegance, and it reminded Gervanno of a swan's.

From around the trunk of that neck, from beneath the width and length of triangular head, something emerged. It was...a man. Gervanno closed his eyes. He should not have seen this much, but having seen it, remembered what he had been taught upon another desperate field. It was the demons who looked like men who were most to be feared.

He was thankful that at this remove he could not clearly see the creature. But vision and hearing were different; he was certain that no one was spared the sound of the words that emerged over the panicked cries of horses, the curses of men, the screams of women and their children.

"Who is your leader?"

And to Gervanno's great surprise, to his lasting shame, Evaro, aged and wide, stepped out of the slowly gathering crowd and spoke. "I am." His voice, too, could be heard.

"Ah. Come forward, then. I would speak with you."

Move, Gervanno thought. But he didn't. He could see Silvo in the distance, could see his back, his drawn sword, the unnatural stiffness of his slender shoulders. He should be there, beside the boy.

Or the boy should be here, beside him.

But it was late, now. For that. For everything.

"You will forgive us for our conveyance," the creature said. His voice was Northern winter, Northern ice. "And for the nature of our interruption. We come in haste," he added, "and we mean to offer no threat."

No one believed it. And everyone wanted to. Even Evaro. Especially Evaro. But the master of the caravan did not speak.

"We search for something that was taken from us by Northern thieves," the creature continued. "It is an heirloom—an old sword. It has little practical value, but it is held in esteem by our Lord, and we mean to retrieve it. We believe that it was taken by road to the Empire, and from the Empire to the Western Kingdoms, as you call them. To the Kingdom of Breodanir. Where do you travel?"

"To the Western Kingdoms," Evaro replied. "But we have taken no cargo, and we did not pass through the capital of the Empire."

"And you have met no others upon the road? You have taken no passengers?"

"None."

Fire. The wagon nearest Gervanno's hiding place suddenly burst into flame, and the horse that had not been uncoupled now screamed its terror. And pain, Gervanno thought, cringing.

"Understand," the creature said, voice sterner and colder, "that our time is of value here, and we are unwilling to waste it. We will search, and we will ascertain the truth of your words."

He thought that the demons would come in number then, but he was mistaken. The creature stepped into the heart of the train, and he lifted his fine, long arms. His face was now clear to Gervanno's eyes. Clear, beautiful, cold. He spoke words in a language that sounded only vaguely familiar to the ear; the syllables were strangely fluid and they did not linger, could not be pinned down and held captive by something as simple as memory.

It seemed to go on forever.

Gervanno, understanding something that he could not capture with words, wanted it to continue, because when it was done, night would fall. He was as certain of it as he had ever been certain of any death.

But the syllables broke at last, and the creature's arms slowly folded. "It appears, mortal, that you are correct. You will forgive us for doubting your word." He walked past them all, making his way to the great winged creature upon which he had apparently ridden. The folds of his cloak—if indeed he wore one—shifted as he leapt astride the winged beast's back, disappearing behind the fold of its sinews.

The creature lifted head, snapped jaws almost lazily around the standing trunk of a newer tree. Wood splintered, and small tongues of flame consumed it. Great claws dug new furrows in the earth as the creature forced pinions to unfold; what had not been damaged in its fall was now destroyed as it rose to join its hovering brethren.

Evaro said nothing.

No one spoke. They were captive now, witness to the rise of legend.

But they found their voices again when the fires began in earnest.

IN AN HOUR, it was over. The winged demons spared no one; they hunted like hawks, like eagles, their eyes catching the movement of men, of fleeing children, of scraps of sundered canvas. Each of these were raked by fire; the creatures did not again descend to earth. Nor was there need. Their fires were hotter than torch, and they burned almost instantly anything they touched.

Black and grey punctuated the road; Gervanno could see the trees that remained standing inches from the trees that no longer existed, their roots alone left as proof that they had grown at all. The wagons burned lazily; the horses lay broken upon the ground.

And swords lay there as well, dropped or clutched.

He did not move.

He did not cry out.

He had taken shelter, and shelter informed every part of him; he was hunted here, and only by his absence in the first landing had he evaded the death that now claimed every member of Evaro's caravan.

When the shadows had at last disappeared from the ground, he drew breath; he did not hold it, and he did not move. Twice those shadows returned. But not a third time.

In the late afternoon, in the long shadows of forest approaching dusk, Gervanno at last unfolded.

He had survived the demons a second time.

But the second time was infinitely more costly than the first had been; there he had been surrounded by soldiers. Here?

Surrounded by the dead. By the dead he could see, and the dead he would never see again. He offered no song, no warrior's cry, no beat of hand against the steady skin of drum. His survival here did not speak of victory; it spoke of the taint of cowardice.

And there was only one way to quell it. Death.

Or duty.

Although he traveled in the North, it was the custom of the South that now informed him. Shaking, he began to gather what he could see. He put names to faces, where faces existed; he gave names to the wind, where they did not. And there were so many names, here. The caravan was not large enough—could never be large enough—that any single member was unknown to him.

HE WORKED THROUGH THE NIGHT.

If he had felt fear of the night before this day was done, it was gone. Something else consumed him. If his Lord was a terrible Lord, he was not the only god to which Gervanno owed allegiance, and in the night, when the terror of the demons did not reign, the Lady did.

To the Lady he offered water. To the Lady, he offered wine—for no old soldier went without, even if the wine was poor for drinking. And to the Lady, last, he offered the blood he had not shed in defense of the caravan.

Gervanno's people were no longer a desert people, but they had come, legend said, from the desert's heart, and it was the ablutions that held their power. A gift of liquid. To this, he added other water, in silence.

His tent had not been spared, and the night was chill; the work warmed him, but it was a bitter warmth.

Only when he had finished, only when he had offered his apologies to each and every man, woman, and child that he had failed, did he look to the future that he inexplicably had.

He was almost at the outskirts of the Kingdom of Breodanir. Sylvia had said so, and he trusted her words now that he would never have the gift of more of them. By moonlight and starlight he found the road, and he began to walk it, girded now with two swords and the small items he could scavenge.

Death? Aye, he could have chosen death, and that would have been cleaner. But having chosen life instead, he now walked toward a duty he had thought discharged at the end of his life as a soldier in a distant land.

He walked into a land where clansmen built grand houses for dogs, and clanswomen ruled, bearing his terrible word, his news: demons had reached into the expanse of the kingdoms to the north of the Dominion of Annagar.

CHAPTER ONE

The kingdom that Sylvia had described was not the one Gervanno
first encountered. She had seemed so certain there would be
grand houses for dogs in abundance. Perhaps there would be, in cities
or larger towns. Gervanno had passed through no cities.

He wanted, for the sake of the memory of her generosity and prick-
liness, to see those grand houses, those dogs—even the improbable
women she believed ruled these lands.

He had passed through no towns or villages either, seeking to avoid
them where possible; he spoke good Torra and decent merchant cant,
but he wasn't certain the citizens of the Hunter Kingdom would understand the latter well. He had no hope they would understand the
former, which was the second reason he sought a city.

He was certain denizens of smaller villages, like his own people,
would be both suspicious of strangers, and unfriendly, considering the
condition he was in. He was not important; he was not powerful; he had
neither the bearing nor the clothing to play at being either. He couldn't
command obedience; he couldn't even command civility.

Slaves were not kept in the North; he was unlikely to be captured or
sold as seraf to a ruling lord. It was a small comfort. But strangers could

still be killed, especially one who looked like a straggling bandit. Best to avoid the risk.

The lands here were much like the verdant lands in Averda, although the trees were wilder and the weeds endless. The air was cool, the shadows along the road chilly; they were also constant, as branches above his head sought sunlight.

The road itself was good. It had been built for merchants, but was called the King's Road by anyone who traveled this far to the north and west.

By Evaro, who would never walk it again.

Gervanno wasn't willing to risk the villages. He would take the risk of a city only because the news he must carry was so dire, the warning itself so important. And in a city he had a far better chance of blending in; cities were full of so much that was strange.

He had never been fond of cities. They were too crowded, there were too many people one had to be very, very careful not to offend, there were too many scents, many unpleasant. But it was in cities that the highest of authorities resided, and in cities, he might find men to whom he could pass word of what had happened to the caravan, and warning of what was to follow. What must follow, given the presence of demons.

In cities, one might find the Widan—or whatever they called the Widan in the North. He labored under no illusions. If strength in numbers was necessary, there was no safety simple numbers guaranteed. Not for men like Gervanno. No, they needed the Widan or perhaps the Hand of God. But none of the latter would be found here, so far from Annagar.

He had chosen the life of a caravan guard because he'd never wished to see demons again. His father had been furious; they had barely spoken civil words before he had left on his first merchant tour. Gervanno, as his father, had always been a soldier, but border skirmishes with the Terrean of Mancorvo were small battles between men. Yes, they could kill the careless or the unlucky, but they were almost like the squabbles between young siblings in comparison. He could feel pride in them, if he survived, and he could take lessons from the mistakes that hadn't quite killed him.

One war, one battle, against things that were not men—broken land and broken bodies and far too many ablutions offered to the Lady to pray for her mercy upon the fallen—had been more than enough. His nightmares retained those experiences. And here, in the near-wilderness of the North, new nightmares, worse by far, had been added.

He was practical. If he found a city, he might find merchants from the Dominion, or merchants who intended to travel to it; he might find working passage to his homeland. He would need that work; few of the supplies had survived the fire, and if he husbanded them, he would nonetheless need some way to continue to feed himself. Half of his clothing had not survived the demonic fire, either.

He was dirty from road travel, soot, lack of sleep; the soot, he had attempted to remove, but it clung to creases in clothing. He retained his sword, and he had taken, as well, the sword of young Silvo. Although it was not a particularly fine sword, it had belonged to Silvo's father. He would return it to the boy's family, if he survived and made it back home.

The rings and necklaces—those that fire hadn't deformed and melted—he had taken as well, with a prayer for forgiveness. He would sell them where needed, until he found someone more powerful who could take the news that he carried, absolving him of the responsibility. The rest he would offer the Lady, with gratitude. The dead would forgive him, and if they did not, they could have their say when he joined their number, caught in the howling winds above the Sea of Sorrows.

HIS FIRST SIGHTING of a dog wouldn't have impressed Sylvia. It might have annoyed Evaro, as the dog was more unkempt than Gervanno himself. Perhaps dogs here had rank and hierarchy, the way men did, and this dog, like Gervanno, wasn't worthy of a grand domis, a rich, feted life. It was mangy. He wondered if it were rabid.

Unsheathing his sword, he watched; the dog ran towards him, but stopped at the sight of the naked blade. This close, dirt resolved itself in brown and grey. Patches of dark color weren't the black of dirty fur, but the drying brown of blood. The dog was injured. Without examining the animal, Gervanno had no easy way of seeing the extent or severity of those injuries, no guesses as to what caused them.

The dog was clearly aware of the sword as a weapon, but comfortable enough around people that it didn't turn tail and flee. Instead, to Gervanno's surprise, it started to whine, a high-pitched, pathetic sound better suited to small puppies, not that this was a large dog to begin with.

Had the dog not been injured, Gervanno would have immediately put up his sword. This close to the animal, he could see that it wasn't as mangy as he'd first assumed; where there was no matted blood, the dog was actually clean.

"I've got nothing to feed you," he said, moving his sword aside without sheathing it. The dog immediately padded closer. "I wish Sylvia could have seen you. It would have been one of the few times I'd been right. Where are your owners, then?"

Tone conveyed some meaning, if Torra did not. The dog turned on heel, and then glanced once over its shoulder as if ascertaining Gervanno would follow. He hesitated. Bedraggled as he was, approaching strangers with sword in hand would do him no good. Approaching strangers while being herded by a pet might.

But this pet had been injured. Clearly it took some comfort in the presence of an armed stranger; its whining had ceased. Perhaps the dog had been injured defending its people?

Perhaps the demons that had destroyed the caravan—and all of Gervanno's companions—had somehow made their way to a small village. He froze, his knuckles whitening enough he could barely feel his hand. Forcing himself to breathe was difficult; he could hear roaring in his ears, could see the landscape waver in front of his eyes. He couldn't run. He could hide; here, the trees by the roadside were deeper, taller, their trunks wider.

The dog came back, circling Gervanno, just outside of the reach of his blade. It took up whining again. Sylvia had believed the dogs in the Hunter Kingdom could talk; she would have been disappointed. And concerned, Gervanno thought. She would have seen the injury, seen the dog was neither feral nor rabid, and offered it water, possibly food. Evaro would have complained loudly but affectionately, because Sylvia always said she couldn't abide dogs.

He didn't know what Sylvia would have said in response. She would never respond again.

Terror washed over him, through him, left him struggling for long moments to breathe. But breath came back, and with it, clearer thought.

If the dog's master had been attacked by demons, there was nothing Gervanno could do. He knew: nothing was exactly what he'd done. He shied away from the thought, righted himself, and continued. Against demons, his sword meant nothing. It might comfort Gervanno to have it, but it would make no difference.

If the dog's master had been attacked by humans, the sword *would* make a difference, but it might be a bad difference, because anyone who had just survived that attack would react strongly to sword-wielding intruders. He needed to set the weapon aside for now if he wanted to take the risk of meeting people who knew this country, these lands, far better than Gervanno himself.

With effort, he sheathed his blade. The dog stopped whining and made a series of little jumps that implied it approved. It then, once again, took the lead.

THE FIRST THING GERVANNO NOTICED, apart from the dog, was the road itself. The shapes of shadows ahead were different than the shadows beneath which he'd passed while on walking. He'd spent some time off the road, but even so, something was strange. It wasn't monstrous; there were no moving shadows that spoke of wings and fire and death.

When he had first accepted the job as a guard, he had been told, by Evaro himself, about the new dangers of following the merchant road. He had listened with only half an ear; he had seen the battle in the Averdan valleys. Had seen the demons, revealed, all subtle attempts to corrupt abandoned. He had even survived the magic by which they broke the very earth, coming from the edge of a forest through which the armies had passed days before in numbers too great to count.

Evaro, not a warrior, had managed to maintain a somber expression while Gervanno answered his questions about that battle. It became clear to Gervanno that the merchant didn't understand the truth of battle on any level; the battle had been won, hadn't it?

What else mattered?

No, Evaro's concerns had been about the rumors and the reports that traveled between merchants—friendly rivals and bitter enemies, both—about the roads. About the changes that could come upon whole caravans, or their surroundings. Rumors, often delivered in hushed whispers, had a depth of power, a weight, that facts seldom did.

This was the first time rumor had met fact in his travels.

The road Gervanno had been walking had shifted. It appeared to be the same road, a road with cracks and a handful of hardy weeds. It would be — would have been — his job to scout ahead if it seemed safe. If it didn't, it would be his job to protect the caravan while Evaro attempted to find a safer way forward.

The dog butted the side of his leg with the top of its head; he reached down to place a palm across warm, short fur, asking for patience without the actual words. If the dog belonged to the people here, it wouldn't understand most of the words Gervanno habitually used.

Maybe its owners were generally silent; the gesture worked. The whole of this land was unfamiliar to Gervanno, but he was observant by nature; there was unfamiliar and there was strange. The new trees ahead on the road were strange, different from the trees at his back.

The trees at his back had trunks and branches of greyish brown; their leaves were green, and fringed. He knew that those leaves would turn as the seasons did, and if he passed this way again, he might see red and gold.

The trees ahead had bark of ivory with flecks of grey banding, and the leaves were ivory as well, with hearts of brilliant green. They were also older trees, judging by the width of the trunks. The two — the familiar and the unfamiliar — did not mingle; it was as if the land itself had changed.

He couldn't imagine the dog had come from the land beyond these strange trees. He couldn't see how it could have come from anywhere else. It was a puzzle that didn't immediately lead to fire and death, and as such, it was a mercy.

The dog whined and slowly inched forward, as if it could sense what Gervanno sensed. It sniffed the road, barked sharply, and retreated to the relative safety of a total stranger. Gervanno knelt to examine the dried blood without touching more obvious wounds. Friendly dogs could often snap in fury when injured.

The dog whined again, but this time, the tail came up; it started to sniff the pack Gervanno carried.

"I barely have enough food for myself," he told the animal. But he didn't say it in a threatening way, and in the end, as if Sylvia was still standing over his shoulder, he did open the pack, untying strings but keeping the dog's head away from the insides of the bag. "How long have you been out here? Where is your master?"

"That is a very good question," someone said.

Gervanno froze, sword in sheath, one knee on ground. He looked up to see the speaker, and then readjusted his gaze down, to the road flanked on both sides with the wrong trees. The dog growled at the creature who had spoken.

A fox.

It was a fox, with ears a third the size of its delicate face, and fur of gold, harvest gold, sunrise gold.

SYLVIA WOULD HAVE BEEN SHOCKED into silence, but it wouldn't have lasted long; she had oft behaved as if silence was a subtle, but besetting, sin. Gervanno had never thought to miss her constant chatter, so much of it was nagging; he missed it now. He was almost certain she would have had something to say to the fox.

He rose very slowly, once again placing a hand on the dog's head.

"Is he yours?" the fox asked. He seemed content to sit across the invisible boundary that divided the road.

"No. He found me and seemed content to either follow or lead."

"And you are?"

"Gervanno. Gervanno di'Sarrado."

"Interesting. Perhaps I have lost my bearings, but that name does not belong so far to the North in mortal lands."

"I was not born here," Gervanno replied. He spoke formally, as he had not done for many months now. Although the fox wasn't a clansman of power and wealth, Gervanno had the certain sense that power was not defined the same way by talking animals who nonetheless radiated...he failed to dredge up a word from the mess of his thoughts. But he felt instinctive awe in the presence of this animal—awe and danger. He bowed to the fox—a proper bow, not a Northern merchant bow. "My apologies. I have been traveling on the road in isolation and my manners have all but deserted me."

"They have, but I am not a merciless creature. Not today. Have you come to find the dog's owner?"

"I was passing through when the dog found me. I would not recognize his owner if I saw him."

"Possibly not. These lands are changing, as you appear to have discerned. I have seen people who do not belong here—your people or as close to you as makes no difference—in my travels. I thought to observe them, but I was hunting different creatures, and I did not observe with care.

"They are not yet lost, but they will be. Why have you not moved?"

"The trees you stand between seemed strange to my eye. Perhaps they are natives of the Northern forests, but they are the only such trees I have ever encountered." He hesitated, but the unblinking eyes of the fox grew brighter and somewhat colder, for all that they were golden light. "I felt as if I would be walking into a different land if I continued to move."

The small head tilted to the side. "And so you would. So you would. I cannot yet walk the road you now stand on." There was command in the tone; by that alone, Gervanno knew that this talking animal was a creature accustomed to power.

"If I cross this boundary, can you lead me back? I have word that must be delivered to the highest possible authorities. Failure to deliver it would be disaster for these lands."

"But if they are not yours, why do you care?"

"Even foreigners do not deserve the deaths the demons will cause."

The fox sat upright. "Demons? *Demons*?"

Gervanno nodded.

"You encountered demons in your mortal realm?"

Mortal. He marked the word.

"I traveled with a merchant caravan."

"I did not ask that."

Gervanno heard ice again. Heard it, accepted it. He knew he was safe if the fox could not come to him; the fox's words implied it. But if he knew, he didn't *believe*. "Apologies," he said. "We were met on the road by large, flying creatures. They had wings like a bat's, but far, far larger, and they breathed fire. But they were ridden by demons, commanded by demons."

"And you recognized them? Do you encounter them often?"

Gervanno almost closed his eyes. "Only once before." At the fox's nod, he continued. "In a battle, a war, in the Terrean of Averda, demons came, and in great number. They broke the earth, and the men who stood astride it."

"Yet you survived."

"I do not know how." His voice was softer. "Many did."

"Well, this is certainly interesting. There is only one significant battle of which I am aware—a battle between your country and the Empire."

He nodded. "That was how it started, but not how it ended. I saw demons there, and I saw them here. But here, we had no defending army, no Widan, no Hand of God."

"And it is of demons you wish to speak? You wish to bring word to others?"

Gervanno nodded again.

"Then I should allow it. You said they flew? That there were large, flying creatures?"

"Yes, lord."

The fox tutted. Gervanno might have been speaking of mosquitos, the fox was so nonchalant. "It appears they have awakened difficult things. Very well."

"The demons were searching for something," Gervanno said, as the fox rose and began to turn, once again, down the far side of the road.

The fox paused, and then turned to look over his shoulder. "How do you know that?"

"They demanded it. Before they burned the caravan to ash. They said they were looking for a stolen item of value or concern to their lord."

The fox immediately turned again. "I shall be very, very displeased if you are lying." He was such a diminutive creature that the threat of his displeasure should have been amusing. It was not.

"It was a sword. It was a sword they sought. We didn't have it. They destroyed a wagon before they were satisfied that we were telling the truth."

"And then you were of no use to them, of course. Worse than no use. But you managed to escape."

It was an act of terror and an act of shame. Gervanno knew this. But even so, there were things that must be done before he could make peace with both shame and guilt. One of those things was to deliver word of the attack to people with greater knowledge and power than his own. The other was to deliver Silvo's sword.

He said none of this to the fox, certain that one man's shame and guilt were of so little relevance that the fox would merely be annoyed.

"Very well. I deem it important that you deliver that word to your lord or the lords of these lands. I myself will have to take word to my lord." He tilted head again. "You are *certain* they said sword?"

"Yes."

"It just so happens that I have some curiosity about the very same sword." The fox smiled, exposing glinting, perfect teeth.

"You also search for the sword?"

"In a desultory fashion, you understand. I have not been *asked* to search. But my search brought me here. There is a scent on the wind that the dead cannot follow."

This made no sense to Gervanno—but in a more rational frame of mind, none of this would make any sense. He wondered if he would ever find that frame of mind again. Something had broken in him during the battle in Averda. Perhaps it might have mended, in time. He had intended to escape the horror of one war, as if war was contained, geographically, to the Dominion or the Empire. He understood, now. The war had not ended, and might never end, no matter how far he ran or walked.

"You do not look entirely well," the fox told him, sniffing air as if it was not only the look of Gervanno that was suspect.

Gervanno bowed, expression grave.

The fox exhaled, a huff of impatient sound. "I accept your gesture as a sign of respect." He did not tell Gervanno that such gestures were unnecessary or irrelevant; had he, Gervanno would not have believed it. "Yes."

Gervanno blinked. Bowing, he had time to school his expression. Had he asked the fox a question? A favor? No. He might be exhausted but he was not a fool. "My apologies, lord, but I do not understand."

"You asked if I could lead you back to these lands if you chose to join me. The answer is yes."

Gervanno rose and met golden eyes, glowing eyes. In the South, eyes of similar color in people were considered a curse in most places. Certainly by Gervanno's family. Only in the North were such people accepted, even venerated, as the scions of the Northern gods. Perhaps creatures such as this were the reason why.

"You have said these lands will not last long."

"No—not here. In other places, you would be lost. But the North is curiously stubborn; the voices of the wilderness are muted here, so much so that subtle, quiet voices are lost. Ah, I believe I understand your confusion.

"People of these lands are lost within the folds of the encroaching wilderness. That wilderness is good for me, of course, but it is not so kind to mortals, if it is aware of their presence at all. You have done me a favor in your ignorance, and I will not have it said that I do not discharge even minor debts.

"If you wish to reunite this dog with its master, I will lead you to them. If they do not attempt to harm me, I will lead you all back."

"To—to what lord will you carry news of the demons?"

"To my Lord," the fox replied, more stiffly. Gervanno could not imagine a creature such as this swearing fealty to anything, although he could not say why. "She will be vexed, but intervention on behalf of insignificant, foreign mortals may mollify her somewhat." He glanced at Gervanno, sniffed, and turned back down the road.

His shadow was longer, taller, wider, than his form suggested; perhaps that was why Gervanno had instinctively resorted to the manners reserved for, and demanded by, the clansmen of power and note. Tyrs and Tors, all.

The dog whined at Gervanno's feet, circled him, and then, when it was clear Gervanno meant to obey the fox's unspoken command, followed.

IT WAS NOT that Gervanno trusted the fox. His trust, however, seemed irrelevant. While the fox could certainly be lying, Gervanno privately felt that, to the golden creature, mortals such as Gervanno weren't innately worthy of expending that much effort for. The dog by his side had intended to lead Gervanno somewhere, and that somewhere seemed to be down the road he now stepped foot on.

He didn't understand how the road could continue seamlessly through a forest so starkly different, but the road was undeniably the same. He felt no difference beneath his feet, although the wind shifted instantly as if aware of the boundary Gervanno couldn't otherwise sense.

The fox moved slowly, its steps stately. "Can you use that sword?" he asked, without looking back.

"I can."

"Good. It's possible you may require it."

"As long as we're not fighting demons," he muttered under his breath.

"There are far greater dangers to you and your kind than the dead."

That was the second time he had referred to the dead, and this time Gervanno understood that he meant demons. Demon-kin. "Why do you call them the dead?"

"They are. They are no longer a living part of the wilderness that once birthed them. They made a choice, long ago—a foolish, fevered choice—and they were banished along with the lord to whom they had given the whole of their lives."

"And they want revenge?"

"Revenge? For what?"

"You said they were banished."

"That is perhaps too slight a term; I felt the longer explanation would weary you." By which he clearly meant himself. "The young are easily wearied, and not a single one of you lives to be more than young. Regardless, what vengeance could they desire? They were given a choice and against all pleading and advice, they made it.

"Let me offer you a warning, child."

It had been a long time since Gervanno had been called a child. *Na'Gerva*—his mother's voice, returning when she could not. The winds were unkind, today.

"Do not trust the love that you feel for those who are birthed in the wilderness. It will almost certainly lead to your death, but before that death, to endless, barren misery. The gods do not love as mortals love; they love as gods must. Come, we must not dawdle."

THE GREEN of northern forest gave way to ivory and gold beneath a sun that seemed to have grown distant, given the chill of the air. Gervanno kept one hand on the hilt of his sword as he moved from walk to jog. The dog followed at his heels, timid in the presence of the fox; not that Gervanno blamed it.

He drew sword when he heard shouting, the tenor of some of the raised voices implying *scream* would be the better word. "You're certain there are no demons?"

"They could enter these lands at the moment, the earth is so weak," the fox replied. "But no, they are not here. Lesser kin would be expelled and greater kin are impossible to miss. Although the earth and the water reject them, the wind is capricious and the fire answers *any* call."

"They attacked not far from here as the crow flies."

"They are not constrained by simple distances. Perhaps you did not realize it, but their attack must have coincided with the blending of two lands. You were lucky," the fox added. "To control both their mounts and the landscape requires far more will, more intent, and more power. I am surprised that you survived. Did you flee?"

"No. I hid. I hid and failed to make a sound."

"That should not have mattered."

"The fires were high, and loud, and perhaps they mistook me for one of the dying."

"Perhaps. I feel that this carelessness will not work in their favor."

Gervanno snorted before he could stop himself.

"You find this amusing?" The question lacked a warning note; the fox seemed only curious.

"I am one man. How could I be relevant?"

"Mortal lands do not work the way the wilderness does."

"The difference?"

"There is will, in the wilderness. Intent. Force. The lands are often claimed by rulers, and those rulers are never mortal. Their will is known; their names are heard. Within the boundaries of their lands they are at the heart of their power. Were you in lands claimed and owned, you are correct: you would be irrelevant.

"But the mortal world is not—yet—the wilderness. If one god is intent upon subjugating mortal lands, he must, in the end, use mortal pawns, for there is power yet in mortality to withstand the will of a single god. The dead are not gods; they cannot know everything, cannot understand everything, they set their eyes upon.

"They miss things, Gervanno. They miss people like you."

Gervanno shook his head. "I did nothing. Every friend I had on the road was slaughtered and I did nothing. I did not try to fight. I did not try to defend them."

"Why would you? You would have died." There was no doubt at all in the fox's voice. "It is wise to know when resistance is necessary and when it is futile."

Gervanno couldn't explain. He might have made the attempt, but the shouts and screams grew louder.

Above the sound of that shouting the fox's voice was nonetheless clear. Even as they approached and the human voices grew louder, the fox's gently spoken words rose above them.

But the roar that rose above human voices also drowned out the fox's.

"That is unfortunate," the fox said, raising his voice for the first time. "You are *certain* you know how to wield that sword?"

WHEN GERVANNO REACHED the end of the road—an abrupt end, as if the road itself had been cleaved in two and part of it had simply fallen away—he knew he was in trouble. Had it not been for the fox and the raised and panicked voices, he would have come to a stop at the road's sudden end.

That he didn't was a surprise that caught up with him as branches, lower and no longer held at bay by the maintenance such a road required, smacked against his shoulder, his head, tangled in his hair. He knew he would be lost here if the fox disappeared.

It didn't matter, now. He charged ahead, sword in hand—charged as he *should have* done when the caravan had come under attack and he trembled, frozen, in the bushes, unable to draw sword or move or breathe. Unable to fulfill his duties.

It would have killed you. You know it. How would your death have prevented theirs?

It wouldn't. It wouldn't have. But he could have gone to face what awaited him after his death, and his voice would not, in whatever land the dead occupied, wind or desert sand, be raised in screams of anguish. He understood, now, why the dead screamed.

He understood that these people—these shouting, screaming people —were not his duty, could not be his kin. He didn't even understand all of the words they spoke so swiftly or brokenly.

But he understood the roar, the growl: the language of beasts. He couldn't stand against the demons, but he could stand against the flesh and blood of a wild animal. Even if that proved wrong in the end, it might be a relief: he could die on his feet, sword in hand. He could die the death he had always assumed would be his.

If he saved lives while doing it, perhaps that would tilt the balance in his favor. It wouldn't redeem his honor—but it would mean that somewhere in the world, even here in foreign lands, someone whose life he had briefly touched would remember him as something other than the coward he'd become.

He followed the fox through pale forest, his vision obscured by branches and trees. He expected to reach some kind of clearing, but he had done his share of bandit hunting in his youth; trees and a lack of clear space didn't prevent him from finding—from almost tripping over —a crouching old man whose arms were wrapped tight around a very young child. The child was weeping, but silently. The man was pale, older than Gervanno—perhaps the age of his father or uncle—but alert to more than his own pain or fear. His eyes widened as they met Gervanno's.

The child continued to cry in the rough grip of the man's arms.

Gervanno slowed. "Where?" he demanded. "Where is it?"

The man raised an arm, momentarily releasing half of his hold on the child. He pointed, and added, "Hurry."

Gervanno was certain then that the old man had once served in battle. The cerdan had Silvo's sword; he could arm the older man. He considered it briefly as he looked in the direction the older man had pointed. Yes, he had an extra sword.

An extra sword might help, but in the man's position he wouldn't surrender the responsibility of a child too young for speech for the opportunity to strike whatever animal it was that now roared in fury. He didn't know if the older man realized what the fate of that child would be if they were to be lost in this forest. He didn't ask. The child was not his burden to bear. He shouldered the burden he'd chosen and passed the man.

But he paused, turned, and set his own sword on the ground by the older man's feet. He wouldn't leave Silvo's sword, but he could use it; he could use it in exactly the way he'd told the young man a sword *should* be used.

The older man's brows rose, but lowered just as quickly; the child was looking at the sword, tears momentarily interrupted by curiosity.

"I'll come back for it later."

The child's caretaker nodded once at Gervanno; the nod was grim, but the gratitude genuine.

Gervanno then unsheathed Silvo's sword and began to jog in the direction the older man had indicated.

The dog followed at his heels. He'd remember that, later: the dog had followed.

———

WHEN GERVANNO HAD BEEN YOUNG—A little older than the crying
child the man was obviously protecting—he had seen a tiger. He wasn't
the only one to have laid eyes on it, and he remembered it clearly when
so many memories of that age had dimmed so much he could barely
recall them.

Then, as now, people were shouting or screaming. He might have
done the same, but his grandmother, his Oma, had grabbed his shoulder
in her iron hands. He could hear her voice now, although he couldn't
easily recall her lined face.

*Do not run. Do not scream. You'll attract what you don't want—its attention.
Let the men deal with the tiger.* But he could see the bodies of men—blood
covered, gore spattered; he could see the men who'd drawn swords, the
men who carried torches, could hear the screams and groans of the
injured. He felt their desperation as fear, and fear made sense; he
himself had been terrified. But the nature of that fear—the fear of failure, of the cost of failure paid in blood and lives—had been beyond his
understanding.

Until the war in Averda, facing demonic opponents, the tiger had
been the most terrifying monster of Gervanno's life.

That fear returned, but at a remove.

A tiger was here—as large as his memories had made it—colored in
silver and pale gold stripes, mouth red, claws red. Claws. He didn't
glance at the dog, didn't check the shape of dried, matted fur, of injury.
He knew.

Just as there had been when he'd been a child, there were men with
weapons here—but those weapons weren't swords or spears. They were
pitchforks, axes, whatever they could find. There were bodies, as well,
bleeding out; if the tiger had intended to feed, he wasn't being left in
peace to do it.

He understood now what he hadn't understood as that terrified
child.

Maybe he should have wielded Silvo's sword all along: it was a
reminder. An accusation, yes, but a reminder of what he himself should
have been. The tiger was in profile as he approached its flank, sword
ready. A sword was not the right weapon for such a beast, but it was
better than nothing.

Let the men deal with the tiger.

Yes. Yes, Oma.

Lifting voice, Gervanno shouted, loosing the rage and humiliation of fear, of failure, and of a deep and enduring anger.

The tiger heard it and turned in that moment. Gervanno was well back from the group who were fighting against it to the best of their abilities. He hoped this would buy them enough time to escape, to regroup. And why? They were foreigners. They were not his people. They were not the people to whom he had pledged his service.

But in the face of a tiger, weren't they all the same?

The tiger leapt.

GERVANNO WAS THROWN off his feet. He crashed into the nearest tree and struggled to regain his footing. But the tiger wasn't there; the tiger hadn't been the source of the blow.

The tiger certainly hadn't shouted, "Fool! Get out of the way!"

He shook himself, his ears ringing as he blinked.

Something stood between Gervanno and the tiger. No, someone. Lithe in the way of the young, slender in a way that even Silvo was not. He could see bound, silver hair, the narrow width of shoulders, the hint of prominent shoulder blades. And he had heard the voice: a girl, perhaps on the edge of becoming a woman. She carried a sword, just as Gervanno did; even stunned, he hadn't surrendered his grip on the hilt. He was lucky he hadn't injured himself with the blade.

Before he could think more others joined her: a young man, hair the blond of the North—and in actual armor—and dogs. Many dogs. The man approached; Gervanno froze when their eyes met. Gervanno's were the brown of the South; the young man's were the gold. Gold in the South was the color of demons, or so it was believed; in the North, those with golden eyes were called the god-born.

Nothing about the young man looked demonic to Gervanno; nothing about his mien, his actions, triggered instincts that been so viscerally honed.

All of Sylvia's stories came back to him as he stood.

In the North, those with golden eyes were respected, in some cases revered; they were not exposed at birth, abandoned to the death that awaited helpless infants.

Pride would not allow him to retreat. A girl with a sword stood between Gervanno and the death he had intended to face. He started forward, and a long pole blocked his path.

"Don't get in her way," an older man said. Gervanno glanced at him; his hair was dark with strands of silver to soften the color, his eyes brown. He wore green, just as the younger man did. "If you want to help, help us gather the injured and the dead. If she's right, we don't have much time."

Gervanno was a man accustomed to taking commands, to obeying them; the man who spoke was clearly accustomed to giving them. Even to a foreigner, an outsider. He responded almost before he was aware of just how much of a relief it was to be given orders.

He had expected that his appearance would cause him some trouble. But the circumstances were dire, and in an emergency, he was considered human, not bestial; he was, for the moment, one of them.

He did what he could. The dark-haired man turned to bark orders to the people who had been fighting—and losing—against the tiger, and they, like Gervanno himself, responded instantly. Or perhaps they did what they needed to do regardless; the fallen were theirs.

He did help. They didn't even look askance. They didn't recognize him, but they recognized the man who barked orders. And they recognized his companion as well. Four people had come to this forest; four people had clearly come looking for these people, these villagers. Four lords.

He wanted to look back when he heard the tiger roar; all of the men —and women—helping to lift the injured and the dead did. But he understood the urgency of time, and understood as well that somehow dogs and properly armed Hunters—for this was the Hunter Kingdom— had the tiger under control. He moved.

———

HE HAD an arm beneath the shoulders of a man who was bleeding from left forearm and leg; the bone of the forearm had been exposed, and Gervanno thought it likely that the man would lose the arm, if he didn't lose his life. But the man, younger than Gervanno but not as young as the two younger Hunters, was conscious.

"Call the dogs back," one of the two older Hunters said.

"The animal is fleeing."

"Nenyane thinks we'll lose the dogs if we don't call them back. She's not concerned with the beast."

Gervanno was surprised. He could understand all of what was being said. It was the tongue merchants on the road spoke. It was oddly accented, to be sure — but it was clear, even if he wasn't the intended audience.

The older man, the man who hadn't spoken first, grimaced and nodded. The Hunters had brought stretchers and small wagons, as if they expected to cart the casualties off the field. Gervanno returned to the work of aiding the villagers, and eventually all of the people who couldn't walk were retrieved and set on the wagon. It wouldn't be a comfortable ride, but the alternative was worse.

IT WAS THE GIRL, the sword that remained in her hand, red with blood, who led them back to the road that had ended so abruptly. Gervanno knew none of the people who had managed to lose themselves in the forest, but he glanced back, frowning. The frown deepened.

"You're missing two people," he said.

The silver-haired girl frowned and looked at him; he saw, for the first time, the color of her eyes. They matched her hair, but seemed to glint as if they were new steel. Her lips compressed. "Who?"

"An older man and a young child. They were farther back in the forest, away from the tiger. I passed them on my way through."

She turned to the young man, the light-haired man.

That man exhaled. "We didn't pass them on the way here."

Gervanno shook his head.

Someone — Gervanno didn't clearly see who — said, "It's Phillip. Phillip and his granddaughter. He's not here."

"I'll go," one of the two older Hunters said.

The young woman shook her head. "If he's ventured further into the forest, we've lost them. If we don't get back on the road — back to the safe point — we'll be lost with them. We need to get everyone here out. We can't risk everyone for one man and one child."

A whisper passed between the villagers, but no rebellion. It would be the whole of their argument.

But the dog — the dog he'd forgotten again until this moment, started to whine.

Comparing this mutt to the dogs that clearly served the Hunter Lords was almost impossible; they weren't the same type of animal in any way. The dogs that served the Hunters were glossy-coated, regal, and far, far larger than this stray. But that suited Gervanno.

"I'll go," he heard himself say. "I'll recognize him. I left a sword with him in case he needed it."

"Did you not hear what I just said?" the girl snapped.

He nodded. "I have no ties to your people. If I'm lost, it won't make a difference."

The man who gave orders, the man who seemed to be in charge, turned slowly, frowning. "I am Corwin, Lord Maubreche. You are in my lands. Or you will be, when this passes. Who are you?"

"Gervanno. Gervanno di'Sarrado."

"I accept your offer. We will owe you a great debt should you find my people and return to these lands."

Gervanno bowed. He rose slowly. "I would not have you in my debt for such an action. I have only one reason to be here, and only one duty I must carry out. It is to pass news of an attack on the caravan of a merchant to someone who will know what to do with it."

Lord Maubreche turned to the man who seemed to be his peer; they exchanged no words.

"Tell me."

Gervanno moved away from the gathered crowd, lowering his voice. "I worked as a guard for the caravan. It was attacked by creatures I have seen only once before in my life in the South—during the war between the Dominion and the Empire. Demons, who rode great, flying creatures. Those creatures breathed fire, and the fire destroyed every-one. Everyone but me."

It was the girl with the sword who turned on heel, silent, her face whiter. If she had been pale with fear, it would have made sense to Gervanno. She was not afraid. He thought her white with rage. "When?"

"Nenyane." Lord Maubreche lifted a hand in the direction of the silver-haired girl. "Where?"

"On the border closest to the King's Road, near where the road went strange. According to Evaro, we had just crossed it. They were looking for a sword."

"Very well. If you do not return, I will see that word travels."

"He should come with us," Nenyane said. "We need a fuller report and we've wasted enough time; he can't give it to us here."

"We can investigate, or call for others to investigate." Lord Maubreche glanced at Gervanno. "Go. Go and bring them back if they still survive."

HAD Gervanno ever been as disrespectful to a ruling lord as this girl was, he would be dead. Had any of the ruling lord's relatives, save perhaps only his heir, his kai, been one-tenth as rude, they would also be dead. He had been told that the Empire, the Free Towns, and the Western Kingdoms—of which Breodanir was one—were far more forgiving, but had never fully understood the truth of it until now. The young woman could not have made her displeasure more clear if she had called her lord—for he was clearly in command—a fool. Loudly. Gervanno was almost surprised she had not.

True to his word, Lord Maubreche marshaled his forces: the dogs, the three subordinates, and the injured, exhausted villagers, guiding them toward the safe part of the King's Road.

People streamed past Gervanno as he considered the unsafe section of the same road. He stopped one. "Apologies but—do you know who this dog belongs to?"

"Probably one of Keller's strays."

"Keller?"

"Haven't seen him. Probably in the part of the village that wasn't made strange."

It had been a stray? Gervanno looked down at the dog. Given the dog's behavior, it was a stray who'd been treated well enough by Keller, whoever he was. "You should go back," he told the dog.

The dog's tail began a frenetic back and forth that made clear it understood none of it, and Gervanno didn't have the time to argue with a dog. He began to stride back down the road, into a forest of ivory, lengthening that stride as he picked up speed.

HE KNEW ROUGHLY where he'd seen the older man, arms tight around a young child. He came to the abrupt end of the road he had followed and stopped there, instinct telling him that the road now ended in a different place. Where before it seemed as if the stone had been sheared in half, and one part discarded completely, the break now looked different. He could now see the King's Road, but it was blurry, as if seen through dirty, smudged glass.

Or perhaps as if stone were a weave, a cloth, and the ends had been damaged enough that the cloth was fraying.

"You are very foolish to return here," a familiar voice said.

Gervanno turned towards the voice of the fox. "I passed an old man with a young child on my way to confront the tiger."

"Tiger, is it?" The fox chuckled. This time, however, he did not set foot on the road—either the frayed, smudged version, or the solid one. "You really are an oddly cautious mortal. I have taken a liking to you."

The creature might have said, *I will kill you the next time we meet*, to less effect; Gervanno was instantly on his guard. Even so, his hand didn't stray to sword hilt. He wondered if the Lady's hand had guided him to the fox—or the Lord's. Wondered if he was meant to prove something about himself to either the night or day, the merciful or the merciless.

The fox chuckled, and this Gervanno felt as if it were a tremor in the stone beneath his feet. "But your caution will be for naught, if you hesitate. You have come to seek the man and child, yes? I know where they are. I can lead you to them."

"At what price, lord?"

"Oh, very good, very good. The old man's life is of little value to me, but the child? Children are meant to be shaped and formed. She might become someone useful, in the end—but mortal children are *so* fragile."

Gervanno's sword hand remained by his side, but it took effort. Perhaps it was the wilderness. Perhaps it was the shock of seeing a young woman snap so rudely at the lord who ruled her. Perhaps it was the loss of the honor he had, in his own rough way, prized all his adult life. Whatever caused it, he was angry, and the anger was a deeply rooted thing.

But men controlled anger; children allowed anger to make their choices.

"And it would be years before she could be useful, I think. For my kind, your years pass in the blink of an eye—but we are now tied in many ways to your time, not our own. I feel you might be more useful to me. I cannot easily travel in your world, not yet—although the time is coming when I will no longer be constrained.

"You might see the end of days, little mortal, and be unaware of the majesty of it. But I digress. I will lead you to the two you seek—if you decide quickly. If you do not, I fear you will all be lost in the wilderness." As he spoke, his fur began to gleam, as if he had swallowed sun's light and could not contain the whole of it.

"What must I offer in return?"

"You are stubborn, I see. I wish a minor thing. The girl that intervened in what you call the tiger's fate—I am *very* interested in her. Ah, no, do not make that face; I have no desire to harm her. I have no desire to be seen by her or known by her, not yet, if ever. But I wish more information."

"I know nothing about her; she serves a lord of these lands, not my own, and she is unlikely to offer me information."

"Tsk. I do not want what *she* says about herself; I want what *you* observe. I am willing to lead you to the old man and child, and I will also lead you back to the edge of these lands before you are lost in the overlap. All I want in return is that you observe her for as long as you can, and share your observations with me when next we meet."

"I will not spy—"

"Given her temperament, spying will not be necessary, if by *spy* you mean some sort of clandestine observation."

"Why are you interested in her?"

"I could hear her. I can hear her now; her voice is loud—but it is fading as she exits this place. Well?"

Gervanno exhaled, glanced once at the dog that seemed determined to follow him, and then stepped off the road, into the trees of ivory bark, ivory leaves. The fox was waiting for him.

"Give me your hand."

Gervanno did not hesitate; he offered the fox his left hand.

"You are right-handed, then?"

"Yes."

The fox nodded, opened its delicate mouth, and bit that hand. Teeth pierced the mound of palm and the muscles between thumb and finger. It was brief but painful; Gervanno felt fire enter his veins, as if the creature's bite was poisonous. The fox immediately released Gervanno's hand, but the pain of the bite remained.

"My apologies if I cause you discomfort; we do not have the time to

do things more gently. Now, come." And speaking thus, the fox turned
and began to move between the trees.

GERVANNO'S WAS EASILY the greater stride, but he found he had to jog
to keep up with the fox, who did not appear to be exerting himself at all.
His hand burned, and the flesh around the multiple small incisions
seemed to swell. He thought he understood what was happening, what
would happen: this ivory forest wasn't meant to be in the middle of
Lord Maubreche's territory. Somehow it was; it had overlapped the
lands the fox called mortal lands.

But it was now being peeled away, as if it were complicated clothing, and what would remain in its absence were the lands that were
meant to be in this place. Mortal lands, probably a mortal village.
Farms. Homes. Those who stood here when the lands separated would
remain in the wrong forest, with no way home. The fox belonged in the
ivory forest. He could not walk in normal lands.

Gervanno felt some relief at the thought; the fact that the fox felt he
soon could was a thought for another day. If Gervanno survived
this one.

A DISTANT ROAR almost caused Gervanno to freeze.

The fox tsked loudly. "Hurry. I have no desire to fight the lord of
these lands, and if you do not move, I will be forced to do it. Let me
offer advice: do not fight the lords of the lands through which you pass.
Those lands are the seat of their power, and they will be stronger there
than in any other environment. It is no small wonder to me that mortals
stood on the verge of extinction for so long."

Gervanno noted that, although the fox did not pick up speed, his
steps left impressions in the dirt beneath the trees—impressions that
Gervanno's feet did not, although he was far larger and, in theory, far
heavier.

Thought, however, fled as he saw the iron hair of the man with
whom he'd left his own sword. The man looked up to see Gervanno, the
dog, and the fox. He still held the child, but against his chest, her head
against his shoulder. She was sleeping.

"I've come to find you," Gervanno said. The man held sword in one hand, child in the crook of the other arm. "Lord Maubreche and his people have come; those who survived the tiger have been led back to their homes. I was given permission to return to find you, but we have no time. If we do not leave now, we will never return home."

The distant roar sounded again, but it was closer. Gervanno labored under no illusions; he could not kill the tiger, not on his own. The only safety offered this man, his grandchild, and Gervanno himself was flight, and it was vanishing. If they lost the road, if they lost the way back, they would be the tiger's prey, and no rescue, no aid, would come.

He had a sword; the older man had a sword. He had a single dog, but he knew the mutt wasn't equal to even one of the lord's dogs, having seen them; they were fearless. Only the confident and the naive were fearless.

Gervanno desperately wished, at this moment, he were either. He had seldom had command of men. He knew his strengths, knew his weaknesses. But he knew, as well, what this man, exposed and vulnerable because he carried the child, needed.

"Follow now. We have enough time to make the road, but it will be tight. If I tell you to run, run, and run in the direction I point." He spoke without fear. He spoke with certainty. Neither were a reflection of his actual feelings—which would do the old man no good. They'd do Gervanno no good, either. He seldom thought of his father; the old man's anger at Gervanno's perceived desertion was an anger to which he did not wish to return.

But he thought of him now. In a crisis, his father said, a bad decision was better than no decision.

How could that possibly be true? He'd wondered, and wondered. Skirmishes hadn't given him the answer. The battle in the Averdan valleys hadn't given him an answer, either. But this moment did. How ironic, to reach a visceral understanding so far from both war and home.

The older man needed decisiveness. He needed to be told what to do to reach a safe place in which he might set the child down. His fear was high because of the burden he carried; Gervanno had no doubt that the man would give his life to preserve the child's, and no doubt whatsoever that the man knew, if he died, the child would follow. What he needed was authority. Commands he could focus on, commands that rose above the fear driving him.

Gervanno could give him that. Needed to give him that, regardless of outcome. The tiger roared. Gervanno began to move. He kept the old man to one side; he didn't surge ahead as instinct told him he should. He'd come here to find the man. He didn't intend to lose him.

But the tiger roared again, its voice louder, closer. Gervanno's fear gave him the impression that the roar contained words, syllables. Language here didn't matter; if the tiger found them, the entirety of that language boiled down to death.

The dog ran beside him, surging a little ahead, but never so far that he left Gervanno and his charge behind. Gervanno wasn't running blind; he was following the glimpses of small footprints impressed into earth.

The third time the tiger roared, Gervanno was certain he could feel the beast's hot breath on the back of his neck. Given the speed at which the older man moved, he probably wasn't alone.

"Can you see the footprints in the ground here?" he demanded.

The older man looked down without missing a beat. "No."

"Fox footprints—small, but deep."

"Fox? Yes. Yes I can see them."

"Follow those. Follow only those—they're the only road out for us. If I fall behind, don't look back. They'll take you to your people."

THEY RAN side by side until the tiger roared again. This time, Gervanno could definitely hear syllables coalesce into words, into a language Gervanno understood.

How DARE you?

Other words followed, descriptions of a death that would be welcomed and embraced because what would precede it would be so terrible, death would be a blessing. He'd needed no incentive to flee, but had he, words from the mouth of an enraged, deadly beast would have provided it.

He ran until he could hear and feel the tiger's feet at his back; he slowed, then, turned, blade ready, as the man he had come to find pulled away, obeying the final commands Gervanno had given.

The tiger was yards away, but the yards closed before Gervanno could fully come to a stop as the tiger leapt. In the sunlight, claws and fangs glinted, proof that the beast was more than beast, if the color of fur — silver and gold — hadn't made that clear.

———

FOR THE SECOND time on that long, strange day, Gervanno's life was saved by an intervention that came from the side — his left side. He was hit and sent stumbling. He thought the strange young woman had come back; he was wrong.

It was the fox; the fox had leapt, as the tiger leapt, and landed before the tiger could — the fox was closer. This time, Gervanno didn't crash into a tree.

The fox spoke. Gervanno couldn't understand a word he said. He was surprised at the sound of the golden creature's voice — it was the equal of the tiger's roar, encased in a body a tenth the size or smaller. No, it was louder.

"Do not be a fool," the fox said, in a much more familiar tongue. "Run *now*. You are useless to me dead!"

Yes, Gervanno thought, command was essential to those who had followed commands to the best of their ability all their lives. Gervanno obeyed.

Chapter Two

The roar of the tiger receded, as did the roar of the fox. Gervanno put distance between them, widening his stride as he followed the tracks the fox had deliberately put down.

It was awkward to run, arms laden with the living burden of another person, even if that person was a child; Gervanno closed the gap between himself and the man he'd ordered to continue. He then kept pace with him until he could see the road again. The road, however, was shrouded in fog; the sunlight that implied clear skies in the ivory forest dimmed and vanished.

He didn't pause to sheathe his sword; he had one hand free. He didn't tell the older man to sheathe the sword he carried, either—they didn't have the time. The fog was thickening and he understood viscerally that the moment they lost sight of the road, they were lost.

Instead, he grabbed the man's wrist, risking injury, because it was the wrist of the arm that held Gervanno's sword against bitter, final need. He then picked up speed, a final burst of it, dragging the man with him as his foot hit road, hit familiar stone, before the stone was too obscured to be seen.

His steps echoed oddly in his own ears, as if his boots were steel against stone, not the leather he knew them to be. He couldn't hear the older man's steps in the same way, couldn't feel them as if they were heavy impact; were it not for the wrist in his hand and, consequently, the awkwardness of running, he would have assumed he'd lost his companion to fog and strange magic.

But he could certainly hear the healthy lungs of a child waking from sleep to the frightening and unfamiliar. He had never thought to find the sound a comfort, having no children of his own.

It was the sound of life. It was not the scream of a dying man, a young man too shocked by mortal injury and pain to hold on to the dignity of his station. It was not the cry of bewilderment at impending death, or the fear of it. And it gave Gervanno the strength for one last, awkward burst of energy, of speed.

THE FOG CLEARED SUDDENLY, as if it were a physical curtain; between one step and the next—both wide and hurried—it was gone. Gervanno and his companion, crying child in arms, stood on the King's Road, beneath a gently clouded sky. Their shadows were longer than they had been; the day was stretching toward its end, and the sun would soon color that sky as it set, making way at last for the beneficence of the Lady's night. But that time was not yet.

He stumbled to a stop, as if he had jumped, not run, and released the older man's wrist as he did. The man handed Gervanno his own sword, instead of casting it aside; he then wrapped both arms around the crying child, bending his head over hers as he drew her to the center of his chest and held her fast, as if she was the most precious thing he had ever carried.

She quieted, but it took time.

During that time, Gervanno looked for the dog. The dog was there, just ahead of where the two men stood, panting heavily, tongue exposed, its head slightly tilted to one side. When their eyes met, the dog trotted over to Gervanno and stood by his side, as if this was the most natural thing in the world.

Gervanno turned to look down the road that had led to ivory forest and tiger. All he saw was the King's Road the merchant caravan would have traveled on its route to the King's City. The ivory trees were gone, replaced by the trees that girded the road that had led to them.

"Apologies," Gervanno said to the man. "I am Gervanno di'Sarrado. This dog found me. I hear he was a stray someone in your village took in."

"Probably one of Keller's, then." The man lifted head from the quieter—but awake—child's. "I'm Ronson, around these parts."

"You're part of the village?"

"Aye. Brookton's been my home for over a decade."

"Then you know the way back from here."

"I do. If we can reach it. Morning was…rough. Woke to trees. I mean, those white trees. They were where my house was. My house was gone. I live with my daughter and her child—this is Nessa," he added. "Nessa, can you say hello to our friend?"

The girl glanced at Gervanno, and then buried her face in her grandfather's chest.

"She's a bit shy. Nessa and I were surrounded by strange trees. Nessa's mother wasn't there." He shook his head and looked down the King's Road, which continued into the distance until it rounded a gentle curve. "You have children?"

Gervanno shook his head. "Even if I did, they'd be home in the Dominion."

"You're far from home, then."

"Very far," Gervanno answered. "I was a merchant caravan guard. The caravan was attacked. I survived. Most didn't."

"You were attacked by enough bandits to wipe out a caravan? Here, in Breodanir?"

"Near the border."

Ronson exhaled; he kept his tone light, mindful of the child. "We don't have much, but it doesn't look like you're used to fancy. Come with me—I'll at least give you a meal as thanks."

Gervanno nodded. "I'd like that."

"I owe you more than a meal, but some debts can't be repaid."

"It wasn't—"

Ronson's smile was lopsided as he lifted a hand to stem the flow of words. "I know. I wouldn't have been fool enough to do what you did, but sometimes fools are God's people."

GOD'S PEOPLE OR NO, a meal wasn't what awaited Gervanno when Ronson led the way to Brookton. The dog, the mutt, trotted ahead of Gervanno, and broke into a run as the first of the buildings visible from the road appeared. Ronson's home—if it still existed—was, as Ronson explained, out the other side, past the small town hall and the elder's home.

But between Ronson and his possible home stood familiar people: Lord Maubreche and his aide, Nenyane and her companion. And dogs. So many dogs. Pale, grey-coated dogs, brown dogs, patched dogs; they were taller by far than Gervanno's companion. Cleaner and heavier as well. When Ronson walked toward them, Gervanno by his side, all of the dogs turned heads to stare at him.

The silence was unnerving.

It was broken by a scream—a good scream, but nonetheless loud, shrill—as a woman broke through the pack of dogs and raced to close the distance. That, he thought, would be Ronson's daughter, Nessa's mother. Her eyes were red, dark crescents underlining them; she'd clearly been weeping. She all but flew, arms wide, and Nessa began to wail, launching herself into her mother's arms. Her mother caught her and held her as if she would never let go.

Ronson, however, failed to introduce Gervanno. A mother's desperate greeting would be forgiven in these circumstances, even in the South, were not the lord of these lands present. This lord did not seem to find the interruption displeasing.

At the lord's side stood the silver-haired young woman Gervanno suspected was perpetually angry. Her sword was sheathed, her mouth shut, but her gaze fastened itself to Gervanno as if she, like Nessa's mother, intended to never let him out of her sight again.

"We have much to thank you for," Lord Maubreche said. He surprised Gervanno; he offered a bow. It was Northern, not Southern, in form, but it was exact, precise. To his right, his aide offered the same bow; to his left, the pale-haired youth did likewise. The young woman simply nodded.

Gervanno, however, shook his head. "I offered, I was not commanded."

"Ronson and his granddaughter are part of Brookton, and Brookton is my responsibility. We came late."

Questions arose instantly, but Gervanno was an old hand at this: none of them escaped his mouth.

"You have word you wish delivered to the appropriate authorities."

Gervanno nodded.

"Lady Maubreche is in constant contact with those varied authorities. Let me offer you the hospitality of Maubreche as gratitude for your aid in Brookton." Gervanno knew an order, no matter how prettily it was cloaked, when he heard it. He heard it now.

"I would be honored," he replied. There was no other answer he could have offered.

"Very well. We're finished in Brookton. The land should be stable, now. Do you ride?"

"I do."

"Good." He turned to an old woman. "We'll need one of the messenger horses."

The old woman's network of wrinkles barely moved. "Darren," she snapped, "you heard the lord."

"We'll send word for one of the Mother's daughters to visit Brookton, but events such as these are widespread across Breodanir."

"And they won't arrive in time to do any good." It wasn't a question; the words were heavy, clipped, anger just beneath their surface. Anger, Gervanno thought, or sorrow. He knew that the northwest was not Annagar, but was constantly surprised by it. No village elder in the South would have dared to speak their mind so openly in their lord's presence.

Lord Maubreche had no answer to give the older woman. He nodded his acknowledgement of unpleasant truth.

"Just what is happening?" The old woman wasn't done yet.

"We cannot be certain," Lord Maubreche replied. Another surprise, another reminder that Gervanno was in completely foreign lands. "The Order of Knowledge is studying the phenomena in an attempt to understand both why it happens and how to prevent it. In Breodanir—and only in Breodanir—those changes can be reversed if they are caught in time. Brookton should be safe, or as safe as it can be in such troubled times, for now.

"But we must depart to bear word to Lady Maubreche. Is there word you would have us carry?"

The woman snorted. "Not now, no. Petty land disputes don't seem to matter much if we can't even be certain the land we wake up in will be ours. Tell her we know our priorities."

"Thank you."

Gervanno waited for a horse to be brought. He could infer certain things from Lord Maubreche's interaction with the village elder, and it brought Sylvia back to him as an almost primal force. Although it seemed impossible to a man of Gervanno's birth and upbringing, it appeared there was truth to the stories that Sylvia had told with such relish.

And once again, he was determined to see it, to witness it in her stead, who would witness nothing again.

GERVANNO DISCOVERED, to his dismay, that there were subtle differences in the way Breodanir horses were trained. He felt a level of embarrassment that would have been at home in the heart of his much younger self. Men knew how to handle horses, even those that could not easily afford the full upkeep of such a treasure. He had claimed to know how to ride, and was being proven, if not a liar, then something close.

The desire to excuse his incompetence came and went; he controlled it enough to offer his apologies for the differences in equine training that must have existed.

Lord Maubreche accepted this without question, and Gervanno adjusted, aware that he was dirty, fragrant, unshaven; and that he nonetheless had the genuine gratitude of this lord. Gratitude was best seen at a distance.

The only other difficulty was the dog. The dog came running when Gervanno mounted the horse, barking in that way that suggested it was ill-pleased or felt ill-used. Gervanno had assumed the dog had run off to its master, and would remain there, but it seemed the dog had other ideas. Among those was shouldering its way through the vastly larger and better-behaved giants that clearly served the lord of this land.

One or two of those dogs growled; none of them attacked.

"Is he yours?" the pale-haired youth asked.

"No—he found me on the road and tried to lead me to what I assume were the missing people. His owner is someone named Keller."

The young man's smile was full of warmth. "I don't think the dog agrees."

"He'll get tired of following us and return to his master," was Gervanno's gruff reply. As he had already been wrong about his ability to ride, the thought that he might be wrong about the disposition of a dog that had been a stray when it had been found by this Keller was almost inconsequential—which was good, because he was wrong about the dog, too.

The dog followed the lord's party, which included Gervanno, all the way to that lord's home.

THE DOMIS—AH, no, manor?—of Maubreche was visible from a distance. It occupied a great deal of land, and if it did not tower above the landscape, it nonetheless made itself known. It was an enormous, two-story dwelling, with a small nod to a third story in some places, the stone pale at a distance. The road that led to the manor was in almost perfect repair, but while Evaro would have been impressed and pleased with that road, it was not the road that impressed Gervanno.

It was the garden, the grounds, the miles of greenery that seemed to be carefully husbanded and tended. He seldom saw gardens of note, even in Averda; they were the province of the wealthy and powerful. That wasn't different in Breodanir—but had a similar garden been situated in the Dominion, it would have belonged to the Tyr'agar himself.

He was silent in a wonder that allowed no envy.

The dog tried to pee on a bush.

IT WAS clear that both the garden and the dog were so completely normal to the Hunters that neither impressed or annoyed. The dogs that served the lord were led away by that lord; the horses were handled by servants.

The pale-haired youth approached Gervanno as he dismounted. "I didn't have a chance to introduce myself. I'm Stephen of Maubreche, and this is my huntbrother, Nenyane. Welcome to the Maubreche estate. If you wish it, we can take you on a tour of the grounds; Maubreche boasts a maze and a garden that is unequalled in Breodanir." With quiet pride, he added, "Or any other country in the world."

"I would like that," Gervanno began.

Nenyane, however, cut him off. "Is this the time to offer a walkabout? We need to speak with Lady Maubreche, and we need to hear what this man—"

"Gervanno di'Sarrado."

"Gervanno has to say. He said demons destroyed his caravan. He was the only survivor. What if they followed him?"

The growing irritation visible across Stephen's face froze in place and vanished. He turned to Gervanno, bowed, and said, "After you have been debriefed by Mother, I will offer to take you around the manor and the gardens." It was a half-surrender. "Without my hunt-brother."

Breodanir customs were stranger than Gervanno had realized. He was certain that Nenyane was a young woman by the pitch of her voice and her particular impatience, but Stephen of Maubreche—Stephen, no styling of lord or par or kai, as it would be in the South—had clearly called her *huntbrother*. Gervanno did not ask questions; he did what he always did in a possibly dangerous situation. He observed. If his observations didn't lead to immediate understanding, that was irrelevant. The purpose of observation such as this was to ensure that Gervanno gave no unintentional offense.

He did, however, say, "If possible, might I bathe and shave? I do not wish to offer offense to the Lady by my presence."

It was Nenyane, who considered a tour of the grounds a meaning-less waste of time, who wrinkled her nose. "Fine."

It was Stephen who, in the name of hospitality, attempted to soften his huntbrother's ill-mannered sense of urgency. "Perhaps it is not only a bath you require. It is late, Ser Gervanno; I am certain, given the debt we owe you, that Lady Maubreche would be willing to put off a formal meeting until the morrow. I, too, am in need of sleep."

Gervanno hesitated for a moment. Was this a subtle, Northern test? But he could not believe that, given Stephen's expression. He nodded, grateful.

GERVANNO'S CLOTHING was meant for the road and the various merchant compounds in the cities in which the caravan stopped to trade. It was not meant for meetings with important people—people whose umbrage could lead to either injury or death. The clothing itself was in heavy need of competent laundering, but the spare set was far less fragrant, less obviously dirty.

He was led by a servant to the room in which, he was told, a bath would be brought. It was; a large, heavy basin in which a man might sit if he drew knees to chest. Water was brought, and water boiled to add heat to what otherwise would have been tepid. The servants also offered him aid should he require it, but he could sense both avid curiosity and anxiety, and dispensed with that aid. He wasn't a child, to be tended by adults because he was incapable of cleaning himself.

His hair was a mess. He was almost certain he would find things living in it, and took care to thoroughly wash it until those possible things had been drowned. He considered the newly clean hair with trepidation, but decided to braid it in the style of the North rather than bind it in the style of the South—that style was reserved for warriors, for men who defended their homes and their lands from intruders.

Gervanno had left that life behind.

———

THE ROOM in which he found himself had a bed and, further, a large mirror. He could shave without one, and often had; Sylvia was far better at pointing out spots he'd missed than any silvered glass could be.

Ah, he would have said she was a nag to end all nagging, a maternal figure who carried the power of all such women in balled fists. He would have said he would be glad to see her back for the last time. Were all men such foolish liars?

His hands shook and he waited until the tremor passed before he continued to shave; the last thing he wanted from the endeavor was nicks and cuts left by haste.

When he finished, and finished cleaning the blade and carefully returning it to his pack, he stood back, examined himself in the mirror, and grimaced. Here before him was a man who most closely resembled the man who had fought in the valleys of Averda against his own people, those who had chosen to ally themselves with demons. And here, too, the man who had survived demons; he could not with any accuracy say he had fought against them.

He could not meet his own eyes for long. Even the attempt had wearied him. He set Silvo's sword in the corner of this enclosed, almost suffocating room, and headed toward the bed.

———

1ST DAY OF EMPERAL, 429 A.A. MAUBRECHE ESTATES,
KINGDOM OF BREODANIR

Stephen met Gervanno at the door to his room; in the domis of the lords of the South, a seraf would have done so. Nenyane was nowhere in sight.

Stephen's clothing made clear that he was scion of the land's ruler. It was of fine cloth, expensive cloth, and if the dyes themselves weren't the costly dyes Evaro sometimes transported, it mattered little. The colors the Hunters wore were predominantly green with some brown, and the edging in slightly different colors. He thought they might be Maubreche colors, but could not be certain.

"We weren't sure what to do with your dog," the young man said, as if the mutt would be Gervanno's first concern. "He doesn't seem used to grooming, but we fed him and cleaned him to the best of our abilities. He's in the kennels, and you can see him either before we meet Lady Maubreche or directly after. Unless you wish to have him present."

As if the dog were of great value, great use. As if the dog were an actual friend and companion.

"Thank you for your consideration. I will see the dog after my meeting with the Lady. Unless you believe the Lady considers the presence of dogs an important matter of etiquette."

Stephen's smile was brief and rueful. "Oh, she does. She considers it poor etiquette for the dogs to be present unless she is dealing directly with a Hunter Lord—a man like my father. She would be delighted that you show such forbearance, were you Breodani."

Gervanno bowed, hiding his own smile. He rose. "Your huntbrother is not present?"

"I apologize for her manners. She wasn't always this bad, but the changes that Breodanir has undergone—the changes that threaten Maubreche—have left her almost permanently unsettled." An interesting choice of word, and far milder than Gervanno would have used—but the boy was talking about family, so perhaps he too might have underplayed things. "She will be waiting, just as patiently as she has been since you've met her, with Lady Maubreche."

"She's very sensitive to the mention of demons."

"As am I," Gervanno said. He paused and judged a small risk was safe. "As all men should be, in the face of such creatures."

Stephen exhaled, and Gervanno realized the young man had been tense, nervous, as if afraid of the judgment of a lone foreigner from Annagar. A lone, insignificant foreigner. "I wanted to personally thank you for finding Ronson and Vanessa. I know they're strangers to you, but we lost people to the shift of land there, and the survival of two people also assumed to be lost was..." He searched for words. "It's the unlooked-for good news that can sometimes offer the most solace to the grieving; it can be one of the very few things that can break through their pain.

"We owe you a debt, and it is a debt that we hope to repay in some small fashion. We cannot repay it in full but we are aware of what we owe you." Stephen tilted his head, and added, "Perhaps far more aware than you yourself are."

HE WAS OFFERED BREAKFAST, his companion Stephen, in a modest room with a small table and windows that occupied at least half the available wall space; it was bright and simple.

"I'm sorry if you missed breakfast with the rest of my family—most of us thought it best to let you sleep."

"Most?"

"My huntbrother believes sleep to be a waste of time if something is wrong." He grinned as he spoke. "Lady Maubreche understands, however, that sleep is necessary, given the events of yesterday; she also believes that food is necessary if one is to maintain sharp wits."

THE ROOM to which Gervanno was led, after the surprisingly congenial breakfast of bread and eggs, was a very large room, its colors, as the clothing of its lord, in somber greens and browns over a floor of grey. At the far end of that room, in one chair, sat Lord Maubreche. Beside him, in the larger and more ornate chair, sat a woman Gervanno assumed was Lady Maubreche. To his surprise, there were no obvious guards present. The man who appeared to serve as Lord Maubreche's aide stood to one side of his lord's chair.

The silver-haired, perpetually angry young woman stood to one side of Lady Maubreche's. Two younger men stood beside her. Family, he thought. Perhaps brothers to Stephen? They didn't have the look of Nenyane about them.

"I am Cynthia, Lady Maubreche," the Lady said with a smile that didn't quite reach her eyes, which was oddly comforting, it was so familiar. "Please approach comfortably. You might note an absence of the guards you no doubt expect; we consider you an honored guest. If you consider our trust ill-informed, you must forgive us; you risked your life to save our people without pausing to negotiate a fee. Reason to distrust you could not be more difficult to find."

He froze for one long moment as he realized that Lady Maubreche was speaking *Torra*. His mother tongue. But she spoke it as a Tor or Tyr might; it was far too complicated, too perfect, to suit a man like Gervanno. It was true, he thought. Sylvia had, once again, been right.

This woman was Tor'agar here. Possibly Tyr'agnate. She was *lord*.

He felt his spine stiffen, felt his shoulders reset into a perfectly straight line. He wished he had properly styled his hair, wished he had clothing suitable to his own status when standing in the presence of a lord.

Even a lord who was, as Sylvia had claimed, a woman. The steel in her, the certainty, was so clear she was like a drawn blade. Ah, no, like a swordhaven, a place where blades might come to rest between necessary battles. Nenyane at her side was a naked blade — a blade drawn in anger or panic.

He offered Lady Maubreche the bow he would have offered his own lord, or his lord's lord. He held it for as long as etiquette allowed; longer might seem like an implied criticism, an act of sarcasm.

"I do not wish to trouble Lord Maubreche," he said, speaking in Torra himself. "I am aware that the Dominion is far from Breodanir, and our language has not spread widely here."

"You will not trouble Lord Maubreche," she replied, with a hint of amusement. "It is true his Torra is not the equal of mine." The man beside Lord Maubreche coughed into his hand. "But were he to be tasked with diplomatic matters, it no doubt would be." The smile ebbed from her face. "I believe there are things you might say more clearly in Torra than in what is widely called the merchant tongue.

"Matters of war and battle were oft deliberately and delicately discussed by those who spoke your tongue — as if it were a language invented in the heart of battle. And it is, I fear, of war we must speak."

To Gervanno's surprise, three of the seven people in the room, if one did not include Gervanno himself, seemed to understand Lady Maubreche's fluently spoken Torra: Nenyane, Stephen and the lord's aide. He knew that Evaro considered Breodanir an important destination, and knew further that Evaro was not the only merchant who regularly traveled outside of the borders of Annagar. But he had not imagined commerce would be so important that the rulers would consider it necessary to learn his tongue.

"Please," Lady Maubreche now said, "tell us what occurred. You spoke of demons on the road, and the loss of an entire caravan to those demons. We believe you and wish to know the details. I have allies in the Order of Knowledge—it is in some ways analogous to the South's Widan, but it is an organization that has strong ties to the heart of the Empire. They will be very interested in the word you bear, but they will have questions for me and I will not be able to answer them well if I am not apprised of the facts as you experienced them."

Gervanno bowed. To tell them what happened, he would have to face the very obvious fact that he had survived. He was a guard. He had been hired to protect the caravan—and the people who owned it—from outside attack. That he was alive and they were dead would be proof of malfeasance. Proof of cowardice, of the lack of honor that made any man trustworthy.

He wished, then, that she had chosen to summon him at night, for that was the Lady's time, when frailty might be, if not forgiven, then at least understood.

Had the events not been so large, so important, and were this kingdom not facing the threat of the demonic, Gervanno would have taken his shame to the grave before he exposed it. But if he had little of honor left, a slender strand remained to him. The powerful needed to know—and it would start with Lady Maubreche.

He kept his voice steady, kept his posture straight; he began to speak as if he had been called in to be debriefed by his Tor at the end of a skirmish that had almost been disastrous. He had survived that. He would survive this.

SHE INTERRUPTED SELDOM, and when she did there was no accusation in her words; she merely asked for clarification of details. He could give them too easily; the weight of that day was one he would bear for the remainder of his life. He did not think he could forget no matter how hard he tried.

He stopped himself once, as well, when Nenyane of Maubreche stiffened, when her hand fell to a sword hilt that Gervanno couldn't believe was decorative. He had now reached the part in which the demons had made their demand. They were looking for a specific sword they believed was being transported to Breodanir.

"Nenyane," Lady Maubreche said, although the young woman hadn't chosen to speak.

Nenyane maintained her silence, but as Gervanno took up the thread of his story, she stiffened again and this time, before Lady Maubreche could speak, she chose to leave the chamber.

Stephen, however, kept his gaze on Gervanno; it moved only to Lady Maubreche before returning.

When Gervanno at last fell silent for the final time, Lady Maubreche nodded head. "I am uncertain that you will not be asked to speak with a member of the Order of Knowledge in person. Would you be willing to do so?"

"You said they're like our Widan."

She nodded.

No sane man, no man who wished to survive, wanted to interact with the Widan; their arts made them wild and strange. It was to the Hand of God that he would have gone, in haste, had the attack occurred in his homeland.

"I will speak with whoever you deem both knowledgeable and powerful enough that they might begin to work at countering this threat."

She nodded her approval, and rose. "I offer you the hospitality of Maubreche while I correspond with my contacts in the Order of Knowledge. You have had a difficult time, and I see that you were injured."

He blinked. Injured?

"Your hand."

Ah. "This was not the work of demons; it was the work of an animal I stumbled across when...when the lands grew strange."

She then turned to Lord Maubreche.

"The beast escaped," the Lord said, almost surly. "We thought it best that we retreat with the people from Brookton before the way was closed."

The Lady's gaze went past her Lord to the man at his side. "Arlin?"

He nodded, his face almost expressionless.

"I imagine it was a close-run thing?"

"As you have always said, it is the results that matter. Nenyane was against pursuit, and she was joined by Stephen. Corwin considered the possible fate of the villagers, and concurred."

The Lady's smiled grew sharper, but she spoke no further words on the subject.

"I have a few questions about the caravan you traveled with." Her attention returned to the Southern guard.

"I will answer to the best of my abilities."

"It is not a test, but as you have also seen, demons have not been our only—or even our primary—concern. You traveled with a caravan through the Free Towns?"

"Yes. We traveled to the Empire from the Dominion, stopped there for a week, and then made the journey from the Empire through the Free Towns, to the border of Breodanir. Evaro—the caravan leader—intended to stop in Breodanir, and then return home."

"You responded well to the changes in Brookton. Did your caravan have some experience with similar changes during your travels?"

He hesitated. "Only in Averalaan. But in the merchant compounds there, similar stories were told. Evaro only half-listened. I was new to caravan travel when I joined him, as were many of the guards. A merchant life is not for everyone."

"Averalaan?"

"Evaro said the entire city had been replaced—but to my eye, the people in it were much like people anywhere. There were no tigers, no demons, just ..."

"We heard word of the substantial changes in the capitol city of the Empire; I have not witnessed them myself, but those words have been substantiated."

"It was a city unlike any city I have ever seen—but its citizens seemed to consider it, if not unremarkable, at least normal. That wasn't the case for your villagers."

"No. In our experience, and in the experience of many of Breodanir's demesnes, the changes often occur further away from where people live; it's seldom such turnings have taken the King's Road.

"You will no doubt be asked about your experience in Brookton, but the Order of Knowledge is likely to focus predominantly on the demonic. The demons have not been our concern in recent years." He noted the qualifier. "But the turnings—as we often call them—have taken more lives than demons in our immediate history. I must withdraw now and being to write—and bespeak—those whose knowledge and experience with the demonic is far greater than my own.

"Once again, I offer you the hospitality of my house while we await the replies that are certain to come."

Gervanno knew a dismissal when he heard one. He bowed, deeply, to Lady Maubreche, rose, and walked down the long stretch of carpet to the doors at the end of the hall. The doors rolled open in the hands of two young people. Before he left, he turned toward Stephen and was surprised to see the youth halfway between mother and himself.

"Can we visit the kennels?" he asked of the Breodani lord's son.

Stephen's smile widened. "Of course!" In a much quieter voice, he added, "No request you could have made would please my father more."

Ah. "And not Lady Maubreche?"

"She is fond of my father's dogs, but they're not her concern. There were six people in that room—well, maybe five and a half—who take responsibility for the dogs, and perhaps two who take responsibility for external politics."

"Two?"

"My mother, of course, but Arlin—my father's huntbrother—often helps."

THE FIRST THOUGHT Gervanno had when he approached what Stephen had called a kennel was: *Sylvia, you were right.* If the dead were trapped in the winds of the distant South, she would not see proof of her conviction; he would witness it for her and perhaps, if her anger at his failure could be escaped, he would tell her.

The kennels were not the equal of the manor in which people worked and lived, but they were not small; they occupied a large stretch of land, and each of the three buildings was larger than the house in which Gervanno had been born. The roofs rose above the single floor and glassed windows allowed sunlight to enter the building, as Gervanno saw when Stephen opened a door clearly designed to allow horses to enter and leave.

The dogs appeared to have been waiting for their lord's son; they leapt up from where they were sitting or lying and converged on the young man. They had noticed Gervanno, but paid him little mind.

All but one, and that one, a mutt half the size of the Hunter Lord's dogs. Gervanno knelt as the dog hung back, attempting to avoid the much larger, much better-fed and -kept animals. He looked for obvious visible signs of mistreatment, as if the mutt were an awkward child prone to being bullied, but saw none. Only the previous injuries could be seen—and his fur had been cleaned well enough that they were far less visible than they had been when the two had first met on the road, in the lee of what Lady Maubreche had called the turning.

The mutt trotted toward Gervanno, slowing when he reached the Southerner's side. Unlike the Hunter's dogs, he didn't leap up immediately, and there was no high pitched, rapid barking.

"Good boy," Gervanno said, in his own tongue. Over his shoulder he added, "What breed of dogs are these?"

"Alaunts," Stephen replied, as the dogs, content with the short strands of fur they'd left all over his clothing, came to rest on either feet or butt. "Except for those two; they're lymers. Scenthounds. Alaunts are bred for size, for speed, for endurance. They're necessary partners when we hunt."

"You hunt often? In the South, hunting is frequently done using birds of prey."

"What a bird of prey can take down can't feed a village," Stephen replied. "But in the King's City, some of the lords also hunt with birds of prey." Gervanno had the sense that Stephen didn't entirely approve.

"You hunt for food, then?"

"It's one of the duties of the Hunter Lords of Breodanir. Hunter Lords were given gifts by Breodan, in order that the majority of his people not starve. This land is not what it was when Breodan led his people to it. The villagers know how to unmake the carcasses brought to them; to strip fur, to use the leather, to smoke and preserve the meat. In the winter, that meat becomes essential, especially in a bad year." He smiled. "I'm certain it isn't what you're used to."

"We do not get your winters, no. But Averda is verdant. The farms are, weather willing, abundant. Should I leave the dog here?"

"If you want to take him for a walk, he can join us—unless you've thought better of touring the grounds?"

Gervanno smiled. "No. I can think of few things I would rather be doing."

HE HAD SEEN no sign that the dogs spoke, but was unwilling to consign Sylvia's certainty to foolishness, which was ironic, given how often he'd done so while she lived. He couldn't bring himself to ask Stephen, even in Nenyane's absence. He was both guest and outsider; it was unsafe to give offense or present oneself as ignorant.

But on the grounds through which Stephen now led Gervanno, he felt ignorant, regardless. Ignorant and almost awed, as if he had stepped into a turned land, wherein one might see wonder and subtle magic: not winged, fire-breathing beasts who served as mounts for demons, but something that reminded him, viscerally, that not all wonder and awe was reserved for, felt by, those who faced immediate death.

He was almost afraid to speak; he thought, if he tried, he would babble like a callow youth, or worse, a child. He had seen hedges once, in the garden of the Tor—had seen the way they were planted and clipped—but those hedges were a green wall. These seemed to serve a similar function in places, but there was a sense of captured life about the sculpting that made of living things a perfect canvas, a perfect form of art: it would change, because plants grew. He had no doubt, seeing first the head of a young deer, and second, the ears of a fat rabbit, that the gardeners who tended these would sculpt that growth, that obvious proof of life, to imply many different lives, all in green, all in leaves.

Stephen said nothing, as if waiting for questions, but Gervanno had none; there were no words that would not somehow be rendered pointless if words themselves were neither expected nor demanded. The dog was likewise silent, but he seemed content to chase Gervanno's shadow until it paused, and then to sit in it until it once again moved.

Still, Gervanno struggled to remember manners and etiquette. "You must have an army of gardeners."

Stephen's smile was odd. "Yes. But come to the maze; the maze is the work of a single man." The smile dimmed. "His life's work, I think;

he has long been gardener to Maubreche, but I fear the time of his retirement is coming."

Such was the nature of wonder, of awe, that a man who had almost lost his life — and had lost the lives of all of his friends — could still feel the specter of the retirement of an unmet stranger as a visceral loss. He wondered what Sylvia would have said, had she been standing here. She probably wouldn't have been impressed — or rather, would have walked away before she was forced to show that she was.

Evaro, however, would have remained, just as Gervanno did.

He wondered if Silvo would have been too young for awe in this situation. The boy would be awed by martial prowess, and perhaps envious — but a garden? Would Gervanno himself have been so awed in a youth that seemed increasingly distant?

But even thinking it, he continued to follow Stephen's deliberately slow pace. He stopped again, frozen in place, as he encountered a standing figure, carved in green and the almost invisible brown of slender branches. This, he thought, would have impressed Silvo.

A man stood, shield covering half his body, sword — a sword! of leaves! — in his hand. He gazed out, above the heads of both Hunter and foreigner, his expression grim, as if he could see the approach of the enemy he had been born to fight. Gervanno glanced at Stephen, but the young man's eyes had widened as well. This, then, was new. New to the grounds, the gardens, new to a youth who had spent his life in the shadows of this wonder.

"Moorelas," Stephen whispered. "Do you have stories of Moorelas in the Dominion?"

Gervanno shook his head. "Who was he?"

"He was a mortal man who wielded a sword forged by gods to kill their enemy. It was the dawn of our age, according to the wise. He rode with the four princes of the White Lady's court — and he did not return. Betrayed, in the end, by three of those princes, he failed to kill the god we do not name."

"You called him Moorelas?"

"He's sometimes called Morel, but in the Empire, Moorelas is the most common name."

"We have children's stories of a warrior who was chosen to bear such a sword, such a task — but Moorelas was not the name he was known by. He was known to be fearless. He did not fear demons."

"No, he wouldn't—while he lived and fought, there were no demons."

"There have always been demons. In our stories, he rode out against the Tyr'agar of all demons, the very heart of their forces."

Stephen said nothing, a signal that he disagreed but understood his duties as a host. Gervanno surprised himself: he liked the young man. Such a person was above his approval, beyond any need for it, but he thought Sylvia would have liked the boy as well.

He turned away from that thought, toward the sculpture, thinking of the ways in which stories of bygone heroes and their tragedies and triumphs were almost always about men who had taken up sword, men who fought. They were never about gardens and grounds such as these; never about the losses and the grief of that swordsman, that paragon. As if such paragons must be above simple humanity.

As he wished he himself could be, could have been, and might be in future.

He bowed head.

"IT IS early for you to bring a guest to the maze," a new voice said. Something in its tenor made clear to Gervanno that this voice, soft and carefully modulated, belonged to the Master Gardener. He developed an instant appreciation of the fact that the word *gardener* did not mean, in Breodanir or Maubreche, what it would have meant in the South.

Stephen turned toward that voice. "Yes. He was in Brookton during the turning. We almost didn't make it in time. But he went back when the ways were closing, and he found two of our villagers—Ronson and his grand-daughter—and returned them to us."

"I see. I am the Master Gardener," the man said, turning to Gervanno. His eyes, in the light of fading day, were silver; they seemed imbued with light from within. That light reminded Gervanno of sun off blade. Instinct had saved his life many times in the skirmishes of his youth; he had learned to trust it, because fighting against it had proven costly too many times.

Now, his instinct spoke of death. It was death to offend this gardener; death to cross him. Gardens were not fortresses, but this one, by the presence of its master, was.

Gervanno had practice standing in the presence of men whom it was death to offend. He offered the Master Gardener a precise and complete bow. Had he intended to converse or listen—had he been offered that privilege—he would have knelt, straight-backed, head slightly bowed. He would not have raised voice unless asked.

Here, there were no mats, nothing on which to kneel except the grass itself, or the path they had left to approach this Moorelas. And it was not a custom in the North or in Breodanir, regardless.

"I am Gervanno di'Sarrado."

"You are far indeed from home, although Stephen's ancestors and yours once roamed the same lands in the distant past."

This surprised both Stephen and Gervanno.

"How did you come to be in Brookton?"

Gervanno would have glanced at Stephen for guidance, but did not wish to look away from the Gardener while being addressed by him. He considered his meeting with Lady Maubreche before he replied.

"I was a guard for a merchant caravan."

"Ah. Whose?"

"Evaro di'Pierro."

"Evaro is here?" The Gardener's expression was neutral, but his voice was slightly warmer.

"No. Evaro was caravan master. The caravan was apprehended on the road by demons who rode flying creatures; they burned the caravan to the ground."

The eyes flashed silver again, but this time the light wasn't a glint; it was a fire.

"Lord Stephen?"

"We found no evidence of the demonic in Brookton, but have no reason to doubt Ser Gervanno's words. Lady Maubreche will have the report confirmed. She is likely already attempting to raise her contacts within the Order."

"Did the attack seem random?"

It was an odd question. "They were looking for something." The Gardener waited, his eyes narrowed. "A sword."

"A sword?"

"They had word that a sword was being taken to Breodanir. They were looking for means of transport. We did not have a sword of note; all of our swords were in our hands or scabbards. But there was no fighting." No, just death.

The Gardener's gaze turned to the Stephen he had just styled *lord*.

"It is time, Stephen. Time for you. Time for Nenyane. Soon, even Maubreche will not be safe." He turned once again to Gervanno. "You bring ill news indeed, but warning is always of value. Please feel free to make yourself at home in the gardens I have tended." He paused, frowned, and looked around that garden, as if only then realizing what had stopped the visitors, what had drawn their attention.

"It is more martial than most elements of this garden—a reminder of a war that has perhaps never ended." His smile was brief, bitter. "I would not have it be my last working before I, too, must depart. I shall leave you both to your visit." But even speaking thus, he too turned toward the sculpture he had created, to stare at the face of the warrior who had perished so long ago, no truth could be known of him.

THE DOG that Gervanno had not named—perhaps in the hope that he would return to a better master—was not allowed in the dining room. None of the dogs were, by order of Lady Maubreche. She disliked, she said, watching her family struggle to stop their dogs from begging at the table, because the dogs knew better and did it regardless.

Lord Maubreche clearly felt this was insulting to the dogs, or perhaps insulting to the Hunters; his response implied that Hunter control of their hunting packs was perfect.

Stephen and the younger son said little, although the younger boy—Robart—seemed as offended as his father. If Gervanno understood correctly, the second young man was Robart's huntbrother. Mark's face was as devoid of expression as the oldest Huntbrother present, Arlin. These two, Gervanno had learned, had been adopted into Maubreche. He found it hard to believe; they were so clearly part of the family and so obviously valued and loved.

Nenyane, however, openly snorted at the Lord's claim of mastery, and even pointed out occasions in which *perfect* control had somehow gone disastrously wrong. She, too, had been adopted into Maubreche. But she lacked any obvious signs of gratitude for the home she'd been offered. She was prickly, defiant, difficult.

And also accepted.

Regardless, Gervanno had no desire to bring the dog to the table he was to share with Lady Maubreche. It was her hand that ruled, here. He believed that she was, as stated, grateful to him, and therefore indebted. But no wise man responded to gratitude of that nature with base demands. Gratitude was delicate and easily torn.

"Did you reach the magi?" Nenyane asked, as dinner was brought to the table by silent servants. Gervanno had not eaten with men of rank more than a handful of times, and found the difference in utensils and the demands of foreign manners intimidating. The food itself, however, was not, and he was embarrassed when his stomach began a loud and undeniable rumble.

Lady Maubreche raised a brow, but her accompanying smile was warm. When she turned to Nenyane, however, that smile cooled. "Our guest," she said, with emphasis on the second syllable, "has no doubt been eating rations meant for the road. I do not consider your question appropriate discussion material for his first dinner as a guest."

Even the defiant Nenyane fell silent—and remained silent for the rest of the meal. It was the first time Gervanno felt some sympathy for her; he, too, considered her question the only relevant question, and it had been forbidden.

The food, however, was welcome. He ate too much, as if looking ahead to the road and the return of scant meals.

3RD DAY OF EMPERAL, 429 A.A. MAUBRECHE ESTATES, KINGDOM OF BREODANIR

If dogs did not talk in Breodanir—the one thing about which Sylvia had been proven wrong—they weren't silent. Gervanno was surprised they could be heard so clearly, given the distance from the manor to the kennels, a word that did not do justice to the building itself. He woke, rolled out of bed on the side farthest from the door, cursed because his sleeping brain had not adjusted for the height of the bed from the actual floor, and landed poorly. His sword was already in his hand.

Silvo's sword was propped against the wall.

He'd overslept; it was well past dawn. Clearly he'd needed the sleep. The panic caused by dogs and their alarm had driven all thoughts of sleep from his mind. He heard no human cries, no screams, no commands, and laid the sword across the bed while he hurriedly dressed. While it was possible to wield sword in any state, it wasn't optimal to do so in nightwear.

He was once again armed when he heard the first of the shouting. It was controlled: urgent, but not panicked, not yet. He opened his door and entered the hall, narrowly avoiding a collision with an older man.

The man was unflappable. "Every living person currently in the manor is gathering by the back doors. We've been ordered to retreat to the grounds. Please follow me."

"What's happened?"

The old man didn't answer, and Gervanno fell in beside him. He needed a guide; he had no idea where the back doors were. Stephen had taken him on a tour of the grounds but he wasn't certain he could replicate that journey, he'd been so profoundly affected by what he had seen there.

But he did see the reason the dogs could be heard so clearly: they were in the manor itself.

Lady Maubreche was waiting for the old man and Gervanno. She nodded at both, turned to speak to two women who carried young children—one a babe in arms—and began to stride toward the gardens. She clearly expected to be followed.

Once again, Gervanno acknowledged her power here. She had not raised voice, and did not appear to be armed, but the old man by his side immediately relaxed. He was alert, yes, but it was clear that he had handed responsibility to the greater power.

One dog, a sleek, black giant, remained at Lady Maubreche's side. Ah, no. It stayed a body-length ahead of her, as if it were an honor guard. The only noise it made was the unavoidable sound of paws against stone.

Lord Maubreche was surrounded by five large dogs. He stood waiting for his Lady at the edge of the grounds, Arlin, the man Gervanno now understood to be his huntbrother, at his side. The Lord's expression didn't change as Lady Maubreche emerged from the manor, but the huntbrother's did. He was relieved.

"What is the emergency?" Lady Maubreche demanded.

"Nenyane."

This answer made little sense to Gervanno; it appeared to make far more sense to Lady Maubreche. She paled, her hands curling briefly into fists. Turning to the old man, she said, "Are the rest of the servants out of the house?"

"You have the last two," he replied, "unless the pages fail to return."

"We'll wait," the huntbrother added quietly.

She nodded and began to move again. She said nothing when Gervanno drew his sword. Neither did the two mothers. They were as pale as Lady Maubreche, but more determined—of course they were. They carried their children as they followed.

The word *Nenyane* appeared to have had the same effect on them as it had had on Lady Maubreche. They appeared to understand, from just that name, what they were facing. They moved more quickly, widening their strides and attempting to keep the sudden knowledge, the visceral fear, from their expressions.

The babe in arms didn't notice the effort, and began to wail.

CHAPTER THREE

I f Gervanno had marveled at the grounds and the hedge-work of the Master Gardener, he had expected that in time of war that wild majesty would fade into the background. It did not. Instead, he felt—as he had on the King's Road—that the landscape had shifted beneath his feet, that things would become stranger, more dangerous, far less predictable as he moved.

Lady Maubreche, however, did not shorten her stride. She did not run—he understood that would be beneath her dignity—but she moved as fast as that dignity would allow. The wind moved through her skirts and hair until the moment she reached the entrance of what he realized was a maze—a maze whose walls were green, growing, and shaped in the most astonishing ways, as if leaves and slender branches could be the materials of a tapestry that implied the colors of war. He could not help but gaze at them, and forced his eyes, time and again, to return to Lady Maubreche.

But when he stepped foot beyond some invisible demarcation, wind stopped. Silence reigned. Had he not stepped onto a road that had become, between one step and next, surrounded by strange trees, and had there not been such urgency in his hosts, he would have hesitated here. He could not say why.

But he wasn't terribly surprised to hear the high, yappy bark that had grown somewhat familiar over the course of the past few days; nor

was he surprised to see the smaller, scrawnier version of a commoner's
dog come bounding down the path toward him. The great black dog
that served as both scout and protector glanced back once at the sound.
Gervanno would later swear that the black dog shrugged before once
again returning to its duties.

The dog Gervanno had still not named, not having the rights of an
owner, came to a halt in Gervanno's shadow. He compared the two: the
Hunter's dog with its healthy coat, its size, and its determination to
fulfill the duties assigned it by its Hunter, and the mutt who appeared to
believe that if he cowered close enough to Gervanno, he'd be saved. The
difference could not be more pronounced.

"Follow, then," he told the mutt, as he sped up. He did not want the
humiliation of being lost in the maze—a humiliation that Lady
Maubreche would clearly never face. One day, in some distant future,
he wanted to return; he wanted the time to bear witness to the marvel of
what the Gardener had created.

He stole glimpses as he moved—he was accustomed to taking in his
surroundings even when battle had been joined—and had a certain
sense, as he did, that there would be no future time, no gentle stroll, no
second chance to absorb the marvels and return to them simple awe.
Things that grew changed, if they were not kept in check, and he felt,
viscerally, that they would not be kept in check for much longer.

Or perhaps he had walked under sorrow's cloud for so long he saw
its shadows everywhere. Living things that were lost did not return,
except in memory.

The mutt barked; Gervanno moved more quickly, catching a
glimpse of skirts moved by a stride that would have been difficult in
Southern clothing. The baby's wail had quieted into a hiccup-laden sob;
he could hear the soft murmur of indistinct syllables surrounding it, a
mother's voice providing comfort, or trying.

He came at last to the entrance of the last part of the maze; he knew
it for what it was because Lady Maubreche had come to a complete
stop in front of two young people: Stephen of Maubreche and his huntbrother, Nenyane. The Nenyane whose name had been passed between
the Lord and Lady as if it were a foreboding, even a curse.

He understood why in that moment.

She stood, sword in hand, eyes the color of new silver, before age
had left a gentling patina to provide a hint of warmth. Her hair was
deplorably long, and it was, further, unbound, but the stillness of the air

that surrounded all of the people in this enclosed space was not hers; wind pushed hair from her face when it touched nothing else.

He had seen her back in Brookton, or in what Brookton had almost become. He had not seen her fight. But watching her now, the truth that women *did not fight* was lost, was made a lie, and he was certain that truth was forever lost. Had Gervanno encountered this young woman on any field of battle he had, by duty, chosen, he would be dead.

She seemed to look through Lady Maubreche and the two servants she had guided to this place; her gaze settled on Gervanno, and then dropped to Gervanno's four-legged companion. But she noticed his own naked blade, and seemed to almost approve. The opinion of a foreign girl should have meant nothing to Gervanno. The opinion of a blade master, however, had value that could not be put into words. Guided by instinct formed from a life of practice, he bowed to her; he bowed low.

He rose when Lady Maubreche spoke, although her words weren't meant for Gervanno's ears.

"Where are your father and Arlin now?"

Silver hair blew back in strands; the wind was stronger.

Gervanno found himself holding his breath, and exhaled.

It was Stephen who answered the question, his expression odd, almost distant, as if he was now observing something so far away no other eyes could see it. "They've taken a stand near the oldest fountain."

"A stand?"

"They've found—or been found by—one of the invaders."

Lady Maubreche paled, but her color was the only thing about her that changed; she had perfect control of her expression. "One?"

This time, it was Nenyane who answered. "There are two of significance."

Lady Maubreche's hands curled into fists. "Are there more than two?"

"There are lesser demon-kin, but Corwin can handle those—he's on Maubreche soil, very near the heart of Breodan's power."

Demon. Demon-kin. Gervanno's knuckles were whiter than the Lady's, but hers gripped air and his, a sword. He felt rage rise at almost blinding speed, and could not easily discern whether that rage was at himself or the demons. Chasing rage was guilt, and the guilt was many-headed.

Had the demons somehow tracked him here? Was he the reason

that the lords of this land were now under attack? Would their deaths be on his head?

And beneath that fear, something else rose: this was his chance for a bitter redemption. This was not a slaughter, but a battle. If he joined it, if he made a stand against those demons, perhaps he would earn the death he should have faced on the road to this kingdom. He could never recover the honor lost by the sudden visceral cowardice; he could not defend those it had been his *duty* to defend, but if he faced the death that should have been his—that *would have* been his—he could join the dead, could apologize, could make some small peace with his failure.

But first, he had something to say. "My apologies, Lord." He bowed to Lady Maubreche. "I did not realize that I was being pursued. If I have led them here—"

Nenyane, ever ungracious, snorted. "You think they're here for you?"

"I was the only survivor of the attack on the caravan. I am therefore the only witness."

"Demons have practiced subterfuge where they've the will and self-control," she replied. "But the time is coming when a witness—a single witness—will be irrelevant. If you feel guilty, don't. You're not the reason they're here."

He found it hard to keep pace with her words, but Stephen repeated them quietly in Gervanno's mother tongue.

"How many insignificant demons?" Lady Maubreche demanded.

Again, it was Stephen who answered. "Six. They look similar to dogs in shape and form. I'm not sure if that's deliberate." To Gervanno, he added, "If they chose those servants as companions, they meant to come here. Not to follow you, but to attack Maubreche."

Nenyane turned to Gervanno. "Lady Maubreche can keep everyone in the maze safe. All of the servants know it—and we know it, too. Will you remain behind and guard her?"

He felt redemption slipping from his grasp.

"I will not require his services, as you have just pointed out," Lady Maubreche then said. She turned to Gervanno. "It is a poor host indeed who asks guests to take up swords in defense of the host's home."

And felt it return.

"They are Hunters," the Lady continued, voice softening until he could almost see the mother lurking behind the ruler's eyes. "I ask that you aid them where possible. And if you find my younger son, tell him his mother has commanded his presence in the maze." This last was colder.

"He's with Corwin," Nenyane said. "He and Mark."

She exhaled, relief and fear blending, as they so often did. She opened her mouth, but the words she spoke in her carefully controlled tone were drowned out by the lowing of horns. Everyone froze at the sound, except for the babe in arms. Any attempt at further words was lost to a grim silence. Lady Cynthia physically guided both servants holding children past the two who had stood guard at the maze's entrance; she joined them as the horn sounded again.

Horns had been used as signals—horns, drums, things that made noise loud enough to be heard over the din of battle. The particularity of these calls was unfamiliar to Gervanno, but the sense of them was not: battle had been joined.

It said much about the power of rule here that although Stephen and Nenyane tensed and stiffened, they remained where they had been standing until the Lady nodded. Only when that silent permission had been granted did they move. Nenyane leapt down the corridor that had led to this sanctuary. She landed without a sound and was almost immediately lost to a corner formed by hedges.

Stephen followed, moving as swiftly as she had.

Youth, Gervanno thought, with just a touch of envy. He ran, instead. The one good thing about this self-adopted dog: he didn't get under Gervanno's feet. And he didn't join the baying howl that rose in the distance, either. The Hunters' dogs, like the horns themselves, were obviously a signal that battle had begun.

The field was the wrong field; there were no banners, no drums, no companions by whose side he had fought for many years, and trained for more. A manicured, perfect, almost opulently *green* place meant for the leisure of the powerful and the wealthy was not a field that matched any of Gervanno's prior experiences.

It was always a bad idea—or so Gervanno had been told—to let the enemy decide the field of battle: they made their choices based on what was best for both their method of attack and their eventual victory.

But he thought, and hoped, that this advice, tendered him by a man who had died in the Averdan valleys, was wrong.

WAR MADE, or perhaps revised, rules. No two battles were the same. All lessons that had not been absorbed well enough to become instinctive could be shed or broken beneath the weight of survival's imperative. Those who survived their first battles could assess the value of, the necessity of those drills, those lessons, could learn how to better reinforce their roots.

Those who died did not learn those lessons, but their deaths underlined the import of them.

Gervanno had not been trained to lead. Would never be trained to lead anything more than a handful of men. He was cerdan, but he was not high-born; he owed allegiance, loyalty, and service to his Tor'agnate. That Tor owed allegiance to the lord he served, and that loyalty was a chain that began—or ended—with the Tyr'agar: the ruler of the Dominion. Gervanno's position had been, and would remain, so far from the Tyr'agar he would be invisible, faceless.

He had learned to follow orders. He had learned to survive the following of those orders so that his death would not reflect poorly on the men he served. He had taught those who served beside him—for they did not serve him directly—to do the same.

He wondered if those who had survived the final battle in which he fought would have done as he now did. He followed a young woman by the stream of her silver-white hair, struggling to keep up. He gave the lead to her, and knew he would leave it in her hands until the moment she found what she sought.

The howl of dogs in the distance quieted, as did the call of horns. Those sounds grew distant as he ran. No matter how he widened his stride, Nenyane was ahead, always ahead, as if running were as simple, as sustainable to her, as breath. It was natural to follow her here, where all things had become both strange and familiar. He wondered if it would have been as natural were he standing—or running—on Averdan soil.

But he remembered the single glimpse he had had of Kiriel di'Ashaf —self-named—in the valleys; the sight of her had been enough to freeze the blood of both Gervanno and the men he was old enough to lead. What would that distant, terrifying woman do if confronted with Nenyane?

He had been taught that women were softer, weaker; that women could not wield sword and step onto the battlefield. In his youth, at Nenyane's age, he had believed it. He could not believe it now; experience had given him the ability to read the subtle signs that spoke of power. Perhaps women had been denied the battlefield for reasons other than inherent weakness.

WHAT DO we call a fearless man? His father's voice. His father's voice, offered from the certainty of childhood memories, for he did not think he would hear it again while he lived.

A hero? he had asked, shorn of certainty; it had been such an odd question.

In the shallows of dusk, in the time between the reign of the Lord of the Sun and the Lady, doubt and uncertainty could be voiced — but carefully. Even as a child, he had known that.

His father had shaken his head. He was not displeased with the answer; he had clearly expected it. But it was the wrong answer.

A corpse.

Gervanno had not understood the answer, not then. Men were supposed to know no fear; it was one of reasons he yearned for distant adulthood. If he became an adult like his father, he would finally be free of fear.

Fear serves a purpose. Understand it. It is a weapon, but it is a far deadlier weapon than even the swords of the mighty. Use it, hone it, absorb it with care. It is fear that makes us men.

How? How can fear *make us* men?

His father had been silent for long enough Gervanno thought no answer would come. *You think of fear as a single thing, as the result of cowardice. That is why you cannot understand. But you will. You are my son. Your mother is my wife.* He had used a Northern word, a merchant word. *I would not be the man I am now had we never met; I would not be the father I am now. She changed the world, for me.*

This, Gervanno had heard before.

I fear to lose her. Do you understand? Can you imagine a world without your mother in it? She is shade. She is shade to the merciless heat of the sun. She is an echo of the Lady's mercy, and that echo resonates throughout the day.

It was only at dusk that his father could speak so.

I fear to lose you. I fear to lose the domis we built as a family. It is that fear that defines me; it is to avoid what I fear that I assess and make the choices I make. I am not driven mad by the fear; fear does not push me into terror. I am aware of the ways in which it might. I am aware of what your lives would be should I throw away my life on a field seeking glory.

You dream of glory, his father added. *But you do not see the cost of that glory to your mother. You will be told, time and again, that honor is a warrior's breath, a warrior's blood. It is true. Understand that honor does not mean glorious death. Do not die, Gervanno. Do not throw your life away in order to attain the honor that is only given to those who can never tarnish it again.*

Do not forget why you fight.

But never, ever allow fear to become terror; never let yourself become fear's tool, fear's pawn.

HE HAD BETRAYED HIS FATHER.

First, when he had chosen to accept employ with Evaro. The war was over, and the need for soldiers—those that remained who could still fight—was ebbing. Gervanno's decision was not an act of abandonment. He was a free man; his abilities, such as they were, were the only skill of value he could offer. He wished to retreat—perhaps forever—from the war that he had barely survived. He could fight, yes; could wield sword well, better than most men of his station. But that skill meant nothing to demons, and the sword that was—that had been—his pride had proven ineffective against them. What use sword when the edge dulled against demonic skin without leaving even the trace of a wound?

Merchants faced bandits—the desperate and hungry, often soldiers as Gervanno had once been. Those, his sword could cut.

But he had betrayed his father in a deeper way as just such a merchant guard: terror had taken the whole of his mind, his will, his ability to move or fight or even flee. It had rendered him, in the moment, a helpless child. Fear ruled everything because on a visceral level there was nothing he could do. Nothing but die.

He did not yearn for his father, as he would have done at a very young age.

No, he dreaded him, now. The first betrayal was a choice; it was a choice men could make. He could stand his ground and weather the fury of the older man; he'd weathered so much conflict in his life.

But the second betrayal?

No. He would sooner die—here, now, on his feet—than ever confess to his father. If there was any affection remaining in that old man, it would break. It would break him more certainly than even Gervanno's death. And it would bring a permanent stain, a dishonor, to the Sarrado clan. Death before dishonor.

He ran, and discovered again that no man could successfully outrun himself.

WHEN NENYANE CAME TO A HALT, Gervanno was winded and deeply embarrassed to be so; Stephen was not. The young man was alert, armed, as ready as Nenyane herself appeared to be. Had Gervanno, in the passage of months, become so feeble?

He had no further time to dwell on his inadequacies—he would have time later when he once again returned to the road. Now, the odd shell of such self-doubt was shattered: he could hear the sounds of swords. Worse, he could *see* it, even if he could not yet see the wielders or the combat itself. If steel clashing against steel was thunder, the lightning here was red and blue, streaks of color that rose from a field he could not yet see, stretching for sky before they faded.

He approached the two as they stood; he could see Stephen's grim expression in profile, but Nenyane's back was a wall. He asked no questions. It was clear that Stephen knew who at least one of the combatants was; his face was pale, shadowed not so much by fear—fear would at least make sense—but grief.

Red lightning. Blue lightning. The silence between them emphasized the unnatural storm: there were no voices, no shouts, no horns, no howling; there was nothing at this distance. This distance was safe.

Safe or no, Gervanno was unsurprised when Nenyane once again began to move. What caution she had chosen to exercise by coming to a halt at all was a silence of assessment; she had no intention of avoiding the demons. Neither did Stephen. As Nenyane, wordless, moved forward, he followed in step—as if they were not two people, but one, spread between two bodies.

Perhaps because she reacted as if demons were somehow expected, somehow *normal*, Gervanno's visceral fear failed to paralyze him; his treacherous feet moved—and moved quickly. Nenyane knew where she was going. Gervanno could see the source of the brilliant light that spoke of battle, but it was beyond hedges; reaching it would take longer if he lost Nenyane and Stephen.

He did stop when they rounded the last corner. Grass ended in a long, slightly curved flower bed, and beyond that there were three things: stone, a large fountain, and two men.

One wielded a burning blade, a thing of red that made fire both compelling and terrifying; the other wielded a blade of ice or lightning, a shining blue that had no analogue in reality.

He forgot fear for a moment, forgot war. Forgot that things beautiful could be so ugly, so deadly. The demon wasn't monstrous to the eye: his body was lithe, long, flexible; the movement of his feet so precise, and yet so fluid, he seemed almost to dance. His hair was longer than Nenyane's, and likewise unbound; it moved around him as if to emphasize his grace, his precision.

The face of what Gervanno had been taught was evil had never looked so compelling; he felt his mouth dry as he gaped.

Were it not for the demon's opponent, Gervanno might have remained frozen, but the demon's opponent was very alike: nimble, agile, graceful, his blue blade moving as counterpoint to the red, the nature of lightning and the nature of fire not quite one thing but not easily separable. His hair, too, was unfettered, and in those brief seconds where they drew together, their hair intertwined as if trying, in some fashion, to bind the two together.

Gervanno had seen sword dancers in his childhood, and seen them again in his youth, both long vanished. He had never, ever seen a sword dance with the power of this one. He knew that if one of the two slipped, they would be injured—badly. There was no illusion in that; if one looked at the silent expressions of the two combatants, it was clear that what waited at the close of this dance was death.

Yet on the face of the demon—identified only by the fires with which demons seemed so comfortable—there was something very akin to joy.

On the face of his partner in this dance, joy was absent. In its place, sorrow. It was the sorrow of loss—a loss that has been, finally, accepted; a loss that the bereaved have railed against, wept against, and endured. *The dead will not return.*

The hand on his sword grew slack as Gervanno watched. There was no opening for him, here. No way to interrupt what should not be interrupted. Perhaps, should a dancer fall or fail, he would have a role to play. Perhaps not. In the moment, he felt small, clumsy, overwhelmed by what he knew he'd been privileged to witness.

Nenyane, however, was not Gervanno; she was not of the South. She had, he thought, never seen a sword dance; she did not understand the way that the blade's edge, wielded between two such as these, could be an expression of trust. The greater the trust, the greater the matching of skills. In the greatest of pairings, the consequences of a single mistake could be profound and permanent.

There was no trust here. He understood that. But he could not shake the certainty that in some distant past, some other country, there had been.

Nenyane leapt. Stephen followed far more slowly this time, as if he, too, witnessed this combat as Gervanno did. There was no opening for either the Maubreche Hunter or Gervanno, but Stephen seemed to feel little fear as his huntbrother raised sword. Gervanno had never seen a sword dance of three. He would have said it was impossible.

But he had known that Nenyane was a sword master; had seen something in her that immediately granted recognition, but did not immediately offer reasons for it. He thought her very like the two who fought now, although she lacked the perfectly matched height of the other two; her hair, shorter as well, flew in the same wind that carried the weight of their blades, the lightness of their steps.

Ah, he thought. Their steps. Half of the time, they did not bother to touch stone. Nenyane did, leveraging the momentum gained by pushing off the stones that surrounded the fountain itself, leading to the glassed doors of the northern manor. He could see her reflection in those panes, dimmed by red and blue to her grey presence. Her sword did not glow; it did not scatter light as if light were sound and fury.

Stephen's dogs spread out, keeping a distance from the fighting itself; they moved when the combatants moved, at no orders Gervanno could hear. It was not the time to think of Sylvia, but he did; Sylvia was seldom wrong. These dogs did not speak in a way she would have immediately grasped—but they could be heard by their masters.

This fight, he thought, was not his fight. There was no room in it for him, no necessity for his presence. But he remembered the brief words that had come in answer to Lady Maubreche. "Lord Stephen," he said, granting the son of the ruler a title he did not use himself. "My blade is useless here. But it might be of aid to Lord Maubreche and the people he now protects. I do not know where they fight—but I believe you do. Can you—ah, no, can one of your dogs—lead me there?"

Stephen's brows rose, a slight motion that implied he had all but forgotten Gervanno's presence. But they lowered again and the dog that was brown, black, and white immediately returned to his side. "This is Patches," he said. "Patches will lead you there and return." He hesitated, and then added, "Thank you."

IT DID NOT PAIN Gervanno to turn away from what was not, in the end, a sword dance. It did grieve him to lose the opportunity to see Nenyane of Maubreche display the skills he was certain she possessed. But Stephen had silently concurred with Gervanno: his skills, rudimentary in comparison to hers, were not necessary there.

They might be necessary for Lord Maubreche and his huntbrother. Or perhaps even for the sake of the dogs that were clearly so prized they were, to the Maubreche clan, as valuable as proud cerdan. Patches could run, and did, as if the ordered absence from the side of her master must be made as short as possible without obvious disobedience. Gervanno followed with more ease; he'd regained his breath while watching the sword dance of the two, demon and man.

He found it disturbing that he saw nothing demonic at all in the man who wielded the red sword. Perhaps that was why he could not find the terror that had destroyed all sense of his own honor on that single day Evaro's caravan had been destroyed. Had his father failed to hear about the caravan's fate, and his son's humiliating survival, he would have nevertheless been disgusted at the way Gervanno had gawked—the word his father would have used—when in the presence of a mortal enemy.

Beauty was skin deep. Beauty was just another tool in a limited arsenal. His father would have expected Gervanno to remember it: only mawkish youth confused beauty with honor or respectability. Those things were defined in other ways. Yes, beauty did not immediately mean that a person was ultimately unworthy—but possessing beauty was like possessing hair. Some men didn't.

The last leg of the escort became unnecessary. If there were no flashes of unnatural lightning, there was noise—a lot of it. The dogs growling or barking, the lower, louder growls of what Gervanno assumed were not and could not be dogs. He could not hear Lord Maubreche or the man called Arlin, but he could hear the sound of something glancing off steel, and at a distance, a roar of pain and fury co-mingled. Not, he thought, a human sound.

He had been so impressed by the hedges here, but found them the impediment he had feared they would be should battle be necessary; they might serve strategic purposes, but it was difficult to see through or around them.

It was less difficult when fire rose from branches and leaves in a sudden, consuming blaze. Elements of the landscape were lost in an instant, and when the furious blush of orange and white flames vanished, when smoke rose and was carried away by howling wind, he might have been standing on the plains of Averda.

He could see the demons. One among them looked almost human, but the half-dozen that stood—and fought—on four legs did not. Not even at this distance could he mistake them for dogs or other natural creatures; they glistened in the fire's light as if their bodies were made of polished chitin, and their teeth were far, far longer than the fangs of the dogs they resembled in passing.

The almost-human demon turned toward the newcomers in this combat; the beasts that flanked him did not. They were focused on their quarry: Lord Maubreche, Arlin, and the younger son, Robart. Mark stood back from the three; he was white with fear, his chest noticeably rising and falling far too quickly.

Gervanno was no longer a young man, no longer a youth, but he saw a mirror of himself in Mark.

Mark, whom the dogs did not obey. Mark, who served at the side of the second son of the Lord of Maubreche. He had training to offer his Hunter, but nothing exceptional beyond that—and the training had failed, was failing. Gervanno had been that youth on the first battlefield he had ever encountered, but he had found his footing in the barked orders of his leader; even if he had had, in that precise moment, no known way forward, his feet had begun to move, regardless.

Mark had not been trained in the same way, that much was clear. But Robart was standing, armed, beside his father, his eyes narrowed and oddly glinting; they looked very like his father's or Stephen's. Mark's didn't have the same odd glint.

Neither did Gervanno's.

It was to Mark that Gervanno was naturally drawn. He moved quickly, losing his guide as the multi-colored dog veered to the left at great speed. She had done her duty, and made haste to return to the master she served.

GERVANNO DID NOT REALIZE IMMEDIATELY that the skies were no longer shifting to red or blue or some combination of both. The fight that caused that aurora was no longer his concern; he could not affect its outcome. He could possibly affect the outcome of this one, in a mundane, entirely mortal way.

Mark was without commander here, without leader; he had frozen in a spot to the side of, and behind, his Hunter and his lord. Anyone his age might have been overcome with fear—Gervanno had far more experience, and fear had overwhelmed him on the road. That terror had probably saved his life—but it had preserved none of the self-respect that men needed if they were to ever stand on their own two feet against their enemies.

He knew the first battle was over when he saw the blur of silver hair, the glint of long, straight sword so common in the Empire and the Western Kingdoms. Nenyane had taken to air as if air were solid, physical; she landed two yards ahead of Lord Maubreche, finding a place for herself between his bristling, silent dogs.

Behind her, running at speed, his stride wide, his footfalls only slightly heavier, was her Hunter, her brother. Stephen of Maubreche, sword in hand, came to stand at the side of his huntbrother. No blood added color to the exposed flats of either of their weapons.

ROBART GLANCED, briefly, at Stephen and Nenyane; Gervanno thought he had been seen, but his presence—or absence—was irrelevant to the youth.

Nenyane's was not.

Nor was it irrelevant to the demon who seemed to hold the leash of the others.

Eyes wide, sword wavering, the demon turned to face her, as if she had become the only thing of import in this burning garden.

She was not. Lord Maubreche moved as swiftly as the demon's attention did, his own dogs fanning out around the demon dogs. Arlin

joined not the Lord but the dogs, as if he were part of the Lord's pack;
Robart joined Arlin. Mark failed to move until fire enveloped the grass
on which he had been standing, motionless. He moved then, and moved
quickly.

Movement returned some sense of immediacy to the surroundings
Mark found himself in. It put him in range of the demon dog to the
furthest left of the central demon, one of the two that Nenyane had
considered significant.

Gervanno was well aware that the insignificant could kill. He was
aware, as well, that Nenyane required none of his aid. He therefore
headed toward Mark, sword readied; the first blow he struck, he struck
across the front shoulder of one of the gleaming, armored beasts.

He had some experience with demons; he leapt back as the sound of
sword against chitin resonated, sending a tremor up his arm. But there
was blood on the sword, dark and red. These creatures were not like
most of the demons that had amassed on Averdan soil. Here, Gervanno
could make a difference.

The consequences of the attempt would be the same in either case:
he could possibly die. But here, that possible death seemed to serve an
actual purpose. He could stand. He could fight. He could use the skills
that he had honed all his life and they would make a difference.

It was a blessing, unlooked for at the very whisper of the word
demon.

His attack, the blood it drew, the way he avoided the snapping jaws
of the creature whose attention he'd gained by causing such an injury,
served a second purpose: a slap in the face to the young man who had
almost been consumed in demonic fire.

Mark drew sword—drew it well enough it was clear he'd undergone
training—and shifted stance, coming back to himself, the emergency at
hand, and his ability to influence it. Fear shifted focus, loosening its
grip.

Together, Gervanno di'Sarrado and Mark of Maubreche stood side
by side on the field—and that felt right to Gervanno. He understood
that neither he nor Mark were at the heart of the battle; they were not
generals, commanders, or Widan. But he had never been that, in any of
the skirmishes he'd experienced in the past.

Nenyane of Maubreche was at the heart of it. Nenyane and the
demon. Even Lord Maubreche pulled back—three times—when
Nenyane rushed in. Stephen of Maubreche was watchful, waiting; he

stood by Arlin and Robart. Only once did he lift hand to grab his younger brother by the shoulder, but no words followed that simple gesture.

Gervanno noticed all of this only when the creature he and Mark faced had finally succumbed to their joint attacks, its body—as all demonic bodies did—crumbling as they watched, chitin and fang becoming, in a matter of few seconds, ash. He turned then, as Mark did, seeking new opponents.

What he saw was Nenyane of Maubreche.

He saw her blade trace an almost visible arc in the air; could almost hear it whistle with the force of her swing. Fanciful, yes—but at the heart of fancy, truth.

What it had taken him and the young Maubreche huntbrother long minutes to achieve, she achieved artlessly, casually, her disregard for the threat of the four-legged creatures so apparent no one could mistake it for anything but contempt.

Two of the demons died, beheaded, in one stroke; she had not appeared to look at them at all. She had eyes for only one demon, and in turn, he had eyes for her. He was wary of the Hunter Lord; the Hunter's dogs were wary of him, and they kept their distance. The demon could not behead them in like fashion, could not entirely ignore their presence.

His blade clashed against hers twice, but the third time her blade slid across the length of his, the weight of the blow allowing edge to carry beyond the demonic hilt. First blood was hers, and if the blow was glancing, it nonetheless left a wound; the demon did not recover quickly enough to prevent it. The shudder of red fire followed first blood.

Gervanno watched.

It came to him as he did that Nenyane could have fought the demon near the fountain with as much agility, as much grace, as the opponent the demon did have; that her bladework would be equal to that demon's; that there might be, in the back and forth, the same deadly grace, the same wild beauty. But no, he thought, watching, it could not. She fought with a rage and fury—cold fury, yes—that did not allow for detachment.

She fought as if she had encountered demons before—just as Gervanno had done—and had managed to survive. Her battle was personal.

He was vaguely certain that nothing he could do would earn the depth of her enmity, and absolutely certain that he would not survive it if he somehow managed. His mouth was dry, and he realized, belatedly, that he was not afraid for Nenyane of Maubreche; he was almost afraid *of* her.

Mark withdrew as Gervanno watched, breaking their brief alliance as he returned to the side of his Hunter; Gervanno could not move, and felt no desire to try. As if this dance of blade and fury was a gift, he bore witness, not for the sake of his dead traveling companions, but for himself, for the sake of the war that must come — soon — to envelop them all.

He was not surprised that the demon fell to the girl's sword; he was slightly surprised that it took as long as it did. Only when ashes stood, briefly, in the form of a man before crumbling, just as the demonic dogs had crumbled, was he once again free to move.

SILENCE REIGNED in the wake of the demon's fall. The four-legged demons were also dead, their bodies gone to ash as if they, and their master, had been a fever dream. In the distance, he could no longer hear the clashing of two impossible swords; that fight, too, had ended. Of course it had. Nenyane and Stephen were here.

It was Stephen who turned to the Southerner. He offered an odd bow, a Northern bow, and said, "We are once again in your debt." He did not mention Mark by name.

Nor did Gervanno, although he understood. "You have offered me the grace and freedom of your domis as if I were an honored guest. Or perhaps even a distant blood relation. If I have managed to repay that welcome, even in a small fashion, I am grateful." He surveyed the ruined grounds and thought, again, about the cost of war. So much beauty had been destroyed in scant minutes. It would be replaced — the Maubreche clan seemed wealthy enough — or regrown, but both things would take time, and what stood in place of what was gone would never quite be the same.

"I will inform my mother that it's safe to return to the manse." Stephen glanced at Gervanno, as if extending an invitation.

Gervanno nodded and followed as Stephen moved away.

THE FOLIAGE beyond the wide area in which the demon had chosen to attack was green; it had not been touched or damaged. Were a visitor to be deliberately led on a path that avoided that demon's destruction, they might remain ignorant of what had been lost.

The sole advantage offered by that destruction, for one unfamiliar with Maubreche, was the ease with which one could choose a direction; here, with hedges once again standing in strategic locations, it become far more difficult. Familiarity was required. Stephen had the familiarity that Gervanno lacked, and would continue to lack, unless he somehow became part of the Maubreche household.

On some level, truly serving as a Maubreche cerdan was compelling. But the sword in his hand was Silvo's, a constant reminder of the responsibility he had undertaken. The blade must go back to the Dominion, to Silvo's family. There was only one way it might arrive there, and be conveyed with the respect and honor that was Silvo's due —if a man without honor who had failed in his duties could be such a conveyor.

LADY MAUBRECHE WAS WAITING, her expression impassive. While the servants—people similar to Gervanno, transposed to a different culture —were both visible and audible in their relief, she gave nothing away. Looking at her eldest son, she said, "The intruders?"

"The intruders have been repelled. Permanently."

Her nod was crisp, offered without hesitance. She then turned toward the servants. "Camden, see that everyone returns to their posts." To Gervanno, she offered a grave nod. "We have offered poor hospitality indeed, to see you burdened with our defense. Please join us in the hall before we offer you a meal, and perhaps the more traditional hospitality for which Maubreche is known." The last words were offered with a hint of a smile, and that smile contained approval.

He felt callow, young, when that approval warmed him. He returned perfect bow for nod, and he held that bow a fraction of a moment too long, to emphasize respect. Only when her skirts moved past the line of his vision did he rise.

Stephen was waiting for him. "When she tells us to join her in the hall, she means immediately."

"Of course."

"She isn't angry with you," Stephen said, correctly divining the source of Gervanno's discomfort.

"Unless I am mistaken, such attacks do not occur often."

"No."

"Perhaps she believes that the demons were searching for me."

Stephen shook his head. "I doubt she believes that, but she accepts it as a possibility given the news you bore. It would be better for Maubreche if your suspicions were true."

"Which is why you don't believe it?" The words left his mouth before he could properly assess the harm they might cause. He knew better than to speak to the eldest son of a lord in such a familiar fashion.

But if Gervanno knew better, Stephen did not. His smile was slender and offered with a hint of weariness. "Yes."

THE SECOND AUDIENCE with Lady Maubreche was comprised of the same people as the first, but Lady Maubreche now appeared to be leading a council of war. Gervanno was led—by Stephen—to a hall which contained a large table, across which was laid a map. The map had been pinned in many places, the pins slender and possessed of small, colored flags.

Lord Maubreche and his huntbrother Arlin were to one side of the table, accompanied by the second son, Robart, and his brother, Mark. Nenyane, arms folded, left foot tapping in the universal signal of impatience—an impatience that would never have been shown in such august company in Gervanno's youth—looked up.

To Gervanno's surprise, her gaze was fixed on him, the assessment bold and without compunction. "You're not terrible with a sword," she finally said, the words grudging.

Had Gervanno not traveled through foreign lands at Evaro's side, he might have had to struggle not to take offense at the words; the familiarity in them was almost astonishing. It was not that he had not heard similar judgments before—he certainly had. But they had come from his commanders or his father and uncle, people who had both the right and the need to see him properly trained.

Lord Maubreche looked across the table to their visitor. "Nenyane speaks roughly," he said, his voice more measured. "But it is seldom that she offers such a compliment."

Nenyane shrugged. "It's not a compliment. It's a simple statement of fact."

This amused Lord Maubreche. It did not appear to amuse either Arlin or Lady Maubreche in the same fashion, but it was clear they agreed with Lord Maubreche—it was rare.

Gervanno approached the table and the map it contained. He had seen maps with entirely different geography laid across folding tables, but he had never been invited into important councils of war, not even when he was given the responsibility of supervising small groups of men. Decisions taken in rooms such as these were relayed to those whose rank did not offer a say in such councils.

"We are waiting for one more person," Lady Maubreche said. "I apologize for the delay; he is oft difficult to find when he is otherwise occupied, and damage was done to the grounds. He will join us soon."

SOON WAS ALMOST AN HOUR LATER. Gervanno inferred, from brief snatches of conversation, that they waited for the Master Gardener. He marveled at the Breodani—at people who allowed their councils of war to be led by a woman, and who waited upon a gardener before important discussions could begin.

But he better understood the waiting when the door opened upon a familiar man: the man who had engaged the demon on his own; the man whose fight brooked no interference, and required no aid. Long silver hair, unbound, fell down his back, and his eyes, grey in the light streaming into the room from large, high-reaching windows, swept the room, pausing only briefly on Gervanno.

He did not bow to the Lord or the Lady. He looked weary, angry, resigned.

Respect did not seem to be the social coin of this land. Or perhaps such a sword master was not required to pay it. "I have seen to the grounds, but with constant interruptions, I cannot repair the damage done."

Gervanno almost backed away from the table, but as the Breodani seemed unoffended—and entirely unsurprised—by both his tone and his words, he relaxed.

"Nenyane believes you recognized at least one of the intruders," Lady Maubreche then said, without preamble.

"Does she?"

Nenyane snorted. "I do. I don't care what he's called, and I don't care why you recognized him."

"Nenyane," Lady Maubreche said.

Nenyane's jaw snapped shut. She turned to glare at Stephen, who had said nothing, and whose eyes remained fixed on the surface of the map, as if to draw physical shape from the flat lines drawn there.

"It is true that it is not recognition that is the most relevant point here," Lady Maubreche then said. "But if you did, you might better be able to answer our most pressing concern."

The Master Gardener nodded, grim now. "They are searching, Cynthia. You know this. I am certain that Bredan has informed you. Ah, or perhaps not. You have not entered the heart of the maze in well over ten days."

"I entered it today, as you well know."

"And did you choose to bespeak the Hunter God there?"

Her eyes narrowed; for the first time, Gervanno could see small cracks in her discipline. "I did not. The Between is not a comfortable place for most mortals to occupy. Had the intruders reached the heart of the maze, I would have invoked sanctuary. And that is not the matter for which I have convened this meeting."

"It is the matter that is most relevant," the Gardener countered. He then turned to Gervanno. "You lost your companions of the road to demons. Tell me, did you recognize your attackers?"

Did he? His impressions of that day of slaughter were of wing and flame—but a demon had ridden upon the back of one of those winged creatures. "I confess I was not attempting to study the demon that seemed to be in control." He exhaled slowly, struggling to maintain proper posture, proper breath. "But no, I do not believe either of the two demons you consider significant were the ones in charge of the attack on the caravan."

The Gardener then turned to Nenyane. "Well?"

Her gaze seemed focused on a distant point beyond the Gardener's shoulder, but there was no fear in it. If demons were her enemies—and clearly, that enmity ran deep—she considered them natural enemies, just as Gervanno would have once declared the Mancorvans his foes. She felt no awe of them; she granted the powers they clearly displayed no more than a tactical nod.

He did not understand her, but felt, for the first time since he had dragged himself off the last battlefield in Averda, that if she were his commander—if she were his companion—he could face the demons not as almost-gods, but as foes he had some chance of defeating. His father would have been both outraged and enraged by the thought: his son, hiding behind a *girl*. But his father had not seen her fight. What would the old man have made of her blade work?

Gervanno shook his head to clear it. Nenyane was not Averdan. She was not a leader of men. She was as elemental as sandstorm.

How strange, then, that she should be huntbrother to Stephen of Maubreche. But perhaps not; Stephen's eyes were golden, and in the home of Gervanno's childhood and youth, golden eyes were a sign of the cursed; they were often considered demonic in origin.

Evaro, however, had never believed that. Sylvia had actively snorted with derision the first time Gervanno had encountered a golden-eyed woman, a daughter of the Northern Mother, and made the sign to ward off evil. Perhaps because of his familiarity with the caravan, Gervanno had come to believe that the Mother and the Lady of the Southern Night were simply different cultural names for the same god, and that had brought him some uneasy comfort.

There was no Northern analogue for the Lord of the Sun. Gervanno had asked Evaro and Sylvia, and both had failed to answer, their thoughts suddenly private and far less accessible. He had never asked them if they believed in the gods of the North; it was clear on some level they did, and that might have become a source of conflict between Gervanno and the caravan leaders. Better not to know.

"Nenyane," Lady Maubreche said. If stone had spoken, it would have had the same timbre, the same implacability.

Nenyane shook her head and returned to the present. "They weren't the demons that attacked me when I was a child," she replied. "I'm not sure either recognized me at all."

"Then you think the point of the attack was?"

"What it's always been," she replied, with an uneasy shrug. "This is the heart of Bredan's territory. This is the heart of the Breodani world, whether the King acknowledges it or not. They can't easily destroy the maze heart, but the maze becomes irrelevant if you're all dead. I couldn't invoke it. Mark couldn't. Only those with Maubreche blood can."

The Gardener glared at Nenyane; he clearly found her answer wanting.

Gervanno didn't know enough to judge the veracity of it. But he knew that Maubreche—and its many servitors—believed in the power she claimed resided at the heart of the maze.

The Gardener turned to Lady Maubreche, the annoyance falling from his expression, although to Gervanno's eye it lurked beneath the surface of it. "It is not the maze or the sanctuary they fear."

Lady Maubreche raised a hand, palm out. It was a command.

And the Gardener was clearly a man who could survive open disobedience and disregard. Gervanno did not, viscerally, understand those from the North or the West.

"It is possible they do not understand Nenyane's significance. I myself did not, when we first met. But the sanctuary is trivial. If the allies of the god we do not name come to Breodanir through the Western Kingdoms, they could, with effort, crush the kingdom—and the effort would be small. We do not understand why the enemy remains in the frozen North, but we know he is gathering his armies as we speak.

"If they destroy the kingdom and scatter its defensive forces, what matter if Bredan's sanctuary stands? It is a small patch of land, upon which no human cities—or even small villages—could be founded. At most, it is the equivalent of a fortified closet. It is not the sanctuary they fear.

"Bredan is gone. He is returned to his place across the divide. He is, as all the gods, sundered now from the lands in which mortals dwell and live. And die."

The silence that followed his words had weight, teeth; Lady Maubreche was pale with it. Nenyane was not; she had reddened. Lord Maubreche and Lord Arlin looked down at the map—clearly there was a history between the members of this family that Gervanno had not seen and did not understand.

"It is Stephen, son of—"

"*Enough.*"

The Gardener fell silent. It was therefore Nenyane who spoke next. Gervanno was frozen in place, staring—as the lord of these lands had chosen to do—at the surface of the marked map. It was an awkwardness heightened momentarily by fear, the tension was so thick.

"Silence does not change fact," the pale-haired huntbrother told the woman who, if Gervanno understood the adoption correctly, was her mother.

"He is my son," Lady Maubreche said. "The raising of him has been mine."

"And the scarring was not at your hand."

Stephen, beside Gervanno, tensed instantly, the line of his shoulders and neck frozen.

"But the Gardener is right: it is Stephen for whom they search. They know—they must know—that he is god-born. Bredan's son."

The Gardener reentered the conversation. "He is one of a very few human children born to the God, and of those few, he is the only one who has survived."

"The Hunter God—"

"Do not play games, Cynthia. The Hunter God was your god while he was harbored, much diminished, in these lands. It was because of his nature, because of his oaths to the people who served him, that he founded this land. And it is through the power of sacrifice—his, and his people's—that the land was fecund. He is the God of the Covenant. He is the god of oaths.

"And the human children of his blood are oathbinders. It is the oathbinding, the binding covenants, that the demons wish destroyed, for their god understands the full measure of that power, even be it in the hands of frail mortals."

"I know what the God wants," Stephen said, lifting his chin to meet the eyes of the Master Gardener. "And I will not give it to him." He turned on heel and walked directly past the Master Gardener to the door through which he had entered.

Lady Maubreche opened her mouth and closed it again. She did not command her son to return; nor did Lord Maubreche. Nenyane's eyes had narrowed to slits, and after a moment she turned to Lady Maubreche, tendered her a surprisingly graceful and correct bow, and then followed her Hunter.

The Gardener did not likewise depart, and it seemed to Gervanno that he was just as angry as the Maubreche family—but he understood that the chain of command was in Lady Maubreche's hand, not Stephen's or Nenyane's.

"The time is coming, Cynthia. Soon, your hand will be forced. I have come to tender my resignation; there is a greater burden of service I am forced, by circumstance, to undertake. Your oldest son and his huntbrother are part of that burden, but I am not their keeper.

"You've seen the change in the lands in just the past year. You almost lost Brookton."

"Were it not for Nenyane's *necessary* presence here, there would be no *almost* about it. Maubreche needs Stephen and Nenyane." This, too, had the feel of a well-worn argument—an argument that neither side had won. Gervanno glanced, briefly, at the door, desiring escape from the business of a family of which he was not part.

But that was the South in him, and he was not in the South. In some families, simply witnessing the disrespect and the weakness of emotion would have been an eventual death sentence.

"Then you will have to come to terms with their absence. You have a visitor; he has been sent by the King."

Gervanno's head shot up; Lady Maubreche's eyes narrowed. Before Gervanno could speak—and it would have been a struggle—she said, voice almost flat, "Lord Grayton is here?"

"Lord Grayton has just reached the perimeter of the grounds."

She bowed head briefly, and then lifted it. "My apologies, Ser Gervanno. While your input in this discussion was sought, it must be put off. Lord Grayton is Huntsman of the Chamber—the King's right hand. He seldom visits, except at need—and when he does, he carries the King's commands."

Lord Maubreche left the table's side. Arlin remained. "I'll go," he told his wife.

She nodded, her lips a slender, white line.

CHAPTER FOUR

Cynthia's office was located down the longer and less public gallery; it was to that office that she had retreated when Corwin left to greet their guest. She had made no arrangements to greet a man of Lord Grayton's stature, but as he was a Hunter Lord, those arrangements were often made by her husband. Corwin, however, had not been expecting Lord Grayton's arrival. Although the demonic attack remained Maubreche's primary concern, subjecting Ser Gervanno, to whom they owed a debt, to Lord Grayton would have been neither desirable nor wise.

To have Lord Grayton arrive without warning was not a good sign. If he came on Hunter business, he would interact with, deal with, Lord Maubreche himself, but the Huntsmen of the Chamber served the King directly. The King, Master of the Hunt, did not hunt; he governed, alongside his queen.

This unasked for, unwanted visit had been an approaching shadow for the better part of the year.

If Lord Grayton carried word from the King, it was not for Corwin that that word was meant. It was for Lady Maubreche. It was for Stephen's mother. She was not above hoping that the matter was a Hunter matter, but she was above praying; prayer had never been of benefit.

Stephen. She closed her eyes, lowering her chin as she waited.

SHE HEARD the approach of one of the servants—Heather, she
thought, by the cadence of the steps. Heather was older than Cynthia,
and far too senior to be sent as a page. She did not rise until Heather
—and it was Heather—stopped in the door frame. She tendered
Cynthia a bow that was so perfect, she might have been in the
Maubreche manse in the King's City, pausing in the door of a crowded
parlor.

This was never a good sign.

"Lady Maubreche," Heather said, which was, if possible, even
worse. "The Keeper of the Keys sent me to inform you that your presence is required."

When Heather used this tone, she meant to keep her distance—and
that forced Cynthia to maintain her own. She stiffened, but rose,
straightening her skirts.

BENEATH THE GLITTER OF A CHANDELIER, she saw a man dressed in
Hunter greens beside the Maubreche Keeper of the Keys; the deep, if
dusty, forest shade. These colors were heightened with a slash of grey,
the color of the winter hunt. Even had he chosen to wear clothing that
did not denote his rank, she would have recognized him.

Corwin was not present, and his absence destroyed the tiny thread
of hope she'd been unconsciously—and unbecomingly—husbanding. It
was not Corwin's company she desired now, but his huntbrother's,
Arlin. The absence of both men implied a request on the part of Lord
Grayton. Ser Gervanno was likewise absent, but that absence, at least,
was a comfort. The only one.

Lord Grayton, Huntsman of the Chamber, was not young; he had
the scars that years of service to both King and land brought. He had a
right to the colors he now wore.

He wore them, however, for a reason, and as if to underscore that
reason, he tendered her a bow. It was a bow meant, in its entirety, for
the Lady of the manor; Hunters in general did not otherwise note
proprieties better served in a drawing room.

"My apologies, Lady Maubreche," he said, as he rose from his bow.
"But I have been instructed to wait upon your reply." As he spoke, he

drew a scroll case from the folds of the jacket he wore, and held it out to her.

She was not surprised to see the seal it bore: the King's. Her hand was steady as she extended it. "Depending upon the nature of the message, such a reply might require some time."

He nodded, sliding hands behind his back. The dust of the road, and the effect of sun, had changed his complexion.

"If you will wait," she said, "please—avail yourself of Maubreche's hospitality. There are baths here, and beds; there is food and water. Your horse?"

"She has been stabled."

"Good. It is not yet dinner, but I would be pleased if you would join us in a few hours. Your dogs have been seen to in the kennels?"

Lord Grayton nodded. "Weslin sees to them now. I apologize for the lack of notice. I was sent with little warning from the King's City. I have come to speak to you about your son."

She did not stiffen. She did not tense. Nor did she ask him which son, as she had two; she knew. He knew that she knew. The time for tact had passed, although she had used every possible variant of it in the past several months. "Very well. Allow me to attend to the correspondence you were tasked with delivering." Turning to Camden, the Keeper of the Maubreche Keys, she nodded. "Your rooms will be prepared. Allow me to read the King's message, and to formulate a response at his command."

———

SHE DID NOT BREAK the seal of the case until she had almost reached the safe harbor of her study, such as it was. Having broken the seal, she intended to read what lay within it. Lord Grayton had issued no commands in the name of the King, but it wasn't necessary; he was to wait for a reply. A reply, therefore, had been demanded.

She thought she could guess what lay within this missive, and contemplated it in chaotic silence. Guessing, however, was not necessary. Better to face disaster, to understand its full extent, if one hoped— however slenderly—to mitigate its effect.

She did not, however, read the letter. She had not even managed to remove it from the case when she looked into her study, and froze.

"Lady Maubreche."

The Master Gardener stood to one side of her desk.

SHE WAS silent for one long beat; he did not belong in the manse, and certainly did not belong in her study.

"You have not come to the maze," he said. "And time grows short." One glance at the case in her hand caused his eyes to narrow. "And perhaps you will understand why, soon. Perhaps not; the ways of mortals are not our ways."

"Why are you here?"

"Have I not said that time grows short?" A hint of impatience marred his features. Those features now felt foreign, unfamiliar, as if the garden and the grounds had defined him for the entirety of her life; outside of that context she did not know who he was, did not recognize him.

The gardens did not define him now. He wore armor; he carried no sword. His hair—had she not seen his hair before?—was unbound. But no, no, she thought; she had.

He had come to the maze the first time the demons had attacked Maubreche. He had come to watch Stephen and his huntbrother fight. She had not forgotten. And yet, she had, as if memory could not comfortably contain the truth of what she had seen.

"Bredan no longer hunts the wilds of the King's preserve. What he built here I have maintained. What he desired, I have fulfilled. But the work left to be done, I cannot do while I remain." There was, about his voice, something that hinted at joy, and something that simultaneously hinted at sorrow, although she could not be certain, then or later, what it was. "It was never his intent that I remain here; it was a task offered me for the duration of my exile."

"Exile?"

"Even so, Lady Maubreche."

"And you now return home?"

"Ah, no. We believed, your god and I, that I would be summoned; that I would have no choice but to leave, for I have other duties to fulfill, and they are the reason for my very existence." He bowed. "But no such summons came, and I have waited, I have listened, I have prepared. I thought perhaps..." He fell silent. "It is never wise to anger your gods, Cynthia.

"He waits, now. Come to the maze."

She did not reply.

"Come to the maze," he repeated. "And allow me to take my leave of you—and your line—there. I ask it as boon, who has asked nothing of you or your kin."

CYNTHIA WONDERED, as she left both scroll and study behind, what it said of her that she refused to be moved by the compulsion laid upon her by a god, but could not refuse the request of a gardener. The fact that the gardener was in the study and the God—the God's influence— in the heart of the maze must tell in her favor, for she had no doubt at all that the Master Gardener could, should he so decide, forcibly remove her to the maze.

But she knew, as well, that he would not.

"If I had refused you, would it delay your departure?"

A smile touched his face. It was warm as sun in the bitter, bitter chill of winter. "You are no longer a mortal child, to be so bold with questions. Even were you, that child did not waste time asking questions to which she was certain she knew the answer."

Cynthia bowed her head, chagrined; she felt, for a moment, very much that long-ago girl. But time passed, will it or no.

"Lady Maubreche?"

Had she forgotten that she had guests? Ah. "Lord Grayton."

Lord Grayton's attention was all but fixed upon the Master Gardener.

Cynthia said, simply, "This is the man responsible for the creation —and the upkeep—of the maze for which Maubreche is known." She spoke softly, was aware that softly was the correct way to approach the older man. *Weslin, where are you?* The thought was sharp, but internal; she could recognize, in the sharpening of Lord Grayton's focus, the sudden thrum of his stillness, that he had called the Hunter's trance.

She heard a door open down the hall; she heard a heavy, rushed tread with which she was not instantly familiar. Weslin, Lord Grayton's huntbrother, joined Lord Grayton, looking harried.

"Apologies, Lady Maubreche," he said, tendering her an exact bow. Cynthia thought the bow was meant to hide his actual expression; it gave him a moment to compose it. He could not have failed to notice the Master Gardener.

"I have been given a task that I must complete before I join you both."

"And that task?" Lord Grayton all but demanded.

"To speak with Breodan." It was the Master Gardener who replied. "And all gathered within the confines of Breodanir must, in the end, obey the Hunter God."

He did not, she thought wryly, understand Hunter Lords. At all.

LORD GRAYTON'S wariness was slow to fade, but she watched it recede because he insisted—by presence alone—that he accompany her. Weslin's expression, while guarded, was also almost an open book; he was embarrassed, both for her and by Lord Grayton. This was blessedly familiar. How often had she seen the same semblance of frustrated composure on Arlin's face? Even Robart's younger huntbrother showed signs of it from time to time.

To be huntbrother was not, and had never been, an easy task.

She remembered—

She bowed her head a moment, although the path toward the maze was familiar enough that she did not halt their procession at all.

"Gods are not mortal parents," the Gardener said, divining— although it was not, in Cynthia's opinion, difficult—the direction her thoughts had taken.

She did not reply. At her back, the Hunter Lord and his hunt-brother had fallen silent, although Weslin's silence was the silence of awe and unease. Lord Grayton had seen this maze before, and even had he not, his personal dignity outweighed any expression of awe. Nothing would dwarf a man like Lord Grayton. His determination in that regard was second to none.

But that was unfair. She knew it. And she knew that, should she command it, he would remain in the manse. By law, she had that right. But society was not governed by law alone, and such a command would have ramifications in the near—and perhaps far—future. She had trodden the byways of Hunter pride with the care all such women must tread them. And she was tired of it.

Tired of it, and afraid, conversely, of its ending.

The Master Gardener did not appear to notice their companions. "I will miss this place," he said, his voice so soft it shouldn't have carried.

"Will you not return?"

"When one joins an army, one's intent is only partially relevant. But we go to war, Cynthia."

She felt an absurd comfort in her unadorned name.

"We?"

"We. The Breodani. Those who dwell in the kingdoms to the south, to the north, to the west. The small settlements you call the Free Towns. And the vast bulk of the Empire. Beyond the Empire, and beyond the Kingdoms, the people of the Dominion have already begun to engage in their dangerous, necessary skirmishes. If there are mortals anywhere who have not been touched by the shadow of war, it signifies little; those shadows will give way to reality, and the truth of what they face.

"Understand: a god walks this plane."

"And he is your enemy."

"He is the only enemy." The Gardener's voice was cold, then. Cold, hard; he lifted his chin and gazed to the north, as if his vision could reveal what Cynthia's could not. And she was grateful for the lack.

"And your role?"

"I have never been leader," he replied. "Nor am I leader now. But even those of us who cannot command vast armies have their roles to play, and those roles might turn the tide of a battle we cannot avoid."

"Can we win it?"

Lord Grayton cleared his throat. "Lady Maubreche, to whom do you speak?"

She glanced at the Master Gardener; his lips were turned up in a thin, wintry smile.

"My apologies, Lord Grayton."

"Apologies are irrelevant and unnecessary. I desire some explanation; it is the reason I was chosen to deliver the King's message."

Not here, she thought. But she had long since learned that proper time and proper place were often the pipe dreams of a weary heart, a way of setting aside responsibility and unpleasant duty. Life did not, had not, guaranteed enough respite that she could choose all of the parameters of an encounter, and even when she had, those plans went awry more often than not.

"I have not yet read the King's message. I am certain, once I have—

and once I have had time to compose a considered reply—we might discuss its contents."

Weslin winced, the shift in expression slight and easily banished—but not, obviously, easily suppressed. His eyes, more than his Hunter Lord's, made clear to Cynthia that Lord Grayton was party to the message he carried in some fashion.

Hunter Lords, she thought.

In the distance, she heard the sound of a dog's voice; a lymer's call. Her own dogs—ah, no, the Maubreche dogs of both generations—were with Corwin, Robart, and Stephen.

Weslin's flinch returned and settled more deeply into the lines of a pained grimace.

"I would not advise that here," the Master Gardener said, before Cynthia could frame far more politic words.

"They are his dogs," she said quickly. "He is their master. They will do nothing at all without his permission."

The Master Gardener did not look away from Lord Grayton. Weslin did; he met Cynthia's gaze with his own, and whatever he sought there, he found. It did not entirely calm him.

"Lady Maubreche," the Gardener finally said, breaking an increasingly brittle silence. She thought him finished, but no, that would have been too simple. "Lord Grayton. Understand that you are now walking upon lands blessed by Bredan. It is here, in the heart of this living tapestry, that the voice of your god is clearest.

"Understand, as well, that Lord Stephen," he said, placing emphasis on a title that Stephen had not, in the eyes of the King, earned, "is Bredan's only living son. If you wish to speak of his disposition, of his place, of his duties, I would advise you—with as much emphasis as you will tolerate—that this is not the place to do so. Lady Maubreche is a Hunter, at heart. She serves the Hunter God. But she is mortal, as are you. What she might accept in the privacy of her study—or yours, should you possess one—is not the province of the God you serve." Emphasis on the last word.

"She has been called to the maze. If you wish, you may allow her to bespeak her god in private, but if you are wise, you will allow her to choose the words and have that discussion without interruption. Gods are not mortals; they are not mortal parents. But as any parent, they value their offspring."

Cynthia was half afraid that Lord Grayton would tell the Master

Gardener that he had no business—as servant—offering advice of any kind to a Lord. To her relief, he bowed head a moment, an acknowledgement that did not require the framing of tactful words.

But the lack of words made clear—if further clarity were needed—that the King's message, the King's chosen messenger, was concerned with her son.

Stephen.

How much more, she thought, containing the bitterness and the echoes of a pain that never quite died into stillness, *will you take from me? How much more will you destroy?*

Mist rolled in from all directions; she lost sight of her feet, which had been easily seen a moment before as she bowed her head. She looked up; met the flashing silver of her gardener's eyes. No, not hers, she thought. He had never been hers. But he had been a part of her home from the moment she first drew breath. He had been part of Maubreche for the entirety of her line's existence, a constant in war, in peace, in struggle, and in times of plenty.

He would leave. He would leave Maubreche.

And the God said, *Yes.*

THE MISTS ROSE, obscuring boots, grass, and the fountain that lay at the heart of the maze. It obscured the last of the hedges, the last lesson of history, near or far, before that history opened into the maze heart. She could see the Gardener; she could no longer see Lord Grayton or Weslin, which was a small mercy.

A larger mercy would not be granted, and she did not beg. She understood what the God could, or could not, achieve, and gods were not mortals; they did not have mortal hearts. But she watched, now. She waited.

The Hunter God emerged from the rising mists. He was the shape of a man, but antlered, and far taller than any man Cynthia had ever met. She could not clearly see his eyes, but his eyes were not all of one thing; there was a constant, subtle shift in shape and color. The antlers, however, were solid; the height of his shoulders, the length of his arms; his feet were obscured as were her own.

He shocked her. He bowed.

She was left wordless with sudden fear.

"You did not come," he said, when he rose. "I called. I would have offered warning."

She found her voice, then. "Would the warning change anything?"

"No, as you are aware. I am in my realm, now; you are in yours. There are rules and covenants that bind us."

She swallowed. "You are the God of Covenants and their bindings. If the god you do not name now walks this plane, why does he still live?"

"He did not bind himself to this covenant. Had he, we would not be here now. He walks. Standing here, I can feel his passage across the frozen wastes in the North. We have time, Cynthia, but even in mortal parlance, it is scant."

She drew breath. Exhaled. Straightened her shoulders. Her hands were fists by her side, but she could not prevent that. "Why," she demanded—and it was a demand, not a simple question; her tone was not that of a supplicant. "Why have you not accepted Stephen's oath?"

"Have I not?"

"He is not Hunter Lord; Nenyane is not huntbrother. In the past— before your return to your own godly lands—the oath was simple; it was a rite of passage, no more. But no less."

"Oaths were not meant to be rites of passage."

The ground beneath her feet rumbled. She felt it, and felt the fear of it settle into the pit of clenched stomach. But if fear of the God existed —and it must, in this place—there were other fears that were more profound, more visceral.

"Yes. You fear for our son."

My son. *My* son.

"He is not a child, even by mortal reckoning, and the oaths sworn— or not sworn—are not, in the end, my choice. They are his. He would swear the Hunter's Oath—and has. It is not the Hunter's Oath that prevents him from the title you desire on his behalf. It is the huntbroth-er's oath."

"Nenyane won't swear it?"

"She will. Stephen will not accept it."

Silence, then.

"He will not allow her to enter that covenant."

Had Corwin been right, all those difficult years ago? Had he been right to suggest a normal huntbrother—a boy such as Mark?

"If it eases you at all, no. Stephen will accept no huntbrother but

Nenyane, and even were he willing to do so, he will not allow the hunt-brother's oath to be uttered in a fashion that is binding."

"But—but *why?*"

"He is your son as much as he is mine—and he understands both why you named him, and why you lost the man for whom he is name-sake. I killed Stephen of Elseth because he fulfilled his oath. And I would have killed him, in the end, had he not."

Silence, then. Profound and terrible.

"They will call for him, Cynthia. They will call. If you do not heed that call, I might protect him here until the world ends—but I, too, have made oaths and vows. You might break your vows and survive, if they were not made to me or to Stephen; I cannot. My very nature would destroy me.

"The King will call him, and he must obey. The Priests will bespeak him. They will cajole and demand—as Corwin himself as done, in your absence. If Nenyane makes the huntbrother's oath, I will accept it. I have counseled Stephen; I have asked that he do what must be done.

"But I am parent, not master. The compulsion to obey me, for those who bear my blood, is strong. He will no longer speak to me, even as you speak now; he has become a wall. And we do not have time, in the end, for that wall. Lord Grayton understands that Stephen is important to the Hunter God. He understands that Stephen is important to all of Breodanir, and possibly beyond.

"He does not understand that Stephen can be both of those things without being a Hunter Lord; no more does the King of these lands, or his august Queen. They will need strong Hunters, now more than ever; the boundaries between the wilderness and the tame preserve of mortal lands have faltered. You have seen the results. Understand that in a decade, there will be no mortal land left.

"Regardless, my Hunter Lords are necessary, now. And no Lord of power, or possible power, can be overlooked."

THE MISTS of the Between receded, and with them, the God, the father of her oldest child. The father that had scarred her son for life.

She stood alone, confined by anger, by resentment, and by duty to that god, to these lands, to the enemies of the Breodani against which the God stood. Standing farther away were Lord Grayton and Weslin,

utterly silent. If they had bespoken gods in the Between before, they
had not done it often enough that the remnants of awe did not cling.

Cynthia had.

She turned to the two men. "I request a moment of privacy," she
said, voice soft. "The matters that brought you here will then be
addressed."

They glanced at the Master Gardener, but the resentment in Lord
Grayton's eyes had faded; it would not return again before this day was
done. They saw Cynthia, for the moment, as the scion of Maubreche,
the true blood heir to the family closest to Breodan. The King was
distant, loyalty to his commands loosened for the moment.

She knew it would not last.

But many things were ending on this terrible, quiet day. Many
things. She turned to face the Master Gardener. His eyes were silver;
his hair, platinum. He wore tunic over mail armor, and that armor
seemed almost to glow. Emotionally, she could not imagine that the man
standing before her had ever lowered himself to wield gardening shears,
although intellectually she knew he had.

He bowed to her, then. It was a perfect bow; it implied fealty and
obedience—neither of which had been on display earlier. It depleted
hope, and she had so little of it left.

"It has been an honor to serve Maubreche," he said, as he rose.

So very little. She looked at the maze, formed by the hedges he had
so carefully sculpted. They would be, in time—scant time, she thought
—simple hedges laid out in the pattern of a maze; the wonder and awe
they had inspired, both within Maubreche and its many visitors, would
be lost to time and imperfect memory.

"It has been my honor to serve your father, and his father; it has
been my honor to serve you, mother of Stephen of Maubreche, the last
of the foretellings."

"Where will you now go?"

His smile was almost gentle, but his expression was cool, remote.
"Where would you have me go, Lady Maubreche?"

"I would have you stay, if it were my preference that guided you. It
is not, and we both know it. If I have been your titular lord, you have
never served me."

He shook his head, offering her a slender smile. "That is both true
and untrue. Five generations ago, your forebears would have been
shocked at the respect I have shown you. We are both what we are,

Cynthia. And we both have duties to which we must attend, no matter our desire."

"Will you tell me that this is somehow your desire?" She glanced at the grounds, as if they were almost irrelevant.

"Would you believe me if I did?"

"To my knowledge, Master Gardener, you have never lied to me; lies are oft political or social necessities, and you have never been beholden to either."

"In that you are wrong—but the laws to which I am beholden were ancient ere you were born. I would stay here," he continued. "I would stay and husband my creation, negotiating with nature as I always have. But it is time. It is past time. I offer you a boon for the years you have allowed the tending of this maze, these grounds; they were a purpose when purpose was needed."

She met his gaze, held it, and looked away. "I want my son to be safe." Her words, her voice, was low.

"Yes. Understand—if yesterday's events do not make this clear to you—that he will not be safe in Maubreche for much longer."

"Tell me that he will be safer in the King's City, if you can."

The Master Gardener shook his head, his expression grave. "Would you have me lie, now, at the end of my service? The time for safety has passed. There is nowhere Stephen will be safer than in Maubreche. But if he remains in Maubreche, the safety of a far greater number of people will be at far greater risk.

"They, too, face danger—and face it unaware. He is Bredan's son. What he can do, he must do." He bowed head a moment, and breeze ruffled strands of his hair. "But I will do what I can to defend him until he realizes what he must do, must become. I will travel with Stephen and Nenyane; my presence will break no Hunter laws, no oaths.

"More than that, I cannot offer."

"It is not a boon you grant to me," she said, for she had always been shrewd. "It was what you intended since you first announced your retirement."

The Master Gardener nodded, the smile across his lips warmer and more genuine. "You have always been insightful. I am not sure that has been a kindness to you. But I require permission to travel as part of Maubreche."

Cynthia considered the man before her dispassionately. She had not seen him fight, but knew he could wield sword as well as Nenyane—

because Nenyane knew it. Nenyane granted the Master Gardener a subconscious respect, and always had, although she had been suspicious of him — as of everything — in her first year as huntbrother.

But he served Breodan, he served the God of the Covenant. He wanted what the god wanted, not what Cynthia wanted.

What, then, did she want? Ah, it was hard. What her son wanted was to be free of the curse of his blood. Had he not been god-born, he would *be* the heir; he would be Lord Stephen. He would perhaps not be the son Corwin had expected, but he would be the son of Maubreche, and that would be enough.

She could not have that, or rather, Stephen could not. But she wished — how she wished — that his very nature did not cause such stark divisions within him. He could not change the circumstance of his birth. Nor could Cynthia.

Perhaps what she wanted for him was peace — the peace of acceptance, no matter how bitter it might appear at a distance. One could not live peacefully for long when at war with one's self. One could not live peacefully regardless when the god they did not name stirred in the distant North, readying his army, but Cynthia had learned, early in her tenure, that when facing external conflicts, internal conflicts had to be kept at bay. She had been older than Stephen when that lesson had become firmly entrenched, but she understood why, in Stephen's case, such resolution remained out of reach.

She exhaled. "I will give you the requisite permission, the requisite assignment of duty. Protect my son where protection is possible."

The Master Gardener nodded.

"But I will ask a boon that you have said you are willing to grant. Bring him home. Bring him safely home."

"I will do everything in my power to do so." He bowed again, and this time did not rise until she commanded it. "I watched you grow, Cynthia. You were always willful, but you were observant, intelligent, strategic. You understood where the boundaries of your duties and responsibilities lay, and you did not try to step over those boundaries. But you were, in your quiet way, bold, and you were beset by curiosity. That has not changed.

"I will miss you."

CYNTHIA CONVENED a meeting with her family in the austere confines of the audience chamber in which the citizens of Maubreche pleaded their legal cases before her. She knew how to be impartial; she'd had much practice. She could set aside the personal weight and burden of her own concerns. Here, in this room, she was Lady Maubreche, arbiter of the justice offered to the citizens of Maubreche. Not even Corwin could gainsay her here — nor did he try.

She knew, however, that were he to make the attempt, it would be on a day like this one.

Ser Gervanno had been asked to join them for the evening meal; she had something to discuss with him as well. If Breodan had not mentioned him by name, what he had spoken of included Gervanno: demons and the changing of the landscape from the familiar to the dangerously foreign.

But he was not in the audience chamber, nor would he be, and she had much to discuss with her family. Lord Grayton, paler than he had been when they had first met, had retreated with Weslin for the time being; they would join the family for dinner when this discussion was over.

Stephen and Nenyane arrived first, and took positions in front of the throne but as far apart from each other as manners allowed; clearly they had not yet resolved their argument. Cynthia was not unaccustomed to this; her husband and his huntbrother sometimes took time to resolve their differences as well, and they were fully adult by any measure.

Robart and Mark came next, but they stood together, nearer Stephen than Nenyane, which was wise. Stephen's control of his anger was generally far better than Nenyane's. Robart was very like his father.

Robart would be heir. Younger son, he was Hunter Lord, although just newly.

Stephen was not. She accepted that Stephen would never be. The acceptance had come slowly and with pain; he was an excellent Hunter in every possible way. But the earliest of the oaths that Hunter and huntbrother swore, he would not swear. She had hoped that would change with time; she had no such hope now.

She met Stephen's gaze and held it; his expression was grave. He understood what Lord Grayton's visit to Maubreche meant. So, too, did Nenyane. Cynthia could guess what their argument had been about; she'd heard it so often as they aged.

No, if there was difficulty, she expected it from only one person. She looked away from her sons as the door opened, and that person entered the chambers. He marched to the throne, Arlin behind him.

Without preamble, Cynthia said, "The King has summoned Stephen and his huntbrother to the King's City." Before Corwin could speak, she raised hand. "He will be going without Lord or Lady Maubreche, and he will remain in the King's City for a length of time not to exceed three months."

"Pardon?"

"Lord Grayton's message was quite clear. Any hope I have of failing to understand what the missive contained was removed by the clarity of the directive. The King is concerned about Stephen's status. He wishes to have our son instructed in the hopes of making clear just how dire the need for Hunter Lords in the kingdom has become."

"He has passed every test of competence, every test of note, every hunt required," Corwin snapped.

"He has not. The earliest and the most important of the ceremonies has never been completed."

"It doesn't *matter*."

"It matters to the King. We rule Maubreche, but Maubreche is part of Breodanir—unless you have some foolish notion of seceding."

Corwin fell silent. The King was a good ruler, and the kingdom, well-governed. Aside from this one blight in his life, Corwin had few complaints. "I will accompany him."

"You will not. If you wish to come up with a pretext for visiting the Master of the Game, you must do so with subtlety. The King has made it quite plain that Stephen is not to be present as a guest. This is not a diplomatic mission. He is not there to plead Maubreche's case in any fashion; he is there to plead his own. If you choose to accompany our son, you do so in direct conflict with the King's politely written command."

Corwin fell silent. "Take the dogs," he finally said to his son.

Cynthia's hands tightened. "This is not the Sacred Hunt."

"He is a Hunter," Corwin replied, with both ice and heat. Stephen had not participated in the Sacred Hunt. He could not. By law, he was not yet Hunter Lord.

Arlin stepped toward them both, but kept his hands firmly entwined behind his back. Cynthia felt a surge of affection for this man, who would always be torn between the two people he loved most in this life.

It was Nenyane who spoke the words that bubbled beneath all of the surfaces made of pain and anger—or perhaps just pain. People expressed pain in their own ways, after all.

"He is not a Hunter Lord. If he were, we wouldn't be forced to leave."

Stephen winced. "Nenyane—"

"No. It's the truth. He doesn't have the obligation to take his hunting pack with him—I'm not sure he even has the right. Until he is fully Hunter Lord, he cannot choose his pack; the dogs belong to you."

"He is the *Hunter's son*," Lord Maubreche snapped, his jaw clenched so rigidly it was a wonder any words had escaped at all.

Cynthia bowed head for a long moment. Lord Maubreche was Stephen's father in any way that mattered. Any way except blood. He did not often refer to the God whose blood Stephen shared, the blood that had been the cause of so much conflict. That Corwin could say so now meant he was standing at the edge of his parental cliff. This son, this god-born child, was Corwin's, had been Corwin's, from the moment he had allied himself with Maubreche, thereby accepting all of the responsibilities that came with that power.

She would have stopped him if she could; she accepted that she could not. And she looked at her son—hers—to see his shuttered expression, the paleness as color was leeched from compressed lips. Corwin was not the only person who avoided all mention of Stephen's blood father.

Corwin was not obliged to be publicly deferential to one of his children—and Nenyane was very much that, huntbrother or no. "He is the Hunter's only son. He will not go to the King's City and stand before the Master of the Game without his dogs."

Nenyane, Cynthia thought bitterly, was, in most of the ways that mattered, the Hunter of the pair. She had the temperament, and less desire to control displays of annoyance than even Corwin on his worst day. Cynthia had once thought that Nenyane would mature out of it, or mature into greater social control. That had never happened. If she was to be sent to the King's City with Stephen, it likely never would.

"They're not legally his dogs!" Nenyane had never loved the dogs the way the hunters did. It wasn't in her.

"He chose them. They chose him. They obey Stephen above all others. They are his in any way that counts."

Stephen lifted hand and placed it, firmly, on his huntbrother's shoulder.

"No, Corwin," Lady Maubreche said quietly, coming to someone's rescue. Stephen's, perhaps. Nenyane's. Even Corwin, for whom this conversation was nothing but frustration and pain. "Laws matter. In the King's City, any dogs that accompany Stephen are not Stephen's; they are yours. Hunter Lords do not travel without their dogs. Stephen, be he Breodan's offspring or no, is *not* Hunter Lord."

"In every way but one, he is. You haven't seen him hunt. You don't understand. But I have, Cynthia. I have, and I am Hunter Lord. There is no dog alive that would not heed his commands—even mine.

"The King is not pleased, no. We knew he wouldn't be. If for no other reason, he *must* have dogs of his own."

Nenyane was not convinced. "You aren't being called to the King's City. We are. The plans made for us there are made in their entirety because *someone* will not accept the huntbrother's oath. The King knows this. The Hunter Lords know it. The dogs probably know it as well. Since the reason we've been summoned is the lack of the oath itself, the dogs fly in the face of the Hunter laws that somehow govern this kingdom. We can't take dogs."

It was Mark who said, "You just don't want them because you don't like them."

Arlin winced.

Nenyane, however, did not. She turned to Mark. "They take too much time and too much care. We are not going there to hunt. We're going to—" she glanced at Stephen. "Actually, I have no idea why we're going. I think it's a waste of time. We could have solved this years ago."

"The King's commands are never a waste of time," Lady Maubreche said. Quickly, too, as if to forestall Lord Maubreche's agreement.

"You haven't observed many rulers in your life, have you?" Nenyane countered.

Stephen tightened the hand on Nenyane's shoulder. "It's irrelevant," he told his huntbrother. "We're not going to see other rulers; we are going at the pleasure of the King. Unless we spend the next few days doing nothing but argue, in which case we're going exactly nowhere."

Nenyane was very much Hunter Lord in temperament. Stephen was not. The reversal of roles discomfited his father. His mother, however, had always accepted it. She had known instantly what Nenyane's opinion would be, but Nenyane was not Lord Maubreche, and her word, not command. It wasn't Nenyane she had to convince, but Corwin, Lord Maubreche.

Cynthia watched Arlin for a long beat; his expression and the posture he adopted were often a weathervane. Ah. She wouldn't succeed. Not today.

So much pain here, so much regret, so much anger and resentment, parceled as they were between the various people she loved. Stephen would feel, watching them all, that he was the cause of it. Had always been the cause of it, even before his birth. Cynthia hated it. Hated it, and as all hated things she could not personally change, accepted it grudgingly.

Nenyane would not budge without Stephen's intervention. Corwin would not budge. Arlin had no purchase; Corwin's pain, his fury, were too deep.

All of the Maubreche family looked to Stephen now, even his mother.

———

"I WILL TAKE FOUR DOGS," he said. "Four. It is not a full hunting pack. Traveling with four dogs does not imply that I believe myself to be Hunter Lord. But..." He trailed off.

"But in Maubreche, at least," Nenyane said, taking up the words he could not bring himself to say, "he is acknowledged Hunter Lord. The villagers use the title that he has not, by the King's law, earned. And he told you not to allow this when you encouraged them," she added, her voice sharpening, "He said it would cause trouble in future."

"Stephen didn't care about the title. He *tried* to stop the villagers from even using it. There was no way the King wouldn't eventually hear or know. And it was wrong."

"He is a Hunter Lord in every possible way —" Corwin began.

Nenyane cut him off; she was the only other person who could.

"He has the abilities of the Hunter Lords, yes. But oaths exist for a reason and he hasn't sworn them. It was wrong. Let us go to the King's City. Stephen has to make his peace with his reluctance — and when we return, we'll own the title properly. He'll take four dogs. I'd prefer zero. You'd prefer eight. But he's right. Eight is a minimal hunting pack. It will send the wrong message."

"He has sworn his oaths to the Hunter God. The Hunter God is the arbiter of his value, his worth. And he is of great value to the *God we all serve.*"

"The oaths he has—or has not—sworn are personal and private. They define specific duties he has undertaken. They are *not* the oaths the Hunter Lords swear to the Master of the Game, and you already know this. This isn't about his *merit*. He has that. We all know it. This is about the law. The oaths of the Hunter Lords are deeply important to Bredan.

"And you are not the King. You are not the God's Priest. You are Hunter Lord, yes. But you don't get to decide what is—or is not— acceptable in any lands but your own." And even in his own, her tone implied, he was on unstable ground. "I don't agree with your position. But I don't agree with Stephen's, either. We could dispense with this. We could have dispensed with this years ago. And now we no longer have that option.

"We will therefore go to the King's City with four dogs, which will not insult the King and his priests, and will not offend Maubreche."

Corwin's silence was oppressive.

Nenyane, however, did not seem concerned. She turned to Lady Maubreche.

Cynthia nodded. "Four dogs," she agreed. Her tone made clear that the agreement was grudging; it was a compromise, not an ideal solution. She glanced, once, at her husband.

Lord Maubreche, Stephen's father, nodded brusquely, his hands in fists.

IF GERVANNO HAD HAD any polite and reasonable method of avoiding dinner that evening, he would have taken it. Had he been a guard, he would have arranged to have his duty overlap the dinner. There were many polite, and therefore safe, ways to avoid accepting an invitation that was almost certainly offered out of the obligation of the duties of a host, but none were available to him.

He had spent the day traversing the grounds, the mutt at his side. He had also been offered a tour of the manse, which he accepted; tours were not a place where speech or conversation was demanded, unless the person responsible for such tour was the ruler of the lands.

But there was a distinct downturn in the mood of the various servants whose path he crossed. They were polite to a fault in his presence, of course, but it was the non-verbal cues he observed. That and the whispers that sprang up as he passed by. The servants were worried.

Lord Grayton's presence had been noted, and it had cast a pall over Maubreche.

Gervanno had been offered clothing suitable for dining with people of power, but it was Northern clothing. He accepted it, however, uncertain whether the offer was laced—as such offers would have been in his homeland—with subtle command. He could guess that Lady Maubreche was not concerned about the state of the clothing he did possess; he doubted—highly—that Lord Maubreche even noticed. He had been called into their presence prior to this, and he had noted no condescension, no judgment, from any who dwelled within the Maubreche manor.

Lord Grayton, therefore, was a man whose opinion mattered to Maubreche. A man of power in this foreign land, whose rules of power Gervanno was still struggling to learn.

Servants came to aid him in the fitting of the Northern clothing. Gervanno did notice the fabric, the stitching, the thickness of the cloth, and the fit of it; Evaro had been at pains to teach the caravan guards which wagons were to be given defensive precedence should bandits attack.

He was not surprised when someone came to his door to lead him to the dining room; he was surprised when he opened the door to Stephen of Maubreche. His huntbrother was not in evidence. He offered the youth a nod, and Stephen returned it.

"You will have heard that we have an important guest," Stephen said, in Torra. "He was sent by the Lord of the lands—the equivalent of your Tyr'agar. He is highly valued by the King, and he's delivered a command to Maubreche that cannot be denied."

Gervanno waited.

"Lady Maubreche feels that your mission will be best served in the King's City." He hesitated, and then added, "My huntbrother and I will be traveling to that city very shortly."

"When?"

"In three days at the latest. We would leave at once, but as we are expected to remain in the city for a few months, some packing is required. Will you accompany us on the road?"

This was more than Gervanno had hoped for. He nodded immediately.

"Nenyane, myself, and the Master Gardener will be traveling with four of the Maubreche dogs. Will you travel with yours?"

Gervanno blinked. "The dog is not mine; he found me—or I found him—when the road went strange. I'm not sure who his owner is."

Stephen shrugged, a half-smile on his lips. "He believes his master is you," he offered.

"And the concerns of the owner?"

"I don't think they matter. No one in Brookton claimed ownership of the dog, and the dog seems to follow you. If it's not clear, the Breodani are a people with a high respect for dogs."

"Your dogs and that dog are almost different species."

"Yes. But yours is still a dog. Think on it. We can kennel your dog with ours, but yours is small enough it might be acceptable to innkeepers on the road."

"You'll stay in inns?"

"That's our intent. It will depend on Nenyane." He turned and began to walk—slowly—down the hall. Gervanno fell in beside him. "Nenyane is sensitive to the demonic and demonic influence; if she feels our presence will jeopardize civilians, we'll camp instead."

"I'm accustomed to camping."

Stephen nodded. "Lord Grayton can be imperious, and he has very little in the way of humor, but the King respects him, and Lord Maubreche respects him as well. He does not speak Torra, and if you are willing to accept a translator, you might be more comfortable speaking in your native tongue."

"I can speak the merchant tongue well enough."

"Yes. The choice is, of course, yours."

Much could be forgiven a foreigner with no knowledge of the customs of power. Gervanno nodded and continued to follow Stephen.

LORD GRAYTON WAS NOT MAGNIFICENTLY CLOTHED, in Gervanno's opinion—an opinion that was largely the result of travel alongside Evaro and Sylvia. But his posture spoke of certainty; he was a man who was accustomed to wielding both power and the respect that power should command. He was not a large man, but the confidence he radiated more than compensated for lack of physical size.

He had been seated to one side of Lady Maubreche; in the Dominion that would have been the place of honor. Across the large table from Lord Grayton sat Lord Maubreche, his huntbrother at his side. Gervanno now understood that all Hunters had huntbrothers; he assumed the man beside Lord Grayton fulfilled that role here.

Beside that man sat Stephen, and to Stephen's side, Nenyane; beside Arlin was Robart, the second son, who would be styled par in the South, and to his side, Mark. Gervanno was left with a seat at the foot of the table; it was the correct Southern position for a man of low birth who had nonetheless been called to grace the presence of his lord.

But the food was not Southern food; nor was it common Northern fare. He could not discern which foods were meant to be eaten by hand, and which by the various utensils that girded the sides of the plates like weapons—weapons that could only hurt the wielder in this specific case. His lessons for travel on the merchant roads had not covered the etiquette of the powerful; not here, not in the Empire. In the Free Towns, power was vastly more subtle, but it was also harder to offend.

As he had always done, he looked to others for cues. He watched how they ate, what utensils they chose, what they ate first. Nenyane, however, he passed over. She was a force of nature, a natural talent so rare it was clear that all behavior was tolerated. Gervanno was not, and would never be, her equal. She was also part of this family. The Breodani did not seem to value blood ties above all else; she was clearly kin, a difficult daughter to the ruling clan.

Stephen, however, seemed to understand that he served as silent guide here. He was slow and methodical, his gestures and utensil choices very easy to follow.

Dinner conversation was extremely polite. Lord Grayton was mostly silent; he did ask Stephen a few questions, but kept most of his conversation confined to the head of the table. Servants came with food, and servants cleared the food that remained uneaten when it was time for the next round of dishes; Gervanno ate all of his food, in part because he didn't wish to offend the hospitality offered by his hosts, and in part because it was food and food shouldn't go to waste.

He didn't speak a word until Lady Maubreche looked down the length of the table at him.

"Ser Gervanno, we are grateful that you chose to join us. We owe you a great debt for your intervention in Brookton, and it is an embarrassment to our house that we must ask a further favor of you." She spoke entirely in Torra.

It became clear that Lord Grayton's huntbrother understood it, given his reaction; Lord Grayton merely looked mildly irritated.

"I will do my best to undertake any favor you wish to ask," he replied with care. He was grateful that it was Stephen who had come to guide him to the hall.

"I have arranged for a meeting between you and a member of the Order of Knowledge in the King's City. I will give you a letter and a token by which your identity will be known. You have information of import to convey to them, and I believe it in the best interests of the Breodani that you do so in haste."

He swallowed. He now had Lord Grayton's attention.

"I am uncertain of the customs of the Dominion," she continued, "and I hope you will forgive me if I overstep the bounds of a host. We would like to hire you to guard the small party that will be leaving Maubreche in three — or four — days."

Lord Grayton frowned at the word *four*, but said nothing.

"We will negotiate your fees on the morrow; I will prepare all the documents you might require after that. If you choose not to accept employ, I will still furnish the necessary introductory paperwork — your news is of great import to the Order of Knowledge; it is not of lesser import to the Breodani. Even if your story is not delivered directly to the King himself, know that the King will be grateful that your first impulse was to carry word of demonic attack — within the borders of Breodanir — to those with the power and knowledge to make use of it."

She then turned to Lord Grayton, lowering her voice.

Gervanno was left with the uneasy specter of future negotiation. He had negotiated his employ with the caravan, but he had done so after talking to two acquaintances who had served Evaro in previous merchant missions. He had never negotiated in a circumstance such as this: she was lord of these lands.

He was not even one of her people.

The lords of the Dominion saw to the housing and pay of the warriors who served them; the prices were fixed and men did not haggle. Not in such situations. Lady Maubreche, however, seemed to expect something along those lines. He wondered, then, what service *meant* to those who dwelled within the borders of Breodanir. It could not be a country without soldiers of its own.

But he was landless, now, his home abandoned when he had chosen to take to the road to avoid demonic wars and pointless death. Although Lady Maubreche did not look his way again, he bowed head to her.

THE GARDENS at night were both more impressive and less. Gervanno, unable to sleep, had at last escaped the confines of his very Northern room, headed down the stairs, and out the back doors — pausing only to glance at his reflection in the ostentation of glass that stretched from floor to ceiling.

In the night, with moon providing most of the illumination, his eyes adjusted to the silver-grey in which moonlight had dyed most of the greenery. The mutt came with him; he had been allowed to share his room. This wasn't Gervanno's desire, but Lady Maubreche had offered it as a kindness, even if she knew the dog wasn't legally his.

The dog, however, was happy to be outdoors, even in moonlight. His examination of the various hedges and plants seemed more thorough, but also more playful; he went and came back, tracing an oddly wide oval around Gervanno's movements.

He was not surprised to see Stephen of Maubreche in the same gardens, although Stephen's much more impressive dogs were nowhere in sight. Nor was his huntbrother. Had Gervanno better night vision, he would have withdrawn to allow the young man his privacy. But the dog apparently considered Stephen of Maubreche another interesting bush, and Stephen recognized the dog.

He turned to Gervanno; in the shallows of night, Gervanno couldn't immediately see his expression. But he could see the clear outline of posture, and the way that posture shifted upon realization that company — no doubt unwanted — had arrived.

"You couldn't sleep either?" Stephen asked, opening conversation to prevent awkwardness on the part of the interloper.

Gervanno nodded; it was safest. "And you?"

"I've seen these grounds and variations on these gardens, for the entirety of my life. I don't remember a time when they didn't exist."

Ah. "The Master Gardener will accompany us to the King's City. I believe he intends to remain by your side while you reside there."

Stephen shook his head. "He can accompany us; he won't be allowed to remain by our side. The dogs, yes. But not a guard. Not in the King's residence."

That made clear that Gervanno would not be allowed to remain, either. He was surprised at the feeling of disappointment; in the South, the lords—and their sons—were escorted by cerdan as a matter of course. No lords divested themselves of their surest guards.

But Gervanno was not Maubreche cerdan, if they even had them. He would not be considered one of those trusted guards, regardless. The Master Gardener, however, would, and he, too was to be denied.

"I'm grateful that you've accepted my mother's offer," Stephen continued, the words shorn of both pride and distance. Although the light was scant, Gervanno no longer needed it. He understood the tone, and the vulnerability that was only ever exposed during the Lady's time.

"If the decision were in my hands," he replied softly, "I would be honored to serve Maubreche." To his surprise, he meant it. "I do not know why you are being summoned to the King's City. But if there is conflict between your family and the Tyr'agar, and you have doubts, I have none."

Stephen turned to face Gervanno.

"My father would have approved of you. And if he was less set in his ways, of your mother—women do not rule in the Dominion. He would have trusted your lord. If you find yourself in difficulty with your Tyr, I will remain in the city. Reach out to me; perhaps I can help."

The words left his mouth and hung in the air; they were followed immediately by internal condemnation. Help? How? Had he not survived the demons because he had been paralyzed by fear? He tensed; the dog came to butt the side of his left leg, as if he had spoken the words aloud.

"Thank you, Ser Gervanno," Stephen said. His soft voice contained genuine gratitude, and that gratitude stilled the voices the demons had left him.

CHAPTER FIVE

S teel rang against steel in the courtyard before the watchful eyes of
the sole Maubreche guard, hired—somewhat ridiculously—to
protect Stephen and Nenyane of Maubreche. Were Gervanno serving
as cerdan in the Dominion, his presence would have made far more
sense—but only by the side of at least three other men determined to
perform the same duty. Lack of cerdan was a symbol of either overweening confidence or absolute trust.

Lady Maubreche, however, had openly offered the worry of a mother's heart; she intended her children to have at least a modicum of
protection. Gervanno winced as a blade went flying; he did not otherwise move.

Apparently, the common courtyard of an inn was an acceptable drill
yard, as long as one's practice didn't range across the drive. Perhaps it
was only acceptable if the guest was the son of a ruling Hunter Lord;
Gervanno had not seen any other people attempt to use the courtyard in
such a fashion. He was grateful for his travel with Evaro and Sylvia; he
had learned much of the various customs of the lowborn and highborn
throughout the North.

Maubreche dignity required not only four dogs as opposed to the eight Gervanno had been informed were a full hunting pack, but apparently a carriage as well. Carriages required horses, and the one used by the two Maubreche children—larger than those that might be used in the Dominion—required four.

Gervanno approved of the Maubreche stables, although his opinion had not been asked, and he was not fool enough to offer it. They treated their dogs better than they treated their horses, though; Gervanno's father would have been outraged by their foreign ignorance. Since they treated their horses *well*, Gervanno had no complaints—but a family that prized dogs over horses would have sat very, very poorly with Gervanno's father.

His father, Devarro di'Sarrado, wouldn't have liked their weapons, either; he had a distrust of double-edged weapons, and considered the lack of the longer, curved edge graceless. Training in double-edged swords therefore had come on the field, away from the watchful and irritable eyes of his father. Gervanno would never be an expert in that weapon, but he recognized mastery, regardless.

"You seem taken with Nenyane," the Master Gardener said. Gervanno had not asked the man's name, and the man had not offered it.

"As do you," he replied. He did not consider himself equal to any of the people he now traveled with; the closest perhaps was Stephen of Maubreche, but Stephen was a powerful lord's son. No good had ever come from familiarity with the scions of the powerful, but he found it hard to keep his distance from Stephen.

The mutt barked at his shin, or perhaps the insect that had landed on it. Stephen's dogs were both bored and silent; they watched their master without apparent concern—but without resentment, either.

Stephen and Nenyane occupied the courtyard of the inn at which they had stopped; they were practicing their swordwork. The swords were not practice blades; Gervanno was surprised to see them wield actual weapons. The Master Gardener, however, was not.

"Nenyane is a sword master. She will not be recognized as such by those who are not extremely adept with the blade—but she has no desire to be recognized or judged. As you may have noted, she is a strict taskmaster."

He had. If nothing else had made clear that *huntbrother* meant brother, it was her lessons that drove the point home. She was not kind in her disappointment, and apparently Stephen's swordwork was a patchwork of those disappointments, blended on occasion with accidental competence. The young man, however, seemed accustomed to this.

"Do they ever injure each other?"

"Never."

Gervanno's respect grew.

"Nenyane can stop her blade instantly; Stephen is not yet master enough to wound her. But he has improved tremendously since the early years."

"When did they start?"

"She was, I believe, eight or nine years of age. She did not approve of the trainer hired by Maubreche." He smiled as he said this, as if remembering. "She was willing to have Mark or Robart train with the man, but not Stephen. Stephen was hers, and she expected better of him."

"Pardon? You mean that *she* trained Stephen from that young an age?"

"Indeed. She took the risk of challenging the lord to a bout to prove that she was competent. I do not recall that he was best pleased by the challenge, but he could not argue against the facts. Nenyane was a far better swordsman than Lord Maubreche, even at that age. She was allowed to tutor Stephen."

"I am surprised Lady Maubreche allowed it."

"She has always been a pragmatic woman. She could have refused, but they would have engaged in the lessons regardless. It was not something Nenyane could leave alone."

"Have you known her long?"

The Master Gardener's smile was slender, his expression momentarily far too grave. "Yes. I have watched her since she arrived in Maubreche. You have seen some of the work I did as Maubreche's gardener."

Gervanno nodded.

"It is, or was, both the history and future of the Maubreche line, a line beloved of the Hunter God. Now, it stands entirely as history, and as things historical so often are, its shape and its truth will be lost to time and growth. But she was not part of that living tapestry—and yet, absent, I deem her to be at the very heart of my final work." He glanced at the mutt by Gervanno's side. "You should name your dog."

Gervanno had surrendered. He did not understand all of the rules of

ownership in a country in which dogs were prized more highly than
most of the citizens, but he understood that for the moment, the dog
considered Gervanno his master. "So I've been told. I will do so before
we reach the King's City." He frowned. "How long will they continue?"

"I am uncertain. Not more than another hour."

Gervanno shook his head, chagrined. "I could not have kept up the
intensity of this lesson in my youth for that long."

"Or now?"

"I am older. I definitely could not keep up now."

"Well," the Master Gardener said, "give it your best."

Gervanno's brow folded in confusion.

"If you are hired as guard to Maubreche during such troubled times,
she will want to take your measure in the only fashion she trusts." His
smile was not entirely kind.

"And not yours?"

"She has already taken mine."

Gervanno's legs locked in place as Nenyane lifted hand to call an
end to Stephen's exercise, turning toward Gervanno as if her Hunter
was already irrelevant. She waved him over.

"I am not comfortable or competent with your Northern style of
blade," he said, in an attempt to stave off what he was certain would be
upcoming humiliation.

"Use yours." He had had trainers and teachers who were less terse.
He glanced down at the dog by his side, then squared his shoulders and
reached for his sword.

TO WATCH Nenyane at a distance was to watch the most dangerous of
natural storms; she was a force that could not be countered, the like of
which he had only rarely experienced. Nenyane of Maubreche belonged
on a battlefield, or would have could she but take commands. He
thought she would be the equal of any demon, even those who flew. He
could not stand beside her, and would not be called upon—ever—to
guard her back.

To cross swords with her was an entirely different experience.
Gervanno had been prepared to receive the criticism—blunt and
annoyed—that Nenyane's brother had received, and in this at least, he
was mistaken.

But he was given little time to admire the grace or speed of her movements, little time to evaluate the strength of arms that seemed, to the eye, far too slender to justify the weight of her swings, her thrusts. She was fast—faster, he thought, than she had been while sparring with Stephen—but he let his own instincts take control here, parrying her blade or stepping quickly to the side while also returning her blow.

He had thought to be worried *for* her, given the length of his blade, the curve of it, the reach in comparison to her own. He had thought, somehow, that he must underplay his skill, his hand, that he must husband his strength and keep it in reserve for the moments when it was truly necessary.

But he had thought all of that as he walked across the courtyard to take Stephen's place; he was surprised when Stephen patted his shoulder, in either sympathy or encouragement. The Northerners tended to be far freer with touch than those of the South, at least when it came to non-kin. He faced Nenyane, bending slightly into his knees.

She did not, however, charge; she moved, circling, her steps light and graceful, her blade an extension of her arms, her movements. He had no further time to assess. She didn't charge or lunge in a predictable way; she moved, and moved quickly, steps in and out as if she were fencing—a type of swordwork that seemed relegated to the Imperial elites.

Had Gervanno no experience watching sword dancers at work, he might have been overwhelmed. Had he no experience fighting younger, more lithe opponents, he would have immediately lost.

As it was, he had no time to think, to overthink, to strategize; he moved as she moved, catching small hints of her intention in the blur of her movements. He parried, he avoided, he used the movement greater weight necessitated, pivoting rather than leaping, minimizing all motion to the exact amount needed, no more.

He almost struck her twice, the edge of his blade so close to her skin it was miraculous that she avoided injury; he himself should have borne a hundred small cuts as her blade skirted cheek, chest, arm. But she did not draw blood. Did not allow blood to be drawn.

He lost track of time as time slowed for him. It slowed in the same fashion when he was on the battlefield—on any field save one. She did not speak a word, did not call him on his mistakes, did not congratulate him on his successes. In her silence, so different from the familial interactions with her Hunter, he could almost hear a song, wordless, voiceless, but rhythmic.

He stopped when she put her sword up, almost without warning; he responded in kind, a beat behind her.

"You'll do," she said softly, her skin glistening—as Gervanno's almost certainly was—with sweat. He knew that her words would be among his most treasured of memories in some distant future, if he survived. And if he did not? They would be among his most treasured while he lived, regardless. The praise of the praiseworthy, as his father would have said.

A hint of the attachment he had had to that father in his own childhood returned: he wished that Devarro di'Sarrado could have seen Nenyane of Maubreche wield a blade, and he wished he could have witnessed his son, Gervanno, hold his own against her.

"YOU LIKE HIM," Stephen said after dinner when they'd withdrawn to their room.

Nenyane shrugged. "He's good with his sword. Better than he thinks he is."

"And that's the only reason?"

"Almost all of the men I meet are far worse with their blade than they believe they are. And they assume I'm far, *far* worse with mine. There's a reason Cynthia forbade even friendly challenges in Maubreche." She needed less sleep than Stephen, and they had both bathed before they'd dared the public dining room. Dogs were allowed in the rooms in this inn, but the hunting packs were generally offered the quieter kennels.

Nenyane braided her hair at night. Stephen preferred to keep his short enough it didn't require fussing. Nenyane preferred that as well, but her hair would not stay short, no matter how closely it was cropped. To avoid causing the servants distress, Lady Maubreche had decreed an end to such experiments.

"That's a good enough reason, I guess."

"Meaning it's not."

Stephen smiled as he lay back into one of the two beds in the largest of rooms in the inn. "I like him. We often fail to see anything of interest in the same person. I was curious."

"You won't like the answer."

"Will my like or dislike change it?"

Nenyane snorted. "He was the only survivor of the caravan massacre."

Something in her tone silenced Stephen; he focused on listening.

"I was the only survivor of demonic attack. I don't know if he survived the same way I did. By running."

Stephen nodded, the nod more felt across the Hunter bond than seen; the room was darkening quickly at the flight of day.

"But if that's why, he'll carry it: the guilt of it, the certainty that he should have died with his friends. He knows who they are, or were. I don't. But...I feel like I carry some of the same weight, even without memories. I know how the weight feels. I know he'll carry it no matter what I say or do."

Her lips turned up in a feral smile. "And I know that given the chance, he'll stand to face the demons if he has a reason to face them; he'll want them dead. I want them dead. It's like we're comrades in a hidden war."

"It's not going to stay hidden for long," Stephen replied.

"No. But, as I said, he's better with a sword than he thinks he is. That part's probably the most important."

15TH DAY OF EMPERAL, 429 A.A. THE KING'S ROAD, KINGDOM OF BREODANIR

The King's Road, as it was called, cut across the demesnes of the Hunter Lords who ruled them. Gervanno noted that the demesnes that did not have easy access to that road tended to be among the less powerful of the lords. He did not wonder at cause and effect; Evaro had taught him—and taught him well—that commerce was the underside of power in the Northern world. Honor, dignity, respect—they could be suborned by the desire for wealth. Gervanno did not argue with Evaro, but did not point out that the same rules were true in the South. In the South, however, that wealth had to be gained in ways that did not tarnish the honor of the clans that sought it.

Only the Voyani were exempt, governed by their own rules; to Gervanno, they were very like organized bandits. They did not care for the things that made the South what it was; they operated under laws that were invisible to men of Gervanno's birth and standing. They were not, however, wealthy in the way the Tyrs and the Tors were.

But he knew that the Hunter Lords did not fight for territory; the territory their families had been given at the dawn of Breodanir had the strength of myth behind them. The Hunter Lords themselves might be rivals—or worse—but their conquests were not measured by the increase of the size of their territories. There were exceptions, but those were rare, and they involved the King. Hunter Lords were not terribly fecund, and if a line passed without issue, the land would return to the King's hands. It was the King who decided who would succeed the lost family. Even then, the boundaries of the territories were preserved.

It was because of the Sacred Hunt.

Evaro had made allusions to that hunt, but did not fully understand it himself. When he could be pressed to speak of it, he spoke only in the dusk or the time before dawn, as if his words could somehow be heard by the gods the Southerners worshipped. The Hunters, he said, were offered as sacrifice to their foreign god. On a single day, each territory must surrender its Hunters, and the Hunters would then be hunted, until the God found his prey.

It happened every year.

There was no way to substitute another citizen for the Hunter; to fail to attend the Hunt itself meant all power, all titles, and all land were immediately forfeit—what honor the Hunter possessed was tarnished beyond repair. The hunt, for this year, had passed, and if Gervanno understood correctly, Stephen of Maubreche could not be offered as such as sacrifice. He was not qualified; he was not a lord of these lands.

Robart, the younger son, was.

Stephen had been called to attend his King because the King hoped to change, or to force Stephen to change, his status within the Kingdom. Nenyane thought it was a waste of time—both hers and his—and the two argued one-sidedly about this constantly, genuine anger in the cadence of familiar words. Gervanno, surprised at first that such failures would be discussed around relative strangers or non-kin, quickly grew used to the way the two interacted. He thought nothing could stop Nenyane when she was determined.

In that, he admitted he was wrong. Stephen could stop her; he simply refused to engage. He did not raise voice, did not add a cutting edge to his tone or his words, did not meaningfully react in any way at all, except to acknowledge her advice and her speech. Gervanno had some experience with cold silences; his mother was master of them, and he knew they could be used to great effect. Stephen, however, did not incorporate a wall of silence into his own defenses.

He could endure Nenyane's anger without descending into obvious anger himself. It was not an approach that Gervanno had ever considered, but he considered it now, as the King's City drew closer. He had been hired to see the two Maubreche youths to the King's Palace; beyond that he had been given no formal duties. He would be released from his short service, with pay that would cover his food and shelter in the city, and a letter of introduction, complete with a heavy, silver ring meant to prove that he was the bearer for whom the letter had been written.

To that person, Gervanno would disclose his experience with the demons.

Lady Maubreche did not tell him not to speak of the maze and the demonic attack that had driven most of the Maubreche household to seek shelter there, but she focused on the news of the attack on the caravan. He understood what that focus implied. All families of note had their secrets.

He would need to find a guide when he at last saw Stephen and Nenyane to their destination; he was surprised at how little he anticipated the theoretical freedom. He had spent one day crossing swords with Nenyane of Maubreche, and he desired another, and another, and another.

He had not deserved the first opportunity. He would not ask for more.

STEPHEN OF MAUBRECHE had made clear to Gervanno that Nenyane was no longer required to suggest names for any of the Maubreche dogs. Gervanno understood why. But he had a dog he had not purposefully acquired—a dog that had come to him without exchange of either coin or certificate, the latter for which he would never have paid. The dog had followed him from almost the moment they had first met, and it followed now, another mouth to feed.

But he wished a name for the dog, and therefore chose—at dinner— to ask Nenyane's aid.

Stephen almost choked on the mouthful of food he'd been swallowing. He managed to find his voice. "I would not recommend that."

"Were I possessed of a dog worthy of the Maubreche stables—ah, no, kennels—I would no doubt take your advice. But I have an accidental dog, and the dog does not seem likely to abandon me. It is not a dog worthy of a grand name." No more was Gervanno, although he had dreamed, in his distant youth, of proving himself worthy of exactly that. "No offense will be taken at any suggestion, should Nenyane choose to offer one."

Nenyane glanced at Gervanno, and then down, to the side of the chair the mutt now occupied. None of Stephen's dogs were in the inn, but that was Stephen's choice; the inn permitted the presence of dogs.

"He's not much of a dog," she said, blunt in her appraisal.

"He suits his owner," Gervanno replied, voice low.

She frowned.

The Master Gardener, still unnamed, had chosen to join them at the dining table, although he could not be said to take great enjoyment in the food, which he eyed with either disdain or suspicion. He watched Nenyane, his expression neutral.

Nenyane glanced from dog to master and back, while Stephen watched her in some surprise. Gervanno inferred that she had taken no time—or care—in the naming of either Steel or Patches, as if the names were irrelevant.

"Leial," she finally said. "I'd call him Leial."

"If he were yours?"

"No dog will ever be mine. No horse, either. I'd call him Leial because he's yours."

The Master Gardener's brows rose slightly. "Leial?" he asked the Maubreche huntbrother. "An interesting choice of name." To Gervanno, he said, "It is an old name, an old word; the current closest equivalent is 'loyal' or 'loyalty,' but it loses some essential part of the meaning." He did not ask Nenyane how she knew it or where she had learned it. His comment invited response without demanding it, and Nenyane did not choose to respond.

"Is it a common name?" Gervanno asked.

"No. But I think it apt in this case. Leial is the loyalty that is given, not demanded. It is a word that implies service, the truth of service. It is entirely in the hands of those that give, and the recipient is honored by that giving."

He thought it a highly pretentious name for a mutt, but accepted what he had asked for. In truth, he felt grateful. The dog's name was a slender bridge between the sword master and the man who desired to, but could not be, her student.

16TH DAY OF EMPERAL, 429 A.A. THE KING'S CITY, KINGDOM OF BREODANIR

Gervanno did not care for cities, but had learned to both navigate and tolerate them. In cities, there were caravan compounds to which merchants were directed; he would be here alone, on foot, and would have to find them for himself. There were children in the streets here, and among them, he hoped to find one who could serve as a reliable guide in return for some of the coin Lady Maubreche had offered him.

But before he could do that, he would have to see his two charges to their destination. That destination was the King's Palace, the building that presided over the city itself. The architecture of the Western Kingdoms was not the architecture of the grand palaces and residences of the Dominion; there, light and open space was adorned, always, by a hint of the wilderness—the artful placement of trees, of still lakes, of gardens that did not resemble the more regimented gardens of Maubreche.

In the King's City, there was far less greenery evident in the streets upon which the gates opened; the trees were sparser, and seemed much more haphazardly planted. The weeds in the road were more prominent. But in this city, he could see men, surrounded by dogs—Hunter dogs by size and the sheen of their coats. Some of the Hunter Lords were older men, some Gervanno's age; one or two were the age of his father.

He had not expected to see so many here. He knew they gathered in the month of Veral, but Veral was past. Perhaps he did not understand the society and the responsibilities of the Hunter Lords yet. But the Hunter Lords appeared to trace a path to—or from—Stephen and Nenyane's destination. The Master Gardener sat beside Gervanno. Gervanno was not required to scout ahead; he therefore remained in the carriage and watched the streets in part because it was his duty as a guard, and in part because they were new.

"Have you been to the King's City before?" the Gardener asked.

"No. This is my first time. It was to be Evaro's final destination before we returned to the Dominion."

"It is a mortal city," the Gardener said. "But there remain pockets of history, girded and guarded by the palace itself. They are difficult to access if you have no business in them, but they are worth visiting if you can."

"Will you not remain with them?"

"I will not be allowed to remain within the palace as their attendant. The Dominion has serafs, and the serafs are considered part of the lord when it comes to the space they are intended to occupy; there is no like understanding here. Here, slavery is illegal. My presence—or yours—might be considered a subtle insult to the Queen."

Gervanno frowned but accepted this. "They have no servants?"

"The palace has pages and servants who attend to the functioning of the palace, yes. Those servants are palace servants, under the command of the Keeper of the King's Keys. In the Empire, they are often called stewards; I am uncertain what they are called in the Dominion. It has been long since I have traveled in the South, and things have changed markedly since that time.

"Perhaps we will see it again. Come, we are almost there."

THE CARRIAGE's driver dropped them off in front of the gates beyond which the palace lay. He would follow the road; the carriage and its horses would be housed in the yard and stables meant for the use of visiting Breodanir nobility.

Stephen stopped before he entered the palace gates. Nenyane stopped a beat later, turning to look back at her Hunter with character-istic impatience. It was the expression Gervanno would always later identify with Nenyane, because it was so particular to her.

Stephen turned to Gervanno. "We will be resident within the palace for some months. If you encounter difficulties before your departure, please, *please* reach out to us. We are in your debt, and some measure of aid in return would ease that burden."

Leial barked in Stephen's direction, although he remained at Gervanno's side. Stephen's dogs glanced at the mutt, but otherwise ignored him. Stephen bowed to Gervanno—and to Gervanno's surprise, it was a bow in the Southern style. He then turned to join his hunt-brother. She glanced once at Gervanno, and offered him a nod, no more. She then walked through the gates, her Hunter at her side; she did not look back.

"I, too, shall take my leave," the Gardener said softly. "If you wish it, I can guide you to the merchant compound and the associated inns. I assume you will look for employ for your return trip."

Gervanno nodded.

"Take care while in the city."

"I've been in cities before."

The Gardener did not smile; his expression was grave. "Perhaps you are not aware of the more subtle ways in which the winds in a city can change. Or perhaps you have nothing against which to compare. But the winds here feel subtly off, and I think if you have business in the King's City, it is best for you that you finish it quickly."

"Stephen and Nenyane will be here for months."

The Master Gardener glanced back, to the palace. "Will they? When storms come, many are swept off the decks on which they stand. No, do not turn. They are no longer your concern—but the information that you came to pass on must be passed on now, while there is still a chance it might arrive to those in power before it becomes entirely redundant."

"Who are you?" Gervanno asked, his voice a bare whisper.

"Not yet, Ser Gervanno. But perhaps, if you are unfortunate enough to cross my path again, you will know." He bowed, as Stephen had bowed, although the movement lacked the stiffness of something unfamiliar. "Come, I have tasks to accomplish as well. Let me take you to the merchant compound."

"Is there an inn you'd recommend?"

The Master Gardener grimaced. "No. None, however, are known for murdering guests. I would say that you might want to avoid certain places if you were accompanied by Hunter dogs, but your dog will raise no eyebrows."

"Will they be all right?"

"They? Stephen and Nenyane? What do you think?"

"I feel it foolish to worry about Nenyane's safety," Gervanno confessed. "But were she a child of a ruler in the Dominion, half of the words she speaks would have disgraced her family for at least two generations, and she would be unlikely to survive it."

"She causes friction, yes—her very existence is already an affront to the more conservative of the Hunter Lords. The priests, however, are torn. Stephen is Bredan's offspring; it is known. But Stephen has not completed the first of the Hunter vows, as you may have heard.

"Some priests feel this is Bredan's judgment on Stephen's choice of huntbrother. Others, better informed, do not. They accept Nenyane with great reluctance, and as you can imagine, her general manners do not ease that grudging acceptance." The Master Gardener's smile was almost rueful.

"You approve of her."

"You do not?"

"Her manners would be her death in my country; her swordsmanship would barely guarantee her survival. Regardless, it is not mine to judge." He hesitated. But he did not expect to see the Master Gardener again; nothing he said would return to haunt him. "But were I offered the chance, I would serve under her while I could still wield blade and draw breath. I have never seen a swordsman so perfect."

"A woman?"

"A swordsman. Nothing else matters."

"She will be fine. She is impervious to criticism she does not feel is relevant—and that, to Lady Maubreche's continual despair, would be almost all of it."

16TH DAY OF EMPERAL, 429 A.A. THE KING'S PALACE, KINGDOM OF BREODANIR

The King's Palace was one of the oldest buildings—and the grandest—in Breodanir. Portions of it were modern, although the architects had taken great care to harmonize the new with the old; portions of it, mostly invisible from the gates or the streets, were not. On the interior, the demarcation between the old and the new was more obvious; one could almost feel, walking between one hall and the next, the descent of age, of antiquity, the cold and spare grip of history.

The King's inner chamber, the Chamber of the Hunt, was old; it was not meant to be a public space. But here, from the gatehouse, that chamber and what lay beyond it were invisible—and very few of the Breodani would have cause to visit it, regardless. Only the Hunter

Lords and the Priests could be called there; all other difficulties were resolved in the Queen's audience chambers, which saw much more use.

Stephen, however, was not here as a Hunter Lord. He had passed the tests set for succession. All but one. And that one, he would not pass.

This was not the first time he had visited the King's Palace; he had come with his father and younger brother, to be introduced to the man who ruled the Hunt, and therefore ruled them all. But he was not here today as his father's son. His father, Lord Maubreche, was Hunter Lord, and he had the right to use the second entrance.

Stephen was not.

Unless an exception was made, he would never become one. He glanced down as Patches headbutted his leg. The dogs had also come to the King's Palace before; they knew the kennels and the extensive runs built for the care and the exercise of hunting dogs, and they fully expected to be taken there. And fed.

Stephen knelt by Patches's side, which immediately drew the attention of Sanfel and Steel; Brylle, calmer, was looking straight ahead, as if he didn't expect that those kennels would be immediately available.

From the front gate, the road branched; to the right the road was crowded with people from all walks of life: merchants, craftsmen, foreigners. The left road, almost empty, was meant for the use of the Hunter Lords and their dogs. Stephen bowed head for one long breath. He had never entered the palace through the doors meant for everyone but Hunters, but he had no right to take those doors, now. Had he been willing to accept the earliest of the huntbrother vows, he would not have been summoned to the city.

He would stand—and fall—by the choice he had made, forcefully and viscerally, as a young child. Nothing that affected that determination had changed. Nothing would.

He rose, indicating in silence that his dogs were to follow.

"Where are you going?"

"We aren't Hunter Lord and huntbrother," he said, voice soft. "We're just regular people."

Nenyane snorted. "You were summoned in person by the Master of the Game. If we're not Hunter Lords, we're still Hunters."

Stephen shook his head, not bothering to look back. He took his place in the line of people who were waiting for permission to enter what was, no doubt, a very crowded public hall.

"Most of these people are here on Queen's business."

Stephen nodded. "Most, but not all. Some must be here to petition the King. We're one of those people."

"He *ordered us* to come here."

"And so we have." He exhaled. "This is the road we've chosen."

"*We* didn't choose it. *You* did."

"Are you going to walk it with me?"

"If I don't strangle you first, yes."

"Then this is where we start." He hesitated. "If you want to wait outside, you can. I'll call you when you're needed."

Her glare was all of her answer.

THEY WERE AN HOUR IN LINE. The dogs were, of course, well-behaved, but they were restive, and not all of the people in line were accustomed to the presence of four Hunter dogs at such close quarters. They tried to make room, which in this case meant pushing themselves further into the people ahead of them, or lagging further behind. Most of the Breo-dani understood that the dogs were not—unless their Hunter was in danger—a threat, but clearly many of the people in line were not Breodani.

Nenyane disagreed. "They're probably city people. When do they see Hunter dogs? The King doesn't hunt the way the Hunter Lords do; he doesn't feed the people here the way we do in the demesnes. He couldn't. There are too damn many of them."

The dogs then sat, or in Brylle's case, lay down, across sun-warmed stone. They rose only when the queue moved forward, and once again sat or lowered themselves to the ground when the line paused. In this fashion, the Hunter dogs presented less of an immediate threat to those unaccustomed to dogs. Or so Stephen hoped. It was interesting, because it was not something of concern in the Maubreche territories; the dogs were part of the ruling lord's entourage, and no one feared them. Could the dogs kill? Yes.

Would they? No. Not unless someone was foolish enough to attack their master. The lethality of the dogs, to the villagers, was the lethality of a sword, a bow, an axe: it was in the hands of the man who could wield them. Here, the fact that Stephen was master and Stephen was in complete control had the power of rumor, not the certainty of experience. He wondered if this would change, and felt his first pang of home-sickness.

But the line did move, haltingly, toward the open doors, and beyond those doors into a large room; the room had benches along the walls, but the benches were occupied. Stephen continued to wait until he reached a very large, very long desk; he handed the seneschal the King's letter.

The man's brows drew in toward the bridge of his nose; he looked at the missive, and then at its bearer, with something approaching confusion. Stephen, however, had spent years learning at the feet of Lady Maubreche and Arlin; his expression was pleasant, neutral.

"Move your dogs toward the west wall. I'll send for the Keeper of the King's Keys."

NENYANE WAS NOT PLEASED. She had never liked crowds, and in situations in which entire villages gathered to greet their lord, she had always chosen to stand well back.

"They're not greeting us," she snapped. "They're just coming for the food."

As there was some truth in this, Stephen declined to argue, even if his huntbrother was now spoiling for a fight. Crowds, and being in the middle of one, had long had this effect; she grew agitated and surly when forced to endure them. Stephen had offered to allow her to remain outside the doors, and therefore felt her growing anger was unfair.

"You saw his face. He was confused—and annoyed. I told you this isn't the entrance we should be using."

We are not here as Hunter Lord and huntbrother.

"We're here as the children of Maubreche at the King's command."

We're here because *we're not considered Hunter Lords. This is the entrance we should be using.*

"We'll be waiting here until they close the gates!" She turned toward the hall; the light from doors, pinned open, was a glare of grey and white.

Nenyane—

"You can wait here if you want. There are too many people for me."

She turned on heel, a gesture familiar to anyone in the Maubreche residence. Stephen grimaced.

Unfortunately for Nenyane—or perhaps the rest of the people who waited their turn to speak with the seneschal—the annoyed turn-on-heel march was interrupted by a wall of people. Or person, in this case.

She was slender; people often assumed she was a few years younger than Stephen at first glance. Until she opened her mouth, most assumed she was fragile, slight. After she opened her mouth, they thought her brittle. Stephen, who had sparred with Nenyane for half his life, could not make that mistake.

Annoyed by his thoughts, Nenyane began to march into the crowded room. When she ran into someone who was a head taller and at least another body-width wider, it was the stranger who bounced. He didn't lose his footing, but it was close. Stephen cringed; the stranger was young, large, and dressed in Hunter greens—and he was angry.

Nenyane stopped and turned toward him. "I'm sorry, I didn't see you."

He snorted. "You didn't see me. You just ran across the hall without paying attention."

"Yes."

Nenyane, please.

The stranger had stepped closer; he now looked down—from superior height—at the Maubreche huntbrother. Stephen's hands became involuntary fists.

"Do you not know who I am?"

"Should I know every random young Hunter in the kingdom?"

Nenyane, this isn't the place.

I didn't start it. "Or maybe you're not actually a Hunter. Because if you were, you'd know that this is the *wrong entrance* for people like you."

Stephen was grateful that neither his mother nor his father had chosen to escort them to the King's City in person. He could imagine his mother's expression, and flinched even though Lady Maubreche was a safe distance away. His mother had always had ways of hearing about every social infraction.

The stranger froze, his hands bunching in fists. Someone behind him moved to the side—and one stepped in front, a brown-haired young man. He didn't look at the Hunter; he looked at Nenyane, who was much smaller in stature. She never seemed small or diminutive to

Stephen; if most people considered her both at a first glance, the second glance cured them.

But it was also true that certain people tended to overlook her because she was slender and young. If she failed to live up to—or down to—their expectations, things got far uglier, far more quickly. Nenyane had never cared. She was clearly not about to start now.

"Who are you to tell me which entrance I should be using?"

"Someone who doesn't like crowded rooms. I didn't see you. If you're trying to tell me that I should pay attention to every breathing body in this hall, you could start with yourself. You didn't see me."

"I did."

"You didn't."

"I did—I expected you to correct course."

"Why? If you saw me and I didn't see you, you should have been the person to move."

The Maubreche dogs rose from the floor, far more alert—and far less resentful—than they had been moments before. Stephen's wordless *heel* kept them in place. It helped. He had not properly constrained his worry, and they responded, as they always did, to it. His father, even in the most ill of his tempers, did not lose control of his dogs. Stephen knew the dogs served him—naturally, without effort on his part—but their service nonetheless required self-control.

He worked to calm himself because the dogs, in this cramped, crowded place, required it.

The stranger with whom Nenyane had collided was wearing Hunter greens, a forest green that was granted to those who had passed all of the many tests on the way to becoming a lord of Breodanir, as Stephen would not. Nenyane was not incorrect; this entrance was not meant for Hunter Lords. His hair was black, almost as dark as Gervanno's, but his skin was pale, except where it was heightened by the red of anger. Before him stood his huntbrother, hair a mousy brown; he was a full six inches shorter than his Hunter, his eyes lighter. In build he was slender, almost coltish; his Hunter was not.

One of the huntbrother's eyes was underscored by yellowed skin, the color the echo of a bruise. His eyes were downcast; this changed as Stephen watched. His head came up, his eyes widening.

The Hunter had lifted a fist.

Nenyane did not appear to notice. Appearances could be, and in this case were, deceiving. She noticed. Nothing in her stance changed, but she dropped her right hand to the hilt of her sword. "I've apologized for not seeing you," she told him, looking up to meet his eyes. "I'm not sure what else you want from me."

"Respect."

"Oh, I'm giving you the respect you've earned."

Nenyane.

She didn't answer. Stephen moved, and with him, the dogs; he came to stand beside his huntbrother, as the four dogs sandwiched them.

It was the dogs the stranger noticed. He stared at them, his fist tightening, his anger shifting.

Nenyane's smile was bright, sharp; there was a hint of the wild in it. Stephen froze. Anyone who lived or worked within the Maubreche demesne would have recognized that look, and attempted to get as far away from it as physically possible, while Stephen ran interference.

Nenyane, stop.

I'm not doing anything, she replied, the internal voice almost cloyingly sweet when compared to her normal voice. *Unless you'd like me to just stand here and do nothing while he hits me. I am allowed to at least dodge?*

Before Stephen could answer, the pale, slender huntbrother stepped between Nenyane and the raised fist of his Hunter.

"Get out of the way," the Hunter said, voice a growl of anger.

The huntbrother didn't answer in an audible fashion.

"*Move.*"

Stephen had watched his younger brother, Robart, and Robart's huntbrother Mark exchange blows before; they had started at the age of eight, and continued to the present day. But the fights had been fairly even; Mark could give as good as he got. These had diminished with time, but those scuffles and this one were different. Stephen had had no sense that Robart and Mark would be divided in the presence of outsiders. They were brothers.

He did not feel that these two were. Not in the same way.

No one in Maubreche was foolish enough to interfere in the conflicts that arose between brothers. Nenyane was huntbrother, therefore that rule still applied. Stephen was almost at a loss as the unknown Hunter turned the edge of his ire toward his huntbrother—as his huntbrother had no doubt intended.

Nenyane was aware of this, and it soured her mood. If she was supremely confident in her ability to handle an intemperate young Hunter, she was less sanguine about that Hunter's huntbrother, who looked as if he had already been on the losing end of at least one fight.

Stephen tensed. On her own behalf, Nenyane was irritable but amused. On behalf of the unfamiliar huntbrother, less so, which would be a disaster. Nenyane taking an altercation seriously was something no one wanted.

He was uncertain what he would do, or would have done, had a cold, cutting voice not intruded. "What is happening here?" The voice wasn't loud, but it cut across the noise of milling crowd, and it demanded attention. Even Nenyane's.

Stephen turned toward it and saw the silver edging around forest green: this man was a Huntsman of the Chamber, a Hunter Lord who directly served the King. *No,* Stephen thought, as he offered this man a perfect bow.

I'll send for the Keeper of the King's Keys.

This man was the King's keykeeper—the most trusted of the King's trusted servants. Lord Declan. Stephen had met him once before, in a childhood that seemed impossibly remote. Nenyane was slower to turn toward Lord Declan, and therefore slower to bow. Borrowing Sanfel's eyes, Stephen saw that the unknown huntbrother was bowing.

The Hunter was not. His fist was no longer raised, but his arms were folded across his chest. Stephen had thought him close to enraged while facing Nenyane; he realized he'd been wrong. This Hunter glared at Lord Declan as if the King's most trusted servant was a mortal enemy, a person against whom vengeance must be taken.

The keykeeper was not impressed, but did not appear to be surprised. He turned to Stephen. "Rise. In future, Stephen and Nenyane of Maubreche, please come to the Hunter's entrance. Lord Ansel, Heiden, please accompany me."

"To where?" the Hunter demanded.

"To the rooms in which you will be staying—and studying—during your tenure in the palace."

THE FIRST OF these rooms was not a bedroom or a bedroom suite; it was a spacious great room. Stephen would have preferred the former; he desired a bath and a few moments to shave and make himself presentable. But Lord Declan was a Hunter Lord; he expected Hunters to be far less fastidious about their personal appearance, unless they chanced to have an audience with the Queen.

The Queen, however, did not interfere with Hunter business unless it overlapped the adjudication of the laws over which she presided. Drunk Hunters starting a melee in public was frowned on. Drunk Hunters killing a non-Hunter was a crime.

Stephen was aware that the fact that he was in this great room, with its chairs carefully arranged around a fireplace that was not at the moment in use, was of little relevance to the Queen. He fervently prayed it remained that way.

But the great room itself was already occupied.

Although the circumstances were grim, Stephen felt an instant lightening of mood; he recognized both of the occupants of this otherwise empty, cavernous room.

"Max! Alex!"

Max rose instantly. Alex rose slowly, and offered Lord Declan the bow that Max had apparently forgotten. The two, Stephen and Max, met in the room's center as they moved toward each other. Stephen's dogs moved with him; Brylle was practically puppy-like in his behavior, but he had always adored Maxwell. Maxwell returned his regard.

"Your mother let you bring your dogs."

"My father insisted. He wanted eight."

Alex, who had more quietly joined them, winced. "Our mother and father would have let us bring dogs — but they're *his* dogs. Lady Elseth, however, absolutely forbid it."

Max's mother was not Lady Elseth; his grandmother was. If she'd hoped to retire upon the marriage of her son, Gilliam, those hopes had been dashed. Espere of Elseth was not, and could not be, confined in the role that Hunter Ladies adopted; in her hands, the governance of the demesne would have frayed completely. Lady Maubreche, whose view of those who abandoned responsibility could be said to be dim if she were otherwise in a good mood, nonetheless liked Lady Espere. Her respect, however, was given to Lady Elseth, a woman she had known for almost two decades, and whom she admired without reservation.

But Lady Maubreche had always expected that Gilliam's children would suffer difficulties.

He had not one son, not two, but three — and two daughters, besides. They had all been born on the same day, within a span of hours; the oldest was eldest by fifteen minutes; the second oldest, a daughter, by ten; the third, a second daughter followed, and after her, two sons.

Those two, Max and Alex, had been almost identical; eye color, hair color, and even weight, as measured by midwives who had been allowed to tend Espere on sufferance, and might be forgiven for making small mistakes. Gilliam, Lord Elseth, would not leave her side.

The oldest son, William, had taken a huntbrother at the same age his father had been when Stephen of Elseth had entered the Elseth family. Stephen of Elseth, dead many years, still cast a long shadow. Lady Maubreche agreed, but added, "some shadows are beautiful; they are shade in the most punishing of summer suns."

William's huntbrother, Lucas, had been trained to within an inch of his life by Lady Elseth, for Lord Elseth had no huntbrother William could shadow and observe. But perhaps because she had lost a son, Lady Elseth was also indulgent and careful.

The daughters, Ingrid and Justine, seemed to take to the territorial duties of the demesne as if they'd been born to it. They were their grandmother's grandchildren, not their mother's daughters.

Max and Alex had been the joint runts of the litter—which Espere had once said in public at a large dinner gathering, to the deep chagrin of Lady Elseth. They had been small for their age through their childhood, and that had not changed until they reached the age of thirteen.

But they had not taken huntbrothers.

Their father, Gilliam of Elseth, had dutifully set out to find huntbrothers for his sons. He knew what a huntbrother was, what it meant, and why huntbrothers were important. But he knew the pain of the loss of a huntbrother, and perhaps in the end he failed to push this one necessity harshly enough; he already had an heir who was properly positioned within the society of Hunter Lords.

Espere did not see the need for huntbrothers, but she often didn't see the need for Hunter Lords at all—unless it was her lord.

Stephen had, many times, overheard the discussions about these problems that passed between his mother and Max's grandmother. The older woman's fear for her grandchildren could not always be contained behind a mask of perfect silence.

Max and Alex could hunt. They could run prey farther and faster than even the older lords. They were uncannily competent; they could call the Hunter's trance from a very early age—far earlier than Stephen of Maubreche or Robart had, as if that state were their natural state.

Max and Alex were smaller than their brother, of a height with their sisters, but they were quick, bright, and curious about things that generally didn't involve other people.

Gilliam considered Stephen and Cynthia family. More significantly, so did Espere. Max and Alex therefore accepted Stephen as if he were a litter mate. They were also comfortable around Nenyane, whose bluntness and lack of the social grace so prized by the Hunter Ladies often caused social ripples. They didn't care that Nenyane was not a boy; they had known, almost instantly, that she was Stephen's huntbrother.

For her part, Nenyane was neutral toward the two; she called them the twins, although they were essentially quintuplets. But neutral, with Nenyane, was good.

I don't hate them.

No. No, she didn't. Stephen hugged Max—a bear hug that lifted Max off his feet—and then set him down beside Steel. Steel, unmindful of manners, leapt up, placing both paws against Max's chest, as if Steel were a pup, and not the leader of Stephen's small pack.

"You were sent here, too?"

Stephen nodded, and added, "Probably for the same reason you were."

It was Alex who answered. "How long do you think we're going to be here before they accept that we're failures?"

Lord Declan cleared his throat—loudly and almost theatrically for a man of his station. "You are not considered failures; you are considered troubled."

A grimace passed between Max and Alex, but at least Max kept his thoughts to himself. Stephen had learned early that obvious displeasure was better than obvious *spoken* displeasure.

Ansel—ah, Lord Declan had called him *Lord* Ansel—had entered the room like a thundercloud. He glared at Nenyane, but clearly had enough anger left over to spread a miasma of resentful contempt. His huntbrother stood behind and to the side, head bowed as if he were studying his feet and had no intention of noticing anything else. Or of being noticed.

"We're troubled," Lord Ansel said. "Being here at all is a waste of time. I don't know about these puppies, but I'm already a Hunter Lord."

"You are a Hunter Lord," Lord Declan replied, "who has made clear he will forgo his duties in the next Sacred Hunt."

Ansel said nothing, his lips compressed tightly enough the edges had whitened. "You've pulled me from Bowgren at a time when Bowgren *needs* its Hunters. There's no one but me."

"Lord Bowgren is Hunter Lord; it is his territory, until he passes—not yours." The words were blunt, the tone icy. Lord Declan was not pleased.

You should have just let me hit him.

You were the one who was going to be hit.

Nenyane snorted rudely; the sound immediately drew Ansel's attention.

"You have something you want to say?"

"Sure—but I've been told it's inadvisable."

Lord Declan's gaze went from chilly to glacial before the last of Nenyane's syllables had tailed off.

Max and Alex, however, were now looking at Lord Ansel; they had drawn their shoulders back, and their gaze was almost unblinking. Stephen knew the look, he'd seen it so often; he moved almost instantly to stand between them, placing a hand on either shoulder. As quietly as he could, he whispered, "She's never going to be in danger from someone like him."

"Not while we're here," Max replied, less quietly. His voice was pitched low. Sadly, it was the low of a dog's growl. Alex, who was more socially adept than his brother, was silent—but silence and the ability to mime good manners didn't prevent his gaze from being as sharp as Max's.

"Why are you even *here*?" Ansel demanded—of Nenyane, as if Lord Declan was invisible or irrelevant.

"Don't ask me—it certainly wasn't my idea. It's a waste of time. Even yours."

Ansel took a step forward.

Max took a step forward as well.

"*Enough*," Lord Declan said, stepping into the center of what was not quite a fray. "Nenyane is Stephen's huntbrother."

"She's a girl!"

"Thank you for pointing out what we must have failed to observe ourselves."

"How messed up is that? And the other two? Why are *they* here?"

"That is irrelevant, Lord Ansel. They are here—as you are—at the

King's command. Consider your own difficulties before you attempt to judge others."

"So they're *difficult* Hunters?"

"They are of the Elseth and Maubreche families. They are Hunters; they are not yet Hunter Lords. But they have passed every test of aspiring Hunter Lords save one. Maxwell and Alex are Hunters without parallel within Breodanir; were they to agree to swear the only oath they have rejected, they would not be here at all.

"You have passed all of the milestones that grant you the title—but you have made clear that you will not attend the Sacred Hunt at the King's command, rendering the title meaningless. Or worse."

Stephen was silent. He had heard the words—less angrily spoken—the first time, but the meaning had been very slow to take root. If Lord Ansel refused to honor the duties of a Hunter Lord, he would be stripped of that title. While Lord Bowgren was alive, Ansel would likely remain within Bowgren—but if Lord Bowgren passed away, the new Lord Bowgren would be someone of the King's choosing, unless Ansel had a brother.

Stephen knew himself lucky; Maubreche had Robart, and Robart was likely to become Lord Maubreche in time.

Ansel did not reply to Lord Declan's words. Lord Declan, absent huntbrother or the presence of Lady Declan, therefore continued. "You are, Lord or no, a far more dire liability to both Bowgren and yourself at the moment."

"The Sacred Hunt hasn't been called yet," Ansel said, voice low. Low the way growls were low. "Until then, I'm Lord Ansel."

"And if you now intend to dismiss your *vow* as a momentary lapse of either grief or temper, I am certain the Master of the Game would be content to allow you to return to Bowgren. Your stated intent, however, mars any past accomplishments. You are perhaps the most significant failure in this room."

Had Stephen been at home, he might have covered his face with his hands. He was not. For one rigid moment, he was certain that Lord Ansel would attack Lord Declan, and that certainty grew when the pale-haired, bruised huntbrother once again stepped forward, to stand between Lord Declan and Lord Ansel. This time, he did not turn to face his Hunter.

Instead, he offered Lord Declan a very low, very deep bow. "I am Heiden of Bowgren, Lord Ansel's huntbrother," he said, as he rose.

Lord Declan glanced at Heiden, at Heiden's bruised face.

Ansel did not hit Heiden. He looked through him, as if the hunt-brother was invisible. No doubt the huntbrother might have wished that were true. But Ansel then returned to Nenyane.

Ah, no. It was to Stephen he now looked. "You have golden eyes."

Stephen was tense enough that he couldn't tense further. "Yes," he said, before Nenyane could answer. "I do."

"And you're a Hunter? You? I haven't heard that any of the Maubreche ladies were god-born." He said the word with the contempt often expressed by the Breodani; the Breodani tolerated the Imperial gods, but they did not *respect* them; respect, such as it was, was given only to Breodan.

Breodan, the god the Easterners called *Bredan*. God of oaths.

"No. The only member of Maubreche who is god-born is me."

"Which god, then?"

"Breodan," Nenyane snapped. "Not that it's any business of yours."

"Breodan? You're saying you're the son of the Hunter God?" He continued to speak to Stephen, as if Nenyane—like Lord Declan—did not exist.

"He is the son of the Hunter God we serve," Lord Declan replied, before Nenyane could. His warning glare passed through Nenyane's profile as if she were unaware of his presence.

"The Hunter God *we* serve? The Hunter God who murdered Barrett and left Lord Bowgren—my *father*—a living wreck?"

It was Stephen who answered. "Yes. I'm sorry."

CHAPTER SIX

M ax and Alex dropped all pretense of social conversation; they flanked Stephen, their sudden silence a warning. Steel stood to one side of Max, but the rest of the dogs came to join their Hunter as he, golden-eyed, met the dark eyes of Lord Ansel of Bowgren.

Heiden of Bowgren did not move; he stood, back to his Hunter Lord, eyes as dark as his Hunter's. There seemed to be no anger in him, just weary grief; he looked pale, injured, and exhausted. And yet, he stood between the angry Bowgren Hunter and Stephen. Their eyes met briefly, and it was Heiden who dropped his gaze, as if the weight of carrying it had become too much.

Nenyane stood alone, closer to Heiden but to the side, as if she considered Ansel a trivial danger. Which was fair; she did. It was Heiden for whom she was now concerned, and that concern was edged —as it always was, in Nenyane's case—with anger. But if she had failed to acknowledge Lord Declan, she was aware of him. She was certain Ansel's visceral rage would break against the wall of Declan.

Stephen was less certain. Lord Barrett of Bowgren had died in the Sacred Hunt of 429. He had fulfilled the huntbrother's oath, and in so doing, had left behind his Hunter and his family.

Some Hunters did not survive the death of their huntbrothers. No huntbrothers survived the death of their Hunters, should that death occur during the Sacred Hunt. This was not the only reason that

Stephen had failed—and would continue to fail—to accept Nenyane's oath as huntbrother. He understood, had always understood, what the oath entailed; he knew what the cost of failing it would be.

The complicated ceremonies of the Hunters and their priests, in this one case, served as an oathbinding. Lord Barrett had sworn an oath at the age of eight; he had fulfilled that oath, and in so doing, had saved Lord Bowgren's life.

But Stephen was well aware of what grief that deep could do to the living. Some Hunters survived. Some did not. Lord Bowgren clearly had not recovered from Barrett's death, and grief had given way to an anger that his son, his heir, had absorbed whole.

Lady Elseth had lost both huntbrother and husband to the Sacred Hunt; she had lost a son, a huntbrother, to it. She had continued to govern as her remaining son, Lord Elseth, shed rage and grief with the passage of time. Stephen had always considered the strength of the Breodani to be rooted, and grounded, in the women.

But he had grown up in the shadows cast by that same loss. The death of Stephen of Elseth shadowed Lady Maubreche; it was from that Stephen his name had been drawn, as if to prove that life continued in the face of the most painful of deaths. She had loved Stephen of Elseth.

It was Arlin who had explained the fact of his birth, the fact of that loss, to Stephen; Corwin had known and Corwin had always accepted both the love and the sense of abiding grief. The Breodani rulers were people steeped in loss.

"Lord Ansel, remedial lessons in the history of Breodanir are clearly in order," Lord Declan said, breaking the tangled silence.

Ansel turned toward Declan, as if the Huntsman of the Chamber were a mortal enemy. "I am well aware of the history of Breodanir," he said, voice low, guttural.

"Are you? Are you aware that we are given the blessing of Breodan as rulers to succor our people? That it is the Sacred Hunt itself that makes Breodanir fertile?"

Ansel failed to answer.

"Lord Barrett understood his duty to both God and people. He took his place in the Sacred Hunt as huntbrother to the ruler of the Bowgren lands."

Ansel glared. He opened his mouth, but closed it again without ejecting words, aware—as Stephen was aware—that Lord Declan had, decades past, lost his own huntbrother during the Sacred Hunt.

"You dishonor Barrett's sacrifice. You dishonor his death. You dishonor the reason for that death—and the reason that Hunters are granted lands to rule. We are not the Eastern Empire; we are not the Southern Dominion. Duty has always walked hand in hand with power, here.

"Lord Barrett came when the king called; he hunted at the side of his Hunter Lord. He died in his Hunter's stead. And because he did, the lands can be cultivated, the people, Breodani all, will not starve." Lord Declan's expression was neutral; his tone was not. "If you feel that Lord Barrett died for no reason, you have failed to understand the heart of Breodanir. If you say that his death was pointless murder, you are insulting *my* huntbrother's sacrifice.

"Do you understand?"

Stephen thought, for one silent moment, that Ansel would argue further. Stephen himself had argued against such necessary deaths as a child—as if only his own grief, his own needs, had primacy. As if just anyone could be sacrificed to the Hunter's Death so that the people he loved and needed could be guaranteed to survive it.

His mother had not been amused. His father had been truly angry.

Just as Declan was now angry.

Arlin, however, had said, *he's a child, Cynthia. He's a child. Of course he's afraid of losing his family to his—to the God.* Arlin, who would, should he prove true to the oath that had brought him from the streets of the King's City to Corwin's side, become the sacrifice the God demanded.

Stephen, however, had never dared to argue that point again. And as he had grown, as he had seen the grief and loss permeate the families of friends and allies, he had come to understand that, to the Breodani rulers, life was predicated on death. He knew—they all knew—what the cost to the people of the kingdom had been when one King had failed to call the Sacred Hunt because foreigners had said it was barbarous and he was too weak to remember that he was Breodani.

And he knew, as well, what the cost to the Hunters had been when the delayed Hunt had finally been called. Not one death, but many, all savage. He had not, could not, understand that. It was not the fault of the Hunters that the Hunt itself had not been called. Some Hunter Lords supported the lack of that hunt, because they served their king, not their god. But some had had reservations, and those numbers had grown as the land itself grew parched and barren.

History accepted those deaths as the price of the king's decision.

Stephen was not history; he had been a confused and angry child. What even the Priests could not demand of their god, Stephen could. He had gone to the heart of the maze. He had called the God. And he had demanded an explanation. It wasn't their *fault*. Why, why, in that first Hunt in years, had he killed *so many*? Was it anger? Was it vengeance? Those Hunters had done nothing wrong.

And do you think that only those who deserve death die? That all deaths are just, that all loss is fair?

He had not been so young a child that he believed that. But he had been old enough to argue. "You killed them. Accident didn't kill them. Illness didn't kill them. Starvation didn't kill them. *You* did."

Yes. But I did not kill them as punishment, although that is how such deaths were perceived. Understand, Stephen, that the mortal plane—the lands in which you can safely live—is no longer hospitable for gods. What gods require has been removed, almost entirely, from your world.

And gods hunger. Gods require sustenance. Without that sustenance, they cannot long retain what you view as sentience. What we become without that sustenance is primal; we are a force, like unto tidal waves and earthquakes. I did not kill them in anger, but in hunger; when that hunger was assuaged, there were no further deaths.

"And one death a year is enough?"

It is. Understand that I am not, now, where I was in regards to my people at that time. I am no longer a god who walks the mortal plane. But the covenants that altered the land of Breodanir remain, and without the loss of that life, the lands will become what they once were before I led the Breodani north.

Stephen had grudgingly accepted that, in the Between. He accepted, as well, that although he was given Stephen of Elseth's name, he was the God's son. Breodan-born.

But he had seen clouds of loss for the entirety of his life, in his mother and in his godfather, Gilliam of Elseth; he had seen how loss had almost broken Hunters; how it had destroyed huntbrothers. He thought there must be a better way, a different way, but he could not conceive of one on his own.

He watched Ansel, watched Lord Declan, saw the familiar coloration of loss. Ansel remained silent in the face of Lord Declan's anger, but the older man's wrath seemed to bleed some of the rage from the younger Hunter Lord.

Lord Declan mastered his anger, turning from it toward the rest of the gathered Hunter youths who had been summoned to the King's

City. "The pages will take you to the rooms you will share while you remain in Hunter's Redoubt. Breakfast, lunch, and dinner will be served in the dining hall, one room over. It will be served on time. Should you fail to arrive on time, you will miss that meal.

"Your schedules will be decided after we have assessed what you do, and do not, understand. That assessment will require some remedial lessons—and those lessons will take place within a classroom, not upon the field."

If the edge of Ansel's anger had been diminished, the anger itself remained. Lord Declan looked to Ansel, as if expecting argument. Ansel managed—barely, if one judged by expression—to curb speech, if not the emotion behind it.

"You are all no doubt aware of the difficulties that have swept across Breodanir in the past year."

The silence shifted in texture; Ansel abandoned rage. All of the gathered Hunters watched Lord Declan as if somehow the Huntsman of the Chamber—older and far more experienced—could divulge answers, or better, desperately needed solutions. All except the Maubreche Hunters, who knew no answers, no solutions, would be forthcoming.

Lord Declan took the silence that followed his question as assent. "The Order of Knowledge has been studying the changes with an almost unheard-of speed and urgency." Ansel grimaced. The Breodani did not trust the men and women who called themselves mage-born. It was at the behest of so-called knowledgeable foreigners that Breodanir had almost perished decades past. Stephen even understood that the intentions of those foreigners—the end of the barbaric Sacred Hunt and the lives lost to it—had been good.

But the results had been catastrophic. The mage-born, the magi, did not then understand all that Breodan had wrought. He was not certain they understood it now; the priests viewed the magi with the remnants of anger.

"There are many theories for why these events have begun to trouble our lands—and information has arrived that makes clear it is not only Breodanir that has been so troubled. Breodanir, however, has weathered the changes better; it is why the magi are here.

"They believe that it is *because* our lords are tied to the land—by oath, by Sacred Hunt, and by the blood shed in that hunt..." Here he paused to glance at Ansel, as if waiting for interruption. When none was forthcoming, he continued, "that Breodanir has not been so heavily affected."

Ansel inhaled. Exhaled. Inhaled. Once again, Lord Declan paused, no hint of annoyance across his features. This time, however, Ansel spoke. "We lost an entire village. We lost half of a second village. Bowgren *has* been 'heavily affected.'"

Declan nodded. "Bowgren is not the only demesne to have lost villages, but it is among the most extreme—to date. The magi believe that we, as a country, will face similar losses in the future—the near future.

"The Queen accepts this. She has been much in their counsel, as has the King." He turned to Stephen. "Maubreche has not suffered the same losses."

Nenyane shrugged, the motion instinctive; she was, for a change, listening carefully to what Lord Declan was saying. "We almost lost Brookton; it was close. We've lost one hunting lodge—but it was early enough in the season, none of our servants were lost with it."

"How many people has Maubreche lost?"

Nenyane frowned. "Less than ten; when the lands beneath Brookton shifted, some of the villagers were lost to the primal forest, some to the creatures that roam it."

Lord Declan nodded; clearly he was aware of this. He turned to Max and Alex. "Elseth has been likewise fortunate."

Max shrugged and left words to Alex. "Our mother can sometimes sense the shift in the land."

Ansel did not consider Max an authority figure; he had no trouble interrupting him. "How?"

Alex and Max exchanged a wordless glance. Max shrugged. Alex, however, said, "She is beloved of Breodan, and she is sensitive to changes in the territories of Elseth."

"Can you sense what she can sense?"

"Not nearly as well as our oldest brother, William. But yes, if we're close enough." Alex turned toward Lord Declan and offered a short bow. "Apologies for interrupting you."

Lord Declan nodded, as if the apology were necessary. This predictably annoyed Nenyane. "The sensitivity is not something that can be taught," the Huntsman of the Chamber told Lord Ansel. "We have spent some time speaking with Lady Espere and Lord Elseth; the magi believe the ability is part of Lady Espere's essential nature.

"They do not believe, however, that that sensitivity would extend to other demesnes. She is good at sensing disturbances in Elseth; she seems to lose that instinctive awareness when she is in lands she does not consider her own."

Max nodded; Alex was silent.

"We are curious to know whether Maxwell and Alexander show evidence of similar sensitivity, but that is not the reason they are here." He then turned to Nenyane. "Lord Maubreche and Lady Maubreche have also been in the Queen's counsel. Lady Maubreche is not Lady Espere of Elseth; her awareness of the change in the land is what would be expected of any similar ruler.

"But Maubreche has not suffered losses to the extent that other demesnes have." He now turned to Nenyane and Stephen. "You are Breodan's son," he said to the latter. "The Priests have confirmed it, were there any who might doubt. Lady Maubreche is unwilling to expose you to the councils of the Queen, and she has been supported in her stance by the priesthood.

"You are not, therefore, here to attend the councils of the Queen. If some pressure is brought to bear, you will report to me and I will speak with those who seek to apply it. Is that understood?"

Stephen nodded.

"It's not because of Stephen that Maubreche has been safe," Nenyane said.

Stephen's natural manners prevented a cringe.

"No? Perhaps you would care to share your opinion further."

Nenyane shrugged, shifting slightly on her feet as she turned to fully face Lord Declan. "Not really."

Max coughed, lifting a hand to cover his mouth as he turned away. Alex threw Stephen a sympathetic side glance.

Lord Declan looked as pleased with Nenyane as he had been with Ansel. Stephen stepped forward, leaving Max and Alex at his back. "Nenyane isn't good with words," he said, as if she were Hunter, and he huntbrother. "If you have questions, perhaps I could answer them."

"I have no questions to ask of you at this moment; the assessment of which I spoke does not directly touch upon these issues." Lord Declan exhaled. "I had heard she was, in temperament, very like a young Hunter Lord; I see that was not an exaggeration."

Stephen winced.

"I have no complaints with pragmatism or practicality," Lord

Declan continued. "But Hunter or no, there are vows that those who become lords of demesnes in Breodanir are expected to both make and uphold. The very heart of those, the earliest of those vows, is the beginning of the actions that bind us to the lands we must both protect and defend. Where those vows have faltered, the land has faltered. The truth of that is seen most clearly now.

"In my time, in the life I was raised in and to, the matter of vows and oaths did not have the primacy of action; they were almost entirely ceremonial. But after the Sacred Hunt in which Stephen of Elseth lost his life—in a foreign Empire, not within the King's Forest—things changed. Hunters and huntbrothers failed in those early ceremonies. The oaths between Hunter and huntbrother were rejected.

"I see I have surprised some of you; I have not surprised Stephen."

Nenyane moved to stand between Stephen and Lord Declan.

Nenyane, don't. He doesn't mean anything by it.

She ignored him, as she often did when she was at her most protective. And in some fashion, he knew he deserved it. He was god-born, and that had been the one thing that had, in the end, scarred him permanently. He did not deny his father; he would not, and could not, do that. But he did not obey, either. He did not call him father. In any true sense his father was Corwin: Corwin, who had married into Maubreche to continue its name and legacy.

In order to stop Nenyane from snapping at Lord Declan, he said, "I am not surprised, no. Breodan is Bredan of the East. He is both the God who saved our people, and the God of oaths and covenants. While he hunted in our world, he was not entirely himself, and the oaths sworn were therefore largely ceremonial. Those that were offered truthfully became true oaths; those that were not were air.

"But he is not here now in the same fashion, and he will not consecrate an oath that is offered in either fear or bad faith. That he can consecrate oaths, at a distance, is some part of the covenant made with the sleeping earth; no other oaths but this single oath can be offered and accepted—or rejected—in the same way." Could they, a god-born son would have been irrelevant.

Lord Declan met and held Stephen's gaze. "I see. You are therefore aware that the acceptance of the huntbrother's oath frequently occurs when the Hunter and prospective huntbrother are older than was once traditional."

Stephen nodded.

"Or in rare cases, not at all."

He nodded again.

"And so we come at last to the reason you are all here: you will not allow the huntbrother's oath to be sworn. Maxwell and Alexander will not accept huntbrothers. Lord Ansel will not participate in the Sacred Hunt."

Max said, before Alex could stop him, "We don't need huntbrothers. We have each other."

"That is not the will of Breodan."

"If Breodan truly disapproved, we wouldn't be able to call the Hunter's trance. We wouldn't be able to bond with Elseth dogs. We wouldn't be able to hunt as Hunters do. We can do all of that. We've more than passed the rest of the tests. We could run game against any Hunter Lord in the kingdom, and win."

Lord Ansel snorted.

Lord Declan did not. "Remedial lessons, indeed," he said.

"It's true of Stephen and Nenyane as well," Max continued, dogged in his defense of those he considered kin. He glanced at Ansel, but offered no defense of that Lord—a young man who had passed all of the priests' tests and who had earned his colors. A man who defied the single duty that defined the ruling Hunter Lords. Neither the scions of Maubreche nor Elseth would do the same, if somehow accepted and called.

As if Max hadn't spoken, Lord Declan continued. "The fabric of Breodani society, and the wheels of its power, rely upon the ceremonies created by Breodan himself, at the dawn of Breodanir. They are like unto laws. There may be reasons why a man steals food, and some of those might be acceptable to the ladies who sit in judgment over the crime itself—but a god is not a governor, and the rules of a god are not flexible. Were we to allow those in power to fall foul of the rules that have kept Breodanir safe and fecund, we might damage the country at a time when it is already coming under siege by forces we do not understand.

"I will not argue against your ability to fulfill your duties as Hunters; each of you have proven your skill in that regard. But we cannot have doubt, we cannot have deviation, at a time when the faith of citizens in the safety provided by the rulers of the demesnes is already being shaken to its core.

"It is for that reason that you have been called to Hunter's Redoubt, and for that reason that you are to remain here while we assess. If any of you would care to alter your position now," and as he spoke his gaze became glare, "you may return to your demesnes. I am certain your absences will be felt more the longer you remain here."

Stephen and Alex offered identical winces almost instantly; Nenyane was angry. So was Max.

"If you brought us here to threaten us," Nenyane snapped, "you're making a big mistake."

Max, who had opened his mouth, shut it.

Ansel, however, had to split his glare. He clearly agreed with Nenyane, and hated that Lord Declan had forced him into that position. Hands in fists, he said nothing, but the white edge around his compressed lips made clear his silence was a struggle.

Heiden did not lift his head.

"You will forgive me if I do not consider my words a threat; at worst, it is meant to be incentive. You are not imprisoned, you will not be starved, and aside from your classes, you will have freedom of the King's City. But you are required to attend the lessons. Meals will be held in the dining hall in the Redoubt; you are expected to attend.

"I will, of course, join you for meals." He cleared his throat, loudly, and the door opened to a page. "Please lead the Hunters and their hunt-brothers to the rooms that they will occupy during their stay here." He paused, and then added, "Stephen, you will personally see your dogs to the royal kennels."

Nenyane was grateful. Max, however, seemed slightly crestfallen; he had no doubt intended to borrow at least one of the four Lord Maubreche had seen fit to send with his son.

THE ROOMS in which the so-called students were to stay numbered three. Hunters and huntbrothers were expected—given the presence of two beds—to room together. Max and Alex were fine with that, as it was what would have happened anyway. They had always been close— as close as Hunter and huntbrother might have been had they been raised together from infancy. Lady Elseth often despaired of the two, who had not taken well to etiquette lessons. Max had always been openly defiant; he growled and argued. Alex, much quieter and much more compliant, offered defiance in a way Lady Elseth found harder to navigate—he smiled, he *thanked her* for sharing her wisdom and experience, and very, very politely apologized for his inability to agree or comply.

It was a trick that had surprised Stephen the first time he'd seen it, but he'd been impressed by the results, and had adopted the tactic. Nenyane, younger, had snarled in frustration.

"That's had nothing to do with my age," she snapped. She was pacing the floor, tracing the three sides of the bed that weren't pushed up against wall.

"There is no point in worrying about Heiden," Stephen knew why she was pacing. "Heiden is huntbrother."

"Is he? Is he, though?"

"He's our age. He has to be. Ansel is a Hunter Lord; it means Heiden's oath was accepted." Stephen swallowed. "If he intended to be forsworn..."

Nenyane turned instantly. "There is *nothing* you can do about it. And it's the huntbrother's oath. Forsworn is decided in one way, and one way only."

"You're worried about him," Stephen replied, voice cooler. "Why is it acceptable for you to worry, but not me?"

"I'm worried that he's being beaten to within an inch of his life by his Hunter—and I *can* do something about that. You're worried about something that will never happen, given Lord Ansel's stated intent. If Ansel doesn't participate in the Sacred Hunt, he'll lose his rank—but Heiden can't be forsworn.

"He can, however, be beaten to death at any time. It won't break Ansel's vow."

"It will."

"It *won't*."

"Hunters swear oaths to huntbrothers."

"Yes—but you know those oaths aren't accepted *as* oaths in the same way. The ceremonial binding—the slight echo and attenuation of Bredan's power—only applies to the huntbrothers. It's *why* you won't let me swear that oath. I'd swear it today. I would have sworn it when we first met. I'd swear it tomorrow—any tomorrow you care to name.

"That was always the deal: life of luxury in exchange for loss of that life *if* it protected the Hunter—the true person of value."

This was not the first time they'd had this argument; it was old enough now that all of the directions it might go were well-worn and too easily trodden. They had never had that argument within the King's Palace.

It was seldom that embers of anger could be found in the ashes of a recurring, consistent argument. A pity, then, that this was one of those few occasions. "That was *never* the point of that oath!"

"It was — on a purely pragmatic level, it *absolutely* was."

"We were meant to have *brothers* who had once lived a life harsher than ours so we would never, ever lose sight of the people we were meant to succor, to protect, to *feed*. It was a way to make absolutely certain that power didn't become what it is in almost every other kingdom!"

"Oh please. Do you think most gods even understand the difference? Bredan knew that it was the healthy, the strong, the *Hunters* who could feed the people, and he knew that among those people were those who were practically useless. Better for his people to sacrifice one of them instead of the healthy, strong person."

Stephen chose a different avenue of defense. "And how do you qualify for that? How are *you* a better sacrifice than *me*? You know a large part of Maubreche's defense now is you."

"I'm talking about *intent*."

"And you'd swear that oath, understanding the intent?"

"Yes!"

Before Stephen could reply, the door opened; Alex and Max stood outside, looking in. "Are you two at it again?" Max asked, walking in. Alex waited.

"Come in," Stephen told him. "You've heard it all before."

"We've said it all before," Alex replied. "Well, except for the bit about appropriate sacrifices." He glanced at Nenyane's narrowed eyes and winced. "You're sure?"

Stephen nodded.

"Close the door behind you," Nenyane added, in a far less friendly voice.

Alex entered, and did as Nenyane bade. "What do you think is going to happen, here?" he asked of Stephen.

"I think we're going to be poor students," he replied. "Unless you think there's any chance either you or Max will change your minds."

Max looked about as happy as Nenyane at the question. "I'm willing to swear the huntbrother's oath."

"But not willing to accept mine," Alex added.

"We don't *need* it. We don't need strangers between us. We never have. We'd be less effective."

It was true. Max and Alex hunted side by side; they could, as Hunters could, see from each other's eyes. As both were Hunters, they could both call the Hunter's trance; huntbrothers couldn't. They could switch the burden of that trance between each other so seamlessly it was hard for outsiders—and Stephen included himself in that number —to tell who was, and who was not, under its influence.

Stephen and Nenyane were likewise blessed; Stephen had a Hunter's endurance, but it lagged far, far behind Nenyane's; she could run all night without pausing for things as simple as food or sleep.

Nenyane shrugged. "It's not that we need the oath either," she admitted. "But it would make our lives in Breodanir simpler."

"It would," Alex said quietly. "But you have Robart and we have William. I don't believe Lord Ansel has a brother who could inherit; I'm not certain he has a sister who could marry a second son, the way Lady Maubreche did. The situation for Bowgren is more dire."

"Would you swear the oath if you had to inherit?" Stephen asked.

"What do you think?" It was Max who answered.

"I think Alex would accept your oath if the alternative was to leave Elseth without heir."

Max shrugged. "I'm not Alex. He's always been like Nenyane."

Nenyane's brows rose into invisibility beneath the line of her hair.

"I mean—he's always been willing to swear the huntbrother's oath," Max hastily clarified; none of the four thought Alex or Nenyane were remotely similar in personality. "But...I know what it means. I know the only thing that matters to the Hunter God in relation to that oath. You won't accept Nenyane's oath for the exact same reason I wouldn't accept Alex's. I'd swear it," he added, which surprised Stephen.

Alex smiled. "It doesn't matter. I won't accept it from Max, either. Neither of us are heir. If one of us had to become Lord Elseth..." A shadow crossed his normally pleasant expression, passing slowly. "We have options that Lord Ansel doesn't."

"They brought us here to change our minds, didn't they?" Nenyane asked.

Max shrugged. "Our father was against it. Our mother feels we'll be true to ourselves no matter where we are. Our grandmother, on the other hand..."

"Lady Maubreche holds her in the highest respect."

"I don't think that makes it any better. Would your mother have you swear those oaths?"

Stephen looked down, to floor. "It would make her life much less complicated. But no, if she has a preference, she has never made that demand. She understands what the cost of it would be."

Silence shifted in texture in the room. "Nenyane and Mark are also her children. Demanding the acceptance of such an oath from one of her children would be a type of favoritism that she cannot show."

"I'm certain it does happen," Nenyane said, her tone implying strong agreement with Stephen's statement. She walked over to her bed and sat on it. "What are the two of you going to do?"

"Be good students," Alex replied, leveling a glare at his brother. "You?"

"Stephen will, as usual, be an excellent student." She folded her arms. "I'll try. I understand that Maubreche's prestige is tied to our performance here. But we all know that nothing—for us—is going to change."

"What about Lord Ansel?" It was Alex who asked; Max bristled at the name, just as Nenyane had done.

"His is the most serious crime; he's passed all of the tests. He's a Hunter Lord—until the next Sacred Hunt is called. After that, he'll lose his title, and lose his right to inherit Bowgren.

"If the King is concerned with those of us who have not conformed to the necessary strictures, it's Ansel who represents the biggest—the most shocking—loss."

"Are there historical examples of Hunter Lords who have refused to attend the Sacred Hunt?"

All eyes turned to Alex.

"Why are you all looking at me?"

Nenyane snorted. Stephen, however, said, "You're the person most likely to have an actual answer. I suppose we could ask Lord Declan."

Alex's turn to snort. "There are no historical examples of such Hunter Lords, no." He paused, as if waiting for Max to snort; his brother faithfully did so, rolling his eyes. "But there have been cases in which the Lords were injured outside of the Sacred Hunt; they were required to attend, but they were not required to participate fully in the hunt. There was no recurrence the following year. One or two of the Lords who were injured in this fashion may have faked injuries—but again, it happened only once, so historical opinion is divided.

"In Ansel's case, his outright refusal is in no way similar." Alex frowned.

Max snorted again, this time more loudly. "You can't honestly believe that Lord Ansel is refusing to Hunt because he's afraid for his huntbrother!"

Max, as Nenyane, had noticed Heiden's demeanor, posture, and the yellowing around one of his eyes. While it was perfectly plausible that Heiden had been injured in the line of duty, it was difficult to believe.

Stephen shook his head. "It seems doubtful—but both are young enough that the oath—the huntbrother's oath—was genuine. It had to be, to be accepted at all. We can't judge."

"I can," Nenyane said.

"I don't have a problem with it either," Max added.

Alex and Stephen exchanged a glance; Alex shrugged. "I would say, for the moment, that neither Lord Ansel nor Heiden are our problem— and it would probably be best for all of us if we kept it that way. Max is my brother in every sense of the word, but it doesn't mean we haven't tried to pound sense into each other on rare occasions.

"I don't think you and Nenyane have." There was a slight rise in the words implying question—but a question that could be ignored if the listener found it too intrusive.

"Not for a long time," Stephen replied. "She could be really rough when she was teaching me how to use a sword. My father was amused. My mother...was not."

Max winced. "Lady Elseth would have been furious. My mother would have stepped in to send us both flying. Her motto is that the only person allowed to hurt her children is her."

"Gilliam?"

"Not even Gilliam. She has enough of a temper that it's never been Father who's terrifying."

Alex, smiling, nodded.

"If she wanted you to swear the oath, would you swear it?" Nenyane asked.

"She'd never ask," Max replied, with certainty.

Stephen concurred. "We have to take the dogs to the kennels," he told the Elseth brothers. "You can follow if you want—I don't think, aside from the lecture, they have any further plans for today."

Hunter's Redoubt, as the wing of the Palace was called, was almost empty, and the emptiness made the halls seem foreign and cavernous. The floors were stone, as were the walls; even light footsteps echoed here.

Stephen entered the hallway, followed by Nenyane and the two Elseth brothers. There was no angry shouting coming from behind the closed Bowgren doors.

"If the Hunter promises to respect and value his huntbrother, can he also become forsworn?" It was Alex who asked, and he asked the question of Stephen.

"I've never asked. But...I suspect the heart of the oath is the huntbrother's oath, not the Hunter's." He knew why Alex had asked. Was the oath fair? No. But Stephen had long since given up on the hope that gods would be fair. Better to expect fairness from the weather or from natural disasters.

Alex fell silent as they left the wing that would be their home in the palace. That silence surrounded them until it was broken by the noise of a busier hall, a far more crowded gallery. Hunter's Redoubt was not the only wing of the palace, after all; the palace itself was the heart of Breodanir diplomacy, and the Queen's halls were larger, grander, and far more elegantly appointed than the halls Hunters were expected—and entitled—to use.

Here, men and women of notable wealth and power, or notable talent, came to entreat the Queen. None of those people were Hunter Lords. Most were accustomed to both Hunters and their dogs, although the dogs were not given full run of the palace unless the Hunter had been commanded to attend the Master of the Game—the King himself.

Nenyane tensed as she always did when the crowds grew too dense. Max and Alex did not, although it was Alex who glanced around the hallways, absorbing the color and scent of people in various styles of clothing, and listening for snatches of languages he couldn't immediately understand. Max only paid attention to crowds when he sensed hostility; there was, as yet, none. He therefore paid attention to Steel.

Max could speak with his father's dogs as if they were his own. Alex could as well, although it took more effort for him, as he lacked his brother's deep interest. But Lady Espere was not Lady Maubreche. The idea that Max and Alex, who lived at home, had any need of a pack of their own did not occur to her. Stephen's godfather, Gilliam, was the leader of the pack; a dog pack did not break up into rival packs.

So Max was without dogs of his own.

"So are you," Nenyane said, although Stephen hadn't spoken aloud.

Both Elseth sons were accustomed to this. Nenyane could speak through the huntbrother's bond, but instinctively disliked it; she felt it implied she had something to hide.

Stephen, attempting to spare Max, nodded and attempted to divert his train of thought. All four of the dogs he had brought with him were technically Corwin's.

But in Stephen's case it was a technicality, a legality, that did not encompass the whole of the truth. Since birth—since before birth, given his mother's tales—the dogs had served Stephen, had responded to Stephen, had obeyed Stephen. Corwin could—and was frequently forced to—bring them to heel, and Stephen learned early never to interfere with his father's commands.

The fact that he could, should he so choose, had therefore caused surprisingly little tension.

It wasn't the same for Max. Stephen therefore let Steel flank Max with a small and hidden gratitude.

THE FASTEST WAY TO leave the palace was the door at which they had first arrived, but leaving through that door was the longest outdoor route to the kennels. Stephen was not entirely familiar with the layout of the King's Palace; he had seldom been called upon to visit the King, and he had done so at his father's side, as son and possible heir of Maubreche.

The first time, he had been proud. Proud of his father, Corwin, and proud of himself for being given permission to stand beside Lord Maubreche as if Stephen himself were a real adult. That child had long since vanished. If his first visit had been a bright and shiny excursion, full of hope and a child's burgeoning pride, this one was predicated on failure: Stephen's failure to conform to, to accept the rules of, the Breodanir Hunters. His father was not here, and in future, it would not be Stephen who stood beside him.

The only grace note in the summons was that Robart had not likewise been called. Robart, whose sense of youthful rivalry had slowly given way to confusion—why can't Stephen be Lord Maubreche?—and from there to a dull, but growing, resentment. His younger brother had been, if not his closest companion, companion nonetheless. But, as Robart grew, as he passed the test that Stephen himself would not pass, he had become far more frustrated, far more resentful.

"I'm god-born," Stephen had said, at the height of one of their later arguments. "My responsibilities to the god are not the same as yours."

"And that means you can't be a Hunter? That's garbage!"

Every word that Corwin and Cynthia refused to use against their oldest son, the younger son felt free to say. Sibling interactions became tangled. Robart resented Nenyane for a while, but eventually and grudgingly surrendered that anger; she couldn't help being born a girl — and she was more than competent; she could outrun Robart and Mark on ground hunts. She didn't tire. She was exempt from the sword lessons the younger Maubreche brothers had to endure, by her own desire and the demand of the sword master who felt he had nothing to teach.

And nothing to learn.

Nenyane snorted loudly. She had not been impressed by the sword master's skill, and her anger had been mollified — slightly — when it was pointed out that the use of a sword in a hunt was a last-ditch measure of self-protection at best. To Robart and Mark, skill with sword was merely raising their level of competence enough that they would not humiliate themselves — and therefore Maubreche — with their ignorance.

Robart, however, had pointed out that Stephen didn't have to take lessons. Stephen had been forced to admit that his teacher was Nenyane.

Mark, instantly, had attempted to draw Robart's attention — silently, through the huntbrother bond. The sword master chosen by Lord Maubreche was good, and was likely to be far less harsh in his criticisms and his lessons. They both knew what Nenyane was like.

And they both knew that it wasn't Nenyane who was the problem; it was Stephen. Stephen preferred this: they were, or rather Robart was, angry at Stephen, not his huntbrother. But the seed of resentment had grown in the past year. Robart had wanted, as a child, to be Lord Maubreche. Perhaps he wanted that now — but not this way. Those had been his words: *not this way.*

Stephen's reply had infuriated him. "The only other way is my death — is that what you want? Rulership isn't a trial by combat. It isn't a test of competence in hunting. For the Hunter-born it's an act of necessity — one that can, and does, lead to death. Would you have me die, instead?"

"Yes!" Robart had stomped off.

Mark, however, had remained. "He doesn't mean that. He's just..." The Maubreche huntbrother had squared his slender shoulders. "It's been hard for him, to live in your shadow."

Stephen had nodded. He knew. He only barely stopped himself from demanding, of Mark, if Mark thought that Stephen—who cast that shadow—had had an easier life, an easier time, than Robart. But that would have been unfair, and he had known it.

"But he's always looked up to you, as well. You're *Breodan's* actual son. You're the only person in this kingdom called Hunter-born that the foreigners from the Empire accept as god-born. The priests treat you with actual respect. Robart always believed that you—Stephen—would become the strongest Lord Maubreche the kingdom has ever seen: respected, feared, obeyed.

"You were important enough that in the end, Nenyane—a girl—was accepted as your huntbrother."

"Father had to fight for that."

"Yes—but he succeeded." Mark exhaled. "He doesn't understand why you're walking away from the only life he's ever wanted. He thinks it means you don't respect it. You don't care."

"What do you think?"

Mark bowed head. "I think you do care. I don't understand—I can't —what it's like to be you. But Robart...won't understand it. He doesn't want to be Lord Maubreche because it means you intend to abandon us. He won't be Lord because of his own worth; he'll be Lord because, to you, it's not worthwhile."

Nenyane had moved in to intervene, stepping away from the wall against which she'd been leaning.

Don't.

He doesn't understand.

His oath was accepted. Breodan knows that Mark is truly and completely huntbrother. But Robart doesn't *understand what that means.*

And you want him to be ignorant? Is that it?

I don't want to build a wall between Robart and the brother to whom he's closest. I don't want anything I say to sound like an accusation or an excuse. Please, Nenyane. Please leave it alone. She had, but resentfully; Nenyane had never been a person who surrendered with grace.

ROBART WAS NOT HERE. Robart, Maubreche's best hope for future continuity. Robart, who was certain that Stephen intended to abandon his duties. Not for the first time, Stephen wished that his actual father had been Corwin; that gods had not figured in his existence, in his life.

"You don't intend to follow Bredan's will, either," Nenyane helpfully pointed out. Her voice was louder than usual because the hallways through which the Hunters and Stephen's dogs now walked were far more crowded.

Max and Alex remained silent, although it seemed to take some effort on Max's part.

Stephen, for his part, failed to reply. This was not a conversation to be held in a public space, and even if it were, it was the continuation of an argument without conclusion, both participants having staked out their territory years ago, buttressing it against any shift in position. Nenyane, restive, wasn't content to let it go; he could feel her frustration.

And he could feel it suddenly shift, as if she had been standing on the edge of a cliff and the wind had blown her off.

He reached for the dogs instinctively; their posture shifted and changed, just as his did. The Queen's gallery through which they were walking became both disaster and backdrop. He knew Nenyane well.

There was death here.

Max and Alex responded just a beat behind the dogs, because Max, sensitive to Hunter dogs, understood instantly what Steel's posture meant. Stephen shifted gaze, bouncing between the eyes of dogs that were now facing outward in all directions. Most Hunters could also seek the advantage of their huntbrother's vision. Stephen avoided that in all but specific emergencies because Nenyane didn't see the world the way other people did, and her viewpoint took effort to untangle and understand. There was too much color in her vision, too many details that Stephen, through his own eyes, couldn't naturally see.

It was the reason she could do what she did for Maubreche when it came to the incursions that she called the wilderness.

There was no incursion here.

Stephen leapt to the side as a man separated himself from the gallery's normal occupants; he noticed only that the stranger wore relatively expensive clothing in an ostentatious way, as if demanding to be noticed. What the Maubreche Hunter noticed instead was his blade; it was narrow, longer than a normal knife, and in keeping with his brightly colored shirt and jacket.

The knife passed through one layer of Stephen's clothing, but went wide on the second attempt; there was no third. He had not drawn sword or weapon himself, but the weapons he did have—Hunter weapons all—were moving and sentient. Steel's jaws snapped around the man's weapon wrist; the man's expression did not change at all. He pulled a second knife.

Nenyane sliced clean through that wrist.

Blood sprayed instantly, hitting not only dogs and Stephen, but some of the people who were passing by and were not as quick to notice the movements of a stranger. Alex was out of the splash radius; Max was not.

Some people began to scream, some to shout, and many to panic; this was a public hall in the palace, and not all of the visitors were Breodani. Some feared the dogs and some the girl whose clothing was spattered with blood. The man went down to the rest of the dogs. Stephen shouted orders—more to be heard by strangers, and to be seen to be obeyed—but Nenyane wasn't a dog.

"Don't kill him—we want him alive for questioning!"

Even that came late. Nenyane had never cared to leave assassins alive, if the demonic could be said to be alive at all; in her opinion they could not.

The Queen's Guard converged on them from both sides of the hall; they were faster than Stephen had expected. Swords were drawn, and orders snapped; the screaming and shouting banked at the sight of armor and tabard, both.

Belatedly, Stephen realized that Alex and Max were both wielding swords; neither had struck the attacker, but it was a bit late for that. Nenyane looked about for something on which to clean her blade, but finding nothing, shrugged and wiped its length across her shirt.

Not for the first time, Stephen was grateful that his mother was safely in Maubreche—safely, for him and Nenyane.

THE DOGS DID NOT MAKE it to the kennels, in large part because their master did not manage to leave the palace. Nenyane, in the absence of threat, had resumed her studied nonchalance. If it had been a simple act, that would have been fine; it wasn't. Nenyane considered the dead assassin finished business; he wouldn't be coming back.

Stephen, however, considered him a source of possible information, or he had been when still breathing. He chose to keep the words to himself because they, like any words employed in arguments with Nenyane, had little to no effect, and he did not wish to be seen scrapping with his huntbrother in front of strangers—all of whom were on the edge of anger themselves.

Lord Declan had been summoned to the Queen's gallery in which the guards detained all four of the Hunters. The guards looked askance at the dogs, but in truth, not severely; they understood that these were Hunter dogs, and their master, detained, was not to be allowed to deliver them to the kennels. In normal circumstances, the dogs might have been escorted there by one of the resident Hunter Lords, but these were not normal circumstances, and the dogs were not of a mind to be separated from their master; they had made this embarrassingly clear.

The Huntsman of the Chamber never looked happy; Stephen was privately certain he was incapable of something so simple. He was not yet angry, but his expression implied he was very, very close.

The Queen's Guard had clearly apprised Lord Declan of the circumstances that necessitated his presence in the gallery where blood and body had yet to be cleared away. He bent to examine the corpse, and then rose, looking toward the four Hunters as if the body was no longer relevant. "What happened here?" he asked, his voice the wrong type of soft.

No one answered. Glances were not exchanged, but Stephen was certain some discussion was happening between the Elseth Hunters. For his own part, he and Nenyane were silent; the only thing he asked of her was that she leave the talking to him.

She agreed.

"We were on the way to the kennels," he therefore said, pausing. Lord Declan continued silent. "When we reached the Queen's gallery, one of the passersby—that one—attempted to stab me."

"Attempted."

"We noticed. I narrowly avoided the first strike, and the second was wide; Steel caught his wrist."

"And the missing hand?"

"He drew a second weapon, possibly to defend himself from the dogs. Nenyane cut off his hand."

Lord Declan turned to Alex. "Alexander, do you have anything you wish to add?"

"No, sir. Everything happened as Stephen has said. Max and I had time to draw weapons, but not time to use them."

"None of you seem particularly upset." It was the man in charge of the Queen's Guard who spoke.

"This is not the first time someone has attempted to assassinate me," Stephen replied, his voice even. "I imagine it won't be the last." Almost defensively, he added, "Lord Declan doesn't seem particularly upset, either."

This was not the right thing to say; he knew it just after the last syllable left his mouth.

"I am ill-pleased," Lord Declan then said—to the guards. "But Lady Maubreche made *quite* clear that her son has, indeed, been the intended victim of similar attacks in the past—in Maubreche. I *assured her* that he would not encounter that difficulty in the palace.

"Clearly my confidence was misplaced."

The Queen's Guard reddened; he offered no further implied criticism. "We were not informed of either this assurance or the need for it."

"An oversight, I'm certain. I have cause to speak with the Queen later in the day, and I will make certain to impart all necessary information to her at that time."

Stephen exhaled slowly.

"It is possible some exception about the placement of your dogs will have to be made," Lord Declan continued. "For the moment, I want all of you to return to your rooms."

"HOW MANY TIMES HAS THAT HAPPENED?" Max asked, when they had put enough distance between Lord Declan and the Queen's Guard.

"It hasn't happened that often—" Stephen began.

"Five."

Max glanced at Nenyane. "Five. How old were you when it first happened?"

"I don't remember—" Stephen began.

"Ten."

"Do you want to have the rest of this conversation?" Stephen snapped.

"It'll be faster and more accurate," Nenyane snapped back.

Stephen tried to rein in his own frayed temper. *I don't want to give them more cause to worry than they already have.*

"You just don't want them to worry about you."

I don't need Max and Alex to think of me as some sort of frail treasure that has to be protected!

"They don't think you're frail. Look, you're god-born, they know it. They know which god, too. They're going to understand that there are some gods and some people who *don't* want a god-born son of Bredan to survive. It's better that they know—you were attacked in the heart of Breodanir, in the King's damn Palace. If it can happen here, it can happen anywhere."

Max opened his mouth. It snapped shut audibly before words could escape.

It was Alex who therefore intervened in the apparently one-sided argument. "Nenyane's right. We're not going to think less of you—but if this is what you might face, both of us need to know." He glanced at Max. "I think this is probably the reason neither Father nor Mother made any attempt to argue against the King's demand. They must have known that you'd be sent here as well."

Stephen said nothing, but he absorbed Alex's words.

"You know our father thinks of you as his nephew. He doesn't care that you've got golden eyes. To him, you're the son of Stephen of Elseth —his huntbrother, dead before you were born."

Stephen swallowed.

"So does Cynthia," Nenyane said quietly. "Stephen, in her eyes, has three fathers. But Stephen of Elseth is—for her part—the reason for his existence. Not Bredan."

Alex nodded. "You're the only thing that remains of his Stephen. He couldn't protect his huntbrother. He couldn't save his life.

"And he can't interfere in Maubreche—Lady Elseth has made that *quite* clear. But he'd be here, if he could. He'd defy king and God— because the God killed his huntbrother. He understands why," Alex continued, voice dropping, "and he accepts it. But it's complicated. We're probably here because he couldn't be."

Nenyane shrugged. "You'd have had to come anyway; there's no way you could have avoided the King's summons."

Max said, "I'm not so certain of that. Elseth doesn't need us to *be* Hunters; we have William and our sisters. They could have chosen to disinherit us—Mother knows we don't care about it. We're not willing to follow their rules if it means we have to replace each other with strangers. Father doesn't care much, either.

"William sometimes resents it, but mostly, he supports our decision. And he *is* Lord William, and Lucas is a good huntbrother to him—William can be a little wild when he starts to lose his temper.

"And none of that matters. Mother and Father didn't argue against the King's demand when Grandmother presented it; they nodded and accepted the King's word, as if they'd always been so obedient." He grimaced. "They must have known that you'd be summoned as well."

Max glanced at the dogs. "I think we're meant to be part of your pack."

Nenyane snorted. "His dogs are much better trained than you."

Alex laughed; Max no doubt had thoughts. He didn't, however, choose to share them with anyone but Alex. "I know it won't bring much comfort to either of you," Alex said, the laugh relaxing into a smile, "but it's comforting to us. We were confused when we were sent away. We didn't understand why.

"Now, we do. Come on, let's head to your room."

"You can head to your own rooms," Nenyane said.

Max shook his head. "We need to plan."

CHAPTER SEVEN

Planning took second place to cleaning up. While Nenyane herself was not concerned with small amounts of blood—her words, as neither the Elseth brothers nor Stephen considered the stiff stretches of dried blood to be small in amount—they were in Lord Declan's domain, now. While they weren't under the auspices of the ruling Lady—in this case, the Queen herself—they were expected to conform. Outsiders' eyes would be upon them on occasion, and they could not be an embarrassment to the Breodani in front of powerful foreign dignities.

Stephen was likewise bloodied, but first saw to the cleaning of Steel's fur. This was practical; Steel, like many of the dogs, disliked to be scrubbed, and the blood was not going to come out without effort. His clothing would be drenched in the aftermath, and there was no point in having two sets of clothing that required laundering.

Alex and Max likewise left to change, but they were far more efficient, not having dogs to clean. Or Nenyane.

"I heard that."

"The assassin is dead. A walking reminder of his existence—and the pall it casts on the Queen's Guard—is not a good idea. Lord Declan was, I believe, genuinely embarrassed."

"He should have been."

"What would you prefer as the alternative? Me confined permanently to my room, except when under the escort of the Queen's Guard? Press this, and that is almost certainly the outcome we face."

Nenyane had no problem with this. "It's what would normally happen in this circumstance."

Frustrated, his arms shaking from more than the effort of cleaning one dog—and beating his own bloodied clothing for good measure in the water that remained—he said, "How do you know? How can you even consider yourself an expert in something like that?"

It was the wrong question. He knew it, but he was not as calm or accepting as he had attempted to be when in the presence of the Elseth brothers.

Nenyane was always certain of her opinions. Always. Nenyane, who could not *remember* any part of her life that did not begin as a child in Maubreche, except for the attack of the demons. She made assumptions about the life she had led, absent memories trauma had clearly destroyed, and she couldn't be moved.

Stephen understood that she didn't remember. As a child, he hadn't cared. She was the huntbrother fate had given him, and he had no intention of rejecting her. Nenyane became Nenyane of Maubreche.

Nenyane had always cared.

It was the wrong question. He knew it, but could not take it back. The anger, the frustration, died, snuffed out like tentative candlelight in strong wind.

She knew. She heard it all. If Stephen didn't always pay mind to Nenyane's thoughts, she was ever aware of his; in that, she was truly huntbrother. He expected anger.

Would have preferred anger.

"Nenyane—"

She turned toward the door. "I don't know. I've *never* known." He was wrong; she *was* angry, but all of her anger was turned inward.

"It's never mattered," he said, rising, half-dressed, arms wet. "I didn't mean—"

"You did. You meant it."

"I didn't mean it that way. You know I've always trusted your instincts."

"But that's all they are. Instincts. Instinct without explanation, without actual information others might assess and believe."

"It doesn't matter. You're not their huntbrother—you're mine."

She turned back to him, her eyes dark, her expression somber. "You understand that people aren't the only assassins you'll face. That you're not just a Hunter Lord—that you might, if you continue in this way, never *be one*. You know I recognize demons—but not in the way you recognize things. You don't doubt me. But I can't tell you why I react the way react. I can't explain it to *anyone*.

"I *can't plan*." Her voice was almost a whisper. "I can't *remember*. Your mother called the magi; they couldn't help with my memory either. Whatever I once was—it's lost. And with it, information *we need* if I'm not to lose you—" She stopped, her shoulders down, her body gathering briefly inward as if she had shouldered a weight she could not carry. He knew she would turn, open the door, and walk out, because Nenyane shared tears with no one.

BY THE TIME Max and Alex joined Stephen and his dogs, Nenyane had not returned.

Alex took one look at Stephen's expression and closed his mouth before he could ask about Nenyane. Max and Alex were closer than most Hunters and their huntbrothers, but they understood all of the ways in which disagreements and conflict could cause more pain, not less, to those who were close. Given the events—an assassination attempt, without warning, in the King's Palace—they knew tempers or fears could run high.

Nenyane didn't have fear, in their eyes.

Stephen knew they were wrong. But her fears didn't include human assassins; nor did they include demons. Fear was not what demons invoked in Nenyane; she passed almost instantly beyond fear into a bitter, raging fury.

Max surprised Stephen. "She's worried about you," he said, his voice uncharacteristically gentle.

Stephen looked toward Max; Steel rose and padded in the Elseth Hunter's direction.

"She'd never have accepted the huntbrother's oath if you were the one who had to swear it. If she swore the huntbrother's oath, Breodan would accept it. He would have accepted it practically the first day you met. Our father knew it. It's why he accepted her at all."

Alex grimaced. "He'll never trust Evayne, and Nenyane came to you through Evayne. But he accepts that Nenyane's not Evayne. Should we go find her?"

Stephen shook his head. "She won't thank you; if you're lucky, she'll tell you to go away."

"Unlucky involves violence?" Max asked.

"Only if you're Stephen of Maubreche," Stephen answered. "She actually likes the two of you. She would never have left me alone, otherwise."

Max shrugged, awkward with the secondhand praise. "She knows you have the dogs."

"You think she trusts the dogs with my safety?"

"She should. Speaking of dogs, should you send one of the dogs to her?"

"You know what Nenyane's like with the dogs — that hasn't changed. She's just...worried."

Alex nodded; he expected attempted assassinations to have that effect. Stephen didn't correct him. While Nenyane didn't consider assassins trivial, it wasn't the assassination that had pushed her out the door. What she wanted now was distance, privacy.

Distance was very, very difficult to achieve between Hunter and huntbrother; it had been perhaps the hardest thing the young Maubreche Hunter had had to learn.

He almost envied Max and Alex, because he was certain they didn't require it.

He could not comfort Nenyane. Her lack of any memory whatsoever had not concerned him immediately. But her pain and frustration at the lack of memory was continuous.

We're defined by what we've done, she had snapped. *Who we are is based on what we've done. I have* no idea *who I am — don't you understand that?*

You're my huntbrother. You're Nenyane of Maubreche. As if that was all she had to be. As if that was all that mattered. He almost winced, remembering his own youthful certainty. But it had been earnest, honest; she was his huntbrother, the most important person in his world. He could not understand, then, why the lack of memory mattered.

Any time events involving demons or what Nenyane called the wilderness occurred, echoes of that rage and pain would return to her. He could not draw her out of them, could not drive those thunderous clouds away. Worse, he could not join her there. She demanded distance.

What if she did remember her past? What if she had a family—a different family, one she loved and to whom she might feel her duties lay?

She had never sworn the huntbrother's oath.

He had never let her.

She was not an orphan, as huntbrothers almost always were. Or perhaps she was—Evayne had rescued her from demons, after all. Perhaps her family was dead, and, shattered by grief and the attack itself, she had lost all memory of them. But if they lived? If they lived, could she return to them? Would she want to?

His fear was a child's fear—it was for himself, not for Nenyane. And it was a fear, in the end, that he simply endured until he grew older and he could fear *for* her as well.

"Stephen?"

Stephen shook his head, a half-smile on his lips. "I knew, the day I set eyes on her for the first time, who she was, who she was meant to be: I knew she would be my huntbrother, or I would have no huntbrother. She was so scrawny, back then. She looked like a starving orphan. She almost never spoke; she avoided everyone in Maubreche who wasn't me. She didn't like the dogs—they were smelly, there were too many of them, it took too long to care for them and, in her opinion, they weren't *necessary*."

Max bridled instantly.

Alex, however, chuckled. "That hasn't changed much, has it?"

"She's learned to be quieter about it. She's a lot like a Hunter in temperament, and she's practical. Her attitude has changed; she accepts my dogs grudgingly as partners she can trust. She just thinks they're unnecessary."

"Dogs are never unnecessary for Hunters," Max growled.

Stephen nodded. The dogs had never been troubled by Nenyane's opinion of their relative worth. "She has no memories of her life before she arrived in Maubreche." He paused, and then corrected himself. "She has no memories beyond being attacked by demons. Being pursued by them. She assumes—we all assume—that it was the injuries she took from the demons that destroyed her memories.

"Evayne found her. Evayne saved her."

"That doesn't mean you should trust Evayne." Alex's voice was soft but focused.

Stephen knew. His godfather, Lord Elseth, still blamed Evayne for the death of his huntbrother over seventeen years ago. "But when we met, when I knew who she would be to me, I didn't understand that it was somehow important for her to mean something to herself." Alex winced, which caused an echo of the same response in Stephen. "She's never recovered the memories she lost. Mostly, it doesn't affect her. I used to think that meant she didn't care, because I didn't care. She was Nenyane of Maubreche to me.

"But sometimes I wonder who or what I would be if I had no memories. Sometimes I wish I didn't."

They knew.

"Not remembering wouldn't change facts, but if I had no memory, Nenyane would have sworn the huntbrother's oath and I would have accepted it. I wouldn't be here now."

Alex bowed head briefly. "It's what she wants."

Stephen shook his head. "She wants it because it's practical. She's never cared for the King's City, and she tolerates the Hunter hierarchy only because she has respect for Corwin. To her, the oath is materially true. It's not so much that she's mine, but that I'm hers. She would kill to protect me."

Given they had all had to clean blood off their clothing and the assassin, dead, could not be questioned, they knew.

"But she would die to protect me as well. An oath therefore changes nothing practical for Nenyane. I know who she is. Sometimes I want who she *is* to be more important to her than whatever it was that she was."

"Not fair," Alex said quietly.

"I know that. I know. But when she's in pain, there's nothing I can do for her. Nothing I can try. I know her better than I know anyone, including members of my family. I know her anger, I know her frustration, I understand her intensity. But knowing that doesn't make things like this easier—for her. There is nothing she wants from me when she's like this; nothing I can offer that will provide comfort.

"The only thing I can do is—" He froze.

"Stephen?"

He turned toward the door, Max and Alex all but forgotten. Patches caught the edge of his jacket in her teeth as he leapt forward. It caused him to stumble; he ordered the lymer to release him, and she did—but she barked, the sound underscored by a brief, high pitched whine.

Nenyane accepted the dogs grudgingly, as the dogs accepted her—but they understood that she was, in a very integral way, the heart of the pack to Stephen. Aside, but never separate.

"What is it? What's happened?" Max and Alex were watching him, echoes of the morning in their expressions.

"Nenyane—Nenyane is..." he could not bring himself to finish the sentence. Nenyane was *weeping*. He tried, although it was uncomfortable, to see through her eyes, to get some sense of where, in this palace, she was. Her vision had never felt natural to him, and he knew—from discussions with Arlin—that this was highly unusual.

But even if it hadn't been, he wouldn't have been able to see much; her eyes were now closed. She was caught in the grip of a grief so intense it would have been painful to experience in any circumstance. It was worse now, because he had never felt a like grief from her. Even in her fear at the possible loss of her truest self, she had never grieved like this.

He opened the door and sprinted into the hallway, assassins and Lord Declan's commands to remain within the Hunter's Redoubt forgotten. The dogs leapt up and followed, flanking him—this hallway was built wide for Hunters, and all Hunters had dogs. At his back, he could hear the more human steps of Alex and Max.

There were two men in the Queen's Guard uniform who stood at the entrance—or the exit, in this case—of the halls in which the recalcitrant Hunters were housed. They opened their mouths to speak—to perhaps stop them—and Stephen sprinted between them before they could close ranks.

He did not call out to Nenyane through the huntbrother bond. If she responded, she would tell him to go away, to leave her alone. Normally, he would do just that; she had always been a person who needed to be entirely alone with her emotions when they were overwhelming. But never in Stephen's prior experience had those emotions involved such overwhelming grief and loss.

The Queen's Guards didn't immediately pursue the three Hunters; perhaps they had not been informed that said Hunters were confined to the wing by the man who ruled it. Stephen knew, dimly, that Lord Declan would not be pleased—but his displeasure was a distant concern. If Nenyane was aware of his approach at all, she made no sign;

she did not insert herself into his thoughts, did not tell him to go back to their room.

The halls were not empty; as the three Hunters and their dogs—all running as if they were on a ground hunt and had found their quarry— left Hunter's Redoubt, they were forced to thread their way through the more populated public halls. The halls in which an assassin had apparently lain in wait for Stephen of Maubreche.

Threading one's way through forests was simpler because the trees didn't move. Stephen had, regardless, expanded his awareness of his surroundings; he had called the Hunter's trance here, where he hunted nothing.

Moving people were therefore not an issue he faced; he was aware of all of them, of their walking speed, of their footfalls, of their breathing, their brief words, their silence as three young men and four dogs blazed past them.

He did not slow, did not stop, until he could see his huntbrother's back with his own eyes. Then, having arrived, he froze—as if all the awkwardness of another person's naked grief had waited to slap him across the face only then. Nenyane was all but alone in the hall; there were few other people present, but most strangers did not stop by the side of someone who was so clearly and so openly in the grip of such strong grief.

Stephen understood this as well; it was his reaction. Grief of this nature was private, and weeping so openly broke all of the boundaries established for polite behavior between strangers.

This was a hall that led to the Queen's Chambers, the most opulently appointed state rooms the King's Palace boasted; appointments were generally required to walk this hall at all. Adorning the walls were paintings and statues, gifts given by the powerful, many of whom were not Breodanir natives. It was in front of one such statue that Nenyane stood. Her arms were by her sides, her head tilted back— as it would have to be if she wished to view the statue's face.

It was not a statue Stephen recognized; he assumed it was Imperial in origin, as much of the maker-born work in Breodanir was. Perhaps because he was suddenly at a loss, he looked more carefully at the statue. It was of a man, larger than life, the details in proportion; he stood, facing outward, both of his hands on the pommel of a great sword, point to pedestal. He wore armor, and folds of cloth, expertly suggested by the artist, fell partly over his left shoulder, and partly down his back, unseen at the angle from which Stephen viewed him. His hair was long and braided; he had no beard. His eyes were not of stone, but sapphire; they caught light at an odd angle, almost as if they were alive, as they surveyed the hall and its occupants. There was no anger in the graven expression, but no peace, either.

Alex and Max had come to a stop behind Stephen and his dogs. No one moved. Not even Nenyane, as if she was, for the moment, entirely unaware of her surroundings—and she had never lacked awareness, even in her sleep. The whole of her attention appeared riveted to this one statue in a hall adorned with art.

"It's new," Alex said quietly. At Stephen's bewildered expression, he added, "that statue. It was a gift from the Order of Makers. It represents Moorelas, or Morel of Aston, as he is sometimes known."

"How do you know that? I thought you never left Elseth."

"You don't have my grandmother," was the wry reply. "She still has hopes for us."

"For Alex," Max corrected his brother.

Alex grimaced but didn't disagree. "We come to the city more frequently than you do." He looked at Nenyane. "She hasn't seen it before."

Stephen shook his head. The movement, following Alex's gentle commentary, eased the almost stricken tension that kept him in place. He moved toward Nenyane, while Alex, Max, and all four of his dogs remained behind. A growing sense of urgency added speed to his steps, although they were otherwise silent.

She turned, just before he could touch her; he had reached out, instinctively, with both arms—to Nenyane, of all people. Her face was wet, her eyes bloodshot, her nose running. Her eyes, however, widened. She froze, and before he could change his mind, Stephen wrapped his arms around her and drew her toward his chest, no longer afraid of her grief, no longer afraid of how she needed distance. As if she had stumbled at the edge of a cliff, he reached out to grab her, to stop her from falling.

She buried her face in his chest, and he was reminded of his first sight of her: too slender, too fragile, too brittle, eyes darkened, expression grimly silent. He had been determined to hold on to her, to protect her, from that moment, if not in those words. As a child, he could say and do things that an adult would have to consider and reconsider given the harsher consequences for adults.

In the moment, he was that child again.

And in that moment, she was the child she had never been. She wrapped her arms around his body, the strength of her grip giving lie to the visual implication of frailty, of weakness.

She sobbed. It didn't matter; bathing Steel had left his clothing wet, and he'd run out of his room so quickly he hadn't had time — or inclination — to choose more appropriate attire.

"Your mother would be so angry," she said, her voice muffled, her arms tight. "I'm sorry."

He shook his head, his chin brushing her hair. "It was my fault." Her arms tightened. "I'll pass out if you squeeze any tighter — and you'll be stuck dragging my unconscious body back to our room."

She shook her head again. "I know Max and Alex came with you — I'll make them do it. I'm sorry," she said again. "It's not — it's not just the assassins. It's..."

He almost rushed in with words, but held them back, some hint of the person he was now once again asserting itself over the raw emotion and reaction of his distant childhood self.

"Don't die," she whispered. "Don't die on me. Don't leave me behind."

"I won't die."

"Promise. Promise me you won't die?"

He was the son of the God of Covenants. He could not make a promise he was not absolutely certain he could keep. He wanted to, here and now; he wanted it desperately. "I'll do everything in my power to prevent it."

"I don't care if I die," she whispered. "I don't care if I die first. But this time...this time..." She stopped, drawing in a ragged breath, pulling herself back to the end of the reach of his arms to look up at him. "When did you get so tall?"

"Two years ago?"

"I was willing to swear the huntbrother's oath," she said, after a pause for breath. "I was willing to swear any oath that meant that if I failed you, if I failed to protect you, the cost would be my life."

Said so nakedly, so plainly, it was painful to Stephen. His arms stiffened; he couldn't prevent it. In a far quieter voice he said, "I don't want to lose you, either. You're my huntbrother. You are the only person alive who will ever be my huntbrother. I know you don't care about your own survival; you never have. Ever. It's the one thing about you that always worried Father.

"Promise me that you won't die, either."

She looked at him, tears once again falling down her cheeks. "I won't die," she told him, none of his own doubt about the swearing of oaths evident in her expression.

They had always been different people.

He wanted to know why she had wept, but she was close enough now that he knew what her answer would be: *I don't know*. He could feel the confusion that underlay the weight of sudden, unexpected grief; was certain it would, if touched at all, turn to anger and the self-loathing that always accompanied lack of memory.

"If the two of you are finished," Alex said, "we should probably make a reasonable attempt to obey Lord Declan's commands."

LORD DECLAN WAS NOT IMPRESSED by the so-called attempt.

He was not a man to raise voice, as many did in anger; he was a man whose volume dropped precipitously. It reminded Stephen very much of dogs: when they growled, their voices low and rumbling, they were at their most dangerous.

Nenyane, for once, was subdued. Had Ansel been called to the great room, she might have rallied; Nenyane had always shored herself up with enmity when the situation was dire. She could find no enemies, no rivals here, except perhaps Lord Declan himself—but even exhausted as she was, their mother's lessons made clear just how poor an idea that would be.

She therefore endured, Stephen by her side, although she did move out from the shelter of the arm he had laid across her shoulder.

It was not obvious to Lord Declan that she had been so upset. Stephen thought that might be deliberate on the Hunter Lord's part, but was uncertain.

"I believe I made myself clear: Stephen—and therefore Nenyane—is expected to remain within Hunter's Redoubt. I have been informed that you leapt past the guards; you did not even take an escort we are reasonably certain we can trust with your safety. Understand that any injury you take here will reflect poorly on both the King and the Queen. Perhaps you have not met our Queen."

All four had, of course, but Stephen's encounter had been in distant childhood, before his refusal to participate in the earliest of the Hunter ceremonies. He could not clearly recall her face.

In the demesnes, the women ruled. Their Hunters were far too involved in the duty and responsibility of the Hunt itself to properly attend to the governing of their lands, although often they just didn't care about governing; the Hunt was all that mattered. Stephen knew there were rare cases where Hunter Lords interfered with their wives' governance, but it happened seldom; the Ladies had been educated and raised with just such governance in mind. Hunters had not.

The Queen, in all ways, was a special case. Her husband did not join the Sacred Hunt; he called it. He called it, and all of the ruling lords who wished to retain their title and lands answered that call.

The Queen could lose neither husband nor son in the Sacred Forest; when the Hunter God hunted his own, the King and his progeny were not the ones who faced the Hunter's Death. In theory, this meant the King was perfectly capable of ruling as Lady Maubreche did. But if the King was not called to the Sacred Hunt, he was nonetheless Hunter-born, and he—and all male heirs—were expected to pass each of the tests that Hunters must pass to assume their place among the Hunter Lords; they were expected to provide the bounty of their hunts to the people in their personal demesnes.

It was the Queen who interacted with the governing ladies; the Queen who wrote political missives and dealt with foreign dignitaries; the Queen who was expected to understand—and speak—several languages. Governance was not simple; the title itself made knowledge necessary, and the consequences of mistakes more severe.

Had Stephen been her child, those consequences could be kept within the family; he was not. And Cynthia of Maubreche could stand toe-to-toe with the Queen—with any Hunter Lady—without flinching or backing down. If Stephen died here, the Queen would bear the brunt of Maubreche's wrath—and that wrath would not be inconsequential.

Lord Declan's mention of the Queen was very like a father's *wait until your mother finds out about this*. It was a way of underlining displeasure at a forbidden activity. Lord Declan did not intend that the Queen should become involved as judge and jury; it was a Hunter matter.

Or perhaps not. "The Queen's Guard is aware of the incident, and the Queen is displeased that Nenyane dispatched the assassin; from the reports of the guards, his death was not necessary. What little information can be gleaned from a corpse has been gleaned — but the magi were summoned to examine the body.

"I am not counsel to the Queen; I am therefore not fully apprised of the contents of the report the Order of Knowledge tendered the Queen. The King, however, is, and he is now highly concerned. Do you understand?"

Stephen nodded, just as he would have nodded had he been called into his angry mother's presence.

"It is the Queen's opinion that you should not have survived the assassin."

Nenyane tensed, shaking herself free of all grief, all confusion, at the certainty in the soft-spoken words. She did not — yet — take the comment personally. "Is the Queen's opinion based on the report the Order of Knowledge made?"

"That is my current assumption." He turned to Max and Alex. "I believe you were included in the order to remain in the Redoubt. I may, however, have been unclear."

Max stopped himself from shrugging, but given his expression, it was close. Clearing his throat, he said, "The assassin wasn't after us." His tone, softer and far more respectful than it usually was, softened the argument in the words.

"I do not believe the assassin is relevant to my orders. In Hunter's Redoubt, I am the ranking Hunter Lord; the wing is under my purview. My word, where it is not illegal, is law. Perhaps you are under the impression that you are here on vacation. The fault in that misapprehension is no doubt mine. I intend to alleviate it now."

"The Queen feels it highly likely that the assassin could have killed you all."

This time, Nenyane snorted.

To Stephen's surprise, Lord Declan glanced at Nenyane and nodded. "Indeed. The Order and its various mage-born disciples have long misunderstood the strength of the Breodani. Report or no, you are adults, and you have passed all of the tests that involve purely physical endurance and strength. The Queen, however, holds the mage-born in high regard, and she is less involved in Hunter matters than either Lady Maubreche or Lady Elseth.

"But it is the Queen's Guard who has been tasked with your protection while you remain here. An exception for your dogs has been made. They will not sleep in the kennels; they will, however, be fed there. You have the King's permission to retain the use of your dogs within the Redoubt."

Stephen nodded.

"The Queen has also consented, but the Captain of the Guard is not best pleased."

Nenyane, about to let loose a volley of words that would humiliate Lady Maubreche, snapped her jaws shut.

"You have something you wish to contribute?" Lord Declan asked her, his expression chilly.

"He has *me*. The Queen's Guard was slow to react." The words, carefully modulated, still contained heat; she did not think much of the guards. "Too slow. The dogs were faster. I understand that the King's Palace *is* the Queen's palace — but I will not put the feelings of the captain of her guard above my Hunter's safety."

"Indeed." To Stephen, he said, "The King was impressed with both your dogs and your huntbrother; impressed enough that he pled your case. The Queen consented to have you be responsible for your own safety." Lord Declan's hands crept behind his back. "She has, however, placed a condition upon that consent."

Nenyane tensed. So did Max.

"She wishes to meet with you both." He glanced at Alex and Max. "In my opinion, she would not be displeased to meet with the Elseth brothers as well, although she is more familiar with them." He paused; Stephen was almost certain the hands he clasped behind his back had tightened, but didn't move his dogs into a position where he might see through their eyes.

"When does the Queen wish to meet with us?" Stephen asked, before Nenyane could.

"Given the unusual nature of the attack within her own walls, she has said she will meet with you at your earliest possible convenience."

"Now?" Nenyane asked, while Stephen was still processing the words.

"Indeed."

"Can Stephen eat first? None of us have had lunch." Nenyane's expression implied she would accept a refusal. Four of the five people in this room knew how misleading that implication was. She had chosen food because it was the only available avenue for argument.

"You have missed the morning meal," Lord Declan replied, his eyes narrowed as they met Nenyane's. Perhaps Lord Declan was more perceptive than Stephen had expected of someone who appeared to be so autocratic. "As the oversight was caused by today's incident, a meal will be readied in haste—but such accommodations will not occur again. Both Lord Ansel and Lord Heiden came to the dining room at the expected time; they will not be joining you."

Stephen exhaled, the tension leaving his brow and his shoulders. He glanced at Alex, not Max; Alex nodded grimly.

THE MEAL WAS silent because the Hunters were given fifteen minutes in which to consume the food that had been plated and set in front of them. Lord Declan joined them at the table, although he did not likewise receive a plate from the servants; clearly he, as Ansel and Heiden, had eaten at the appropriate time.

This meant, however, that there was no discussion and no planning. Any discussion would, under Declan's shadow, be artificially polite at best, and neither the Maubreche nor the Elseth Hunters had the stomach for that. They ate quickly and more or less neatly—with more being Stephen and Alex and less, Max; Nenyane barely touched the food she had all but demanded be served.

That was for you. You need to eat.

He was surprised—as he often was—when she chose to speak through the bond. *You need to eat as well.*

I've never had the problem with hunger or sustenance the rest of you have.

You need to eat as well, he repeated, shifting emphasis slightly. But it was true that she weathered hunger better, even given sustained exertion.

She glanced at her plate. *Not hungry.* This was quieter. *I just killed a man.*

Stephen fell silent, appetite vanishing as the weight of her words sunk in. She had just killed a man. She was Nenyane; he had never expected that the death of an assassin would affect her in any way at all.

She had killed demons before; her rage and fury left no room for regret, no room for anything but grim satisfaction. Demons were not men, and the assassin was not a demon. Stephen forced himself to eat because Lord Declan was present, but he felt relief when Lord Declan rose and declared the hasty meal at a close.

———

"YOU DON'T HAVE TO COME," Nenyane told Max as she rose. "The Queen is likely to be angry by the end of the meeting."

"You intend to offend her?" Alex asked, voice a whisper that evaded Lord Declan's ears only because that lord had already reached the door.

"I never intend to give offense — offense is something that's taken," Nenyane replied. "I will be on my best behavior, but Lady Maubreche seldom feels my best is up to scratch. Lady Elseth might be grateful if the two of you are well clear of the Queen's annoyance."

Max shook his head. "We're coming. We have no idea who else might be lying in wait in the hall."

Nenyane approved of Max, which is why she failed to point out that, had Stephen's safety been entirely in Elseth hands, he would likely be dead.

———

LORD DECLAN LED the Maubreche and Elseth Hunters to the Queen's third audience chamber — the chamber in which she entertained Breodanir lords. Many of those lords — Stephen's father among them — considered the ostentation of the largest audience chamber required for and by foreigners distasteful; there was too much expensive color, too much noise, too much pomp, for too little substance, in their vocal opinions. History played against well-placed foreigners, in this: it was the foreign intelligentsia who had convinced a weak — and despised — king that the Sacred Hunt was quaint superstition.

Almost a third of Breodanir's Hunters had been lost to the Hunter's Death when the Hunt was finally called again, and their descendants did not forget. Perhaps, in time, they would.

Regardless, the Queen intended to hold audience with the children of Hunters, of Hunter Lords; she did not choose to impress them with the finery for which Breodanir was not known.

The hall that they traveled to reach the third audience chamber was narrower than the public gallery, although the ceilings were as high. Stephen was grateful that Lord Declan's route bypassed the hall in which the foreign statue with sapphire eyes stood; he did not want Nenyane to see it again. Not yet. Perhaps not ever.

The halls of God's Reach were decorated with weapons and

tapestries, the longest of which depicted the Sacred Hunt in which the God's fury at the forsworn had been unleashed. Nenyane passed it by without comment; Stephen lingered. It was Stephen who earned Lord Declan's glare. Nenyane, abandoning subtlety—not that she had more than a passing acquaintance with it—grabbed him by the arm and dragged him away.

———

To STEPHEN'S SURPRISE, he recognized the man who waited at the modest—and closed—doors. Iverssen, a Priest—perhaps *the* Priest—of Breodan. The King did not have a huntbrother, but in any practical sense, it was Iverssen who served in that role. The priesthood, historically, had both weight and power, but part of that power had been cut off by the monarch who had chosen to suspend the Sacred Hunt. The failure of Breodanir in the wake of that decision, and the loss of so many of the Hunters after that king had perished and the Hunt had been called, had restored the priesthood's power—but they had been careful to make that power subordinate in all visible ways to the King's authority.

Or so Iverssen had once told Stephen, when the Priest had traveled to Maubreche to visit, as he had done frequently when Stephen was a child.

He came to see you, Nenyane said. *Because you were god-born—you were proof that Bredan was a genuine god.*

We always knew that.

Yes—but the Imperial scholars didn't.

Alex and Max bowed instantly; they clearly recognized Iverssen as well.

Stephen offered the priest a deep and respectful bow, in part because he genuinely respected Iverssen, and in part because a bow meant he did not have to speak or greet him in a more casual way.

Nenyane offered Iverssen the same deep bow. Inasmuch as she respected any authority, she respected Iverssen. Or perhaps she simply liked him; he wore authority not as a mantle of command, but a burden of responsibility.

"It is good to see you all well," he told them. "But it is not to me that you should tender such respectful bows. The Queen waits."

Alex and Max offered identical nods. Stephen joined them.

"Is the King here, then?" Nenyane asked. Had she been speaking to any other Huntsman of the Chamber, Stephen would have wilted.

"As you surmise by my presence, yes—but it is the Queen's audience chamber, not the King's. Be as mindful as you can of your manners; the King is King, but Hunter at heart, and the Queen is... not." He said the last apologetically; it was clear to Nenyane that he referred obliquely to Lady Maubreche's expectations of good behavior in the presence of the Queen.

She nodded, the nod grim but not stiff, and Iverssen himself opened the doors.

Lord Declan offered the Priest a stiff bow. "I will return to Hunter's Redoubt," he said. "I have not been summoned."

As a Huntsman of the Chamber, Lord Declan should have had blanket permission to attend the audience; his decision to absent himself implied one of two things, the latter being a smidgen of cowardice. Then again, as a Hunter Lord of note, he took great pains to avoid stepping on any area of governance that overlapped the Queen's.

MUSIC FILTERED into the hall before Stephen had a chance to set foot across the worn threshold the door had created by opening. It was soft, almost plaintive in tone, the melancholy of the tune recalling, for Stephen, the long walk past a tapestry that occupied the greatest part of the hall. In it, mourning had been captured—mourning at a distance, when the grief and pain of loss had dimmed enough that one could lift voice, could speak, could perhaps not dwell only on the pain of that loss itself.

The notes made, of this hall, this chamber, this place—God's Reach —a testament to the sacrifice of those upon whom the health of this nation depended. He felt gratitude at the unfamiliar tune; felt certain that here, in the heart of the rooms of Breodanir's Queen, a musician of the Breodani existed.

But the man playing an instrument seldom seen in Breodani hands was not of the Breodani, to Stephen's knowledge, although he stood beside the Queen's throne and one step behind—a position that implied that he was both honored and trusted.

Stephen entered the room, his gaze drawn to Queen and not musician, although he could not shut out the music itself, no matter how softly it played.

He approached the throne and knelt before the Queen; the King occupied a throne at her side, but it was the lesser throne; he wore no crown here, crowns being a contrivance meant to establish authority with foreigners who did not understand the weight of the role the King served as Master of the Game. The Queen's forehead was likewise bare.

Stephen might have remained as he was, caught in music, in memory, in the certain sense that here, here walked history as it reached with one hand for the present and the other for the future. But Nenyane, who had walked at his side to reach this position of both supplication and profound respect for the burdens of rulers, did not kneel.

Instead, at his back, he heard a sound so distinct and so familiar he reached instantly for the eyes of his dogs—the whisper of steel against scabbard.

Stephen froze, too shocked to form the words that might have stopped his huntbrother; she had, indeed, drawn sword. Her eyes were flashing—literally flashing—as if they were a perfect blade's edge reflecting light. She leapt up, and up again, and the still air carried her.

It carried her directly toward the man who now played his instrument in the Queen's shadow. Her sword came down—down to ring on stone and cut instantly through a carpet that was probably worth more than Stephen's life would be after this moment had passed.

"What is she doing?" Max said, lifting voice as if the attack itself were shocking and disgraceful—which it was. But he also drew sword as she leapt, and he turned immediately toward Stephen. Alex was a beat behind. The only visiting Hunter in the room who had not—and would not, damn it—draw weapon was Stephen himself.

The dogs were bristling.

"Nenyane!" he shouted, abandoning the necessary show of respect owed the Queen as her due. He knew he could not catch his huntbrother, could not stop her—not as he was. He summoned the Hunter's trance, the truest test of the ability of the Breodani Hunters, his awareness expanding, his reflexes sharpening. Not even in nightmare had the possibility that Nenyane would do this in the Queen's presence occurred to him.

He froze a second time; although Nenyane had come to ground, her sword crashing against stone and echoing into the sudden silence, the musician was no longer in the path of that sword, even though she had moved blindingly swiftly.

No; he was, to Stephen's shock, in the air, his leap carrying him farther from Nenyane's blade than her own had carried her forward.

He was not a demon; Stephen was certain of that. Nenyane did not feel rage, not precisely; she felt visceral danger, visceral threat. The musician might have been another assassin, so fast, so determined, was her attack. That thought brought the dogs instantly to Stephen's side, where they formed a wall between the stranger and their master.

Nenyane's second leap took her closer to where the stranger stood, but the stranger once again leapt the moment she did, as if he could read the direction and the intent of her attack. This time, however, she twisted while following the arc of her intended trajectory, and her blade cut his clothing before he leapt clear.

In the distance, he heard shouting, and the shouting contained anger and incredulity. The Queen had spoken.

Nenyane did not hear her. Stephen understood, then, that although he had not sought Nenyane's vision, he was bound to what she could see or hear. At the moment, that was the stranger. When her sword caught clothing—a gaping sleeve, this time—the stranger finally set aside his instrument; into his hands came twin blades, and as they did, the air carried him in a way it did not carry Nenyane. Nor did the instrument, so carelessly dropped, hit the ground immediately.

Nenyane! Nenyane, stop!

She heard him, but chose to ignore the words, so focused was she on her chosen enemy. The Queen rose from her throne. Through Patches's eyes, he could see that that august figure was pale, her eyes so narrowed he would not have been able to see their color were it not for the trance itself.

"Nenyane of Maubreche!"

Her voice echoed in the ceiling above. The King, however, neither rose nor attempted to speak. These were the Queen's chambers, the heart of the Queen's territory.

Nenyane could ignore her Hunter; she'd had years of practice. Ignoring Lady Maubreche, however, had never been as easy; she could do it only when Lady Maubreche was not present.

The timbre of the Queen's voice was a ruler's voice; Nenyane slowed. She did not put up her sword; she twisted in air and came to land, on both feet, in front of her Hunter, her blade pointing outward, ever outward, toward the musician.

If Stephen had been horrified at her attempt to kill the man—and he was—he could now almost understand the why. The musician, armed with twin blades, remained a long moment in the air above the ground, gazing down at Nenyane, his eyes as narrow as the Queen's. Stephen thought them brown, or perhaps hazel, but the color was irrelevant.

Wind moved the musician's hair, golden curls streaming away from his face; air carried the fullness of a grown man's weight as if the man himself weighed nothing. Even the instrument itself had been brought with care to ground, as if the very air understood its value.

Without turning to face the Queen, Nenyane said, "He's an assassin. He's dangerous. How comes he to stand by your side in such a position of honor?"

"He is an assassin?" The Queen replied, the tone of her voice implying scorn. "He is a *bard*. A bard from the renowned Senniel College." But further words failed to emerge as the Queen looked up to meet the bard's gaze. "He is an honored guest. Sheathe your sword."

"I was not aware," Nenyane replied, the sword remaining in her hand, "that bards from Senniel College had learned how to master the wild air."

"As you suspect," the bard in question replied, "they have not. The mastery of the air—and mastery is an inaccurate word—was not taught me in my years at the college."

"Nor your mastery with weapons or combat, either," Nenyane said, voice cold and low.

"No. I am not here to assassinate your Hunter."

"You bear a mark I have seen before."

The man stiffened for the first time. He then exhaled, nodded, and sheathed the blades he had drawn only when direly pressed.

The Queen resumed her seat; Stephen was surprised to see the King's hand upon her wrist, although the King did not speak.

"It has been long indeed since that mark had any but personal meaning."

"You came for Stephen."

The bard did not deny it. "I did. I was not expecting him to be so exact a representation of his father." He turned to Stephen, then, and came very lightly to ground; his feet made no sound as they touched stone. "You are son to three; one is dead. It is of that father I speak. Stephen of Elseth."

"You knew Stephen of Elseth?" Stephen asked.

"Briefly. I was once sent here to save his life. Were it not for the color of your eyes, I might feel that I had traveled not only to Breodanir, but through time itself."

Nenyane snorted. Some of the sense of immediate threat drained from her.

Nenyane—sword. The Queen is angry. She ignored Stephen, but that came naturally. It was the Queen that was Stephen's urgent concern.

"Someone has already—in this palace, on this day—attempted to assassinate Stephen of *Maubreche*." Nenyane spoke the last word with force and heat, as if spitting out an accusation.

The bard glanced past her, to the Queen on her throne; what he saw there confirmed the truth of Nenyane's words. "I had no hand in that attempt. Stephen survived."

Stephen winced.

"The assassin of whom you speak—"

"Was dispatched," the Queen told the bard. "By Nenyane of Maubreche."

"He bore the mark you accuse me of bearing."

Grudgingly, Nenyane nodded.

To Stephen's surprise, the bard bowed to Nenyane; he bowed low, but rose of his own accord. "I have seldom encountered a sword wielded as expertly as you wield the one you bear. Were I not who I am, I would be dead, and the diplomatic tangle that followed would be borne by your lords."

She was enough in control now that she did not immediately deny that the monarchs were her lords, but it was close.

"Or perhaps you did not fully understand. The bards of Senniel College frequently serve as messengers at the direction of the Twin Kings."

Stephen froze.

Nenyane didn't. "And you are here as messenger for your Kings?"

A glimmer of a smile touched the eyes of the bard. "Yes."

Nenyane exhaled. She offered no apology for the attack, but it seemed to Stephen that none was expected—from the bard.

"I see that Maubreche has been absent from court for *far* too long," the Queen said. The coldest of Breodanir winters could not touch the ice embedded in those words, but clearly she had been well apprised of the Maubreche huntbrother. "Please accept my personal apologies for the grave discourtesy you have been shown."

"No apology is necessary," the bard replied. "I did not mean my words to threaten political consequence. This is far from the harshest of greetings I have encountered—and I have survived them all."

"It is the harshest greeting of a *personal guest* I have ever witnessed," the Queen replied.

The bard bowed, as if he were Hunter-born. He then rose at the Queen's command and walked to the instrument that lay on the ground; he retrieved it with care, the gap in his sleeve flapping as he adjusted his hold on the rounded bowl of its body. To Stephen's eye, he was calm. Nenyane's attack might have been, his expression implied, an ordinary occurrence. He did not seem to consider that attack either offensive or threatening.

"Stephen of Maubreche," he said quietly, "I did not expect to find you in the King's City. I paused here to deliver word to the Queen; my destination was Maubreche. It appears that, were it not for this encounter, I would have missed you entirely. I am grateful to have met you." Before Stephen could reply, he turned to Nenyane, "Bright blade, I am grateful, as well, to meet you in this place, by this young man's side.

"I will not tell you to protect him; it is clear that that is your focus. Nor will I tell you that it is necessary; nothing I could say to you now would make things more clear than they have already become. But I hope you will permit me to speak with Stephen again, ere I depart."

Nenyane met his gaze. "Who are you?"

"I am Kallandras of Senniel College," he replied.

"That is not quite the name I hear."

The bard's eyes widened; when they narrowed again, his brow was creased. "It is the only name I now own; I am not certain what you hear, but perhaps you have a touch of the seer-born in you. *I give you my word, Nenyane of Maubreche, that I mean Stephen no harm. Where it is possible, where I am present, I will defend him with my life.*"

There was a cadence to the spoken words that Stephen would not have been aware of were Nenyane not his huntbrother, an odd resonance that made the hair on the back of his neck rise.

Whatever it was, he felt Nenyane relax—inasmuch as she ever did when people other than Stephen were present.

"Were Stephen to allow it, I would have you swear a binding oath," she replied, voice low.

Stephen froze.

"But he will not allow it. I will nonetheless accept your spoken words as truth." Her smile was slender, as exquisite as the edge of her blade, and just as friendly. "I have been rude. I am Nenyane of Maubreche, huntbrother to Stephen of Maubreche." She then turned toward Max and Alex; Alex had sheathed his blade—probably when the Queen had raised voice. Max, however, had not. Nor did he until Nenyane at last sheathed her own.

Lady Elseth was going to be at least as unhappy as Lady Maubreche in the near future.

The Queen rose. "It appears," she said, her voice without warmth, "that my informal audience with two of *my own people* will have to be put aside."

Iverssen winced, but said nothing; his face was pale. He had been as shocked as the Queen. The King, however, was watching the bard closely, brow slightly creased. Before the Queen could continue, he rose. "Kallandras of Senniel, we offer you the hospitality of our palace. Understand, however, that that hospitality must come second to the safety and concerns of the Hunters who form the backbone of our governance.

"Nenyane of Maubreche, you have permission to remain by Stephen's side as guard; the dogs will, of course, be allowed to attend you as if you were in your own home."

The Queen turned her head toward her husband; what she saw in his expression seemed to bleed some of the icy rage from her own. She exhaled and turned her attention back to the young Hunters. "Stephen and Nenyane, you are dismissed." As they bowed to her, she added, "I would like a few words, however, with the Elseth brothers."

CHAPTER EIGHT

"That went as well as could be expected," Iverssen said, when the door to the Queen's audience chamber was firmly closed behind them, and they had retreated several yards. "In future, if possible, Nenyane might offer *some* warning."

Nenyane was not of a mind to listen, and she was therefore not of a mind to let the Priest know she'd heard his softly spoken words. As they'd been addressed to Stephen, this might have been plausible had she been anyone else.

"I recognize the bard," Iverssen continued, when neither Maubreche Hunter spoke. "He is both respected and admired by the Queen. It is his unruffled response that will likely guide the future consequences; one might think random strangers attempted to murder him frequently."

Nenyane opened her mouth, but snapped it shut without allowing words to escape. To Stephen she said, *He's an assassin.*

Stephen flinched; he had the headache that usually accompanied his attempt to see anything through Nenyane's eyes.

"I do not believe the Queen will bring the matter up with Lady Maubreche, given the bard's reaction." He glanced at Stephen. "And it is true that you resemble Stephen of Elseth strongly."

"Why did he say he was here to see Stephen?" Nenyane demanded.

"I am afraid you will have to ask him, if you feel it is safe to meet

with him again in person." Iverssen slowed, forcing Stephen and
Nenyane to likewise shorten their strides. "I have known you both since
you were children, and I will be honest: you have presented far more
difficulty than even young Lord Ansel. But I have never known you to
act without cause. I am certain that Kallandras of Senniel will have
some of his own explanations to tender the Queen.

"He will certainly have to explain himself to the King."

"He didn't do anything wrong, though," Stephen pointed out.

"The King is not a fool," Iverssen replied. "His instincts have always
served him well. He is more politically adept than most Hunter Lords,
but he has their visceral instinct. He did not believe Nenyane's attack
was groundless, which means he does not believe the bard harmless."

Stephen shook his head. "I wouldn't say he was harmless, but I
would say he didn't mean *me* harm. If Nenyane attacked every person
who could plausibly harm me, the palace would be awash in blood."

"I am not going to stand still while in the presence of—" She bit
back the word with effort. "We should never have left Maubreche."

"The King summoned us," Stephen replied. He had seldom seen
Nenyane remain so unsettled. The assassin, the statue, and the foreign
bard had combined in a dangerous way.

"I suppose," he said, as if in thought, "the Queen's assertion that all
of us should have died at the hands of the first assassin is closer to
truth—"

"Was I there?" Nenyane snapped, shedding instability to replace it
with genuine annoyance.

Iverssen gave Stephen a side eye, but held his peace; he did not fully
understand Nenyane, but expected that Stephen did.

"If your reaction to someone you thought was the assassin's
companion was so swift—and given that the bard appeared to be able to
walk on air as he willed it—the assassin presented a genuine threat.
Max, Alex, and I are not as good with sword as you are, and when
you're fully engaged, we can't match your blade. The Queen hasn't seen
you wield a sword—"

"Even if she had, she'd disregard it. She wouldn't recognize mastery
of the sword."

Iverssen coughed, but the cough didn't stop Nenyane. She retreated
into the comfort of a familiar tirade, and did so with a passion she had
attempted to quell since childhood. Breodani swords were not swords.
Breodani sword masters were unworthy of the title. Breodani Hunters

would be better served with clubs. Iverssen grimaced, but made no attempt to stem the voluble flow of Nenyane's most shared opinion.

And Stephen felt the uncertainty, the instability, recede as she found her footing on well-worn, solid ground.

IF LADY MAUBRECHE was to be spared the details of the aborted meeting between monarchs and subjects, Lord Declan clearly was not. Iverssen bowed to Lord Declan as he reached the great room, his two charges by his side. Lord Declan glanced at Iverssen; Iverssen was silent. Stephen had employed similar silences in his time, and clearly Lord Declan recognized this one.

"Go, join Ansel and Heiden. It appears we will have an interrupted first lesson, but I have no wish to waste the rest of the day."

Nenyane grimaced. She had no desire to join Ansel. Neither did Stephen, but he felt he was perhaps being unfair. They hadn't started out on the best foot; none of the Hunters sent—in disgrace—to Hunter's Redoubt had been in any way happy to be here. People, he reasoned, expressed unhappiness in different ways.

Nenyane snorted. "He's an ass," she said, dismissively.

"He's an ass who has effectively lost two of his three parents to the Sacred Hunt. Barrett and Lord Bowgren."

"You are not your father. It is not at your feet he should lay that loss."

Stephen nodded. It was not a loss to be laid at the feet of any save Breodan, the architect of the magic that kept Breodanir and its people alive. "But he'll lay it at the feet of the people for whom Barrett, in the end, was sacrificed—and that's far worse."

Nenyane shrugged. Nothing Stephen said would rehabilitate Ansel in her eyes. She could think of very little that would. "Barrett chose. He *chose*. He was truly huntbrother. He laid down his life to preserve the life of his Hunter." And she would do the same, her tone said.

He understood, then. Ansel's crime was this: he denied the truth of the attachment between Lord Bowgren and his huntbrother; he denied the respect that Nenyane granted the man who had died.

THE GREAT ROOM was broken into several parts. Ansel and Heiden were seated at the end of the rectangular space, farthest from the fireplace that stood in the center of the room. There, tables and chairs had been pushed together, and it was clear that the recalcitrant Hunters or would-be Hunter Lords were meant to treat this as a study room. At the end of the wall, beyond the tables and the chairs—two of which were occupied—stood a wall of bookshelves; books occupied perhaps half of that space, and by the look of the well-worn spines, the current group of Hunters were not the only ones to have used the room in this fashion.

Stephen had not heard of Hunter's Redoubt before, but its existence made sense to him. If the Hunter Lords of Breodanir had been given a sacred duty, they were not identical people; in any gathering, there were men and women worthy of respect or contempt.

Stephen was aware of the history of the governors—the Hunter Ladies who ruled in all but name. He was aware of those women who, having been trained to power, had refused to cede it upon the deaths of their husbands. While the conflicts that arose from those decisions were not called war, they had nonetheless caused death. Women governed, but the titles revolved around a living husband, or a living, unmarried son—a son who was Hunter Lord, or likely to become one. It was the possibility of death, the willingness to become Breodanir's sacrifice, that was the root of power in the demesnes.

Stephen was uncertain what the fate of Bowgren would be. Historically, Bowgren would become the King's responsibility, and he would pass on that responsibility to a Hunter Lord—a second son from a different demesne—whom he felt would carry its weight properly.

Ansel was here because he was heir to Bowgren; heir to a demesne which had, in his living memory, paid the ultimate price the Sacred Hunt demanded. He had no intention of honoring the oaths that Hunter Lords swore to uphold. He had made that clear; the clarity of his declaration should have removed him from the line of succession. Perhaps to honor Barrett's sacrifice, the King had summoned Lord Ansel.

Stephen wondered if he would feel as Lord Ansel now did if Arlin had been the one to die in the Sacred Hunt. If, shadowed by that loss, Corwin became so unhinged he resented his lands and his people—the reason that the Sacred Hunt existed. The reason that Barrett had died.

Nenyane snorted. "No."

"I don't know that for certain. I *believe* I wouldn't—but I haven't faced the loss that he has."

"I'm telling you, you wouldn't."

"You're not exactly objective."

"And you're exactly stupid!" Nenyane's voice rose, as it usually did when Stephen had annoyed her.

The two so-called students at the back of the room looked up. Ansel, seated, sneered; Heiden once again returned his gaze to the tabletop, as if the weight of looking at the world was too much to bear. Only when Ansel pushed his chair back from the table and rose did Heiden lift his head, his eyes darkened by dread. One of them. The other was darkened by bruising. It had been less prominent the first time, but a new bruise had been laid over the old one.

Nenyane noticed immediately, and her expression shuttered, the squabble with Stephen forgotten.

"Oh, do continue," Ansel said, as he strolled toward them. "I didn't mean to interrupt you."

Nenyane was not in the most stable of moods. "I don't argue with my Hunter for the amusement of strangers; I'm sure you don't beat your huntbrother for our amusement either."

Nenyane!

She ignored Stephen, focused as she was on Ansel; in the moment, all uncertainty was once again compressed and set aside. Ansel was an enemy—just not a dangerous one.

Ansel's expression grew grim, the sneering playfulness shattered by what was, at base, an accusation. "I do not beat my huntbrother." His voice was low.

"Oh? Then the doors and walls here must be very, very uneven—he didn't get that black eye on his own."

Nenyane—this won't help Heiden. Stop it.

Ansel stepped forward, hands in fists. Heiden, who had remained seated, practically leapt from his chair; it teetered and crashed to the floor behind him as he sprinted to close the distance between that fallen chair and his Hunter. He did not deny what Nenyane had said— possibly aware that it wouldn't be believed—but he stepped neatly between the Maubreche huntbrother and his Hunter. This time, however, he faced that Hunter, holding his arms out to either side as if to shield Nenyane.

That's not it, she snapped, her interior voice resonating. *It's not me he's protecting. It's Ansel.* After a beat she added, disgust in her voice, *His Hunter doesn't deserve him.*

We've come to blows ourselves.

We were children. *Cynthia would* murder us slowly *if we came to blows in front of any witnesses but the dogs, now.*

Any discussion between Ansel and Heiden was likewise private, but Stephen could see Ansel's knuckles whiten in the extended silence. He prayed silently—he who knew better than anyone just how futile that was—that Ansel would not hit, or attempt to hit, Heiden. He was certain that Nenyane would respond in kind, and he was under no illusion here: Ansel was not, size and weight notwithstanding, her equal. In any other circumstance, she wouldn't have noticed him at all.

And Ansel knew it.

Nenyane would not hit first; she had no qualms about hitting *back.* Ansel's relative strength—his apparent strength—changed none of that. There were things Stephen could ask of his huntbrother, and things he couldn't. Allowing herself to be treated as a victim was one of the latter.

As it happened, Lord Declan was, once again, someone's unwitting savior.

"I see the Bowgren Hunters have come to greet their Maubreche counterparts."

Everyone froze, and everyone turned toward Lord Declan—everyone except Nenyane.

Ansel spoke first, and with surprising resentment. "I see that the vaunted Huntsmen of the Chamber play favorites here, just as they do in all things."

Lord Declan glanced at Ansel.

"Both Maubreche and Elseth evaded *mandatory* lunch, and they have been absent at the start of a class you assured us was just as mandatory."

"I consider their reasons acceptable. I consider the reasons for your current behavior to be far less so."

"If you intend to tell us what your *rules* are, they should be consistent. I, at least, am fully Hunter Lord; they are not."

"My rules," Lord Declan's voice had become distinctly chillier, "have not changed. The Elseth and Maubreche Hunters were summoned into the Queen's presence, at the demand and command of the Queen herself. We are subordinate to her governance—*all* of us."

That stopped Ansel's tirade, or at least interrupted it. Heiden, however, did not lower his arms, and Nenyane did not look away.

"And the Elseth brothers?"

"While you are not in a position to demand answers, I will tender them; they remain with the Queen at the Queen's pleasure. The Maubreche Hunters have been returned to my keeping.

"And as we are on the subject of rules, there are now new restrictions in place for your tenure in *Hunter's Redoubt* as my students. You will not leave the halls without supervision—mine, or a Hunter I designate—during the daylight hours. You will remain within your rooms at the end of the day."

Ansel's jaw dropped, his skin mottled. "Am I now a criminal? I am fully adult. I have consented to be 'taught' by you, in accordance with the whim of Lady Bowgren, but I have not, in that consent, agreed to accept pointless and unwelcome *insult*. I have committed no crime—I am not a prisoner, and I will not consent to become one!"

"The rule applies to all of us," Nenyane pointed out.

"Even the vaunted god-born, the favored son? The son who conveniently absents *himself* from the Sacred Hunt?"

Stephen exhaled. Nenyane, temper already frayed and destabilized, was getting angry. Her anger pulled him away from the pangs of guilt she most hated.

"I am willing to join the Sacred Hunt," Stephen said, his quiet voice nonetheless clearly audible. "I have performed every hunt, passed every test demanded of those who would serve—and rule—as Hunter Lords. There is only one oath that I will not suffer to be sworn. And you understand why. Isn't that the heart of your refusal to join the Hunt?"

Heiden froze.

Ansel glared past his huntbrother, as if he could no longer see him.

"*Enough*," Lord Declan snapped, sharpening the tone of his voice rather than raising it, as shouting might be beneath his august dignity. "The rules apply to all Hunters who have not been summoned at the command of the Queen. Max and Alex are in her chambers now; they have been apprised of the change in rules, and they are well aware of the reason for them."

"So everyone was told but the only legitimate Hunter Lord?"

Nenyane had had enough. "Legitimate? You made clear your decision to abandon the responsibilities and duties that *come with* that title. You're far less worthy than *any* of the four of us!"

Nenyane—stop—that's not what—

"I won't. Look at his huntbrother. Look at his face!"

That face was ashen, the bruising around the eye far more apparent as Heiden lost color. To Stephen's surprise, he pivoted, turning from his Hunter to face Nenyane of Maubreche, lowering his arms as he did.

To Nenyane's surprise, Heiden's expression was grim; there was obvious anger in it for the first time.

"Ansel is my Hunter," he said, voice low. "By my own choice. Stephen knows. I offered my oath, and my oath was *accepted*. Whatever difficulty we've had, it's *ours*. Not yours. Not Lord Declan's. Not even the King's. *Ours*."

Ansel placed a hand on Heiden's shoulder. To Stephen's surprise, Heiden shook it free and continued to speak. "I will never interfere in your relationship with your Hunter. I will try hard not to judge it. I ask that you extend the same courtesy to us."

Nenyane lost the fire that had carried her. She ignored Ansel, focusing instead on the huntbrother. Because she was Nenyane, she said, "I was worried. For you."

Heiden exhaled. "I know. Sorry." The tension left his frame, the momentary anger bleeding into pale stillness.

Nenyane exhaled as well. "An assassin made an attempt to kill Stephen when we were on the way to the kennels."

Heiden's head shot up again. "An assassin? Here?"

Nenyane nodded.

"What happened to the assassin?"

"He's dead." Stephen couldn't see her smile, but could feel it. Cold, brittle, it covered an anger that was far closer to the surface than Heiden's now was.

"But...why? Why Stephen? He's Breodan's son."

"It's because he's Bredan's son. Or did you believe that Bredan's son would be respected and exalted by everyone?" The question was an accusation aimed entirely at Lord Ansel, although Nenyane didn't look at the Hunter Lord at all.

Heiden's color improved; he flushed, which was enough of an answer to her pointed question. "Did the assassin poison himself to avoid capture?"

She was annoyed by the question; she felt it naive. She did not put this into words. "No. I killed him. We missed the meal because we were meant to take the dogs to the kennels before we joined you. We won't miss another meal—or lesson—unless we're washing blood out of our clothing again."

"Does this happen often?" Ansel asked, as Heiden opened — and closed — his mouth.

"Not every day, no. And none of the other assassins were human."

Silence, then.

THE SILENCE that descended upon the Bowgren and Maubreche Hunters remained. Movement — and there was movement as the awkward group returned to the table at which whatever lessons Lord Declan meant to teach would be taught — returned, but it was unbroken by words.

Lord Declan did not look best pleased with any of them; Stephen thought it unfair that most of his glare went to Nenyane, given it was Ansel who'd started the conflict. Nenyane, predictably, didn't care. She took a chair with her usual grace — none at all — and flopped into it, leaning against the back as she stretched. This was, more or less, her posture during any lesson taught by Maubreche tutors.

Lord Declan's expression made clear that he was not those tutors.

There's nothing he can teach us at this stupid table. There's nothing he can teach us in the field. We're here until he gives up. If your mind could be changed by simple lectures, we wouldn't have to be here at all. It's the same for Max and Alex. The only person here who might be influenced at all is Lord Ansel — he has more to lose.

You could treat him with the respect our mother expects.

From me?

Stephen surrendered. If the worst that Lord Declan had to contend with was Nenyane's graceless posture, Lord Declan could be considered lucky.

Alex and Max returned perhaps fifteen minutes later. Alex caught sight of his fellow students and walked a direct line to the table, Max in tow. Max looked as frustrated as Nenyane felt, and took a chair with just a touch more grace. The Elseth brothers then looked to Lord Declan.

"It has been a trying day, and a highly unusual one, even for the Redoubt."

No disagreement was offered. It was probably the only statement the Huntsman of the Chamber could make that would be universally agreed upon.

"You are here for a reason. Your families are not—yet—in disgrace. It is our hope that over the three months you are students within the Redoubt, you will come to understand the urgency both of our situation and your own. The Kingdom relies on its Hunter Lords. At any other time in our history, we would have had more flexibility, especially with Bowgren. Lord Ansel has undertaken all of the tests required of a Hunter Lord, and he has passed them with ease.

"As, it must be admitted, have the Elseth brothers and the Maubreche pair. It is possible that the Elseth brothers are without peer in those tests; the King was highly—and unusually—impressed. In the case of Maubreche, Nenyane is...outside of our norms. She has been accepted as Maubreche huntbrother. Were it not for the lack of the oath, she would not be here at all. Nor would Stephen.

"But you have all seen and experienced the difficulties that Breodanir as a kingdom has faced in the past year. You have lost people, you have lost part of your hunting domains."

"We haven't," Nenyane said.

Lord Declan exhaled. "You have come close, if the Queen's records are to be believed. Lady Maubreche and the Queen—as most of the ruling women—have been in constant communication since the first incident was reported. Today, I wish you all to discuss the difficulties your demesnes have faced."

Silence.

"This is not a voluntary exercise. It will also make clear—to me— how much, or how little, you understand of the gravity of the situation."

Ansel, Nenyane, and Max instantly bridled. Lord Declan clearly expected this; he was unmoved—and severely unimpressed—with their reaction, but waited for it to pass.

He'll be waiting a long damn time, Nenyane snapped. Stephen thought the one thing they might gain from this long and needless schooling was this: Nenyane was far more willing to speak in the relative silence of the Hunter's bond than she had ever been at home. Perhaps this would continue—it would bring Lady Maubreche great joy.

"Some parents feel the need to protect their children from disasters over which they feel the children will have no control. This is not, as half of you seem to think it, a pointless or needless request. Lord Ansel, as the most senior person present, I would ask that you begin."

Ansel was utterly silent. None of that silence was caused by fear.

Heiden once again kept his gaze firmly fixed on the table, and on the hands that rested, palm down, against its surface.

"Bowgren," Lord Declan continued, into the unbroken silence, "has been more severely affected by the changes than many of the Breodanir demesnes."

Ansel's jaw tensed; his lips were white. He continued to be silent.

"Perhaps you are not aware of the difficulties Bowgren has faced."

Heiden closed his eyes.

Ansel stood, shoving himself back from the table. The chair teetered precariously before crashing to ground. "I am more than aware of the difficulties Bowgren has faced. Bowgren has been crawling with agents of the so-called Order of Knowledge—at expense to Bowgren and with no useful information extracted." He glared at Stephen. "Our lands are not as blessed as Maubreche's lands."

"It has nothing to do with that," Nenyane said, continuing her insouciant slouch as if Ansel's anger was irrelevant.

"And you know more than the magi?" Low words, low voice.

"Lord Ansel, you will resume your seat," Lord Declan snapped. "Nenyane, you will speak in turn, when you are called."

Nenyane's shrug appeared to annoy Lord Declan more than either her spoken words or Ansel's anger. "Permission to speak?" she asked, in the wrong tone of voice.

"Perhaps you would care to enlighten us, where the magi have not," was the severely voiced reply. "You have my permission. Lord Ansel. Your chair."

"You were correcting Lord Ansel."

"I was correcting his assumption that somehow Stephen is so beloved of Breodan that Maubreche lands are safer. The relative safety of our lands—and they are *not* safe—has nothing to do with Stephen's parentage."

"He claims to be our God's son," Ansel snapped.

"A claim," Lord Declan interrupted, "that has been substantiated fully by the priesthood."

"What do you think gods are?" Nenyane demanded of Ansel.

His brows drew together across the bridge of his nose. "Gods. They're gods."

"Yes, but what do you think that means?"

He stared at Nenyane as if she had asked an extremely stupid question.

One of us is extremely stupid, yes.

"Nenyane, perhaps you would care to offer your opinion."

"Gods once existed in the lands we consider dangerous to our people. The lands were almost part of what they were; they responded to the whim and dictates of those gods. The gods were creators and destroyers, both, and those of less power gravitated to them, to worship, to love, or to hate."

Ansel turned to stare at her, his expression one of studied disgust. Stephen was grateful that Nenyane chose to find this amusing; the alternative would be a disgrace to Maubreche.

But ignorance isn't?

He wanted her to stop, not because he thought she was in any way wrong, but because answering the question would only cause more questions to arise—and those questions, Nenyane could not answer.

"Some time ago, the gods who walked this world chose to abandon it—for their own reasons. They left the world to us, and the world itself became what we are: mundane, the natural dangers barely an echo of the days when gods walked the lands. Those gods were bound by oaths made to Bredan—to Breodan, if you prefer.

"But Bredan himself did not enter into those binding covenants. He was called by his people, and he came at their call, to lead them to lands they could call home. What he discovered was that the lands themselves had been altered; he could not exist here, among mortals, as he had once effortlessly existed.

"He went to his Priests, those who could bespeak him without becoming ensnared by divinity. And he bade them make a choice. What the land required here, what the ancient sleeping earth required, he could no longer give it—not and remain sane. He understood the price that must be paid—to that ancient earth—and he explained this to those Priests who had called upon him.

"*Once a year, on the edge of sanity, the God must hunt. Once a year, on the edge of sanity, blood must be spilled.*" She shrugged. "It was an act of sacrifice; he wished to know if the people could maintain it. After what I presume was much discussion, they agreed; better to lose one person a year than to risk losing all."

"And how exactly do you know this?" Ansel demanded. Lord Declan, watching Nenyane, nodded, granting permission to speak after the fact.

"I'm Stephen's huntbrother. When Stephen is called to the Between,

I go with him. I've heard what the God has to say." She folded her arms as she leaned back, staring at Ansel. "If you have a problem with what I've said, maybe you should take it up with the Priests."

Stephen was grateful for Ansel's presence; Nenyane considered him hostile, and no matter how much she hated questions about her knowledge—because they led, inevitably, to her lack of a known past—she would not show any of that weakness in the face of a would-be enemy. She wouldn't allow herself to feel it at all.

Because it's not a weakness when dealing with someone like him. He's looking for a fight. I'll give it to him if he doesn't back off.

Ansel was not the only person present spoiling for a fight.

"You disapprove of the choice?" Lord Declan asked her.

"No. One person instead of many? It's the right choice. Clearly the Priests felt it was the only choice. But Bredan understood how this might, in future, be abused; he therefore offered power to those who would participate. The Hunters' deaths during the Sacred Hunt fulfill the oath just as well as the huntbrothers' deaths would. But the huntbrothers, chosen because of their position in society—physical infirmity, perhaps, or age—swore a different oath.

"The huntbrothers were meant to bear the brunt of the sacrifice, the cost of it, because in those lean and early years, the strong were meant to survive and serve. The Hunters hunted. The Hunters fed those in the lands they ruled. Those who could not hunt could not feed the Breodani, when feeding the Breodani was most important for their survival.

"But he knew, as well, that people seek power, and that the further from the truth of starvation and desperation people grew, the more that natural need for power would transform into something less...pure?"

"*Pure* was the word he used," Stephen replied.

"So that the Hunters would understand the cost of that power, the cost of that sacrifice, he asked that those who stood in for Hunters be exalted; they be raised as Hunters, and they help in the fulfillment of the duties Hunters must undertake; that they be acknowledged as equals. They must willingly make the choice.

"Much of that knowledge was lost when the priesthood came under attack—demonic attack, we now believe—centuries ago, and the meaning of ceremonies and sacrifice was almost lost. The oaths huntbrothers took to their Hunters were not always accepted by the God, but when they were genuine, they were binding—a consequence of Bredan's covenant with the ancient earth.

"Now, they are not accepted if they are not meant. That was the mercy he offered the powerless, in the earliest of days; no oath would be accepted were it not genuine; no oath would be sanctified when offered in fear by those who had far too much to lose should they refuse."

Ansel stared at her, his gaze moving to Stephen and back, his expression twisting in confusion, in anger. Beneath that, curiosity existed—but as if curiosity was a weakness, he could not frame the questions without belligerence.

"This is *not* what huntbrothers were told."

Nenyane nodded. "It is only in the past seventeen or eighteen years that the truth has become more widely known—because Bredan no longer walks the lands of man; he has traveled across the divide that separates us from the gods. But he will not accept the oath offered by huntbrothers who do not speak the words with intent and meaning.

"It is why so many ceremonies have begun to occur later in the lives of young Hunters, and why some huntbrothers cannot form the necessary bonds with their Hunters. But once Bredan takes the oath, once he accepts it, there is no flexibility.

"Bredan is the God of Covenants. Break oaths sworn that he has blessed, and you will die. There is nothing—no healer, no secondary magic—that can prevent that." She exhaled. "Barrett of Bowgren clearly loved Lord Bowgren. But had Lord Bowgren perished in that Hunt instead of Barrett, Barrett would have followed on his heels. When faced with death in the Sacred Hunt, he paid the price as he had once sworn to do." A glimmer of compassion touched her expression. "I would hate the God for the rest of my existence if Stephen had died in the Hunt. I would never, ever forgive him.

"If I were the Hunter, and Stephen the huntbrother, I would never allow him to swear the huntbrother's oath."

Lord Declan glared at her, but added no words.

"Our father isn't so keen on the God, either," Max said.

"No. Stephen of Elseth died—killed by the Hunter's Death."

"In a foreign country."

Nenyane nodded. "I've always thought it incredibly cruel," she continued. "To find people to love, to find people with whom you'll be closer than anyone else, and to sacrifice those people for the sake of strangers and villagers. The sacrifices face death. The death is instant. Those left behind face endless silence and loss. But I'm not a god, and the decision is not in my hands.

"Bredan was afraid that some men of power would randomly sacrifice anyone else in their own stead, that those sacrifices would be
unwilling. And the people who would be sacrificed were Breodani, all.
They were the reason that he came when called. They were also his
people.

"He's probably right," she added. "If I could preserve Stephen's life
by sacrificing a total stranger, I'd do it. I wouldn't regret it at all."

"You would," Stephen said, with some heat. "I would never forgive
you."

"But you'd be alive, and you'd still be a Hunter," she snapped, more
heat in the words. "The gods don't care if I die. Bredan would care very
much if you did."

"He's not a human, he's a god—I'm the human and I would care."

Lord Declan cleared his throat. Loudly.

Everyone turned to look at him, except Stephen. *I mean it.*

Nenyane shrugged. *So did I. There's no point in lying about it.*

*I don't want you to lie—I want you to understand the true cost of what you
just suggested.*

Believe that I understand the cost.

Lord Declan cleared throat again. "Stephen."

Stephen turned toward him.

"We have clearly strayed far from the topic I wished to introduce,
and I would like to return to it now. Lord Ansel, please tell us what you
know about the difficulties Bowgren has faced in the past year."

Ansel had been caught, momentarily, by the argument between the
Maubreche Hunters. He had actually paid attention to it, his gaze
narrowed and focused. He had not resumed his seat when Nenyane had
begun to speak of the nature of Breodan, and it was clear he had no
intention of doing so at Lord Declan's command.

"This is a waste of time," he said, voice low. "You already know
everything Bowgren has faced. You've no doubt received reports. If you
want them to know, you can tell them yourself." He turned from the
table and stormed down the great room and out of the doors.

Heiden did not rise; he did not follow.

"Very well. As Lord Ansel is reluctant, I will ask Heiden to answer
my question."

Heiden's gaze seemed fixed to his own reflection on the gleaming
tabletop; he sat frozen, as if he had not heard Lord Declan, his expression rippling subtly. He was, no doubt, speaking with Ansel. He winced

twice, but lifted his head, his bruised face in keeping with his expression.

"Lord Ansel," he said, his voice firm, "is not wrong. You already know what Bowgren has faced." It wasn't a question.

"Indeed. But Maubreche and Elseth do not."

"And it is so important to force Lord Ansel to revisit the pain of loss that you insisted he relay information you are capable of relaying yourself?"

Nenyane was surprised by Heiden's tone. Stephen was less surprised, but understood; today, Heiden had indicated he was capable of anger, something neither Maubreche Hunter would have guessed given his prior behavior.

He had stepped between Ansel and others — Nenyane in particular — before, but never in anger, never in a way that somehow excused Ansel's behavior. Heiden's interventions up to now had underscored the risk that he himself appeared to be taking to protect Bowgren's reputation as a family. It was familiar territory; it was what huntbrothers did, what they'd been trained to do.

Nenyane's silence was loud; she had never taken well to such training. The burden of diplomatic response was Stephen's to shoulder. Alex performed those duties for the Elseth pair. But Heiden had always seemed so cowed, so afraid.

It appeared that Lord Declan was also somewhat surprised. "It is important, yes. It is important for me; I do not fully know what Lord Ansel knows. I do not know if his current reluctance to follow Hunter norms and rules is predicated on ignorance."

Heiden was not impressed with Lord Declan's statement.

Stephen thought he understood Lord Declan's reasoning, but privately agreed with Heiden.

"It is not predicated on ignorance." Heiden's words were well-modulated, but a thread of steely — and surprising — anger continued to run through them.

"Very well. I accept that your knowledge of your Hunter is deeper than my own. Your responsibilities with regards to him, however, are very different. I would have you tell us the difficulties Bowgren has faced in the past year. If you feel I am being unfair, know that both the Elseth and Maubreche Hunters will likewise be called to give similar accounts."

Heiden nodded, some of the anger draining from his posture.

Clearly, Heiden was not a person given to displays of temper; he once again looked down at his reflection. His hands trembled slightly.

"Bowgren has lost the entirety of one village. We weren't aware of the difficulties sweeping Breodanir; the loss came early."

Lord Declan nodded.

"We spent some time searching for any trace of both the village and the villagers; Amberg was not a small village, and it was in the heart of our territory. Lady Bowgren immediately sought the counsel of the magi; she was much in conference with the Queen and members of the Order of Knowledge. Lord Bowgren..." He exhaled, turning away from whatever he'd been about to say.

"Lord Barrett died in the Sacred Hunt called at the start of this year. His death caused upheaval in Bowgren—as I am certain you are aware."

The nod Lord Declan offered was slower, and for the first time, the Huntsman of the Chamber looked away, his piercing gaze seeing, for a moment, some silent history. He was older. That history, given his peers, must inevitably include more than one loss.

Stephen's mother had been quietly clear that some Hunters did not survive it; time did not lessen grief or rage; time did not dim pain. "Yes," she had said, although he had not asked. "Our God is cruel. It is a subtle cruelty, and we bear it—we who cannot Hunt and who will not, therefore, die in the line of our duties. Too many mothers have had to bury their sons."

Fathers lose their sons, too. Stephen had only pointed this out once.

Lord Bowgren's situation, Lord Bowgren's grief and anger, was not unknown to any of the Hunters in this room. But knowledge was not experience. The losses that had affected Stephen's life were now a melancholy that struck his mother on difficult days. He had not seen her when grief and loss were new; hoped never to see it in life, but did not pray. He knew how pointless prayers were. Who better to know it, who had once groveled and pled with a god in person, to no effect?

Nenyane reached out and placed a hand over his. She said nothing. Stephen nodded.

"In the absence of Barrett, Lord Bowgren was...not as active as he might have been. During that time, Lord Ansel attempted to carry out the duties previously undertaken by Lord Bowgren. It was Lord Ansel who discovered that an entire village was missing." Heiden swallowed.

"We thought it was the maps, or maybe our memory, our panic; we were not the equal of Lord Bowgren when...when Barrett was alive.

"But we were right. The village was gone. Strange trees had grown up in its place, and from that small forest came beasts unlike any we had encountered in Bowgren before. They could be hunted and killed—we could do that. But hunting and killing them did not bring back the village.

"In confusion, Lady Bowgren went to the capital to speak with the Queen and the Queen's foreign counsellors. What she heard there aged her, and she returned to us, and to Lord Bowgren, with what she had learned." He closed his eyes. "Lord Bowgren heard but did not respond." He fell silent; Stephen thought he was done.

Lord Declan simply waited, his head slightly bowed as if concentration were required to catch all of Heiden's softly spoken words.

"I think, in some fashion, he felt it was the demesne responding to Barrett's death—just as he had. Nothing was to be spared."

Lord Declan closed his eyes.

Heiden broke the lengthening silence, squaring his shoulders and attempting to come back to pragmatic facts. Stephen was not certain he could have done as well. "Three months ago, we lost half of Clearbrook—but not in the same way. Half of the village...half of the villagers... had been replaced by statues. We recognized some of them."

Nenyane opened her mouth and shut it.

"The magi," Heiden continued, as if failing to notice Nenyane's effort, "told us that the villagers had not been replaced. The statues were what remained of them."

Nenyane opened her mouth again. Closed it with less force.

What is it?

I think those villagers can be saved. But—I can't say that, can I? The bitterness was back. *I'd have to explain why I think that or how I know—and I can't answer, even when I ask it of myself. I'll look unhinged, and that won't reflect well on you.*

On Maubreche?

On you. If I had ever learned to lie, we could offer the information and make something up that would at least justify further investigation.

"It was not like the loss of Amberg; the magi who came interrogated the villagers. Half of the villagers had simply become statues within their own homes or on the paths that surround the village.

"The Priests came with the mage-born; I believe the King sent them.

They spoke for a long time with Lord Bowgren; after that, they asked to speak to Ansel. To Lord Ansel."

Stephen looked down at his reflection across the table.

"It didn't go well. I think they hoped to offer advice—but their advice sounded like criticism to Ansel. He is the only son of the line. He understands that in future he is to become Lord Bowgren—or rather, he understood it.

"But the Priests seemed to imply that, were Lord Bowgren more present, more aware, the damage to the villages, the damage to the heart of Bowgren's territory, would have been less severe."

Nenyane said, before Stephen could stop her, "They're not wrong."

Heiden's head snapped toward the Maubreche huntbrother.

"Maubreche has survived what would have become similar losses because Lord Maubreche is present. He has been much on the road for the past year, and not simply for hunting, although he does not neglect the necessary hunts. When he is within the vicinity of a turning, he can feel the shift in the earth itself—and if he is near enough, he can push it back.

"We are not part of the wilderness. Were it not for Bredan, our tenure here would have no meaning to those ancient and wild forces. But Bredan himself built the binding that protects Breodanir—and if it is thin, if it is all but unheard by the encroaching wilderness, it exists if we can reach it."

Lord Declan turned toward Nenyane, just as Heiden had.

"I am not saying it is Lord Bowgren's fault," Nenyane said, voice softening. They were not words spoken at Stephen's silent behest; he had not had the time. "I understand how the Priests might come across that way. There are events that we almost missed; we nearly lost half a village, not to stone, but to the wilderness; it crept into Brookton when we were too far away. We weren't guaranteed to reach Brookton in time.

"But the reason Maubreche has been less affected is Lord Maubreche. If Lord Bowgren is bowed to immobility by grief, you wouldn't have that."

"Can Stephen affect the land?" Heiden asked.

"Not as well as Lord Maubreche; Corwin is lord, and the land recognizes that. Don't ask me how," she added, but without the sharp edge of defensiveness to mar the words.

"Even if Stephen is Breodan's son?"

Nenyane stiffened, but accepted the question as it had been offered. "Even so. Stephen is not—and will likely never be—Lord of Maubreche."

"That is not yet decided," Lord Declan said, an edge in his tone.

"It is not yet *accepted*, Lord Declan," she replied. "It has long been decided." She folded her arms and met his stony gaze without apparent concern. "Heiden, do you have anything else to add?"

Heiden shook his head. "There have been other incidents, but none so dramatic. We've lost a handful of villagers to sudden changes in the road; most now avoid the King's Road, where it crosses our territory—it seems to be the most unstable. Ansel had been trying, in the absence of both Barrett and his father. Lady Bowgren has never faltered. But Bowgren still faces difficulty—and Ansel has been called here, at a time when Bowgren can least afford it."

"Tell me, are those your words or Ansel's?"

Heiden met Lord Declan's gaze and held it.

It was Lord Declan who looked away. "If what Nenyane says is accurate, it is not Lord Ansel who can provide the necessary relief, but Lord Bowgren."

Heiden flushed, his eyes narrowing. "Perhaps," he said, his voice brittle but otherwise quiet, "you have not heard a single word I have said—all spoken at your command."

"I have, boy. Do you think I have no experience with men such as Lord Bowgren? Do you think I have not watched what the Sacred Hunt takes from us, year after year? Do you think—" He paused. Silence descended, and remained in place until Lord Declan once again broke it. "There are some for whom grief is, if not lessened, then held in abeyance by the responsibilities owed to the demesne. I know Anton; I believe that he will return to Bowgren in time.

"Regardless, it is with his permission that Ansel is present. His and Lady Bowgren's. You believe that Lord Bowgren has abandoned his duties. Were that true, neither you nor Ansel would be here. Perhaps it is Ansel's absence that will finally motivate him to move while carrying the burden of his grief.

"Grief is like any other unbearable weight. Carry it for long enough and you develop the muscles to continue to do so, until the weight itself —never negligible—becomes bearable."

"Or it kills you," Nenyane said. "If you have that choice."

Lord Declan was unamused. "What choice?"

"Death."

"Enough. *Enough*, Nenyane of Maubreche. This was not the purpose of either my example or this discussion."

"If you've experienced the losses incurred by the Sacred Hunt, you know *for a fact* that some Hunters do not survive that grief, that loss." She shifted position in her chair, her back straight, her hands trembling in her lap.

"If Lord Bowgren had no intention of surviving, he would not have allowed Ansel to be sent — or brought — to the palace."

"That's *exactly* what he would do — he needs a functional heir! The King didn't *ask* permission. He gave a command."

"And were he forsworn, that command would not have been obeyed."

Nenyane, stop. Please.

She was not of a mind to listen. "Lady Bowgren has not fallen to grief the way Lord Bowgren has, for which you should be grateful."

Heiden said, "Lady Bowgren loved Barrett. He was the bridge between Lord Bowgren and Lady Bowgren; he was the heart of their interaction. She is shattered."

"She is — she is shattered the way any woman who loved husband might be shattered. But she is not what Lord Bowgren is; the loss seems unbearable but it is not the same loss. It is not what you would suffer if you lost Ansel — if, in fact, the loss of Ansel would *be* a loss, given —" She did stop herself, at least, from finishing a sentence that did more than cross a line. "It is not the loss I would feel if Stephen died."

LORD DECLAN'S silence was brittle and cold. This time, Nenyane allowed it to spread, swallowing the words she could not take back. They had been spoken with a visceral heat — more akin to growl than words — but the dogs had remained by the wall, watching with disinterest.

When at last Lord Declan was ready to grace them with words, he continued as if Nenyane hadn't spoken; to be fair to Lord Declan, this was often what happened in the Maubreche manor as well. "Most Hunters do survive. Max and Alex have some experience with what the loss can do to a Hunter — their father, Lord Elseth, is now without hunt-brother. He hunts alone."

Max coughed; Stephen looked down at his hands.

"Do you wish to add something, Maxwell?"

"My father doesn't hunt alone." He carefully ignored the look Alex shot at him, as he was no doubt ignoring the words only he could hear. "When our father goes on his hunts, our mother goes with him."

Heiden's brows rose.

To Heiden, Max said, "Our mother is not Lady Elseth; that honor and duty is carried by our grandmother."

Lord Declan's look soured. He was clearly aware of this fact, and just as clearly disapproved. But his disapproval was without fangs, here; Espere was accepted by the Priests; she was accepted by the Queen. Lady Elseth might have wished for some help, some clear path to retirement—but perhaps not. She had been raised and educated all of her life to become the ruler she now was.

And Espere had not. Stephen seldom asked Espere about her childhood; her answers—when he was of an age where such questions would not be heavily frowned upon—had made little sense to him. He had only asked because she, too, was a child of Breodan, and technically his older half-sister. But her eyes were not golden eyes, and if she had been cursed, as Stephen had been cursed, that curse had never burdened her.

She was a protective mother, but not a terribly attentive one, and the lessons she chose to teach her children had far more to do with the hunt and the land than the lessons one would generally expect when one's mother was wife of the lord of the demesne. Lady Elseth, however, made up for that benign neglect. Max preferred his mother's lessons, as did Alex, but Alex found use in the information offered by the various tutors Lady Elseth had employed during their childhood; he had taken to those lessons less reluctantly than Max.

"Stephen is like us. Our mother is not. But she's sensitive to the lands her lord rules, and sometimes she stares off into the distance as if she can see the approaching storm. When she calls our father to action, he moves instantly. Even so, we have lost more people than Maubreche has lost in the past year.

"In Elseth, strange creatures hunt; they are not demons, according to the magi; they are natural creatures, and in a different time, they might have been hunted as we hunt the beasts of our forests—for sustenance, for hides. But they are not so easily met by the dogs, and we have taken some losses in the attempt to contain or eradicate them. For some, their natural prey appears to be humans, and in the absence of those, the beasts upon which our villages depend.

"Our father has never taken another huntbrother—as most Hunters, he has been offered that option and has rejected it outright. But he is not alone the way Lord Bowgren is now alone." Max stopped, then.

Lord Declan exhaled. "Very well. I had hoped that this discussion might move Lord Ansel to consider more carefully the consequences of his bitter rejection. Perhaps it will happen when he has taken time to think."

Heiden's expression made clear to Stephen that Lord Declan hoped in vain—but he did not think Lord Declan foolish enough to believe the possibility he advanced.

"Every demesne in Breodanir is facing these difficulties; Bowgren's losses are among the worst. The magi who serve at the Queen's pleasure have been much on the road in an attempt to curb or contain the incursions; there has been some success, but far more failure. The nature of the incursions varies too widely.

"But that is enough, for the day. Tomorrow we will discuss those strategies that have been at least partially successful."

Nenyane immediately left her seat.

"I have not said I am finished, although perhaps my words imply that. We are finishing with this particular discussion." Lord Declan's expression was pinched and severe.

His face is always like that, Nenyane snapped.

"We will now move on to the next step of this discussion. I have a guest who will conduct the more technical aspects. You will remain here while I tell him we are now ready for his instruction." He rose, glaring Nenyane back into the chair she'd been in such a rush to abandon.

Heiden, however, lifted hand.

"Yes?"

"I would like permission to get Ansel. If the information is important, if it's relevant to Breodanir, I'm certain he wouldn't want to miss it."

Nenyane snorted.

Alex, however, watched Heiden with a look of quiet concern.

"You are his huntbrother; I am certain you can tell him without leaving that chair. You can, can't you? The bond between you is not so damaged that he cannot hear you?"

Silence. Stephen stared at his hands; he, like Alex, felt concern for Heiden. Max, he was certain, had spoken of Espere entirely because Lord Declan intended to make Elseth a *good* example, in contrast to Bowgren. Perhaps Lord Bowgren deserved to be made a bad example; Stephen was almost certain Ansel thought so—but Heiden didn't, and Heiden was the only representative of Bowgren present.

"Lord Declan," Nenyane began.

The lord rose. "I expect you to be in your seats when I return." He turned and walked, at a measured pace, toward the far doors.

"I can't hit him, can I?" Nenyane asked, when the door had closed on Lord Declan's back.

"Depends," Max said, shrugging in irritable agreement. That was a trick of his. "Do you want to go back home again, ever?"

"You can't," Heiden said, which surprised them all. He looked across the table at Nenyane, his expression absent the bleak humor that adorned everyone else's. In a softer voice, he added, "It's hard enough to stop Ansel." His shoulders slumped, but he looked up at Max, and added, "Thank you."

"For what? I was only speaking the truth."

"Truth can be either a weapon or a comfort. Barrett used to say that —that it's not truth itself but how you deliver it, how you use it, that's important." He swallowed. "Barrett was the heart of Bowgren. His loss destroyed Lord Bowgren—but it injured the rest of us. Especially Ansel. I know Ansel hasn't made a good impression."

"Will he come back?" Nenyane asked.

"I know it looks bad," he said, talking now to his reflection on the table. "I know he doesn't come across well. But he'll come if there's any information—at all—that might lead us to our missing village."

Nenyane snorted.

"But he wasn't always like that. This is new—this is just loss and pain. This isn't what he's like. Barrett would be more upset about how things have changed than he probably was at his own death. I've tried," he added, voice dropping so much they had to strain to catch his words.

"I've tried, Barrett. I've tried to hold things together—but I'm not you."

Nenyane opened her mouth.

Nenyane, don't.

She snapped her jaws shut. Nenyane was not a comforter; on the few occasions she felt she should be offering comfort she became intensely uncomfortable. She herself did not ask for, had never wanted, comfort. In the early years, she didn't seem to understand the purpose of those who made the attempt, and she viewed them all with suspicion.

With time she had come to better understand the need, but not how to fill it. She mostly avoided trying. Something about Heiden, however, had caught her attention from the first.

She opened her mouth again, but was rescued by the sound of the door as it opened to allow Lord Declan and his guest to enter.

All of the words Nenyane had so painstakingly attempted to gather were lost in that instant. For one long moment, there was nothing in the room but Lord Declan's guest. Not even Stephen.

CHAPTER NINE

N*arianatalle. Fanniallarant. Taressarian.*

The names echoed, the syllables extended, attenuated. He did not speak them; by the White Lady's command, none of her people could. It was physically impossible. But she who set all laws was not burdened by them; she had spoken their names. It was in her tone, her voice, the softness of Summer momentarily denying the chill of the almost endless Winter, that they echoed in his thoughts.

Grief was too slight a word, too scant, to encompass the whole of what he felt—but he listened, regardless; it was all that was left him of the three who had once been his closest kin, his truest companions. They had faltered at the end—as he himself had almost done—out of love for the White Lady.

Perhaps she knew. But even knowing, there was no forgiveness in her. They had failed her. He had been part of that failure. Everything she had granted them, every gift, had returned to her; they were, who had been his closest companions, now simply a part of the White Lady's power.

Only Illaraphaniel, of the four princes, had survived; only Illaraphaniel, of the four, had obeyed. But one of four was not enough—had not been enough—to succeed, and thus the enmity between the White Lady and the god they did not name had grown roots and branches, deepening and strengthening with the passage of time.

He, who was eternal, nonetheless felt the passage of that time; it was grim enough that he envied mortality. Age was not a choice; infirmity, when it came with age, not a choice; the struggle of mortals was acceptance of both; eternity was not, had never been, theirs. Not in the flesh.

In the grim confines of the Kingdom of Breodanir, he felt age keenly. Age and loss. The power in this kingdom was predicated upon the willingness to face loss in pursuit of vows made—and blessed—by Bredan. He did not understand the full measure of the covenant Bredan had created in this kingdom, but could see the edges of its effects. Muted, mortal, it should have been inaudible, for the many voices of the wilderness had gained in strength over the passage of a simple mortal year or two.

Perhaps his long, long exile had irretrievably damaged him in some fashion.

Sigurne was in the East, in her Tower, bowed with an age that had not yet diminished her determination. He was almost reluctant to leave her side, but understood that she had the right to demand it of him. He wondered if this reluctance was akin to mortal fear: she was aged, and she might pass before he could see her again, could make his reports, could watch—and even admire—her response to what was delivered. But what she commanded, what she demanded, was necessary.

Thus, he was here, to speak to children about the changing of the land and what it might presage; to show them, with arts magical, images of the most dangerous of the creatures they might face. Should he attempt to catalogue them all, they would age by a decade and the lesson remain incomplete; the wilderness was a constantly changing force.

But his journey here had given him the information required to shorten that lesson. He was an exile, but in exile, he was nonetheless not mortal; he could hear the lands wake; could hear joy, wonder, and raging fury. He could identify the familiar—if long unseen and unvisited—lands that were strong enough, whole enough, to encroach upon Breodanir. He therefore knew what the mortals here were likely to face in the near future. Should the future stretch out a mere handful of mortal years, he was certain even the covenants created by Bredan to succor the Breodani would be destroyed, and against what would follow, the mortals had little hope. He himself could stand against the lords of the wilderness as they woke from their long slumber, but he was one, and they, many.

And the time was coming when mortal countries would perish, their meager history lost to the tide of things ancient. Thus had he informed Sigurne, but she had disagreed. They had argued, but as colleagues will, refining their arguments iteratively as the heated discussion wore on.

In the end, he had agreed to go west to the Free Towns and from there to the Kingdom of Breodanir, which seemed to suffer fewer incursions than kingdoms further to its west. Sigurne wanted answers. He had given her the answers it was in him to give, but she wanted—of course she wanted—something upon which she might act, or instruct others to act.

A god who walked this plane created Breodanir, he had said, annoyed. *That god is no longer present, nor will he return. We cannot imitate what he achieved; we, neither of us, are gods.*

Could the Firstborn?

Silence, then. The White Lady was one of the Firstborn.

Go to the West. Aid them where aid might be of use. If the kingdom can stand as a bulwark against the breaking of the barriers that sundered mortal from immortal, strengthen it as you can; there will be those who flee across the borders who might find safety in Breodanir.

They would find safety in Averalaan.

They might never reach it; we are so far away. But yes. Yes, Jewel will take those refugees who are wise enough to flee before it is impossible.

He did not say that the wilderness was not the only danger they would face; but to Illaraphaniel, it was the lesser danger, the lesser threat. The god they did not grace with name was in the North, and if he amassed his forces there, they were not for show; he would move, and move soon, even by mortal reckoning.

The Queen of Breodanir was not as inclined as the magi to consider the incursions to offer little true threat; she had been much in contact with the Order of Knowledge in Breodanir, and the Order, therefore, had been much in contact with Sigurne Mellifas. Sigurne had sent some of her mages to Breodanir—those that could travel swiftly and had some hope of arriving without collapse.

But of course it was not to succor the Breodani alone that she sent them; she knew that, in Breodanir, some trace of genuine resistance could be found, and she tasked the mage-born she chose with discovering the why and how of it. Illaraphaniel felt he had offered all of the necessary information: the covenant of Bredan. But Bredan, as Sigurne had pointed out, was gone, and the country itself remained resistant.

He had studied little of the Breodani, but thought he understood what kept the wilderness in check—in a small fashion, an almost insignificant fashion. Sigurne had not been pleased with this reply, but she seldom was; she wanted solid answers upon which she could stand. Academic guesswork was not an acceptable substitute.

Sigurne was in Averalaan, and as all people who dwelled within its towering walls were, safe. But beyond those walls the rest of humanity lay, and no such safety could be guaranteed.

She knew that the incidents, which had seemed so random—and remained so—were growing in number, and she envisioned a day when everything beyond Averalaan's walls was a tangled wilderness that meant only death or loss for her kind. While she supervised the magi— she hesitated to use the word *rule*, although Illaraphaniel felt it a quibble —it was her duty to protect those faceless, nameless mortals.

Ah, people changed, even the intense, bleak Sigurne. In her youth, in her prime, and even in the beginning of the age that had crept up on her, her one concern, her *only* concern, had been the demon-kin. He wondered, often, if that was what had drawn him to the remarkable, pragmatic, determined young woman: she had been willing to give her life, had been certain her life would be the coin with which she might buy the death of the mage in the distant North who had summoned, and kept, the demon-kin.

Had she begged for mercy, he would have walked away; she would have remained in the hands of the Order of Knowledge, their judgment the only one that mattered. But she had faced him, eyes clear, shoulders drawn back in silent, ferocious triumph. It was not that she wanted death, but she had understood, at that young age, that there was a price to be paid. If her life was the coin, she offered it without hesitation. Success mattered; survival had not.

She was bold, then: bold enough to use him as a tool, a means to an end. They were not her words, of course. He doubted that she had considered it in that fashion at all. But she had been the first thing— perhaps the only one, aside from one god-born student—to truly catch and hold his attention in his long exile.

And as he walked into the room to do the duty she had demanded of him, he stilled. He froze.

Thus it was, after the passage of long, long centuries, that he once again met the child, witness to his greatest—his only—failure. He knew her at once, although if questioned, could not have easily answered the how or why of that recognition; there was nothing about her appearance, nothing about her slender, trembling body, that was remotely familiar to him. Had he passed her by on a crowded street, he would not have given her a second glance—if he had bothered with a first.

But that was wrong. He was certain that he would have stilled in those streets just as he stilled in a room that suddenly seemed too mundane. He waited for her words, who found he had none to offer.

He waited in vain.

One of the children rose, and when he did, Illaraphaniel moved, disentangling himself from the viscera of memory.

"MERALONNE APHANIEL?" Lord Declan said, rising a beat behind Stephen.

"Apologies. I have been on the road, and look it; I am not perhaps at my best. But the Guildmaster felt we had little time to waste, and I am one of the few who could be expected to travel to Breodanir quickly and survive the toll such travel demands." He bowed, the movement fluid and far too graceful to Stephen's eye. Pale haired, pale eyed, something about the man reminded him of Winter in Breodanir—a new winter, the snow untouched as it made the world a single color.

Stephen could see him. And he could see, as well, what Nenyane saw when she looked at him—she had not once looked away. His head ached, as it did when Nenyane looked into the heart of the wilderness. Were it only that, he would have resumed his seat. But he felt, in Nenyane, what he had felt after she had stormed out of their room and wandered into one of the grandest of the public galleries, there to stop, to stare, to weep, although she could not say why.

He thought she might know, now—and he was suddenly afraid of it, whether for her or for himself, he could not say. He moved to stand in front of her, as if to shield her from her sorrow. He had no sense, however, that this man was the cause of it, not that it mattered.

The magi, for he wore the medallion of the Order of Knowledge, moved his gaze to Stephen. His brows rose.

"You are Stephen of Maubreche."

"I am."

"How come you to be in this place? This is not where you are meant to be."

"It is where the King commanded me to travel."

The magi seemed almost confused, the expression not at home in the contours of his proud, Winter face. That was what Nenyane saw in him: bitter, endless Winter. Or perhaps not; perhaps he was a reflection of ancient, endless sorrow, endless loss.

"You should not be here," the magi said again.

"This is *exactly* where he should be," Lord Declan replied. "He is Breodani and, as all Hunters, he must obey his King. Your criticism is both unwarranted and unwanted; it is not the reason you were tasked with attending us."

The mage ignored Lord Declan.

"And you?" he asked, looking past Stephen's shoulder.

Nenyane did not hear him.

Stephen turned toward her then.

She blinked, her brow furrowed in a confusion he had not seen in her for over half her life in Maubreche.

"Why are you here?" the mage asked.

"She's my huntbrother," Stephen said. "She's here because I'm here." There was defiance threaded through the words; he struggled to mute it. He did not like the magi, but knew this was unfair.

"It is," Nenyane said, speaking slowly, as if language had become unfamiliar and she was struggling to remember how to use words. "Illaraphaniel, why are you here?"

"Is this boy your choice? How came you to meet him? Where did you meet him? Where *have you been?*"

"Enough," Stephen's tone would have failed his mother's test of manners. "You have no right to question her. No right to question us."

He knew Nenyane did not share this sentiment. For the first time, the past that she couldn't remember became viscerally relevant.

"Only to you," she whispered.

"We have been searching," the mage continued, as if Stephen had not spoken. "All this time. How came you to Breodanir?"

"You'll have to ask Evayne."

The mage stiffened. "She brought you here?"

"She rescued me and brought me to Maubreche, where I have remained."

"And you sought the god-born?"

Nenyane shook her head; Stephen felt a sharpening of something in his huntbrother. "I am his huntbrother, Illaraphaniel. And he is *mine.*"

The mage stared past Stephen, as if Stephen were transparent.

"And you have once again chosen a mortal? Did you not learn—" He stopped himself. "I did not travel here with any expectation that I would find you."

"No, of course not. Finding me, not finding me, both are irrelevant. I am here, where I have chosen to be, and I will not leave unless and until Stephen does."

"And Stephen will not leave," Lord Declan said, the words both more measured and more angry. "I do not understand your line of questioning, but it is both inappropriate and unwelcome; I am certain the Queen would not find it amusing."

"No, probably not." To Stephen's surprise, the mage reached into his sleeves and withdrew a pipe. "She is not known for her sense of humor; she finds very little amusing, these days." As if the presence of the pipe were not enough, the mage proceeded to light it. And smoke it.

"Stephen, return to your seat. I am assured that the mage has important and useful information for the Breodanir Hunters."

Stephen hesitated.

Later, his huntbrother said, her inner voice muted. *We'll talk later.*

THE MAGE TOOK A SEAT, pipe in hand, at the head of the long table. Or rather, given its orientation, at the foot—but his presence inverted the natural order.

"Breodanir has some natural immunity to the incursions of the wilderness, but it is scant immunity, and it will not hold."

"Bredan's covenant," Nenyane began.

"It is tied to the earth, as you must know, but that earth is not fully awake—and if the waking of the earth might afford protection to the boundaries of your kingdom, it will be very costly. Bredan as God could invoke and command the earth—but the earth was sleeping; he bespoke its dreams.

"Dream or no, the earth remembers Bredan's command and Bredan's oath—and it remembers and honors the sacrifice of blood. But if the memory is deep, it is narrow, and other things, remembered and beloved, are beginning to wake, to lift voice."

"You speak of things beyond my knowledge," Lord Declan said. No one else spoke. Heiden was watching the mage carefully.

"It will become common knowledge soon enough." Meralonne exhaled rings of smoke, and then spent further time exhaling smaller rings that rose through the larger ones.

Max was amused. Alex might have been amused, but he was worried that Lord Declan would mark the attitude.

"I do not know what you know of the magi," Meralonne continued. "But the study of Breodanir is not my area of expertise. The study of things ancient, the lore that is all but lost to tides of human ignorance and war, is. The events that now occur are not specific to Breodanir, and it is for that reason that I have been asked to speak with the Hunters.

"I had not expected to speak to students, but perhaps, as the world once again unfolds, we will all become students of greater or lesser power. I am concerned, however —"

"You have made your inexplicable concerns clear; it is not to us that you must plead your case, but to the King." Lord Declan's voice was sharp but certain. The mage had annoyed him enough between the first blown ring of smoke and the last that he spoke without the patina of respect.

"It is the Queen who is most in counsel with the Order's master."

"This, however, is a matter concerning Hunters, and that is beyond the Queen's purview."

"Very well." The mage set his pipe aside; it floated in the air scant inches beyond his hand. Stephen had seldom seen magic practiced by the mage-born; he was fascinated. So was Alex.

He's not mage-born, Nenyane said quietly. *And his magic, while it might be mistaken for the magic mortals who are born to that power wield, is not their magic.*

He serves the Order of Knowledge.

Nenyane was silent for a beat. *I don't think that's possible,* she said, familiar frustration in her tone. Stephen knew better than to ask her why.

Do you think he came here hunting us?

...No. I think he did come at the Queen's invitation. But we need to be cautious, now.

Stephen almost missed her words; he would have, had he relied on normal hearing.

The mage began to speak, and mist rose, as if the smoke he had exhaled had returned to ring his hands and the portion of the table those hands occupied.

Not even Declan could appear disinterested as the mist began to move, and eventually to coalesce, as if the mage's spoken words were forcing it to cohere into shapes—and colors.

"In my travels here, I have noted the edges of lands that were once sealed away from humanity by a wall that was nigh impassible. Only twice a year did those walls weaken enough that people might enter the wilderness—or escape it. The wilderness is not geography as you understand it; it is both fixed and ever-changing. I cannot draw you maps that will retain their value; even what I tell you now might be changing as I speak. But in mortal terms, I believe that the information I have come to convey will be helpful.

"The Queen asked me to speak to the Hunters of three demesnes gathered here: Maubreche, Elseth, and Bowgren. I have words for the Hunters who rule over the other Breodanir demesnes, but they are less relevant to you."

Alex stiffened, but remained silent.

"I will assume that scions of each family now sit at this table."

Heiden cleared his throat. "Lord Ansel is not yet present," he said. "But he is almost here, if you would be willing to wait."

Meralonne APhaniel nodded.

It was less than five minutes later when the doors opened on Ansel, who walked quickly to the table to take a seat beside his Huntbrother. Heiden looked relieved.

Meralonne then began to speak again. "I have traveled through Maubreche and Elseth, but spent little time there; there are traces of the wilderness, but they are too scant to fully identify. If difficulties develop further, I will return. But Bowgren is closer to the borders of the kingdom, and in Bowgren the wilderness is not so much echo as roar. You have noted difficulties in Bowgren?" He turned to Heiden to ask the question.

Ansel lifted chin, then. "I am Lord Ansel of Bowgren," he told the mage, leaning slightly across the table. "If you have queries about Bowgren in the absence of Lord Bowgren, they are to be addressed to me."

"Very well," the mage replied, voice dry as tinder, eyes crinkled in corners suggesting amusement at Ansel's tone. "Lord Ansel. I am known for my manners—or rather for their lack; the mechanisms often escape me when I am concentrating on important matters.

"Have you noted difficulties in Bowgren?"

"We have."

"If you do not care to have them discussed, I will not discuss them; I am here at the request of your Queen, not your King, and I have information that may be of aid to you, inasmuch as knowledge is of aid when the forces you face are overwhelming. That knowledge is freely given, and as all gifts, it may be honorably rejected."

Nenyane snorted and rolled her eyes.

"You feel differently?"

"You have more patience with word games than I do. You were about to show us something."

"I was. I believe Bowgren is experiencing greater difficulties because the lord of the wild lands that subtly overlap Bowgren is a power who has long resented the separation decreed by the gods, and she is ever pushing against the boundaries created by the covenant of those gods. The power of the gods was the greatest of the powers that once influenced and shaped the world—but their greatest power, their greatest act, was to leave it. They understood—"

"How do you know this?" Ansel demanded.

"I told you—it is my area of expertise and study."

"And how can you study gods?"

"Lord Ansel," Lord Declan said, the name a command to silence.

Ansel exhaled, but obeyed. It was close, though; Stephen wondered if Ansel would remain in the great room for the duration of this class.

The mage nodded when it was clear he would be allowed to resume without further immediate interruption. "But if the powers of the gods were unquestioned in these lands when the gods walked them, no spell is eternal; time touches all things, and the gods are no longer present to repair what they first built. The machinations of our ancient enemy have strained those barriers almost to the breaking point; they are far weaker than they once were.

"When they break, when they fully fall, you will no longer recognize the lands in which Breodanir has stood for centuries."

"What enemy?" Ansel demanded.

The mage frowned. "There is only one enemy of great significance; were it not for his actions, the barriers would not have been weakened." He glanced at Lord Declan.

"Your enemies are not always our enemies," the ranking Hunter said. "If it pleases you, answer Lord Ansel's question."

"A god we do not name walks this plane. I am surprised that this is not better known; were it not for the interference of Lord Gilliam and Lord Stephen of Elseth, the entirety of the Empire would have been lost in moments, with the rest of the continent to shortly follow.

"But they were mortal; they were not magi, not Firstborn, not gods. They interfered with the long ceremony meant to summon the god we do not name to the plane from his abode in the Hells."

Stephen glanced at Nenyane.

"The summoning succeeded, but the god was greatly weakened; he was forced to flee before his avatar was destroyed and he was once again banished to the Hells. He has been attempting to recover what strength he can—but the lands as they are now cannot easily support a god—any god.

"The Breodani in particular should understand this: it is because of the nature of the lands—created so that mortals with scant power might survive and grow—that the Sacred Hunt was necessary. It anchored Bredan, who is called Breodan in the Western kingdoms."

"Our father did this?" It was Alex who asked; Max was silent.

"Has he never spoken of it?"

Max shook his head. "We know only that Breodan killed Stephen because Stephen called him on the day of the Sacred Hunt, from the heart of the Empire."

"Yes. And the God came, as he was bound to come, at the call. It was because the God was there, because Stephen of Elseth died, that our enemy was driven away, weakened but not dead.

"We do not yet have the power to stand against that god; weakened though he was, he is not an enemy that we can easily face. He has gained ground since his summoning—but we, at last, have begun to move. A City of Man has risen in the East, in the heart of the Empire of Essalieyan, and against its walls, the armies of that god will break.

"Other cities might stand against our enemy for some time, but none of those cities is within Breodanir. And I have allowed myself to be distracted. Have I answered your question?"

Ansel frowned. "You say it's the actions of that god that have indirectly caused the problems we now face?"

The mage nodded. "The gods built walls; the lands through which they had once roamed freely were hidden, and the paths to reach it, hidden as well. But they were hidden behind walls that mortals could not see, could not touch, could not disturb; for most, the existence of those walls passed into history, lost even to the children's stories that retain some grain of truth.

"The geography of the wilderness is not fixed, although paths exist between the lands ruled by the wild lords or the Firstborn. None of those lands are safe for mortals to enter. But in Bowgren, the paths lead to a lord even the Firstborn feared. She is awake, now, and she is moving."

"Does she serve the god you won't name?"

"No. Should you encounter her, and should you survive long enough to ask her that question, you will wish you had not. But if she does not serve, she is willing to ally herself with the powers she cannot subvert, destroy, or command. What she does now is not in service to our enemy —but it will aid him, nonetheless."

"His kin feed on fear and pain. Literally. It is the sustenance they require."

"You speak of demons."

"I do; He is the Lord of the Hells. But his eye is not yet turned toward Breodanir."

Nenyane said, "It is."

The mage did not contradict her. He paused, as if to grant weight to the two words. "If that is the case, it is essential that some action be taken, even if Sigurne Mellifas might consider that action reckless. I do not believe that to be the case, but if you have encountered the demon-kin, understand that they—like we—have been searching."

"They weren't looking for me. They've been hunting Stephen."

"That is not surprising. He is not the only Bredan-born mortal, but he is one of the very, very few who have survived. If they have come for Stephen, it is not because he is Breodani; they would seek him in any country in which he dwelled. But it is not for Stephen alone that they search."

"We can discuss this later, if at all," she replied, terse now.

Stephen was surprised when the mage nodded gravely.

"I have oft been accused of being easily distracted. As you can see," he added, reaching for his pipe as it floated by his hand, "there is some truth to be found in that accusation.

"The barriers in the lands ruled by Bowgren have been severely weakened with intent by the lord, who seeks entrance into the mortal realm; she does not wish the hunt to pass her by, and if she is first to fully emerge, she might establish herself strongly enough that the god in the North will be forced to parley—or so she likely believes. It is clear that, among her servitors, there are those who can trace the narrow path, walk it, and reach Bowgren; the stone villagers are evidence of that.

"But she herself cannot, yet. Had the overlap of her lands and mortal lands occurred in any other country, that country would already be lost; it is only because it occurred here that she has not made her mark. If Bowgren falls, I believe you will lose half of Breodanir within a year—and all of it within three." As Nenyane opened her mouth, he lifted a hand to forestall her words. "If Lord Bowgren has felt he is a failure in comparison to the lords of other demesnes, understand that what Bowgren faces is far graver."

Ansel's expression shuttered.

The mage turned back to Nenyane. "Have you passed through the Bowgren demesne?"

"We've had no cause to cross it. The King's Road from Maubreche does not pass it at all."

"A pity."

Ansel opened his mouth, his eyes narrowed. To Stephen's surprise, he snapped his jaws shut before ejecting words.

Nenyane continued to speak to the mage. "What is attempting to enter Bowgren?"

"I will not speak the name here; you should be well aware that names have power. Have you heard of the Bowgren village in which half of the occupants were turned to stone?"

Nenyane's nod was slow. She had not looked away from the mage since he had entered the room; it was as if he had become the only visible person present. "I assumed that one of the stone-born had escaped into the village."

A ripple of movement spread across the table at her words. Whatever it was she had assumed, she had shared with no one, including Stephen.

"Would the damage not have been greater in that case?"

"If it wasn't hunted down."

"None of the Breodani have ever hunted the stone-born. It is quite likely that, had the Bowgren Hunters made the attempt, they would have been lost as the villagers were lost."

"Can you save the villagers?"

Ansel tensed. Heiden appeared to hold breath. Stephen realized that the answer was important to both—and felt ashamed that he had not immediately assumed it would be.

"Perhaps the question you wish to ask is: can they be saved?"

She snorted, leaning back in her chair and folding her arms, as she often did when she had not fully decided whether to be blackly amused or angry. "Fine. Can they be saved?"

"Possibly. It is not as simple as hunting down one wild creature. You were called to the King's City, but I believe that Bowgren should have been your destination."

"The King," Ansel said, "believes otherwise." He spoke with edge and heat; there was no anger for the mage in his expression, but Ansel always had anger to spare.

"I have not yet been called to justify my recommendation to the King; I have, however, been granted that permission by the Queen, who now shares my concern." Although Meralonne spoke to Ansel, his gaze returned to Nenyane. "Regardless, I intended to focus my lessons today on the difficulties Bowgren faces. The wild difficulties; if there are others, they are no part of these lessons. Lord Ansel of Bowgren will assess the information I offer within that context. With your permission, Lord Declan?"

Lord Declan nodded, aware—as they were all now aware—that the mage considered his permission almost irrelevant.

Pillars of mist began to solidify across the table. The mage was creating a diorama, his materials raw magic and will. First came trees of varying heights; at least a third of those trees had been felled by storm. Or worse. A road appeared between those trees; Stephen did not immediately recognize them as native to Breodanir, but his experience was grounded in the forests and lands of Maubreche.

Nenyane, however, rose. She glanced at Ansel and turned once again to the mage. "Where did you see this? No, never mind—when?"

"Three days as days are counted here."

"Were you on that side, or on this one?"

"I was at the border of both."

She was agitated, and because she was Nenyane, didn't trouble to hide it. But it was to Stephen she turned, her eyes wider and darker. "We have to go." The words were low.

We can't just walk out of the palace against the King's express commands.

"We don't have time," she continued, her voice soft in the wrong way, the effort to speak privately beyond her.

"Will you both *be quiet* and let him finish?" Ansel growled, rising, as Nenyane had risen, from the chair he had been uncomfortably occupying.

Meralonne's smile was brief, and offered to Ansel. "Thank you. You can see the damage caused to the forest here."

Ansel nodded, the movement jerky but controlled.

"It was caused on the other side, not in Breodanir—but it was an act of almost mindless destruction. The creature that destroyed those trees destroyed them in an attempt to break through."

"Break through to Breodanir?"

The mage nodded.

After a longer, more thoughtful pause, Nenyane said, "Who is controlling them?"

The mage's smile deepened. "First, let the Bowgren Hunters see the creature."

"They'd have already seen it if you weren't wasting time trying to be so dramatic."

Lord Declan's cough was a clear warning—as clear as Lady Maubreche's reproving glances in similar circumstances would have been. Nenyane failed to notice. This was genuine; the mage had all of her attention.

"Very well." The mage gestured, and emerging from the mist at the foot of the table came a creature that Stephen had never seen before, not even in the older story books in the Maubreche library. It was large enough that the trees seemed like new or young growth, although given the girth of their trunks, this was not the case.

Its body was covered in pale, silver fur except for the underbelly, exposed when it rose on its hind legs, which was black and reflective. It had the expected four legs, but another two in the front that were like the claws of mighty birds; its tail was a fan of light and fur and...feathers. What was more distinct, however, was its head—it had two. One was a beast's head—like unto a great cat, although it had two horns, and the other an eagle's, made large and oddly colorful.

"It has three," Nenyane said. "And the fact that you can't see the third is the only good thing about this image."

The mage was watching her carefully.

"Is this the lord of the wilderness?" Ansel asked, as focused now as Nenyane.

"This? No. They are strong enough in their own right to captain lands in the wild, but the lord of these lands is very much a power. In order to survive, they serve, but service to the lord who defeated them is…peculiar and all-encompassing; they could not now end their existence if they desired their own death."

"Is that creature responsible for the villagers of stone?"

"Yes."

"And the village we lost?"

"No. I believe, having traversed Bowgren, that the first loss of a village was similar to the losses Maubreche and Elseth have—barely—managed to skirt. But the stone villagers are the work of this creature."

"It turned the villagers to stone."

"Yes. But they did not or could not remain within Bowgren. They are flexible in ways their lord is not, and they can tread further on slender pathways than she, but they are leashed, and unless that leash is broken, they must obey their lord."

"If we kill its lord, will Bowgren be safe?"

"There is no certain safety, now, but I judge you would be as safe as any other demesne in Breodanir."

They knew that the mage's definition of safety was not their own.

"Can you kill the creature's lord?" Nenyane asked the mage.

"Not with ease, no. But in this I have unlikely allies."

"*Will* you kill her?"

"That is an entirely different question."

Nenyane folded her arms. "We don't need you."

A pale brow rose. "You feel that you can kill the lord of that land on your own?"

"On my own? No. But I won't be on my own."

"Stephen of Maubreche will not be of aid to you."

Her smile was natural, unforced. "His is the only aid I require. It would be easier if you accompanied us—but that might be too much to ask of you, given your history."

For the first time since he had entered the room, the mage's expression flickered, the easy condescension broken, for a moment, by a glimmer of genuine anger.

Nenyane—

No, let me do this. I can see something—I can almost see the past.

Can you see when you might have faced the monster the mage conjured for us?

No. But I can see him. Illaraphaniel. I can see hints of the wilderness. I know I've fought by Illaraphaniel's side before — as ally. And I know... Frustration colored her words; the glimpse of the memories she so desperately wanted fading before she could give them the anchor of words.

You're certain he can kill the lord who controlled this creature?

She was. But a hint of doubt plagued that certainty. *We could do it together,* was her compromise.

He wants something from you.

She shook her head. *It's not me he wants it from — it's you.*

Stephen's shoulders dropped.

Yes, she said, voice grim. *If that's the price he demands, we'll go alone.*

"What do you want from her?" Ansel asked, making the same assumption Stephen had. "Is it something that Bowgren could grant you instead?"

"No. The resources that Bowgren possesses will not be of aid in the war to come."

"And the resources that *she* has will?"

"Tell me, Lord Ansel, have you ever seen Nenyane's swordwork? Have you seen her fight?"

Lips compressed to prevent an intemperate reply, Ansel gave a curt shake of the head. Stephen thought he was at the limit of his self-control — but he thought that because of Heiden, whose posture very much mirrored Stephen's at the moment.

"Then I will not spoil the sight for you. But in a contest of pure bladework, she could hold her own against even me."

"Bladework is not generally expected of the magi," Lord Declan said. His elbows were on the table, his hands steepled beneath his chin.

"The expectations of fools are not my concern."

"I am not generally considered a fool."

The mage nodded.

"Do you believe you can be of aid to Bowgren? The image you have shown us is, I admit, intimidating — it is not in keeping with the strange animals reported in other demesnes."

"No. But as I said, the problems you face, the whole of the world will face, in some fashion. Breodanir has some base protections, and against most of the denizens of the wilderness, those will hold for some time — longer, certainly, than they will in the kingdoms to the West. But

Bowgren's enemy is not simply the disintegration of the walls that kept the ancient lands hidden from your own.

"Sigurne Mellifas, the Guildmaster of the Order of Knowledge, has no desire to see Breodanir fall; if I explain the situation, she will agree with me, and may even second my services to Breodanir for the duration." He turned to Ansel. "I would require your permission to interfere in your lands—or possibly your sire's permission. Nenyane would require a like permission."

"And Stephen of Maubreche?"

"If I understand correctly, she is considered his huntbrother; where she goes, he will naturally follow. Is that not true of you?"

Max and Alex held their peace. But Alex watched the mage, Max, Ansel.

Ansel turned to Lord Declan. "I will return to Bowgren."

"You will return to Bowgren when you have asked for—and received—the King's permission. You did not come here for a holiday, but for a very necessary purpose," Lord Declan said, the words measured even in his obvious displeasure.

"Then I will seek the King now."

Heiden's spine curved toward the table. He spoke through the hunt-brother's bond; whatever he said caused Ansel to wheel in rage. His response was as silent as Heiden's communication, but his hands were white-knuckled, and he took a step toward his huntbrother's chair.

Nenyane leapt lightly from floor to table and landed on the tabletop in front of where Heiden sat.

"Get out of the way," Ansel said, voice low, words evenly spaced in a growl that would have done an angered dog proud.

"Make me."

Stephen almost covered his face with his hands; Alex certainly did. He rose instead, as Max did; his dogs, relegated to the far wall, rose as well.

"If one blow is thrown in this room—*one*—I will have you jailed for no less than three days," Lord Declan snapped, speaking in the same overly punctuated tone Alex had used.

The mage rose. "I have little else to convey before speaking with your King. I understand that Lord Ansel wishes to speak with the King as well, and if I may avail myself of his company, I would be grateful if we might travel together; it has been long since I have been in the palace, and it is far too easy to get lost on the way." He did not seem to be in the least concerned with the beginnings of an altercation.

Nenyane bent slightly into her knees as she watched Ansel.

Ansel brought his rage under control, although it remained visible. He struggled to pull back far enough to find words to offer the mage. "With Lord Declan's permission, I will guide you."

"Permission is not granted. The magi has the Queen's permission to seek the King's counsel. You do not."

"I'm a Hunter Lord."

"Indeed. But by your own declaration, that status is in question or you would not be here. The privileges granted Hunter Lords are exactly that—privileges."

The mage nodded, intensity replaced by something suspiciously like boredom. He rose. "I will take my leave. Should the King desire it, I will return."

"I'm Lord Ansel *of Bowgren*," Ansel said, as if the mage hadn't spoken.

"And if what the Order of Knowledge believes is true, it is Lord Bowgren who is necessary, not Lord Ansel," Lord Declan replied, in the same tone. "Perhaps the mage's visit to Bowgren will provide the anchor your father requires to find his feet again."

Ansel's hands were fists, his arms trembling. Stephen wasn't surprised when the Bowgren Hunter drove one of his fists into the hardwood of the table, but winced on his behalf anyway.

"And what of Bowgren's people? What of the villagers who are under threat? What of the demesne—and the people—who depend *on us* for safety?"

The words surprised Stephen, where the violence to the table had not. He had felt, listening to Ansel, that Ansel resented those villagers, because it was for their sake that the Hunters agreed to be hunted on a day when one of those Hunters would perish.

He probably does, Nenyane said, making the effort to contain the words between only the two of them. *I can resent and love at the same time. It's not hard. I gave Robart a black eye once, after all.*

Family is different.

How? Yes, he's angry that Barrett died. But he's a Hunter Lord and he takes the responsibility to feed and protect Bowgren's people seriously. Bowgren's losses probably seemed like a personal failure to him. Until Illaraphaniel.

Why do you keep calling him that?

Illaraphaniel? His name? She was silent for a beat, and then said, "I know his name."

Everyone at the table glanced at her, but only briefly; Ansel's rage seemed far more of a danger than Nenyane's stray, out-of-context comment.

Stephen knew her well enough not to ask how or why, but he wanted to know. He was certain the mage had been introduced as Meralonne APhaniel. The name she knew was similar, but not the same. She had never met him during their life together; there was no way Stephen could forget someone like the mage. In height, in build, in coloring, he reminded Stephen of the Master Gardener who had toiled for centuries on the Maubreche grounds.

Although the Gardener's work was oft viewed by visitors, his age—or his apparent lack of age—was never discussed. Once or twice, older Hunter Lords, men who had encountered the Master Gardener on prior visits to the former Lord Maubreche, had made comments, but those comments remained hanging until it became clear, even to Hunter Lords, that the question itself was unwelcome or awkward.

Yes, Nenyane said softly. Stephen realized only then that Nenyane had never asked. *They resemble each other because they're...* The words fell away. *The Master Gardener didn't recognize me. Illaraphaniel does. Why?*

Stephen had no answer to give. He had questions, and he attempted to keep them entirely to himself. What he wanted to know was who the mage thought Nenyane was. Although he had always known that Nenyane had had a life before she'd become his huntbrother, the knowledge had been safely theoretical.

Now, he felt two things: uneasy, and guilty for feeling uneasy. He had never considered himself possessive or jealous by nature, but he felt a twinge that might be either of those things.

Nenyane ignored this, focused on the problem at hand. "Bowgren's people are in danger, yes. The mage has made clear he thinks they face the greater danger—and if Bowgren falls, Breodanir might follow."

"Will follow," the mage said, once again possessed of a lit pipe. "But I will see myself out. I am certain I will speak to you all again." His gaze fell on Nenyane.

Ansel remained on his feet as the mage departed. He remained on his feet after the door had once again closed, the mage and his illusory magic gone as if they had never graced the table.

He then turned toward the closed door, walked toward it, opened it, and walked out. The slamming of the door echoed in the silence of his wake.

HEIDEN REMAINED SEATED, his shoulders drawn in and down, as if Ansel's fury, Ansel's barely contained violence, had been left in the room when Ansel himself had departed.

Nenyane wanted to follow the mage, but was aware that that would put her in the same general category as Ansel; only her instinctive dislike of him kept her seated.

Max and Alex were the calmest people present, if one didn't include the dogs.

Clearly Lord Declan remained unamused by both mage and student; his lesson, such as it was, had been clipped and short.

"Today's discussion did not go as planned for obvious reasons," he finally said, leaving his seat. "I would have you go to the library and study the laws that govern the Hunter Lords for the remainder of the day. We will convene again in the dining hall." He, too, left the chamber, no doubt bound for the King, to whom Huntsmen of the Chamber had instant access if they felt such access necessary.

He did not slam the door behind him.

The minute he was no longer contained by the room, Nenyane rose and began to pace. "We need to talk to the mage," she said.

Alex and Max exchanged a glance, with a brief stop to look at Heiden, who said nothing. It was, as usual, Alex who spoke first.

"What do you want to say to him?"

"We need to go to Bowgren."

Heiden stiffened then, and finally lifted his head. Stephen found him hard to predict; he shed fear the way dogs shed hair, but the fear was complicated, some turned inward and some, out.

"Lord Bowgren would not welcome the aid of outsiders." The words were stiff and formal.

"Lord Bowgren isn't the only person in Bowgren, as you well know," Nenyane countered, not much bothered by a distant lord she'd never met.

You've met him before.

"Was I paying attention?"

Stephen surrendered. "Probably not. You weren't very old. But if you don't remember him, it means you didn't hold him in your usual immediate contempt."

Heiden looked almost shocked.

"Ignore it—that's just the way she is," Alex said quietly. "She doesn't mean anything by it." To Nenyane, he said, "When?"

"The mage is right—soon. We could leave now, and maybe take the royal messenger horses if we needed to arrive quickly."

"We can't horse all of us that way, and we've also got the dogs. Bowgren is on the edge of Breodanir. We *can* ride, but we can't ride the horses to exhaustion and switch them out with any certainty."

Heiden turned to stare at Alex. "Lord Declan hasn't given any of us permission to go anywhere—and if he hasn't, we don't have the King's approval." He seemed almost shocked.

Stephen sympathized, but was accustomed to Nenyane and the Elseth brothers. He was happy to have Max and Alex with them, but when the three were all pointed in the same direction, one had a slightly better chance of talking them out of their intended plans than diplomatically persuading a forest fire to stop burning.

"It's better to beg forgiveness than to ask permission," Max said. "You've heard that, haven't you?"

Heiden's expression made clear he had not.

"You don't have to come with us," Nenyane told the Bowgren hunt-brother. "I mean, I know you're of Bowgren, but the creatures we need to counter aren't. Yet."

"But the mage said he required Lord Bowgren's permission."

Nenyane shrugged. "He might. We don't. What the mage wants to do won't be done entirely on Bowgren lands—but he's right. If we're not there soon, there will be further losses, each worse than the last, until there's nothing left to lose."

Heiden stiffened, as if slapped.

Nothing in Nenyane's brusque words had caused his reaction; that was clear to everyone in the room. Everyone in the room was bound to a brother; they recognized the signs of Ansel's distant anger.

"Ansel followed the mage?"

"Ansel," Heiden said, voice a whisper, "went directly to the King. Or tried." He rose. "I have to go."

No one argued. Not even Nenyane, although she came closest.

Absent Heiden, the four chose to retire to the library in Hunter's

Redoubt, where they might continue their discussion without the appearance of breaking the rules they had chosen not to follow.

After a very subdued dinner, with very little decided, they retired to their chambers to sleep, or in the case of at least two of them, to try and fail.

17TH OF EMPERAL, 429 A.A. *HUNTER'S REDOUBT, THE KING'S PALACE*

Breakfast was remarkably silent. Lord Declan appeared to be as much in need of sleep as Stephen felt, and he did not remain to offer the delinquent Hunters his usual lecture. He was called to the King's Chambers and went instantly, advising the six to practice useful self-study and self-reflection.

The ramifications of the assassination attempt echoed in the near empty halls of Hunter's Redoubt. It was felt in the visible presence of a bristle of Queen's Guards. Max and Alex carried the weight of the caution; only half of their attention could be prized from the alert watchfulness they had adopted.

There were many practical elements to consider if the intent was actually to leave for Bowgren immediately, the first of which was permission and the likelihood it would be granted. Neither Ansel nor Heiden chose to join the Elseth and Maubreche Hunters, and without them, the discussion could not quite descend into the purely practical. If permission were granted, the rest of the practicalities could be left in the hands of the various royal services. If permission were not granted, the practicalities became the problem of the scions of two lords: Maubreche and Elseth.

No one wanted an angry Lady Maubreche or Lady Elseth; Max and Alex weren't concerned about the reaction of either of their parents, although they winced when their oldest brother was mentioned.

"We'd like to avoid speaking with the Queen if at all possible," Stephen told the Elseth brothers.

"Agreed—but I assume you have more than the usual reasons."

Stephen glanced at Nenyane, who shrugged. "I'd like to avoid the guest I tried to kill in the Queen's audience chamber. He's an assassin. He just wasn't sent for us."

The Elseth brothers usually avoided questions that would set

Nenyane off, but Alex was clearly still unsettled by the attack. "How did you know that?"

"Because I'd just killed an assassin who *was* sent for us." She exhaled. "For Stephen."

"Same difference," Max said. "But why would you assume the bard was an assassin?"

"Because he bears the same mark." She folded her arms. "Stephen couldn't see it on either of the two, either." Jaw clenched, she added, "I'm not impressed with palace security."

"That might work in our favor." Alex's expression became his usual thoughtful frown as he processed the information.

"How?"

"We'd be out of the palace while the assassin is in it. Breodanir has bards, but—"

"He was an Imperial bard from Senniel College," Stephen told the Elseth Hunter. "He was surprised by Nenyane, but he wasn't offended. Nenyane of course believes if no offense was taken by the bard, the Queen should likewise be unoffended."

"And hunting dogs should grow on trees."

"It would be more convenient—would we still have to train them?"

Nenyane glared at everyone.

"I didn't say anything," Max pointed out. "But even I would think twice—or a hundred times—before attacking a foreigner the Queen considers a guest *in front of her throne*. You couldn't wait?"

"If the assassin was sent for Stephen, no. Stephen would be dead. I will not take that risk over something as petty as good manners and social politics."

Stephen raised a hand. "There's nothing to be gained by arguing about it. We all know it was intemperate. I mentioned it because the Queen isn't going to be an easy avenue of approach. At the moment, she's inclined toward anger."

"Do we need the mage?" Alex asked Nenyane.

She started to say no, but closed her mouth before the single syllable could escape. "We have a chance of success without him, but it's a much smaller chance. He's not bound by Breodanir customs in the same way we're supposed to be—but he'll accompany us. It's clear that that was his intent."

"Will he stay away if we don't want him?"

She shrugged. "I'm not certain. He was never one to take orders, but he was willing to work toward a common goal, unlike—" She froze, as a name that had almost emerged drifted away before she could voice the syllables.

Her frustration, her rage at her lack of memory when memory was becoming increasingly important, was palpable, almost another presence in the room.

Steel lifted head, rose from the floor, and padded across it to reach Nenyane.

"Go away," she snapped.

He dropped his large head in her lap—probably to prevent her from rising. The dogs didn't serve Nenyane the way they served Stephen, but they understood her place.

"None of us can approach the King directly. We'd have to get Lord Declan's permission," Alex said.

Nenyane nodded, but added, "He'll discuss it with the King."

"You're certain?"

"He has to. Even if he doesn't believe the mage, he can't afford to dismiss the mage's claim out of hand; there's too much at stake if the mage is right."

"You think he's right."

"I'm certain."

Max and Alex exchanged a glance. It was Max who spoke. "Lady Elseth has merchant connections in the city. It's possible—probable, even—that we could borrow or rent their horses; we could certainly pick up necessary supplies before we head out."

"You know the merchants?" Nenyane asked.

"Alex does. He's traveled here with Lady Elseth a number of times."

"Alone?"

"Mostly. Oh, I was with him, but she's given up on me." Max grinned. "They had problems telling us apart, so I could fake Alex if I had to. You've never had that problem. Sadly."

Nenyane shook her head, her hand scratching the spot behind Steel's ears. "Move, you stupid dog. I have to go find the mage."

"We're not supposed to leave," Alex pointed out. "Today, at least, Declan is going to be paying attention; if he isn't, his guards will."

It was Max who said, "Just wait for the mage to return. What? He couldn't take his eyes off Nenyane for most of the class he attempted to teach. He'll go to the Queen, and if he convinces her, the King—we should ask Heiden if the mage, at least, was granted an appointment."

Nenyane shook her head. "Don't ask him about Ansel. Ansel's not entirely stable, and Heiden will bear the brunt of his temper if he loses it."

"You're certain they're actually Hunter and huntbrother?" Alex asked Stephen.

"They seem to be. I don't understand how."

"The huntbrother's oath—the one you won't let Nenyane swear—can it be broken?"

"I know it won't be accepted if it isn't genuinely meant. If I had to guess, it would be Ansel who would be forsworn—but the oath was created when the country was created, and it was meant to preserve the Hunters, not the huntbrothers. Heiden could despise Ansel—but if he was willing to die in Ansel's stead in the Sacred Hunt, the God would consider the oath to be unbroken."

"If Max treated me that way…"

"The two of you would start a brawl," Nenyane said. "Heiden's significantly smaller than Ansel." She hesitated and then added, "I think Heiden chooses not to fight back—but he's still doing what he can to protect Ansel. Or protect Bowgren. Ansel's angry.

"But he clearly does care about Bowgren. Angry or not, he does care about the people he'll one day rule."

Alex nodded; Max said, "Not if he keeps his word and refuses to participate in the Sacred Hunt, he won't."

Silence again. Alex broke it. "Let's figure out what we'll need at a minimum, both with and without the mage."

THE DINING HALL at dinner was silent.

Lord Declan sat at the head of the table; he had arrived early, but by how much, no one could guess. The dark circles beneath his eyes accentuated his naturally dour expression.

We're not late, are we? Stephen asked.

Nenyane shook her head. They walked to their seats, as did Max and Alex. Alex had done some reading toward the end of their so-called study period, in part because he wasn't certain Lord Declan wouldn't test them on the reading.

Stephen, however, had been properly tutored by both scholars and priests, and had had no need to study those particular books; he could answer Lord Declan's questions with ease. Nenyane, he could feed answers, but Max and Alex were on their own.

Lord Declan waited for perhaps ten minutes.

The door opened, and Heiden entered the room, walking quickly because he knew he was on the edge of late, and likely to fall off the wrong side. He was alone. Ansel did not follow.

Nenyane's hands became fists; she almost rose and left the room.

Heiden's left eye was red and swollen, the left side of his mouth swollen as well.

I swear I'm going to kill him.

Remember: you blackened one of my eyes.

I was ten. I only did it once. The other time was not my fault—you ran into the branch.

Stephen was certain Nenyane's reaction was the right one, but he knew better than to interfere in an altercation between huntbrothers, unless asked for help.

"Heiden," Lord Declan said, inclining chin. "Where is Lord Ansel?"

Heiden, silent, took his chair and bowed his head to limit the visibility of the swelling.

"Does he intend to join us?"

Silence again, shoulders shrinking inward.

"I see. That is unfortunate. We have guests." Lord Declan lifted hand and the page that customarily stood to one side of the door bowed to him, and then opened the door.

Standing in its frame were two men: the mage Nenyane called Illaraphaniel, and the assassin she had tried to kill in the presence of the Queen.

CHAPTER TEN

The bard entered first. He offered Lord Declan, at the head of the table, a very graceful Imperial bow.

"I believe you've met at least two of the people present?" Lord Declan asked, expression grim, but lips oddly quirked, as if he could not help but see humor in their previous meeting.

"Indeed, I have had that pleasure and privilege," the bard replied. "Lords Stephen and Nenyane."

Lord Declan was not churlish enough to correct him. "Maxwell and Alexander are of Elseth, and Heiden is of Bowgren."

"Ah. I was informed that a Lord Ansel would also be present?"

"You were informed correctly, but apparently there has been some altercation."

"A pity. His presence, given the current difficulty, would be welcome." Speaking thus, the bard looked to Heiden, who failed to meet his gaze — or anyone else's.

Nenyane's jaw tightened. "Why would it be of relevance to you?"

Nenyane, careful.

The bard turned to her, the hint of smile implied by the corners of his mouth. "I have come from Senniel College at the behest of the Bardmaster; I am to witness the changes in the lands to the west of the Empire, and tender a report. I was informed that Meralonne APhaniel would likewise be traveling, and if the situation merited it, I might aid him where he thought my aid would be of use."

"Does she know what you are?"

"I am Kallandras of Senniel College, Master Bard. I am frequently sent on missions that she feels no one should be able to survive."

"And you always have."

"To date, yes. I am not a god; I am merely a talent-born mortal." He turned to Lord Declan. "Apologies if I have interrupted anything."

"You were given leave to attend us by the King; that is good enough for any Breodani." He stressed the word *any*, but did not deign to glare at Nenyane.

He shouldn't be here.

That's not for us to decide.

He's dangerous.

Ironic, coming from Nenyane. Her gaze moved to the mage; he stood behind Kallandras, as if waiting for the bard to seat himself. Once again, his gaze was on Nenyane. She was far more careful this time; her glance strayed to him, but did not remain.

"Please, join us." To Heiden, Lord Declan said, "Inform your Hunter that matters of Bowgren are to be discussed at the table; perhaps that will provide incentive to join us."

Heiden nodded, but made no further reply.

Meralonne, as Kallandras had called him, took the seat at the foot of the table; Kallandras, perhaps aware of Nenyane's bristling suspicion, took the seat farthest from her—to the left of Lord Declan, and beside Alex.

Stephen wasn't hungry. He thought Nenyane ate because a dinner knife was nonetheless a weapon in her hands, and she wanted one. Drawing a sword, unless attacked, would cross a line.

That's the problem with our so-called bard, she said. *He's too fast, too aware of how any room can be a battleground. I might not have time to draw sword if he attacks in earnest—and it won't be me he'll attack.* She held her peace, enough in control that she could speak this way; it had always taken effort on her part.

He won't.

She accepted his certainty, grudging any of her own. *If the mage lights that damn pipe again, I'll stab him.*

He'll wait until after dinner.

When we've eaten and nausea has worse consequences. She wanted to get up and storm out; she envied the strength Ansel's rage had given him.

That's not strength.

He didn't care what anyone thought. He passed beyond worry.

Stephen shook his head. *That's not how I define strength. It's the opposite —whatever it takes to remain in control of his anger, he's lost it.* He glanced at Heiden's bowed head to emphasize the point.

Nenyane exhaled. *You win. And the second black eye was not my fault. You can blame the trees. I will not attempt to kill the assassin with dinnerware—but if I tell you to move, move instantly.*

Stephen nodded. His dogs rested against the far wall. They were bored and restless—they'd been cooped up inside for too long. The royal kennels had exercising runs for the Hunter dogs who stayed there, but as the dogs had been given permission to remain with Stephen, they hadn't made use of those runs. He glanced at Max, and almost asked if he'd take the dogs for exercise, but Lord Declan cleared his throat.

"Perhaps you wish to discuss your meeting with the King." He spoke to the seated mage.

"There will be very little to discuss if we are not able to raise a reply —a swift reply—from Lord Bowgren or his absent son." The mage's response was clipped; he was clearly annoyed.

"Can we just assume we've had a reply, and it allows us to do what we need to do?" Nenyane's question was almost—but not quite—a demand. Stephen could practically hear Lord Declan's brow furrow.

"We could, but I answer to Sigurne Mellifas, and I can assure you she would be displeased were we to act without the requisite and necessary permissions."

"I'm not asking you to skirt rules. I'm asking what your plan of action is should we be allowed to act in Bowgren."

"And you will find out when the Breodani choose to take the situation seriously enough they are willing to tender a reply."

Nenyane was annoyed.

Alex, catching Stephen's eye, shrugged. Permission, while preferred, was not necessary. Stephen nodded.

The meal itself was, therefore, a mostly silent affair, although the bard did attempt to keep what passed for conversation going. The annoyance of the mage, the annoyance of Lord Declan, and the annoy-

ance of Stephen's huntbrother made that conversation difficult; Stephen
and Alex, however, did their level best to aid Kallandras.

The dinner came to an end with nothing resolved, for Ansel did not
return. Not only did Heiden refrain from speaking, he barely lifted his
head for the duration, and the moment the first guest rose, making plain
his intent to leave, Heiden rose as well and scurried out of the dining
room.

---

*17TH DAY OF LATTAN, 429 A.A. MERCHANT QUARTER, KING'S
CITY, KINGDOM OF BREODANIR*

Traveling the merchant routes as he had, Gervanno was familiar with
the accommodations offered—and paid for—in the North. He had
become accustomed to the chill, northern cold so different from the
desert cold with which he was thankfully only passingly familiar. But he
found the inn's room dark and almost airless, with its closed—and
locked—doors. The interiors could be warm and cozy if a fire were lit,
but he felt confined by the small space he could afford.

The dog, Leial, did not appear to feel likewise stifled; he had found a
patch of sun, and had curled up beneath it, breath even, as the sun
descended. Gervanno had never had dogs of his own—and had never
truly desired one—but he understood the upkeep and feed of animals;
he could afford to feed the unkempt mutt. The inns were accustomed to
the larger hunting dogs, and had kennels for their use, but Gervanno
felt the kennels were for show; he could not imagine the Maubreche
Hunters leaving their dogs in them unless in an emergency.

Leial would be unlikely to remain in the kennels, and dogs were
allowed in the rooms, with the caveat that damages done by domestic
animals would have to be paid for by their owner.

This was the first time he had been in a foreign city alone. In Brookton, where he had first encountered the Maubreche Hunters, the
villagers had treated those Hunter Lords with respect. No, more than
respect: they were honored. Gervanno knew the difference between
respect paid in fear and respect that was genuine; he had grown up in
the Dominion's version of Brookton, although he was not seraf, to be
owned in his entirety by a ruling clansman.

In the city, however, with its mix of foreigners—he himself being one—that respect was muted, possibly even begrudged. Those noting Leial had reacted in different ways; some had mocked the dog, some had mocked Gervanno, and some had been friendly. One or two, however, had made comments about Gervanno's dog; they were willing to accept the dog because it wasn't a *Hunter's* dog. The sneer in the single word housed resentment, envy, even anger.

This, Gervanno understood. It was the resentment of those who believed they were without power, and it was voiced only in the absence of those they believed had it. He did not interfere or argue, settling instead on a silent look of confusion as his best shield.

Swords were not the only thing in which he had been schooled in his distant childhood. The merchants' compounds and their surroundings were not a place meant for Hunters; if Hunters had power, they were nonetheless not the driving engine for the commerce that kept Breodanir markets stocked. This was not their place.

Gervanno almost regretted it. If he was not, even in his homeland, of a rank that would allow him to consort with lords, he had nonetheless felt welcome in Maubreche. He shook his head ruefully. It was not just that. His hands trembled briefly at the thought of the sparring match he had faced against the best swordsman he had ever known. He wondered what her reaction would be to those who disparaged her Hunter; while Gervanno's understanding of Breodani law was extremely spotty, he doubted that she could simply cut the man down to make a point to those who might be tempted to show a similar disrespect.

It would not be against any laws in the Dominion, although the young Leonne Tyr had been attempting to bring some taint of Northern law into the laws that governed the South. Gervanno's father had mixed feelings about this—but the kai Leonne had, in the end, brought the Sun Sword to the demons who threatened Averda; he had fought a war, the war had not killed him, and he had emerged as the ruler of Annagar. Tainted by the North or no, he had proven himself. That was enough for Gervanno, a lowly cerdan who had faced demons on the same battlefield, had lost comrades, had miraculously survived.

Two years ago, he had fled the battlefields for which he had been trained; had come to the North with—of all things—a merchant caravan, and there had discovered that the demons had broken something in him. A second time, far, far more ignobly, he had survived.

A second time, his companions had not.

Leial lifted head and rose, tail wagging, head slightly lowered as he butted Gervanno's leg, as if the dog could understand Gervanno's thoughts and the direction in which they were leading him. He rested his palm against the top of the dog's head.

This morning, after some argument, he had made an appointment to speak with someone in the Order of Knowledge, although that appointment had been gained only by dint of Lady Maubreche's letter. Prior to the reception of that letter, he was given the suspicious stare reserved for outsiders of little wealth. Foreigners. Were it not for the circumstances under which he had left home, his experience in the King's City would have made him yearn for it.

But he was no longer a youth with naive ambitions. He was a disgrace who hoped, in whatever small way he could, to atone for his cowardice. For the fact of his survival.

He was not expecting a knock at his inn door, and rose slowly, willing the unexpected visitor to go away. Leial, however, did not seem overly concerned, although he swiveled head toward the door, almost as if he could see beyond it. When the knock was repeated a second time, Gervanno lifted his scabbard but did not unsheathe his sword. He then made his way to the closed door.

"Yes?" he said, raising voice so that it might be heard through the wood.

"Master Gervanno?"

He made haste to open the door, then. In its frame stood a familiar figure: the Maubreche gardener. They had parted ways a day prior, but it felt much longer. "Please, come in."

The Master Gardener raised a brow at the sword, still sheathed, and Gervanno shrugged. "Not all inns are friendly or safe to one who travels alone."

"I imagine they are not." The Gardener stepped into the room as if it were a hovel with only half a roof to keep inclement elements out.

"Why are you here?"

"I have come to give warning, but I must not tarry."

"Warning?"

"Someone has entered the King's City. Ah, no. Something has entered the city."

Gervanno paled. "Demons?"

"At least two; neither, at this point, are significant threats. Were they to catch you unaware, they might do damage, but your sword skills are good enough that the damage would be slight unless you were sleeping."

This was not as comforting as the Gardener clearly intended it to be.

"They do not, to my admittedly scant knowledge, seek you."

He had seen the damage done by demons who had had no knowledge of who he was; they'd had no knowledge of who any of their victims had been.

As if aware of Gervanno's concern, the Master Gardener said, "None that I can detect are of the power of the demon that attacked— and destroyed—the merchant caravan. But if he was following the Breodanir road, he is also of concern. Were he unveiled, were he to use his full power, even the mortal mages would be aware of his presence. They consider themselves alert, and inasmuch as they can be, they are watchful."

Not watchful enough. "Can the demons arrive unseen?"

"Not these ones. But the greater danger they pose is their ability to don the appearance of mortals. I believe a mortal is with them—one who works in concert with the distant Shining Court."

Gervanno frowned.

"I do not expect you to hunt them; nor do I expect you to locate them. Were you in your own lands, I might make that request, but you are in Breodanir, and as you have no doubt discovered, it is very difficult for outsiders to gain the attention of the powerful here."

Gervanno grimaced. "It was ever the same in our own cities." He set the sword aside on the small table that occupied a corner of the room. "If you don't expect me to find them, to hunt them, why do you offer this information?"

"You have stumbled across many things wild and dangerous in your time in the North; while it is not probable that you will cross their path, it is not impossible, given your one duty in the King's City. You are a foreigner; you are not Breodani. Play to that; hide what knowledge you have gathered. Men of power will oft overlook men without similar power; it is wise to be so overlooked, now."

"I have an appointment to speak with the Order of Knowledge tomorrow, by grace of Lady Maubreche's letter."

The Gardener was silent for a long beat. "I would stay with you, but I cannot do so in safety."

"They are surely not hunting you?"

"If they were aware of me, they would—or perhaps they would flee." The Gardener offered Gervanno a rare smile.

Gervanno nodded. Any desire for sleep had fled with the Gardener's warning; an uneasiness stabbed him, but the figurative blade remained where it had been seated. "How did you know where I was?"

"I told him, of course."

Gervanno wheeled instantly, once again reclaiming his sheathed weapon. The Master Gardener said, "Do not draw blade." The Gardener then turned in the direction of that voice, a flicker of annoyance crossing—and leaving—his features.

They both faced a small, golden fox. Gervanno lowered his sword. He recognized the creature to whom he owed a great debt.

"Eldest," the Gardener said, offering the fox a fluid, perfect bow. "I had not thought to see you in the heart of a mere mortal city."

"You wonder why this particular mortal can see me? He and I have met before, in a forest that almost overwhelmed mortal lands."

The Master Gardener glanced at Gervanno briefly, but his gaze returned to the sheen of gold that was the fox.

"He is not mine, but I am aware of his presence, and he of mine." To Gervanno, the fox added, "The mortals in this city cannot see me yet; I walk the forests, even here. I have a cub that walks the streets in a more natural fashion, and I have been observing his progress." His whiskers fluttered as he wrinkled his nose. "I am surprised that you are still here, Caralonne. I know that you have always been safe in the lands of those chosen by Bredan, for your lord will never cross them without warning, except at need. Did you not sense the arrival of your lord?"

"I did. I wished to offer warning to this man before retreating."

"You take a great risk to do so. Why?"

"He was guest in my small garden for a short time, and he was of aid there. I merely discharge a slight obligation. Will you walk with me?"

"You do not want my company or my counsel; you wish to separate me from the mortal."

The Gardener bowed, accepting the fox's observation as the polite refusal it clearly was. "Eldest. He is not as we are. He has a duty to discharge; I would see him fulfill his obligation and be quickly free of this place."

"To what end? The North is not his home, but the South faces its own danger. The Deepings have grown increasingly wild; even I will not cross them, now, unless at great need."

The Gardener stilled. "To what do you refer?"

"The tangle is moving," was the quiet reply. "We are not certain to what end, but we fear that its influence will spread."

Silence, then. Gervanno felt his ignorance keenly, but knew better than to expose it in the presence of the powerful. He had no doubt that, of the three assembled in this tiny, humble room, he was by far the weakest.

"I should tell you, as well, that Namann has left our Lord's city."

Distaste crossed the Gardener's features. "Your lord accepts him, then."

"She is remarkably straightforward in that acceptance, but she is largely mortal. I do not believe she even understands the effect he has on those who are not. Let us hope that she can contain him when he is far from her influence."

"Does he come to this city?"

"Who can say?" Fur rippled, catching and reflecting light from a source invisible to Gervanno. "Not I. But my cub might have insight, there."

"I would ask a boon, Eldest."

"You wish me to leave this mortal out of my games?"

The Gardener nodded.

"I found him first," was the amused reply. "Perhaps I should have let him lose his way. But no. I thought he might be of use to my cub in the near future, and you cannot offer to take his place with Illaraphaniel so close."

At the mention of the name, the Master Gardener stiffened. He bowed head, as if to contain his expression, but it was clear to Gervanno: comingled desolation, loss, and bitter yearning. The Gardener did not reply. Instead he turned to Gervanno. "You have an appointment with representatives of the Order of Knowledge. It is my hope that one of those representatives, Meralonne APhaniel, will be the person to take your report. You will need to practice little caution if that is the case.

"If it is not, practice far greater caution. For reasons not clear to me, those mortals who choose to affiliate themselves with the *Kialli* are oft considered mages of some power." He nodded to Gervanno, but offered the fox a full bow. "I will take my leave."

"HE HAS CHANGED GREATLY since our first encounter," the fox remarked, when the Gardener had left. If Gervanno hoped that the fox would follow, those hopes were to be dashed; the fox sniffed in distaste and said, "This floor is rough and uncomfortable." He then lifted head.

Gervanno understood the comment as the command it was; his Oma had been wont to make her demands in just such a fashion. He knelt to lift the fox from the offending wooden planks. To his surprise, the fox fur was cold, the slight body, heavy. A reminder that talking animals were not, in any way, animals at all.

"We met a handful of days ago, but perhaps he remembers me because of the demon attack upon the grounds he tended."

The fox tilted his head, his large, golden eyes unblinking. "You fought?"

Gervanno in his youth would have felt the prickle of shame. "I fought." He was no longer that youth, and if he envied the naive belief he had once possessed in his own strength, he knew that belief would never return.

"Did he see you fight?"

"I'm not certain. My focus and attention at the time was not on the Gardener." This much was true.

"It's an odd reaction, nonetheless. Perhaps he is unsettled; Illaraphaniel does not generally travel this far to the West. Should we visit him?"

"Visit this Illaraphaniel?"

The fox nodded. "It is best to offer him warning: Caralonne is close."

Gervanno was both tired and confused. "My apologies, Eldest. I do not understand."

"No, of course not. But I am feeling generous at the moment; my cub has amused me. I will therefore explain. Ah, you will have to carry me, and you will have to follow my directions."

Gervanno, apprised of the presence of demons in the city, had no desire to wander through its streets. Not when he carried a fox that couldn't be seen; he suspected that the fox would insist on verbal answers to any question he might pose, which would make Gervanno seem not only foreign, which he could not avoid, but also insane.

He had no avenue to refuse the fox, who, in spite of having bitten his hand deeply enough to draw blood, had nonetheless led him out of the wilderness before it vanished in the sudden fog, stranding Gervanno in a land in which mortals did not dwell. The Sarrado clan paid its debts.

"May I set you down in order to open the door?"

The fox lofted nose in the air. "If it is absolutely necessary. You will find, however, that it is not necessary if you choose to trust me."

"And I am to be replaced so quickly?" a new voice said.

Gervanno, arms full of fox, could not easily draw his sword, but he turned in the direction of the voice. A man in a grey cloak, eyes glinting as if of steel, leaned against the wall closest to the door, his arms folded, his lips an odd line—not quite smile, not quite frown.

"I have no intention of replacing you," the fox replied, his voice warm with, what sounded to Gervanno's ears, genuine affection. "I was perhaps bored, and I caught sight of an old friend. I followed him here, and he led me to this dingy little hovel and its mortal occupant.

"To my surprise, I recognized the scent of the mortal's blood, having tasted it once, and I chose to join them."

The stranger lifted hand to the bridge of his nose, which he pinched. Gervanno smiled at the gesture. It seemed comfortingly familiar; his uncle had oft been reduced to expressing his frustration in the same way. "If he has injured you, I ask you to forgive him; he finds mortals strange, and he continually overestimates their base strength." The stranger's accent was Northern, Imperial.

"But not yours?"

"No. In my own fashion, I serve him. I am certain it will come as no surprise to you that he can be a most trying master."

What surprised Gervanno was the man's tone. The Master Gardener had treated the fox with a respect Gervanno was certain he did not show the mortals who, theoretically, owned the grounds upon which he toiled.

"My manners have seen little use of late," the man continued. He smiled, the expression warm. It was in his eyes that cold remained. "I am Jarven ATerafin."

It took Gervanno a moment to realize that the stranger was speaking in Torra. "Gervanno di'Sarrado," he offered in response. He glanced at the fox in his arms, hoping the stranger would understand the lack of a proper bow or greeting.

"You are far from home. What brings you to this city at this time?"

"I had business to conduct and information to deliver to the Order of Knowledge in the King's City."

"I could not help but overhearing my master offer to lead you directly to one who serves the Order of Knowledge."

"Meralonne APhaniel?"

"The very man. The Guildmaster of the Order of Knowledge has seen fit to send him out of Averalaan far more frequently in the past year."

"Do you know him?"

"Our paths have crossed more than once, and neither of us are worse for those encounters. He is not, however, a man I would ever wish to anger. I assume you know how to use that sword."

Gervanno nodded. "Not as well as I once believed, but better than I once feared."

Jarven ATerafin uttered a brief bark of laughter. "If you wish to get that mage's famously scattered attention, carrying my master will accomplish that."

"Jarven." The name was sharply spoken.

"You wish to surprise APhaniel? You? I do not think it can be done."

"I have word to convey to him, and it is convenient to do so in this fashion."

Jarven's smile was sharp. "Convenient."

"Please ignore him," the fox told Gervanno, "and carry on."

"Might he hold you while I open the door?"

"I told you, trust me and you need not touch the door at all."

Gervanno relented. He clearly, and perhaps undeservedly, had some sense of dignity; he did not wish to be seen bouncing off an inn's door. The sense that the fox had a sense of humor that would find such embarrassment amusing was strong.

To his surprise—and relief—the fox's words were true. He could walk through the door to his small room without opening it. He wondered if he could also walk through walls, but did not put this to the test; he returned to the room itself, clumsily retrieving his pack, the second sword he carried, and his keys.

The dog, silent until this moment, whined.

The fox turned toward the dog and uttered a growl that was louder and deeper than should have been possible given his size.

Leial's belly hit ground. He rolled, exposing underbelly and throat, the coward.

"You can't follow now," Gervanno told the dog; he wanted to pat him to offer comfort, which was almost ridiculous, given the situation.

The fox's student—for the older man's interaction implied heavily that that was his role—bent knee and place a hand on the dog's head, and the dog rolled over again, lifting that head in Jarven's direction.

"We'll be back. Or your master will be. Be patient." He rose, glanced at Gervanno, and nodded to the fox. He then walked—without fox in arms—through the closed door.

THE EVENING STREETS were dark and, nearest the merchant compound's many inns and taverns, crowded and noisy. Some of the noise would become ugly; there was alcohol in the air. But the young men who reeked of it were not Gervanno's men, nor his students; they were not his problem. This was especially true because they did not seem to notice his presence at all.

"They cannot see the forest," the fox said, voice a rumble. "But my lord says that is for the best, although frankly I do not see how."

"She fears you might take offense at the lack of respect, due to their ignorance, and destroy them," Jarven replied, smiling. "And she is who she is: she does not wish the merely foolish and disrespectful to perish."

"I have never understood why."

Jarven's smile was slender but Gervanno judged it genuine given the shape of his eyes. Between the two—talking fox and the man he referred to as his cub—Gervanno would have taken his chances with the fox; there was something about the man that spoke of death.

Perhaps he allowed the size of the fox—and his current position in the cradle of Gervanno's arms—to lull his sense of caution, or perhaps, because the foes against which he had trained his sword were human, he could instantly recognize that this Jarven was not a man upon whom it would ever be safe to turn his back.

"You don't like my cub?" the fox asked, exposing a throat that was paler than the gold of the rest of his fur.

"I do not know your student," Gervanno replied. "But were you to group the cerdan with whom I have trained or with whom I have served in his presence, I would consider him the deadliest foe in that gathering."

"Did you command them?" Jarven said; he seemed neither pleased nor insulted by Gervanno's observation.

"In the last war between the Empire and the Dominion, I was considered experienced enough to guide younger men."

"Experienced enough?"

Gervanno, arms full of fox, shrugged. "In the Dominion, that simply means I have been in many battles and have survived."

"I imagine survival is the telling part." He frowned. "Do not disappoint me by being one of those earnest young men—at your age, it is not a good look."

Gervanno blinked.

"You were about to say, modestly, that it comes down to luck."

As that was, indeed, what Gervanno had been about to say, he felt a minor flash of annoyance. "It is not considered earnest, ATerafin, but good manners."

"You are carrying a talking animal while walking—invisibly, I might add—through the streets of a foreign city, and you are concerned with good manners?"

"I have been informed that the denizens of the wilderness are to be treated with respect; in my country, modesty and humility are considered part of that respect when conversing with another."

The fox chuckled. "Jarven, stop teasing him. He is entirely correct, and in the wilderness, he is far more likely to survive random encounters with the lords of the various lands than one such as yourself."

"Respect is given where it is due," Jarven countered. "And I am not so powerless that I bend knee for everyone who styles himself my superior. Perhaps I might offer the patina of bent knee or fear."

The fox shook his head. "You are remarkably good at mimicking actions or emotions you do not feel, yes. I still find the ability quite refreshing; there was a reason I chose you."

"And a reason I chose you, although your damnable tests make me feel that I was the kindest and gentlest of mentors in comparison."

Gervanno highly doubted that the students who had labored under this man would agree. There was something about him that put Gervanno on edge.

"I believe we are almost there," the man now said. "Would it trouble you greatly if I attended your meeting as well?"

"I have no appointment with the man in question," Gervanno began.

"Don't be ridiculous. *I* am here," the fox said, "and I have personally escorted you; he will of course condescend to listen to what you have to say. I am not unknown to him."

"I am curious to see what his reaction will be. You are far from home, and far from your Lord's side."

The fox's tail tickled the underside of Gervanno's jaw. "She is my Lord, she is not my master. While her rule over the city in which she dwells is impossible to contest, that rule becomes far more theoretical beyond the boundaries of her forests, her lands."

JARVEN ATERAFIN WAS GENUINELY AMUSED by the foreigner serving as a personal conveyance to the Eldest, as he was generally called. He himself found the fox amusing, interesting, and irritating, almost in equal measure. But power could lessen many personal flaws, and the fox was powerful. Jarven had always respected power, to a greater or lesser degree, his respect being dependent upon how easily that power was broken, diverted, or subsumed.

Powerful people oft played dangerous games. Jarven had, as a youth, desired a seat at their table, a full hand in their game. He had played similar games, with deadly results, as a young, brash man, and except for the wealth involved, could not see a structural difference between the monied and the dens that roved the streets of the inner holdings. Linguistic differences, yes, and differences in social context — but no substantive difference. If he was going to risk his life for reward, he intended to do it at the most expensive tables in the land.

But he had discovered, as he aged, that boredom was also a factor. He had served the Twin Kings as security, but by and large he had spent his time swatting the equivalent of flies, he did his job so well. From there, he moved on, coming to rest, in the end, in House Terafin. That, too, bored him, but as he was no longer a young man with burning ambition, he settled there, almost content.

Almost content until the moment the *Kialli* had come into play, and demons had upended the boards across which games of power were — and had always been — played.

Almost content until the new Terafin, young, far too earnest, and unequipped to handle the job into which she'd been placed by the

Terafin Jarven had served for the duration of his time in the House, had become something other. Something far more powerful and far more strange. To her side, then, had come the denizens of a wilderness he was still struggling to master—inasmuch as the wilderness could ever be mastered.

She was considered a power in the new world. The fox spoke to and of her with respect, or what passed for respect in his mind; the powerful came to greet her, to pay the respects she, as lord of the wilderness in which the whole of Averalaan was now set, was due.

The demons could no longer enter Averalaan. Where they had crept in before, wearing human face, human guise, or literally living human flesh, they were gone. Only if the city itself fell would they return. Jarven, therefore, had no remaining opponents against which to test his newfound power at home.

It annoyed him. He had bound himself to the fox to gain what the fox had offered: power. The strength of youth, if not the appalling ignorance of it. But no, even that was wrong. He was, in all ways, young again, and the ignorance he had all but stamped out as he gained experience had returned with a weight and a severity he felt he had never experienced. It lit his days with an inner fire that had almost been extinguished by the ennui of arriving at the pinnacle of power.

The Eldest, the fox, was a demanding master, which was not a problem except in one way: the final transformation of Jarven into something stronger and more physically powerful was being withheld. He had set Jarven a task, and Jarven, shorn of the usual arsenal of tools at his disposal, had failed to achieve it. Yet.

But he had tested himself against minor demons and the strange denizens of the wilderness, and if he had been injured—and he had—he was always the survivor. That, at least, had not changed. He was not to be one of Jewel's many advisors, and while he doubted the quality of the people with whom she condescended to confer, he had a small spark of affection for the regent she had chosen: Finch ATerafin. His final student, at least for the next several decades.

Still, there was no gain to be had in the games that would be legal now within Averalaan. If Jewel, if The Terafin, did not condescend to declare herself Queen over all of the city—and she did not, deferring in all ways to the Twin Kings—the wilderness treated her existence as the declaration she would not make.

Her abominable winged cats had the run of the city, and they were swifter, larger, deadlier than they had been when they had first appeared at the Terafin manse. The black one had whined and hissed his way through an infantile demand that she allow demons in, because the cats were bored.

It was the only thing Jarven shared in common with them, but he would die before he gave voice to the sentiment; in spite of Lucille's constant nagging, he *did* have some sense of personal dignity. He was surprised to find himself smiling. Of all of the people who had occupied the official Terafin offices during Jarven's tenure, Lucille was perhaps his favorite. Why, he could not say. She was much like the current ruler of the House whose name she bore, and ferociously competent in the job she had chosen. But the entirety of her ambition had been the smooth running of the Terafin Merchant Office. She had had no desire for greater wealth or greater political significance; the job of office manager had been her only calling.

He had tested her, of course. Many might claim, when they sought employment, to be interested or invested in the office, as Lucille had claimed. Of very few was it true. He might have continued his small tests, his small offers of greater power or greater authority, but she had put a firm stop to that—by threatening to quit on the spot if he did not desist.

He had laughed freely, which had further soured her expression. And he had decided then and there that he would keep her in the Merchant Authority offices for as long as he lived. If what the fox offered was truly within his power, he could not. He would outlive her, he who had been old when she was young. In theory, the office was still his, although it was now shared with Finch; the events of the past year had made political struggles seem quaint and irrelevant.

That would not last; it never did. People became accustomed to new rules, new lives, and as they did, they returned to their games. Only against The Terafin would those games not be played, but Finch was not The Terafin.

He shook his head to clear it, surprised at himself. In a dim past, he remembered his sudden anger when he had discovered that Finch was subject to assassination attempts. How *dare* they? If she had not been as promising as many of his apprentices, she was nonetheless his and under his auspices; he took the attempts very personally.

She had survived. And were she to remain in Averalaan, she would have no need of either Jarven or his protection; she had Jewel, now. A flicker of irritation came and went. If he were honest, and that was not his particular strength, Finch was a puzzle that he had not fully pieced together before the world had changed.

And Haval, humorless as always, had seen—in Finch—what Jarven himself had failed to see. His pride rankled at the very idea. Perhaps that was why he had not surrendered the Merchant Authority office entirely. He still did not see what Haval had seen and, until he did and could, he was unwilling to surrender the board.

But Lucille, Finch, and Haval were not here in this tiny, godforsaken kingdom; Jarven was. As was Jarven's prey.

Meralonne APhaniel was not that prey, but Jarven's curiosity was keen; he therefore followed in the steps of his chosen master—or at least his chosen master's personal conveyance.

GERVANNO CARRIED the fox and obeyed his commands, all of which involved directions. He passed through the merchant compound, and past the inns and taverns that had been built around the area where the caravans sheltered while the merchants bought, sold and traded. He had not spent much time in the city streets; he had mapped out the route between his inn and the Order of Knowledge, husbanding what coin Lady Maubreche had seen fit to gift him. That coin would have to carry him east and south, to Silvo's home, and from there…he shook his head.

"You are worried?" the fox asked.

"No, Eldest. I am nervous, but it was never considered wise to interact with the Widan."

"Widan?"

"I believe our Widan are equivalent to your mage-born, and it is to meet one such that I am now walking."

"Why ever would you avoid the magi? They are considered both wise and powerful by your kind."

"Those without power are not always best served by the presence of the powerful," he replied.

"You are reconsidering your decision to accompany me, then?"

Gervanno considered the question with care. "No."

"You feel you had no choice?"

"I had a choice."

The fox's chuckle was louder; his small body shook as chuckle became laugh. "Yes. Yes, you did. Survival is predicated on the choices we make. But I told you: my Lord does not approve of senseless death. Had you attacked me, she would consider the loss of life on your part deserved, but you did not—and would not. It is a gift of knowledge I give to you: those who serve my lord cannot casually kill you without consequence."

"And the man who calls you master?"

"He does not serve my lord, although theoretically he has vowed to do just that. But his vows to the House Terafin she rules are pleasant air, a passing breeze, no more. To truly bind one such as Jarven, one of two things are required."

Gervanno nodded, waiting for enlightenment as he continued to walk.

"The first: have something he wants. It must be yours to give, and yours alone; if it is a simple object, or even a complicated one, he will find some way to sneak around you and take it for himself without your permission."

"And the second?"

"An oathbinder."

"What is an oathbinder? I believe I have heard the word before."

"It is as it sounds. When an oath is made in the presence of an oathbinder, and when it is consecrated, those who swear the oath are bound to it. Should they break that oath—knowingly or unknowingly—they will die." The fox tilted head. "You are not one on whom I would waste the price of an oathbinding."

"Oh?"

"Some part of you dies when you fail to keep the oaths you have sworn. If it is possible, you will live up to those oaths, and if it is not…well."

Gervanno knew the route to the Order of Knowledge, but did not know it well. He assumed that the fox did—why, he was uncertain. But even his scant knowledge of the layout of this city made clear as he walked that it was not the Order of Knowledge that was their eventual destination.

"I am not ready to leave the city," Gervanno said, voice soft.

"No, not yet. But the man we seek is not in the building from which you came earlier. He serves the Order of Knowledge, but he does so in his own fashion, and he does not care for the buildings and offices here. To my eye, there is almost no difference."

Jarven coughed theatrically. "My master's eye does not acknowledge differences that would be apparent to most men. The building granted the Order of Knowledge, while considered reasonable by the standards of Breodanir, is small and confining, and it is lacking the one thing that would tether the mage to an interior office: Sigurne Mellifas, the Guildmaster."

"You know of the man we seek?"

"I know him, yes. If it is true that demons have entered the King's City, there is no safer place to stand than behind Meralonne APhaniel."

Gervanno did not argue; he had no facts on which to structure argument. But he thought of the sword master, Nenyane of Maubreche, in silent disagreement.

GERVANNO HAD BEEN SCHOOLED WELL by both his father and the cerdan who relieved his father of training when Gervanno came of age: avoid the Widan. As a young man, he had not understood the why of it, for the Widan were often old men with no sword skills to speak of. That had changed the first time he had seen the Widan use their power upon the battlefield, where the arts practiced by them in the secrecy of their order had been brought to bear against the enemy.

Gervanno had been proud of himself—ah, youth—and the skill with which he wielded his sword. In that one moment, all pride had vanished; he felt awe and terror in equal measure. Over the years that followed, he had picked up the pieces of his former pride; he was not Widan, and did not have their skill, but he had a part to play in the defense of his home. There was a reason Widan seldom entered the battlefield: they were few. Cerdan were many.

He had never been called upon to speak directly to the Widan; he had never been considered significant enough. Insignificance, then, was a type of protection. He closed his eyes, and walked that way for some minutes. He was less than insignificant, now; he had proven himself a coward, and by dint of cowardice, he had survived a fight that should have left him dead. It was thus humbled, thus almost broken, that he approached a man he would have made haste to avoid at any other time in his life while carrying a talking animal and walking beside a man upon whom he would never turn his back.

That man stood between two streetlights, arms folded, head slightly bent as if he intended to catch a few minutes of elusive sleep in the lee of coming battle. Behind him, the buildings of this modest section of the city rose; above him the moons hung, large and small, bright and dim, as if he alone were worthy of their steady regard.

This man was not Widan as Gervanno knew them.

He wore robes, but beneath those robes, the glint of metal could be seen: chain links, to Gervanno's eye, not the heavier plate sometimes beloved of the North. It was his hair, however, that first caught the cerdan's eye: it was platinum, long, unbound, and its color suggested not age but otherness. Once, only once, had Gervanno seen something this beautiful—and he had understood in that moment that beauty was death.

The fox did not seem troubled; the stranger upon whom Gervanno would have hesitated to turn his back was likewise unfazed.

"APhaniel," Jarven said, offering the mage a brief nod as they approached. "What a surprise to find you here. You are far from home."

The mage, thus named, looked ill-amused. "I could say the same of you."

"You could indeed. It is my hope to be done with this tiny kingdom in the very near future."

"Jarven," the fox said, its voice lower, deeper. "Do not embarrass me."

"Yes, yes." Jarven rolled his eyes. He then offered the mage a deep bow.

"He has spirit and boldness." The fox's voice resumed its normal volume. "It is what drew me to him in the first place. But the bold must have the ability to survive their boldness."

"So far, I have not disappointed you, have I?" Jarven rose.

The mage was unwilling to listen to the reply. "Why have you come, Eldest?"

"It is not entirely on our own business; Jarven's test is his to pass— or fail." There was a warning in those words.

The mage, however, did not take from that warning what Gervanno would and did. "If not on your own business, can I assume that the mortal who now carries you through the farthest reaches of your lord's forest has business that coincided with your own?"

"I am uncertain. It is not the first time I have encountered this mortal, and he has word he feels he must convey to a greater authority. Although he has made an appointment to speak with someone in the Order of Knowledge, I thought, as you were here, he might relieve himself of that burden now."

The mage then lifted gaze from Gervanno's chest—or what he clasped loosely against it—to Gervanno himself. "The elders of the wilderness are not known for their grasp of social nicety. I am Meralonne APhaniel, a member of the Order of Knowledge; much of my work to date has been done in city of Averalaan, at the heart of the Empire. You are?"

"Gervanno di'Sarrado."

"You are far from home, if I understand the styling of your name."

"I signed on as a guard for a merchant caravan. It is of the fate of that caravan that I wish to speak." He had the entirety of the mage's attention then, as if the mage could see what lived in Gervanno: shame and loss.

"Very well."

Gervanno began to speak. He would have dropped his gaze, but he found the light of the mage's gaze compelling, as if it would not be safe to look away unless and until the mage did.

———

"You survived."

"I was the only survivor. I froze by the roadside, and they did not see me or hear me through all of the chaos."

"Tell me, would you recognize the demon who led the attack?"

Gervanno nodded.

"This is not good news," the mage said, finally looking away from Gervanno; his gaze fell upon Jarven ATerafin. "Were you informed?"

"No, it is news to me as well." Although the words were grave, the tone was off. If the mage considered the news of import, the man...did not. "Surely you expected something? The god we do not name has not been idle or sleeping."

"Of course we expected something, but not this. I am grateful now that Sigurne thought to send me to Breodanir. You do not perhaps understand the significance of the demon's attack," he added, speaking to all present.

"And you do?" the fox asked, lifting head.

The mage ignored the question, turning his attention, once again, to Gervanno. "How did you come to the King's City?"

It was not the question Gervanno expected.

"You said you were found in Brookton, in the Maubreche demesne."

Ah. "I traveled with the son and daughter of Maubreche, as a guard, until we reached the King's City."

"Alone?"

"No, there was one other." He hesitated. "The Master Gardener of the Maubreche grounds also accompanied us."

"Ah. That is why he was here. Have you seen him since your arrival?"

Gervanno nodded.

"Have you seen his gardens?"

This time, a simple nod would not suffice. "I have. They were unlike any garden I have ever encountered. When the demons attacked, it was the loss of the garden, the damage to the grounds, that seemed almost the greatest loss—we lost no lives to that attack. But he will not remain within the city..."

"He cannot, while I am present. If I could but speak with him, I would feel at ease for the first time in centuries." The light in the mage's eyes dimmed as they narrowed; he shook his head. His reference to centuries did not strike Gervanno as odd in any way; this mage, unlike the Widan Gervanno had encountered in the past, was Other. He was not as the Widan were—or Gervanno himself.

"No, he is not." The fox's voice was soft. "You are an odd creature, Gervanno di'Sarrado. You are strangely perceptive for one of your kind."

The mage chose to ignore this—or perhaps he did not hear. Regardless, he continued. "Nenyane and Stephen have a significance that is far larger than the borders of a single, small country. If you were their guard, you have my gratitude. The report you conveyed contains information I must impart to the Guildmaster, but I will offer information to you as well, who carried the greater burden.

"You said the demons were searching for an artifact—a sword—that they thought was being transported into Breodanir from across its borders."

"That is what I recall hearing, yes. I may have misheard."

"You did not. They have been searching for some time, but that search has clearly intensified. They do not wish word of that search to reach our ears, or perhaps the ears of mortals who cannot and will not understand the whole of its significance. It is best that they do not know we know, although the time for ignorance is passing.

"I therefore ask that you keep this information to yourself. Speak of the demons, yes. Speak of their search and the destruction they left in their wake, if you must. Do not speak of what you believe they were searching for."

"I would hear more of it," Jarven said, the words cocooned in a different kind of quiet.

"You have heard everything of relevance," the mage replied, his voice all of Winter. "Unless this task is a task set you by the one you call master, I bid you leave its strands alone."

"I do not believe Sigurne would agree. As you well know, strands of information form a web—and no single strand can be assumed entirely irrelevant until the web can be seen in full." He glanced at Gervanno. "Have you already approached the Order in Breodanir?"

Gervanno nodded. "Lady Maubreche wrote an introductory letter, indicating that the meeting was of some urgency."

"I would consider it unwise to attend the Order of Knowledge at this time. You have spoken with one of its members—a mage of the first circle, renowned for his unusual character."

Jarven's smile was thin; it did not reach his eyes, although his voice was almost conciliatory. "I am certain you did not travel to Breodanir to attend to bureaucracy, but if you wish information to be hidden or excised, that is the wisest course of action. You have been involved in not one, but two demonic attacks."

He had been in the war in which demons had been disgorged into the valleys of Averda, but offered no correction.

"Or alternately, I would be willing to place myself at your service for the duration of the interview. I am an old man, and harmless, but I am ATerafin and clearly cognizant of the doings of the Order of Knowledge."

Old man. Harmless. Gervanno frowned, wondering if Jarven ATerafin thought him a fool. The fox chuckled.

"You are unintentionally insulting our guest," he told his student.

"Am I?"

"He has seen you walk by my side; how can he then accept your claim to be both old and harmless? Even before we encountered one another, you were not toothless; I do not imagine even your death would be enough to render you harmless."

Jarven laughed. "How much damage might a dead man do?"

"I shall ask young Finch."

Jarven stiffened.

"Or perhaps that man you so enjoy teasing? Haval? I am certain he would tell me all of the contingencies you might have left in place in the event of your passing."

"I doubt he would be aware of all of them. Very well." Jarven assessed Gervanno with a gaze that gave lie to harmlessness. "I am here to hunt a mortal who consorts with demons. Having done careful research, this is not the kingdom my target would normally choose; he has access to wealth, and he is accustomed to the respect given the hierarchically significant.

"He could never hope to become hierarchically significant in Breodanir; he is not Hunter-born. At most he would occupy the position of a wealthy foreigner, condemned to be an outsider. As are we. But he is here." He turned the much sharper gaze toward the mage. "And if the demons hunt something of value, if they have reason to believe it is in Breodanir, that such a thing might be found, it would not be beyond belief that he, too, would arrive.

"He failed, in Averalaan. The scope of his failure is known. The lord of the House he once served—for a value of service that involved betrayal—has handed down her decision: she is The Terafin; I, merely ATerafin. His survival is considered a stain upon Terafin. The laws of Breodanir are not the laws of the Empire; by the laws of the Empire, he has been condemned. There will be no trial. There is only judge and executioner."

"Who is the man you seek?" The mage seemed unimpressed by Jarven's information; the question felt perfunctory to Gervanno's ear.

"I will give you the name, as it will mean little; if he is a fool—and he is—he is not enough of one to use it openly. He was once known as Rymark ATerafin."

"Why do you believe he might be found within the Order of Knowledge?"

"He was once trained there, in Averalaan's Order. He was a mage of middling significance. His potential was considered significant, but he did not associate greater power with greater effort; he associated greater power with hierarchical significance. He did not therefore rise to the heights his former masters had foreseen; his interests lay far too much in the political.

"He is here, somewhere."

The mage said, "You are certain?"

"As only those under geas can be," Jarven replied. "I have been given the duty of eliminating him by two different beings: one, the golden fox Gervanno now carries; and the other, the Sen of Averalaan. He caused harm to the House she values; he has lost the House Name, and any possibility of succeeding her."

"There will be no successors," the fox said, his voice much chillier. Gold gave way to silver in his shining eyes.

Jarven's expression skirted disrespect, in Gervanno's opinion, from the wrong direction. The fox, however, seemed intent on the man's words, which did not seem disrespectful at all.

Jarven's tone as he continued barely shifted, so focused was he on his quarry. "If Rymark is here, he will no doubt be somewhere affiliated with the Order of Knowledge; he will have both power and greater convenience that way. But he is canny, and his experience with the *Kialli* and their subterfuge far greater at this point than my own. Yes, before you ask, I resent it. Should you be willing to maintain the appointment you have made, I could travel with you."

"I am not in favor of that. The magi are well aware of the nature of the threat we face when that threat involves the demonic. You are not — all rumors to the contrary — demonic," the mage said. "But the previous iteration of demonic intervention did indeed involve members of the Order in Breodanir. Unless the situation changes markedly, I believe it would be best that you cancel the meeting. If investigation must be done, I will personally see to it."

Gervanno knew a dismissal when he heard it, but he carried the fox, and the mage had offered the fox obvious respect. If the fox was not his lord, his was the greater power. Gervanno was accustomed to becoming invisible while standing in place when he escorted people of significance.

The fox, however, nodded. "Be cautious, Illaraphaniel. We see the End of Days, and either your demise or your absolution, in the near future; even mortals will reckon it swift beyond our measure."

CHAPTER ELEVEN

Had the meeting ended there, the evening would nonetheless have persisted as one of the strangest in Gervanno's life. But if his recounting of the destruction of the caravan had discharged the burden of the duty he had chosen to carry, he was not free to simply bow and retreat from the councils of the powerful; he carried the fox, and his only attempt to return to the inn had been stymied when the fox's small jaws had attached themselves to Gervanno's hand.

It was a warning; he drew no blood. The meeting with the Northern mage had ended, but the fox made clear, with teeth, that he still desired the convenience of Gervanno's service.

Gervanno therefore stood, fox in arms, as he awaited the fox's permission to return to the inn. To return, he thought, to the tattered remains of his life, and his final duty: to travel to the Dominion, bearing Silvo's sword to the younger man's family, where it might, in the fullness of time, be passed on.

He had no thoughts for his own future, but felt, in the presence of these three, that even had he, the future seemed to have no place for someone as ordinary, as unremarkable, as Gervanno of the clan Sarrado. It had been decades since he had listened to and marveled at the stories told to and by children, but realized now that he had loved them as a child because they did not exclude him. He might grow to be the heroic warrior. He might grow to be worthy of a sword that could withstand the brunt of demonic attack.

That had not happened. And perhaps that was how any man emerged from childhood: reality chipped away youthful daydream until only embarrassment at ever having those childish beliefs remained. Here, for a moment, those childish stories stirred, and he felt the tug of the roots that they had grown from, could hear his mother's voice, his Oma's, his Ono's — a low, gentle bass that enlivened any telling.

Could he but return home with any vestige of honor remaining him, what might they have said about what he had witnessed outside of the Dominion?

"Perhaps," Jarven said, "you might let Ser Gervanno put you down."

"I am not yet finished, or I would," the fox replied.

"Is there something on which you wait? I fail to see it myself, but you have always considered me short-sighted."

"That is incorrect. I have considered you appallingly short of patience, and that is evident now. If you are bored or restive, you may leave; I will see the mortal safely returned to his hovel."

Jarven bowed, the fluid motion containing the respect his words lacked. As he rose he said to Gervanno, "If you intend to arrive at the Order of Knowledge at the appointed time, having discharged your duty to convey information, I will accompany you."

Gervanno had no desire for this man's company, although he was certain the stranger's knowledge of the danger the demons presented was far greater than his own. But given the existence of demons, perhaps a dangerous ally was better than none.

"I feel it is unnecessary," the mage said.

"The man has asked for — and received — an appointment. If for no other reason, it would be good manners; it was Lady Maubreche, after all, who recommended him, and if there is discontent with his absence, it will be Lady Maubreche's reputation that is tarnished." Jarven then nodded to the mage, bowed — again — to the talking animal he called master, and withdrew.

His final words remained with Gervanno. He did not serve Maubreche, but felt indebted to that house; he had no desire to diminish Lady Maubreche's standing in any fashion.

That left the mage, who was silent for a long moment. "Tell me," he said, as he looked into the distance, "about the Maubreche grounds.

Spare no detail. The time is coming when those grounds will revert to what they once were. I have never seen them, and if it might now be safe to visit, time does not allow for such trivial indulgences.

"I see I have surprised you." The mage withdrew a pipe from the folds of his robe. "Think you that such gardens are of no interest or concern to one such as I?"

It had not occurred to Gervanno to think it until asked. "You are a warrior," he finally said. "But in the South, in my home, warriors of renown cultivate beauty where they can—it is a reminder that they have not become so enmeshed in the battlefield that life itself has no value." He hesitated, but the mage turned toward him then, and what he saw in the mage's face shifted the ground beneath his feet.

"I once wanted," the mage said, voice soft, "to garden. To grow. To husband the growth of living things. In my youth, I did these things. In my distant youth, I walked the great forests, and the hidden; I spent time in the Green Deepings, and in the Stone Deepings; I traversed the Tidal Deepings. The Lady I served—and serve still—valued things of beauty, and she was content to allow it.

"But war shadows all things, and the great war became the whole of her focus, and therefore, the whole of mine. Almost." The word was a whisper. "Tell me, then."

Gervanno nodded. He spoke of the grounds, and as he did, he allowed the wonder of that distant childhood to creep into his voice, his words. What he had noticed, what he had found most affecting, was the subtlety of the Gardener's work; the brief, green hints of the life that might be found in the forest, where prey was cautious and tentative. He talked last about the living tapestry that spanned the wall of Maubreche's maze, for he felt, walking it, that the past had never died. It was contained in this place, cultivated, husbanded—as if the Gardener had seen it all and wished, in his own fashion, to preserve the truth of it.

The mage smoked pipe, but the scent of pipe smoke was oddly comfortable, oddly familiar; it added a touch that made him seem almost human.

When Gervanno at last fell silent, the mage nodded. "Thank you. You have given me a gift, and if you do not understand the value of that gift, it does not lessen the debt I feel." He exhaled a pale stream of smoke, and the breeze pulled it away from his lips. "Eldest, will you return him to his inn?"

"I will. But I believe the last of your guests has arrived, and I would hear what he has to say, if it pleases you."

Gervanno was unfamiliar with the mage, but nonetheless was certain the fox's request did not please him. He was silent as he met the fox's eyes—gold to silver, both bright, their colors sharp and glinting. Or perhaps that was only Gervanno's fancy, who had spent much of his life on fields of battle—almost everything was reduced to things that caused death, in order to better avoid it.

Here, he had hoped to avoid the chaos and the terror of the battle-field the Averdan valleys had become. And here, he had experienced far worse.

"Very well," the mage finally said.

The fox nodded, as if the outcome had never been in doubt.

"She has grown in power, if you can walk the forests to reach this place."

"Or I have. I did not rule in the wilderness, but I believe, had I the desire, I might have." The mage's expression was skeptical, but he did not disagree with the fox, who continued. "I dislike being trapped in one place—it is too much like growing roots. Let the great trees rule and lead, should they desire it; I hunt, Illaraphaniel."

"It is no wonder to me that you chose Jarven as your student."

"You do not care for the mortal?" When the mage failed to respond, the fox chuckled. "That is all to the good; you see what I first saw. He has so much potential."

"Perhaps. He has adapted, and he is not entirely reckless—but he is reckless. Thus far, that recklessness has endangered only Jarven, but it grieves The Terafin, your Lord."

"It does not *grieve* her, it merely annoys her. But she has never felt she could rein Jarven in; at best, she could ameliorate the damage he might do. It was ever so with the lord my Lord once served. He does not serve her, and we have no oathbinder to enforce the oaths that otherwise remain lip service."

"We have an oathbinder—one that has survived."

"I am not so certain of that. We will see. Is that why you were sent?"

"No. I was sent to evaluate Breodanir's defenses against the wilder-ness; as you must know, if you have traveled this far, those defenses are stronger here than they are elsewhere." As the fox opened his mouth, the mage lifted hand in a shooing motion. "Yes, I am aware there are

pockets of resistance elsewhere, but they are not as significant as Breodanir's.

"But I have found, and will protect, the oathbinder. And I have
found something of greater value to the White Lady, hidden in this
country that still fights the total collapse of the walls that were built to
separate the wilderness from the mortals. I do not know why, but I see
another hand in it."

"Not a hand you are fond of, I see."

The mage smiled. "We have all taken perilous students in our time
because of the potential we see in them." More, he would not say;
instead, he looked to the sky. Gervanno followed his gaze, as did
the fox.

In the folds of air, ringlets artfully arranged—and rearranged—by
the wind's moving currents, stood a man Gervanno had not met before.
He seemed mortal in a way the mage did not, and there was a silence to
his presence that spoke of danger, of death, but that danger was not the
danger Jarven ATerafin might pose.

Of the two, he was not certain that Jarven would emerge victorious,
should they tangle.

The man who stood in air a moment leapt lightly forward, his feet
touching the stone upon which Gervanno stood. "Well met, APhaniel,"
he said to the mage. He then glanced at Gervanno, and at the curve of
Gervanno's arms. "Eldest." He had not offered the mage a bow, but
offered the diminutive fox one—and it was deep and familiar. Ah,
Gervanno thought, surprised. It was Southern in form, Southern in
grace.

He then rose. "I am Kallandras of Senniel College; I am far from my
home. But you are far from yours as well. I see you have been afforded
a position of singular honor."

Gervanno could not offer Kallandras an appropriate greeting; his
hands and arms were full, and a bow would be awkward, if the fox
allowed it at all. "I am Gervanno di'Sarrado; I was born in the Terrean
of Averda, but came here as a caravan guard."

"You must have seen much in your journey. Even I, for whom the
roads were once familiar, have found the voyage here astonishing, so
much has changed." His gaze fell once more to the fox. "Have you
carried word for me, Eldest? My master is not yours, but the opinion of
your lord carries a great weight, regardless."

The fox sniffed. "You are so graceful in your manners, respect imbues your very words. And yet you know that there is no such message. You are sly. I personally approve. I am here because I wish to know what you discuss with Illaraphaniel, for I feel the wind, and it whispers his name both in the mundane, mortal streets and in the wilderness, low and high. The wind is cold," the fox added, voice softening. "But it is no longer bitterly so; Summer, long thought lost, has returned to the wilderness.

"It is on the Summer paths I walk, with permission of both the Summer Queen and my lord; it is the Summer paths I have extended to reach all manner of places. Even this one. But here, there are familiar scents on the breeze, some quite foul. So I will offer you this, although you have not asked it, in appreciation of the grace of your offered respect—it is the one thing Jarven lacks. The foul stench of the dead is stronger here than it has been on most of the slender paths I have walked.

"The dead play games with the almost-dead—the mortals over whom they have much influence. I do not know what they seek; were they to attempt to behead the rulers of this realm, I cannot see how it would be of benefit to them." The fox stretched. "But if, as you say, there is an oathbinder here, I better understand the necessity of subterfuge. I would have assumed that the mortals would simply hire assassins—competent assassins, I hasten to add."

"Ah. They have made that attempt, Eldest. The assassin is dead. The oathbinder is not."

"I see." The fox nodded. "I will not question you further; there are things it is unwise to say, and less wise to know." He looked up at Gervanno, stretching his neck. "You may return me to your hovel, now. I have seen enough." To the bard and the mage, he nodded head. "We will no doubt meet again; I perceive a howling in the wilderness, and it will reach even your ears before the month is out."

GERVANNO WALKED SLOWLY through the streets; they had begun to empty as the sun descended. Only as the merchant compound's outer borders came into view did the streets once again become crowded; off-duty guards took to the taverns surrounding that compound. It was here that Evaro would have led his wagons, had any of them survived.

"What do you believe the demons seek here?" he asked the fox.

"You are greatly daring," the fox replied. "But you have shown me a modicum of respect, and you are somewhat resourceful. You heard me speak of oathbinding, yes?"

"Yes."

"There is only one god—the God of Covenants, of oaths—who was capable of oathbinding. In the presence of that god, two parties could swear binding oaths. They are not the blood oaths of the Firstborn; those are binding in a more subtle way. Be wary of them, should they be offered to you.

"But binding oaths are absolute. You swear an oath, and if it is judged genuine and it is consecrated, the cost for the breaking of that oath is the existence of the one who broke it. Gods are not exempt from the cost," he added. "Nor are we, scions of the true wilderness. The oaths are a danger to those who have sworn them should they prove false, and that cost, that consequence, exists; not even the god who consecrated the oath can alter the consequence of its breaking.

"It is one way to kill a god," the fox added, chuckling. "But I cannot foresee a situation in which a god would now be bound; there are almost none who still walk this plane. Mortals, however, those with divine blood, can serve as a conduit to their parent's power: when they accept an oath, or accept the validity of oaths sworn in their presence, they bind the swearers, and the consequences of the breaking of the oath are then borne by the forsworn, be they mortal."

"Demons?" Gervanno asked.

"That is less certain, in my opinion; the demons are not truly alive."

He had seen them; they did not suit any definition of death he knew.

"Perhaps we will eventually receive an answer to the question. It is not that possibility that engenders fear in the *Kialli*, in my opinion. If they hunt the oathbinder Illaraphaniel has found, they will likely perish. My own Lord does not, I believe, fully appreciate the consequences of binding oaths and their long use; I am under no obligation to assist Illaraphaniel in his chosen role."

"But you aided me," Gervanno said softly.

"Yes—but that was entirely an action of my own choosing, my own whim. I might just as well have left you in the wilderness, and in a different frame of mind, I would. But we are ruled by a very unusual lord, and perhaps her attitudes are reflected in some small fashion in my impulses. I do not feel you owe me any great debt; you might value your life highly, but it is just another mortal life to me.

"Ah, no, perhaps that is inaccurate. I am not at all certain that you value your life. My own cub values his highly. I thank you for your aid; I dislike the feel of your mortal roads. If we encounter each other again, I may grant you a small boon of your choosing." He sighed loudly.

"Did the bard give you information?" Gervanno asked.

"What do you think?"

"I think information was conveyed, if unintentionally."

"You have a good eye. My cub may have mentioned that he has a test to pass. What judge would I be if I could not see the parameters I cannot myself set?" His grin was toothy. Gervanno offered the Lady a silent benediction; she had placed the fox in his path in a helpful way, but had not made of the fox a teacher or a master.

STEPHEN WAS NOT YET asleep when he heard the knock on the door to the rooms he shared with Nenyane. Nenyane was already across the room before Stephen slid out of his first attempt at sleep, sitting up, swiveling feet onto floor, and finding the slippers nearest the bed.

Nenyane was not alarmed; she was alert, but she recognized the knock, or perhaps the steps that led up to it. She opened the door to Alex, who was not dressed for sleep.

"We might have a problem," he told her.

She opened the door fully, and he slid into the room. Stephen was surprised to see that Max wasn't with him.

"Max has gone ahead," he told them, before either could ask.

"Ahead? Ahead where?" Stephen shrugged himself out of his gown, reaching, in a poorly lit room, for clothing.

"You know you've been forbidden to leave Hunter's *Redoubt* without permission and a suitable cadre of guards," Nenyane said; she too had changed clothing, and in much less time than it had taken Stephen. Less stubbing of toes as well. Nenyane's nighttime vision had always been second to none.

"They're trying to keep people out," Alex offered, "not keep us in. Heiden's not on that list, but at this point, the guards are likely looking for Heiden. We don't have much time to slip past their net before it's reestablished." As if there was no question that they would at least make the attempt.

"Why did Heiden bolt?" Nenyane asked, glancing out the door. She grimaced. "The Queen's Guard are already repositioning themselves. Do you think Heiden got caught?"

"I don't know why he bolted. Max followed him." Alex exhaled. "We went to his room to talk about the situation in Bowgren. We wanted a clearer idea about whether or not Ansel—or Lord Bowgren— would welcome or resist the aid of outsiders.

"Ansel wasn't in their room—no surprise there. He didn't come back after dinner. But Heiden was clearly aware of where Ansel was, or where he was going. He wasn't cagey; he was like a very polite wall. He did not deny that Bowgren is in serious trouble. Nor did he deny that Lord Bowgren is not what he was; grief has almost rendered him immobile."

"He didn't say that."

"No—I did. I asked. He didn't seem offended, and he didn't seem upset—the only time he showed serious annoyance is when Max asked about the black eye in a way that cast aspersions on Ansel. Ansel may be out of control, but Heiden hasn't given up on him yet." He spoke with emphasis to Nenyane.

She shrugged. "What happened?"

"We don't know. He was halfway through a sentence about some of Bowgren's difficulties when he stopped; his jaw dropped, and I'd swear his eyes were halfway out of their sockets. His color is always a bit blanched, but it got worse instantly. He ran to the door, opened it, and took off at a run down the hall.

"The Queen's Guards ordered him to stop. He didn't. But he was aware enough to easily evade them because he caught them unaware. Max lagged behind a bit, allowing the guards to leave in pursuit of Heiden—they made quite the ruckus—before he followed."

"He said nothing?"

Alex shook his head.

Ansel, then. Ansel was in trouble—or was causing trouble that wouldn't be easily hidden, if it could be hidden at all. Stephen guessed the latter, but was uncertain. Panic was not Heiden's usual response when Ansel's self-control was spiraling downward—and Alex had clearly described panic.

Nenyane disliked Ansel, especially when Heiden was visibly injured. But she didn't dislike Heiden, and Heiden—if he managed to evade the Queen's Guards, who had been stationed near the *Redoubt* in greater numbers—had vanished into a city he probably didn't know well.

You don't, either, Stephen pointed out.

It's a city. How dangerous can it be? I don't care if we don't find Ansel. But I think Heiden might be in trouble.

Stephen had no doubt that Nenyane could evade a handful of guards with ease. He knew her well; she was going. She wasn't asking permission.

"I'll head out," Nenyane told them both. "I'll distract the guards. You two head to wherever Max is; I'll meet you on the way." She paused and then added, "Take your dogs. Alex, I'm leaving Stephen in your hands until we meet up again. There shouldn't be difficulty— assassins tend to look for routine, and this is not routine."

Alex didn't offer to go in her stead; he understood why they were being split this way. He knew where Max was, because of the hunt-brother bond; Stephen knew where Nenyane was—or would—for the same reason. They could speak to each other at a distance if communication was required. If Alex took the lead here, if Alex served to distract and lead the guards astray, that communication would be broken.

Stephen wanted to send Steel with Nenyane; she declined. He had no time to argue; she was on the move.

GERVANNO EXPECTED noise as the hour grew late and men had had the time to drink far too much. Their descent from boisterous to dangerous was oft predictable, and he was well aware of how giddy exhaustion could descend into rage. It was for that reason that he often avoided drink. He glanced down at the fox; he recognized the street through which he was, unseen by the rest of its occupants, walking.

"Might I take a slightly more circuitous route? It is loud here, and likely to be chaotic."

"Mortal chaos can oft be both surprising and amusing," the fox replied, rejecting Gervanno's request. "Perhaps it will surprise me. I did not spend much of my existence in the company of mortals in their own warrens. You need not worry—I highly doubt my cub would be caught in a simple, mortal fracas."

It was not for Jarven ATerafin that Gervanno worried. He knew, while he carried the fox, he was effectively invisible; he did not seem to cast a shadow in the lights that were now gently illuminating the streets. The streets themselves were in good repair—the merchant compound was an economic necessity to the small kingdom, or so Evaro had said, and the roads that led to and from it were the very path of commerce in that merchant's mind.

He felt a twinge of unease, and as with all unvoiced, unexamined fear, it carried a weight not easily dislodged. He almost took the longer route he had suggested to the fox, but was certain the fox would notice; that creature's eyes were now bright and wide as he gazed upon the density of gathered bodies that surrounded the compound.

Gervanno shook himself. He could not avoid the crowds; he would have to trust that there would be no cause to interact with them. Gervanno walked in the road where carriages and wagons would otherwise be found. Although the fox insisted that collision would be impossible, nothing was lost by maintaining a greater distance. He hoped.

IF NOT FOR ALEX, Stephen would have been utterly lost the moment they hit the city streets. If he had warned his huntbrother that she was not familiar with the city, he'd done so with reason. Neither of them had spent much of their lives in the King's City. Although they'd heard stories of whole neighborhoods considered unsafe, they had no idea which of the many streets led to them. Or away.

Alex knew the city a bit better, having spent more time in it, but Alex had one thing Stephen lacked: Max. Max, on Heiden's tail, hunting the Bowgren huntbrother through its streets. He stayed as far back as he safely could without losing Heiden, but this didn't prove necessary. Heiden made no attempt to cover his tracks. He ran, showing that in endurance, at least, he was hunt-worthy.

"This is not good," Alex murmured, as he glanced at Stephen. "Heiden's going to one of the less friendly parts of the city."

"Less friendly?"

"Some of the people who live in them don't like Hunters or Hunter Lords much."

Neither Alex nor Stephen were in the habit of hiding their backgrounds; both wore the colors they'd earned in the hunts that would, in theory, go on to inform their later lives and responsibilities. In the villages, those colors were known—but so, too, their bearers. Stephen wasn't certain if they would be likewise recognized here, but Alex seemed to think they would.

They weren't going to turn back to the palace to change; they would almost certainly be trapped there if they did.

"Clothing won't make much of a difference if you have the dogs," Alex pointed out. They had taken to the streets at a jog; Alex had the lead because their intended destination was Max. Nenyane was behind, but as she'd promised, not by too much. She had circled around once, but the armored guards were no match for her speed. Even had they not been wearing armor, she would have outpaced them with ease. They had no intention of harming her, so ranged weapons of any kind could not be used.

Alex sped up only once, brow furrowed in a concentration that spoke of worry.

"Where are they?" Stephen asked.

"Merchant compound," Alex replied. This had meaning to the Elseth Hunter that it did not have to Stephen. The cursing that followed, however, he understood.

NENYANE WAS unimpressed with the caliber of the Queen's Guard. She had expected to be farther behind her Hunter when she at last lost them —but she had lost them without notable effort. She looked at the moon, at the way it was framed in Stephen's vision. She did not immediately recognize the streets or the buildings that he moved past, but she did recognize the speed of movement; they were now in pursuit of someone. Max, probably.

What's wrong? What did Alex see through Max?

Heiden's heading to the merchant compound.

And that's set Alex off?

It's not considered a safe part of the city—not for Hunters. Stephen hesitated.

She understood why. The dogs were with Stephen. No one who lived in Breodanir could mistake them for any other kind of dog. *I'll be there as soon as I can.* She glanced at the streets through which she was passing; they were not the streets Stephen had crossed. She picked up speed, widening her stride, lowering her head into the wind.

The wind.

The wind was wrong. Without pause, she leveraged speed, shifting direction slightly as she leapt to the right, toward a gap between two multi-story buildings. The slight shift, given her building momentum, translated into a larger deviation. The buildings were in decent repair; if people lurked between them hoping for bounty from unwary passersby, this was not going to be their night.

She drew sword. Felt Stephen almost stumble in the distance, which annoyed her. *Keep Alex in sight. Do not try to reach me — there's nothing here I can't handle.*

You don't know that.

It was true; she didn't. Something was off, something was wrong. Stephen knew her well. If she had drawn her sword, she had drawn it because she thought she might need it. He had confidence in her — if Nenyane could not defend herself when armed with sword, the situation was extreme. But he knew he was never useless — he had the dogs, and the bond with Nenyane, and they added a tactical advantage in dangerous fights.

Stay with Alex, she snapped. *It's not demonic.*

What is it?

I don't know. The wind is wrong, here. It could be Illaraphaniel.

You'd pull a sword on the mage?

He'd consider it a sign of respect. I mean it. She looked up, then; wind tugged her hair. Wind wrapped around her, like a giant hand, whistling past her ears. She was lifted off the ground. Stephen stumbled, then, which annoyed her further.

Nenyane cut the wind and came to stand in the streets again. The wind was ill-pleased; the noise of it, the roar of it, grew. Debris from the streets rose in its folds, surrounding Nenyane and obscuring visibility. She realized, belatedly, that slicing wind had not been the right choice, here — and that led to rage. At herself, at her failure of a memory. Here, now, that memory might save her pain. It might save her life.

She felt like a dumb beast, an animal, guided by instinct and temper.

Nenyane. Nenyane of Maubreche. The moment she heard the voice above the howling of the wind, she knew. She could hear the layers of it, the weight of it, and she understood that the speaker was bard-born.

Understood who that speaker was. This time, she looked at the wind; she heard its voice, separate from the voice that had dared to speak her name above the wind's howl. And she saw that he stood in the shadow of wings, dark and yet luminous—something that the wind itself did not grant him.

But she had seen the hint of that in the mark that adorned the lobe of his ear. She had seen an echo of it surround the slender form of the assassin she had killed in the Queen's gallery. A word, a name, was on the tip of her tongue; she opened her mouth but could not speak it, could not hold it in place.

"Nenyane, stop." A different voice. A familiar voice. She did not sheathe sword, but she lowered it, ignoring the wind, ignoring the second voice, her eyes anchored to the bard who stood where a mortal should never be able to stand: in folds of wild wind.

Even so, she could not be unaware of Illaraphaniel. He ignored the wind and the wind's anger; it parted to allow him to pass unharmed. Only his hair moved at the wind's discretion, but it was a gentle movement, a caress.

"Nenyane, why are you here? Where is your Hunter?" He lifted hand, raised chin; the wind stilled, the debris falling harmlessly to the street where it became all but invisible again.

"Why are *you* here?" she countered. "And why are you here with an assassin?"

Pale brows rose in concert; eyes silvered and flashed. He was annoyed. Dressed as he was in the tatters of mortal robes, he still expected the respect due him. The respect due a—a...

She knew him, but did not know him. She was certain of one thing: she would return the respect she had received, measure for measure. Whatever he thought he recognized was not who she now was, sundered from memory, sundered from the identity that memory created.

"I am here with a Master Bard from Senniel College; he serves both the Senniel bardmaster and the Twin Kings."

She shrugged. "They're not my kings."

"They are not, but they are kings regardless. Have you forgotten?"

She smiled, then. "Yes. I have forgotten all of the life I lived before I landed in Maubreche. Some part of me recognizes you—but no part of me recognizes your right to command or demand anything of me.

"You are here with an assassin; one of his ilk attempted to kill my Hunter in the King's Palace. I note he commands the wind, which is unexpected."

"You have no memories?"

"No."

"But you knew me."

"I knew your name. I recognized something about you. But whatever I was when you knew me, I am not that person now—and I have no idea how I might become that person again. Maubreche has spared no expense in an attempt to return to me the memories I lost. The mage-born came to examine me, along with priests from various orders. The Mother's children can heal, but they recommended that the healer-born should be called in as well. We could not find one willing to travel; there are, to our knowledge, none now within Breodanir."

"Or none who are foolish enough to announce their abilities."

Nenyane nodded. "If things were not as they are in the wilderness, we might have made the trek to the Empire to visit the healer-born there."

"Perhaps you will find a way to traverse the wilderness to reach that place. I think even walking the streets might feel oddly familiar to you." The annoyance was gone from the mage's face, but it was replaced by something far more distasteful: pity. "As for Kallandras, I did not lie: he is esteemed by the Kings, by the bards, and by the many foreign dignitaries he has entertained in his travels.

"Whatever else you believe of him, he is here at the behest of the bardmaster, and if you are pressed by enemies here, he will fight for you —or," he added, as Nenyane opened her mouth, "your Hunter. Stephen of Maubreche."

"If you came seeking Stephen, if you came because you expect him to be an oathbinder, you can go back the way you came. I won't allow you to even mention it in his presence."

The mage's eyes flashed silver again, narrowing at her tone. This was not a game, for Nenyane. She didn't budge.

"I think," the bard said, alighting, "that this is neither the place nor time to have this discussion. I apologize for interrupting you; I did not expect that APhaniel would choose to engage when we are otherwise occupied."

The mage did not acknowledge the bard's words. "Where do you run?" he asked, instead.

"Occupied with what?" she asked, at the same time.

"There are demons abroad," the bard replied, gazing down the street. "The wind carries the scent of ash and death. If your Hunter roams these streets tonight, it is possible that he will face those demons before we can, if we tarry here."

The mage's smile was sharp as blade's edge. "Come, Nenyane of Maubreche. Fly with me, as you once did." He held out a hand, palm up, the gesture a subtle command. "You are not, now, where you should be."

"And you can take me there?"

"I can. If you are unwilling to trust Kallandras, trust me. We face the same enemy, and I have never wavered."

Nenyane stretched out a hand and placed it, palm down, across the palm of the man Stephen called a mage.

SHE FELT THE WIND, felt its irritation, felt its desire to please. It heard Illaraphaniel's voice as a benison—but it had always heard his voice that way. Mixed into the whisper of its movements, some delicate and gentle, some powerful enough to lift her entirely off the ground, she could hear the sounds of the city at a distance.

And she could hear the whisper of something else, something Other: death. The dead. She had cut the wind's folds, but the anger she heard was far, far older: rage at loss, rage at death, rage at the dead. The walking dead. The returned that were called many things. Demons. Demon-kin. *Kialli.*

The city fell away, the movement of wind so natural Nenyane did not feel the sudden loss of gravity at all. Illaraphaniel did not carry the bard; the wind that enfolded the pale-haired stranger was his own. He was not Illaraphaniel; she could see the struggle to contain the wind's anger in the line of his jaw, the subtle tension of his expression. His lips moved; she could not hear the words, was not meant to hear them. The bard-born could speak in a fashion that even the wilderness must hear, if the bard desired it—but the attention of the wilderness was not something many mortals desired.

She knew all of this. She knew it the way she knew breath, but she did not know how or why. And for just this moment, the pain of ignorance, the humiliation of it, the resentment, vanished as she turned face into the breeze; it was a summer breeze.

A summer breeze, here, where she had expected endless winter.

"Tell me where I must go," Illaraphaniel said, voice soft. "If you know it."

She nodded; a request was not a command. Closing her eyes heightened her hearing and the sense of odd taste that Stephen had always found challenging when confronted through the Hunter's bond. There were only two things that now mattered in this haven of wind and intent: demons and Stephen.

She trusted Alex, trusted the dogs, understood that neither would abandon Stephen regardless of the danger he faced—but in the end, they were not Stephen's huntbrother. She was. And he was *hers*.

"There," she said, speaking to wind and Arianni and bard.

"APhaniel," Kallandras said. "I will go ahead."

Illaraphaniel was silent for a long, long beat. "No," he said at last. "A *Kialli* walks these streets whom you should not encounter alone."

The bard's smile was slender, sharp—the congenial expression had fallen away. "The wind senses him; he is only newly arrived. If indeed the Shining Court intended to infiltrate this city, they will not be pleased."

"Perhaps, perhaps not; were I in their position, I might consider it an opportunity. In the shadow of this *Kialli*, all others might pass undetected if they are cautious."

"Given your companion," Nenyane snapped, "I'm not certain those who are forced to resort to subterfuge would be more of a danger."

"You will learn," the mage replied. "Here, your memory will be of little aid; to my knowledge, you have never previously encountered Kallandras."

She did not correct his assumption. Illaraphaniel trusted this bard. Trust was a simple affair when those offered it were almost powerless in comparison; what benefit betrayal if the betrayed would barely notice, barely condescend to acknowledge it?

As if he could hear what she did not say, he smiled. "In one way, you have not changed—you underestimate the strength of your allies."

"He is not my ally."

"But he will be. If you must see him tested, if he must demonstrate his resolve, I fear it will be tonight. Can you not hear it? The hidden wilderness cries out in rage and fury." Illaraphaniel frowned.

Nenyane could not hear what he could hear, but she felt something different in the air, something both alluring and wrong. "Not all of the wilderness," she whispered.

"No. I fear for the future of your small kingdom if we do not arrive in Bowgren in a timely fashion." He had allowed Nenyane to lead, to move the wind as the wind must be moved, the streets she had briefly studied on her run toward Stephen now rendered irrelevant.

She could see him. Stephen had frequently envied her vision; this was different. She could see him running, where the dogs and Alex were all but invisible at this distance; Stephen was silver light—silver, gold, and pale, pale blue.

"Kallandras," Meralonne said, lifting voice.

The bard did not look to the man he called mage, but nodded. The wind carried him ahead, past where Stephen ran.

"The blade you carry," Illaraphaniel said softly, "is not a blade worthy of you."

"There is no blade worthy of me," she replied, with the natural arrogance that had characterized all matters to do with swords and swordsmanship since her arrival in Maubreche.

He smiled. "No. But that one is *unworthy*."

"It's the only one I have."

"If you allow it, I will replace it."

"You won't be able to replace it in time. Set me down."

The wind lifted her, carried her; she felt it as if it were natural, this movement, this speed, as if she had traveled thus before tonight. She bent into her knees before there was ground to brace feet on, and she leapt from the folds of the wind, landing just a step behind Stephen.

The dogs were not surprised, nor was Stephen; if he did not borrow her vision, he was constantly aware of her thoughts, her reactions. Alex was ahead, but not so far ahead that he was unaware of the moment Nenyane joined them in their increasingly desperate run.

———

ALEX WASTED no breath on a progress report; Nenyane didn't ask. She was in contact with Stephen, just as Alex was with Max; what Stephen knew, Alex assumed she'd know. Max kept pace with Heiden, but Heiden did not speak; he made no attempt to strategize or rein in his growing panic. He understood that Max was almost beside him, but Max was an onlooker, an outsider, not a partner or friend.

"They're heading into streets that are more crowded," Alex called back.

"At this time of night?"

"Taverns, inns, and bored merchant guards," he replied. "Drunk guards. They can't run all-out in the streets now."

Nenyane glanced up. "Tell Max to be careful."

"He hasn't collided with anyone yet. I can't say the same about Heiden." He glanced back at Nenyane briefly. "What are you worried we're heading toward?"

"I'm not certain—but Illaraphaniel and his companion believe we might be facing demons."

Alex slowed. "They said that?"

"I think that's why they're out tonight." She exhaled. "If significant demons are in this city, we *want* the mage to be here."

Stephen said nothing for a long beat. "We don't hunt demons," he finally said. "Let's get in, grab Ansel, and get out."

Nenyane failed to reply.

Alex was not of Maubreche. Most of the time he'd spent in Nenyane's company had been when they were all younger. Alex's father, Gilliam, had been suspicious of Nenyane because she had arrived under the auspices of Evayne, and Gilliam only grudgingly accepted Evayne's right to breathe the same air he was breathing. He did not expect her to cheat, lie, steal—he accorded her that much respect.

But he knew that, should the deaths of every person he had ever loved—or would ever love—be the sacrifice required so that Evayne might win the private war she had devoted her very strange life to fighting, they would all die. She would not hesitate. He did not trust her with Stephen of Maubreche's life—and Stephen of Maubreche was all that remained, in a complicated way, of Stephen of Elseth, dead before any of the Elseth children had been born.

He therefore visited often, dragging Max and Alex in his wake; he had sent Max and Alex to keep Stephen and Nenyane company. The fact that the two youngest Elseth siblings liked, understood, and approved of Nenyane eased much of his worry, but he had given both sons one command: be wary of Evayne. If Evayne appeared out of nowhere again, their father must be informed, and at speed.

She had never encroached upon Maubreche again, and as Nenyane came into her own, she had earned Gilliam of Elseth's grudging approval; the grudging part fell away as he observed her and interacted with her. He trusted Nenyane with Stephen's safety. Alex doubted that that trust would be enough should his father hear of demons. Which

was fair. Alex found the word—and the certainty in Nenyane's voice—
almost terrifying.

This annoyed Max.

It annoyed Max until Max became far too busy to waste any time or
attention on petty annoyance. Heiden had cut through a crowd of
drunk and belligerent men; one had caught him by the collar before he
could emerge. Max had been on his heels, but the crowd through which
Heiden had attempted to pass became a small wall of backs.

Alex could hear—through Max's ears—the sound of ugly, drunken
hostility.

"You think you're better than us? You think you can just hit me and
run?" The voice embodied the sound of resentment fueled by alcohol.

Max didn't wait for Heiden's reply; he heard the first blow land, and
then he, too, broke through the thicket of turned backs.

Alex stopped worrying about demons, then.

STEPHEN KNEW the moment Alex summoned the Hunter's trance—the
gift given by Breodan to his Hunters. Alex and Max were exceptional;
unlike the usual Hunter and huntbrother pairings, both of the Elseth
Hunters could call the trance. It was why they could run prey to ground
better than any aspiring Hunters: they could carry the trance for the
entirety of the hunt, passing the burden of it off to each other.

And they could call the trance while on the move; they could fall
into it while running, as Alex was running now. Without apparent
effort, his jog became a sprint. Stephen lost ground as he, too,
summoned the trance; there was no other way he could keep up with
Alex. Nenyane, who couldn't summon the trance, had never required it.
She slowed as Stephen slowed, confident that she could close the gap
Alex was now widening.

Go with him, Stephen told her, without hope. She had spoken of
demons. She would fight for Max and Alex; she would protect them if
protection was necessary. But Stephen came first, always.

He sped up as the trance strengthened him. The buildings came into
heightened relief as his vision sharpened. The various scents of the city
sharpened as well, but he could easily pick up Alex's, he was so close.
He could not see what Alex saw, but knew that Max—or Heiden—
were now in trouble.

Steel.

The leader of his small pack surged ahead, following Alex. *Patches. Don't lose Alex.*

The lymer caught up to Steel, running beside the leader, the couples that were often used to physically link hunting dogs absent but unnecessary. They understood exactly what Stephen intended; they understood the urgency of it. Everything else was irrelevant.

Sanfel and Brylle flanked Stephen and Nenyane, where the street was wide enough to accommodate them. Stephen had abandoned the walks meant for foot traffic for the width of the road. It was late; the only traffic on it would be carriage traffic. Or so he hoped.

Alex put on a burst of speed, heading toward Max, all other concerns discarded.

GERVANNO HEARD the mass of voices, as he often did; they were a type of aural geography by which he—and most of his kin—navigated the undercurrents of power. To men without power, those currents spelled death if navigated poorly. He therefore heard the ugly laughter, the raised voices, the anger and resentment that, driven by alcohol, had been unleashed. He would have moved away instantly; he had not yet been entangled in those currents. As an outsider, the chance that he would be was high if he was not cautious.

But the fox opened its small jaws and bit his hand. Not hard enough to draw blood; just hard enough to make the silent threat clear. He then released Gervanno's hand. "I think you will regret cowardice if you leave. Fortune favors the bold."

He couldn't be seen while carrying the fox, which made caution almost irrelevant. The only thing that could damage him here was the fox himself.

"My cub is in the streets," the fox continued. "The air is rank with the scent of decay. You cannot smell it? Ah, no, of course you cannot. Do you believe in fate?"

"Fate, Eldest?" He chose the form of address the Northern Widan had used.

"Perhaps it is the wrong word, given the paucity of your language, but it will have to do. Fate is the convergence of coincidences, great and small. Tonight, my cub is in these mortal streets. Above us, the wind whispers Illaraphaniel's name. And on the ground, you, who were called by, and almost lost to, the wilderness. I chose to lead you out on a whim.

"But whim can be part of the weave of fate."

Gervanno did not believe in fate. He knew, however, that his beliefs would have no weight. The fox, delicate in seeming, was master here.

"Do not put me down," the fox said, voice dropping in register. "Unless and until I command it. Your survival depends on it." There was no threat in the fox's voice; if Gervanno perished here, it would not be at the fox's hand. But the shift in timbre implied that survival was not guaranteed. The moon was bright, the night dark; he could see the stars in the northern sky clearly.

He had seen them less clearly on the day he should have died, their light obscured by the wings of enormous, flying creatures with breaths of fire. More terrifying was the man who rode one of them, for it was at his command that the creatures wrought their destruction. In no childhood lessons, no adolescent trials, had Gervanno faced an enemy that could kill him simply by breathing.

In no other combat, no other battle, had he frozen so completely, legs locked by terror, breath almost non-existent. In no other war had survival been the proof of absolute disgrace. He forced himself to concentrate on his breathing; to keep it even and regular took effort and will.

No, he thought. *No, I will not fall to this. I will not fall to this again.*

It was not impossible to fight the demons. He had seen it done. He had seen it, sword drawn; he had not frozen, had not become almost insensate with terror. No, he had watched with wonder. He had watched the best swordsman he had ever seen launch herself at a demon, and he had watched the grace and speed of her swordwork; she lost none of it, even fighting for her life.

Perhaps because he had stood in the long shadow her skill cast, there was no room for terror; she stood on no battlefield, nor in the folds of the Averdan valley; she was not fighting in a clearing off the side of a foreign road. So clear was the image of her, he felt breath return in a rush; he could almost see her in these crowded streets, the people in them as relevant as the lesser demons who had taken the shape and form of hellish dogs.

He could see her sword's edge catch light—firelight, lamplight, and silver moon, her hair streaming past as if it were that moonlight made solid. Behind her came the dogs that characterized Hunter Lords in this land. Behind her ran Stephen of Maubreche.

Gervanno's arms tightened as he blinked.

They were not images he had conjured to shore himself up, to remind himself that he had strength, that the demons could be injured or killed by one such as he. They were here. The Maubreche Hunters were *here*.

And they were running into the crowd, into the currents of anger and ugly resentment without so much as a pause to evaluate.

"Do not put me down," the fox said, the words rumbling. "This is not a fight for a mortal such as you."

"They are mortal—"

"They are not as you are. Put me down, and you will be swept up in the events that must surely unfold—and my cub will be denied an attempt to prove his strength. Our gifts are not mortal gifts, and most mortals wear them poorly. You could not carry my gift and my blood; I believe it would destroy you."

"But your apprentice can?"

The fox chuckled. "My blood gives power, and to those with no understanding of the subtleties and the respect that power requires, the power turns their heads; they become fools who believe that the small gift I have chosen to grant gives them the power to kill me."

"And he does not?"

"He is informed, in all ways, by the latter impulse: he seeks power because power gives him relevance. But he has learned in his mortal life to read the currents of power, to see the truth of it—for without true understanding, how can supremacy be achieved? He is safer from corrosion because the desire already all but defines him. It is why I find him so entertaining: he struggles with ignorance—and masters it."

Gervanno understood, then. "And I am merely ignorant."

"You are the perfect cub for my sister," the fox replied. "I do not believe you to be ignorant; you understand the ebb and flow of power. You understand when your power is so insignificant your death would be poor coin; it will earn no respite for anyone. But your nature is such that you distrust what you sense. You believe that somehow that coin must be spent, even if spent for no benefit at all."

Gervanno only realized belatedly that the fox referred to honor, and its lack of practical value. His arms tightened, whether in anger or shame, he did not know. "Honor," he finally said, reaching a decision, "is life. What is a life without honor?"

"I am not troubled by simple philosophy. Life is life, Gervanno. It is survival. There are activities which make life more pleasant, and activities which make it less pleasant—but that is true for any living being. If honor means you walk to your death, I am afraid I cannot see the value in it." The fox chuckled. "Jarven is not a cub who follows the path of honor. He keeps his word, but he does so because it is useful to him to be seen as a man who does.

"Were there to be no consequences, he would abandon it in a heartbeat; he would not look back. But that is not what you are. You have given me your blood, and I retain the faint taste of it; I would not, at this moment, take more of it. I believe I understand what you are. And so we are here, where the worlds are close enough that I might witness what occurs in these streets without actually walking them.

"And you might do the same, while you carry me; it is a gift I grant you for no reason other than whim." The fox lifted head, stretched neck, and sniffed, whiskers twitching. "The air grows rank with the scent of death and ash. No, no—not that way. Almost I would gift you as I have gifted Jarven—but the cost would break you, and at the moment, that would not amuse me.

"To the right, Gervanno di'Sarrado. To the right, but do not put me down, or you, too, will be swept away."

Gervanno had no desire to stand—or walk—as mute witness. He had done so once, and if it had preserved his life in the moment, it had almost destroyed it in the aftermath. If the fox considered survival tantamount, Gervanno could not quite agree: it was shameful that he survived in such a cowardly, diminished way. Were it not for Maubreche, were it not for the chance to prove some small worth that might justify his survival, were it not for the scions of Maubreche, who could—and did—stand against the demonic, he was not certain where he would now stand.

Only Silvo's sword, only the determination to return that blade to Silvo's kin, would remain. He was not certain it would have been enough.

Perhaps the fox was right; perhaps honor was irrelevant. It must be, in part, because Gervanno still lived. But he believed that if coin was to be spent, as the fox put it, it must be spent for a purpose; there was no other redemption, no other *reason*, for his survival.

Perhaps the yearning for justification made him dizzy; perhaps the unusual events of this night had uprooted Gervanno's vision, his sense of place, his very reality. But as he walked in a direction not guaranteed to take him back to the normal, small room for which he had paid good coin in advance, he felt the subtle shift in wind, the introduction of different noises.

As if in answer to questions he had not known he was asking, they passed by, Nenyane's blade no longer a glint in the distance; they were close enough to touch, to grab, to hold on to: Nenyane and Stephen of Maubreche. They did not see him; no one in the streets did—and the streets had gathered more of a crowd, that crowd becoming uglier by the passing second, as crowds sometimes did.

His arms tightened; he shifted the fox's body so that he might, if necessary, draw sword. And he began to run, all thought of the safety of an inn forgotten.

CHAPTER TWELVE

"Do not put me down," the fox said, in a voice that was far deeper, far louder, than its small form should have allowed. "Even the dead leave a scent on the wind; they have their own particular version of ash, of dust, of grief and rage and pain, an echo of what they were in life. This one is familiar to me.

"I do not know what drew him to Breodanir, but even in death, he is not someone you can face and survive."

Gervanno did not see demons, but he did not doubt the fox's words; Nenyane was not fleeing, she was running toward something. He could no longer see her back, nor Stephen's, but he saw the shape of the Maubreche hunting dogs, so magnificent in their training, their focus, the sheen of their coats.

He was grateful that his own dog was safe in the confines of a closed inn room. If Leial had chosen to attach himself to Gervanno like a mangy shadow, he was neither trained, nor obedient, both things that were crucial in combat.

"Mortal," the fox said.

Gervanno slowed his sprint; he began to jog toward the edges of the crowd.

"Listen to me. I will not give you another chance."

"Eldest, you are not the lord for whom I would lift—or discard —blade."

"Oh?" The fox grew heavy in the crook of the arm to which Gervanno had shuffled him. He would have to set the fox down to fight and knew it, but he now used the fox's gift to run through the crowd; to ignore its density, to ignore the possible consequences of collision. They did not yet exist. Stephen was hampered by the crowd. Because he carried the fox, Gervanno knew he would catch up.

Nenyane was less hampered than her Hunter; one might have thought she ran through dense crowds every day, sliding through the space between standing bodies. But she was, in turn, hampered by Stephen; she would not leave him behind.

There was a third young man in clothing that resembled the Maubreche Hunters; that youth shouted something in Stephen's direction. Stephen nodded. A friend, then, or perhaps an ally.

But the crowd began to turn toward Stephen, toward this unknown youth; some of the people drew daggers or long knives. The Maubreche dogs moved in, then, and if knives could be drawn on young men, their wielders were far less confident when facing dogs. People backed up, retreating into other people; a wave jostled the crowd through which Gervanno now passed.

"Tell me then, before I abandon you to your foolish fate, who that lord might be?"

Gervanno could now see Jarven ATerafin. He stood in the crowd, but he interacted as much as Gervanno himself did; he could see, in the darkness of illuminated, crowded street, a faint luminosity surrounding the older man.

"Nenyane," he whispered. "Nenyane of Maubreche. You will never see a sword master of her skill again in this world."

"Swords," the fox sniffed. "I have never understood the need for them." His voice shifted back into the higher, softer pitch. "But you have clearly seen this would-be lord, and I am curious. I will therefore allow you to proceed with fewer consequences."

At any other time, given the nature of this unusual excursion and the creature he carried, that might have stopped Gervanno; he understood instinctively that the fox's claim to be the greater power was valid.

"She will not take me," he said, his voice soft and laden with both yearning and regret. "She serves, she does not rule."

"I serve and I rule; I fail to see the contradiction."

"Eldest, you must forgive me—but I do not believe your use of the word *service* bears any close relation to my own. I am but mortal."

The fox uttered a bark of laughter, "Very good, very good; no doubt you are correct. It is always a problem—to choose those with fire and ambition who desire the power I offer and know how to leverage it, or to choose those with antiquated and mortal morals. The one will, in time, be put down, for they lack humility or gratitude, and they will attempt to prove they have grown in power by attempting to kill me; the other will serve willingly and almost completely—but they are not surprising, not *exciting*.

"Jarven will almost certainly attempt to unseat me, in your parlance, in the future. He will die," the fox added, the cheerful anticipation in his voice disturbing, "but sometimes the cubs can be astonishing in their cleverness; I carry one scar from such a cub. I was proud of him, but that indulgent pride is not something over which one would be expected to sacrifice one's existence.

"I have had servants with your sense of honor," he added, "in the distant past. Perhaps there are many reasons I avoid them."

Gervanno listened with half an ear; half of his attention was on the crowd, and on the two people he meant to reach.

"It is too sad, when they perish—and mortals do perish. I am not a god, to prevent that for eternity."

Nenyane was far faster on her feet than Gervanno; even in a youth that felt distant now, he had never been her equal. But she could not run through people as Gervanno, fox tucked in the crook of one arm, could. He did not draw sword, not yet; it was—as he was—invisible. He imagined that any sword he carried would pass through anything without leaving so much as a scratch; he was certain, as he moved through, rather than around, several people, that the same would be true of any weapon they could draw, could they but see him.

He slowed as he reached Stephen's side, Nenyane's back in plain view. He wasn't certain what he had expected, but this was a drunken brawl. Weapons—daggers and long knives—had been drawn in angry, but unsteady hands. Whatever she needed here, it was not Gervanno's intervention.

He could not tell whether or not what he felt was relief or emptiness.

ALEX WAS TENSE; he moved almost as quickly as Nenyane, but his attention was focused on reaching Max. Stephen's was focused as well but there were too many people here; the sounds and smells were almost overwhelming, filtered as they were through the Hunter's trance. The speed and endurance the trance provided were welcome, even necessary, but a city was not the place to hunt without practice and training.

None of Stephen's training involved hunting people.

People are just animals that talk, Nenyane snapped in disgust.

The reason for that disgust became clearer. Stephen reached the edge of a crowd that his huntbrother had already penetrated. The dogs flanked him, heads low, voices dropping into the soft growl that was the only warning they would offer.

Men turned toward them; one carried what looked like a makeshift club, the other drew a dagger. They snarled at Stephen, some mix of cursing and resentment, but did not attack. If people resented Hunters —if they resented the nobility—they feared the dogs that defined them.

A cry of rage and shock rose above the voice of the crowd, stilling it momentarily; it was followed by a scream that broke into sobs and pleas. Stephen did not recognize the voice. He recognized the cursing that followed, though; it was Nenyane's.

We've got trouble.

He could see that, risking her vision.

Ansel stood at the center of the crowd. His clothing was torn in two places, and he was surrounded by men who might—at one point—have been jeering or taunting; they were silent now, but it was the silence of drawn breath. Someone lay on the ground at Ansel's feet, face down; he had lost an arm. Ansel wasn't armed with a sword.

Nenyane was.

The screaming stranger, who had learned that there was a paper-thin wall between hunter and hunted, was not the only person who had fallen. Beneath Ansel, the Bowgren Hunter's feet placed firmly to either side of his prone body, lay Heiden.

Nenyane looked up as Stephen borrowed her vision; they could both see Ansel's face, twisted in rage, darkened by the fear that Ansel would never publicly own. A tuft of hair above Ansel's shoulder could be seen; Max was there, at Ansel's back.

Alex slowed only when he reached the inner ring; the people gathered here were facing in, toward Ansel, Max, and the fallen Heiden.

But the circle itself had broken; people were turning toward Nenyane, silver-haired and armed with a sword that had just seen use.

It's self-defense, she snapped.

He did not argue, but could have. No one here, drunk and armed as they were, had a hope of endangering Nenyane.

Talk to Ansel. Tell him Heiden is alive — but in need of medical attention.

Stephen wasn't certain that Ansel would hear any words that left his mouth. He thought the only person he would hear was Heiden — but it was clear from Nenyane's vantage that Heiden was not going to be speaking any time soon.

The dogs cleared a path; Stephen did not take it, aware that the sides could collapse in on him should the mob's shock at a fallen comrade transform from horror into the rage that seemed to be lurking inside that fear.

But as the dogs parted the crowd, Stephen could see Ansel's face through his own eyes; he let Nenyane's go, because his eyes had started the painful tingle that the huntbrother bond always gave him when he tried to see as she saw.

Ansel's fear, Ansel's fury, he recognized, but only in their attenuated echo: he had seen them on the faces of his godfather and his mother, each feeling silently that their loss was the greatest of losses, but willing to take comfort from those who shared some semblance of their pain. Without thought, he shouted, "He's not dead! He's not dead yet!"

Ansel knew. His knees were bent, his head forward, his lips drawn over teeth that, flat and mortal, nonetheless suggested a cornered beast. He intended to defend his fallen huntbrother against any and all who might cause him harm.

Stephen understood, then. The loss of Barrett had broken Lord Bowgren, and Ansel feared — Ansel was certain — that the loss of Heiden would do the same to him. Stephen would not accept Nenyane as oathbound huntbrother because he understood what the cost might be. Alex and Max would never allow each other to swear the oath for the same reason.

Ansel, in youth, had — because in youth, loss was distant, impossible.

But Bowgren would lose its heir, here, because if Ansel had allowed Heiden to swear the oath, and that oath had been accepted, he had never intended for that oath to be invoked. He could not allow Heiden to sacrifice himself — even if that was Heiden's desire — because it would shatter him. He would not go to the Sacred Hunt, and when he missed that hunt, he would lose the title, and eventual stewardship of Bowgren lands.

Nothing the King could say, nothing Lord Declan could teach, would alter that course. Until the next Sacred Hunt was called, Ansel was Lord Ansel of Bowgren, but only until then; the King would have to find another Hunter, a second son of a different family, to take the Bowgren lands when Lord Bowgren at last met his end. He would appoint a new heir.

Stephen had never liked Ansel. He had thought that Ansel would be a bad ruler, a bad lord, his temper was so much in control of his actions. But he realized, as he met Ansel's warning glare, that in spite of this, he did not want Ansel to abandon Breodanir. He did not want Ansel to lose Bowgren. Some things could be changed, but some could not; the rules and laws that governed the nobility were based on oaths and bindings created before the country existed—and, in the hands of a god, they could not and would not be changed.

Nenyane was angry at Stephen; she was angry at Heiden; she was furious at Ansel, whose rage had driven him to this place, this part of the city, and this encounter. She was disgusted with the people who crowded Ansel, and who had clearly intended him harm, but disgust did not have the power of rage behind it.

Rage, on the other hand, had not caused loss of an arm. Stephen labored under no illusions here: the likelihood that the injured man would be taken to a healer in time to mend the damage was low; the temples were closed, and the Mother's children were always in high demand for childbirths and other emergencies.

He heard a whisper of sound, distinct from the noise of the crowd, as if a weapon was being drawn from a sheath, and looked in the direction from which the sound had come. There, on the edge of the crowd, he saw a man. The man wore a cloak that was the color of night, and boots of a similar color; beneath the cloak, hints of reflective light, suggesting armor, could be seen. That, and the drape of silver hair, so much like Nenyane's in color.

His fear of the mob fell away; the mob threatened injury, but it was not certain death. The stranger was.

Nenyane felt the shift in his thought, the changing wind of fear; she had never had difficulty when looking through Stephen's eyes, and did so now. She saw what he saw instantly. Disgust and anger fell away as something deeper and far more visceral rose to displace them.

The stranger had not yet seen Nenyane, but he would. There was nothing Stephen could do to prevent it.

"Alex," he said, his voice pitched low. "Get Max *now*. We have to leave."

"Ansel?"

Stephen nodded. The path he had cautiously chosen to avoid, he now ran through as Steel leapt ahead, toward Max. "Ansel—grab Heiden. We need to leave *now*."

Ansel snarled, his gaze sliding off Stephen's expression to the crowd that still ringed them, hemming them in. "They'll hurt him."

"It won't matter soon—no one standing here is safe."

Ansel opened his mouth to spit out words, but Nenyane was already in mid-air, her blade at shoulder height. Ansel didn't see Nenyane. He did hear her blade crash into stone as the target of her strike leapt clear. Everyone heard it, although some few were too invested in bringing Ansel down to pay attention.

Those that did saw a man—a stranger—jump to the side to avoid being bisected by a sword they had already seen used to such terrible effect.

But the leap did not carry the stranger to ground or cobbled road; he rose, instead. From beneath the fold of the cloak he wore, wings snapped out—dark wings, and long. They carried him a man's height above the gathered mob. In the distance his eyes were red—not the color of blood, but the color of fire. It was all the warning he would give, and Stephen thought it unintentional; that gaze was focused on Nenyane.

"What is this?" Although his voice was soft, the texture of it implying velvet, it carried above the shouts, the cries, the sounds of panic as men who had become aware of the demon attempted to flee through each other, their fallen friend forgotten. Were it not for Stephen's dogs, the young Hunters might have been trampled in the rush. As it was, Stephen took advantage of it; he bent to lever Heiden off the ground.

Ansel had seen the demon. The rage, the fury, drained out of him, but it did not leave fear in its wake; it left a sudden clarity of expression, a single purpose. He grabbed Heiden's other side and, together, he and Stephen pulled Heiden to his feet. The Bowgren huntbrother was not conscious, and did not regain consciousness when lifted.

Stephen and Ansel therefore became his legs. Stephen was at the end of the safe use of the Hunter's trance, but didn't set it aside, not now. Steel had Max in view; Max and Alex pulled up the rear, their retreat far less panicked, less loud, than the rest of the mob's.

Don't you dare come back, Nenyane said. *It's not me they're after. It's never me.*

But she was wrong. The demons had almost killed her once before; they might have succeeded had Evayne not come to her rescue. "Alex! Help Ansel!"

Alex shook his head, understanding immediately what Stephen intended: to go to his huntbrother. "She'd kill me, and she's far more terrifying than you are." The words were light, but the expression grim. "She'll survive."

"Not this one," Stephen shot back. But Alex didn't move to take his place. He began to run ahead, as if to scout; Max pulled up the rear. In the center, Stephen and Ansel struggled with Heiden.

"IF YOU ARE willing to trust me," a familiar voice said, "I can unburden you."

Ansel looked up at the sound of the Master Bard's voice. Kallandras of Senniel College, wingless, nonetheless remained suspended in the air above them.

Ansel was willing to trust Stephen because he had no other choice. He was entirely unwilling to trust a foreigner, and one who appeared to be mage-born to his eye. He said none of this, but his posture, and the tightening of his grip, spoke for him.

"Pardon me, Lord Ansel. I did not mean to unburden you of your huntbrother. I meant merely to join Nenyane of Maubreche in her fight. She has chosen a poor enemy in her rage, and it is neither the time nor the place to reveal her prowess yet."

"Too late," Stephen told the bard. He didn't raise voice, but knew enough about the bard-born to know it wasn't necessary; Kallandras would hear him.

"It is not too late if the creature dies here," was the soft reply. "But his death must be attributed to another."

"You?"

"I am not alone, and my name does not have the weight, the value, of my other companion." His smile, slender, seemed genuine if chagrined.

Stephen was not possessed of Nenyane's distrust of the bard. He had seen the bard fight—Nenyane had tried to kill him, and he had managed to hold his own. Stephen thought the bard could do far more than hold his own were he to fight in earnest. He had not fought to kill or even injure Nenyane; he had simply fought to avoid dying.

Nenyane was so far gone in her focus that she had nothing to add; even the usual irritation at Stephen's thoughts was absent. She was like this when she fought; nothing could distract her. No, he thought, amending that. She was like this when she fought demons.

She fought one now.

"I would be in your debt if you would go to her aid," he told the bard. "But her opponent is a demon."

"I am aware of what her opponent is. And this is not a minor demon, to be sent to cause mischief in the streets here. I do not think Nenyane is equal to this fight; not in her current state. APhaniel?"

If the mage was present, he offered no reply.

"Take Heiden back to the King's Palace," the bard continued. "Do not leave it until and unless we return. If we do not, if there is danger, go to the Priests; there is a place within the palace in which you will find strong protection for some time. They will know." He rose, then, and the wind whisked him away; he bent into it, as if he were accustomed to flight.

Stephen felt Ansel relax.

"I'm sorry," Ansel murmured, which was far more shocking—or would have been in any other circumstance.

Stephen shook his head. If apologies were necessary, they were not due Stephen; they were due Heiden, who could not hear them.

"I didn't believe you. About the demons." Or not.

Stephen made no reply. The tone of the bard's voice made clear that many things might be abroad tonight.

WHEN GERVANNO SAW the wings of the stranger unfold, suspending his weight in the air, when he saw the color of the man's eyes, he froze in place, as he had frozen once before.

"I told you," the fox said. "Do not put me down. The stench of the dead is strong, now."

"Where is your cub?" Gervanno asked, to prove that his voice, at least, remained in his control.

"You cannot see him? He has indeed become more adept at walking this narrow path."

"You can see him?"

"I am always aware of where he is. I am uncertain that he will join this fray—but I wish to bear witness regardless." His golden gaze was focused on just one person: the same person that Gervanno's eyes sought, his gaze flicking between many things to absorb, in his rush, the lay of the battlefield. "She is the master you would choose, if she would accept you." There was no question in the fox's voice.

None in Gervanno's nod.

"You cannot be of aid to her here, but there is one abroad who can. Ah, no, there are two—how odd. One is mortal, but the wind sings his name."

"The other, Eldest?"

"The other," the fox replied, almost purring, "is the reason your gardener had to flee this mortal city." He chuckled. "My cub is annoyed."

Gervanno tensed, which should have been impossible. Movement returned to his legs, his lungs; things that had frozen in place began to move once again.

"Do not put me down," the fox snarled.

"I must, Eldest. I will not approach the demon; I will guard the young Hunters. I was tasked with their safety by the rulers of Maubreche, and I will do my duty. But I would not deprive you of the sight of Nenyane of Maubreche; mark it well. You will never encounter another as adept with a blade as she."

"You wished to hide," the fox said, the voice deepening as Gervanno's arms began to shake in response to the odd, almost physical rumble.

"Yes. But if this demon is afield, there will be others—lesser, and less dangerous to one such as you. But not less dangerous to Stephen of Maubreche. They have hunted him before; I encountered demons in the heart of Maubreche, there to take Stephen's life."

"I will *bite you*." The fox no longer sounded like a fox; nothing about his voice suggested a creature of diminutive size. His jaws remained fox-like; small, the teeth sharp. True to his word, he bit down on the mound of Gervanno's hand—but it was not the dominant hand. Teeth broke skin, as they had broken skin once before.

"I have killed men for less," the fox then said, the need to speak forcing him to release Gervanno's hand. "But I am not yet of a mind to kill you; as I said, my lord does not approve of the killing of mortals except at need. You will never present enough of a threat to me for such a justification.

"I will therefore allow you to survive what is almost an insult. This forest would have guaranteed your survival, but it will not guarantee the survival of those on whom you must spend the coin of your endless honor. I feel nostalgic, and yes, you are correct; the taint of death is strongest here, but I feel its vines across this city. Go, then. We will meet again if you survive your folly."

Gervanno examined his hand briefly; the teeth had not cut deeply enough that the bleeding could be considered a genuine injury. He drew sword and bent at the knees, setting the fox down with as much care, as much respect, as a warrior in a hurry could muster.

Fear of demons slowly underwent a transformation into fear for Stephen. He knew that it was Stephen's safety that was of paramount importance to the sword master who would never accept him as student; it was the only thing he could offer her.

And he had not lied to the fox: he had accepted the duty of seeing the two Maubreche Hunters to safety. The black, wide wings in the night sky promised death.

Maybe, this time, the death he faced, the death he might earn, would offer some sliver of redemption. Maybe this time, if he continued to move, continued to *fight*, fear would not rob him of every vestige of the man he had once believed he was.

———

THEY COULD NOT MOVE QUICKLY CARRYING Heiden between them, and Heiden did not wake.

"He's alive," Ansel told Stephen. Alex and Max were slowed by their need to bracket the injured Heiden and the two who'd become his legs. Steel flanked Max, but Patches moved on ahead. Stephen had no need to command them; they understood what he wanted, and they gave him what they could—they always had.

The streets were not empty; the mob had thinned as panic broke the crowd and sent it skittering in every possible direction. Alex had chosen the road that would take them to the King's Palace; Stephen and Ansel, less familiar with the city, followed.

Had he not been looking through Patches's eyes, he might have missed the three men standing sentinel in the road. But Patches froze at the scent of blood, new blood, too much of it, immediately ahead.

It was human blood.

At the feet of the three men lay half a dozen people, all dead. Stephen called Patches back, and stopped instantly.

Max said, "Those aren't men." He was not under the effect of the trance; Alex was. Alex's sense of smell was therefore almost as good as Patches', but he could see far more clearly, even given the night sky.

"No," Stephen replied. "Ansel, we're going to need to fight here. Can you stay with Heiden?"

"Until I can't draw breath," Ansel said, voice low.

Brylle and Sanfel moved toward Patches.

"WELCOME, WELCOME TO OUR LITTLE GATHERING," the man in the middle said. "It has been quite the evening; we did not expect to encounter you here, in the streets." Shadow spilled from the man's lips as he spoke. His jaws began to elongate; Stephen could see blood in his widening mouth. "You have eyes of gold in this festering, mortal land, and we have been searching for you."

Nenyane was not here. Stephen did what he could to shut all avenues of communication that connected them. He knew that she had left to fight the greater demon, and he faced the lesser, even at three to the one. Stephen was concerned; he attempted to keep that worry to himself. Nenyane wasn't rational when it came to demons. The only thing she did not abandon was her skill with the sword. But he knew that the demon she faced was a match for her, and in any evenly matched contest, there was risk.

He drew sword. Max and Alex drew long knives; they hadn't armed themselves with swords when leaving the palace. Stephen went almost nowhere without one; Nenyane would not accept it. It had always been easier to acquiesce, where Nenyane was concerned, and Stephen had never liked unnecessary conflict.

But this was not unnecessary.

He was not Nenyane's equal with a blade. She had been his only teacher; he knew he was far, far better than most of the Hunter Lords who deigned to learn. Swords were not used for hunting; were it not for Nenyane, Stephen would be no better armed than either Max or Alex in the face of their enemies.

The demon with the elongated jaws laughed; he lifted a hand, and Stephen saw that it, like the creature's jaws, was elongated, fingers curving into long, ebon claws. To the demon's side, the two who might, at a distance and in terrible lighting, be mistaken for men, moved toward Stephen, as if the dogs that stood before him were irrelevant.

All of the dogs were crouched, growling. The street lamps provided little illumination in this stretch of road—they were broken, the glass that protected the magestones providing illumination shattered, the magic that imbued the stones dispelled. Stephen, in the grip of the trance, did not require their light.

Like the creature they apparently obeyed, the hands of the two that now approached bore long claws; their faces were far more bestial than they had been only moments before. But the one in the center retained some semblance of humanity; it was the central demon that was, therefore, the larger danger.

He did not make the mistake of thinking the lesser danger was irrelevant. Nenyane would have—but to Nenyane, it was.

ANSEL HAD DRAWN A WEAPON—A sword. He had laid Heiden carefully against the road, and now stood—as he had in the middle of the growing mob—astride his prone body. This time, he faced demons, but these demons were not the ones that had driven him to the street, to the tavern, and to drink.

He made no move to join Stephen and his dogs; he stood sentinel.

He was now preternaturally aware. He was, therefore, the first person to see the man who raced toward the demons in the street, sword in hand, off to the left where, during daylight, people would walk. The Maubreche hounds had no reaction whatsoever to the approaching stranger. Whoever this man was, the dogs both recognized and accepted his presence.

The stranger ran past Ansel and Heiden, and past Max, who

pivoted in his direction, only to be cut off by Steel. Max growled—literally growled—a wordless warning. The stranger failed to hear it.

He slowed slightly when the two demons approached the dogs, their spines now curved, their feet spreading as they adopted a shape that boots could not disguise; long claws, almost like a bird of prey's, left runnels in the cobblestone. Ansel watched the stranger.

Stephen nodded as the stranger came to a stop at his side—in the position Nenyane of Maubreche might have occupied. But no, Ansel thought; Nenyane would have been on the ground ahead of the dogs. The stranger lacked her confidence—or her rage.

Ansel recognized that rage; it was possibly the only thing he and the Maubreche huntbrother shared. But she had abandoned Stephen for one fight, and Stephen was now faced with three enemies, not one. Ansel would never have made that choice.

Never.

But he watched the stranger's back as if the stranger, in his desperate, deliberate rush, was the only person—excepting Heiden—present.

GERVANNO DID NOT ALLOW fear of demons to freeze him; he would not. He did not slow. Instead, he allowed fear *for* to move him, to guide him, to rise to the surface and remain there, held by will and desperation.

The two young Hunters who had taken this road with Stephen of Maubreche weren't armed with swords, they were armed with long knives—the reach of which would not be equal to the long claws the demons had sprouted. He gave them the respect due their rank: they were Hunters. But they were not here with dogs; they were not here with swords. This was not a battle for which they were prepared.

Even so, they had chosen to flank Stephen, facing forward, knives ready.

He could not worry about them; if worry was spent, it would be Stephen's worry. Gervanno's role was different, now.

It was Gervanno's sword that parried the first rush of claws, Gervanno's sword that drew first blood. He could control the length of swings, the wildness of them, in order to accommodate comrades and allies, but he stepped in front of Stephen as he parried, becoming the whole of the front line for a moment.

The dogs came in from the right side, focused on the demon whose shed blood proclaimed the true start of combat. The dogs were strategic in their attacks; they worked in concert. But they worked to harry the demons that Gervanno faced; they focused on the demon who had lost half a hand to Gervanno's twist of blade. The fool had chosen to parry —if it could be called that—with his hand.

Stephen, however, was not far behind. He moved to Gervanno's left, sword readied, as the second demon moved in the same direction. They discovered, almost at the same time, that the two legs on which the demons stood were just as flexible, just as extensible, as their elongated arms. Stephen's jacket was shredded as those rear claws ripped through it; he was fast enough to avoid losing the arm. More than that, Gervanno didn't see.

His attention was split between the demon directly in front of him and the third demon, who had not yet moved. He could see that demon only in brief, brief glimpses, the one he faced moved so quickly. But here, in motion, he had the reflexes survival of many battles had given him; he did not have to think about where he placed his feet, about how he dodged, about the length of the reach of the demon's claws—its weapons.

He knew when the third demon raised arms; he knew, from the gestures, that the battlefield was about to be transformed; he felt the rise of hair across the back of his neck, the only part of his body not too sweat-covered to allow it. He shouted a warning—in his mother tongue —as he threw himself to the side, covering distance by force of momentum.

Fire blossomed in deadly petals where he had, seconds before, stood his ground.

But the demon he had faced was not troubled by the fire; nor was he now intent on finishing Gervanno. No, it was to Stephen the creature turned, as if Gervanno was irrelevant, as if he were already dead.

Gervanno rose silently and leapt back into the fray. His first strike— a feint—was parried by the creature's legs. Those legs were Gervanno's target; he twisted the arc of the blade, putting weight and momentum into that twist. His blade struck mid-thigh, and carried through bisection one of the legs; his blade slowed on the bone of the second leg. He yanked his sword clear.

The demon did not topple, as a mortal man would have. The blood that darkened the already dark street seemed red to Gervanno's eye.

The dogs brought the creature down, but did not remain within reach of arms that had not yet been cut away; they bit and harried and retreated.

Gervanno did not make the demon's mistake; he moved in while the demon struggled to regain one-legged balance, and he removed the creature's head. Then, as he had seen on a battlefield once before, the demon dissolved. Blood and flesh became ash, and the ash scattered, dissipated by a sudden gust of wind. The demon was dead, the ash a brief scent before it, too, wafted away on a breeze far too weak to move Gervanno.

He did not join Stephen; against the single opponent, with the weight of the dogs and the ability to leverage multiple viewpoints simultaneously, he believed Stephen could handle himself. Had to believe it. The third demon was once again gesturing, legs planted, arms raised. As Gervanno walked toward him, he could see that the creature's eyes were red, but they reflected some distant light, giving them a silver cast.

He expected the demon's fire; he did not expect it to break the street beneath his feet, but he was ready, and he moved, and moved again. He had discovered, in the dim and terrible Averdan valleys, that the creatures themselves were very much like the Widan. They could not aim or cast their spells instantly—all save a very few, against whom Gervanno and men of his talent stood no chance at all.

He was not yet close enough to the demon. He rolled, coming to his feet, sword in hand—a move he had practiced so often he could do it now without thought, although his sword master's curse at his clumsiness, and his observation that Gervanno was so incompetent he'd cut off his own legs in the middle of battle, echoed as he did. So much of the past was a web, a weave; disparate strands of thought remained caught in the memories that made of the past a place in which roots could be grown.

And these roots led him to the Widan, as it had oft led him to the archers, to those who could stand at a safe remove and kill.

But the Widan were not swordsmen; they were not cerdan. Their strength, such as it was, relied on distance; on the protection, conversely, of cerdan like Gervanno. Demons were not Widan. As Gervanno approached, the demon smiled, his face cracking as he discarded even the appearance of a mortal man.

Gervanno almost went down. The wind roared at his back, as if it intended to push him into the sword the demon had drawn: a long, red blade of flame and steel.

No. It wasn't wind.

"Go back to Stephen!"

It was Nenyane. Somehow, Nenyane had arrived. If he had been unwilling to leave the third of the demons to Stephen, other training took precedence; his body was already moving to obey the command of a greater leader on the field of battle.

"I mean it—go back. Do *not* leave him!" She did not look back. Gervanno did. He did not feel that she meant to imply that he was useless or incompetent; it was the opposite. Stephen was her Hunter; Stephen was the person to whom she swore the loyalty that only ended with death. She had placed his safety in Gervanno's hands, because she believed Gervanno could protect him.

It was an honor.

The two unknown Hunters made room for Gervanno; they, too, had heard Nenyane's command, and they clearly knew her well enough to obey. If they carried no swords, they understood basics: Gervanno required room to move, to attack and defend freely. Stephen stepped to the side as Gervanno joined him. He remained in motion, tracing a half circle just outside of the range of demonic claws.

Here Gervanno held his ground, observing the way the remaining creature attacked. He had already seen the use of legs as arms; he was not surprised when the jaws widened and the neck suddenly elongated in a snap of motion. Stephen was slower than his huntbrother; he parried the attack, and the demon's jaws snapped shut on the blade itself, yanking it free of the young man's hand.

The demon's arms were already in motion, as were the dogs; they collided.

The demon's head was slowed, sword in mouth; Stephen was not unarmed, because the dogs remained under his control. But the dogs' jaws had smaller, mortal jaws, their necks a set size; they could not kill the creature on their own.

Gervanno could. Sword raised, he slid into the gap created when Stephen leapt back, out of range of claws that would have killed him had the dogs not been present to grab the demon's wrists in their impressive jaws. Gervanno moved then; the demon's neck retracted, but the creature did not release the sword, which slowed it just enough that the neck became a target, like an ungainly, misplaced limb.

His sword passed through it, the resistance expected of flesh giving way almost instantly to ash. Two. Two demons gone. The dogs did not seem to resent the transition between flesh and ash; they turned instantly toward where Nenyane fought.

To Gervanno's surprise, she had not yet dispatched the demon to which she had charged—and that fact made clear that the demon would have been beyond him. The demon had drawn a burning blade, and as he fought, he summoned a shield as well; Nenyane had no shield.

Gervanno hesitated, but only briefly. She had told him to stand by Stephen, and he understood why: she did not want to split her attention. Could not, in fact, afford to do so. Stephen confounded his determination; he moved toward where Nenyane now fought.

One of the Hunters, the strangers, shouted his name; Stephen ignored it.

Gervanno did not dare to lay hand on the boy. He noted with approval that Stephen had paused to retrieve the sword torn from his hand by demonic jaws; he lost time.

He almost lost more.

Gervanno understood why Nenyane had barked her command, then. Demons descended from the darkened skies.

LATER, he might wonder why the demons had chosen to shed all subterfuge; later, he might understand just how dire their decision might be, not just for the Hunters, but for the populace of this city, this kingdom.

Now, he let instinct guide him. He was not a leader of men, here; he was not a commander. As he was in his youth, he was cerdan only: his job was to obey the orders he'd been given, and to survive. The normal fear, the normal adrenaline, of any mortal battle in which he had fought before were present, but the paralyzing, honor-destroying fear was not. How could it be when she was on the field? If she fought on his side, death was not certain—not for Gervanno, and not for the young Hunters.

He had never seen a demon archer, and was aware that the demons who began to descend might have among them a Widan, someone who could cast his dire spells from the safety of the distance flight provided. He had seen some handful of those creatures in the Averdan valleys, and he'd lost men to them—he therefore knew that the wings that bore them aloft were limbs that could be just as deadly as claws or weapons.

He barked that warning to Stephen. Stephen's dogs moved, two to the rear of their party; Stephen understood the danger instantly. The demons, when attacking on the ground, were forced to face them, to direct their attacks in a frontal way. From the air, there were no such constraints; they could attack from above, or swoop in from behind. Gervanno made a rough count: eight, nine. The formation of Hunters, with the two non-combatants at their center, could not be further tightened in a way that allowed for safe use of a long sword.

He glanced, once, at Nenyane; she was almost a blur of motion. So, too, her opponent; the demon had no time, no space, to rain further fire upon them. Gervanno grimaced as the demons in the air flexed their wings. Their legs and feet were very similar to the two demons killed in the streets. They had no intention of landing if they could harry—or kill —the humans who could not take to the air to level the battlefield.

It was difficult to look up and look forward; difficult to defend two fronts. Stephen had his dogs, and the dogs helped, but Nenyane was fully engaged with the one demon Gervanno considered the most powerful. To cerdan, to men like Gervanno, even the least of the demons were deadly.

His training and his experience had not prepared him for partially aerial combat; he knew how to seek cover when archers were on the field, but archers were more predictable. They had to be avoided, where possible; they could not be countered with a sword. The aerial demons could be, but when they attacked from above and from the front, Gervanno considered his chances slim.

The two Hunters on the field carried long knives; they had no dogs. They were incredibly agile; they could avoid the attacks aimed at them from on high, but those attacks lacked full momentum. It was only a matter of time.

But if he could hold the line until Nenyane was done—the outcome was never in doubt—some of the Hunters might survive. The demons seemed focused on Stephen—just as they had been when they had attacked the Maubreche manor. The dogs had drawn back, toward Stephen; they faced Nenyane. Stephen had raised chin, his eyes—as Gervanno's—darting between those demons who circled above, and those who were now choosing to land.

The demon Nenyane had engaged shouted an enraged command; if the language was impermeable, the meaning was not.

One demon attempted to land at Gervanno's back—at all of their backs—in the center of the circle. The lone Hunter who had not joined the line was armed with sword; he did not wait for the creature to settle, but lunged, his blade moving not to center or head, but to the spread wings.

More than that, Gervanno did not see; while that Hunter stood, the demon would not attack their backs. He was not alone, here. In this kingdom, this strange, Northern place, they were not civilians.

Fire drew his attention briefly, a splash of angry red and orange as Nenyane of Maubreche drove her blade through her enemy's shield. The breaking was a clap of thunder, and the cry that followed, haunting while it lasted.

The blood on Gervanno's blade evaporated as the demon he faced lost its head, and thereafter its corporeal form. He moved now, aware of where Stephen's sword was, where Stephen stood, and what he fought. Twice, his blade arced up to catch the lower limbs of hovering demons; they could attack him, but could not find enough purchase in air to deliver a killing blow.

There was no third time.

Wind blew down the streets, a sudden gale that tore sound and debris from the surrounding road. The demons in the air were caught, briefly, in its folds; their attention turned from the Hunters and Gervanno to their own defense as they struggled to retain their formation—and failed.

They were blown toward Nenyane, toward the demon who commanded them, before they could right themselves; they did, as their leader shouted. Gervanno did not understand the command, and this time, could not immediately intuit meaning.

One of the young Hunters, however, also shouted, and Stephen looked up. Gervanno noticed the boy lower his long knife, although it remained ready, and risked looking up in the air as well.

Above them, a man stood, blades in hand; they were not swords, nor were they long daggers, and to Gervanno's eyes they were very dark, as if the steel were pure carbon. The man's hair was golden, and far too long for the battlefield to be unbound as it was; he could not see the stranger's eyes. But he recognized the man he had met while he carried the golden fox. Understood, then, why the fox had tolerated him.

Stephen turned to the cerdan. "He's a bard from the Empire," he said, raising voice over the roar of wind. "And he's on our side."

GATHER AROUND THE FALLEN HUNTER.

Gervanno was in motion instantly, the command was so clear. So, too, Stephen, his dogs, and his two under-armed comrades. The Hunter in the center, the one who stood sentinel over the fallen, had been injured by a sweep of claws from shoulder to hip bone; Gervanno could see blood bead in the gap made by rent fabric.

Bard. Ah. He remembered. The bards were not Widan, but they could make themselves heard, clearly, at any distance. They were a tool of the Imperial army, and a greater part of the reason why the Imperial army had been so tactically organized from the start of engagement to its end.

This man *flew*, canting his body forward as if gravity were irrelevant, and the demons in flight came to him, not entirely in control of their own wings.

His weapons met claws and broke them; the sharp tines of blades cut tracks across demonic wings. The demon thus injured fell, listing; the wind did not carry him, but drove him groundward, to where Gervanno waited.

The demons now struggled to evade the air that had turned against them; they evaded the man at their center and found purchase on the broken stones of this Breodani street. There, they were met by dog and sword; the bard's attacks seemed designed to drive them to earth in ones and twos, although ash rained down from above where the demons were not skilled enough to avoid the bard's weapons.

Gervanno was not surprised when Nenyane joined them; she came in behind the demons the Hunters faced, her blade bisecting two in an arcing sweep that seemed impossible given the length of her sword. On the return, her blade cut heads, and ash was her raiment as she stood facing her Hunter.

Stephen said, "You're injured."

Nenyane shrugged, her grudging gaze rising to air, where the bard stood. Only when the last of the demons had fallen did he condescend to land.

"I don't trust you," she snapped. "But I owe you."

The bard offered her a deep bow—a respectful one. "In the war to come, such debts will be irrelevant. We fight the same enemy, Nenyane of Maubreche, with the skills at our disposal."

"He is not at your disposal."

The words made little sense to Gervanno, but Nenyane was bristling, her blade readied as if she intended to launch herself at the bard. Stephen caught her sword arm, as if he, too, saw what Gervanno saw. He did not speak.

"Come. Meralonne has not yet finished, and the streets are not—as you have seen—safe. I hear horns. The King has rallied the Hunters who serve within the King's City. It is best that you not be among them, if I understand your position here." He paused, and turned to Gervanno, to whom he offered a perfect Southern bow. He did not speak. Did not claim prior knowledge, as if aware that the Hunters might not know of Gervanno's strange service to the fox.

Stephen said, "He is Gervanno di'Sarrado; he traveled to the King's City to speak with the magi about the loss of an entire caravan on the Breodanir roads, but he traveled with us at Lady Maubreche's behest, as a Maubreche guard. He wished to deliver warning to authorities better equipped to deal with them; Lady Maubreche wrote an introductory letter. We...parted at the King's Palace."

"Did you know that he would be here this eve?"

Stephen shook his head.

Gervanno cleared his throat. "I will bespeak the Order of Knowledge on the morrow, if the appointment still stands, given the evening's work." He turned to Stephen. "I will see you to the King's Palace."

Stephen nodded. To Kallandras, he said, "This is Lord Ansel of Bowgren, absent from the dinner to which you were invited. We came to find him."

"I see Heiden of Bowgren was injured."

Stephen nodded.

"Very well. With your permission, I will form part of your escort as well."

"It's not necessary," Nenyane said, her voice just one side of polite. "Gervanno is with us, and the demons are once again silent. Or do you hear their voices on the wind?"

"I hear only one."

Nenyane closed her eyes. For a moment, she listened, but no more. "I hear Illaraphaniel," she whispered. "He will not be overpowered here. But there is a strangeness to these streets, some hint of mist and hidden paths that was not present before."

Kallandras's eyes narrowed. "I do not sense it."

"No? Ask the wild wind, Master Bard. The wind most certainly will." She turned to Stephen.

Alex exhaled, sheathing his knife. "We might be able to return to Hunter's Redoubt without being noticed if the King has called the hunt; Lord Declan would certainly be required to join them." As if Alexander's words were an incantation, the sound of horns pierced the air.

Gervanno was not familiar with the call of the horns in Breodanir; he felt them as a clarion call, a battle cry. Stephen's dogs stiffened as if they were one creature, and they turned to their master, as did Nenyane.

Stephen shook his head. "Heiden must be delivered to safety first." He tendered the bard a Northern bow.

IF NENYANE HAD DEEMED Kallandras's presence unnecessary, it mattered little; the bard followed. He had sheathed his weapons, and Stephen noted that the moment he did, the sheaths vanished; he could perceive no trace of the dual weapons the bard had wielded.

Steel paced by Max's side; Alex led. When Stephen fell back to once again aid Ansel with Heiden, the Bowgren Hunter grunted a brief thanks. Heiden stirred twice, but did not wake—and wakefulness would have been a blessing to those who struggled with dead weight.

But as he listened to the sounds of the horns, he could trace the direction of hunting, of possible battle. He could hear the shock of lightning in the clear sky; could almost taste ashes on the breeze that cooled his cheeks. People came to windows although it was dark; he was almost certain that the young and curious would be lurking at street's edge across the city before the sun rose.

He hoped they would survive it.

He wanted to join them, which surprised Nenyane; he felt a core of ice that was Maubreche's ancient anger to Nenyane's burning rage. But Alex and Max weren't armed to hunt, and they had no pack; Stephen had only four dogs, and his sword. In his rooms would be other weapons meant for the hunt, but no Hunter carried them through the streets for any other purpose.

Nenyane offered to take his place when he flagged; he had carried the trance for too long, and Heiden's weight was an increasingly difficult burden. He shook his head. Ansel was only barely content to accept Stephen's aid; he might still refuse Nenyane's.

WHEN THEY REACHED THE GATEHOUSE, the gates were open; the Queen's Guard was out in force, although Stephen assumed many of their number would be in the palace, protecting the Queen for whom they'd been named.

Gervanno stopped at the gates.

To Stephen's surprise, Kallandras turned to the Southerner. "Come. We have passed beyond the point of appointments and the social niceties the Order of Knowledge demands in return for the power they wield. Meralonne APhaniel will return, and it is to him you must speak; if he takes your report, the Order of Knowledge in Breodanir will accept it."

"Grudgingly," Alex added.

"Yes, but that is the nature of pointless hierarchy and unwanted rivalry. In times of peace, it is wisest to observe them, but this is no longer a time of peace."

Nenyane's eyes narrowed. "You don't trust them."

Kallandras nodded, his face a mask.

It was to Nenyane Gervanno turned.

"We're not allowed to have guards—King's rule," she said.

"If it pleases Gervanno, he may join me. I have never been forbidden guards." So speaking, the bard smiled. It was an almost glittering smile, and reminded Stephen of blade's edge when caught in momentary light.

CHAPTER THIRTEEN

The Queen's Guard were, as their increased presence suggested, on alert, but the disruption caused by the King's Hunters had shifted their protocols somewhat. In the late evening hours, the occupants of Hunter's Redoubt were meant to be ensconced in their otherwise empty wing. That they were not, and that one of the six was clearly injured, did not incur pointless criticism; they knew that demons had invaded the streets of their city.

These young men—and Nenyane—were Hunter-born, Hunter-bred; they had been in the streets of the King's City, and they had seen combat there. Stephen thought it likely that older Hunters, fully Lords, would enter the palace in the same way as the hours progressed toward dawn.

Kallandras and Gervanno drew far more attention than the scions of Hunters, the difficult future generation brought to the capital in hopes they would cease to struggle against the imperatives of their duties.

Gervanno was willing to withdraw; this was not his place, and he knew it. Kallandras, however, was not willing to allow it. He was a gentle, charismatic, affable wall. He responded to barked orders and obvious suspicion—the Queen's Guard present at this guard post clearly did not recognize him—with an apologetic nod. It implied that the authority of the moment resided entirely with the guards.

Stephen watched almost in spite of himself, wondering if there were lessons to be learned from the social dance Kallandras now performed with such grace. But he still carried half of Heiden's weight—or perhaps a third, if he were being honest—and he wished to return Heiden to Hunter's Redoubt before more questioning started.

Ansel seemed to flag here, as if entering the palace had been the only goal that had kept him moving. Chagrined, Stephen realized that Ansel himself was injured. It was not a terrible injury, but there was blood, and the clothing he wore was ruined beyond repair.

With the permission of the guards, they made their way to their rooms.

Alex veered off before they'd properly entered the wing. "I'll call a doctor. Given events, they're all going to be awake and waiting."

"I'll stay," Max replied.

Nenyane almost volunteered to accompany Alex; she didn't. She did not trust the security of the palace, and she considered the possible risk to Stephen to be the greater danger. "We should have kept Gervanno."

"We're not allowed personal guards," Stephen replied.

"That's going to change. It has to change. It's you they were after. Again."

Stephen had no argument to offer. What he felt at the moment was not fear for his life, not dread of demons, but guilt. Raw guilt. Had he remained in Maubreche, the entirety of the city would not be infested with demons now. Maubreche had protections that the King's City did not possess, and people who had nothing to do with gods or demons would die tonight. Had already died.

He thought it highly unlikely that Maubreche's oldest son would be allowed to retain a foreigner as a personal guard, but there was no point in arguing with Nenyane in this mood; she latched on to anything in her defiance, and Heiden was not yet in his bed.

Lord Declan was not in the wing. Nor were there servants; even the guards that had been stationed there to make certain the Hunters remained safely in their rooms were absent.

"This is the point at which security must be tightened, not abandoned," Nenyane snapped, grinding her teeth. She remained as Alex ran off. Stephen sent Patches to follow him; he wanted a view of the events, and Patches could provide it. It was the reason Max stayed behind: the exchange of information.

Heiden was no longer bleeding, but hair was matted to his head where a large contusion had risen and would no doubt bruise. Ansel's

wound on closer inspection wasn't deep; it would heal, and likely leave
no scar.

"You two should get some sleep," Ansel said, voice gruff, eyes on
Heiden.

"Alex has my dog," Stephen replied. "And Max isn't bedding down
until Alex clears the gauntlet."

Ansel nodded, expression drawn. It was grim, which was not unexpected, but it showed exhaustion clearly; the rage that seemed a permanent part of the Bowgren Hunter's face had momentarily been drained.
"What did we see tonight?"

"Demons," Nenyane replied.

"You think they were here for Stephen."

"I think they've been hunting for him. Gervanno—the Southerner
with the sword—thinks they were looking for something else. It could
be both things at once. But..." she exhaled. "The demon that joined us
just outside of the tavern? That was no minor demon. He was *Kialli*,
and he is powerful." With the demon at a distance, she could be more
reflective, although it took work. "Were it not for the bard and Illaraphaniel, I'm not certain we would have survived."

"You're certain the mage survived?"

She nodded. "Kallandras came to us because Kallandras believed
Illaraphaniel—sorry, you know him as Meralonne—was equal to the
task." She exhaled far more air than she had apparently inhaled. "He
saved your lives."

Stephen turned his attention to Patches, and through Patches to
Alex. "There are a lot more guards in the halls the Queen occupies," he
said. "But they allowed Alex to enter the halls. The infirmary is there—
and as you suggested, the medics in the palace have been fully
mobilized."

"Is the infirmary empty?"

"Not entirely, but I don't think the occupants currently in beds are
there because of the demon hunt. Alex is explaining the situation—and
we have a doctor on the way."

"Already?"

Stephen nodded. "They're expecting exactly this trouble; they're not
questioning Alex. At all." He turned to Max. "I think Ansel and Heiden
will be in good hands."

Max understood. "Go. Sleep. We'll keep watch for now."

I'm not tired, Nenyane said, but privately; she knew Stephen was. *I can keep watch.*

You will, her Hunter replied, as he turned and stumbled from the Bowgren room to the Maubreche rooms, two of his dogs by his side. Steel, he left—by command—with Max.

18TH DAY OF EMPERAL, 429 A.A. THE KING'S CITY, KINGDOM OF BREODANIR

The innkeeper was bleary-eyed and, not surprisingly, given the location of the inn and the terrible events of the evening, awake. Having seen the Maubreche Hunters to relative safety, Gervanno apologized to the bard. He had left his dog in the safety of the inn, but safety would tip into starvation if he did not return to retrieve him.

To his surprise, Kallandras accompanied him. "You are not entirely familiar with the city, and you will not be able to enter the palace if you are not by my side."

Gervanno was almost embarrassed. His excuse had been his need to collect his belongings—but he had not directly mentioned the mongrel who had adopted him.

Leial was waiting, skittish, by the door; he had taken to opening the door slowly to avoid hitting the dog. To his surprise, Leial lowered head and exposed teeth as the dog caught sight of Kallandras. "Leial, no." He knelt beside the dog, dropping a hand to his head. Soft growl became whine; Leial crouched fully to floor and rolled over, exposing belly.

"This man is our ally," Gervanno continued. Leial had accepted everyone Gervanno had encountered without hostility until now.

Leial barked.

"You are certain the palace will accept Leial? He is not the purebred hunting dog familiar to the Breodani."

"I am certain. Come, collect your dog. We should return."

GERVANNO ENTERED the palace in the wake of the Master Bard. As cerdan, he was accustomed to silence; he served as guard, and words of import were to be imparted only by the person he was guarding. Kallan-

dras of Senniel—and what a place Senniel must be to train those gifted
in music and language with weapons such as the ones he bore—spoke.
And spoke. And spoke. Had Gervanno been asked, he would have said
that the Master Bard was a man of few words; clearly, his first impression left something to be desired.

In the end, however, Gervanno di'Sarrado, scion of Southern
warriors, was granted permission to enter the King's Palace at a time of
war, or as close to war as the Breodani had come. He was present as
companion to, and guard for, Kallandras, the Imperial bard, two
foreigners whose presence at this time caused natural suspicion. The
Queen, however, was above suspicion, and they were—it was made
clear—her guests.

Accustomed to sleeping before or after battle, Gervanno had no
difficulty ignoring exhaustion. He followed the bard past the bristle of
Queen's Guards. The bard seemed to know the layout of the palace; he
had no difficulty finding the rooms granted him for his personal use.

"These will be your rooms as well; you are expected to attend me
while I remain here." The bard's lips lifted in an odd smile. "You will
perceive that I require no guard. I will speak to the Queen when the
situation is less dire; I believe she can convince the King that your presence would be beneficial to the Maubreche Hunters."

"And you?"

"I would not have detained you otherwise. Nenyane seems to trust
you; she will never fully trust me."

Gervanno shook his head. "You saved Stephen."

"His death was not certain, given both your presence and hers."

"His survival was not certain either. Until you arrived. Had the
demons chosen to land and attack from the ground, the chance would
have been greater." He hesitated.

"You have questions?"

Gervanno shook his head. "I am from the South. Questions beget
answers, and no wise cerdan wishes to hear the answers of the powerful; even knowledge offered in words can lead to death."

Kallandras's smile deepened. "As you say."

"But if you will entertain less dangerous questions, may I ask why
you are here?"

"That is not a less dangerous question. The Maubreche Hunters can
answer it. If you choose to remain by their side, it is our hope that they
will travel to the demesne of Bowgren."

Gervanno's lack of familiarity with the geography of Breodanir frustrated him now.

"But you said you were granted an appointment with the Order of Knowledge."

Gervanno nodded. "I wished to inform the Order of my encounter with demons on the road to the King's City—but Meralonne APhaniel suggested that duty had been discharged when I informed him of events." He hesitated.

"You are concerned with Jarven ATerafin."

"Not specifically—but his suggestion that my absence from the now unnecessary appointment might cause Lady Maubreche, or Maubreche itself, to lose face is one I had not considered. I feel I owe Maubreche a debt, and it is poor payment of that debt to cause a stain—however small—upon the family's honor."

Kallandras nodded. "Member APhaniel's concern was not with the repetitive nature of offering two separate reports. His concern about the possible damage to the reputation of a Breodani family with whom he has had little interaction—if any—would, as you suspect, be small to non-existent, given the nature of the enemies we face. It is...discomfiting to have the *Kialli* act so openly; they have, in the past, been prone to subterfuge, unless they feel unassailable.

"But there are possible reasons for drawing such open attention. If you feel it necessary, attend the appointment, assuming that the Order will honor it. Given the events of last eve, they might be stretched too thin; caution is advised."

"If the purpose of my appointment was to speak of demonic invasion, I feel it unlikely that the appointment itself will be cancelled; it speaks to the heart of this evening's events."

Kallandras nodded. "With your permission, I would like to accompany you."

Gervanno, aware of the magnitude of the debt owed this bard, a man as foreign as he in the Kingdom of Breodanir, said, "I accept your company with gratitude. You have clearly dealt with these mages, and I have not; it was not our way to mingle with Widan."

Leial, silent until this moment, padded over to Gervanno's knee and placed a paw on it, as if demanding attention.

"You could, should you desire it, find a suitable home for the dog. The safety of a pet on the roads we will travel is not guaranteed."

Gervanno exhaled. In theory, that was his desire. But Leial had found Gervanno on a road he considered subtly dangerous, and the dog seemed determined to follow.

"I see that you do not. Very well. You have the option of kenneling the dog; I agree, however, that might ruffle the feathers of some of the sticklers. I am comfortable with the presence of the dog in our room; you will have to see to his needs."

Gervanno nodded. Leial withdrew paw and sat, tongue hanging out, eyes the shape animal eyes were when they had decided that food was their most dire and pressing concern.

"Later," he told his dog. "Master Kallandras has more to say, and I must hear it. It affects both of our futures."

Kallandras smiled and continued. "Meralonne APhaniel is of the Order of Knowledge, but he personally serves the woman who rules over the whole of the Order. She is famed for her deep and abiding hatred of anything demonic: the kin themselves, or those foolish mages who seek to summon them to make use of their power. Any word Meralonne receives, she will hear—and she will take those words deeply to heart. We can discuss this later, should the need arise. I would tell you to sleep, but your dog would be disappointed."

Gervanno nodded.

"Should you leave the palace, tell the guards upon your return that you are the personal guard of Kallandras of Senniel College; a page can guide you back."

FINDING food for Leial was not enough of a distraction. Gervanno was exhausted, but exhaustion provided no bulwark against the shadow of demons; those shadows had become so omnipresent he thought himself inured to them. It was a polite fiction at best, a lie at worst.

He was aware of the number of dogs in the streets—hunting dogs from whom mangy strays retreated. He was aware of armed men, men in armor, and men in the colors Hunters wore. He had taken some pains to familiarize himself with the hierarchical use of their colors, but that was simple necessity: to know how to treat those with power, one must recognize the subtle signs that denoted it.

These dogs, these men, had been simple civilians on the city streets even a day before; they had been unconcerned with the presence of foreigners. They were not unconcerned now. While they understood the forms and appearances demons could take, they had the instinctive dislike of the unusual, the strange.

Gervanno therefore kept his head down; when stopped, he answered questions politely and deferentially. His sword drew eyes, but Gervanno had been unwilling to set it aside, given the presence of demons; he explained that he now served as guard for one of the Queen's invited guests. Leial did not particularly care about manners, and to Gervanno's surprise, the excuse of tending to the dog seemed to lessen suspicion.

Merchants were less likely to evince the same suspicion—and more likely to be somewhat unkind in their bargaining, but they too relaxed when they realized the supplies this foreigner sought were meant to appease his dog.

But there was little in the way of forced merchant cheer in the stalls, and the stalls themselves were few. Those who felt they had a choice had chosen to avoid the city until further notice from the King. The demons had caused losses here—and two deaths. None of the merchants looked askance at Gervanno's sword. Their fear was not of foreigners; it was of things that were not even human.

It was his, as well; he shouldered it. It was for men and women such as these that armies existed, after all; it was to protect what they built and toiled at. He thought it would not be enough; armies did not normally fight within the walls or boundaries of cities.

THE TENSION within the palace was more pronounced, and Gervanno's words upon his return took some time to be delivered, but the recipients chose—in the end—to trust him. Or to trust the word of the bard himself. The advantage to the palace guards and servants was their familiarity with the foreign; one of the pages sent to him addressed him in his own tongue, albeit heavily accented.

It was a gift; his concentration had frayed enough that the comfort of familiar words was a greater boon than he expected, and that page was the one who eventually led him to his temporary home.

ONCE INSIDE THE ROOM, Gervanno headed to the long couch. He paused there to draw and examine his sword, but demonic blood, as the bodies of the creatures who had shed it, did not remain on blade or edge; it required no immediate cleaning, no repairs. He almost could not believe it, given the weight of the encounter—as if demonic blood was special, different. He sheathed sword again, divested himself of boots and shirt, and lay down. Luxuries such as shaving or bathing would wait, would have to wait.

But the demons—and the victims of those demons—occupied his thoughts when he closed his eyes, and he opened them again to dispel their images. The ceiling was a far better sight in the dim light. He had no sense of time, no sense of whether or not the Lady's night—and her mercy—had returned.

Leial sat beside the long couch, and dropped head to Gervanno's chest; he stroked that head as he tried to find elusive sleep. He was cerdan, and soldier; he could sleep standing up. Sleep should have come quickly; no warrior fought well when exhausted.

But it continued to elude him. He heard footsteps, identified them as the bard's.

What Gervanno knew of bards was scant; they traveled. They sang for their keep. Those rich and powerful enough sponsored them. The bard no longer remained in the outer chamber in which Gervanno had sought refuge. But as Gervanno listened for movement beyond the closed doors, he heard, instead, the strains of music, a stringed instrument that was not samisen. He heard the drift of voice, clear as a newly struck bell, and he heard the familiar refrain of his childhood, a time when the world had seemed—to an ignorant and loved son—safe.

It was the cradle song.

The sun has gone down, has gone down, this night
Na'Gerva, Na'Gerva, child
Let me take down my helm and my shield bright
Let me forsake the world of guile

Moon's light, moon's comfort; he could see silver light when he closed his eyes. Silver light and elusive, momentary peace.

He slept.

*18TH DAY OF EMPERAL, 429 A.A. THE KING'S PALACE,
KINGDOM OF BREODANIR*

When Gervanno rose, it was to a meal that had been brought to the
room; he was almost embarrassed to see the food because he had slept
through the interruption. He could not say why, and it worried him, but
he was accustomed to keeping worry from his expression. He was
grateful for the food; he had not happily anticipated a meeting with
Northern mages on an empty stomach.

He did wonder, as he glanced at his face in the long, rectangular
mirror above an empty fireplace, whether he might find clothing that
looked less like it had been worn on the battlefield.

His biggest concern, however, was for his dog—a dog he had not
possessed before he had crossed the border to this country.

The bard was awake; he was shaved and clothed in a way that
implied battlefields were the farthest thing from his daily life, and
crossed only because of the lays and epics he might deign to sing.
Gervanno had no doubt the bard's voice could make those battlefields
and their consequences crushingly real should he so choose.

He ate; the bard joined him, but ate less ravenously.

"You acquired your dog in Breodanir?"

Gervanno hesitated. "If you are determined to accompany me, I will
offer you the tale while we make our way to the Order of Knowledge.
You will not doubt either my sanity or the situation—which is as much
as I could ask, given the events that all but define Breodanir to me
now."

LEIAL ACCOMPANIED GERVANNO; the dog was unwilling to remain in
the somber palace, and to his surprise, Gervanno was equally reluctant
to leave the mutt there.

Gervanno had known Kallandras less than twenty-four hours, but
felt as if he had known and trusted him half his life—and in all of that
half, his trust had never been broken. Perhaps it was because the bard
spoke Torra, and spoke it so fluently Gervanno would have assumed it
his mother tongue had his Imperial speech not been likewise natural.

He understood, if he had not fully understood it before, why bards
were dangerous, but accepted it as the price of his life; he accepted that

one who could fly and face demons, summoning the very wind to gain advantage, would find far more of use in the words Gervanno offered than Gervanno himself could.

He did not speak of the manner of his survival of the demon attack on the caravan; the bard did not ask. He offered just enough response to make clear to Gervanno that he was listening and that Gervanno's words and speech were of great import, but never enough to intrude. The story, as it was told—haltingly, and without great organization— was Gervanno's gift, Gervanno's burden.

But his expression grew grave, and graver still, towards the end of the telling.

"If I have added to the burden of either your worries or your duties," Gervanno said, "forgive me. That was not my intent."

"No words you offer, no experience you choose to share, could add to that burden." The bard's voice was soft, but it implied a wall; Gervanno made no attempt to touch it or acknowledge it. "Apologies," the bard added softly, "you are sensitive in a way most of my current companions are not."

Gervanno began to speak of his job as a caravan guard—and of his reason for coming to the King's City in the first place. This was his duty to discharge, although the appearance of demons in the city streets had offered a far more immediate warning than any cerdan's words could.

WHEN GERVANNO FINISHED HIS TALE, he fell into a natural silence as he walked. The bard was silent as well, but it was a companionable silence, and it continued until the moment Gervanno saw the fox.

He was fully capable of pretense; he was a man trained to see, unseeing, the acts and actions of the powerful. But that pretense of ignorance was what was demanded of guards in the South. It was less of a demand in the North. The fox was of neither; he was not human, and the rules that governed respect for such a creature were rules that Gervanno had not fully learned.

He understood, however, viscerally and instinctively, that once sighted, respect demanded acknowledgement. He therefore paused almost mid-stride, stopped in the middle of an otherwise crowded street, and tendered the fox a perfect bow. "Eldest," he said, as the Master Gardener had done.

"Yes, yes. I see you survived your ill-advised run through these dingy streets."

"I did."

"I do not like your companion," the fox then said.

"It is by his grace and the power he wields that my survival was guaranteed. I owe him a debt of gratitude."

The fox's nose twitched. "I do not like the *smell* of him."

Gervanno knelt. He looked to the side and up, for the bard had also come to a stop. "My apologies," he said to Kallandras. "If I disappear, I am nonetheless by your side."

Are you in danger?

Gervanno shook his head. He offered the fox his arms, and the fox, silent demand now met, came to them. Leial growled, voice low, body closer to ground, as if preparing to leap.

Gervanno rose quickly; he had no doubt at all that the dog would die should he attempt to harry the fox.

"We are going to the same place, I expect," the fox said. "Soon. Soon I might reveal myself."

"Why can you not do so now?"

"Because here, there is no wilderness, or very little of it."

"What might change? Forgive me, Eldest, but I do not understand."

"No, of course you don't. Even were I to explain—and in detail—it would doubtless be beyond you. But something is traveling toward Breodanir, now."

Many things, it seemed, had traveled to Breodanir.

"But that is neither here nor there. My cub has sighted his quarry. If he but fulfills the task I have set him, I will gain power here, in these benighted lands." The fox's voice had dropped in register, the growl deepening in a way that belied the delicate form of gold and fur he had chosen to adopt. "Come, come, I am impatient. Carry me to your destination."

"We are going to the Order of Knowledge."

"Yes, yes you are. And you may convey me there while you travel." Golden eyes glinted, their color shivering briefly into the shade of new steel.

KALLANDRAS KNEW THE CITY WELL. If he could no longer see Gervanno, he accepted Gervanno's words. He therefore continued to the grounds on which the Order's building sprawled. It was not as large as the palace, but it was possessed of a tower that seemed taller to Gervanno's eye than any edifice attached to that palace.

"I must put you down, Eldest," Gervanno told the fox. "If I am to fulfill my purpose in this building, I must be visible to the mortals who dwell within it."

"I would tell you that you will regret it, but I am aware that you will ignore my kindly warning where you think it conflicts with your *honor*." The fox swiveled head to look at the bard. "I do not like him," he said again. "He bears the scent of death. Do not trust him overmuch; his loyalties have been given, and they are absolute."

Gervanno might have pointed out that the same was true of the fox; he did not.

"You have met my cub; he is not always careful when it comes to mortal lives. It is the reason my lord views him with some suspicion — my lord is not a fool. But my cub and your companion have what you lack. Mind their words if things become difficult, and we shall meet again.

"Can you not hear it?" he added, voice soft. "The forests are waking, and their whispers pierce my heart."

"WELCOME BACK," Kallandras said, as Gervanno gently set the fox on the ground he appeared to despise.

"Apologies."

"The fox?"

Gervanno nodded. "He is tiny and delicate in seeming, but there is something about him that speaks of, and to, the ages; I am less than a flea in his presence. But I am a sentient flea, and it is neither wise nor safe to deny either his presence or his demands."

"No," was the grave reply, "it is not. And if I understood your tale, you owe a debt to the fox — as does Maubreche. Pay your debts, when they are owed; the wilderness cannot be denied and its memory, if imperfect, is long indeed for slights and offenses."

Gervanno looked at his jacket; the fox had left golden hair in his wake. Were the fox Leial, he would have paused to brush the hairs away, but he was certain the fox was observing him, even if he could no longer be seen.

Kallandras approached the gate guard and offered the name Gervanno di'Sarrado as if he were a Southern attendant, not a Master Bard of renown. The guard nodded him—nodded both of them—past the fence; he barely lifted head. Clearly he was apprised of the schedule kept by various members within the perimeter.

The driveway past the guard booth was easily wide enough to accommodate carriages, and carriages did pass them as they walked, by foot, toward what Gervanno assumed was the front door.

A YOUNG MAN in grey robes was waiting for them when they entered. He called Gervanno's full name, and when Gervanno raised chin and headed toward him, he offered the cerdan a nod of acknowledgement. If there was no respect in the nod, there was no disrespect; he was here for a purpose. His expression changed when Kallandras accompanied Gervanno.

"Apologies, but I am here to guide Gervanno di'Sarrado."

"I am his attendant," Kallandras replied. "Surely you did not expect him to arrive alone?"

For the first time, an expression flitted across the young man's face —chagrin. "I—apologies, I was not informed that Ser Gervanno would arrive with an attendant. I will have to leave you both a moment. If you will follow me, we have a lounge available for expected guests; you might wait there and avail yourself of minor refreshments."

GERVANNO DID NOT AVAIL himself of minor refreshments. He thought the young man sent to meet him guileless, but the situation made him uneasy. He was in close proximity to Widan. He understood that the Northern Widan, the mage-born, were not of the South, but the understanding was intellectual. Widan arts were never arts that men like Gervanno sought to understand outside of the fields of battle.

Men like Kallandras of Senniel might seek that understanding in safety—they were Widan themselves in all but name. Gervanno would never be that.

The bard chatted with the attendant; the attendant offered drinks almost apologetically. The bard accepted what Gervanno would not, although he drank sparingly.

Be prepared for difficulty.

Gervanno glanced at the bard; his lips were barely moving, but words nonetheless filled the space between them. A quick glance at the attendant made clear that the words were heard by Gervanno alone. This was, indeed, a display of one of the North's most significant battle-field advantages. He could not speak in like fashion, and instead raised brow, indicating curiosity.

Kallandras did not appear to notice. He did, however, glance at Leial. The dog had been allowed to enter at Gervanno's side; in Breodanir, dogs were not left at the door. Establishments of note would have been met with less hostility had they demanded weapons be discarded for the duration of any official visit.

Leial was still. The mutt stood in front of Gervanno, but there was a bend to the back that implied crouch, implied readiness. Given Leial was just as likely to flee conflict as to engage in it, Gervanno would have found it amusing in any other circumstance.

He dropped hand to blade when a man he recognized walked through the door, in part because the door had been closed to allow some quiet and privacy in the bustle of the public space of this hall. The man glanced at him, glanced at the placement of sword hand, and raised an iron brow. His lips quirked up in what would have been a smile on another man's face.

Ah, no. It was a smile. But it was Southern at its core; it did not touch the eyes, and it did not denote genuine amusement or congeniality.

"Well met, Kallandras of Senniel," the fox's cub said.

Kallandras did not reply. Gervanno understood that the greeting, the Northern politeness offered, was a simple test. The bard could not see him. Gervanno glanced at his hand; it bore the faint trace of bite marks, a gift from the fox. Or a punishment. He did not yet have enough experience to determine which. But he knew that this man, this Jarven ATerafin, was like—and unlike—the bard from Senniel College.

Gervanno was a normal cerdan, a man whose skill had been taught; he belonged with cerdan, not with men who might as well be demonic, given their abilities. Leial did not care for Jarven, or so it appeared; it was not clear to Gervanno that the dog could see the man. Had he been asked, he would have said it was impossible, but Leial was now as tense as Gervanno himself.

The door opened.

The man who nodded to them was not the same person who had greeted Gervanno upon his entry to the Order of Knowledge; he was far more diffident, more polished. "My apologies, Ser Gervanno," he said. "It appears that Member AGressalis is running late. I have been asked to see you to his rooms."

"And my attendant?" Gervanno asked.

"Your attendant is welcome to accompany you."

"Thank you," he replied. He was not grateful. AGressalis was an Imperial styling; it was not the styling adopted by the Breodani of Gervanno's acquaintance. He glanced at the bard as he rose. Kallandras nodded, wordless, and followed Gervanno out of the room.

Jarven, unseen by any save Gervanno, followed in their wake.

THE MAN LED them through the last of what Gervanno assumed were public halls, given the brisk manner in which occupants moved through them on their way to one or another closed door. At the end of the hall was an arch, and that arch led to winding stairs—tower stairs.

This stairwell appeared to be all of stone; Gervanno's steps echoed loudly, as did the too-long claws of his dog. The bard's step was lighter—not inaudible, but Gervanno felt instinctively that, had he desired to be so, Kallandras could have mounted the stairs without leaving so much as an echo in his passage. Regardless, he felt comforted by the presence of this man. They were almost strangers, but they had shared a battlefield together, and had survived it. Whatever they faced, he trusted the bard to have his back, both figuratively and literally.

At the midpoint of the tower's height, the spiral stairs opened up onto a landing. The stranger led them off those steps. "This way, please."

Kallandras glanced at Gervanno, but said nothing. The glance was enough.

"How interesting," Jarven ATerafin said. Gervanno privately felt the man would use that phrase in the chaos of the battlefield, unaffected by the din of the dying. "You have never visited the Order of Knowledge in this country; I have, and far more often than a man with any intelligence and discernment should be forced to endure.

"Kallandras finds the situation as interesting as I, which is unexpected; I don't imagine he has had much occasion to visit these halls personally. You are, sadly, judged by the company you choose to keep — were I you, I would have chosen a different companion. The bard is known."

And you are not? He could not ask the question. If he wished to discharge the responsibility he had chosen to bear, he could not be seen to be speaking with thin air.

Jarven smiled, as if gleaning the thought, or expecting it.

"It has been interesting to endure my chosen master this past year. I have been known — entirely inaccurately — as a patient man, even a wise one. I have gained knowledge over the decades I have operated within my House, but that knowledge is painfully irrelevant; it almost makes one feel one has wasted one's life, one's youth, in pursuit of the wrong knowledge, the wrong experience.

"I dislike waste," he added. His smile was thin, but it reached his eyes; he was enjoying himself. Or perhaps enjoying Gervanno's inability to respond in any visible fashion. Were it not for the fox, were it not for this man's involvement with that august creature, Gervanno would have — with dignity — acknowledged the man at a safe distance. There was something about him that seemed dangerously chaotic, and that led, on fields of battle, to unintended death. He was a man who was capable of accepting commands when it suited him, and only then.

"In case you are wondering, the rooms here — the rooms to which you are being led — are not offices; they are not meeting rooms. They are meant for the practice of magecraft, the development of spells that must be carefully contained so as not to destroy the building in unforeseen miscalculations. It is seldom that these rooms are used to entertain guests."

Gervanno's nod was brief and shallow, a bob of acknowledgment, no more. He glanced at the bard, whose expression was pleasant but neutral; he did not hear Jarven.

"You have the advantage," Jarven then said. "My master chose to bite you; the bite did not kill. He is now capable of rendering himself visible to your eyes, no matter where he chooses to walk, if he but sees you. I highly doubt the Master Bard would be so foolish as to offer my master a similar opportunity.

"But apparently, this gift allows you to see me. I am uncertain of the full nature of the mechanism. You are wondering why I am here?" The Northerner smiled. "I am hunting, of course. I would have preferred to hunt in the environs with which I am most familiar, but the Lord of the East has risen, and my quarry cannot safely harbor or hide there. It is to kingdoms such as this one that he has been forced to flee when he chooses to leave the Northern Wastes.

"It is difficult for him, now. If he is to prove his worth, he must mingle with mortals—mortals with power, mortals with significance, in the eyes of his lord. There are few." Jarven's smile was slender. "I would not be considered among them." The last words were spoken with amusement. Amusement and an anger that was familiar to Gervanno; he had seen it frequently.

Jarven felt slighted.

Had he the ability to speak, Gervanno might have pointed out that being literally unseen made it difficult for the enemy—or allies, had he any—to offer him the respect of either caution or fear; that his activities were unlikely to be noted or to be attributed correctly. He did not. But if he had considered Jarven dangerous—and given the man's master and the ability to walk literally unseen through halls of power, it was a natural conclusion—he considered him a danger in an entirely different way. When men's egos wielded sword, the arc of the blade became unpredictable.

Jarven could not be relied on as an ally. Were he visible, they might be caught in the same mesh, and their mutual interest—escape and survival—might have forced the man's hand; but he was not. Gervanno had no doubt that, were things to become truly dangerous, the fox's cub would simply observe and walk away; he would feel no compulsion to offer aid.

Only when their goals perfectly aligned would he step in.

The guide opened a locked door. "Please, wait within. Member AGressalis will join you shortly. He apologizes for the venue; he wishes the conversation to remain private, and these rooms will guarantee that privacy."

It was a reasonable excuse, in Gervanno's opinion. It was not, in Jarven's, given his expression. Kallandras nodded; he stepped into the room a beat after Gervanno. Leial hesitated at the door jamb, but followed his master in. Jarven's expression changed when he attempted to follow and found he could not. There was a barrier present—one that

Gervanno could not see or touch—that prevented Jarven's entry entirely.

He was uncertain how to feel about the man's exclusion. But if the man could not enter this room, surely demons would likewise be excluded. Perhaps the reasons for the use of the room were actually reasonable. Or perhaps the room was meant to prevent all noise of combat, of eventual murder, and of possible torture from escaping.

He was not a man given to betting, but he was uneasy enough that he considered the second option the more likely one. He should not have come—but the bard had desired to attend him here. The bard had desired, Gervanno realized, an excuse to enter this building.

Perhaps what the bard sought and what Jarven ATerafin sought were the same thing.

As if he could hear the words, Jarven spoke from the impassible door. "I have been set a goal by my master; my future is contingent upon its completion. Tell the bard—when the time is correct—if he should encounter Rymark ATerafin, that he is *mine*. No other hand must be responsible for his death. I will not take it kindly should stray chance deprive me of my quarry. Nor will I forget should this occur." The last sentence was uttered softly. Softly and implacably.

Gervanno nodded, wondering if Rymark ATerafin was Jarven's brother, uncle, cousin. Northern naming conventions made little sense to Gervanno, although Sylvia had been at pains to explain their significance. They styled so-called family as Houses, and the Houses were not designed around—possibly not always conducive to—blood ties, in some cases. In others, family followed some of the customs and norms of the South—but Gervanno could not easily remember which House was which, the Northern names oft sounded so similar to his ear.

Evaro would have known. Gervanno's role was cerdan, not merchant, and not negotiator. All of the decisions for which he had been responsible had little to do with monied foreigners.

He was not surprised when the door closed behind them.

"This is a cleverly designed room," the bard said. He closed his eyes as he spoke, as if listening for the echoes his voice might make; there were none. Sound was almost unnaturally muted, given the composition of the room: the floors were stone. There were no carpets. The walls appeared to be stone as well, although beams of wood girded each corner; the ceilings were flat.

Leial stood so close to Gervanno he was half-perched on the

cerdan's left foot. Gervanno's hand fell to the hilt of his sword. The attendant had made no attempt to relieve him of the weapon, possibly because to scholarly Widan, or to the mage-born, a sword seemed insignificant. It was not a mistake the Widan of the battlefield would have made.

Or perhaps it was a simple sign of consideration for a foreigner, a man unfamiliar with the rules of the Order of Knowledge, and of Breodanir itself.

Kallandras drew no weapon; Gervanno had lowered hand to hilt of sword. He did not lift it, and would not until the door opened.

The door, however, did not open as someone entered the room. Gervanno thought, initially, it might be Jarven ATerafin; the man exuded a specific stubbornness, a will that could not be suborned by inconvenient, objective fact.

It was not. "My apologies for my caution," the man said. "I am Member AGressalis." He turned to Gervanno. "I believe you petitioned the Order for an appointment, at the behest of Lady Maubreche? We have been much occupied, both last evening and this morn. If the matter of the appointment was urgent, we offer our apologies."

It was his voice, in the end, that sounded wrong to Gervanno's ear; it was too smooth, too deep, too textured. He spoke Torra, which itself was surprising, but so perfectly, so clearly; he used the more exact pronunciation and phrasing men of absolute power might use, dressed as he was in the dark robes and pendant of a foreign Order. It felt wrong.

"Your companion is known to the Order. I am most curious to know how you met, and how he came to travel with you." Thus speaking, he turned to tender welcome to said companion. He continued to speak Torra.

Kallandras answered in Weston, the Imperial tongue. "It was an eventful evening, or so I am told," the bard bowed. "In truth, it is small wonder to us that you could make the time to speak with us at all." The bard's voice was as fluid, as textured, as oddly deep and soft, as the member of the Order.

Gervanno stiffened, although it was subtle. They spoke, these two men, with very similar voices—and Gervanno had cause to know that the bard's was in no way natural. Were the mage-born gifted in similar fashion? He could not be certain; could not remember if he had discussed them at all with either his fellows in the caravan, or the Maubreche Hunters.

"We are much concerned with the happenings in Breodanir," the mage replied. "And much concerned with matters that concern Maubreche, servant of Breodan of old. Time would be made, regardless of the external dangers we face—indeed, if Maubreche calls, it is almost certainly connected. Ser Gervanno, how did you come to receive that letter?"

"It was delivered to me. I encountered difficulty on the passage through the Maubreche demesne, and I was of some use there. The lord of those lands bid me deliver word of my difficulties to the Order of Knowledge."

"They did not choose to deliver those words themselves? How odd."

Gervanno said nothing in response. He felt, at this moment, that it was important to make no mention of Stephen of Maubreche here. "I am a simple caravan guard; it is not my place to question the rulers of these lands."

"And did you arrive in the King's City on your own?"

"I met him on the road," Kallandras said, before Gervanno could answer. "And as I had been invited to perform for the Queen's Court in the very King's City to which Ser Gervanno traveled, I took it upon myself to offer companionship, and perhaps a small amount of guidance in these lands which are so strange to him."

Member AGressalis's eyes narrowed; they seemed to almost flash. It might have been a trick of the light, but there was no source of light Gervanno could immediately pinpoint; no lamp, no lantern, no torches. That, perhaps, was what had made the room itself seem wrong to his eyes; it was lit, but no windows allowed light in, and no light source accounted for the even illumination.

"Very well. Come, tender the report you meant to deliver." This time he spoke with a note of clear command.

Leial barked.

Member AGressalis's expression descended into visible annoyance. "Why is that creature here?" he snapped. He spoke as if he expected an unseen servant to reply; the question was irritable, but it was not directed to either Gervanno or Kallandras.

"May I ask a question?" Gervanno said, surrendering to a suspicion that had hardened so completely he could not talk himself out of it.

The man brought his expression under control once again. "Of course."

"You are AGressalis?"

"Yes."

"You are not, and have never been known as, Rymark ATerafin?"

The mage blinked; Gervanno might have been speaking in a tongue so foreign it was beyond his comprehension.

It was not beyond Kallandras's. Before the mage could tender a reply, the bard had drawn weapons: two. This close, Gervanno could see them clearly; they had not been so well illuminated at the height of night sky. To a swordsman's eye, they were short weapons with wide, pronged guards; there seemed to be little edge on what might, at a distance, seem to be blade.

The mage noted the bard's weapons. "So," he said. He smiled. The smile deepened and lengthened across the width of his face, corners extended up and out as the shape of the face itself stretched almost beyond recognition. "I had hoped to retrieve useful information before disposing of you both. It appears that will have to wait."

"I too seek information," the bard replied, his face absent smile, his voice remarkably calm. "And it, too, will have to wait."

Gervanno drew sword an instant before the demon who had come bearing the appearance of mortal man shed it entirely. Shed was the correct word: he doffed skin, and the blood beneath it implied that it had once adorned a living man. A living mortal. It sloughed off his face, his arms, falling across the stone floor with a wet sound.

There had been a Member AGressalis, at one point. Gervanno was uncertain whether the member was victim or foolish ally; now, it mattered little. Gervanno leapt to the side, leapt clear, his blade clanging against the chitin of familiar claws. Had he been unarmed, he would be dead or dying.

Leial barked or possibly shrieked, the sound was so high; he made no attempt to close with whatever the mage had become.

"This is a remarkable room," the demon said, offering a grin that exposed far too many teeth. "We are aware of you. We are aware of what you bear." He spoke to the bard. "But here, nothing will come at your call. You are without power."

Gervanno had seen the bard's power in action; had seen him—at a distance—close in combat with winged, aerial demons. This demon, however, did not sprout wings; had he, they would not have given the demon the same advantage the demons had in a boundless night sky.

The demon clearly believed the lack of flight, the lack of command over the direction the wind might travel, was key to killing the bard. Gervanno did not. The bard was not a young man, but the age he carried had not yet weakened him. In the cerdan's opinion, Kallandras of Senniel College was a man in his prime: one who had been formed, scarred, and strengthened by experiences that had not yet killed him.

The same could be said of Gervanno.

Leial's barking changed in pitch at Gervanno's back; the cerdan pivoted, bringing his sword to bear at chest height in one sweeping arc. Blood spouted from empty air; it was followed shortly by ash. Gervanno looked for the nearest wall. He could not fight something he could not see. He shouted a warning to the bard, no more; the bard faced the visible demon.

Fear did not deaden Gervanno's limbs; it did not still his movement. He had no time for fear; he had time only for action, reaction; for listening to the sounds of movement, of claw against stone. He knew his swings were wild, but they were aimed in the direction of the noises he caught; the dog's barking should have overwhelmed the quieter noises.

It didn't. Leial seemed to move in the direction of the things Gervanno couldn't see; his barking, high and insistent, was directional. He did not attack the invisible demons—if there was more than one— but he gave Gervanno a chance at survival. A slender chance.

The wall provided the only backup he now depended on, unless the demons could attack, unseen, through the wall itself. He doubted it, given the demon's boast about the properties of this room. He had no time to watch the bard, now; he could hear the sounds of fighting, could hear the demonic roar. The sound of pain and fury must be strategic. Where the demon roared, the small sounds of movement were obliterated.

He took the sounds in as if they were as natural as storm. No armies planned to clash during a downpour that turned a field into mud, but not all battles were planned. Smaller actions were subject to weather, to unforeseen occurrences. Cerdan reacted well or died.

Gervanno made guesses as he remained in constant motion, the wall at his back his only shield. He knew demons took different forms, different shapes; knew that his training had been given over to the study of mortals, the response to mortal tactics. Invisibility was not one of them.

He had no time to glance at the bard. The bard, however, was aware of him. Was possibly aware of the demons Gervanno's eyes couldn't detect. He did not expect to survive; indeed he had taken two wounds, neither immediately deadly. But he would make his death costly. When survival was uncertain, honor demanded at least that much: make them pay for his death. Make them *earn* it.

He was not prepared for the sudden shattering of door; was not prepared for a new combatant to enter the fray. It was the Master Gardener.

No; it was the foreign mage, Meralonne APhaniel.

Had his attackers not been just as startled as he, he would have died, and knew it. Whoever had just destroyed the locked and magicked door was not demonic, and that was as much information as he could afford to take in. The entrance of the Northern mage changed the field of battle.

A wave of light flooded the room in a single instant, as if the Lord himself had descended and carried the fire of his presence—the Sun—with him. Demons were known to plan their attacks for the Lady's time; the silver moon did not burn them; the Lady was no warrior. Gervanno could see the demons, now.

He could see them, and he could see that they were larger, heavier, and slower than their counterparts in the streets of the King's City. They were not armed; they attacked with claws, with elongated jaws. And they burned, in the summoned light, their skin shedding black smoke that rose up, and up again, as their flesh gave way to light.

Gervanno's attacks were not slowed in any way; he took their sudden visibility as the gift it was. Leial fell silent, fell away; Gervanno was no longer aware of where, in the fray, the dog chose to stand.

He moved. Beyond him, he was certain that Kallandras still survived, because the air in the room began to move as well, counter to Gervanno at times; counter to the demons continuously. The wind carried ash, and the ash increased in density; when it fell, it fell to an almost thunderous silence.

Silence.

He looked across the room, then. There, the bard stood, rents in clothing, and a slight gash across forehead—blood beaded there, but did not fall, the damage cosmetic.

"I believe," the mage said, "that I indicated that I would conduct the interview with our visitor." He spoke to ash, or so Gervanno assumed— but another man, pale and shaking, stood in what remained of the door's frame. Perhaps it was he who now received the ire of the stranger.

"Member AGressalis commanded otherwise," the young man said. Or perhaps young woman; given the robes and the neutral timbre of the voice, it was hard to discern. "And he is one of the ranking members of the Order in Breodanir."

"All members of the Order answer to Sigurne Mellifas, and it was she who sent me. I am authorized to speak on her behalf in all matters that touch on demonology. *All.*"

The bard said, "Member AGressalis is dead. If you wish his confirmation, it will be a long time in coming."

"Dead?" The younger mage's voice rose to a squeak.

The mage and the bard now exchanged a glance, the mage's one of studied disgust. "Dead. To *Kialli*, no less. The command you were given was not his, but a demon's." To Kallandras, he said, "You were almost overmatched."

"He was competent, yes. Were it not for his allies, I would have considered it a fair match."

"Fair matches are seldom the province of the *Kialli* when they face the merely mortal. We may be grateful for their arrogance."

Kallandras nodded and turned to Gervanno. "I see I am not the only person to have survived."

Gervanno understood, then. "I survived because you were considered the actual threat."

"You are bleeding; you are not dead. I believe you were underestimated." He offered the cerdan a smile that did not quite reach his eyes, but nonetheless felt genuine.

"I am grateful that you chose to accompany me as guide." Gervanno examined the edge of his blade; demonic blood had evaporated, as it had the time before. He sheathed sword and tendered a perfect, and respectful, bow to the man who had in all likelihood saved both of their lives. "Member APhaniel." He did not understand the mistake he had made, for this man was clearly not the Master Gardener.

Kallandras turned to Gervanno. "I must ask why you asked Member AGressalis if he had ever been known by another name. It is clear that the demon recognized the name; I was quite surprised to hear it from your lips."

"Name?" Meralonne asked. He paused, frowned, and fished about his robes until he had found a pipe in them; he then repeated this action to find leaf.

"Rymark," Kallandras replied. "Rymark ATerafin."

The mage frowned, but continued to fit leaves to pipe bowl. His expression made clear that he both recognized the name and was not best pleased to hear it.

Gervanno exhaled. He had come to deliver word about the death, by demon, of the entirety of Evaro's merchant caravan; he had not come to speak of strange, golden foxes and forests that were like and unlike the forests of Breodanir.

"Why would you ask AGressalis such a question?" The mage asked.

"A man who is clearly under the auspices of a talking, golden fox made clear that he was hunting Rymark ATerafin, and if that man met his end at our hands — or mine — he would consider it a personal affront. I believed that we were meant to kill the creature posing as a member of the Order, given the room and the environment in which the interview was to take place, but I did not wish to anger either the fox or his cub.

"It did not immediately occur to me that I would be facing a demon. I asked because I was certain Kallandras of Senniel could kill the man, and I wished to avoid enmity with one who is…not quite human."

"It is always wise to avoid engendering the enmity of the wild creatures," Meralonne replied, nodding as he set his pipe alight. "But there are circumstances that might prevent it, survival being one. Tell me, who is the cub of whom you speak?"

"He introduced himself as Jarven ATerafin."

Both the mage and the bard exchanged a glance. The mage then pinched the bridge of his nose before he brought pipe to lips.

CHAPTER FOURTEEN

Ansel had no intention of sleeping until he was certain Heiden would wake, and the encounter with the demons had stilled some of the internal rage that kept him moving, often to disastrous consequences.

But Ansel had been injured; his eyes were ringed with dark circles, his color pallid. Alex therefore entered the room. "I'll watch over him," he told the Bowgren Hunter. "He isn't the only person who was injured."

Ansel snarled, but managed to keep words out of the low, guttural sound. His hands were fists—trembling fists—as he forced himself to take a deep breath. He exhaled slowly. "You need as much sleep as any of us."

"I didn't carry Heiden from the merchant compound to the palace. Neither did Max. If I flag, he'll take over. He's in our room," Alex added, "sleeping."

"I won't sleep anyway. There's no point."

"The doctor said Heiden should wake on his own; he told us what to look for when he does. I'll wake you the minute he wakes." Alex failed to add that he'd probably heard more of the medical instructions than Ansel had, but Alex had always been the diplomat.

Nenyane thought it a waste of time, but managed to keep that thought to herself. Her expression made it clear, but she didn't step into the room. Neither did Max; Alex had been entirely truthful. Max had headed straight for bed—and given it was Max, was probably snoring two seconds after he fell over.

Stephen thought Ansel might accept Nenyane's help, but Nenyane wouldn't offer it. She had no intention of leaving Stephen, and Stephen had none of the energy required to persuade her. He understood that for Nenyane, the night of the demonic attack was not over, even given the obvious daylight streaming in through windows. The demons had attacked in numbers, and they had made no pretense of mortality; they had removed the masks anonymity required.

There had to be a reason for that decision.

We don't know enough to even make a guess, Stephen told his hunt-brother. *But if demons continue to attack, we're going to need more sleep. Max and Alex were running Hunter's trance between each other all night; they're almost as exhausted as Heiden and Ansel. I'm going to sleep.*

Nenyane snorted; she knew Stephen well. He was going to bed, yes, but the likelihood that he would actually sleep was small. Nenyane required far less sleep than her Hunter. She had no intention of sleeping at all.

HEIDEN WOKE TWO HOURS LATER. Alex woke Ansel as promised; Stephen could hear steps in the hall as Alex retreated to the Elseth rooms. The Maubreche Hunter almost rose, but Nenyane opened the door and slid out of their room to catch Alex before a door separated them.

Alex immediately offered a report; he knew, if Stephen were awake, he would hear it as well. "His eyes are normal and he doesn't seem to have any unusual weakness of limb. Ansel's wound was shallow."

"Even if it weren't, he wouldn't leave."

Alex nodded. "What do you think is happening?"

"We need to speak with Illara—with Meralonne. If anyone can answer that question, it's him."

"Or the bard?"

Nenyane exhaled. "Or the bard."

"Is Stephen going to be safe here?"

"I don't know. But this—it's like a prelude to war."

Alex yawned his way through a nod. "We're going to need some sleep to fight it."

"Get some sleep. I'll be standing guard."

Alex looked at her, but said nothing. He nodded instead, and headed to his room.

18TH DAY OF EMPERAL, 429 A.A. THE KING'S PALACE, KINGDOM OF BREODANIR

Lord Declan was not at the breakfast table at the appointed time, but breakfast was. So, too, were the residents of Hunter's Redoubt, although none of them—with the exception of Nenyane—looked as if they'd slept at all. Servants were somber and fewer in number.

Ansel was silent for much of breakfast. He lifted head three times as if determined to speak, but words eluded him. Heiden had taken another facial blow in the brawl in the merchant compound and the bruise was a deep purple, but he seemed calmer than he had since they had first met him. He also seemed taller; his shoulders were no longer hunched. That, more than anything Ansel might have said, spoke to Ansel's state of mind.

It was Alex who broke the silence that had settled across the table. "The magi felt that Bowgren faces difficulties far more severe than either Elseth or Maubreche."

Ansel nodded.

"Have you reached a decision?"

Ansel did not pretend to misunderstand. "If the King gives his permission for our departure, we'll return to Bowgren." He hesitated, and then added, "I'm not certain Lord Bowgren will be open to the idea of strangers in our territory."

Heiden glanced at Ansel, but remained silent.

"Would strangers include us?" Alex asked.

"He'd accept Hunters in an emergency." This was said with hesitation. "It's permission for the mage and the bard that might cause difficulty.

"If the King commanded it, he would accept aid. If Lady Bowgren decided that the presence of a member of the Order of Knowledge and an Imperial bard were within her purview of governance, he would likewise accept. Reluctantly." Ansel swallowed. "If you believe the two are necessary, that's their best chance of being granted permission. Lady Bowgren has deep respect for Lady Maubreche and Lady Elseth."

"Not your mother," Heiden added.

Alex grimaced, but nodded. Espere was not, and would never be, a good governor. Her existence as Lord Elseth's wife caused friction in certain quarters. It always had. Wives had responsibilities. Lord Elseth's wife refused to learn or carry any of them. Their mother was not of a mind to care; in that, she was very much like Lord Elseth.

Lady Elseth trained Alex's sisters in the responsibilities of governance; she was already searching for a suitable wife for William, and that wife would eventually undertake Lady Elseth's duties. She had warned William that she was not young and she deserved to retire in peace; William was young for marriage, but not for the preludes to that eventual union.

Alex was grateful that she had focused that attention on William, who was a mere five hours older than Alex and Max. William accepted it with about as much grace as their father did when their grandmother was displeased: he met her head on. Alex and Max preferred to avoid what they could, and Lady Elseth was not so fit that she could chase them down if they managed to get a head start. William never ran from her. It was beneath his dignity.

He shook his head. "Sorry—I started to think about Lady Elseth."

"Is that why you're paler?"

"I love her. She loves us. But she is the most terrifying person in all of Elseth."

Ansel actually smiled. "The same is true of Lady Bowgren." No one was surprised. They waited, the unasked question hanging over the table like a pall.

Heiden answered it. But he answered it without the fear that had characterized their first meeting with the Elseth brothers. "If Lady Bowgren considers both mage and bard indispensable, and if Lord Bowgren can be distracted from the foreign nature of the two guests, we believe we can have you enter Bowgren as our personal guests. You at least will be Breodani, and he will not consider your presence an insult or a threat."

"Because he hasn't met at least one of us yet," Max said.

Nenyane glared at him; Stephen laughed. She transferred the glare to Stephen.

"We will introduce you as friends met in Hunter's Redoubt. He will understand that all of you are in a position similar to Lord Ansel and me. If he questions you, say as little as possible. The advantage for us is that he is likely not to worry about Bowgren's perceived strength—or weakness—in any of your eyes."

Stephen considered Ansel's response, Ansel's sensitivity. Lord Bowgren no doubt shared it, when he cared to do so.

"You want us to come?" Nenyane asked Ansel. Stephen grimaced; Alex had deliberately chosen his words with care to avoid tripping over Ansel's defensive response. Nenyane crushed the value of his efforts, as if she were unaware of the work it took.

But Ansel surprised both Stephen and Alex. He had never cared for Nenyane. It had been a miracle—and not a small one—that the two had failed to come to blows yet. They expected Ansel's reaction to be swift and dismissive. They were wrong on both counts.

Ansel bowed head for a long beat, but no anger followed it, and when he lifted face again, an expression they had never seen clearly had transformed his features. "Yes," he said. "If it weren't for you—if it weren't for your interference—I might have lost Heiden. If it weren't for you, the demons would have killed us all. You gave me back the only thing that mattered." He shook his head. "*I* wouldn't have come for me. I wouldn't have risked my life for me. I was stupid with anger. Why did you?"

Nenyane shrugged. "We came for Heiden. Or with him. He doesn't know the city any better than Stephen or I, but Alex does."

"And after?"

"Did you expect us to just walk away and let you both die?"

"I would have."

Nenyane snorted. "I don't believe you."

Ansel's jaw tightened, as did his fists. Stephen glanced at Heiden; he had come to understand that Heiden was the weathervane. Heiden, however, remained calm as Ansel forced his hands to relax. "It doesn't matter. I couldn't, now. I owe you all too much." His jaw relaxed as his gaze sought the surface of the table. "I've had time to think."

He hadn't taken the time to catch up on missing sleep, given his color.

"I care about Bowgren. Until Barrett died, I *was* Lord Ansel, as I was raised and trained to be. After Barret's death..." He shook his head. "Nothing seemed to matter to my father. And the loss of the village, the loss of villagers in the village we managed to half-save, seemed like it was part of that death, that loss. There was nothing we could do. Nothing we'd been trained to do.

"We knew — Mother told us — that all of Breodanir suffered from the same inexplicable dangers. As if that made it, or would make it, any better." He exhaled. "It didn't. But knowing that we can somehow fight whatever it is we can't see and can't predict *does*. I didn't believe in your demons."

"And now?"

"I'm arrogant enough to believe what I see with my own eyes. If I can believe in your demons, I can believe in the other things you've said. You think we have a chance to somehow stem our losses before they become immeasurably worse. You believe that if we don't, we'll lose not only Bowgren, but Breodanir."

"I want to go home. Now. I want to face the things that threaten Bowgren."

Nenyane nodded. "We'll need at least the mage to have a fighting chance."

"Without him, do we have any chance?"

She nodded. "But it's a very, very small chance, and it requires perfect timing, perfect placement. To even know what the timing or placement would be, we have to be in Bowgren." She hesitated.

"Tell me," Ansel said, his gaze intent.

"In Maubreche, I could sense the movements of the land, the incursions of wilderness."

Ansel nodded. Skepticism and resentment were absent.

"But in Maubreche, we needed Corwin to close them, to stop the turnings. Lord Maubreche," she added. "The Lord rules the land, and the land — mundane in all visible respects — can hear the ruling voice most clearly. Stephen *could* interfere, but not with the same chance of success. Maubreche didn't hear me at all."

"Then how did you hear the wrongness?"

Nenyane shrugged; Ansel had unintentionally stepped on the one vulnerability she had: her own ignorance. Her lack of memory. "I can't explain it. It's like there's a constant sound, a subtle sound — like breathing or heartbeat. I can hear it when it changes."

"Distance?"

"Almost anywhere in Maubreche." She exhaled, pushed herself back into her chair, and folded her arms. "I don't know that I'll be able to hear Bowgren in the same way. I have some hope, but I don't know. I certainly couldn't hear the shifting landscape beyond Maubreche's borders when I was *in* Maubreche. I might be of vastly less use in Bowgren."

Ansel shook his head. "I saw you fight that demon."

"The land isn't shifting at the command of demons, though." She glanced around the table. "Are we going to see Lord Declan today?"

Stephen shrugged. "Why?"

"We need to pack, and we need to plan."

"We've planned," Ansel said, rising. "We need the mage and the bard to petition the Queen; we need the Queen to petition the King and Lady Bowgren. We need the King's permission to leave the city for Bowgren. We need to arrive when Lord Bowgren is...unhappy with the foreign visitors, because if he is, you'll be Breodani, and far more acceptable." He turned to Heiden.

Heiden actually smiled, swollen lips moving awkwardly. "We don't know how to contact the mage," he said. "Or the bard. The Order of Knowledge is our best bet. But I think Nenyane has the best chance of reaching out to them and being answered immediately."

Nenyane grimaced, but nodded agreement.

"And I think, if the King is reluctant, Stephen can talk to the Priests and seek their influence." Heiden frowned. "Will either Maubreche's or Elseth's permission be required?"

Alex shook his head as Stephen said, "No." He rose. "We may not become Breodanir Hunter Lords in our own right," he said, voice soft. "But what we do here will *matter*. I am Breodani, born, bred, raised. I can fail to be Hunter Lord by Breodanir's laws, but still respect those who make different choices." He smiled. "We all can."

All six of the problematic Hunters headed toward the library to continue their first real discussion since they had arrived in Hunter's Redoubt.

"No, really, Lady Bowgren is our spine. It's her we need to convince, and I'm certain we can," Heiden said. He sat cross-legged on one of the library chairs, elbows on the study table. "She's always been reliable." He grimaced, and added, "Lord Bowgren was reliable for all of my life in Bowgren."

"Until Barrett died." Ansel's voice was soft. "But my mother hasn't changed. She's become more herself."

"Terrifying?"

"Pretty much. Until we were called to the King's City, Heiden and I ran most of the hunts for the villages; my father found hunting difficult after Barrett's death."

"How does she feel about outsiders?"

Ansel shrugged. "Less hostile than Lord Bowgren. Probably. She has her pride. But she'll accept you as our friends. Father won't unless he also accepts the mage, which will focus his dislike."

Stephen nodded. He was writing a letter for delivery to the Order of Knowledge, and had started it four times.

Ansel came back to the table with a large book in hand. "Bowgren," he said. He lay the book open across the table, revealing a large map. "This is our demesne."

Nenyane, seated until then, rose. "Where were the Bowgren villages that were lost or harmed?"

Ansel lifted a hand. Alex winced as he brought his fingers in contact with the aged pages, but kept his peace. "Here. This was Amberg, or where Amberg was."

"And now?"

"Forest. The trees were not familiar to us."

Nenyane cursed.

"And the half village?"

"Clearbrook—it's the closest village to the border of Breodanir in our demesne."

"Amberg's in the center, at least on the map."

Ansel nodded again. "If we've faced other, similar losses since we left, I haven't been informed. Would you consider the creature we're meant to hunt somewhere between?"

"If the wilderness were simple geography, yes. The wilderness that encroaches is in Bowgren—but the where of it is less easily pinpointed."

Stephen's attention was split between map and letter.

"Can I ask a question?" Heiden spoke, voice soft. He looked at Stephen, but waited for Stephen's nod. "Why are the demons trying to kill you?"

Nenyane answered well before Stephen could form a cogent response, his relationship with his father was so complicated. "He's Bredan-born. Bredan-born. By Imperial standards, by the standards of the Order of Knowledge, he's the only legitimately god-born son of Bredan."

Heiden nodded.

"He can—if he so chooses—oathbind. The binding is permanent, and once laid, it cannot be revoked. Those who break oaths consecrated by that binding, die."

"The demons want to kill him for that?"

"The binding isn't confined to mortals. It can be used against immortals, and against the denizens of the wilderness."

"Can it be used against demons?"

"I don't know. In any true sense of the ancient world, the demons are considered dead."

"They're not dead."

"They're not alive either. It's an interesting question, and one to which I have no answer. The mage might, but it's been a very long time since an oathbinder existed who could use their god-born abilities. Before Stephen of Elseth died, no oathbinders were born, and those that have been born since haven't survived."

"But the demons clearly believe that the power can be used—either against them, or against the god they serve—in some fashion."

Stephen focused on the letter. When it was done, he rose. "I'll see this sent by messenger service." He left the room quickly, gaze on the floor.

18TH DAY OF EMPERAL, 429 A.A. THE KING'S PALACE, KINGDOM OF BREODANIR

Jarven ATerafin observed the King's Palace from just beyond the gates. A steady flow of people moved through them in either direction, a large number of them in the greens that denoted the nobility of this small Western kingdom. He was aware of the economics of the country from an Imperial standpoint, but the customs themselves had eluded him; they were not a significant source of trade or wealth for House Terafin. He had attempted to alleviate the annoying ignorance with which his prior life had saddled him.

It had been literal decades since Jarven had hunted people. The last time he had chosen to do so, he had done so not out of necessity, but curiosity; he had, at that time, established his competence to the satisfaction of his employers, but wished to see whether or not the man he had chosen to replace him was at least as competent in this one regard.

Extension of life notwithstanding, he found himself rusty. This contributed greatly to the souring of his mood. From his office in the Merchant Authority, he had command of men and women who were — at this remove — possibly better at this than he. Avoiding it because it seemed too much of a bother was one thing; failing was *quite* another.

He did not attempt to console himself; it was an annoying waste of time. He had thoroughly explored the streets of the city. He had more thoroughly explored the Order of Knowledge, and retained an almost architectural understanding of its layout. There were rooms into which he could not walk, walls through which he could not easily pass. He approved of these; he could not easily do either in his own Terafin offices unless he chose to step off the narrow, slender path he had walked to arrive in Breodanir. His test of his own office had been the safest way to gauge the limitations of his new abilities; it had also annoyed Lucille, which was both a pity and an amusement.

He could not, however, be certain how much of the difficulties he faced in his fledgling attempts to walk — literally — through walls were due to the interference of The Terafin; her influence touched the entirety of Averalaan, from the dwellings of the lowest of families to *Avantari*, the home of the Twin Kings.

He shared office space — in theory — with Finch ATerafin; she was at the heart of The Terafin's many councils. Her presence at the desk she occupied — beside his own, much neglected desk — might have made all of Jarven's attempted incursions more difficult than they might otherwise be. The Terafin's power was unknown, but according to the elder Jarven had chosen, for expedience, to call master, it was unlimited within the mortal boundaries of Averalaan.

Jarven was not within those boundaries now, but he sensed a power that felt almost similar in the heart of the King's Palace; the path the fox had set him on did not lead, on any of its multiple branches, through those gates; rather, it traveled around. In itself, this did not annoy him; he was too new to this particular game, this set of tools. It was information.

But the fox had set him one task. He was to find Rymark ATerafin, and end him. Should he accomplish that, the fox would grant the power he had chosen to withhold. Rymark ATerafin was proof of Jarven's competence. It irked him, even now, that such proof might be required, although it was not the first time in his life that his competence had been tested, studied, weighed. He had not, in truth, much appreciated any other such test either—but under every other similar scrutiny, he had been fully confident in the tools at hand.

Here, he had entered the field out of his depth, and was frustrated in the extreme to remain so.

One man, however, was not out of his depth; perhaps two. Meralonne APhaniel and Kallandras of Senniel. The latter was mortal, as Jarven had once been, but graced with talent and combat abilities that Jarven, born in the streets of the hundred holdings, had never honed to such an extent; the other was not. It had long been an unspoken belief that the mage was simply Other: he did not age in any appreciable fashion. But he disliked people in general and did not socialize so much that people would be forced to remark on it.

The Guildmaster of the Order of Knowledge made clear—she whose love of social games and social politics was as dour and faint as the mage's—that she would entertain no questions about Meralonne, and offer no answers.

Such ignorance was therefore accepted as a necessity if one wanted to treat in any fashion with the Order of Knowledge. It was not ignorance that would have been acceptable in any way to the *Astari*, and the *Astari* were beholden to none but the Kings. Even that was murky, a blurring of lines; they were responsible for the survival and safety of the Kings, and where possible, their direct heirs. Their opinion on reasonable risks often clashed with the Kings', and while the Kings did have final say, some decisions were considered either too minor or too important to be left in their hands.

Jarven therefore understood that Meralonne APhaniel was, if not immortal, then exceptionally long-lived. Records about the magi—all of the magi—existed within the heart of the *Astari* domain. Meralonne APhaniel had been part of the Order of Knowledge for well over a century, his joining shrouded in either secrecy or lax record keeping. There was some suggestion that he had been a member of the Order for longer than that, but difficulties within the *Astari*—which were to be expected in any group of people who had been given indirect permission to kill, when killing was deemed necessary—had destroyed some part of the earlier records. He could not attribute the lack of early information entirely to that destruction. Jarven had yet to meet a single person who enjoyed the keeping of those records. The current leader of the *Astari* was single-minded, humorless, and precise; modern records were far more standardized.

As a matter of course, Jarven had therefore always been aware of Meralonne APhaniel. That awareness had not prepared him for the current encounter, or set of encounters.

Meralonne was not human. He was not a man who had somehow unlocked the secret of immortality—a secret for which many, many men would have killed, Jarven among them. He was not a man at all. From the moment Jarven had subsumed the fox's blood—and the fox, his— he had seen the mage as the fox did. The fox called him *Illaraphaniel*, and treated him with a respect otherwise reserved for The Terafin.

Jarven understood why. He disliked the understanding, because it revealed certain weaknesses in his observational skills, and Jarven did not readily accept ignorance when it was his own. Nothing about Meralonne APhaniel appeared human to Jarven's new eyes, his second sight. He was luminous in presence, shrouded, always, in a light with which he seemed imbued. He was not measurably taller than he had once appeared, but if he was present, it was very, very difficult to look away from him. He commanded—demanded—awe, an emotion with which Jarven was pleased to be largely unfamiliar.

What Jarven could not understand was his service to Sigurne Mellifas. She was talent-born but mortal, and that mortality weighed heavily across her aged shoulders now. But she could, and did, keep Illaraphaniel on a loose leash; he served her. Why?

Jarven could be said to have served the Kings in the past; the *Astari* had, in its modern form, conformed to Jarven's design. He could be said to have served The Terafin, although that service was a loose alliance. He had had some hand in seeing Amarais Handernesse ATerafin take the House seat, and it had been, if fraught, not too difficult. Costly, yes —but the cost was to be borne by those foolish enough to stand against her. In neither case had Jarven felt either leashed or beholden.

The fox was the only master he had chosen to serve whose reins were tight; they cut into him, into his sense of self and the freedom that had always been his. He endured because he knew the greater power that waited.

And there was only one way to be granted that power. He had considered what the grant might cost him, and what it might cost to be free of the leash entirely. Jarven ATerafin had already begun to plan. But those plans depended in their entirety on finding the elusive

Rymark ATerafin. The fox had granted him a gift suitable for the hunt he had commanded Jarven endure as his final test: Jarven could scent Rymark on the wild wind. It carried those traces, and he had followed them.

But he had not been able to follow them to their first destination: the bitter, Northern Wastes. It was not the cold, it was not the lack of sustenance — any fool with minor organizational skills could counter either. No, it was the sense that the paths, narrow and delicate, which he had learned to walk, simply ended. There were places the wilderness could not traverse.

He could have stepped off that path, but he had not, for he had seen the Shining City in the distance; it seemed immeasurably large in the vision the fox had granted him, as if it lay at the heart of the world, shining like a second sun. He had been, as he was in the presence of Illaraphaniel, almost awestruck. Dwarfed by its majesty, he had accepted, on a visceral level, that this was not a place for one such as he.

He had resented it immediately, had found his footing, had strategically retreated. But it lurked within him, now. He better understood the folly of Rymark, and those who comprised the Shining Court, for he sensed, at a distance that was only barely safe, the god who was the heart of the city. He was uncertain that he could stand in the presence of that walking, waking god, and remain unchanged; that the god himself would not become the sole focus of his many skills, the sole object of his devotion. This, he accepted more readily. Ego had its place, but if one's ego stood in the way of observation and the acceptance of simple fact, it became a dangerous burden.

There was no such god in Breodanir.

Rymark's position had not changed for months. It was clear to Jarven, and to the master he served, that Rymark had fled Averalaan for the Shining City and the immediate safety it offered. Jarven had never expected Rymark to remain there; the fox had been less certain.

Rymark was human. Mortal. Of what use was such a mortal to a god? Rymark would return to the world Jarven traversed, a world made smaller and simpler by his compact with the fox. And when he did, Jarven would find him. Had, indeed, found him the moment he had begun to move. He had not expected that Rymark would return to Averalaan, and indeed the man had not; he had been stripped of the authority on which his power had, to this point, relied. He was a wanted fugitive, expelled from House Terafin.

But Rymark was not without power. His mage-born power was significant, but he had chosen early in his tenure with the Order to forsake honing it. He was a man in whom ego had weighed so heavily that he could not understand the necessity to labor as lesser men labored. He did, however, understand power, although Jarven was absolutely certain Rymark had no plans, no intentions, and no dreams of somehow surpassing his master to become lord and ruler.

Within Terafin, yes. Within the Shining Court, perhaps; there was lamentably little information that left that place, and very little of it could be considered reliable. Jarven was certain of only one thing: mortals served the Shining Court alongside the demonic *Kialli*. It was among mortals that Rymark might play the game of hierarchy.

The need to prove himself of value without the strings of Terafin at his loose command would drive him out of the Northern Wastes. What Jarven had not expected was that it would drive him here, to this small and largely insignificant Western kingdom. He had come to understand, over the course of two days, what was likely to be the cause: Stephen of Maubreche.

Stephen of Maubreche, who was significant not only to the Shining Court, but to Meralonne APhaniel, to Kallandras of Senniel. If it was in Rymark's interest to kill the boy, it was in Jarven's interest to remain on the fringes of that boy's activities. But Rymark himself had not come out to play; Jarven suspected that the demons sent into the streets of the King's City had been sent at Rymark's command.

All save one.

That one, Meralonne APhaniel had chosen to counter. Meralonne and the bard. Jarven had watched the two—demon and mage—collide in a flash of red and blue, a storm of sword and essence. He had intended to follow the man his master had chosen, in however dimin-ished a fashion, to mark, but he had been almost unable to look away from the aerial combat in which mage and demon engaged, as if he were seeing the blossoming of a deadly flower that would not be born again in his life, no matter how long that life might last. Beauty had seldom been part of the equations by which Jarven had planned a life many would consider long; he wondered if the lack had been due to the life he had led, or if the sudden appreciation was a gift from his master.

Regardless, he had been late to follow Gervanno di'Sarrado. Gervanno, however, had led him straight to Stephen of Maubreche. He felt he now had a dangerous amount of information with which to plan;

he knew enough to begin to see the rough outline of the plans of others, but not enough to make reliable plans of his own.

Had he relied on certainty, he would never have become Jarven ATerafin; timidity served a purpose, but it had seldom served his.

After the demon with whom Meralonne APhaniel clashed had withdrawn from the field of battle, and the demons in the streets had been destroyed, Jarven had lingered in the merchant compound, seeking news of Averalaan; he had listened to the drunken rants of merchant guards and the laborers who were excluded from the nobility of the kingdom; he had gained some understanding of the Hunter Lords who ruled.

And so he had come to the King's Palace, a place he could not easily enter from the paths he had learned with such difficulty to walk. He could circumnavigate the palace; its presence did not obliterate the pathway, as the Shining City in the distant North had. Entry, however, had not been barred in other ways, and while it irked him to be forced to abandon the slender paths of the wilderness, he had options his master did not.

But he had traveled lightly on his hunt, and would require suitable garments with which to approach the King's palace as ATerafin, and at that, the man in charge of Terafin's operations in the distant Merchant Authority. He therefore chose to return to Averalaan; he would need documents, clothing, and some time deliberating his approach as a powerful merchant.

He would return on the morrow.

18TH DAY OF EMPERAL, 429 A.A. MERCHANT AUTHORITY, AVERALAAN

"I feel that you are not happy to see me."

Finch's smile was pleasant, and involved very little warmth. "I am always happy to see you."

"You have not been taking care of yourself, have you? You look peaked."

Finch rose from the desk she occupied, its surface barely visible. She put aside—with meticulous care—the contract on which she'd been working the moment everything in the room flared a brief, bright orange. One of the volumes on the bookshelf remained that color even after Jarven had stepped—from nowhere—into the room. "If you wish to ease Lucille's anxiety, you might have used the door."

"I know full well how to use a door," he replied. "I have not fully mastered newer skills. It is *practice*, Finch."

She exhaled slowly. "Why are you here?" It was not to do the work that had accumulated; to Jarven at the moment, that work was almost irrelevant. She tried not to resent this, but it had been a trying morning, and the day had not notably improved with his presence.

"I require clothing, which of course does not necessitate a visit to the office, although clothing is here."

"And?"

"You have become suspicious of late. I approve."

"I have become overworked of late; I have little time for suspicion."

"There is always time for suspicion if you are doing your job properly." To Finch's surprise, he walked around his desk and took a seat that had been largely empty for months. "I require appropriate documents for entry into the upper echelons of the Kingdom of Breodanir."

Finch frowned. "Breodanir? Is that the Hunter kingdom?"

"Very good! It is indeed. Before you purse your lips any further, I will say that there has been some demonic activity in Breodanir recently; I do not think it has come to an end."

She wanted to tell him that demons were not a game, but to Jarven ATerafin they were. They were almost the only worthwhile game to a man who had made a life playing games he had oft barely survived. She exhaled again, and most of her lingering resentment left her as she did. "At least you're not bleeding."

"Finch."

"We had to replace the carpets after your last visit." Her shoulders relaxed. "Lucille was worried—seriously worried—for a week."

"It's what she does. It is why you like her. What are you looking at?"

"A contract with House Dezmael."

Jarven frowned. "Surely you should have been done with them by now?" He held out a hand, and Finch very carefully placed the heavily annotated and unsigned contract across his open palm.

"I am not Jarven ATerafin, and the lord of Dezmael is set in his ways. He does not treat me with the same respect he has always treated you."

"He is a fool."

"If he is a fool, he is a canny fool. I would far rather deal with foreign kingdoms than our native Houses at the moment."

"Very well. Breodanir exports fur and leather of high quality for the most part; it imports cloth, herbs, and some of the rarer pigments produced in Averalaan. It imports ore and gems as well, but we have fewer of those to offer, as much of our ore is already spoken for. If you wish to write a document that offers to open trade negotiations with the Queen of Breodanir's court of commerce on behalf of House Terafin, I will deal with Dezmael's contract."

"It is not the contract that is the problem."

"Very well. I will deal with Dezmael." Jarven rose. "It will afford me some amusement; the drafting of an initial trade request will not. I will take this…" he glanced at the document, his brows folding, "with me."

"Why do you need to open negotiations with Breodanir?"

"I need entrance to the King's Palace," he replied. She assessed the words without too much deliberation.

"Why?"

"I will be honest," Jarven said, stretching limbs, his expression a study of minor distaste. It was the expression that told Finch he might even tell her the truth. "I have been hunting a man known to you and your compatriots on The Terafin's council: Rymark ATerafin. Yes, yes, I understand the enmity. I am aware of the crimes for which he would pay had he not been wise enough to flee during the upheaval.

"He vanished from the city during the near-cataclysm, and reappeared far to the north and west of Averalaan; I have reason to believe he will not return unless and until Averalaan itself falls.

"The location to which he fled is not one I can enter, were I of a mind to take the risk of entry. But it is imperative that I reach him, and in the past week, he has moved to a location that is far more suitable to confrontation."

"The Kingdom of Breodanir?"

"Indeed."

"He is in the King's Palace?"

"Ah, no, possibly not. But there is a reason he chose to leave the absolute safety of the Northern Wastes, and that reason *is* in the King's Palace. There are rudimentary protections that surround the palace grounds. Were I the Eldest, I would have no simple way of breaching those protections; I am not. I have therefore chosen a more reliable, mundane approach." He walked to the wall, to a space between book-shelves, and placed a palm across it; the wall slid open to reveal a closet. "I will change and return."

"You will use the door."

"Yes, sadly. I will use the door. Dezmael no doubt has informants in the Merchant Authority. I wish to be seen here before I make my way to his office."

Dezmael did not have offices in the Merchant Authority; he had ambitions to change that state. Jarven knew this perfectly well.

"When I return, I expect to be handed the necessary document. I have not spent months waiting for Rymark to lose him because I dallied in Averalaan."

18TH DAY OF EMPERAL, 429 A. A. THE KING'S PALACE, KINGDOM OF BREODANIR

Lord Declan returned before dinner; he strode into the library, his face a shade of grey that implied sleep had been entirely denied him. If he was surprised to find his delinquent Hunters studying at the largest of the library tables in apparent amity, he lacked the energy to express it.

"I am gratified to see you take your studies seriously. We have been, as you are no doubt aware, almost fully occupied with the King's business; no suitable replacement teacher has been, or can be, found; the King himself has led our forays into the streets, and the Huntsmen of the Chamber are fully occupied. I am certain that you are aware of the reasons for that."

They nodded almost as one person.

"It has not escaped my notice that one of you has petitioned the King for permission to return home."

Silence.

"Nor has it escaped my notice that the rest of you have petitioned the King for permission to join him."

Ansel said, "It was my request. I asked the others to join me." He hesitated.

Stephen could see Heiden focusing on the surface of the table, and was almost certain it was Heiden who chose the words Ansel now spoke. But Ansel chose to accept the guidance, possibly for the first time since they had met.

"For what reason?"

"We're a burden to the King's Huntsmen during this crisis—but we wouldn't be a burden in Bowgren. I've had time to consider the words the mage offered us." Stephen waited for Lord Declan to point out that Ansel had avoided being part of that "us," but Lord Declan simply waited.

"The mage felt that Bowgren's crisis was of great import. He requires permission to travel to Bowgren to assess—and possibly aid in the containment of—the threat. I wish to accept that aid."

Lord Declan's nod was slow, but he did not point out that the acceptance of that offer was not contingent on Lord Ansel, but Lord and Lady Bowgren. "That does not require the presence of either the Maubreche or Elseth Hunters."

"No," Ansel said, returning Declan's grave nod. "But they are people I can trust, and they have capabilities that Bowgren does not currently have. I hope Bowgren can make use of them in time to prevent any more disasters like either Amberg or Clearbrook."

"And the four of you?"

Alex said, "We believe we can be of aid in Bowgren."

Lord Declan frowned. "Stephen is at risk. The security in the palace—"

"Is terrible, and you know it," Nenyane snapped. If Ansel was willing to speak with care and a new humility, Nenyane was not. "I'll be with Stephen. The mage will be with him. I believe the bard will also travel at our sides."

"The bard you attempted to kill." Declan did not mince words.

"It was a rare mistake," she replied, unfazed. Had she been Stephen, she would now be red to her ears. "The bard and I have reached an understanding."

An understanding?

He doesn't want you dead. Neither do I.

"You've no doubt spoken with witnesses in the merchant compound and perhaps beyond—you know that the three of us comprise far, far better protection than the Queen's Guard can offer." She folded her arms.

Ansel stared at her, brows rising and folding; she ignored it.

"He is Bredan's son," Nenyane continued. "Bredan believes it is to Bowgren Stephen must travel."

Stephen's gaze joined Heiden's as the tabletop became suddenly fascinating.

Declan exhaled. "We will discuss this further at dinner. I came to inform you that you will have guests then. Apparently one of you sent a missive to the Order of Knowledge; you have received a response."

LORD DECLAN DID APPEAR for dinner; clearly the guests were of enough import that his duties in the streets of the King's City could be held in abeyance for one simple meal. Or a complicated meal, as his pallor suggested this might become.

Meralonne APhaniel and Kallandras of Senniel were ushered into the room. To Nenyane's annoyance, they were flanked by Queen's Guards.

The palace is in a state of near panic, Stephen reasonably pointed out.

And its attendant, pointless suspicion. As Nenyane was frequently the loudest critic of security measures, Stephen found this almost ironic. He did not argue.

All six of the occupants of Hunter's Redoubt were seated at the table, in their best wear. They understood the debt they owed the bard; Nenyane had made clear that they owed an equal debt — or possibly a larger one — to the mage.

Both men offered nods to the gathered Hunters as they took their seats; the Queen's Guard then stepped back, joining the Maubreche dogs.

To Stephen's surprise, Lord Declan appeared to be annoyed.

He always looks that way.

Yes, but usually it's at us.

"Approaching the Queen was unnecessary," the Huntsman of the Chamber said, when all were seated. He must have been exhausted, to speak so bluntly.

"I did not approach the Queen," the mage said. "Be fair, Lord Declan. Kallandras did not approach the Queen. She approached him, as is her right; he is her invited guest. If she is not a Hunter, she governs, and she governs well; she could not but be aware of the difficulties the city faced, and is facing. She is well aware of the disturbances in the demesnes, and she wished to ask Kallandras if he had encountered difficulties on the road, both within and beyond your borders."

The bard nodded, his expression grave.

"The Queen's business is seldom so intertwined with the Hunt."

"She is not a Hunter, no. But she is aware of all of the reasons why the Hunt is necessary. She sent a message — in haste — to Bowgren."

"I am aware of that. You are not under my auspices. The Bowgren Hunters within the Redoubt are."

"I was unaware that her message touched upon them," the bard replied. "If it did so, it was not at my request. Nor was it at the request of Member APhaniel."

Lord Declan clearly wanted to argue, but had gained control of his anger. "You will travel to Bowgren, then."

"We have not received a reply, but if Lady Bowgren invites and accepts our presence, that is our intent." He glanced around the table. "We do not require your students; Lord Bowgren is within the demesne. We made no request to the Queen, and no request was made, to have the students under your care join us. If our request was misunderstood, I apologize; it was not my intent. Your students are young."

Nenyane instantly bristled; Ansel's hands became fists. Both refrained from speaking, to Stephen — and Heiden's — relief.

Lord Declan slowly relaxed. "They are young, yes, although by Breodanir standards they are considered of age. Perhaps you are therefore unaware that Lord Ansel has petitioned the King — during this crisis — for permission to return to Bowgren."

Kallandras nodded; Stephen noted that he did not offer an actual answer.

"And perhaps you are also unaware that Lord Ansel has taken the unusual step of asking for the aid of his fellow students; they have likewise requested permission to join Lord Ansel in Bowgren."

At this, the bard's brows rose a fraction. "I was entirely unaware," he replied. "I am not certain that is wise."

The mage watched the conversation as if he was in line at a merchant's stall while the person ahead of him bickered about price, without apparent concern for the precious time of anyone else in line. His gaze turned to Nenyane.

"I am certain it is unwise," Lord Declan said, "given the apparent target of assassins and demons."

"Your opinion, Nenyane of Maubreche?" the mage asked, as if Lord Declan had not spoken.

"We're going." She folded her arms.

"Will it be safe?"

"As safe as it would be here."

"You will not have the Queen's Guard and the Huntsmen of the Chamber," Lord Declan said.

Nenyane, please.

"But we will have the company of a First Circle mage and Kallandras of Senniel College," she replied, softening her words with effort. "And we will have Lord Ansel and Heiden."

"Do you believe she is required?" Lord Declan's gaze was narrow as he looked at the mage.

The mage, however, had not looked away from Nenyane. His pale brow was furrowed, as if she were a pressing question to which he had not yet found a suitable answer. "She may well be. She is of Maubreche, yes, and huntbrother — but you will not find a better swordsman. It was Nenyane who dispatched the demon who had taken command in the streets. She did so without aid, protection — or injury.

"I did not lie, Lord Declan. The threat Bowgren faces must be contained. If it is not, Breodanir will fall. There is subtle strength in this city itself, but that strength is not mirrored beyond the palace walls, where knowledge of the strongest and earliest of the protections laid have been all but forgotten since the founding. The King's Palace might stand for some time, but mortals require sustenance, and there will be very little to be found if the rest of the country becomes the playground of *Kialli*."

Lord Declan did not insult Maubreche by asking Nenyane to part from her Hunter. "You do not require the Elseth Hunters."

Max stiffened, as did Alex, but it was far less obvious in the latter's case.

"The Breodani have customs and strengths," the mage replied. "My knowledge of these customs is superficial at best. I cannot say with certainty that they are necessary. But if Lord Ansel believes they will be, it is his opinion I would privilege over my own."

Lord Declan raised a single brow. "How unusually humble."

"We seek your opinion," the mage continued, untroubled by the lord's dry tone.

"You seek my decision," Lord Declan's correction caused Stephen to wince. "Please, avail yourself of the food; there is wine should you desire it. I must absent myself for a brief period of time." He rose, offered both guests a nod, and retreated. The Queen's Guard did not.

———

To no one's surprise, the mage considered that decision to be either positive or irrelevant, although he did wait until the door had closed on the retreating Huntsman of the Chamber before he made this clear.

"I apologize for the delay in responding to your message," he told Stephen. "I have been hunting. In Averalaan there are no demons, no *Kialli*. Dangerous creatures of power are human, and hunting them is forbidden by law." His smile was slender. "That is not the case in Breodanir, but those demons that remain, the King's Hunters can deal with; they are, none of them, *Kialli*.

"If you wish to move to Bowgren as a unit of six, we will have to take to the road; my ability to travel at speed cannot fully encompass us all." He turned to Stephen. "A man who was once in the employ of Maubreche is willing to be seconded as a guard for the duration of your tenure in Bowgren. He currently resides with Kallandras. Would that be acceptable to you?"

Before Stephen could answer, Nenyane said, "Yes. Gervanno will not be an encumbrance."

"I see his words were true; you are familiar with him."

She nodded. "He is a competent swordsman."

Pale brows rose. The mage glanced at the bard; the bard smiled. "He is, indeed."

"Very well. I will arrange transportation; the Order will cover the cost."

"Bowgren will cover the cost," Ansel said, voice both quiet and firm.

"I believe the decision would reside in Lady Bowgren's hands, not yours, even be you Lord Ansel of Bowgren."

"Yes. But I know my mother well. She is the head of Bowgren, and she is proud of her position and her governance, prior to the disaster. If we are to travel to Bowgren to aid Bowgren with…the turnings, she will cover the costs."

Heiden said, "You are a welcome stranger, but you are nonetheless a stranger. Trust Ansel's viewpoint in this."

"Very well. It might prevent pointless arguments with the people who oversee the Order's many account books. I will leave you now. Kallandras?"

"I will remain; we have barely had a chance to eat, and food may be less easy to come by on the road."

The mage snorted. "We are traveling with Hunters. Food will be the least of our problems."

"Hunting," Nenyane said, "takes time. Time is the one thing we don't have."

"It is not; we also lack information." The mage hesitated, which was unusual. "I believe there is a strong possibility that the lord we seek in the wilderness has had some contact with the Shining Court. It is unusual for the *Kialli* to announce their presence in such an obvious fashion. I thought it possible that the god we do not name had started to move with his armies; he has not.

"I thought perhaps the demons intended to destroy the surviving oathbinder—and indeed, they did make the attempt. But it was an attempt that suggested opportunism, not deliberation; had it been deliberate…" he trailed off. "They could not have known that Stephen would be in the city streets. They cannot easily enter the palace yet—the historical protections laid into the palace grounds by both Bredan and his god-born Priests require far more power than could be easily brought to bear."

"One of the god's generals was in the street," Nenyane said softly.

"I am aware of that." His gaze sharpened. "I ask, when you are in my presence, that you make no effort to engage the powerful—they are canny." When she failed to answer, he exhaled and reached for his pipe.

Heiden coughed.

"Yes?"

"It is not considerate to smoke while the meal is in progress."

"Pardon?"

"We ask that you refrain from lighting your pipe until we have finished eating."

The mage looked astonished, but his hands—pipe unlit—froze in place. To Stephen's surprise, he burst out laughing. "The rabbit has fangs!"

This didn't offend Lord Ansel, another surprise. He grinned at his huntbrother. "Most people think of Heiden as harmless and easily intimidated."

"As did I. I will have to reconsider my brief acquaintance with him."

The pipe bowl was neither filled nor lit. "There is another possibility. They chose to intervene because they are looking for something else entirely. I did not arrive with any particular secrecy; it is more than possible that they were aware of my presence."

"And your presence would justify an all-out attack?"

"I believe they felt it would be diverting, yes." He met Nenyane's gaze, then. He held it.

"But what could they be looking for, if not Stephen?"

"I am not at liberty to discuss it," the mage replied, his voice unusually grave. "But they are ancient enemies. In the way of enemies who have clashed many times over contested land, we understand each other better than we understand those who have never—and will never—go to war. They seek what I seek, if to different ends; my presence here might have served as an alert."

"And have you found what you both seek?" Alex asked, frowning.

"Perhaps. Things ancient, things wild, are not so easily assessed, even from a vantage of long familiarity."

"And this thing is ancient?"

"Ancient, yes—crafted long before the gods departed this world. Many of those who had a hand in that long-ago crafting have since perished. Their hands will never be raised in such a making again."

"What was it?"

Meralonne's smile was soft. "It is best not to speak of it. The walls have ears. I was leaving before I was interrupted and drawn back to the conversation here. I—with my pipe—will now absent myself. If Bowgren is to take up the cost of travel, things will be much simpler, but I have the freedom to leave as I please; none of you, given Lord Declan's dour expression, have the same uncomplicated freedom." He smiled at Heiden, plucking pipe weed out of his sleeves. He did not light the pipe as he left the room.

"HE TRUSTS YOU," Nenyane said to the bard, slumping back into her chair.

"He is not a person for whom trust is generally relevant," the bard replied. He treated her words with respect, which she found inexplicably annoying.

"He trusts you with Stephen. He wouldn't have left had you not chosen to remain."

"He trusts the protections woven into the ground upon which the King's Palace stands," the bard replied.

She glared, unblinking; he returned the gaze with a small smile. He did not, however, look away. Her expression darkened. "Don't play word games with me."

"That is possibly the only safe field of conflict on which I might hold my own against you."

Five pairs of eyes swiveled between the bard and Nenyane; she was annoyed that Stephen's were among them. "Do you know what he's searching for?"

"No. I have not asked; the business of Sigurne Mellifas is oft far too dangerous for a simple bard to know. When I receive my orders, I follow them; where possible I will come to the aid of those who have once been allies. This is one such occasion. But I was tasked with aiding Meralonne APhaniel should our paths cross and my aid be desired."

She had fallen silent any time Illaraphaniel spoke, straining to catch any syllable that might leave his mouth, his voice was so familiar. She had known him on sight, but the memory of him was almost as absent as any other memory of a time before Maubreche.

She desired to travel to Bowgren; she had not lied. Lying served no useful purpose, so it was not a skill she had cared to learn. Nor would it serve a purpose now. But the words the so-called mage had spoken remained with her, the echoes resounding and gaining volume on the inside of her head.

It wasn't memory; the gods had never been that kind. But it was a thread, a strand; if she gripped it tightly, she might be able to follow it to its source.

She might finally remember enough that she could know who she was.

CHAPTER FIFTEEN

When this room was occupied, it was never fully dark. Even when sun set and the deeper shades of blue came to dominate the night sky, all eyes that were turned toward the manor could see the dim light in the office in which Lady Bowgren fulfilled much of her official duties. In the past year the light seemed, to those with reason to be on the grounds past nightfall, persistent; they might have said it was never extinguished.

That had not always been the case, but since the death of Lord Barrett, the candles and lamps burned constantly, a sign of both vigilance and unrelenting grief. It was a grief that had cast a permanent pall over the demesne of Bowgren; even the village elders felt Barrett's loss keenly. It had been half a year since any flag or banner had not flown at half-height.

All were aware that no one felt the loss so deeply as Lord Bowgren himself.

Anton had yet to recover. Allise, closeted alone in her office, wondered bitterly in the lengthening hours of a day that had been far too long, if he ever would. She was well aware that some Hunters did not. Lord Bowgren's sole heir, her only son, had been sent to the King's

City at the King's request. Lady Bowgren hoped that time there would lessen his anger, his grief, his bitter rage. He was his father's son.

Anton had not cared to forbid it; he had enough sense left to understand that if Ansel failed to attend the Sacred Hunt when called, he would no longer be heir to Bowgren. But his resentment of Bowgren sat uneasily to one side of this certain knowledge. Had he the ability to go back in time, Anton would have refused the call. Barrett would be alive. Bowgren would not now be deprived of the only huntbrother Allise had known.

And Anton would no longer bear the responsibility or the pride of Bowgren; he would no longer face the possible death of his huntbrother every single year. It was the price paid for power, in these lands.

Allise's response was different—lesser, in Anton's opinion, as if his loss, his grief, had no equal, as if the sorrows of all others failed in all ways to measure up. She had been kept so busy by events and losses in Bowgren that she should not have had time to resent this, but resentment had its own cadence; she could not set it aside.

Not for Anton and Allise the reminiscence of happier memories, the grief-tinged nostalgia of all things that had been good in Barrett's time; for Anton good memories led to loss, to a certainty that all good had forever been shattered, destroyed. There was no value in memory when the person upon whom those memories relied would never again be present to create new ones.

She shook head and looked down at the missive she had received from the Order of Knowledge. She had the normal Breodani suspicion of outsiders, but she was also possessed of the hard-won pragmatism of one born—and taught—to govern. The events that had occurred, and continued to occur, in the wake of Barrett's death had no historical precedent within Breodanir. The information such an Order might bring to Bowgren, the possible solutions that might be derived from it, required setting aside prejudices. New catastrophes sometimes required new solutions.

She was—as were most of the ruling Hunter women—desperate for those solutions. Lord Bowgren, in the rare moments of lucidity drink and grief allowed, was likewise desperate. But his desire to strike back at the cause behind the shattering of his life could be silenced only by that drink—or so he claimed. Allise disagreed, but knew her opinion would gain no purchase. Not now, and perhaps not ever.

She faced the dissolution of the demesne to which she had devoted the entirety of her adult life, and for which she had borne a son; she wished bitterly that she had been capable of birthing another child. Even a daughter whose marriage might bring a different Lord Bowgren had been denied her.

She finished the letter she had been penning for hours. The detritus of failed attempts, she swept aside; crumpled parchment lay strewn haphazardly across floorboards and carpets, for she had a second letter to answer. On its surface, it was a far less politically difficult letter: it was from her son. Heiden's words had clearly been chosen with care, for he understood the shadow Barrett had cast upon all of his family. But Heiden could not have sent this letter without Ansel's knowledge, and he could not have penned the contents without Ansel's tacit permission.

She was not of a mind to allow her sons to bring home friends; her first reaction had been shock and even mild anger. But she was accustomed to both—and more, accustomed to showing no signs of either until she had taken the time to fully consider the events that had caused them. And surely the Breodani friends of her sons would be less fraught, less difficult, than the magi.

The magi were outsiders; their words might carry factual weight in very difficult circumstances, but they would carry almost none socially. No one expected the magi to be exemplars of Breodanir. These scions of Breodani demesnes might. Ah, but if these were friends her children had made at school—a school that underlined future failure and disgrace—perhaps they, too, were in no position to judge.

If Ansel was his father's son, Heiden was closer to Barrett's, although they shared no blood. He was closer to Allise than Anton, and had been adept at adopting the lessons, both taught and observed, of Lady Bowgren. If Anton had been isolated and broken by Barrett's death, Ansel was barely better; he had lost both of his fathers. His confusion, his dismay, had instantly given way to anger, to a need to lash out at the cause of his misery. To fight when there was nothing to fight. To somehow win against loss, against death, against facts of life which could not, could never, be changed.

Heiden, she thought, setting aside anger although it remained seated in the lines around eyes and the corners of her lips, needed friends. He needed support. She knew Ansel well enough to know that if he was willing to claim outsiders as friends, it must be at Heiden's urging. Heiden was not Hunter-born; he required company of something other than hunting dogs and the men obsessed with them.

And that was unfair. She knew it, and finally rose, the brief words granting her sons permission only passably finished. Almost, she understood the attraction drink held, for she desired some of that oblivion; her nights had been broken and sleepless, her mornings taken up in the governance of the villages, one of which had vanished without a trace, and one of which was now half-inhabited by statues.

Anton had done only the barest of hunting, and were it not spring, that would be a disaster—but she could see disaster looming in a future that was not far enough away she could set the worry aside.

The curtains, drawn back from the largest of bay windows, seemed to frame the low moon, but that moon was full. If prayer did not leave her lips, it was foremost in her mind. She stood on the precipice, and beneath her feet was the shattered remnant of Bowgren.

Silent, still, she gazed at the moon as if the moon might offer succor; it was a passing thought, a pointless desire, and she could not indulge it long. She took care to curl the letters she had managed to write, to slide them into messenger tubes, and to place them on the tray that meant they were to be delivered on the morrow.

And then, without hope, she lifted what remained of the candle and walked toward her bedroom, her shadows flickering against walls as she moved, her skin too pale, as if she were now a ghost that haunted the manor.

21ST DAY OF EMPERAL, 429 A.A. KING'S CITY, KINGDOM OF BREODANIR

"May I ask what you are doing?" Jarven could keep annoyance from his tone and his expression, but he had not yet learned the trick of not feeling it.

The fox did not look at Jarven; his gaze was firmly fixed on the streets. Or the people in it—in this case, a gaggle of almost genderless children who were running around one of the city fountains screaming their lungs out between bursts of laughter they did not bother to conceal. They were young, but they were young in the way of children anywhere. To Jarven's eye, they were irrelevant; to his ears, they were painful.

"I am observing your young."

"I understand that the use of the genitive in that sentence was meant as a generality, but must point out that they are, definitively, not mine."

"You are out of sorts today, aren't you?"

"I have had a trying day, yes." Walking the path between Averalaan and this tiny, primitive kingdom had been far more difficult than Jarven felt it should be; he could trace a path to the edge of the Northern Wastes with more ease. He did not tire as he had once tired before he had pledged allegiance to the forest elder, but that did not mean exhaustion had become a passing stranger.

"What gave you trouble? I scent no blood." The fox had not once given Jarven his undivided attention.

"If you must know, mortal politics and clothing."

"Mortal politics?"

"I greatly desire to kill a man in a city where murder is forbidden. Demons are far simpler."

"I'm not aware that that has ever stopped you before."

"Oh, it has. Perhaps you cannot see the difference from your lofty vantage. Why are you watching these children?"

"They are young," the fox replied. As this was evident, Jarven waited for a better answer, curious despite his irritation. "We were all young, once. Even you, although perhaps mortal memory is so flawed you have forgotten."

Irritation slowly vanished. "You remember your childhood?"

"I do. It is interesting to me. These children—I am certain you were similar—are not what they will become. To one such as I, observing them at a distance, I might never be able to discern the connection that binds them from this moment to the adults they will inevitably become. If I do not observe them for the entirety of their lives, I will not recognize them—I who forget nothing.

"And perhaps we are like that, we denizens of the ancient wilderness. Were you to have encountered me in what we will call, for the sake of convenience, my childhood—and should you have been lucky enough to survive such an encounter—you would not recognize me as I now am.

"You are living, breathing beings, and as such, you will know change."

"The Firstborn do not appreciably change."

"In the long, long years of their lives? They change, but your lives are too short to see those changes. You are a day of time measured against them; if I remain standing as I am, the children will not appreciably change while I observe them. But they will change, as all living things do." The fox shook himself; sun glinted off fur. It was not the sun under which the children played. "But perhaps you are correct: it is not the time for this."

"I would know more about your childhood."

"Why? It is gone; it cannot be retrieved."

"As you are wont to point out, my life, even extended by your grace, cannot encompass the truth of what you are, what you were, what you will become. But knowledge? Knowledge can be ageless. There are seeds in it, roots in it, that might extend to the time given me."

"Perhaps. Mortals are quick to think, quick to react, but they are not always wise. And they burn so brightly." The fox exhaled.

Jarven's irritation returned, strengthened by the noise. He was not dressed well for this part of town, or rather, was dressed too well. He stood upon the path, one foot in the forests over which the fox kept watch, and one in the King's City; he found it the most difficult balancing act of a long life spent living on different edges. In his hands, he carried a scroll case. It was not the balancing or the impending visit to the King's Palace that annoyed him, now.

"You have been distracted since you encountered Gervanno di'Sarrado."

"Have I?"

"Appreciably so."

"Ah." The fox shook himself. "Perhaps you are right. I should not have bitten him; I should not have imbibed even a trace of his blood."

"If I recall correctly, to do so with me you required not only literal blood but a binding contract of near subservience."

The fox wheeled to face Jarven, eyes wide, brows—silver against gold—raised. "Is *that* what you call it?"

"Perhaps I am being less than ideally tactful. I do not believe you demanded such an agreement with the Annagarian."

"No. But he is not you; he is not my cub."

"May I ask why you chose to mark him?"

"It was a whim, Jarven, nothing more."

"And now you watch street urchins and ruminate on childhood?"

"You are being almost disrespectful."

"Gervanno di'Sarrado is one of those damnable men who prize honor above good sense," Jarven replied. "It is obvious on first glance; a second is not required. On the backs of such men are senseless wars built and carried."

"I agree," the fox replied. "But there is beauty in things that are not practical; beauty in things that exist as they are. Mortals are oft obsessed with their narrow definition of beauty; they find the oddest things compelling. We, too, find beauty in odd places. Perhaps we find beauty in the things that we cannot, and will never be, ourselves.

"Men like Gervanno understand service in a way that neither you nor I can, or ever will. There is a purity in that. I lay no compulsion upon him, make no demands of him."

Jarven was careful now not to roll his eyes, as he had the elder's attention. He was well aware that his master had made demands of Gervanno, and if nothing else of note could be said about the Southerner, the man was not fool enough to deny them.

"As I said, it was impulsive. I did not wish to see him lost to the wilderness. Such men do not easily find a home or a place for themselves in the wilds, and much beauty can be destroyed or lost. I have often found it remarkable that their very essence relies upon other mortals; that others become the setting in which they shine the brightest.

"I have never understood them," he added softly. "But in my time, I have found them oddly moving. Do not make that face. I have offered him no power, no bargain, have laid no geas upon him—I did not have the time. But yes, I am aware of him, aware of the attenuated echo of his presence.

"If you are worried that I might favor him, remember: I chose you. We are alike."

Jarven said nothing.

"Come, come. If your time has been extended, it is still short; do not waste it on pointless rumination." He waited for a reply, and when none was forthcoming, he added, "It bores me."

Jarven offered the fox a bow, brief but deep.

"Where is your quarry?"

"In the city somewhere. I have only barely slept; I can sense his presence but the traces of it have not yet led me to him. I assumed I would find him in the Order of Knowledge, which was optimistic.

Rymark was ever vain and pretentious, but he was never a complete fool."

"Not complete, no—but he chose to stand against my Lord, and that takes a particular lack of intelligence. How do you intend to proceed?"

Jarven's smile was lazy. "I intend to introduce myself to the Queen, of course."

"I fail to understand. She is not your queen."

"No. But there is one place in this city which I cannot enter from the paths you have taught me to walk; I will resort to entering it the regular way."

"I see. Why would you suspect you might find your quarry there?"

"He is, as I said, vain and pretentious. And it appears that hunters such as I—new immigrants to the wild lands—cannot simply enter. He no doubt entered as I will have to enter."

"He is not as you are."

"You are certain?"

The fox lofted nose. "I am *absolutely* certain. He might make a meal should the wilderness hunger, but he bears the taint of the dead like a shroud of ashes."

Jarven frowned. "Do you think he has somehow been granted some part of the *Kialli's* power?"

"No, of course not. They cannot grant that power now. When they were alive, it was not theirs to grant, and dead, they cannot imbue the living in such a fashion, even if they so desire. I merely meant the scent of close association lingers on him. It is unpleasant.

"But do not let me keep you," the fox added, as he turned once again toward the inexhaustible gaggle of screaming children.

FINCH HAD PERSONALLY SEEN to the document carried so carelessly within its protective scroll case. Jarven had perused it; if he trusted Finch's work ethic and competence, there was only so much trust one could expect from an intelligent man. He had considered his options with care. In the past, he might patiently allow plans to come to fruition over the course of a decade, watching as all of the small elements at last fell into place. He had been granted time—time and the strength, if not the appearance, of youth—but he was not foolish enough to believe he had a decade. If optimistic, he felt he had two years. By nature, Jarven was not an optimist.

He left the expensive hotel suite that he'd chosen to book under the auspices of House Terafin; he was dressed to meet royalty, as he had oft dressed in the past. He had considered the elegant flamboyance of clothing with care; he knew, better than anyone, the statement it made. It was not a quiet statement, and if Rymark was somehow resident in, or welcome in, the King's Palace, word would reach him.

Jarven smiled at the thought.

The head of the Terafin merchant arm was a power, and meant to be taken as one. Rymark had never been graceful; no doubt he nursed bitter resentment in this small kingdom. The power he once sought so clumsily was now forever out of reach. He would be, should remain, irrelevant. But Rymark was the target and test chosen for Jarven by his wild master. He was not the target chosen by the woman who ruled Terafin, and in any other circumstance Jarven would have allowed Rymark to slide into the irrelevance his choices had earned.

In truth it had been many, many years since Jarven had killed a man, fewer since he had arranged for a man's death. He wondered how out of practice he was; skills atrophied without judicious use. The thought did not displease him. Decades of House Terafin had blunted the edges his early life had sharpened.

He had a carriage called while he considered Finch's documentation. She understood that, should these documents be agreed upon, House Terafin would be committed to what they offered; she had therefore been cautious and overly conservative. But she had allowed Jarven as much flexibility as she responsibly could; there were several possible avenues of trade, and trade agreements, that could be offered, depending on the outcome of the audience Jarven sought.

Jarven would not, of course, be ushered immediately into the presence of the Queen. He knew enough to know that it was she who effectively ruled; the King was almost a figurehead. All decisions of government with regard to foreign nations were the Queen's dominion. But he expected that he would have to navigate the complexities of bureaucracy; it was a gauntlet with which he was familiar, and at which he was master.

He only required entrance into the palace. If Rymark was not to be found there, he would not be found anywhere in this city. Jarven knew; he had searched. He had traveled to the edge of the Northern Wastes hunting, and had been bitterly disappointed to stall there, seeking safe passage. Or, in the end, any passage that would not be instant death.

But Rymark had traveled south, and Jarven had once again found an ember in the ashes of that hunt. His fear—which was perhaps too strong a word—was that Rymark could somehow traverse the distance between the Wastes and this kingdom; that he would elude pursuit yet again. Jarven did not consider such flight a failure on his own part, but what he wanted could not be achieved if Rymark survived.

He cursed the choice of target, but did so silently; he did not understand it. Rymark was a mage, yes, but not one of great significance; his power had been political, and those fangs had been extracted. The fox, however, would not be moved. Rymark had harmed Jewel in some fashion, and he must pay: the lesser creatures must be made to understand the cost of offending the lord the fox served.

The eldest had said they were alike, he and Jarven; Jarven could not see how. He had served the Twin Kings and The Terafin in his time, but his service had been, as all things were in his life, conditional. Where it was of benefit to himself, he accepted the duties; where it was not, he slid out from under them, seeking greater challenges, greater flexibility.

The fox did not. He served Jewel. She had made no command that the fox, or any of the others who claimed her as lord in the depths of the wilderness, seek and punish those who had betrayed her. He highly doubted the few hours a day she was given to rule had a moment to waste on such edicts. This hunt was not her desire, nor her command.

But the fox felt it; the *Arborii* felt it. What they heard, Jarven could not hear—although he could now hear the whisper of The Terafin's name when he walked the forests she had claimed. He had, by the painful compact between himself and the eldest, become stronger; he was more powerful now than he had ever been. But he knew that the full depth and breadth of the power granted by the association was being withheld until he passed this test.

Had the demonic attack in the streets of the city not affected the security and caution of the palace guards, he might have assumed an alias and entered as a trade envoy of the House he served. And while Jarven could see holes in the security, and a laxity that implied the King had never faced serious threat of rebellion, he nonetheless considered them acceptably competent. He therefore chose to forgo subtlety.

He was Jarven ATerafin, head of the merchant operations in House

Terafin. Rymark, if present in any capacity, would hear his name. Rymark would attempt to gain information: what did Jarven want? Why was Jarven here, now?

But Rymark had never accorded Jarven the respect that was his due. To be fair, very few members of House Terafin did, which had never bothered him. It was always safest to be underestimated, if one cared for safety.

He waited at the gates while the guards examined his credentials; he exited the carriage when they asked. He was diffident, careful, and neutral. But he could feel it, even when he had been seated in the carriage, his feet upon the carriage floor and not the stones of the road: he was entering a territory that did not, and would never be, traversed by the elder. It was owned. It was claimed.

He did not hear a name, but the certainty grew when he was asked to disembark and submit himself to inspection. When his boots touched stone he felt, for a moment, that his entire body had been slapped by an enormous hand; it was bracing, but damaged nothing, not even his dignity.

Yes, he thought. This was the only way to gain entrance to a very unusual building. He wished to explore while he had permission to enter, but was fully capable of denying simple desires. If he explored, he might bypass all attention and notice, some of which he wanted.

Come, Rymark. Come find me.

KALLANDRAS OF SENNIEL COLLEGE made clear that bards were almost elemental in their charm, in the influence they exerted in social situations. Gervanno's grasp of Weston had improved during his time with the caravan, but it required an element of concentration that ill-behooved the guard he had become. He understood that his position was largely deception; Kallandras had no need of guards and perhaps, should the worst happen in the palatial halls, it would be Gervanno who required protection.

But if the position itself was meant as polite fiction, Gervanno nonetheless felt the need to live up to it. Guards were one step above servants, in that they were momentarily visible, but a good cerdan neither demanded nor wanted attention. His clothing was meant for the merchant roads; he had done his best to clean it, but even newly made it

had not been equal to the clothing he saw here. He was therefore forced
to let demeanor cover the lack.

He was observant; all those graced with the honor of guarding their
Tors or Tyrs were, by necessity if not by nature. Observance in the
Empire generally meant suspicion. In the Dominion, it meant one had
to study the flow and movement of power within a given environment.
One could not ask one's lord who was, and who was not, significant; the
question would be a gross overstep, and one from which only the very
young and indulged were likely to recover.

The Kingdom of Breodanir seemed unguarded to Gervanno. People
spoke, often loudly; they laughed too much, moved too much; there was
a sense of a lack of restraint. He had felt this ever since he had crossed
the border as a caravan guard, but had initially assumed it was simply a
difference in hierarchy, in class. Those born seraf were open in such a
fashion among their own kin, their own kind.

His observances as guard had shifted that opinion. There were no
serafs in the Empire—or none by that name. The poor who were nonetheless free felt the lack of gold just as keenly as they might the lack of
freedom; it was not so in the Dominion. In the Empire, however, lack of
status, lack of the blood granted to those of noble birth, was far more
subtle a demarcation than it would have been in Annagar.

Here in Breodanir, the titled mingled with the merely wealthy; here,
even the Queen, in whose large, open court he stood guard, smiled and
indulged merchants and diplomats. And here, the man he theoretically
guarded moved among the gathered dignitaries as if he was the most
welcome of guests. He did not belong here; his demeanor suggested
humility and charismatic deference. He could use his words as benediction, and did so disarmingly.

Gervanno had heard the rumors and the stories of those born with
the curse of voice: that their voice might overpower even the strongest
of men, reducing the martial prowess of the greatest of warriors to an
irrelevance.

All stories had made of those men simple monsters, simple carica-
tures; while some stories spoke of the charm they might wield, it was
always to dire and nefarious ends. He did not doubt that some truth lay
at the roots of these old morality tales, but understood that monsters
were, in times of peril, best set against monsters—and demons, which
figured far larger in the stories of his childhood, were monsters.

But Kallandras of Senniel seemed, to Gervanno's eye, to be a man.

Yes, he had been told that demons—the most dangerous of them—could appear as men, and did; that their beauty was deceptive and used to effect against the weak. Kallandras did not seem ageless to Gervanno, but there was a grace to all of his movements that implied strength.

He considered the people to whom the bard spoke, but there seemed to be no obvious pattern to his various encounters that Gervanno could yet discern. He was certain it existed; certain it was his own ignorance that prevented the pattern from becoming clear. Ignorance, as his father used to say, could be alleviated.

He left off observation for a brief moment when the bard approached a man he recognized. Even dressed as he was in the finest of silks, with the subtle weight of expensive jewelry girding his fingers, Jarven ATerafin was unmistakable. Gervanno watched, closing the distance slightly; his hands remained at his sides as he drifted into the range of their conversation.

"I am delighted to find you here," the fox's servant was saying.

"And I am surprised to find you," Kallandras replied, his voice grave, his lips curved in slight smile. "I had heard you had traveled to the North."

"Oh?" A brief flash seemed to spark from Jarven's dark eyes. "I am disappointed."

"The Terafin mentioned it."

Jarven grimaced. "Her elevation has not changed her base nature; she has always been ineffective at deflecting inquiries."

"The inquiries were not made by me," the bard replied, smiling.

"You are here at the Queen's invitation, no doubt."

"Indeed. It is not the first time I have visited the kingdom."

Jarven looked past Kallandras, his eyes narrowing. "You have a companion."

Kallandras did not look back. "I have, by the gracious permission of the Queen, a personal guard. But I believe you have met."

"We have, under perhaps more trying circumstances. Come, Ser Gervanno, join us."

Gervanno looked to Kallandras for permission. Kallandras, however, shook his head. "As I have said, he is here as a personal guard. To have him interact with the Queen's guest would make of his role a polite fiction."

Jarven raised a silver brow. "I should prefer a polite fiction to a rude one."

"I prefer a lack of fiction where that is possible," the bard replied. His tone was soft, but chillier than Gervanno had yet heard it this eve. "Why are you here?"

"I am here on House business, if you care to examine the paperwork I have carried with such deliberate care."

Kallandras's smile mimicked friendliness without touching it. "Your personal business and mine should not overlap. I do not believe you mean harm."

"Truly? I am losing my touch. In all forms of interaction there are winners and losers; surely you must know that, who have survived so much."

Gervanno did not understand the stilted conversation that passed between these two formidable men, but was grateful to be excluded from it. He sensed that the bard neither liked nor trusted Jarven ATerafin.

Jarven, however, seemed genuinely amused by the subtle animosity. "I am not here to negotiate with a Senniel bard. My kings are the Twin Kings of *Averalaan Aramarelas*, and The Terafin has pledged her allegiance to them; I am forbidden interference where their work is concerned."

Kallandras nodded. "I will leave you to your business."

"Perhaps you might indulge me. I have come to negotiate the bureaucracy of Breodanir, and I find myself at a loss."

"They have far less bureaucracy than the Empire, and much of it is centered in this room. If you seek a Merchant Authority, you will not find it within the walls of the King's Palace; you will not find it in the Queen's halls. If you wish to negotiate a trade deal, it will be done at the Queen's table or not at all.

"There are merchant houses within Breodanir, and they are empowered to make trade deals on their own behalf—you might find them interesting."

"I see." Jarven smiled. "Then perhaps you might aid me in navigating the palace; I hear you have been a guest, and you maintain guest rooms here."

"My visit is drawing to a close," the bard replied. "But should you desire a tour of the publicly available halls and galleries, that can be arranged."

"You intend to leave the King's City soon? A pity. I'm sure I shall miss the pleasure of your company. But I myself do not plan on an extended stay. The length will depend on the delicacy of negotiations—negotiations which the House takes seriously enough that I am dealing with them in person."

Be prepared to withdraw immediately, the bard said, speaking as he had on the night of demons in the city streets. He neither looked toward Gervanno or acknowledged him in any other way.

Gervanno wished he could answer in the same fashion; he could not. The bard had taken pains to shield him from Jarven ATerafin's attention, perhaps because he believed it to be possible.

It was not. Gervanno had, even at the height of the battle, sensed no bloodlust from the bard, no killing intent, although he had killed, if that word could be applied to demons. But Jarven was a predator, and Jarven was hunting. He did not believe himself significant enough to be Jarven's target, but did not imagine Jarven would care if his hunt caused collateral damage that ended the life of a lone cerdan, far from home and family.

He therefore stepped forward and offered Kallandras a very Southern bow. Kallandras understood it as the silent request for permission it was.

Kallandras met and held Gervanno's gaze; what he saw in the cerdan's face was enough. He nodded the permission Gervanno's bow had asked, forgiving the boldness with that gesture. Gervanno rose and turned to the Terafin merchant.

"We do not seek the same things, ATerafin. Neither I, nor the man I serve as guard, will interfere in your hunt, but the hunt is not ours. You seek information without offering information in return, and without that information no aid, whether or not my master desires to give it, can be offered."

The glimmer of amusement left Jarven ATerafin's face. "And you truly mean to depart."

Gervanno nodded. "We have been tasked with a duty; we will undertake that duty with the same focus you have undertaken yours."

"Oh, I doubt that. I highly doubt it. Very well. I would speak with your master in private."

Kallandras watched them both; he nodded. Jarven took a step, and then a second step, frowning. Kallandras waited for a third step that was not forthcoming. "The heart of Breodanir is this palace," he told the Terafin merchant. "It has stood through war and demonic attack since the founding. There are reasons for that."

"I am hardly a demon," Jarven replied, smiling. His eyes glittered, unnaturally bright.

"You must now be aware, ATerafin, that it is not only the demonic that poses deadly threat."

"Very well. Let me dispense with pretense for the nonce. I seek Rymark ATerafin."

The bard nodded, as if this came as no surprise.

"He is in this city; the traces are clear. But they fray as I approach. It is for this reason that I have come on behalf of Terafin. I believe Rymark to be within these palace walls in some capacity."

The bard stilled. "Within the palace?"

"Indeed. You evince some affection for this small kingdom."

Kallandras nodded.

"His past actions revealed both his affiliations and his loyalty; they do not lie with us."

Kallandras raised a brow at the use of the word *us*.

Jarven's brief smile was genuine, but it did not remain. "I am certain he is here. If I am correct, he poses a threat to this kingdom. Demons can enter the palace, correct?"

"There are areas within the palace they cannot enter—not yet."

"Does that rely on the survival of the King?"

"I do not know. I have not asked. It is not of relevance to my position as guest."

"Very well. I do not care about this kingdom, as you are well aware. I care only about Rymark ATerafin. But as often happens when people of power meet, the paths we travel have intertwined, and they may overlap for some time. What takes you from the King's City?"

"The breaking of the boundaries that have held us safe from the predations and interference of the wilderness." Gervanno was uncertain that he would have answered, but it was clear from Jarven ATerafin's reaction that this was information already in his possession.

"That is imprecise. I will allow it. I am aware of the incursion in the streets of this city; I am aware that the Hunter Lords who reside in the capital have been out on the streets at all hours, surrounded by their many dogs. For two days, their horns resounded on every possible wind, but the sounds have become less frequent. If Rymark is here, and the demons arrived here, it cannot be coincidence."

"No."

"I intend to remain as a guest in the palace until the negotiations between Breodanir and House Terafin are successfully concluded. I, of course, am the arbiter of that success. Bards are famously friendly and charming; I am not, sadly, known to be either. I once allowed the hire of a man so dour he could curdle milk simply by entering a room, to make my public appearances seem positively jaunty in comparison.

"You do not have this sad, social problem. Aid me. Find what I seek, and if you cannot, find how it is hidden, how it is veiled."

"And in return?"

"I will make certain, until you return to report to the Queen, that there will be no mysterious assassinations; should demons manage to enter the palace, I will join the Hunters in their pursuit. I will do what I can to preserve Breodani rule."

"You hold no official position," Kallandras said quietly.

"No more do you, yet you are running off on an errand I perceive came from the Queen herself. You are known, Kallandras of Senniel, as a man who could walk into the very depths of hell at the side of an army and remain the only man to emerge after bitter war. I am certain those stories precede you; I am equally certain there is some chance you will add to them here." He glanced at Gervanno, and added, "Those who accompany this particular bard oft pass into fires from which they have no protection. This is the only warning I will offer you."

Gervanno offered Jarven a brief bow, as if in gratitude. This, he could do with ease; it was almost second nature.

"I will investigate as you ask in the short time remaining us," the bard then said. "I will offer you information if I can uncover even a hint of what you seek. In return, I ask that you guard our backs as you are able."

"Do you expect pursuit?"

"If your suspicions are correct, there is a distinct possibility. I will not be traveling alone."

"As you say." Jarven glanced at Gervanno. "Will your guard travel with you?"

"He will. And now, ATerafin, I must leave you to fetch the instrument which marks me clearly as bard in this court; it is one of the reasons invitations are extended, after all."

Gervanno accompanied the bard out of the room. He could feel Jarven's gaze follow them until they had passed through the open doors.

24TH DAY OF EMPERAL, 429 A. A. HUNTER'S REDOUBT, THE KING'S CITY, KINGDOM OF BREODANIR

"We can go," Heiden said, holding the brief letter Lady Bowgren had sent. His hands were shaking slightly, the words the missive contained had been so scant.

"She wasn't happy."

Heiden glanced at his Hunter. "No."

"Did she speak of events in Bowgren at all?"

Heiden shook his head. He could keep worry from his expression; he'd learned that much in his life in Bowgren. But the only person he wished to shield from his worry was Ansel, and that was impossible. He turned to the Maubreche Hunters, glancing at the Elseth brothers as he did. "I don't know what your mothers are like, but Lady Bowgren says almost nothing when she is worried or hard-pressed."

"She didn't want us to come," Nenyane said, the tone half-question and half-statement.

"She has been hard-pressed with the consequences of the turnings; I don't think she wishes to entertain guests of any note."

"Did she mention the magi?"

"Would Lady Maubreche?"

"Yes."

Stephen cleared throat and added, "She would wish to convey some warning to Nenyane; Nenyane is often unwelcoming."

Ansel grimaced but held his peace. He was nervous, and that was as much as Heiden cared to observe; Ansel had come halfway back to his huntbrother. Halfway was better than the distance of fury and fear that had separated them since Barrett's death, but it was delicate. Hope had the sharpest of edges; it cast the longest shadows, and if it shattered, it shattered above the darkest of places.

Heiden had tried to kill hope entirely to be free of that pain. But here he was, and hope—small and fragile—had once again blossomed. He wanted to cling to it, to protect it, to allow it to grow roots deep enough to sustain him.

Ansel was not Heiden; it was not the way he thought. But Ansel now understood the cost of anger and the fear that kept it stoked, and he tried not to fan those still-burning embers. In truth, Heiden was almost afraid to return to Bowgren. Had the mage and Nenyane not been certain that there was something they might do to preserve Bowgren, had they not made clear that Bowgren faced dangers that no other demesne had faced, he would have argued against it.

That, and the fact that they had saved his life—and, more important, Ansel's—had tipped the balance in favor of the return. Ansel now trusted these strangers; running the gauntlet of drunk resentment and demons had proven they would have his back in an emergency. Heiden had trusted them almost immediately, although Nenyane could still be shocking in her bluntness, her lack of social grace.

He wondered what Lady Bowgren would make of her. He was certain Lord Bowgren—as he had once been—would be stiffly disapproving.

He would, Ansel agreed. He did not share Heiden's anxiety. Had his father been capable of offering that stiff disapproval, he would have been grateful.

Silence followed Heiden's announcement. It was a nuanced silence; the Elseth Hunters and Nenyane turned, almost as one person, toward Stephen.

He nodded as if he'd expected the weight of their regard. Rising from the seat he'd taken at the long stretch of now cluttered library table, he said, "I'll ask to speak to Iverssen."

"Not the King?"

"The mage and the bard have petitioned the Queen; they'll be allowed to travel. The King won't interfere with them; permission is entirely in the Queen's jurisdiction. It's the members of Hunter's Redoubt that have no other recourse. But Iverssen is as close to hunt-brother as the King is allowed, and...I'm Breodan-born. He'll speak with me, and if he agrees, he'll bespeak the King on our behalf."

Nenyane rose; Heiden was amused to see the brief cringe cross Stephen's shoulders and vanish.

"What? Iverssen accepted me almost immediately. He'll be fine. Or did you intend to take an escort of the Queen's Guard?" Her scorn was clear. Heiden sympathized—strongly—with Stephen's reaction. He *liked* Nenyane, but she made Ansel look tactful. When a request of this import, this delicacy, was on the table? Heiden would have done his best to make certain her presence wasn't necessary. In this particular situation, it would have been impossible.

But in one way he envied the Maubreche huntbrother: she was so certain of herself. Not for Nenyane self-doubt, and the paralysis that arose from it. She spoke her mind. She declared herself.

Stephen had lived with Nenyane for over half his life, and clearly knew there was no argument he could graciously make that would leave her here, in this room, while he was elsewhere in the palace. To be fair to Nenyane, she had already saved his life once.

But she'd attacked the Queen's guest in the Queen's audience chamber; she'd attacked the bard that had, in the end, been instrumental in their survival. In front of the Queen. The bard had not seemed to take offense, and he had made no attempt to kill Nenyane; he merely defended himself.

He's that good, Ansel surprised him by saying. *He's good enough that he could survive Nenyane without injuring her.*

And Nenyane?

She's good. If I hadn't seen them both fight, I would have said the bard must be the superior swordsman. Ansel then fell silent, as if embarrassed to be caught eavesdropping, which was ridiculous, but very much Ansel of old.

Alex said, "Iverssen is our best bet." Ours. He turned to Heiden. "You've petitioned the King?"

"Through Lord Declan, who made clear that the mage—and the bard—are not reliant on our presence to enter Bowgren; they have the permission of Lady Bowgren. We're surplus to requirements."

Max snorted at Heiden's clever mimicry of Lord Declan's tone. "That's why we're here, isn't it? We're this close to being irrelevant, and our time in Hunter's Redoubt is supposed to cure us of that."

Heiden nodded. He considered it a vain hope in both the Maubreche and Elseth pairs, but he himself now had a sliver of hope for Bowgren. Just enough to cut; just enough to look failure and despair in the face and see its figurative eyes clearly. He understood— how could he not?—what Ansel feared, but Bowgren was uppermost in Heiden's mind. Bowgren, Lady Bowgren, and even Lord Bowgren. Ansel was Hunter-born, Hunter-bred; he was an excellent Hunter. He was known to the village elders, and prior to this past year, he had been respected; they had looked at him as the continuation of the Bowgren line. He had been their future.

He would not be their future if he failed to attend the Sacred Hunt at the King's command. Heiden might go without him, but the line rested on Ansel's shoulders. Heiden accepted the risk. He would always accept it. The price for power was that risk; it defined the nobility of Breodanir in all ways.

He had considered it a mistake to remove Ansel from Bowgren, but repented now. This Ansel was the Ansel he had grown up with, the Ansel he had followed. Bowgren was still of great import to him.

Ansel said nothing; Heiden attempted to think quietly, which was only effective when Ansel's thoughts were elsewhere.

"I hate waiting games," Nenyane said. "Well? Are we going?" She was halfway out the door before Stephen turned and offered a silent apology to Heiden and Ansel. Neither required it.

NENYANE AND STEPHEN were unfamiliar with the minutiae of the geography of King's Palace, but knew that the heart of the Priesthood lay beyond the King's chambers. The small rooms the Priests occupied were rougher and older than the Queen's impressive audience hall. Stephen knew the heart of the Priesthood was the heart of the palace; it was the first structure created before history unfolded and built up around it.

His dogs followed, but they were not the only dogs in the halls as they made their way further into the heart of the palace. Hunters came and went about their business. Given their expressions — grim, focused — that business had much to do with demons and the hunts that still wound their way through the city streets. The students in Hunter's Redoubt had neither received requests for aid in those hunts, nor permission to join them; it had been a remarkably peaceful six days.

Nenyane snorted. "Peaceful? Is that what you call it?"

Stephen was well aware that she felt they were wasting time they didn't have. "We're doing what we legally can."

"Do you think the wilderness cares about your petty laws?"

"No. But the King does. My parents do. I do. I'm god-born, but I'm still Breodani."

"It's Breodanir that will suffer if we arrive too late. You heard Illaraphaniel. You saw what he showed us."

"Why do you call him that?"

"Call him what?"

"Illaraphaniel."

"It's his name?"

"His name—as introduced—is Meralonne APhaniel, mage of the First Circle of the Order of Knowledge."

She shrugged, restless now; Stephen knew he was disturbing the wound that had never, and would never, fully heal. Memory. Nenyane's missing memory. But he had found her fascination with the mage uncomfortable, in part because it had been returned.

"I'm not that fragile!" she snapped.

Stephen nodded, and thought, *Maybe it's me. Maybe I am.*

"You're an idiot."

I am.

"I mean it. You're a real idiot."

He nodded, looking past Nenyane and lifting his head. Down the hall, to one side of a door that looked as if it had survived several battles, was a familiar man.

"Lord Stephen," that man said, offering Stephen a bow. "I bid you welcome."

"Lord Iverssen," Stephen replied. He did not correct the priest's use of a title he had not—and would never—fully earn.

"And Nenyane," Iverssen continued, offering her the same bow he had extended to her Hunter. "We are, as you might imagine, busy; the priesthood is armed and watchful, and I have scant time, but Lord Stephen implied that you face a crossroads." He turned toward the closed door to bow head and lift hands in a silent prayer. He then opened the door, although there was no obvious mechanism for its opening; no handle, no knob, no bar.

"Come, join me. There are things that must be said that are not meant for the ears of others."

Stephen entered the chamber behind Iverssen, and was immediately surrounded by familiar fog: Iverssen had called the god he worshipped from across the divide that separated man from deity. He could not do so in the same way Stephen could; the priest was not god-born. But built into this heart of the Hunter Kingdom were enchantments and promises that had lasted since its founding.

He turned toward Iverssen and saw that the fog was thicker and higher than it often was in the center of the Maubreche maze; it extended almost past Iverssen's waist, and Iverssen was not a small man. His bow had caused his chest to touch that fog, and he held the pose until he was given leave to rise.

It was not Stephen's leave to give or withhold.

My son. Is it now time?

"Time?"

What we built at the dawn of your era could not last; mortality knows both age and change, and things made of it, made for it, must likewise grow and wither. But if there is death, there must be birth, even if mortal birth is strange; it is not a function of will, of desire, of intellect. You are mortal.

Stephen nodded.

My Priest waits. But take up the mantle of your birth, and he will obey you as if you were his king. What would you have of him?

"I don't need to be his king. And you understand why I cannot do as you ask. You know the cost of it."

The cost is born by all who swear my oaths and break my covenants.

"She was *five*. Five years old." His voice low, he raised head to meet the eyes of the many-voiced god.

It was not I that bound her, the god replied. *But once bound, I cannot lift the consequences of the breaking of oaths; could I, oaths might have no consequences except my whim. Many are the people who have sworn oaths in desperation who would seek to rescind those vows; it cannot be done, not even should I desire it. You are the oathbinder. It is entirely upon you to decide which oaths you seek to make binding.*

"I was five," he whispered, his voice soft because he could not otherwise modulate the brief, deep rage that took him.

You are my son. Age is irrelevant to blood and intent.

Silence, then. Nenyane came to stand beside Stephen as mist fell away from her body. In the fog of the Between, she was faintly luminescent. She always had been. But her eyes were narrowed as she glared at the God; she was angry.

You have left Maubreche, the only bastion of certain safety for either of you, Breodan said. *Safety can be found for at time in the heart of the Priesthood — but it will not hold forever. You wish to leave.*

Stephen nodded. He opened his mouth to speak, but Nenyane got there before him, and when she lifted voice, he could hear—could almost feel—the thunder of storm in her words. They were words he did not recognize and could not understand.

She was his huntbrother; he felt the tide of her emotions clearly, but to understand the words he had to go deeper, and the Between was already taxing. He did not wish to collapse in front of the God, and was certain that would be the outcome of making the attempt.

But the uneasiness he felt when he considered Meralonne APhaniel and Nenyane's unknown past paled in comparison to what he now felt, because Bredan turned his gaze to her, and held her glare; it was clear that Bredan did not suffer from any lack of comprehension. When he replied, he replied in the same odd tongue, and his eyes flashed a brilliant white—lightning to her thunder.

Stephen reached for Nenyane's arm, gripping it tightly in one hand, as if afraid she would somehow vanish under the weight of Bredan's gaze.

Iverssen.

The priest, almost forgotten, stepped forward. "My lord."

What my son's huntbrother fears is a danger. Both Stephen and Nenyane must be allowed to travel and they must be free to do so immediately. Hours are now judged by mortal time, which is fleeting and easily squandered.

Iverssen bowed into the mist. "There are, or were, *Kialli* within the King's City."

Given their traveling companion, they will be as safe on the road as they would be anywhere else but in this chamber. Stephen is my surviving child, but he cannot fulfill any of his duties if he remains within these carved stone walls. I judge the risk necessary.

"We would require permission from Lord Maubreche."

Breodan did not dignify the slender excuse with a reply. Instead, he turned his gaze once again to Stephen. *It is the way of mortality to be driven by things invisible to us. I cannot command you. Take the road you have chosen and follow it to its end. If you call, I will come if it is possible.*

Stephen frowned.

The wilderness is waking, and even divided as we are, I can hear its many raised voices. Your voice is a whisper in comparison; were it not for your blood, I do not believe I would hear it at all. Go. Any advice I have to give, I have given to your huntbrother. Do not lose her, Stephen.

"We wish to take Maxwell and Alexander of Elseth with us," Stephen said, raising voice to be heard; the muted whispers of the many voices of the God were neither intelligible or quiet. "Will you also speak on their behalf?"

Maxwell and Alexander. The words were spoken slowly. *Of Elseth. I understand.* The God turned once again to Iverssen. *They are not what Stephen is, nor can they ever become so, but they, too, bear my blood. If they can be of aid, make your pleas to the King you serve.*

Iverssen bowed once again. He rose at the God's command.

You have served me well by serving my people, the God said. *In a handful of your years, if you survive, you will know either the hope that drove us to make our many ancient decisions or the despair against which we labored so long. Stephen and Nenyane are part of that, but they are not the only ones; those whose names I do not know, those who have never been brought before me in the Between, will likewise face the same consequences, for weal or woe. Had I gifts to give, I would offer them now — but they are beyond me in this place.*

All that we have wrought, imperfect though it might be, is here. Go. Bespeak your King. If your own voice fails to move him in the mortal realm, I bid you bring him here, where we might converse at length.

CHAPTER SIXTEEN

Nenyane was silent on their journey back through the mundane halls and galleries that led them to Hunter's Redoubt. She had never liked the Between, where she had always shown the same bluntness, the same lack of tact, that so drove Lady Maubreche to distraction. When younger, Stephen had assumed her resentment came from her overly protective impulses. Now, at a remove, he wasn't so certain.

He didn't ask. He had asked a question that relied on memory once today—and once was already too much.

"Stop worrying at me," she snapped.

He nodded. He had learned—with difficulty in the early years—to better hide his thoughts. That hard-won discipline had all but deserted him during the past few days. "Will the King give us permission to go to Bowgren?"

"What do you think?"

"I think he will."

"Then stop worrying."

He failed to point out that she hadn't, but it took effort, and the rest of their walk was utterly silent.

EVERYONE WAS WAITING in the small library in which they were expected to do independent study during this crisis. Alex looked up as Stephen entered the room, the question in his expression.

"Pack," Nenyane said, before Stephen could speak.

Heiden rose, Ansel remained seated. It was Ansel who spoke. "When can we leave?"

"We don't know yet," Stephen said as Nenyane opened her mouth. "But the Priests will intercede on our behalf. All of us. We want to be able to leave the minute we're given permission; I imagine it will come through Lord Declan if it comes at all."

Ansel rose, then. "I hate waiting. We're already prepared."

Alex and Max rose as well. "We're almost ready."

"Almost?"

"We aren't certain if we can use the royal messenger service horses, and we can't arrange passage if we don't know."

"Did you write to Lady Elseth?"

"Not yet. You?"

Stephen shook his head. "I'll write to my mother when we're certain."

CERTAINTY CAME THREE HOURS LATER. Stephen had been half afraid that they would be summoned to the Chamber of the Hunt, there to offer respect and anxiety to their ruler. He was relieved to discover they would not; word came in the form of Lord Declan. The exhaustion of the street hunts had both paled and darkened his complexion.

"You have been given permission to accompany Lord Ansel and Heiden to Bowgren. The Queen's guest will accompany you, as will Member APhaniel." He ran hands through greying hair as if the decision alone had brought him to the very edge of temper. "I know not what you said to the Priest, but Iverssen was adamant; not even the suggestions of the Huntsmen of the Chamber or the Master of the Hunt held any sway.

"But perhaps it is better this way. You were summoned here to focus on the difficulties Breodanir faces at this time, in the hopes that you would choose not to deepen them. I have made clear to the Master of the Hunt that four of you have made no progress. The two that show some hint of promise are required in Bowgren. Understand what you see, both on the road to Bowgren, and within the demesne. Understand why it is essential that we lose no potential Hunter Lords during this continuing crisis.

"I have not been given leave to travel with you. I cannot give emphasis and weight to the lessons you will undertake on your own. I trust that you—Breodani, all—will understand the weight your choices have, for good or ill. And I expect you all to return to the Redoubt when your duties are complete. You have been given leave to travel; you have not otherwise been released from the King's command." He exhaled. "I have, over the decades, entertained some few students in Hunter's Redoubt. I have lost very few of them.

"Do not join their number."

Nenyane lifted head. "How many of those students chose, in the end, to follow the path set out for the Hunter Lords?"

"Almost all," he replied. "But not all. They found other means of service." He then turned to Nenyane. "Were it not for the support of Iverssen and the insistence of Lord Maubreche, whose credentials are unimpeachable, Stephen would not have been called here at all; we would have set you both aside until Stephen was willing to accept a boy his age as huntbrother. Prove that your father and Iverssen were not in error in their visceral, vocal support of your presence as huntbrother."

Nenyane shrugged. "I have nothing to prove to any of you," she said, no anger at all in her tone. "You are irrelevant to my service."

Alex winced. Stephen forced his hands to unclench. Lord Declan's words had been almost unforgivable, but Nenyane's reply was no less so.

Before Lord Declan could respond, Meralonne APhaniel entered both room and conversation, his voice an almost bored drawl. "She will not be what you desire her to be, Lord Declan—but she has already chosen her master, and nothing you say or do will change that irrevocable fact.

"The Queen has arranged for our immediate use of the messenger service horses. We leave as soon as you are ready to depart."

"The bard?" Nenyane demanded.

"He has gone ahead."

"It is late in the day to begin your trek," Lord Declan said.

"Indeed. But we will meet up with Kallandras at the merchant inn before we leave the King's Road, and from there, we should reach Bowgren within two days if we are determined." He looked around the room, his gaze pausing only on Alex and Max. Max met that gaze head on, but that had always been his way.

"We're going," he said, voice low. "There are no better Hunters than Elseth Hunters when it comes to maintaining the trance. We do not tire."

"Very well. Speed is lost when the number of travelers grow, but I accept what I cannot change." To Lord Declan he added, "You should try it sometime."

Stephen almost choked, but added no further words; he felt just a smidgen of sympathy for the beleaguered Huntsman of the Chamber, a man used to commanding respect by presence and rank alone.

For his part, Lord Declan grimaced, but it was clear he was far less offended by the mage's words than he had been by Nenyane's; he expected nothing good from foreigners.

THE KING'S Road was never empty, but the afternoon traffic was so slow they might have made better speed had they chosen to walk overland. Or so Alex told them.

"Relax," Ansel said, although he looked as impatient as Max clearly felt. "The King won't change his mind. He won't recall us." But he looked at the wagons and horses that now crowded the road. The speed of the messenger horses they rode relied heavily on the road itself, one of the few that was properly maintained across Breodanir.

"It is not the word of the King we have to fear," Stephen said softly, his voice carrying only to Nenyane and Max. "If the traffic fails to move, it's likely that there's another disturbance on the road itself." He turned toward the mage.

The mage nodded, his expression grim. "Nenyane."

She had never particularly liked riding, but moved her horse in the mage's direction; if the use of her name sounded soft to the ear, all present could hear it regardless. She then dismounted, and headed into a crowd made of horses, wagons, and impatient travelers.

"Why did you send her ahead?" Max asked, his tone making of the question a demand.

"She is sensitive in ways I am not," the mage replied, his eyes on the road, not the Hunter. "There have been incidents along the King's Road in the recent past; if the King's Road is—for the moment—impassable, we will have to plan a different route." His eyes were narrow, his lips slightly thinned in either irritation or worry.

Follow Nenyane, Stephen told Patches. The dog darted ahead, attempting to follow the path Nenyane had woven through the restive horses and frustrated people. If other Hunters had taken this road, neither they nor their dogs were in evidence.

The King's Road is owned by the Master of the Game, Nenyane told Stephen as she moved. *The King doesn't hunt the way the lords of the demesnes do. It is the easiest road for the wilderness to breach.*

This close to the city?

She failed to answer, but that was answer enough. Patches reached Nenyane. Most of the people gathered on this road were familiar with Hunter dogs and what they entailed; they tended to give them a wide berth, where possible. It was not possible now, but they left enough room for the dog to pass; if they noted that Nenyane was the dog's companion, they said nothing.

Nenyane herself did not speak, but she seldom did if she was not accompanied by those familiar — and trusted. He could see why she had become tense; there was a lingering emotional pressure in the back of her thoughts, and it came to a head when she saw the strange trees rooted on the road. Literally on the road. They were shorter than the trees that otherwise girded the stone road, and wider, their branches low to ground. Their leaves were a soft, delicate pink; had they not appeared in the middle of a well-trafficked road, Stephen would have thought them beautiful, for there was an odd echo of the Master Gardener's work in their shape, their size.

But the shadows they cast were at the wrong angle, as if the sun that shone on them was not the sun all could see clearly in the Breodanir sky above.

Meralonne APhaniel dismounted, handing the reins of his horse — without a second glance — to Heiden. He had no need to straighten the robes of his Order; they fell in a perfect drape from his shoulders as he gestured. A pipe would have ruined the effect, but it would have been almost welcome, the air about the mage had suddenly grown so cold.

Stephen felt a hint of what Nenyane felt whenever she looked at this man, and he understood then why she called him by a different name: it was older, it was endless.

The mage raised voice, and all of the men and women on the road turned almost instantly toward him. The tone and the strength of it were so strong, he was a force, for a moment, more elemental than raging storm—and just as dangerous.

Alex and Max remained on their horses; Stephen glanced once at both of them, although it took effort to tear his eyes away from the mage. As he dismounted, he wondered what the travelers on the road who saw Illaraphaniel felt, for they could see his face, his expression; Stephen could only see the sweep of his cloak and the long fall of his platinum hair.

But he knew at least one person hadn't turned back at the sound of his voice; she had continued to the edge of the trees, just beyond the reach of the shadows they cast. Patches was two body-lengths behind, and without a direct command from her master, would go no further; her body was low to ground, her throat tangled in the tension of growl.

A growl neither Nenyane nor Patches herself could hear. Patches could hear almost nothing; even the mage's voice, which carried so clearly it might have been a morning temple bell, was faint and attenuated to the lymer's ears.

Tell Illaraphaniel we need to vacate the road as quickly as possible.

Stephen turned to the mage. *He has that in hand. He's...compelling. And he's asked the crowd to return to either their homes or the King's City, if that's where they reside; the road is not safe.*

It's not safe, Nenyane agreed.

When will it be?

I don't know. The trees are rooted in the road; there's no sign of stone. But the presence isn't tentative. It may be a full day—or more.

A day in which food and necessary supplies would not arrive at their destinations.

I'm not sure we will, either. The wilderness here is almost thrumming; if we could hear it clearly, it would be singing a name. Look to the side of the road—the trees are spreading. Tell Illaraphaniel he must *approach with caution.*

And you're safe?

She didn't answer. Stephen moved toward her, but the mage dropped a hand on his shoulder. "She will be safe. Trust her."

He swallowed. "She asks that you have the road vacated."

"We are doing that now."

"But she says the area extends beyond the road; that should be visible." It wasn't. The trees on the road were.

"What worries you?"

He shook his head. "It's…it's hard to hear her. It's hard to hear the people on the road nearest Nenyane."

The hand on his shoulder tightened. "Explain."

"Patches can't hear people speak—not clearly. It's muted, as if Patches herself is losing her hearing."

"Call her back," Meralonne demanded. "And call your huntbrother back while she can still hear you."

"We don't require sound to communicate."

"It is not sound that is being lost. Call her *now*."

Nenyane. The mage asks you to return immediately.

Why?

I don't know what he fears—but it's clear he fears something. Come back.

"What are you worried about?" Ansel asked the mage, an edge in the words.

"Nothing Breodani," the mage replied, without looking at Ansel. "And perhaps nothing at all—but the wilderness is strong, here. You would hear it clearly now if its voice could be conveyed."

"Would I be able hear it if I were in Bowgren?"

"That is the hope," the mage replied, in a tone that implied hope was, and would remain, scant. "There is a force at work here that feels familiar—but that should be impossible. Stephen." The last two syllables were sharper.

Nenyane!

This time, his huntbrother did not respond. The grip on his shoulder tightened enough there would be bruises on his collarbone. Steel growled, body lowering to ground.

Stay, Stephen told his dog. He reached for Patches; nothing in the dog's view had changed. But he could hear nothing at all. Through his lymer's eyes, he could see his huntbrother beneath the boughs of foreign trees, her head cocked to one side as if listening, as if straining to hear.

"She can't hear," Stephen said, exhaling panic. He took three deep breaths. "She's fine—but she can hear nothing."

The mage cursed, the language familiar to those who had lingered as children by the merchant wagons.

"You are lord in your lands," he said, although the target of his words was not immediately obvious. "I leave the road in your hands. Clear it. Clear it as quickly as possible without causing panic." Speaking thus, he leapt up, the air taking him.

Stephen cursed as well, but silently; all eyes had been upon the mage, and if Stephen, as a god-born child, had witnessed his share of magic, demonic and divine, most of the witnesses had not. Before Stephen could speak, the mage drew sword; the weapon was contained lightning, a paler blue than the blue of the sky into which he leapt.

There was almost no wind, but the wind carried him forward nonetheless. Stephen straightened shoulders and called three of his dogs to heel; he left Patches with Nenyane. If he could not bespeak his huntbrother, Patches was his only connection.

As the dogs gathered around the Hunters who had been the magi's companions, gazes fell to them almost naturally; the dogs—too few— underscored their rank, and therefore their import.

Lord Ansel—the only one who had earned the title—sat straighter in his saddle; he lifted voice expecting to be heard.

He was heard. Some of the gazes fastened to Meralonne slid away as the mage moved ahead; they turned to Ansel, who was even now guiding his mount off the road. Because the road was well trafficked, those who had not yet reached the growing, human congestion continued to come toward it. Clearing the road, as Meralonne had requested, was a daunting task.

Alex guided his horse back down the road, where he—and Max, who followed—sat as a living roadblock. Ansel began to move down the side of the road that led to their destination. Stephen joined Heiden, but he saw very little; he was focused on Patches, and he watched Nenyane. He saw the moment Meralonne came into view; she lifted her face toward the sky. Chin aloft, she dropped hand to sword hilt. He tensed. He knew she wasn't out of reach, but it felt—Nenyane standing, hand on sword hilt—as if she were receding, that the distance between them was growing with each heartbeat, each breath.

"It's Nenyane," Heiden said, voice soft. "There's nothing she won't survive."

"It's Nenyane," he countered. "There's nothing she *thinks* she won't survive. She's been injured before." He swallowed, his vision almost entirely given over to Patches. "It's never her own life she worries about. Never."

Heiden bowed head. "She's a huntbrother," he said, voice deliberately soft.

Stephen shook his head. "Ansel doesn't worry about his own survival. It's yours that matters."

"Yes—but Stephen, there are things that I would never do in order to survive. And this? The loss of Bowgren, the loss of the life he spent all of his childhood yearning for, the loss of his people—it's too high a price to pay. I made my choice. I stand by the choice I made. I'm just one person—I don't have the God's gift. I'm not Hunter-born. But Ansel is—and his reach, the effect he might have on hundreds of lives that were once like mine—I don't want him to throw that away when it's always been *my* decision. I want him to respect it. I want him to live with the fear and rise above it.

"Nenyane made her choice."

Stephen was silent for a beat. Meralonne had alighted a yard away, although his feet seemed to rest an inch above the foreign soil. "It's not the same as your choice. Nenyane doesn't care about Maubreche. She tolerates the villagers. She respects Lord and Lady Maubreche. But they could all perish tomorrow and as long as I survived, she would be fine.

"She could die protecting me, and she'd consider it a life well spent. I wouldn't."

Heiden said nothing for a long beat.

"It's not just your choice," Stephen continued. "I understand what you're saying, and I agree—but where there are two people involved, choice and self-determination become blurred and messy."

"You would die for her."

"Yes." He smiled awkwardly. "If you understand that, let me go. I don't know what she's facing, but I don't want her to face it alone." When Heiden hesitated, he added, "That's *my* choice."

Heiden flinched but nodded.

Stephen took to the road.

HE WAS two-thirds of the way toward Nenyane when he felt the shift in the land beneath his feet, although that land remained the worked stone of the King's Road. He felt the shift in the air, as if the breeze was laden with the flowers of a different land; almost, it caressed his face. He bowed head into it as if it were a gale that was almost strong enough to pull him off his feet, moving against the crowd as they responded to the various attempts to vacate the road.

It was true that this was not the first time the road had been subject to a turning—but it had yet to happen this close to the King's City. That it occurred now, on the heels of the incursion of demons, could not be coincidence. But such calculations grew increasingly silent as he approached Nenyane.

She was his huntbrother.

He understood Lord Bowgren's collapse. He understood Ansel's rejection of the Sacred Hunt. It was, in the end, at the heart of his own decision. If Nenyane did not make the huntbrother's oath, he wouldn't lose her the way Hunters throughout Breodani history had lost their huntbrothers. Alex and Max were the same; they were each willing to swear the huntbrother's oath because it was already part of who they were. They were willing to die for each other, to die protecting each other. But they weren't willing to allow the other person to make the same oath; weren't willing to have them suffer the Hunter's Death.

The living person suffered the greatest, the most extended and bitter, loss. Death was easier and simpler to contemplate.

He sensed Nenyane's immediate irritation, although it came without words, without the internal voice which was so much part of his internal landscape he felt bereft without it. Patches could see her clearly; she could see the mage, and did not like him, although she had shown no such enmity on previous encounters.

The mage, however, caused him to stumble for the first time.

Meralonne APhaniel's sword was almost blinding. He bowed. At first, Stephen thought the gesture had been offered to Nenyane, but no — it was offered to a tree of pale pink and wide boughs; it was offered in the shadows that tree cast, so different from the shadows cast by the normal sunlight.

He did not speak — or if he did, his voice, as Nenyane's and Patches, was lost to the shroud of silence. Had the tree been on the Maubreche grounds, the silence would have been almost peaceful.

Nenyane's sword was in hand, but she had not raised it; he could feel the peculiar tension in neck and shoulders that was the clearest sign of her restraint — a restraint that implied great respect. If the mage could not make himself heard, no one could; the bard who might have had the power to do so was either waiting on the other side of this breach or at the inn for which they'd set out. Word had likely not yet traveled.

He almost cried out when the mage lifted blade and brought it down, down, into the exposed roots of that beautiful, peaceful tree; the strike was soundless, but the flash of light—in a clear sky—caused a trembling in the crowd.

The tree cracked down the center, as if the blade had struck not root but trunk; bark flew out, as did wood chips, in utter silence. Nenyane parried those that headed in her direction; Patches was behind her.

There was no sound, but as the tree itself was destroyed and the layers of it stripped away, something appeared to be moving from its heart. It had no clear form, but there was a rippling in the air, and the finer debris that appeared in the wake of the tree's passing, made of petals and smaller shards of wood, floated in the air only in one location.

Stephen continued to move toward Nenyane, but took the risk now of viewing the world through her eyes; Patches's eyes were not enough. What she saw was not what Patches saw; it was not what Stephen himself would see should he manage to reach her side. To Nenyane, the air shimmered in place; the detritus was not necessary to give what appeared to be almost nothing form and shape.

She was surprised by what she saw; her hand tightened on sword hilt. Her mouth moved, but he couldn't hear the words she spoke because Nenyane couldn't. Neither could his dog.

The shimmering, slender cloud could. It turned to Nenyane, paused, and then turned to Meralonne APhaniel. To Illaraphaniel.

Debris rose as if it were cloth. The mage's blade was still; he waited. Only when the movement of petals and leaves had stopped did Nenyane lower sword. The creature spoke. Patches heard nothing but the rustle of leaves.

Nenyane heard speech. In a voice that was built of the mesh of wood bits, small rocks, petals and leaves, the creature spoke a name: "Illaraphaniel."

What Meralonne said in reply was lost; Nenyane could not hear it. But she had glanced at him; Stephen could see his mouth move. He could see the luminosity of silver eyes, the slight luminosity of pale skin. But more, he could see the way the mage wore age: it was mantle, it was strength; it implied eternity in the way distant mountains that might never be conquered did.

Or gods, Stephen thought.

"Why have you come?" The voice was the friction of disparate pieces of wood, stone, petal.

Could Stephen read lips, he would not have been able to piece

together meaning from Meralonne's silent reply; he suspected the
language spoken was not one he recognized.

"Of what do you speak? We are here, where we have always been.
It is your presence that is unwelcome in this place. Why carry you a tool
of war into our lord's land?"

The blade vanished.

"We ask your patience. Our lord sleeps. We do not wish to wake
her; it is to preserve that sleep and peace that we were born. You are
aware of this. You of all people." If floating debris could frown, it did.
"Yes. We have lost some of our kin; it is for that reason that we are
sentinel now.

"But we cannot war in these lands. We cannot disturb her. If we
allow it, what purpose our long existence?" Again there was a pause
where half of a conversation might be. "We did not realize how much
the lands have changed—but we should have; in no other way would
the dead have found entry. We will close the way, Illaraphaniel. But if
the dead at last walk and the barriers crumble, I fear the time of peace
draws to a close."

Stephen heard, in the friction of moving parts, a growing weight of
sorrow.

"Yes. We were promised peace and silence for a time, but we were
told at the dawn of our lord's long slumber that the time would come
when she would at last wake and once again face a world at war. We do
not understand. The gods left, and their effect upon the lands diminished greatly, except—" The rest of the words did not follow;
Meralonne was once again speaking, his lips forming words no others
could hear.

"That is ill news indeed. Help us close this path, this door; it is a tear
in the fabric of our haven, no doubt the results of the dead that walk.
But if the time has at last come, to our great sorrow, we will see you
soon, when our burden and our promise can no longer be carried or
kept."

Meralonne nodded and bowed once again; the bow held something
akin to reverence.

Nenyane sheathed her blade; she stood to one side of the mage and a
step back, as if she guarded him. As if he required a guard. She looked
so natural there, almost as if she had done this countless times before—
and she had. For Stephen.

He reached her side; she glanced at him. Spoke. No sound left her lips, but he knew what she asked: *Why are you here?*

He shrugged as he often did, but forced his lips to move. *Because it's where you are.*

Her eyes narrowed; she was unamused. But she made no attempt to send him away; she almost never did. She then said, *Watch.*

He watched as the cloud of moving detritus slowly fell; watched as the trees, those pink-leafed, peaceful trees, began to fade from view. As they did, sound returned, but it returned slowly, as if it was respectfully aware of the presence of the creature that was even now departing, while petals and splinters and dust once again returned to where they had fallen.

"Will the road be safe?" he asked, and was surprised at the sound of his own voice.

"For now," the mage answered. "But I fear what we will find if we manage to cross Bowgren's borders. This was not a deliberate encroachment on the part of the lord of these lands; it was incidental, the aftereffect of a breach of borders by the servants of our enemy. And where such accidental rents and tears occur, others will be waiting to take advantage of this grey land you call home.

"I am uncertain that this portion of the road will be safe for travel in the near future." He glanced down the road and grimaced; his feet came to touch stone, and the light that seemed centered on only Meralonne faded. "Word will have to be sent to the King."

———

THE INTERRUPTION on the road cost time, and the mage was restless. They had not made it far from the King's City, and Alex had chosen to return to the ruling monarch to deliver word of the disturbance on the road. Max remained; Ansel chose to join Alex.

He turned to Nenyane. "We'll travel in mixed pairs for communication's sake—but I'm leaving Heiden in your hands."

Heiden rolled his eyes behind his Hunter's back, and Ansel pretended not to notice. Or perhaps it wasn't pretense. His gaze held Nenyane's until the moment she offered him a grave nod, shorn of her usual snappishness. That gravity made clear to the Hunter Lord that she understood the import of what he had asked.

And it made clear that he trusted Nenyane with Heiden's safety.

THE ROAD REMAINED CONGESTED, and the roadblock that Ansel and
Alex had engineered more or less held, although no one was happy to
see it. During their absence, Heiden winced twice, but failed to explain
the reason for it; Max winced more.

"Ansel considers the road an emergency," he told them.

"It is," Nenyane said.

"Alex thinks he'll create an entirely different and more personal
emergency if he doesn't curb his tongue."

Nenyane shrugged. "Are they listening?"

"So far, yes. But he's ruffling feathers he doesn't need to ruffle.
There's no Huntsman of the Chamber that doesn't understand what's at
stake." His brows rose. "Lord Declan just spoke in our—in Ansel's—
defense. I think that shocked Ansel enough that he calmed down.
They're sending two lords and a full complement of dogs to take over
the administration of the road."

THE TWO LORDS included Lord Declan. Stephen also recognized the
second lord, a tired and grim Lord Grayton. His hair had taken on the
sheen of iron, which suited the cast of his face. He was not pleased, but
his ire was beneath the surface of a neutral expression, and it was not
aimed at the denizens of Hunter's Redoubt. The full complement of
dogs Max had mentioned, however, was larger than expected; Hunters
traveled with a pack of eight while hunting and in emergencies. These
two traveled with twenty.

Behind the two Huntsmen of the Chamber rode Alex and Ansel.
They dismounted when they reached their companions, while
Grayton traveled ahead to speak with the waiting mage. The mage
was now smoking his pipe, and looked as pinched and annoyed as
Grayton himself. Stephen was glad to be no part of the ensuing
conversation.

Declan, however, came to a stop at his students.

Eight of the dogs flanked Lord Grayton. Twelve remained with
Declan. He dismounted. "I have been guardian and guide in the
Redoubt for over a decade," he said, gazing at them all. "I have never
seen such dangerous disruption. Iverssen was insistent that you must be

given permission to forgo the lessons you were commanded to take, and his words moved the King, where others might have failed.

"But the King bids you remember—all of you—that you are Breodani. Your gifts are the gifts given by Breodan, and those gifts bind you to the lands of your birth while you fulfill the duties set you by our God." He exhaled. "Iverssen said that all dogs, of any pack trained by any Hunter Lord, will harken to Stephen of Maubreche.

"I have not seen the truth of this for myself, and were I the King, I would be less inclined to believe the claim. The King, however, cannot so easily travel at this time. He has survived two recent attempts on his life."

Silence.

"Both occurred in the last three days. He wished to accompany Lord Grayton, but chose prudence, although the decision was not reached quickly. But he understands that the difficulties in Bowgren are of primary concern, and he believes it is possible that the demonic attack and the difficulties to which you now travel might be linked."

Nenyane glanced down the road at the mage who was blowing smoke rings, one inside the other, as Lord Grayton spoke. She then turned her full attention to Lord Declan, something she had seldom done, if at all, during their stay in the Redoubt.

"I will not lie. I find at least three of you very difficult." He turned to Stephen, making clear who one of the three was. "The circumstances of your presence here are unheard of in our history. You have Nenyane as huntbrother. You have the blood of a god running in your veins; your eyes are the gold of the children of foreign gods, and you will not participate in the earliest of the bonding ceremonies between Hunter Lord and huntbrother.

"But perhaps, in the end, there is a reason that these circumstances have come together at this time in Breodanir history: things walk openly that were once the subject of children's cautionary tales. We are men, not demons; our dogs are flesh and blood. We have lost three Hunters in as many days to the creatures we have hunted, and we have seen their power at play.

"Perhaps you were born to travel Breodanir, to do what must be done for the good of the kingdom, and not the demesne into which you were born and in which you were raised. I cannot say. It is Iverssen's belief, and Iverssen can now bespeak Breodan freely should the circumstances demand it.

"The King has chosen to place his trust in the God without whom we would have no kingdom. He therefore sent four of his personal dogs to accompany you in your hunt." Lord Declan then turned to the dogs in their loose formation.

Stephen had seen the cohesion with which the eight obeyed their lord, and understood that the four had accepted, grudgingly, this new deployment at the King's will. They were royal dogs, and those dogs, often symbolic, had been bred or chosen for appearance. But he was certain that they had hunted; if they were meant for show, they were meant to be significant to Hunters, and no dogs could have that significance if they were merely accessories.

"Corran is the black and white. Marrel is the brown and white. Senshal is the gold and white." Lord Declan then turned to the dog that was almost pure white. "Pearl."

The white dog lifted head at the use of the name; she did not deign to notice the tone of command in a voice that was not her master's. But she did look at Stephen, and she did approach him; the three Lord Declan had named stayed back, as if awaiting her august presence.

"She is of Cullan's line," Lord Declan then said. "And as a lymer she has no equal." He did not speak with affection or appreciation. "She was not Iverssen's first choice; she was not his second. He argued against her inclusion; she is temperamental. The King, however, considers her the best of her breed, and he considers your journey into Bowgren of grave import; he would choose no other." Stephen wondered if the hint of apology in Lord Declan's tone was his imagination.

Nenyane didn't. She frowned at the dog, but she often frowned at the dogs. Pearl, however, was unaccustomed to this signal gesture of disapproval. She growled.

Stephen exhaled. "Pearl," he said, his voice flat. The growling banked as the lymer turned to Stephen, lifting nose as if at an unfamiliar scent. "Come."

Patches came to stand by Stephen's side with no command from him, but she did not growl. She watched.

Pearl turned to look over her shoulder at the three dogs with whom she was familiar: Corran, Marrel, and Senshal. As one, they followed in her wake. It was unusual that a pack leader was a lymer, but not unheard of; Stephen simply waited.

She approached him without hostility; he held out a hand, and she nudged it with her nose. Only when her tail began to move did Lord Declan relax, if one could call the subtle drop of tension in his expression relaxation.

"Why do you hesitate?"

"These aren't Maubreche dogs," Stephen said, his voice soft and pleasant, a habit when dealing with unknown dogs.

"You have permission to use them; the King was made to believe that time was of the essence, and did not wish to risk the time it might take for you to travel home for dogs with which you are more familiar."

"What he's trying to say," Nenyane said, with her usual grace, "is that the dogs might not be willing to return to the royal kennels if he hunts them the way he does our own dogs."

"The King is aware that there is a risk; perhaps he is counting on Pearl's famous ego. She is accustomed to both attention and appreciation, and that is like to be absent on the road you must travel."

Nenyane snorted. Pearl growled at her, but did not look away from Stephen.

"The choice is, of course, yours. But you are absent four pairs of eyes that you might naturally use in your hunts, and they might become a necessary component of survival if the lands to which you travel are as compromised as the King's Road has been today. If the dogs become yours in the way Hunter dogs have always served a master, the King will accept the loss."

Stephen continued to hesitate. This hesitation, however, was no longer a matter of ownership. If he had eight dogs, he could send two with Max; Steel had always liked the Maubreche twin, and would serve him with only minor hesitation. If Stephen was short four dogs, Max and Alex were short eight. He expected that Ansel, upon return to Bowgren, would have his own dogs; only the twins would remain deprived of one of a Hunter's greatest assets.

But sending dogs with Max didn't make those dogs Max's. Sending dogs to Stephen was different.

"She looks like she's going to be a pain," Nenyane said, looking down her nose at the white lymer. The white lymer managed to do the same to the huntbrother, if from a lower vantage.

Stephen looked at Pearl. "Well?" he asked, voice soft and even as it always was when he approached dogs.

Pearl sniffed and looked to the side.

"If you wish to return to the King's kennels, return. We hunt where we go and there will be both danger and little rest."

Pearl walked to Stephen's left side and remained there.

"I think she wants to stay."

"I can see that," Lord Declan replied. "But I offer warning. Your huntbrother is not wrong; she requires a degree of maintenance and attention it might be difficult to offer her."

"Did the King send her just to get rid of her?" Nenyane asked.

Max coughed. Ansel looked away. Alex, accustomed to Nenyane, said nothing.

Lord Declan, to everyone's surprise, smiled. "She is of impeccable lineage, and she is as talented as that lineage implies. But it is true that, unlike most of the King's dogs, she has a tendency to choose when and where she will demonstrate that talent. There is very little that escapes her notice when she chooses to work."

Stephen exhaled. "Thank the King on our behalf. We will gratefully accept the gift he offers us in this emergency." His words were stilted, formal. Although he made an attempt to bespeak this lymer, she didn't condescend to answer.

"I will, although the situation on the King's Road will demand most of my time for the next day. Or more." He glanced down the road, and then turned to Nenyane. "Will the road be safe to travel?"

"Not today," she replied promptly. "And possibly not tomorrow. But if the *Kialli* leave off their attacks, it should be safe the day after."

"That is an unfortunate condition, given our present circumstances." She nodded.

"I will leave you, then. You were meant to depart for Bowgren somewhat earlier; I doubt you will be on the road before the morning. Do not let me detain you further."

It was a dismissal, but that didn't bother Nenyane; she wanted far less of Lord Declan's company in her life.

Alex and Ansel waited until the conversation—if it could be called that—between Lord Grayton and Meralonne had reached its conclusion before they once again returned to their horses.

———

WHEN THEY AT last reached the Brass Kettle, strains of a familiar instrument could be heard through a door that had been pegged open:

the bard was, indeed, at the inn. The innkeeper seemed to be listening, but turned instantly as the mage walked through his door, his expression becoming decidedly business-like.

"Bad bit of business on the road," he said.

"It was, and we have lost much time."

"You won't be leaving tonight."

"No. We'll be up at dawn; we'd like breakfast packed if possible."

"Aye, so your companion said. You'll have your breakfast. The mood here was sour until he pulled out his instrument and started to play; he's kept people calm, and that's worth a favor or two."

The Senniel bard played as they entered the large, public dining room; he offered them a nod that did not interrupt his song.

The innkeeper then handed keys to Meralonne.

Meralonne distributed them among the Hunters. "Here. Go to your rooms and get what rest you can; we will leave first thing in the morning. I would leave now, but travel at night is often fraught, and I fear it will be more so this eve." He turned to Nenyane, lifting a brow.

She nodded, her eyes narrowed, and the mage then turned toward the strain of music emanating from the bard's lute, as if her opinion was the only opinion of value the six had to offer.

Alex and Max accepted this; Ansel bridled, but to Stephen's surprise offered no argument. Heiden had already taken the key to the room he and his Hunter would share, and headed toward the stairs that would eventually lead him there. "We'll stow packs in our room and join you in the dining hall, if you mean to eat there."

Stephen nodded; he intended to do the same. But the bard's music followed him up the stairs, and as he walked, he felt the tension leaving his neck, his shoulders, and the rigid line of his jaw. He understood then why the innkeeper had been grateful, for he had no doubt Kallandras had not attempted to charge the man for his work.

"A man who can command the wild air doesn't need to worry about money," Nenyane snapped; she was on edge, and that wouldn't dull any time soon.

Stephen shrugged. "He needs to eat. He serves the Kings unofficially—he's not about to steal food."

Nenyane was not concerned with mundane problems at the moment, but that was fair given the advent of demons and a wilderness that seemed to disgorge creatures that were beyond the realm of even children's stories. She didn't trust Kallandras, but had at least accepted him, which was much as one could ask of her.

"Stop thinking at me," she snapped. "I'm hungry."

Stephen carefully set their packs in easy reach, looked at his clothing, which was relatively clean given how little travel they had actually done, and rose. "Let's join the others."

THE BIGGEST SURPRISE to Stephen was the presence of Gervanno di'Sarrado. Although he had been granted permission to accompany the Hunters, he had not joined them on the road. But he found himself smiling the moment his eyes alighted on the Southerner. If Nenyane didn't smile, she felt the warmth of recognition. This man, she trusted.

He was seated at a table closest to the back wall, but rose almost instantly when his gaze alighted on the two Maubreche siblings; he lifted a hand as if to wave them over. The hand froze in mid-air as he lowered it looking almost chagrined at himself.

Nenyane did smile, then.

Max and Alex were at a table; Heiden and Ansel had joined them, but their backs were to the door; Heiden turned as he noticed the Elseth twins' reaction. Stephen walked to their table; there were two empty chairs. Clearly they did not expect Meralonne or Kallandras to join them.

Nenyane, however, turned to grab another chair. "We've got a friend here," she explained, as she wedged it between the two empty chairs they were meant to occupy.

"Who?"

"The swordsman who came to our aid." She then turned and lifted an arm, waving in the gesture that Gervanno had aborted.

Gervanno offered a deep bow—both Southern and infused with a genuine respect that made him stand out in the crowded environs of the dining room. When he rose, his expression was carefully neutral. He lifted plate and mug and carried them to the table which the Hunter students had claimed for themselves. Nenyane indicated the chair between her and Stephen; he looked quickly at Stephen, as if afraid to overstep the boundaries between Hunter and huntbrother.

Stephen's smile shifted; it was wry as he nodded.

"Ser Gervanno," Alex said, "We owe you a debt of gratitude.

Forgive us if we hope that the manner of repayment involves things more mundane than demons."

Gervanno's smile was instant and deep. "If you will forgive me the same hope."

"Your swordwork is impressive," the Elseth Hunter continued.

"It is my one skill," was the self-deprecating reply. "And as all men, I leverage my skills where possible."

"What brings you here?"

"I was granted permission to serve as Master Kallandras's personal guard while in the King's Palace. Apparently, he encountered some difficulty of a martial nature."

Max choked on his food.

Gervanno was surprised; he had not made his comment with any humorous intent.

"If you need help eating," Nenyane told Max, "I'm here."

"Having seen Master Kallandras in action, I cannot think that a simple cerdan would be much protection," Gervanno continued.

"Will you continue as his personal guard?" Nenyane's brow was raised, but the question was genuine.

"He asked permission as a favor to me," was Gervanno's more guarded reply.

"Does he intend to continue to employ you?"

"In truth I have not asked."

"But you accompanied him here."

"I believe he wished to separate me from a man whose attention I had garnered."

Nenyane's eyes narrowed. This, more than anything else, told Stephen how much she already considered Gervanno hers. Nenyane wasn't one for social interaction except at Maubreche necessity. She had few friends, but those she had were as important to Nenyane as kin. "The man intended you harm?"

"No. No, of course not. He is a man from a house of great repute in the Empire."

"And he's interested in a caravan guard."

"He did not travel with a caravan, no." Gervanno drank slowly. "I chose to act as guard to leave the King's City before I became involved in matters far beyond my experience or competence."

"More so than demons?" Max asked.

"Demons, sadly, are not beyond my experience." His voice was softer.

"Did Kallandras intend that you go your separate ways once you reached the inn?" Nenyane continued, pressing him.

Stephen sighed. "What she wants to say is that we'll be traveling well beyond the King's City toward lands that have been compromised just as Maubreche had been compromised on the day we met. You were of great aid to Maubreche that day, and the experience does not seem to have caused you further harm. If you would be willing to resume your duties as our personal guard, we would be grateful."

Gervanno hesitated.

"I am not Lady Maubreche," Stephen continued, guessing at the reason for that hesitation. "But I am fully capable of hiring guards on my own behalf; my mother trusts me not to damage Maubreche by the hire, and Maubreche will take full responsibility for your pay."

"I did not discuss my disposition with Master Kallandras," Gervanno replied. "But when he finishes here, I will do so. In the event that he considers my services unnecessary, I would—with great joy— accept your offer of employ."

Nenyane nodded, then. She understood that Gervanno could not simply switch masters at his own desire or convenience. She turned her attention to the bard, her expression barely containing her impatience.

He doesn't need Gervanno.

We don't, either.

We did the other night. I could focus on my fight because I knew Gervanno had your back. You're not terrible with a sword. For a Hunter, you're excellent. But Gervanno is good. And if he commits to guarding you, he'll lay down his life in your defense.

I'm not sure he believes that.

I don't care what he believes. She turned to watch the bard, her foot tapping an impatient, but in time, rhythm to his music.

HOURS LATER, if one went by Nenyane's subjective time, or perhaps half an hour if one judged in the usual fashion, the bard finished playing. A plate was offered by one of the many patrons in the inn, and silver crossed it in abundance. The bard bowed and thanked his audience, adding only that he should like to join them in the fine food and better drink the inn offered.

There was applause, and to Stephen's surprise, Heiden joined in.

"Heiden has always been drawn to music," Ansel said, the hint of a smile at play around the corners of his mouth. "I believe the bard intends to join us."

"Not if the mage has anything to say about it," Nenyane pointed out, as Meralonne levered himself off the wall against which he'd been leaning and headed toward Kallandras.

The grim set of the mage's expression made clear that levity was not the correct response to the day's events; this did not stop Heiden.

"We've time for grim and serious—and little choice. We should take the opportunities for joy, however slender and brief it might be."

Ansel closed his eyes. "Barrett said that."

Heiden nodded, although Ansel's eyes remained closed. "Barrett. He would have loved the bard."

Ansel nodded before slowly opening his eyes. "The mage doesn't appear to have learned that lesson."

"The mage doesn't believe he has anything to learn from the merely mortal," Nenyane said. "Eat. The food doesn't get any better when it's cold."

GERVANNO ROSE ONLY when the mage turned on heel and walked away. Food did not seem to be a concern of the platinum-haired Widan. Kallandras then made his way to a table that was now crowded. He glanced at the array of seats, one of which Gervanno was almost self-consciously abandoning.

The bard's smile was without edge. "I would not deprive you of your chair," he said.

"I should not be sitting."

"You are a free man, Ser Gervanno. I did not intend to encumber you when we set out this morning." He glanced at Nenyane, his smile deepening. "Is that perhaps what you desired to hear? Most prefer song."

Nenyane shrugged. She was, Gervanno knew, absent social grace. But perhaps, like Gervanno himself, she had one skill—and that skill caused all other considerations to pale in comparison, it was so luminous. "I would speak with Ser Gervanno if you have released him from service."

"I have, and honorably."

She turned immediately to Gervanno. "Well?"

"It would be my honor to once again serve as a Maubreche guard, if that is your desire."

"Good. Sit down. All the standing and bowing makes me nervous."

Gervanno returned to his chair. He did not expect graceful manners from Nenyane, although had she not lacked them, he might not have noticed. He had been trained by sword masters in his youth who could put the manners of caravan guards to shame in the drill yard; they had never carried that barking disapproval outside of the yard's confines.

Not a single one had been the equal of Nenyane of Maubreche.

He looked at his food as appetite deserted him; it was a happy desertion. Evening was coming, and the darkness of the Lady's night had begun to settle across the horizon, but Gervanno wanted nothing more than to go out to the yard with Nenyane, to cross blades with her, to absorb whatever he could absorb in the time Maubreche was willing to retain his services.

He knew that the choice had been Nenyane's. Stephen offered employ and assurances that his pay would be forthcoming, but neither mattered to Nenyane. It should have mattered to Gervanno. He was a lone cerdan, without friend or family, in this Northern kingdom where demons had shown their hand; some concern for his own responsible survival should be a primary consideration.

But when she rose, when she said, "I haven't had a chance to practice much in the past week. Neither has Stephen," all such considerations were abandoned.

The bard smiled; he had not yet taken a seat, as if aware of what would occur. "I believe it is fast becoming too dark for safe sparring."

"True." Nenyane turned to Stephen. "You're excused from lessons for the remainder of the day. You, however..."

Gervanno rose instantly, the remainder of his meal forgotten. Only once he rose did the small shadow half-beneath the table rise as well, looking very put upon. It was his dog.

CHAPTER SEVENTEEN

Gervanno felt young as he drew sword. Nenyane considered his blade, and considered the practice blades left in the yard as a courtesy for guests who felt the need to exercise. "Can you use these?" she asked, barely keeping disdain from the question.

He glanced at the heavy, wooden blades; they were Northern. If Southern guests came to stay, they were like Evaro; they only barely wielded blades. "As you suspect, they are not my preferred shape or length, but I have used them before."

"Oh?"

"That is inaccurate. I have had them wielded — in practice — against me before. I've seen the real thing, but that wasn't a matter of practice."

"Experience is useful," Nenyane replied, her lips folded in frown as she weighed what was clearly a decision. "Use your own sword."

He nodded. On some visceral level he did not believe he could injure her. He knew it was possible; training mishaps abounded in his youth. But he could not believe it.

He was surprised — and possibly disappointed — when she chose one of the wooden swords.

"Force me to parry," she told him. "And the lesson is at an end."

The practice blade would be at an end, in Gervanno's opinion, but he had long years of practice in keeping his thoughts to himself. He drew blade; he used his own sword, not Silvo's.

She leapt.

Just as the Northern bard had leapt, she seemed weightless, as if she only barely condescended to touch the ground, and at that, only to gain necessary momentum. If her intent was to avoid all contact with his blade at all, she failed—but he realized, as he brought a sword that suddenly seemed cumbersome and far too heavy to bear, that she had said the lesson was over if she herself was forced to parry.

She took initiative; she took the lead. She moved in a constant dance of motion, her trajectory tracing a wide oval in which Gervanno was the heart. She seemed reckless, her arms too wide, her body to open to attack; her speed was her greatest defense. It was a speed Gervanno could not easily counter, and he did not have the excuse of the heavy battlefield armor that often encumbered warriors.

Perhaps he had the excuse of age; he was no longer a youth, with the endurance and focus granted the young. But if lacked that youth, he had the compensating experience of many battles survived, and that experience could be transformed to a canny, battlefield wisdom, could he but take time to think, to assess. Had she been content to simply remain out of reach, he would have had that time. She was Nenyane. She wove attacks between her nimble steps, forcing Gervanno to parry; forcing him to rely on instinct, not deliberation.

No sword master in his experience had chosen to test him by dancing constantly out of reach, each graceful movement a deliberate taunt. Perhaps, had he been his youthful self, he would have grown angry, possibly enraged. He was not that callow young man. He was Gervanno di'Sarrado, dishonored but still alive, still intent on the survival that had so disgraced him.

Survival depended on his ability to stop the opponent who would otherwise kill him. Nenyane had no killing intent, but Gervanno considered killing intent half a myth; he had encountered many killers on the fields of battle, and some handful off of it, and knew well that men could kill without it, as if causing death was a casual matter of course, a daily event with little significance.

Nenyane intended no harm to anything but his dignity, his sense of his own skill. It was needless: he had no doubt at all that she was, and would remain, far more skillful than Gervanno could ever hope to be; that he might, with effort, with will, with practice, stand in the lee of the shadow she cast; he would never stand beside her in her light. He had accepted that as fact the moment he had first watched her fight. Not even in youth would he have believed otherwise.

Those of good skills but lesser quality often underestimated their opponents, especially when those opponents, like Gervanno, had no standing, no noble birth, no power. But the masters? The few he had seen in action, the few with whom he had crossed blades? Never. She did not underestimate him now. She had taken his measure; she had absorbed his ability. He did not think he could surprise her, but for the duration of this lesson, he intended to try.

His blade never reached her; she did not parry, but her flexibility in motion was astonishing. He had seen similar before in the sword dances of his youth, when the two dancers and their blades were so perfectly timed, so perfectly matched, that the blades could pass above the shoulders of one of the two partners, and the partners could bend back in that exact instant, never raising their blade to disturb their motion with the clatter of steel against steel.

Thus she moved, her eyes bright, her expression one of almost feral joy. He did not know what his own expression offered, so intent was he on pursuit.

But he knew the moment the dance was over; the ovals she'd been tracing by movement alone broken as she leapt not within their unetched confines, but out. As she moved, the wooden blade clattered to the ground, forgotten; in her right hand she now wielded blade. Her hair, the same pale color of the Northern Widan's, flew in a similar fashion, as if she was rushing against the wind.

He turned, pivoting, the lesson forgotten; he had no need to draw blade, as she had insisted he wield it.

There, at the edge of the courtyard, he could see the subtle ripple of shadows that were wrong; they were too long for the light cast by moon and fading sun and the lamps that kept the yard lit in the evening hours.

He did not glance back at the inn; did not cast gaze around the yard to see who might be standing in it, working in it. He heard—he expected to hear—the horses. He turned in the opposite direction, sword readied, casting his gaze across the shadows on the ground there; they were, to his eye, normal.

Nenyane's blade struck steel, and the shadows retracted, collapsing inward as they coalesced into an almost familiar shape: a man's shape, if men had wide, dark wings. In the darkness of those wings he saw the glint of light, orange, white, that reminded him of fire.

Of the fire that had killed every man, woman, and child who had traveled with Evaro's caravan.

His hands tightened on blade but he did not freeze; how could he when Nenyane was leading the charge? Demons were death; he knew that. He had lost so many comrades to them. But he would not lose Nenyane of Maubreche here; the demon staggered back at the force of her blow, parrying with a hand against Nenyane's sword. The creature lost a finger, but nothing else. As Gervanno raced to join Nenyane, a red blade shimmered into existence, followed quickly by a red shield, Northern in styling.

Gervanno knew them as demonic weapons. The red light shed had been seen across the Averdan valleys, notable even while one was fighting for survival against creatures who did not wield those weapons. But there were no dragons here, no breathers of fire, no terrified caravan; there was Nenyane.

Nenyane was not afraid. The line of her body had canted slightly forward, the fluidity of her movements at odds with the rigidity of her expression; she was angry. No, he thought, she was furious. He might have worried; fury of this nature was no friend to those who wished to survive the battlefield.

Worry failed to come. He ran—slower by far than Nenyane—his blade readied, his focus on the demon's defenses. She did not command him to leave; did not command him to seek aid, although aid remained one door away, in the confines of the inn. Aid, he thought, or victims; the walls of the inn seemed thin as fine paper, and just as readily burned.

The demon was focused on Nenyane. Gervanno moved wide and came in on its left flank; the demon's shield was raised and lowered in a movement so swift, Gervanno perceived it as a blur of red light. Red light and heat. He leapt clear, but the demon did not pursue; it could not pursue while facing Nenyane.

But he heard the demon raise voice, although the words were strangely unintelligible, and he saw that the demon had not chosen to attack in isolation; from the shadows that remained pooled beneath the creature's feet, eyes emerged, and as they rose from shadow, long-jawed faces joined them, to be followed swiftly by limbs.

He understood that these creatures were in all ways lesser than the demon Nenyane fought, but knew from bitter experience that they were powerful enough to kill a man should that man lack familiarity or caution. Gervanno lacked neither, here. But caution could tip easily into fear, and fear was worse than anger on the fields of battle.

Time slowed for Gervanno; from the corner of his eye, he saw a flicker of light from the inn's door, pegged open to let air circulate and customers leave or enter.

Nenyane had no need to tell anyone to find aid. Stephen's dogs leapt clear of the door, heading unerringly toward where the growing battle raged, Nenyane of Maubreche at its heart. Behind them came Stephen himself—the one person Nenyane did not wish to see endangered in any fashion.

Stephen had golden eyes; Gervanno understood that he was not entirely human. But he had spent enough time in Stephen's company to understand that, golden eyes or no, he was a young man with a strong sense of duty. He was mortal. Without the dogs that characterized the nobility of Breodanir, he had as much chance of surviving as Gervanno himself, perhaps less; if Stephen had encountered demons before, he lacked Gervanno's skill.

Nenyane did not pause as Stephen set foot on the field of battle. She did not glance back, did not raise voice in warning. It was true, then, that Hunter and huntbrother had no need for such communication. He had been told this, had even believed it in some fashion. But he had not fully understood it until now.

He was surprised that she raised voice at all; when she did, she spoke a single word: *Illaraphaniel.*

The mage. The man to whom the fox had shown genuine respect. He had traveled with the Maubreche Hunters to this very inn, had occupied its mundane room, had even chosen to avail himself of a worn pipe.

But Gervanno had not seen him armed, armored, as he now was when he, too, exited the inn. He was not alone; the dining room must have emptied at the speed of his transformation from dusty, irritable traveler to shining warrior, people trailing in his wake as if they were shadows.

Gervanno stepped back as the dogs came to flank him. "Stephen," he said, speaking to the dogs because he knew the Maubreche hunter would hear what his dogs heard, "the demon guards his flank without pause in combat with Nenyane. Send the dogs cautiously if you intend to join Nenyane's battle." Turning, he added, "Other demons have been summoned."

STEPHEN HEARD GERVANNO'S WORDS, but half of them were unnecessary; he could see clearly where the lesser kin emerged. *Nenyane —he summons servants. Can you cut him off from the source of that particular power?*

She did not respond, not with words. Whoever she fought required the entirety of her focus. He had seldom seen demons draw sword and shield, but it was not unknown. If he did not understand demonic rank in any sense, he knew that it was achieved and maintained by raw power.

Light drew his attention as Meralonne came out of the inn. The mage was shining, as if he—and only he—now stood beneath a beam of sunlight in the darkening sky. At his side, shadowed by the light he cast, stood Kallandras. He was armed not with lute, but with weapons.

"He is beyond you," Meralonne said to the bard, voice soft enough that the words should not have carried so clearly to Stephen's ears.

"Perhaps, but we are mortal, Illaraphaniel. What might be beyond any single one of us, might be achievable if we work in concert." The bard's voice was somber. "And I am surprised that I need remind you how varied forms of combat can be."

Stephen focused on Nenyane's combat, and on the demons, lesser, who had not yet joined it. Meralonne's warning to Kallandras—a man who could literally command the very air itself—robbed the evening air of any warmth. He waited for movement from the only person Nenyane had named.

But Meralonne watched the combat, his eyes shining silver, armored but weaponless. "See to the lesser kin," he said, without looking back. "Do not allow the dogs to close with the *Kialli* Nenyane fights; you will lose them all."

He stepped forward into the falling night, and as he did, blade came to hand. Blade, but no shield to bring to bear against a creature whose shield Nenyane could not sunder.

"Lord Ansel," the bard said, although Stephen did not see Ansel until he was called, "Yours is the greatest authority present; see that the citizens within the inn are moved to safety."

Ansel, hand on sword, stiffened.

Heiden, however, said, "We will. Will the inn be safe?"

As if in answer, fire suddenly exploded not six feet from where

Stephen had chosen to stand while gauging the lay of the land. Splinters of wood flew as the door frame and part of the wall shattered. People screamed, shouted, the tenor of those shouts differing; people who had not left the dining room were alarmed. People who had were now afraid.

Ansel immediately turned on heel and barked a series of commands. He expected to be heard; it was clear that he was accustomed to wielding Bowgren's authority. Because he was, he was heard. People's fear did not descend instantly into the chaos of panic. Ansel was lord here, and they turned to him, as Kallandras had intended.

Heiden stood by his Hunter's side; Ansel's acceptance made clear that Heiden was huntbrother. There was only one problem that Stephen could see: there was no ready solution, no ready plan. That would have to change, if they survived.

Alex and Max joined Stephen, watching as he watched; their hands were on their weapons, but they had not yet drawn them.

"The King," Stephen said, "should have granted his dogs to you." Max especially, he thought. Alex was Hunter-born and trained; he loved the dogs that would become his when he was of age. To Max, they were an extension of self; they were almost like breathing. But the twins had each other. They drew breath as if they were one person; he could see the sharpness of their gaze, the subtle shift in stance, that spoke of Hunter's trance.

He nodded as they glanced at him and joined them. They seldom called trance simultaneously, preferring to hunt while passing the physical burden of trance between each other. But the hunt was here, it was now, and they were not guaranteed to survive. Stephen knew; he had centered himself in the Hunter's trance as well.

The summoned demons turned toward the inn. Or perhaps toward the Hunters who now stood in front of the crowd still gathering outside. Their number grew.

"Kallandras," Meralonne said, "I entrust the safety of the occupants of this inn to you. Aid Bowgren."

The bard's weapons trembled for one long second before they vanished. He nodded, grim and silent. If he spoke, Stephen could not hear his words, but Heiden paled and nodded. The bard did not bespeak the rest of the crowd, but stood in front of them watching the changing shape of the demonic battlefield.

Stephen moved alongside the Elseth brothers, blade in hand, his view of the battlefield composed of the visual pieces of information that came from his dogs. It was not their eyes that picked up the most subtle of the changes he felt as he braced himself for the leaping charge of a demon perhaps half his height and double his weight.

No, it was his own hearing, and the tremor beneath the soles of his boots; he could almost hear and feel the earth shift and crack.

Nenyane!

I know. I feel it, too.

He did not turn to the Elseth brothers; he did speak. "The demons are somehow trying to break the wall between Breodanir and whatever lands they occupied before their attack. Step carefully; keep the inn in view."

"And if the turning swallows the inn?" Alex asked, voice so soft Stephen would have missed the words had they not all adopted the trance state.

Stephen offered no answer; he better understood Meralonne's request — or command — of the bard.

Stephen —

He swallowed. *I know.*

The wild earth is not a mortal child. It is far older than even Illaraphaniel and his kin. Bespeak it, remind it; it swore an oath to Bredan, Lord of the Covenant.

He knew. In the sound of cracking, of breaking, he could almost hear the vow made to the earth; could sense the price paid. Breodan could remind the wild earth of its vows, but he no longer walked the plane. Only his children did.

Only his children could.

But the wild earth did not hear Stephen of Maubreche; was barely aware of his presence. It was not unaware of the *Kialli* and the demon-kin, and it raged at the touch of the dead upon its surface. This, too, he could hear.

He could not hear the wind, not yet; if Kallandras was tasked with the safety of civilians, he would not call it; not unless the demons summoned fire.

They won't, unless they're dying. They're trying —somehow— to control the earth. She spoke with contempt, disgust at their overweening arrogance.

The earth buckled beneath the Hunters' feet; they bent instantly into their knees to rebalance themselves.

The earth is angry.

Yes, his huntbrother said, as if the rage of ancient earth was almost quotidian. *Speak to it now; there is only one way to assuage its anger.*

Two, Stephen replied as Meralonne APhaniel at last chose to enter Nenyane's battle. The mage paused briefly, eyes flashing bright silver, to dispatch the lesser kin who stood in his way; some of those had been the Hunters' targets. They became ash almost in an instant; ash and a whining, singular cry that not even Nenyane could hear.

Stephen thought the mage's destruction casual, almost an afterthought. He was wrong. The mage looked to Stephen across the momentary field of ash, and mouthed a single word: *oathbinder*.

The one thing Stephen had promised himself he would never be again.

But Nenyane was right: this oath was not an oath of his making, not an oath he had sanctified; it did not lead to death, or not death as the merely mortal understood it. And if he could not reach the earth in this place, if he could not bespeak it, the inn and its inhabitants would likely pay the price.

"Guard me," he told Max and Alex.

They nodded as one, without question. Questions would follow, if they all survived.

WHAT HE FELT through the soles of his feet, what he heard as distant thunder, made of him a simple witness. They were not elements over which he had any control. Had he been absent, they would have occurred regardless. He could not lift voice to be heard, and even could he, the presence of the demons would have drowned out the slender thread of his mortal words.

But he knew how to reach the earth, how to catch its attention even in its rage. He grimaced and drew his blade across his left palm; blood welled quickly although the cut had not been deep. He then knelt and placed that palm flat against the ground, beyond which shadows pooled and demons roared.

As his hand came into contact with the earth, the sounds shifted; he could hear the rumbling, the crack of stones, the movement of what lay beneath the earth's surface. The demons wouldn't have to do anything to kill every man, woman, and child present; the earth in its fury would do just that if unleashed. It was not yet unleashed, although it struggled for freedom, mindless in its fury.

In any other domain, they would already be dead.

He could not find the words to call the earth, to ask for its attention; he knew that the ancient, the wild, demanded respect, but knew as well that mortal respect had limitations, boundaries, that the ancient did not easily recognize.

He felt Nenyane's sudden alarm; the heat of fire blossomed around him. Before he could lift his hand, he heard Kallandras of Senniel College: **Do what you must do, but do it quickly, son of Bredan**.

He closed his eyes.

The earth rumbled beneath his hand, the movement different from the tremors beneath his knees. He was not prepared to hear it speak.

BREDAN'S OFFSPRING.

He answered without thought, without pause, without the need to think of words through which to funnel meaning. *Yes.*

Why are you in this place? The dead walk, and I will destroy them. But you are son to Bredan, and he is precious to us; be comforted. I will not see you destroyed when I end them. They have woken me. They intend to enslave my heart and to break the lands.

They cannot. Only you have that power. As he said the words he felt them; they were true. His hand—the hand that touched the earth—felt uncomfortably hot. *And I ask you to set aside your ancient—and justified— fury. My kind are frail; the dead might survive or withstand your anger, but my people will perish, who have done you no harm.*

Silence.

The price for the covenants made at the dawn of my kingdom's history have been paid, and paid, and paid, by the blood of my people. We are Breodani, and you are the foundation upon which Breodanir stands. These lands are our lands by the grace of your gift and the blood of our sacrifice. It is a vow I feel, even now. He did not lie. He was uncertain that he could. He could almost hear the echoes of the vow, ancient to him, that bound Breodani to Breodanir. *We have not forsaken it.*

Silence again, but in this, an eddy of a greater quiet, a deeper sense of waking purpose. *Remove the dead. Scrub their taint from the land. I will not allow them to destroy what you have built.*

As the last resonant syllables faded, he felt the earth's intent; beneath his hand, the strands of otherness, the wrongness, frayed and faded. He could feel the earth's anger, the earth's sense of fury at a betrayal that spanned millennia. But he could now also feel what might, in a person, have been a sense of affectionate responsibility; it was fainter by far, because it was—to the earth—too new.

Not for the first time, he wondered what the price of breaking the covenant was for the wild earth; he withdrew his palm before the stray thought could be caught. No Breodani who did not have Nenyane, with her odd flashes of memory, her strange areas of knowledge, would consider the earth itself to be alive. What vows did one make to soil? What succor could one expect from it?

Had he the words to invoke those questions, the earth would have offered its answer.

The shadows at the feet of the *Kialli* from which the lesser kin emerged dwindled, and at their edges, Stephen could now see the faint traces of green: leaves, buds, the slender green stalks of new growth. He thought them wildflowers—a pleasant word for weeds—but as he watched, those stalks grew, and grew again; they were saplings, not flowers. Saplings that might become trees, and whose roots were nestled far more deeply in the earth itself than those of flowers.

Wind blew through the leaves and branches that unfurled, saplings becoming trees as the seconds passed; leaves fell, shaken by wind that rose, and rose again.

Fire blossomed where shadow had pooled.

Nenyane sent a wordless warning, and even that she could only afford because the demon she faced had seen Meralonne APhaniel. It was the sight of the mage that changed the demon's focus. Dark, burning wings unfurled to left and right, bisecting the trees that had grown in an oddly shaped ring around both the demon and his shadow.

Nenyane wasn't happy about the trees: they changed the shape of the battlefield; they inhibited her free movement just as much as they did her foe's. Or perhaps more; she could not easily cut down the trees that had grown at the earth's desire.

But if Stephen had feared the summoning of fire—and he had—he understood that the earth's sense of enmity with fire was more ancient than even its rage and fury at the *Kialli*.

Come away, Stephen. Bring the Elseth Hunters.

His huntbrother had once again closed with the demon. No more lesser demons joined the fray; at least in this, the earth's desire held sway. But she fought. He could not retreat.

As if he could hear what Stephen did not put into words, the bard said, **She will rise above the fray, should it become necessary; the fire cannot harm her, and the earth will not—who better than earth to understand the binding ties between Hunter and huntbrother? Come away, or you will lose your pack and your kin.**

There was no compulsion in the bard's words—words that carried above the growing din of battle. Stephen turned to the Elseth Hunters and spoke a single word: *retreat.* The hunting pack, both dogs he had raised and dogs that had been granted him by the King, withdrew; only Pearl pushed back, but it was slight, more pettiness than genuine resistance. Only when Stephen rose and joined the retreating twins did Pearl concede.

Max opened his mouth, but closed it before words could escape; Alex's hand was on his brother's shoulder. They moved before the trunk of one great tree crashed into the ground where they had chosen to make their early stand.

The bard remained where he had been commanded to stand: in the forefront of a crowd of people. It was a sparser crowd; some people had fled to the road, and some had returned to the inn; the fire that had blackened the wall facing the demon had not found purchase in the wall itself, something Stephen was certain was Kallandras's doing.

Those who remained near Kallandras looked not to the bard but Ansel. Lord Ansel.

Stephen could see a glimpse of the Hunter Lord Ansel had once been, had once aspired to be, the Hunter Lord to whom Heiden had sworn the huntbrother's oath, and to whom Heiden still professed a loyalty that not even anger, violence, and risk of death could easily end. Ansel wore authority as a visible mantle, and people responded to it, in crisis, as if that authority could promise safety.

Stephen had his dogs; most of the people gathered here would assume that he, too, had earned his full Hunter colors. But he had never assumed authority as Ansel now did—perhaps because Corwin had never been broken by the loss of Arlin, perhaps because Stephen had known, from the age of nine, that he would never become Hunter Lord according to the laws of Breodanir.

Whatever the reason, he accepted it; he stood to Ansel's side in a silence that implied he, too, was waiting upon Ansel's commands, although his silence was far more watchful, far more focused on Nenyane.

He made no attempt to see through her eyes; she was always aware of his presence when he did and he knew she could not afford any distraction. Even with Meralonne by her side, he felt no certainty of her survival; he knew only that, were he to join her there in the unnatural, small forest the earth had erected, he would be a distraction at best, a cause for terror at worst.

"Stephen."

He nodded at the sound of the bard's voice, but did not turn to look at him; he looked, instead at the storm of light that broke through the trunks and branches of trees, sometimes literally; he saw blue lightning, red fire, and the flash of distant steel: Nenyane's blade. Nenyane's mundane sword.

In her hands there was no mundanity. He knew; he was her Hunter and her most frequent sparring partner. But only when she fought demons—none so powerful as this winged, majestic being for whom Stephen felt a visceral awe—did he see her differently, did he see her at the distance their disparate skills and knowledge made between them.

There was knowledge that was not in her control, knowledge that she could not easily grasp. But it returned to her in unpredictable waves.

She recognized this demon—a demon she had never seen take form and shape in Maubreche.

He held breath; realized it only when he was forced to exhale. He wanted to call her; he wanted to be by her side, the dogs by his. He was her Hunter. She was his huntbrother.

But she had not sworn the oaths that would bind her by God, law, and custom; he had not allowed it. No. All oaths aside, she was simply Nenyane, and she was determined not to survive him should he die. She did not fear the Sacred Hunt. She feared almost nothing.

But she was, and had always been, afraid that Stephen would die, and in dying desert her. At nine, it had mystified him, but as he took his place as oldest son of Maubreche, as he attended the funerals of Hunters and huntbrothers, as he saw the cost of loss and despair shadow his parents' faces, he began to understand it. As a child did, of course: *How would I feel if Nenyane died? What would I do if I could never hear her voice, never see her, never hunt by her side again?*

The answer, if he had none for himself, the funerals made clear.

He took care not to wonder openly; it annoyed Nenyane. Funerals upset her enough that she had been excused from attending any, and that suited Lady Maubreche well. Although she did not deny Nenyane as huntbrother, it spared the awkward questions and the subtle jostle for social power Nenyane's existence as huntbrother often started.

Fire rose, like lifted veil; earth rose like a wall.

Above them both, wind howled, moving Nenyane's hair, although it did not appear to touch the mage's. The only steel he could see was his huntbrother's; the mage wielded blue lightning, the demon, fire. But the loudest sound in the roar of elements and the breaking of trees was the clash of steel against steel.

The demon's voice he could hear, although it traveled without apparent effort; the mage's voice was likewise audible over all other sounds. Stephen could not understand the language, but understanding wasn't necessary; he heard what lay beneath the surface of spoken sylla-bles: the fury that only follows in the wake of pain, of betrayal, of a loss so vast no words could contain it; of a choice that sundered a people forever.

That sundering lay between the mage and the demon; he was surprised to hear his huntbrother join what was in no way a discussion; was afraid at the sudden surge of rage, of a fury that was so intense it was almost incandescent, almost visible to the naked eye.

Max and Alex froze at the sound of her voice, because it was both familiar and foreign. Nenyane had never been chatty; of the four, she moved most swiftly to irritation or anger. None of her anger had ever been so deep, so seemingly endless.

Perhaps the demons were accustomed to fury; what gave the Hunters pause seemed to have no effect on the *Kialli*. Or perhaps the speed of her blade, her attack, the force of blows that seemed too swift to have gathered momentum, were all he had time for.

No, Stephen thought. If Nenyane was a danger—and she was—it was Meralonne who commanded the demon's attention. Nenyane was almost, but not quite, irrelevant.

Fire did not consume her, although it rose as both wall and pillar around her, as if making the attempt. Wind caught her hair, drawing it back, always back, as if to prevent it from obscuring her vision; more than that was hard to see, she moved so quickly.

But Stephen was closer than Alex and Max; his hands were fists.

"Don't," Alex said. He turned, once again, toward the shadows that lay above the earth.

If the wild earth had offered some protection against the demonic incursion, if it had slowed the spread of shadow and the summoning of lesser creatures, the shadows fought back.

Stephen heard the bard's voice as he knelt; it grew faint as he once again placed a hand against the ground.

HE UNDERSTOOD that the sword that Nenyane had so vehemently demanded he learn was not his weapon here; that combat, such as it was, was now internal, interior—a matter of will, of the volume of will's assertion. He bowed head and once again raised interior voice, enjoining the wild earth to remember its vows—vows far more recent than its ancient grievance against the demons. The demons might survive should the earth lose its focus again; the Breodani citizens would not.

But entreaties did not have the force that binding oaths did; Stephen knew it. It was the God's blood, the God's power, that was necessary here—a power he had used once, and never again. He had reminded the earth of its vows.

It was not a simple reminder that was needed.

He had golden eyes. He had the power of Bredan's blood. But if that power was his to invoke, he had no control over the results, bound as they were to the implacable god. He could accept, could consecrate—if that was the right word—a vow; he could not release someone from it should that vow prove untenable. It was not a gift; it was a curse. A curse that ended in death.

The wild earth was not a mortal; Stephen was uncertain what the results of being forsworn would be. He was only certain that it would be extremely costly for Breodanir. He reminded the earth of its vows. Ah, no; it was not a reminder in any normal sense of the word; it was almost a command.

The earth did not deny him. He had expected some resistance, and the force of his demand for obedience, for compliance, met none. As if the force itself were literal, as if it involved momentum, he pushed through, stumbling into a silence that was shorn, now, of the cacophony of battle.

The earth did not speak in this place, but he felt its presence regardless; it was calm, quiet, still. Instead, he heard, at a great remove, the voices of men. Some were gravelly with age or too much drink, some lighter or higher with youth. They spoke a language he knew, and knew well: his mother tongue. He could not converse with them; he knew that the voices were echoes of people who had once lived, and whose lives had ended in service to both god and earth.

Those lives had been given to the earth that the earth might be fecund, the fields grow the food upon which Breodanir depended; those lives had been given to the Hunter God that he might remember that he was not a wild, elemental force, not a scion of frenzied hunger, but a god: the God who had led the Breodani to these lands, that they might survive and flourish.

The memory of those sacrifices, the earth retained.

It is the gift they offered. The words had no direction. *It is the gift I cherished in the endless silence. Those who could bespeak me — those who did not betray me in their desperate act of suicide — vanished, at the will of the gods. But we are many, we are multiple; no life exists where we do not exist. We were sundered, we ancients, but the shards of what we once were did not — could not — die. Even now, with the weight of geas upon us, we will not die should we be forsworn; we are multiple. If the part of me with whom you speak ceases to exist, I will nonetheless continue in this place.*

But these voices, these precious companions in our long exile, will fall silent forever; they will not be remembered. It is in respect for those that offered everything that I fight, now.

Demons could not command the wild earth, or so Stephen had been told.

No. Almost none can bespeak us, now; not as they are. But there are forces arrayed against your mortal kingdom that are not dead; they are alive and powerful in a way that your kind has never been. Can you not hear their voice?

No. Stephen was not accustomed to the flood of words Nenyane spoke through their bond.

You must learn to hear it, son of Bredan. Think you that the earth is compromised because of the dead? *It is not. But there are forces in the high wilderness that are far more dangerous than the dead.*

Stephen thought of the *Kialli* against whom Meralonne and Nenyane fought.

The earth rumbled; it did not disagree, although the tremor of fury was palpable. He wondered, then, what the demons had once been, when the wild earth had not considered them dead. The answer was wordless pain, and he focused instead on sounds that were not of the earth, not protected by it.

At the edge of his hearing—if hearing was even accurate—he could hear something almost sibilant, a whisper of sound, chill as high winter.

Yes.

The sound grew louder as he strained to hear it; he himself was silent. Silent or no, he knew the moment when he had somehow attracted the attention of whatever it was that bespoke the earth, its voice overlapping Stephen's, its imperative almost the equal of his, of Bredan's, of the covenant that had been paid for, time and again, with the ancestral blood of his people.

Almost, but not quite. This was Stephen's opponent on this field of battle, and he planted his figurative feet in the earth of Breodanir as he demanded—commanded—the trespasser to leave.

The words it spoke in return were not words as he understood them; they were almost music, but the music itself was discordant, the wrongness more felt than heard. Words were unnecessary; there was a primal desire for possession, for ownership, for dominance that he recognized immediately. He responded in kind. Breodanir was *his*. He was Breodani, born, bred; son of the God who had offered the earth the blood of his people in return for the earth's gift of succor, and the cost of that, writ large in Ansel's living memory, would *not* be offered in vain.

He spoke almost without intent.

He spoke with the earth's voice.

The sibilance became roar, the attention of this creature of the wilderness turned, in fury, toward him. Toward the earth itself. The earth trembled as the intruder's voice asserted dominance, control; it trembled again as Stephen pushed it back, more certain of his footing than he had ever been in any other combat, any other argument. He felt neither doubt nor fear, only the strength of his absolute conviction.

These lands were *his*. They were not, and would never belong to any other.

Yes, the earth said, its rumble growing. *Yes*.

The intruder roared in rage, in denial, but the sound was cut short. In that instant, the earth was once again still, the quiet whispers of the long-dead the only sound he could hear. Those people had given their lives to succor and protect Breodanir, just as he would willingly do. This was where he belonged.

But one voice was not in amity with the rest. One vaguely familiar voice adding a note of discordance. He turned toward it.

STEPHEN, enough. Come back *now*.

THIS VOICE DID NOT BELONG HERE; it never would. In the spoken words, Stephen felt compulsion and aggression, but the latter was subtle. Had the speaker intended harm, he would have destroyed it; here, in this moment, he had been granted that power by the earth. The earth to whom the blood of his kin, reaching back through history, had been offered. He felt a hint of Maubreche in this space, a hint of the maze at the heart of his ancestral home; here, demons might rage, but there was safety.

"You *idiot!*"

This voice was not the first voice, and it, too, felt wrong.

Wrong and right. He felt a hand on his shoulder, fingers clenching instantly as they made contact; they were warm. No—they were hot enough to be almost uncomfortable through layers of fabric. "What do you think you're doing? Are you even thinking *at all*?"

He attempted to shrug the hand off; when that failed, he gathered the earth around his body like a shield. But he made no attempt to destroy, to kill; only to remove. The earth's power could do that.

"Come back *right now*. Let go of the earth, or I'll cut it."

He shook his head as if to clear it. *Cut it? Cut the earth?*

I will cut it. With my sword.

The words made so little sense he might have dismissed them were they not couched in so much anger. Ah, no. Not anger, or not anger alone. She was afraid. She was afraid of the earth? No. Afraid of Stephen? No. Afraid *for* Stephen?

Yes. She was afraid for Stephen. Fear made her angry; it almost always had.

He closed his eyes; it made no difference. Here, in the warm dark of the earth, the voices of the Breodani who had walked the Hunter's Road before he had even been born fell silent. It was the silence of the grave. For one long moment he thought the earth had discarded them, and he felt fear of his own.

But no, it had not. The voices returned, slightly lessened in number. He understood, then. The blood that had been shed on the one day given to the Hunter God to hunt was not meant to be the blood of Hunter Lords.

Huntbrothers. People meant to be sacrificed so that the Hunters could feed and build a kingdom for Bredan's followers. In the beginning they had been chosen because they were of less objective use, less value, than the Hunters. They were people without whom a struggling country could survive.

But they were not people without whom their Hunters could survive as easily; to some, the huntbrothers had value and meaning that far outstripped rank and country, home, and even family. He thought of Ansel, then, of Lord Bowgren, bowed and broken by grief.

Stephen was not a scion of earth, to be comforted and protected; he was a Hunter, one not legally fit to be lord. The voice he heard, the anger—and the fear it overlay—was Nenyane's. Nenyane was his huntbrother. Nenyane, whose life he could not cede to either earth or the covenant of his God.

The voices rose and fell, as if they were not echoes or memories; they spoke of their Hunters, their Lords, and they spoke with gratitude and sorrow, for they understood in the moment of their deaths what their loss would mean to their truest brothers.

Stephen!

How could he not know? He had refused to allow Nenyane to take the oath of the huntbrother for a reason. She had come, somehow; she was here. She was with him. He cleared his throat, but found he could not speak. Not with the words that were her preference.

You'll cut the earth? Is your sword a shovel?

He felt her relief, stronger by far than the memories and echoes of the dead. He opened his eyes to night sky and fire that burned in the distance. Ah, the wall of the inn. Stumbling, he rose and headed toward it, but it was surrounded by men and women with buckets.

"It's a normal fire," Nenyane said. "When the demon attacked the inn—at a distance—a fire started in the dining room. The lamps fell and broke. Kallandras has been helping to contain that fire while people work to extinguish it."

"The demon?"

"Gone." Gone, Stephen thought. Not dead. "Illaraphaniel was injured. It was not a fight he could win without his shield. He joined battle because he didn't think I'd survive it on my own." Her snort made her disagreement clear. But words did not capture the odd complexity of thought. Stephen didn't ask her if she agreed. He knew that she did—and she was angry at herself, as she often was, because she considered the lack of power a personal fault.

If she had her memories. If only she had her memories.

"Did you recognize him?" He knew the answer but felt he had to ask.

She surprised him. "Yes." Her voice was soft. "Yes, I recognized him. I've seen him fight before." He knew better than to ask her where or when; if she knew, she would have said so. "Illaraphaniel should have had a shield."

Accustomed to the odd flow of Nenyane's conversation, Stephen nodded. "Why do you think he doesn't have one?"

"If he had one, he'd have used it. He needed it." Frowning, she added, "Oh. You're asking where I think he lost it."

"Both."

"I don't know. I—it's not a question I think I could ask him. But I've never seen him injured while fighting simple *Kialli* before."

Simple *Kialli*. Stephen could not quite keep the words together in his head, they seemed so mismatched.

"So much has changed," she whispered. For just a moment, he could see Illaraphaniel in her mind's eye, and he stumbled; the mage he called Meralonne and the being she called Illaraphaniel were in no way the same. He had seen hints of that grandeur before; he had never seen it fully revealed. "I don't know how we're going to do this. I don't know how we're going to survive if the god is on the plane."

He heard what she did not say. She did not know how he would survive. It was Stephen's survival—or the lack of it—that was the heart of her fear.

"My father said that there were those who were as powerful as gods; they could not leave, as gods did. We'll find them."

She exhaled slowly as if fear was breath and she intended to expel it. "Let's go see the mage." She took three steps and stopped, her back toward him. "You probably saved us. I now understand why the demons want you dead so badly."

"Why?"

She snorted, but still refused to look at him. "You're the oathbinder, Stephen."

"Demons aren't likely to swear binding oaths."

"No. I'm not sure they can—the earth calls them dead for a reason."

He waited for an explanation, but did not approach her.

"It's the power of an oathbinder that you drew on to remind the wild earth of the vows they swore to Bredan, and Bredan swore to them. Where we now stand, the earth is Breodanir's. I think the lands in this region will no longer fall prey to the wilderness."

Stephen exhaled. "It wasn't me—"

"Don't. It was you, and we both know it. The demons will know as well; we can't avoid that knowledge."

"They've been hunting me regardless."

She nodded. "But now they'll hunt in earnest. I don't know what about Breodanir they consider a threat—but something in this kingdom, in these lands, worries them. It must, given who they sent."

CHAPTER EIGHTEEN

The inn did not burn down, but would require extensive repairs. The gravity of the attack, the presence of the demon and the many shadows under its command, had made those extensive repairs seem a minor inconvenience: people had survived. The innkeeper had lost neither customers nor family.

To Gervanno's relief, he had not lost Leial. The dog had not joined the fray, for which he was immensely grateful, but joined his chosen master after the fight was at an end, and the earth itself once again still and silent. Leial was frantic, but relieved, and Gervanno's face—he was foolish enough to kneel—was wet very shortly thereafter.

Gervanno wished to be well away from the inn before the relief of these strangers gave way to reality. But perhaps it would not; perhaps gratitude for survival in the face of certain death would make of the terrible work and the hardship to follow a gift. The dead did not struggle.

He was grim and silent as he aided the innkeeper and his water brigade; he was less silent as he tended to burns, but words were required to treat people, especially the younger ones whose anxious parents hovered—or waited their turn to be examined. It was a reminder—a necessary one—that people died in the face of absolutely mundane happenstance. Death did not require demons and their fell magics, nor did it require battlefields and war.

He had not joined Nenyane in her battle, and attempted to contain his regret, his feeling of shame; he had, however, joined the two Hunters who kept watch over Stephen. The Maubreche youth had been crouched, hand to ground, for almost the entire duration of the battle.

Do not touch him. Gervanno, recognizing the bard's voice, had nodded, but even if the bard had made no attempt to interfere, he would have kept his distance from the young man; it was what Stephen's companions did, and he would have assumed there was reason for it.

Demons had come, summoned by the creature Nenyane fought. If Gervanno considered her blade work unparalleled, he accepted that demonic strength might well overpower it. But he had seen Nenyane fight demons before, and no other battle had caused her this difficulty. Were it not for the intervention of the almost luminous Northern Widan, Gervanno was uncertain she would have survived.

Still, overmastered or no, she attacked, defended, drew some of the demon's attention. Her companion in combat, however, had become the demon's focus as he joined the fray; the creature drew blade of flame, the mage blade of lightning. Where these blades clashed, the sky was briefly illuminated; where they landed, the earth shook.

But the earth had continued its growing tremors. Gervanno had maintained his footing; the Elseth brothers' was less certain. One of the twins was driven, twice, to knee; the dogs, however, stood their ground, darting forth only to attack when the lesser demons approached.

They did not approach often. If the bard had demanded—commanded—Lord Ansel and Heiden, if he had given instructions to Gervanno, he did so with barely a hint of concentration. His attention was focused outward, to the lesser demons; a windstorm that did not touch a hair on Stephen's head, howled around them, slowing their progress. The dogs—and Gervanno—made quick work of them; the Elseth brothers seemed invisibly anchored to Stephen. Gervanno was grateful for it.

He sustained no injuries; nor did the dogs or the Hunters in his immediate view. But he could see that the mage had been injured; that, more than fire or shadow or breaking earth, almost shocked him. The mage, however, sought no medical aid, no aid at all; Gervanno was surprised that he remained, for his gaze traveled out from the inn, as if to trace the arc of his enemy's retreat.

Gervanno finished cleaning and bandaging a young man's arm; the burn was painful but it would not cripple the youth if he took care to keep the injured area clean. Infection was usually the killer in situations like this.

"Do you have any supplies left?"

He lifted head to meet Lord Ansel's gaze; he could see the telltale signs of controlled exhaustion in the young man's gaze, but Ansel's bearing would have been at home among the powerful in the South. "I do. The innkeeper emptied his cupboards."

"Makes you wonder what kind of trouble an innkeeper expects, doesn't it?" This was Heiden, the corner of his lips turned up in a rueful smile. He did not carry himself as a ruler, but rather, the most trusted of oathguards.

Lord Ansel had no answering smile; he was annoyed with his brother. "Heiden thought catching a burning log with his *right forearm* was the most intelligent of options."

"It would have hit a panicking young woman," Heiden explained, without apparent contrition or regret.

"Instead, it hits you — and you have duties to attend to."

"So does she," Heiden said, a frown surfacing.

"She won't be facing demons or worse."

"No — not if we're successful. But...Stephen did something that protected this inn and these people. We may not have the raw power of the demons — we certainly don't have their magic — but we're not unarmed. Regardless, she works in the inn. She feeds herself, and she probably feeds some part of her family — if not all of it. She's not a soldier, no — but not all responsibilities are military in nature. Don't disrespect your people."

Lord Ansel exhaled. "Fine. I deserved that. But if that burn becomes infected and I have to cut your arm off, I'm going to be angry."

"I've always been way more careful than you," Heiden snapped.

Gervanno chuckled, the warmth of amusement drawing their attention from each other. He rose. "You're the last of my patients — no doubt intentionally. If food survived in the inn's larder, I would beg a meal — I ate very little earlier. It is a mistake I have not made in a decade on various battlefields, and I am reminded that there are pragmatic reasons to eat and sleep at any opportunity that presents itself."

Heiden, pale, nodded.

"Join me, then. I believe the Elseth Hunters are returned."

"Stephen?"

"Nenyane seems somewhat annoyed with her Hunter."

Ansel glanced over his shoulder. "We should let them be."

"Oh?" Heiden asked.

"I don't believe *somewhat* is the right choice of word. I'm somewhat annoyed with you. She's angry."

Heiden winced and nodded, rising. The burn was not severe, but it would cause some pain and discomfort for the next few days. Gervanno had no supply of the bitterweed that sometimes dulled pain, but there might be drink in the inn, which would help. But perhaps not. He'd spilled much of it over burns such as this. The innkeeper had not begrudged it.

Heiden was right. Within what remained of the inn's interior dining room, he could see the bustle of soot-blackened skirts and aprons; if people could not now take a chair at a table meant for dining or drinking, they could still eat. Which meant food had to be prepared. They prepared it. It was an act that would no doubt not occur to any of the Hunters present as a necessity.

Gervanno, born free, had been born without rank or the power derived from rank. Had he not chosen to follow the path of the warrior, he would be one of those men and women, hurrying to prepare what food they could offer.

He would be one of the people who felt a deep gratitude for the intervention of the Hunters and their companions. Men like Gervanno, even if he was among the weakest of their number.

A hint of the child he had once been surfaced now, as it sometimes did: he had loved his parents, his Oma, his Onos, and Onas. He had greatly desired to take up the sword to protect them from everything, and he had been young enough to believe that all danger came with intent—that the sword was the only certain protection.

His sword had been no protection at all when it counted most. He had intended to return to the South after delivering a warning; to return Silvo's sword to his family.

To wait until moon reigned and the Lady's face was upon him, and to offer what remained of his dishonored life as atonement for his cowardice, his failure. And here he was, in a foreign country, defending a Northern lordling and offering medical aid to people like his family. He heard the loud, barking voice of an older woman, and knew, if the words were different, if the language was strange, the tone was exactly the same; she was no doubt in charge of the kitchen, and in her fashion, marshaling her forces.

He wanted the food, not because he was hungry, but because it offered this foreign cerdan a glimpse of home, a reminder of what had started him on this road.

He could not now return to the South with Silvo's sword, although he still intended to do so when the task here was finished. Nor did he now feel offering his life—his honorless, valueless life—to the Lady's mercy was his only way forward; he wanted to remain with the Hunters for as long as their battle lasted. In their service, he might be able to lift his head, might be able to see his reflection with something other than unadulterated contempt.

But first: food. Food offered by people he had defended.

If the financial loss of the inn dampened their mood, tonight they were almost celebrating, and he wished to let that celebration envelop him for a brief period, even if he did not entirely deserve it.

NENYANE DID NOT JOIN STEPHEN, Alex, and Max for the offered food. Nor did she vanish into the surroundings, as she often did in Maubreche. Stephen noted that she observed Meralonne with an intensity of focus customarily reserved for Stephen himself. He couldn't decide whether this was a relief or a concern, but chose relief; Nenyane was angry with him.

She knew she was being unreasonable, and was therefore also angry with herself. Anyone who knew her knew that that anger was usually the least comfortable for anyone in her vicinity. But beneath her fury at herself was the shadow of fear.

She understood what Stephen had done—possibly better, on a visceral level, than Stephen himself—and knew it had been necessary. But she also knew Stephen had been in danger; he had almost been lost to the earth's overwhelming presence.

She was therefore also angry at the wild earth. She had no way of bespeaking it, but had she, he was certain she would have offloaded the worst of her temper at the earth itself. He doubted that would go well, and if the earth was angered, there would be few survivors.

"I know that," she snapped, her hands clenching and unclenching. She wanted to storm off, but didn't. Instead, she turned away, in search of Meralonne.

"WHERE IS YOUR SHIELD?"

Meralonne looked up from the bowl of his pipe, half-lined with fastidious care. The meal in progress in front of the inn had little appeal. If the wound he had taken was not insignificant, neither was it life-threatening. It was a bitter reminder of a distant past—a past which he had never entirely left. If the four princes of the White Lady's court had been considered the most powerful of her servants, they had had rivals in their time; those with power close to, or almost equal their own.

Princes and rivals had had contests—some bitter and deadly—to establish supremacy or to change the accepted hierarchy, establishing themselves as more worthy of the Lady's gifts and honor. In their distant youth, that had been the most important of prizes: her approval. Her regard.

How, then, could brothers in arms turn away from that? How could they betray her? How could they be compelled to swear both service and life itself to their enemy?

"It is gone, as you have noted." He did not set the pipe aside.

"And you have not replaced it." This was not a question.

"As you say." He looked up only after he had lit the pipe, setting the stem against his lips. "How much do you remember?"

She shook her head. "I remember you. You and your kin often chose to express your condescension by withholding your strongest weapons —but you were injured. This was not a foe whom you could fight without all of the tools at your disposal. You have no shield."

"No."

"Why? Why have you not replaced it?"

Lips pursed, the mage exhaled rings of smoke and watched them rise and extend. "You do not remember enough, Nenyane of Maubreche. The craftsmen that might create a shield such as I once bore are scattered. Even if they were not, I am in exile; the forges are closed to one such as I. You have no doubt heard, in Maubreche, tales about the Sleepers? They woke, and they are gone now, returned to the White Lady, perhaps in her hour of need.

"But she is not what she was, when we first met, and she will never be that, again."

"Exile?"

He nodded, his expression neutral. "Our enemy has stirred in the distant Northern Wastes; he has gathered power, there. The attack upon the capital of Breodanir indicates that his long, careful patience is almost at an end. You are not ready to face him." He inhaled and exhaled another ring, smaller and denser; he watched it rise. "Nor am I, as you have pointed out.

"But I cannot lay duty aside because I am lacking a shield, just as you cannot, while lacking the memories of your purpose, your birth."

"None of us remember our birth."

"As you say. Your Hunter did well, there—better by far than I had been given cause to believe he would." At her clenched fists, he shook his head. "You were born for a reason, as was I. We did not choose birth, but at the core of what we are, those reasons drive us."

She stared at him. "Exile?" As if no other words had penetrated her caged, restless anger.

"I am not welcome in the White Lady's lands. I cannot return to the White Lady's court. And it is in that court that the shield I once bore was made."

"How can you be exiled?"

"At the White Lady's command."

"But *why*? You exist, you breathe, you fight—had you been worthy of exile, you would have been worthy of death. Why do you still live?"

"Perhaps, in her view, life in exile was the greater punishment." He rose, as if Nenyane's restlessness could be transmitted. "It is what I believed for the long, long years I was condemned to live. But no longer. I see the shape of the future taking form, and I can finally see the threads that link it, tarnished and frayed, to those long-ago events of the past.

"Or perhaps I am simply what I was born to be: I see the hope of redemption. I see the hope of forgiveness, no matter how foolish either hope might prove to be. Do you not see the same?"

She was still, silent as a rabbit made suddenly aware of a predator.

"You were badly injured; given your current state, it is a small wonder you survived. It is your unmaking that most concerns the god we do not name. Do you understand that much?"

She did not answer.

"Would you have your memories made whole?"

She moved, her chin rising, her eyes widening before they narrowed so completely they almost appeared to be closed. "How?" The single syllable was guttural. "You cannot return to the White Lady and her court."

"No healing—for you—would be found in that court. And no safe, gentle healing can be offered, the damage is so complete."

"Who must I seek? Where must I go?" Her arms trembled, her knuckles white; her voice was both soft and low.

"To speak with the dead. The dead that cannot die as mortals die, or even as Firstborn do." He lowered his pipe, his gaze unblinking. "You must return to the place of your birth."

"And where, exactly, would you claim that is?"

The mage glanced in the direction of the voice: Stephen of Maubreche had arrived, no doubt because he was privy to Nenyane's emotions as her Hunter. He did not answer; instead he turned back to Nenyane. "He is mortal. But you had a fondness for mortals, a weakness for them. We never understood it, we who did not age as mortals do.

"You, who feared loss and grief and separation, tied yourself to someone who was doomed, from birth, to fade and die, even should his life be peaceful and calm for the entirety of its duration.

"These are not peaceful times, as those were not. You are here, and you have made your choice, be it unconsciously. You were made for war. What risk will you allow your Hunter to endure that you might be whole enough to fight it?"

"Surely that is up to her Hunter, and not a mage from the Empire?" Stephen demanded. He stepped in front of Meralonne, his back to the mage and his pipe, as if to shield Nenyane from the mage's eyes.

"Is that what you believe?" the mage said, from behind. "Yes, the choice and direction should be yours—"

"Ours. It is *our* choice. You will not coerce Nenyane into doing anything she—and I—do not fully understand; we will not make choices in ignorance." The youth's voice was low, almost a growl of sound. Meralonne was not surprised to see the dogs begin to approach, but they moved slowly and awkwardly, as if they had been forbidden Stephen's company, and nonetheless sought to sneak into it unnoticed.

"Your huntbrother has no memories of life before Maubreche, and perhaps that suited you. But she cannot make a reasoned choice without the knowledge she once had. I might tell her where she must go —and were it within my capability, I might lead her there—but I cannot do what must be done. Only she can."

"If she can't remember—"

"It is only, in my opinion, that she *might*. I offer no guarantees, but Nenyane knows that. When navigating among the dead, there is no certainty, no safety."

"The dead? Dead what?"

Meralonne set his pipe aside; it floated beside him in mid-air. "Gods."

The mage watched the carefully neutral expression the young Hunter adopted as the youth turned, almost resentfully, to face him, assessing. When the mage exhaled, he set the pipe aside. "You are Nenyane's vulnerability, her biggest weakness. If there was a way to separate yourself from her—for her own good—could you do it?"

It was Nenyane who answered as Stephen attempted to marshal his words, to wrap them around his angry, visceral response in a way that muted anger.

"No. Stephen is my Hunter. Stephen is my choice." Her eyes were narrowed as she glared at the mage. "There is only one way to separate us, and I will kill you—slowly—should you ever attempt it. You will join the dead of whom you speak."

This pulled a smile from the mage. There was no amusement in it as he met—and held—Nenyane's gaze. "There is no certainty that I would die." He wondered then what it would be like to cross blades with Nenyane when she was intent upon his death, and felt a brief pang of regret that it would never come to be.

"But I have wandered. There is only one place you might travel to retrieve what you have lost. We travel now to Bowgren, but forces that are gathering in the wilderness—did you not hear their voices?—are focused on that demesne. It might be wiser for you to travel to a different location."

"The enemy is in Bowgren."

"Not yet, little huntbrother, but soon. And you are not, as you are full aware, prepared to face them. Or will you leave the life of your Hunter to my plans, my strategies, my advice? He and I are not the same, and our goals differ. Were I called upon to surrender Bowgren—or even Breodanir—in its entirety in order to better attain my goals, you must know I would do so.

"Travel in your state of half-ignorance, and you are doing exactly that: you are leaving any intelligent decisions to me."

Nenyane's complexion was dark as she glared, unblinking, into his narrowed, silver eyes. Her hand fell to sword hilt and rested there, white-knuckled. Her Hunter took a step toward Meralonne, but she lifted an arm—without looking at him—to block his passage. "This won't be the first time we encounter things I should know and don't."

"But Stephen promised Ansel and Heiden that we would save Bowgren if it was possible."

"Stephen of Maubreche will, of course, go to Bowgren. If he did not sanctify oath, he is what he was born to be; he will not be forsworn. But you do not have to follow. If you leave now, I believe you might rely on instinct to take you to where you must go; I could not guide you more quickly.

"And if you do what must be done, you might return, whole, to your Hunter. This will not be the first battle Stephen will face into which the ancient and the wild seep; it is a simple first step, a test of both you and the readiness of the Breodani. Or you can avoid what you must know is necessary, waiting until the time has passed, and chaos descends upon us all."

———

NENYANE DIDN'T SPEAK. Not a word. Stephen was aware that, were it not for the presence of the mage, the outcome of the demonic attack could have been much, much worse—but he found it hard to appreciate the mage's presence.

The mage watched Nenyane. Stephen had become invisible, as if he had never been part of the conversation, as if he was irrelevant. Perhaps, to the mage, he was—but he would never be irrelevant to his huntbrother. He willed her to tell the mage no.

She did not. Silence stretched between the two: mage and huntbrother. Stephen could hear the swirl of thoughts beneath the surface of her silence, but they were so fragmented he could find no solid purchase.

She wanted to go. She wanted to walk a path that Meralonne implied only she could walk, to reach a destination that might—*might*—give her back her memories. This was her choice to make, even now, with Bowgren under threat, and all of Breodanir soon to follow if that threat was not somehow resolved in their favor.

She had always had moments in which the lack of memory, the lack of personal history, had grieved her, but those moments had grown to occupy more and more of her internal space, fueling a self-loathing that had once existed only in brief flashes.

Tonight it was not brief. It was not easily turned aside, if it could be turned aside at all.

Meralonne was not correct. Stephen had sworn no oath, but he had made a commitment to Nenyane, huntbrother. He expected Hunters to understand the weight of that.

"You are not going alone." Stephen's voice was flat; there was no flexibility in the words. This was the heart of her interior conflict. She knew he would never allow her to head into unknown danger on her own. He had tried all his life to give her the space she required, but in this he would not bend. "You are allowed to make the decisions and choices you feel necessary. But you are not allowed to travel into unknown dangers alone. We're brothers. Where you go, I go. Where I go, you go."

"And if we must walk—for a time—in opposite directions?"

He shook his head. "We choose one together."

"Do *not* fold your arms like that. Only Mother can carry it off." Her frown was a flash, there and gone. "I can't take you with me. You heard what he said."

"Everything he said spoke of risk, of possible death. I don't think he's certain that he can safely go where he feels you must go."

"If he can't, you definitely can't."

"That's a pity, then. Why do you think you can? Because he said you might?"

"I don't know. *I don't know.* But how can we fight and defend ourselves when I don't know what I *should* know? What if something irrelevant to me occurs and I don't see it clearly enough when it's *not irrelevant to your survival?* I recognize the man you call Meralonne. I've seen him fight. I know his blade work; I know his capabilities. I don't know *when* I saw him fight. I know that we were allies; I know that I trusted him. But I don't know why. I recognized the creature he showed us in Hunter's Redoubt. I don't know *why.* I react instinctively; I recognize things but I have no context. I don't know how anything will affect *you.*"

That, Stephen thought, was the heart of her fear of her own ignorance. Stephen's ignorance, she accepted as natural—which had caused more than one heated disagreement in their childhood.

"I need to know who I was. And I need you to survive."

"Which," he said, voice as soft as he could make it, "of the two is the priority?"

"Your survival." She answered without thought, a low growl beneath the words, as if every worry or fear she had accumulated in their life together was trying to claw its way free.

Stephen did not retreat. "My death isn't guaranteed. My survival isn't guaranteed. You know that. You've always known it. We've been hunted by demons for much of our lives; they've come with little warning, and perished the same way. There is no safety, no guarantee."

"What about what I want?"

But he knew this game. "If you wanted just one thing, I might agree. But you don't. What you want is tangled up in your fear for me—it's the thread that winds through every fear you have. You're not capable of choosing just one thing. It changes."

"And you're any better?" she demanded, eyes narrowed, hands clenched. It had been a long time since they had come to physical blows.

"I *am* better. I would let you go wherever you felt it was necessary to go—but I would accompany you."

She spit out a few words that would have caused his mother to pale— the kind of pale that appeared around lips compressed into a tight, narrow line. "And that's *why* we're even in this godsforsaken place? Because you'll *let me* make my own choice and swear *my own bloody oaths*?"

Stephen failed to reply, robbed for a moment of words.

"I was willing to swear the oath. I *knew what it meant*, and I was willing to swear it. I'd swear it *now*. I'd swear it *tomorrow*. It's your choice, and it always has been. You won't *accept* the oath. You won't let me swear it because you're afraid your father *will*! How is that allowing me to make my own choices?"

"You don't care about the oath!" He could not stop his own voice from climbing, just as his huntbrother's had done. His hands became fists, twins to hers; they shook in the same fashion.

"Exactly! I don't care! It won't change anything in my life! I could have done this *one thing* to make yours better—and you rejected it! You weren't willing to live with the possible consequences of my choice so don't talk to me about letting me make my own choices!"

"It's not just about you! The oath comes from you and is accepted by me—but the consequences would be borne by you alone! If you need to go, if you need to risk your life to find the answers you need, I accept that. But I don't accept it has nothing to do with me—because it doesn't!"

A hand fell gently on Stephen's shoulder; it was not a familiar hand. He turned, words cut instantly, and found himself facing the bard. The bard then removed the hand. "Perhaps this is not the time to have this discussion."

"It's not a discussion," Nenyane snapped, "and it's none of your business."

Stephen, however, lowered his voice and unclenched his hands. It took work, but it was necessary because the bard was right.

"Come. Join us for dinner. The mood around the fires is good—but it will not remain that way if the Maubreche contingent comes to blows."

"THAT WAS NOT WELL DONE," Kallandras said softly; he watched the two Maubreche Hunters depart, although the huntbrother had been slow to surrender her anger. He understood that; anger blended with fear grew the deepest roots.

Meralonne had once again taken up pipe, but the familiar smoke seemed to provide little comfort. "I am not Celleriant, to accept your chiding as if it came from kin." His eyes were silver, flashing; his hair moved by no natural breeze.

"Perhaps not. But we will be companions on the road to Bowgren, and on the roads within it, and if I understand anything of what has passed, those two—Stephen and Nenyane—will be necessary there. We have neither the time nor the ability to quickly traverse the endless wilderness."

"She does," the mage replied. "It is not Nenyane that we require here, but Stephen. And if it were Nenyane we required, we would almost certainly be doomed. She is not what she was—and she is not capable of becoming that yet."

"You heard them."

"The entire gathering heard them." A hint of a cold smile crept up the mage's lips. "But I do not hear as you hear. Were I to spend the rest of my existence in the study of humanity, I might mimic your talent, but I will never fully possess it."

"Stephen will not be moved. Between the two, it is Nenyane who will yield."

"And with grace, I see." The cold smile deepened. "I wondered, in the distant past, if she chose as she chose because she thought mortals malleable and less intimidating."

Kallandras did not reply. He did not require the hearing of the bard-born to know that the mage did not lie. He was familiar with Nenyane of Maubreche. "We will depart for Bowgren on the morrow." It was both a statement and a question.

"Were it just the two of us, I would depart for Bowgren tonight. Can you not hear it?"

Kallandras exhaled before nodding.

"Bowgren has fallen farther than I thought possible in this short span of time."

"The demesne has not yet completely fractured."

"No. I will stand watch. You will join the Hunters."

The words were a command. Kallandras, accustomed to navigating the whims of the powerful, nodded as if command were the mage's right.

WHEN HEIDEN CAME to the door of the room Stephen shared with Nenyane, Stephen was awake. As so often happened, the echoes of the interrupted argument had returned, and possible retorts—or responses—returned with it, as if he could somehow change the argument's flow when the argument itself was, if not over, abandoned for now.

"Ansel?" he asked.

"Sleeping. Nenyane?"

"Out speaking with the mage."

"What *is* he?"

"A First Circle mage of the Order of Knowledge." The words were a closed door. Heiden accepted it in a way Ansel wouldn't have, had he been present.

"I came to ask when we should be ready to leave."

"Dawn, I think—if that late. Meralonne is concerned." His Hunt-brother was sensitive to the mage's worries. "Nenyane decided to do without sleep."

"Is she worried the demons will return?"

Stephen shook his head. "Not here, not tonight. She's worried because they shouldn't have been able to attack the first time—but they did, and they arrived by traversing paths that they shouldn't have been able to walk."

Heiden nodded again. Silence enfolded them, but it was not entirely companionable; it was the silence of a person who was now trying to choose their words with enough care they caused no offense. Stephen could have told him it wasn't necessary.

"What did you do?"

The urge to deliberately misunderstand the question was visceral; Stephen put it aside. Heiden was huntbrother, Breodani to the core. Heiden, as Nenyane would have had she been allowed, had sworn the huntbrother's oath with an understanding of what it meant.

"I spoke with the earth of Breodanir. All Hunters do, or can—if they stand in their own demesnes—but Breodan's compact with the earth stretches across the boundaries of the entire kingdom. And our voices, singularly, have trouble reaching the earth."

"And the blood?"

"It helps."

"Is it necessary?"

It wasn't a question Stephen had considered before; he turned it over, examining it. "Considering the Sacred Hunt, blood has been shed, and that shedding is necessary. Outside of the Sacred Hunt, I think blood is the equivalent of a horn call; it reaches the earth in a way our normal raised voices do not."

Heiden nodded again, hesitating. Stephen was uncertain that he would speak, that he would force the question he'd come to ask out. "Will you be coming to Bowgren? Or will you..." Heiden's question trailed off. This, Stephen thought, was why he had chosen to risk knocking on his door.

"We will come to Bowgren. Both of us."

"Or neither of you?"

The Maubreche Hunter shook his head. "Both of us. Nenyane won't run away without warning, and she won't—yet—allow me to accompany her wherever it is the mage feels she should go."

The Bowgren huntbrother's shoulders dipped as Heiden exhaled. "Thank you. I don't know if Ansel will tell you this in words—but I will. He didn't want to come to the King's City. He didn't want to be forced into Hunter's Redoubt. He took his resentment out on you, and he does regret it. But had we not been sent, our return to Bowgren—if it happened at all—would have been very different." Heiden bowed head. When he lifted it, a careworn smile moved his lips.

"I know what it looked like on the outside. I know you were worried for me. But if you didn't see him tonight, you won't understand why I held on, why I clung to hope. He *is* Lord Ansel. He'll be a better lord than the current Lord Bowgren, and he *is* respected by the villagers in our demesne. He's better than his anger, his pain, his grief. And for the first time in too long, he has real hope. He has a sense of purpose.

"And I have Ansel back."

THE INN'S wall had not magically repaired itself, nor would it. But the innkeeper had marshaled his mundane forces to deal with the emergency, and if he was not delighted by the need, he was energetic and grateful to the Hunters who had inadvertently been the cause of the attack. His wife was less sanguine, but took her worry out on the young men and women who had come as laborers, although much of her worry was of the *watch how you carry that, you'll hurt yourself* variety.

She was, however, grateful as well when her attention could be claimed for farewells; she understood some part of what she'd seen, and knew it was a fight for the Hunters and their friends—all of whom had been present.

"And at least it happened in summer," she added. "None of us will suffer under the threat of cold while we work." She'd packed food for the road; Stephen would have felt guilty accepting it, but she handed the food to Ansel. Of course she had; he was the Hunter tasked with keeping the people safe—and calm. To her eyes, Stephen had spent the combat crouched almost to ground, as if fear had robbed his legs of strength.

The bard and the mage were waiting as the cast of the sky slowly changed at the horizon; the mage was impatient, the bard calm and placid. Alex and Max were the last to come down, Ansel and Heiden the first.

The horses were skittish, but the demons had not reached the stables; their own sensitivity had made clear to them that fire and death were close. The dogs, however, were excited—bright-eyed and eager. The notable exception was Pearl, whose entire presence implied immense condescension on her part. She obeyed Stephen to the figurative letter, but made it clear that it was her choice to do so.

Stephen accepted this; dogs had personalities. Nenyane found it almost offensive. She was not in a good mood, and found sunlight at the wrong angle offensive as well.

The King's Road branched into the territory of Margen, beyond which lay Bowgren, near the northeastern border. Stephen had little experience with Lord Margen, although he had met Lady Margen in the capital a handful of times, always in the company of his mother. Lady Margen had presented her elder son when Stephen had been perhaps ten.

"Eleven," Nenyane snapped.

"Does it matter? We'd like to pass through Margen as quickly as possible."

"We should be able to clear the territory, and reach the borders of Bowgren, by nightfall tomorrow, in the best case," the mage said. "We will need to push the horses, but the Queen's messenger service does not fully stable horses in the Margen territory—or the Bowgren territory if it comes to that. We cannot drive the horses too hard."

Ansel nodded curt agreement, bottling words with a restless energy that implied he might run all the way to Bowgren on foot in the absence of horses.

"Lady Margen is among the gentler of the Hunter Ladies I have met," Kallandras then said. "Given the situation in Bowgren, I highly doubt she will attempt to have us stopped at the border."

"Lord Margen?"

"I have not met Lord Margen in person; the lords seldom visit the capital except for the Sacred Hunt, and they are not wont to be social at that time."

"Lord Margen will hasten us on our way," Heiden said, raising his voice to be heard. He had not learned the art of projecting his voice, and his natural voice was on the softer side. "He was—he is—a close friend of Lord Bowgren, and I believe he was not pleased at the King's decision to command Ansel to the capital during the troubles. He will not bar our passage."

26TH OF EMPERAL, 429 A.A. KINGDOM OF BREODANIR,
DEMESNE OF MARGEN

For ease of travel, the mage had elected to follow the roads. The road
that wound through Margen was narrower than the King's Road, but
was intended to allow merchants some ease of passage. In places,
however, it was packed dirt, not the maintained stone of the King's
Road. No rain had softened that dirt enough to turn it into the mud that
made passage difficult, but evidence of such rain persisted in the shape
of the road itself.

Gervanno, traveling from the South to the Imperial capital, and
from there to the Western Kingdoms, had seen roads in far worse
repair, but he had slowed his horse as the sun began its dominance of
the sky. With roads such as these, the danger to the horses was
always higher, and unhorsed, their necessary passage would be
slowed.

Nenyane glanced back. She then slowed her horse to match his
pace, as, over the course of minutes, did the others in this strange party.
Ansel was restive, but did not question the undiscussed decision. If
horses were not dogs, they were nonetheless valuable to Hunter Lords,
and they were treated—where possible—with care.

Nenyane dismounted and said, "I'll go on foot."

Alex, Max, and Stephen shrugged and made no attempt to argue.
The bard was likewise silent. Heiden made a single attempt to dissuade
her. Ansel might have done the same, but when he met her gaze—which
was, by this point, mostly glare—he closed his mouth and glanced in
Stephen's direction. Nenyane was not his problem; she was Stephen's
problem.

Gervanno's mutt joined him, carried in one arm for much of the
journey, which made the ride more awkward than it would have been
had Gervanno not been an excellent rider. Leial was too short-legged to
keep up with the hunting dogs, who were accustomed to long runs. He
understood that the Hunter dogs were working dogs; Leial was not.
None of the Hunters objected to Leial's inclusion.

Nenyane did not keep pace with the horses—she ran ahead of
Ansel, who had taken the lead because these were roads with which he
was more than familiar.

Only when Nenyane was out of earshot did Ansel reposition his
horse. "Can she run all the way to Bowgren?" Before Stephen replied

he added, "I couldn't. I could make it most of the way there if I constantly invoked the trance—but I'd collapse at the end."

"She can run all the way to Bowgren and back, but she won't humiliate the rest of us by running laps around us. She's always been the best runner in Maubreche; I can match her if I call the trance, but only in sprints."

"She can run at that speed all day?"

Stephen grimaced but nodded. "She doesn't like horses. To be fair, horses don't like her much either. They'll carry her if they're well trained."

"Has she always been like that?"

"For the entire time she's lived in Maubreche. Her temper has gotten worse, though." Stephen stiffened.

"What is it? What's happened to Nenyane?"

The Maubreche Hunter looked down the road; its shallow bend robbed him of immediate sight of his huntbrother. "You said we should have clear passage to Bowgren?"

Ansel's knuckles whitened as he clenched the reins of his horse. "Yes."

"There are guards on the road on this side of the border. We have to hurry—Nenyane's annoyed."

STEPHEN REACHED Nenyane's side first, although the rest of the Hunters weren't far behind. The mage and the bard pulled up the rear, aware—which, in the case of the mage, was surprising—that their presence as outsiders could be counted against the Hunters, even the familiar ones.

Six men stood before Nenyane, barring her passage. There was no obvious strangeness on the road at the guards' backs; they faced in, the oldest man present lifting chin at Stephen's approach. "Road's closed," he said.

"We travel to Bowgren," Stephen replied. "Time is of the essence."

"You won't make it Bowgren on this road." The man lifted hand to forehead, brushing aside strands of fallen hair. "She says she's Maubreche."

"She is. I am Stephen of Maubreche." He ordered his dogs forward, to flank his huntbrother; it was a statement. If these men were not

Hunters—and by their colors, they were not—they would nonetheless be familiar with hunting dogs.

"Lady Margen gave the order: the road is impassible until further notice."

"Sten," Ansel said, coming up from behind Stephen.

"Lord Ansel." The man's iron brows rose in surprise. "You travel with this lot?"

"It is to offer necessary aid to Bowgren that they have traveled in haste at my request."

"Your request? We'd heard you'd been packed off the King's City— and at a time like this."

Ansel lifted a hand to forestall the criticism that was almost certainly going to break through the rest of the words. "We've had word—and news—that might greatly alter Bowgren's circumstances. Why is the road closed? Lady Margen seldom interferes in passage between our two demesnes. Is Lady Bowgren aware of it?"

"Couldn't say for sure. I believe she is. You should head to the Margen manor—our lady would be happy to see you, and she might be able to answer your questions."

"As my companion has said, time is of the essence; we had difficulty at an inn on the King's Road, and we hoped to make it to at least the nearest village before nightfall."

The man pursed his lips.

"Tell me what you do know. I greatly admire Lady Margen, but to speak with her will take hours of time we don't have."

The man Ansel had called Sten exhaled. "Have you heard from Lady Bowgren?"

"She gave permission for our return home with visitors."

Stephen turned to look back; he could hear horses on the road. The mage and the bard were mounted behind the Hunters, their horses unmoving, although the bard's didn't seem pleased about it. As the approaching horses rounded the slight curve in the road, he relaxed. The two men in front wore Hunter colors: Margen's Hunters had come.

LORD MARGEN WAS YOUNGER than Stephen's godfather, but older than any of the Hunters present. He dismounted practically before his horse had come to a stop, knees supple as they bent to balance his weight. He rose, and as he did, Margen dogs approached, slightly winded; they had raced here at speed.

Lord Margen's eyes narrowed as he took in the presence of the mage and the bard. Before either could speak, Ansel turned. "They are Bowgren's guests," he said, his voice clear and steady. "One is a mage from the Order of Knowledge, one a bard from the Empire; both are considered wise by the Queen, and they have offered Bowgren their expertise.

"I have accepted that offer." Ansel, too, dismounted, as did Heiden.

Stephen did not immediately recall the name of Lord Margen's huntbrother. "We're happy they sent you back," the huntbrother said, "but things have changed markedly in your absence."

"We haven't been gone for that long," Heiden's usual reticence was absent. He was at home, here. Or perhaps he was at home in a place where Ansel was lord.

Lord Margen nodded. "Bowgren was hard-hit by the chaos; harder than Margen, at least to start. But Margen has now lost the residents of Dunston — they vanished four days ago. I sensed a disturbance, but we did not reach the village in time."

"Was the village close to the Bowgren border?" Meralonne asked.

Lord Margen did not immediately answer the question; he glanced at Ansel first. When Ansel nodded, he exhaled. "Yes. We sent men to Bowgren, to discuss the similarities or differences in the circumstances with Lord Bowgren. The men failed to arrive."

"Killed?"

"We cannot be certain. They simply disappeared, just as the villagers had. And they were my best — trained to notice minute shifts in the landscape and turnings on the road. If they are dead, their bodies are likewise absent; I could track them, but all traces, all scents, simply...ended."

"You closed the road to prevent similar losses."

Silence again. "I would invite you to my home if you are amenable."

"My apologies, Lord Margen, but we are expected at home. We have avoided one difficulty on the King's Road, and another at an inn on that road; I believe we can pass into Bowgren to reach my parents." He hesitated, and then said, "Mounted are the sons of Maubreche and Elseth; they have come as my companions and my comrades."

"Maubreche?" Lord Margren approached Stephen's horse and looked up; Stephen met his gaze.

"You are the one the foreigners call the god-born son of Breodan."

Stephen nodded.

"And the young woman who has caused some consternation among my guards is your rumored huntbrother."

"Yes. Nenyane of Maubreche. I am Stephen."

"The dogs are yours."

"Four of them are from the royal kennels—they are the King's dogs, not Maubreche's."

This, more than even the sight of Stephen's golden eyes, caused Lord Margen's brows to disappear beneath his hairline. They descended almost as quickly. "They obey you?"

Stephen nodded. "The white dog is Pearl, and she obeys at her own pace." He grimaced as he spoke.

Lord Margen chuckled. "Even I've heard of Pearl. If the King sent her with you, he trusts your ability to handle dogs."

"Or he was offended," Nenyane added. She had moved to stand beside Stephen's horse.

This deepened Lord Margen's smile. "Ansel, lad, will you not accept hospitality? We can see you on your way at dawn's first light."

"We'd like to reach Bowgren before nightfall."

It was Kallandras who lifted chin—and hand. "Please forgive my boldness, but I suggest you accept the offered hospitality, Lord Ansel."

Ansel's frown was deep; his brows gathered as if the bard's tongue was momentarily foreign enough he had to concentrate to make sense of the words.

"The wind, even here, is too wild; it speaks of the early fall of night." He looked to the mage. The mage nodded, eyes as narrow as Lord Margen's now were. "I believe Lord Margen has the right of it—if we cross the border now, we will not reach the demesne of Bowgren before nightfall. If at all. And night will not be our friend in our travels; the subtle signs of encroachment might be missed."

GERVANNO LET his hand fall from sword hilt as the Hunters discussed the matter amongst themselves. Lord Ansel was determined to proceed, but his huntbrother was not. The twins allowed their decision to follow Stephen's. Stephen and Nenyane had one of their frequent one-sided conversations; Nenyane was clearly of the same mind as Ansel. But she had ventured into the wilderness in which Gervanno had almost been lost; she was not afraid of losing her way.

Lord Ansel was the highest-ranking member of their group, but Gervanno had long since learned that the South was very unlike both the North and the Western Kingdoms—at least the one he had encountered so far. The discussion was not a matter of rank, although had he been at home in the Dominion, it would be Lord Ansel's words that carried the day.

Here, there was more discussion. Ansel made his desire clear. Everyone understood the urgency. But it was Alex who pointed out that Ansel's information was out of date, and the Margens might offer both information and warning at a time when both would be helpful.

Only after those who desired to be heard were heard did Ansel's shoulders slump briefly. He bowed head, and raised it after a minute had passed.

"Thank you for your offer, Lord Margen. We would be honored to accept."

CHAPTER NINETEEN

The path to the Margen manor was an odd shape; it had not been built by leveling ground, but rather, had been wound around the slight inclines in hills that were half natural stone. Because the lords of the manor had, at one point, decided to move in harmony with nature, rather than against it, the manor itself came into view only when the last bend had been rounded.

Stephen noted the presence of armed guards, rare in Hunter manors; he noted their watchfulness, and beneath that, the need for such oversight. Whatever had happened in Margen in recent days had left its mark upon both lord and servants.

Ansel was at least as grim as the guards. He chafed at the delay; the possible need for it only made it worse.

Nenyane nodded, as grim of expression as Lord Ansel. Max and Alex were likewise silent, but Steel accompanied Max, and dogs had always prevented Max from sinking into either despair or rage.

Neither the bard nor the mage spoke unless spoken to; the journey was almost funereal in its silence, with the exception of Pearl, who clearly felt due respect had not been fully paid. She was a beautifully proportioned dog; among the sixteen dogs gathered here as Hunter escort, she stood out. Stephen imagined she would stand out no matter where she was situated — but sadly, not for appearance alone.

Patches was tolerant, which was the most one could ask.

"I don't suppose we can leave her here?" Nenyane whispered, as the manor at last rose above small hills.

"I don't think the King would be best pleased." It was Alex who replied, on the off chance that Nenyane was serious. As she was entirely serious, Stephen said nothing; better to pass off the otherwise shocking comment as black humor and frustration.

The horses were led to stables, the dogs to kennels; some time was taken in preparing the dogs for rest and sleep, but with the help of Max and Alex — Nenyane being absent — the process took less time than it would at home.

Leial, however, drew stares and raised brows.

"If it would not be too much to ask," Nenyane said, before Gervanno could speak, "we would greatly appreciate if Leial could be treated as a pet. The dog doesn't eat much, and doesn't bark except when demons are present."

The word *demon* dropped like a large stone might into a still pond. Stephen winced, but understood that they were the right words if one's goal was acceptance of a mutt as an indoor companion.

Lord Margen turned to Gervanno. "The dog is yours?"

Gervanno nodded. "I will take full responsibility for any damages my dog might cause."

"You have some experience with demons?"

"Most of that experience — the worst of it — has been within Breodanir."

"Very well."

Lord Margen and his huntbrother then tended to the Margen dogs; this took more time, but was not unexpected.

Stephen glanced — frequently — at Ansel. Ansel's silence was absolute. Heiden shook his head briefly when Stephen opened his mouth; he closed it without speaking.

The mage and the bard did not help with the dogs, but made no attempt to enter the manor; instead, the mage withdrew, finding and lighting a pipe as he faced north. Kallandras joined the mage. Stephen was not surprised when Nenyane chose to join them, as if she were also an outsider, a foreigner.

"WILL we be able to enter Bowgren proper from Margen?" Her hands perched momentarily on hip before dropping to sword hilt and remaining there. She, too, faced north.

"In the morning," the mage replied. "If at all. Can you not hear it?"

Nenyane was instantly frustrated. Stephen could feel her annoyance; she made no attempt to hide it.

"I hear the wind," Kallandras replied, as if the question had been meant for him. "It is angry, but there is a note of keening in its folds that implies a great sorrow, a terrible loss."

The mage nodded, exhaling a stream of smoke. "The earth?"

"I have never been as sensitive to the voice of the earth."

"Ah, no. Of course not. Nenyane?"

She shook her head. "We stand on Margen lands. That much is clear to me. It is Bowgren that is in peril. Why did you agree to wait?"

"We are Lord Ansel's guests. The decision was his."

"Please. Do you honestly believe that it will be safer come dawn?"

"Master your impatience, Nenyane. We are Lord Ansel's guests. Surely you must understand how significant that is at this time?"

"The bard told him to wait."

"The bard *advised* him to wait, and he accepted that advice. But yes, I am aware that the acceptance was grudging. I fear we lost time in the King's City, on the King's Road, and in the inn itself—and it was time we could ill afford. Let us see what Lord Margen has to say. There must be a reason the roads are closed."

"Are there other roads that lead to Bowgren?" the bard asked.

It was Nenyane who shook her head. "There are smaller paths—the villagers nearest the border might use them, but they are not as easily traversed as this road." She frowned. "There is a road from another demesne, but it would take two days to reach, and we would have to pass through Margen regardless. I don't know if it's only the Bowgren border that's closed."

Kallandras nodded. "Come. I think Lord Margen is finished. Perhaps you might ask the question of someone who has answers."

NENYANE DID NOT RESENT BATHING, but resented the subsequent fuss about appropriate clothing. Although they had lived in the King's Palace, they had been exempt from the rigors of "appropriate" clothing. Lord Declan, Huntsman of the Chamber, considered clothing a necessity, but—assuming one wore shoes and shirts—not a subtle sign of respect.

Here, in the presence of Lady Margen, choice of clothing was once again important, as was hair, lack of facial hair, cleanliness of shoes. Nenyane's usual impatience had deepened almost to the breaking point by the fear she steadfastly refused to acknowledge, and complaints about pointless social preening became her only outlet.

They were therefore the last of the Hunters to finally leave their rooms.

Alex and Max loitered in the hall, waiting. They then walked down the hall as a group; at the end of the hall, a young page was waiting to lead them to their destination.

Of their fellowship, only Gervanno excused himself from dinner; it was not his place to stand guard in the Margen dining hall. In the South, it would have been—but Breodanir was not the home of his youth, and he felt that the presence of a foreign guard might actually be considered a subtle insult.

Nenyane was ill-pleased at the idea that Gervanno's presence— Gervanno's sword—could *ever* be considered an insult, and made this very clear. Gervanno, however, seemed gratified by her ire, which was the only good thing to come of it, as Stephen was certain this would not be the last of her ire experienced this eve.

LORD MARGEN TURNED out to be of an age with Gilliam and Corwin, although the years had been kinder to him. Stephen had assumed he was almost a decade younger. Lord Margen's huntbrother, Edwin, was seated to the lord's left. Of the three adult residents, his was the face most drawn and careworn.

One of Lord Margen's sons, Alfric, was present, but he was too young to have a huntbrother. He was almost too young to be at the table, in Stephen's opinion; in Maubreche, when guests were present, he would have been fed in a separate room.

Nenyane, however, nodded in the child's direction, and the child brightened instantly at the recognition. Or perhaps the smile felt brighter because the air at the table itself had passed from formal to funereal.

They took the seats indicated by the servants. Meralonne and Kallandras had been seated at the far end of the table, to one side of Lady Margen. She had chosen to dress as if receiving exalted guests, and even Nenyane was grudgingly grateful that Stephen had insisted on proper clothing; they were merely underdressed, but not disastrously so given their sojourn at speed by road.

The bard and Lady Margen conversed; the mage brooded. At the opposite end of the table, Lord Margen was seated beside Ansel and Edwin; the child sat beside the huntbrother. Heiden occupied the seat beside Ansel, and the Elseth and Maubreche Hunters filled in the seats in the table's middle.

"Lord Ansel," Lord Margen said, offering Ansel a grave nod. "Thank you for accepting our offer of hospitality."

Lady Margen looked up as her husband's words announced the start of the meal, the pleasant expression she had offered the bard falling from her face so instantly the room seemed to drop in temperature.

Ansel nodded, aware — as they were all aware — that *offer* was not the correct word. Having made the decision, Ansel did what he could to accept it with grace — but Ansel was not known for his grace, and if he had changed, he was still Ansel. Heiden was staring at the empty plate set before him, eyes narrowed; it was clear to all Hunters present that Ansel's grace was balanced on Heiden's.

Nenyane, however, was not Ansel; Margen, while part of Breodanir, was not her concern. She turned head toward the ruling power in the room, folding her arms, but allowing her chair to remain on four legs, rather than the customary tilt of two. "Why have you closed the road, Lady Margen?"

"The decision was Lord Margen's," that lady replied, her eyes narrowing until they were the same shape as Nenyane's.

Nenyane rolled her eyes, tightening her arms. "The source of the decision is almost irrelevant. We need to enter Bowgren — we have very little time before Bowgren is fully engulfed by the wilderness, and nothing of what it has been remains in the mortal world."

Stephen was not Heiden; he had very seldom been able to control Nenyane by the simple expedient of pleading. He glanced at Lord

Margen and his huntbrother, aware that Lady Margen's expression would give nothing away. Lord Margen's expression was composed; Edwin's was not.

It was, to Stephen's surprise, Edwin who spoke. "What do you mean?"

Nenyane, please be careful.

I'm here, aren't I?

Servants began to place food on the plates, but all attention was now focused on Nenyane of Maubreche. "You can't be unaware of the troubles Breodanir has faced in the past year."

Edwin nodded, for Nenyane had turned to face him.

"It's likely to get worse before it gets better—if it ever gets better. Even the King's Road is no longer immune to the incursions."

"Incursions?"

"The turnings, if you prefer that word. They aren't attacks— although the practical difference is irrelevant. The lands that we occupy, the lands we call home, were once part of the wilderness, and the wilderness is waking. The lands that are strange to us have their own rules, but perhaps the one element in common is that they can be claimed and ruled. Some lands have no current lord; those are the easiest to deal with. When the two—Breodanir and wilderness—overlap, the ways between our lands can be closed if we arrive in time.

"But not all of the wilderness lacks a master." She hesitated, and for the first time looked to Stephen.

Stephen was not of a mind to take the threads of her explanation and continue to spin them. She had started this; she should finish it. But he was aware that she was an anomaly and Margen was already tense with worry. He exhaled, letting his annoyance with his huntbrother bleed out as he gathered and chose words.

"Word reached the King's City. The Queen has been keeping all reports of the difficulties the demesnes face, and she has taken the most severe of the difficulties to the Order of Knowledge." Lord Margen's eyes narrowed at the mention of the foreign order. "At the behest of the Queen, the magi have begun to examine those reports.

"One of the magi is here. He is Meralonne APhaniel, and his specialty is ancient lore. He passed through Bowgren on the way to the King's City, and he tendered a report to the Queen."

"And that report?"

"I was not present for it, Lord Margen. But APhaniel felt that

Bowgren was in far greater danger than any other demesne—and that it might be preserved if we traveled in haste. The King gave his permission—and his dogs—that we might do exactly that." He exhaled. "I do not know how quickly word travels, but the King's City came under demonic attack very recently."

Lord Margen was a Hunter. "Are the demons involved in that attack situated in Bowgren?"

"We know very little about either."

Meralonne, however, said, "That is now my belief. More accurately, they are situated in the lands that have turned, but those lands are within Bowgren's borders."

Silence reigned at the table until the child broke it. He turned to the silver-haired mage. "My brother went to Bowgren," he said, voice still inflected with the lilt of the young.

Stephen froze.

"When?" Nenyane said, the single word sharp as any blade she had ever wielded.

Lady Margen replied. "Four days ago. He did not arrive in Bowgren."

"You're certain?"

"Lady Bowgren and I have a means of communication that we felt necessary given the troubling times." She glanced at the mage, but did not elaborate. "My son and his companions failed to arrive. Two of the dogs, however, did. One did not survive. After some discussion, the borders were closed between Margen and Bowgren." She glanced down the table at her husband.

Her husband was silent. His huntbrother was pale. "If we had left immediately—"

Lady Margen lifted a hand before Edwin's sentence could be finished. "Lady Bowgren let it be known that she expected Lord Ansel and Heiden to travel to Bowgren. If the roads were not, in our opinion, safe, we should house them here until the danger has passed."

Ansel now looked as happy as Lord Margen.

"Now, tell us what you intend."

THEY DID, although the explanation was fractured, coming as it did from several different sources. Lady Margen paused the explanation only when her husband chose to interject, but her expression made clear that those interjections, while acceptable, were unwelcome.

Stephen, however, understood. Everyone in the room did. Margen was lucky enough to have two sons. One was at the table. One was lost to the wilderness. Stephen could not imagine a circumstance in which the son's dogs would flee, unless commanded to do so by their Hunter.

"What is your older son's name?" It was Nenyane who asked.

Edwin replied, "Brandon. His huntbrother is Aelle." He hesitated, and then continued. "The dog that survived does not speak. She cannot bark, or if she does, her bark cannot be heard."

Meralonne rose, dinner all but forgotten. "I will take my leave of you for the moment." To Nenyane he added, "I will scout across the borders. The road has clearly been compromised, but there may be passage into Bowgren that has not. I will return."

Lady Margen turned her gaze upon the mage as if to argue. What she saw in his expression caused any words she might have offered to die before they escaped. Lord Margen was unconcerned; a mage from the Empire was not his problem. He might be a visitor, but he was no part of a Hunter Lord's responsibility.

"My apologies for my lack of manners," the mage said. "If Stephen and Nenyane care to, they might explain my concern."

Stephen had only barely managed to keep Nenyane in her seat, and it was still an ongoing struggle.

"Remain with your Hunter, Nenyane. I will travel in a fashion Stephen would find difficult."

"I wouldn't."

"Will you leave him alone, given the incident at the inn?"

"...No."

Meralonne gestured; his robes fell away, revealing chain mail that seemed imbued with light. "If I do not return, the ways are closed. How you proceed from here will no longer be in my hands." He turned to the bard, and nodded. The bard remained seated.

Only after he had left the dining room did conversation resume.

"You lost villages and lands to the turnings?" Nenyane asked, pulling the focus of the table back to Margen concerns, her gaze darting between the head and foot of the table.

"We have lost villagers, but the villages themselves we have managed to preserve. Most understand that if the trees or the surrounding foliage grows strange, they are to avoid the paths those alien plants adorn. But the younger children have not yet fully absorbed that truth, and the youths tend toward tests of courage." Lady Margen's expression made clear that she felt courage and stupidity were synonymous in this case. "We have not experienced the losses that Bowgren has faced since the Sacred Hunt."

"You are attempting to make certain you do not."

"As are all lords of all demesnes in Breodanir. Lord Bowgren has not yet recovered from the Sacred Hunt." If he ever would, the tone implied. "And the King's decision to summon Lord Ansel to the capital has furthered the difficulties, in my opinion. We were grateful to hear that he had been released back to Bowgren."

"The land responds to the lords who rule it," Stephen said quietly. "But they are accepted as rulers—by both land and people—only so long as they participate in the Sacred Hunt. Lord Ansel *is* Lord Ansel until the next Sacred Hunt is called. Lord Bowgren's influence would be stronger in different circumstances." He fell silent. "What did the surviving dog do?"

"She is kenneled in Bowgren, but she is not there happily. Twice now, she has attempted to leave the kennel."

"Brandon survives," Nenyane said. Stephen thought it, but kept that thought to himself; he was well aware that false hope was not a kindness.

Edwin's jaw whitened as he clenched it.

"That is our hope," was Lady Margen's quiet response. "I am no Hunter, but both my husband and Edwin reached the same conclusion. If he survives, however, he is beyond Bowgren, in these lands you call the wilderness. And it is in that wilderness that the greatest danger to Breodanir now lies. You have said you intend to face that danger, head on. Are Lady Elseth and Lady Maubreche aware of your decisions?"

"Probably," Nenyane replied. Before Lady Margen could voice what was certain to be disapproval, she continued. "Do you have items of import to your missing sons?"

"Pardon?"

"Items of import. Items that they value, for whatever reason."

"Yes!" the child said. "Do you need them?"

"We might," Nenyane replied, her voice gentling at the earnest desire to be helpful the young boy displayed. Stephen found the exchange confusing, but beneath the confusion he felt unsettled. Nenyane was certain that what she asked for might be of import—but as usual, had no idea *why*. He stayed as far away from the question as he could.

"I can get things—can I get things?" he asked his mother.

"Your brothers might be upset if you take things precious to them. We have no guarantee that those items, whatever they might be, will return unharmed."

"But—she thinks we need them to *find* Brandon and Aelle. And if we find them, that's the most important thing, right?" Nenyane had not said that in so many words, but the child was correct.

Lady Margen asked the question Stephen had tried so hard to avoid. "Why do you believe these are necessary?"

Nenyane's hands did not become fists, but it took effort. "The rules of the wilderness are not the rules of Breodanir's lands. Had your sons gotten lost in a normal forest hunt—I am *not* suggesting that is a possibility, Lord Margen—the items would be irrelevant.

"But in the wilderness, the rules of identity are different. If either of your sons valued objects for emotional and sentimental reasons, that attachment *can* form a bond, a thread that leads from your son to the object itself. It's not guaranteed," she added. Her hands relaxed. She could not tell Lady or Lord Margen how she knew, but the knowledge itself—in this moment—was certain. She focused on that, riding above the expected wave of frustration and self-loathing. "Hunter Lords tend toward the pragmatic, and it may be that the items will not prove helpful. If I were lost in a similar fashion, there would be no such objects of relevance to me."

"You are grasping at straws," Lady Margen said softly.

Nenyane exhaled and then nodded. "I have grasped at straws all my life, Lady Margen, but some of those straws were, in the end, gold."

To her young son, Lady Margen said, "Yes, Alfric. Go and find one item for each of your brothers and return to the table." When her youngest left the table—at a run—she exhaled, the line of her shoulders dropping slightly into a posture that seemed more relaxed. "Allow me to join you, then. I, too, will grasp at straws."

"We will, of course, require your permission to cross the border," Heiden said. "And we will, as Nenyane's request suggests, make every attempt to find Brandon and Aelle."

"If you mean to reach home, you will not do so," was the soft response. "And Lady Bowgren would be grieved to have her only son sent into the wilderness." The subtle emphasis made Ansel's importance to the continuity of Bowgren clear.

"The mage seeks safer passage now," Heiden replied, before Ansel could—and it was clear Ansel meant to. "It would be strategically best if we could choose when and how we enter the wilderness—but as Maubreche has made clear, we intend to enter that wilderness. The mage does not feel we can preserve Bowgren if we do not take the hunt to the lord of the lands that are struggling for dominance." He hesitated, and then turned to Edwin. "We would prefer not to have representatives from Margen join us. We are already unwieldy in number—according to the mage."

"He is my son," Lord Margen said, his voice the low growl of an angry Hunter.

Heiden, however, was accustomed to this. "Yes. And you are Lord Margen. Margen requires its lord if it is not to be overwhelmed by the wilderness."

"Bowgren requires its lord as well."

"Lord Bowgren will not be joining us. He will remain in Bowgren."

"Lord Ansel is heir. He is the only heir; you have no sister by which another Hunter might join Bowgren through marriage."

"Bowgren," Ansel said, all attempts Heiden made to contain him unsuccessful, "is my problem. Were it not for our companions, I would not be taking this risk—and Bowgren would fall. We are not equal to the task of defeating this one enemy without external aid. But we have external aid for the moment, and we must use it. If the mage finds a safe entrance to Bowgren, we will—with your permission—take it. But if he does not, we will take the road."

"Lord Ansel," Lady Margen began.

"I understand that it might cause grief to my mother," Ansel said, cutting her off. Stephen would not have dared. "But I *am* older than Alfric; were I Lord Bowgren, it is a risk I would take, given the circumstances. And we have no time to argue about the finer points of the consequences of failure because, if we do, the lost time guarantees that failure."

"It might come as a surprise," Lady Margen said, in a Winter ruler's voice, "but I did not intend to argue against it. It is clear that you understand the consequences to the long-standing alliance between Bowgren and Margen should you be lost to that wilderness. I am...conflicted, and I must make that clear. Were my sons not lost to that very wilderness—and we have *searched*—I would withhold the permission you seek.

"Were I a responsible ruler, a responsible ally, that is exactly what I would do."

Ansel said nothing, but his expression softened.

"Lesagh," Lord Margen began.

The smile she turned on him was the sweetest smile Stephen had seen in a while. He froze. Alex, across the table, froze as well. "The borders are the responsibility of the lady of the manor," she said, her tone matching her smile. "It is the lord's responsibility to guard those borders that the lady has decided, in her governance, should be closed." The smile deepened.

Edwin was now as still as Stephen and Ansel; Heiden was paler.

"Lord Ansel is Bowgren's only—"

"Of course—and Lady Bowgren is justifiably proud of her heir."

Edwin was now staring at the side of his Hunter's face; he was also no doubt accompanying that stare with words that only his Hunter could hear.

Lord Ansel rose. "We are grateful that you have allowed us to cross the border, Lady Margen; we will do everything in our power to find your sons. If they have vanished—"

"If we find the creature we seek," Nenyane said, her tone the opposite in texture from Lady Margen's, "we will find your sons. But while we eat and negotiate, their time—as Bowgren's—is running short."

"Why do you believe you will find them with our enemy?"

"The dog," Nenyane replied. "The dog who cannot make a sound. There are two ways that might occur in this circumstance. The first— and the far less likely—is that the enemy is already in Margen. The second, however, is that the dog attacked one of our enemies, and swallowed some portion of what he bit off."

Lady Margen rose as well—which was the signal that should have given Ansel permission to rise. "Very well. I will see that food and supplies are available for you. You will go on foot?"

Nenyane nodded. "We have some supplies."

"You intended to travel to Bowgren by horseback. I will make certain you are given supplies more suitable to a forest hunt of indeterminate length."

Ansel, who had risen before her, now offered her a very correct bow.

"You carry the burden of all of Bowgren on your shoulders," the lady said, voice soft. "And I should not add burdens which are not yours to bear."

Ansel shook his head. "Brandon is a friend, and we'll eventually *be* Bowgren and Margen. If you had not made this request, we would look regardless."

Before he could say more—if he intended to, as Ansel was not fond of words better spoken by huntbrothers—the Margens' youngest ran into the room, both of his hands full. He brought his treasures to Nenyane, the person who had asked for them.

"This," Alfric said, handing her an aged, ivory horn, "is Brandon's. It was my grandfather's before he died, and his grandfather's before that. He left it to Brandon, but Brandon often carried it when he went on hunts—he said it was lucky."

He hadn't been carrying it on this one—but he hadn't intended to hunt.

"And this is Aelle's." It was a wooden toy, a horse, carved inexpertly and smoothed in places with time and too much handling. "This was the only thing he brought with him when he came to Margen with my father. He said it was the only thing his mother had left him." Alfric hesitated, and then added, "He would never talk about his life before Margen—but I asked about this toy."

"You've done good work, Alfric. If anything can lead us to your brothers, it's these. I will handle them with care, and I will return them to their owners."

"Promise?"

"Alfric!" Lady Margen said, the shock mild enough it did not appear to be theatrical.

Alfric kept his back toward his mother, his eyes fastened to Nenyane's, as if he thought her vow would be of more value than anyone else's in the party.

She smiled. "Yes. I promise."

Perhaps because Alfric was young, earnest, and desperate, no one corrected either of them. Ansel had already told Lady Margen he would search for her sons; Nenyane's promise merely added gravity to his word.

Only Stephen understood that, in this room, it was Nenyane's vow that would cause problems, if problems were to be caused. She had not come to Stephen because he was an oathbinder, although she had always understood it, but in all of the years he had known her, she had never broken a promise once it was made. She very seldom made them.

He did not ask her why she'd made this one; he knew. If he might otherwise disapprove, he understood that she offered solace not only to the child who so desperately sought it, but to the parents who were far too adult to make such a demand. Lady Margen had strayed dangerously close to that edge, but remained on the correct side.

And Lady Margen's expression made clear that she would have words with her youngest once the guests were safely absent.

27TH OF EMPERAL, 429 A.A. KINGDOM OF BREODANIR, DEMESNE OF MARGEN

Dawn broke; the sky was a blend of approaching sun and pale moons.

Lady Margen's supplies were packed and waiting; Margen servants had clearly had a sleepless night. Lord and Lady Margen had perhaps overseen the packing, for lack of rest, lack of sleep, shadowed their eyes and expressions. Alfric was with them; Lord Margen carried his youngest, who was still dressed in nightclothing.

In silence, the Margen supplies were shouldered. The six Hunters had discussed the possibility of taking one pack animal, but no one thought horses would fare well. Lady Margen, however, had foreseen this issue as well; she had spent all of her life in the company of Hunters—or in the absence of them—and had guessed that they would not risk the lives of those horses. She had offered a mule instead.

Nenyane, however, was against it. While she felt the mule would be less high-strung, if it fled, the mule would take necessary supplies with it. Ansel, in theory the leader of this party, nodded without argument. He knew supplies might be necessary, but he wanted to be on the road.

Nenyane, however, stared out the window—or rather, faced the window. Her eyes, as Stephen approached, were closed.

Meralonne had not yet returned.

"I'll see the dogs readied," Stephen said quietly. Max trailed after him, in part because he was curious about the Margen kennels, and in part because the dogs were part of an everyday routine that Hunter's Redoubt had shattered. Alex remained with Nenyane and Heiden,

Ansel with Lord and Lady Margen. Kallandras remained with the Margen rulers.

Alfric was sent to bed, one nanny trailing behind his very slow progress.

"Should we leave without the mage?" Max asked, knees bent, as he examined Steel's collar.

"If he doesn't return soon." Stephen exhaled.

"Nenyane doesn't want to leave without him." Sometimes Max could surprise with his observations. It was true. The signal Nenyane awaited was the return of the mage. Kallandras was willing to join them without Meralonne, but Stephen had seen enough of the bard in action that he had no fear for the bard's safety.

They were both surprised when Edwin joined them. "Lord Stephen, Lord Maxwell," the Margen huntbrother said. Lord was a courtesy title in both cases, not a correct one.

To Stephen's surprise, Edwin carried a hunting horn. "Some demesnes have calls that are not those used in the Sacred Hunt."

Stephen nodded, as did Max, shifting his attention from the comfort of Steel's presence. Maubreche had not developed their own signals; nor, to Stephen's knowledge, had Elseth.

"I will teach you the calls Margen hunters use to identify themselves in the field. Sound this horn, and Brandon and Aelle will recognize it. They will know that Margen forces have arrived."

Neither of the two bridled at being called Margen forces. Edwin sounded the horn: two notes clipped, almost staccato; two longer, but not so long they took on the fullness of the sound. Lord Margen did not come running, but the Margen kennels became more alert as dogs rose to the Margen call.

"I consider it a waste of effort," a familiar voice said. All three turned toward the sound; Steel, at Max's side, tensed.

Beneath the fading moon, Stephen could see Meralonne APhaniel, sword in hand. He saw then what he realized he had never seen: the mage's blade was dark with blood. As he approached, Stephen could see that it was not only the blade that was so darkened.

Nenyane was out of the house before Stephen reached the mage; she moved at almost blinding speed. The mage lifted hand before she reached his side, and she skidded to a stop at the silent command.

"The borders," he said, "are not passable. There are areas across the border that have not been fully absorbed—but they are heavily guarded by denizens of the wilderness who had managed to slip through the thinning veil between our two lands. They were not interested in allowing me passage." He sounded more annoyed than injured. "And they sought to interfere in my battles with the dead."

The dead. Demons.

"Not all of their deaths were at my hands. If I dislike interruptions, the dead are no different; nay, perhaps they are worse in their response. It is only on the edge of death—my own—that we can meet as we once met.

"We will take the Margen road that was previously barred to us," he continued, as if the news of the presence of demons was irrelevant. "It is safest. The dead guard the mortal lands, but the wilderness is harder to traverse; it is not Scarran, when the barriers are thinnest and the earth almost in slumber."

"You're injured." Nenyane's voice was flat. Beneath the surface of those words, Stephen could sense a coil of emotions, too mixed, too blended, to be easily identified—except for the fear.

The fear was, in texture, almost unfamiliar.

———

THE GUARDS at the border were waiting as Lord and Lady Margen approached. They rode, as did the Hunters, but the Hunters intended to leave the horses in Margen hands when they dismounted. The dogs, perhaps sensing Stephen's apprehension, were jittery; they obeyed, but they mixed a higher blend of sound into their usual barks. Only Pearl seemed immune to anxiety, or perhaps that was the wrong word; she seemed to look down on it. She was here, after all; what could possibly go wrong?

Stephen found it oddly comforting. In as much as Pearl could, she accepted Stephen as her master; she found the presence of the rest of the dogs irrelevant. Steel, at Stephen's silent command, joined Max, as he had done since they had departed the King's City. The only dog that was not his responsibility was Gervanno's.

Taking a breath, he looked down the road past the Margen guards.

Nenyane, however, was no longer aware of the road. She drew sword and leapt forward, past the Margen couple, toward the guards that watched the road.

To Stephen's surprise, a second sword followed—not Meralonne's, and not the bard's odd blades, but the Southerner's. Gervanno was a step behind Nenyane, although he could not match her speed. He was clearly accustomed to running while balancing the weight of his longer, curved sword.

The Margen guards on the road suddenly peeled away to the sides, leaving only one; he raised his arm and lowered it in a sweep of deliberate motion. Fire shot from his fingertips in three parallel lines.

Were it not for Nenyane's blade, Margen would have become leaderless that day. She cut the fire, slicing through the three strands as if they were purely physical. The attacking guard froze for a second, and then wheeled and broke into a run toward them. Above his head, the sky flashed blue, as if blanketed briefly by lightning. The wind came in the still morning; whether it was to bard's call or mage's, it made no difference.

Lord and Lady Margen dismounted; Lord Margen drew sword. Lady Margen did not; nor did she raise voice; she retreated, but did not turn to expose her back. Her face, as it came clearly into Stephen's view, was almost white—whether with fear or fury he could not say.

His Huntbrother leapt from a sprint in the direction of the false guard's back. Without pause, her blade came down in an overhead arc —a move she rarely used because it left her too open. Gervanno was behind her, but not by much.

Lord Margen lifted voice to command his guards forward; Lady Margen belayed his orders. It was Lady Margen's word that held sway. She ordered the men back, and they obeyed, retreating as she had retreated, swords unsheathed and readied.

"There is nothing you can contribute except chaos," the mage very helpfully informed Lord Margen.

The bard said nothing, but Stephen was almost certain the initial separation of the rest of the Margen guards—in silence—was due to the bard's command. He noted that the mage, armed, did not move forward.

"He's not human. He's not human anymore." He could hear Alex's voice at his back as he sprinted toward Nenyane; he did not waste the eyes of his dogs to see what Alex was doing. He knew Max had moved forward, running behind Steel; he was almost certain the deeper, even breathing was that of the trance.

"It is too late," the guard snarled; he had turned to parry Nenyane's strike—with his hand—and he succeeded without losing that hand. His voice was almost bestial. "It is too late for you and your kind."

How far had demons penetrated into Breodanir? Stephen tightened his grip on his blade, moving to Nenyane's right, as Gervanno held her left.

It's not a demon, his huntbrother said. She pivoted as the hands of their opponent shot forward—and forward again, extending far beyond the reach of a mortal man. Where her blade struck, it clanged as if hitting stone; had it not been for the man's grunt of pain, Stephen would have assumed no damage had been done.

But a blow that would have neatly amputated a human arm—and Stephen suspected a demonic arm as well—failed to have the same effect on the creature Nenyane fought. She struck again, and the creature bent elbow, parrying with the one arm, and striking—or attempting to strike, with the other.

His face, however, remained human in seeming; were it not for the unnatural arms, he might have been a treasonous mortal.

It was the dogs who drew first blood. The creature was focused on Nenyane, and the dogs came in from the sides, and from behind; they attacked the legs, Steel leaping up on the man's back as if to topple him. This failed, but the dogs' teeth found the purchase that Nenyane's blade could not.

This time, the creature roared, its human form at odds with the depth of its voice.

Stephen pulled the dogs back as the creature's hands once again extended, claws in the place of fingers. He was unwilling to lose the dogs here against an opponent whose skills and abilities he did not know.

Even Pearl obeyed; the dogs circled, looking for an opening.

Gervanno's sword fared no better than Nenyane's, but it kept the enemy off-balance. Only when Meralonne deigned to take to the skies did the creature falter.

"These are not your lands," the mage said. "They are not the lands of your lord. There is only death for you here."

"From *mortals*? Death at the hands of the vermin for whom the world was destroyed?" He struck out at Nenyane without looking away from Meralonne; she leapt above the strike, pivoting almost in mid-air, the downward arc of her blade parried by his forearm.

"Even so. We do not judge the strength of your lord by your strength. If you do not retreat, I will personally destroy you."

The creature parried again. "In exile?"

"Even so."

"We offered you a home, Illaraphaniel. No exile from the court of your cold queen could tarnish you in the eyes of our lord; you might have had a place at our lord's side."

"Think you that I would abandon the White Lady? Perhaps I will destroy you even if you choose to retreat." Winter was in the mage's voice, but beneath it a cold so intense it felt like heat.

"My lord would never have sent you from her side. The forest would have welcomed you; her lands would know your name."

"Is that what you believe, little foot soldier?"

"Kill me, and my lord will know."

Meralonne's smile was thin, mercurial; it reached his eyes in the worst possible way. "No, she will not. These lands are not hers; you will die here, where you stand. But I feel almost sentimental this morn; if you flee, I will not pursue, and you will not die."

The creature parried Nenyane's strike without apparently seeing her at all. He parried Gervanno's in the same way, but Gervanno had seen the blood the dogs had drawn; his sweeping arc was aimed at the creature's leg.

"Ser Gervanno." The mage's voice held familiar command, familiar authority.

Gervanno froze instantly, as if Meralonne APhaniel was the commander on this field. Nenyane slowed, but did not stop. Nor did Meralonne command her to do so.

Stephen called his dogs. They retreated, backing up and growling every inch of the way. He had to command Pearl to obey; she did, but he was almost certain to suffer for it later.

"She killed your brothers," the creature said, his voice clearer in the absence of many small attacks.

Meralonne, however, shook his head. "They returned to her. They returned to their truest home—as all of our dead once did. Do not treat with the dead. Do not become enmeshed in the schemes of those treacherous enough to betray their lord and creator. Tell your lord this."

"To what end? She desires a return of her lands."

"Her lands have not been compromised."

"They have—they have been caged and contained for eons; it is the first time she has been able to hunt in the mortal realm. She does not intend to allow those paths to be closed again."

Meralonne bowed head. "She and I were never allies, but we were not enemies. It grieves me to face—and kill—her, but if this is the battle she has chosen, my duty gives me no choice. Still, for the sake of the memories of days long past, I would spare you if you retreat."

"He'll carry word to her!" Nenyane practically shouted.

Meralonne did not acknowledge the danger. Or Nenyane. "Once, you would have died before you called the dead your allies, and yet you are here. Go now, or I will allow pragmatism to guide my hand. You cannot hope to stand against me here." He lifted hand in Nenyane's direction. "Let him pass."

"You are not lord here." Nenyane's words were cold.

Meralonne then turned to Lord Margen. He offered that lord a low, perfect bow. "Lord Margen, I am a stranger in these lands, and I ask a great favor. Although this man has encroached upon the border of your lands in service to the enemy, I ask that you grant me his life; allow him to return to his home. I will be in your debt. Grant me this boon, and in turn I will do everything within my power to find what you have lost and return it to you." As he rose from his bow, he was glowing. It almost seemed that he had swallowed moon's light and made it his heart —if the rest of his body had suddenly become transparent.

Nenyane snapped her jaws audibly shut; she glared at the mage's back. She was the only one who would, in this moment, have dared.

Lord Margen did not answer immediately; he turned, instead, to his Lady. She stepped forward. "If you feel it wise, APhaniel, we will grant your request in return for your service."

"Lady." He bowed again, and then turned back.

The creature glared at the mage, but in the end he turned and walked down the road, his form dwindling beneath the night sky until he could no longer be separated from the shadows of night.

———

ANSEL AND HEIDEN WERE SILENT, but Ansel was not still; he paced, as a caged beast might, deprived of freedom. But he said nothing, although silence clearly took effort, until the person who had imitated the Margen guard could no longer be seen. He then turned to Stephen.

Stephen nodded. "Are we ready to leave?"

"We are," the mage replied, sorrow sliding from his face as if it had been an Artisan-made mask.

It's not, Nenyane said, her interior voice a blend of empathy and anger. *But he is not like you—sentiment and sorrow may drive his decisions, but they will not stay his hand. Have you not seen him fight the* Kialli? When Stephen failed to answer, she continued. *There is method to his mercy; yes, he desired to stay his hand. But the dogs could do what I failed to do; he is wounded, and in his retreat he has left a trail the dogs can follow.*

As if he could hear their conversation, Meralonne turned to Stephen. "It is time, I believe, to hunt in earnest."

Stephen's dogs were the only dogs present who would accompany them on this hunt, and Pearl was impatient to be off, her nose to ground, her shoulder blocking Patches when Patches attempted to join her. Stephen separated them, but Patches was disgruntled; only if he let them both start their hunt would there be any peace.

He glanced at Max and Alex; they both nodded, shouldering the packs they had dropped when Nenyane had closed with the creature.

Meralonne took the lead; Kallandras, accompanied by Gervanno, took the rear. Between them, the Hunters fell into their own ranks; Ansel and Heiden followed on the mage's heel, Alex and Max were a yard behind them, and Stephen and Nenyane took the rear, closest to the bard.

If the road vanished, they would likely to be forced to proceed single file—but the dogs would frame the Hunters, regardless, on either side, and the two scenthounds would run ahead. It was the scenthounds who would decide the speed of progress, here, and one of them knew it.

STEPHEN KNEW the moment they had passed beyond the borders of Margen into what should have been Bowgren; he could feel a curious *snap* in the air, as if the threads binding him to the land of his birth had been suddenly severed; as if a subtle melody, heard so much in the background it seemed silent, fell truly silent.

Alex and Max noticed something as well; Ansel and Heiden did not. Stephen wondered if the twins were affected this way because of their mother, but did not ask—in part because there was some danger the mage would answer. Nenyane was on edge. Her eyes, when they met Stephen's, were faintly luminescent; beneath the skies of these foreign lands, she almost resembled the magi at his most intimidating.

It was perhaps thirty minutes before she was willing to sheathe her blade; Gervanno had sheathed his the moment they committed to take the wild road. The Southern guard was watchful, wary, but absent the physical signs of tension that were clear on Nenyane's face.

By this time, even Ansel and Heiden were aware that they had crossed into a turning, rather than avoiding it. Everyone was. The morning sky had given way to night, daylight colors bleeding into the muted silver of night sky, starlight, moonlight.

"Will he head directly to his lord to make his report?" Alex asked.

Nenyane shrugged. "I'd say it's likely, but it's not certain. There are some lords to whom failure should not be reported if one wants to survive. But I would guess that he is bound to that lord; he will do what he is commanded to do, and he will return to her with his report.

"The beast that Meralonne showed us in Hunter's Redoubt is leashed and bound in a different way. Left to its own devices, it would not serve at all—and I would guess that the power necessary to compel it requires significant focus.

"The creature we're tracking is not the equal of the one that petrified half of Clearbrook. He will either return to his lord, or he will go to ground in a place that he considers temporarily safe. Either will give us information. We're hoping for the former for obvious reasons. I think Illaraphaniel assumes the latter more likely. If there's a safe place—one that provides some small protection from the lord, we might be able to take advantage of it." She exhaled some of her tension. "If Meralonne chooses to attack anyone in these forests, leave him to his fight unless he calls for aid."

Nenyane wouldn't. She had always been a do-as-I-say-not-as-I-do person.

"He hadn't called that fight," she replied, the irritation in her voice entirely familiar.

Stephen nodded. "I don't think he considered the creature a threat in any substantive fashion."

"Perhaps the mage is not what the rest of us are," Gervanno said, stepping up to join them. "Something immune to blade would be a threat to most of us." The Southerner looked ahead. "The road ends soon."

Stephen looked up, to the night sky. He stilled.

"Yes," Nenyane said, although he had not spoken, "there are three moons."

"Are there always three moons in the wilderness?"

She shook her head. "Only in a handful."

"Why?" It was Alex who asked.

"Because the lands conform to the desire of their lords, where their lords have the will and power to shape them. The lord of these lands is old; she is almost the age of Meralonne's lord." She frowned. "Yes, it might look beautiful to you—but think of the third moon as the lord's eye. While the skies are clear, it is not our friend."

Stephen nodded. The dogs had not yet lost the scent of the creature's blood, and approached its tracking as if the world had not shifted beneath their feet. Only Gervanno's pet remained with them, or rather, with Gervanno himself. But the dog Nenyane had helped to name was silent as it kept pace.

Pearl and Patches followed the scent past the point where the road dissolved. Between one step and the next it faded, to be replaced by plants and saplings that grew beneath the boughs of tall trees. It was hard to judge color, given the darkness of night sky, with one exception: a type of flower shed a luminous blue light. These flowers, gently glowing, appeared in different places, as if surrounded by a sea of night grey.

"Do not touch the flowers," the mage said, his voice blending with the exact same instructions from the bard, spoken at the same time, syllables overlapping.

"Are they poisonous?" Alex asked.

"In a fashion, they might be. If the flowers deign to be picked, they will demand a price in return for the picking—and it is not a price mortals were meant to pay."

"How do you know this?" Alex turned toward the bard. Stephen knew Alex would ask more questions than any other Hunter present. He'd always been like this; it was tolerated by his mother and father, and encouraged by his grandmother.

"I have traveled these lands in the past," was the soft reply. Soft or no, it carried. "When I was perhaps only a year or two older than you."

"Did you pick a flower?"

"No. I take care not to touch anything in a wilderness claimed by a master. I would not hunt here, except at need, and what I hunted—what we hunted—were the traces of the dead. No land accepts the dead with any grace; most whose lords are strongly rooted will do all in their power to eject or bury them. Our intrusion was in all ways a lesser evil; their sympathies with our cause led to their grudging hospitality.

"Understand, however, that lords of these lands are, in some fashion, similar to our kings. They set laws, but those who dwell within their boundaries may well attempt to break them; if the lord offers hospitality, their citizens might attempt to kill us regardless."

"Without consequence?"

"Ah, no. I did not say that." A hint of amusement underlay the bard's words. "But those who break laws have their own reasons in our lands, consequences notwithstanding. It is not so different here."

Alex nodded; his silence, however, was momentary. Stephen knew he had questions—an endless line of them—and was now caught between which to ask first. "What do the flowers offer, that they demand a price for the picking?"

"I have never picked one, and cannot therefore say. These flowers are not the dominion of the land's lord; she did not bring them into being and she cannot fully uproot them. The evidence that she has tried can be clearly seen; these flowers, left to their own devices, grow in an expansive field, and their light beneath the night sky eclipses moon's light; they can blind the lord's eye in the darkness.

"Do not squander your life in idle curiosity."

"Too late," Max muttered under his breath.

Alex's eyes narrowed in his brother's direction. "Is there anything else we should avoid?"

"Yes. But chief among those would be these lands at all. Nenyane," the bard added, "have you the items given you by the youngest Margen?"

Nenyane failed to answer, annoyed by the question; of course she had them. She understood their value to both the young child and the Hunters they sought. She had no like toys, no like memories, and perhaps because of her lack, she treated these things as if they were of incalculable value.

"They cannot be used yet," Stephen said, aware that Nenyane had no intention of answering the bard.

"Apologies. What she intends, I have never attempted; I am unaware of how they might be used."

Stephen would have asked his huntbrother, but the dogs suddenly tensed; his attention was instantly consumed by their handling. Alex fell silent, and Max, accompanied by Steel, turned toward Stephen. A silent question passed between them; Max nodded.

The tension of the Hunters passed up and down the line; Lord Ansel joined Stephen and Max. "You found him?"

Stephen nodded. "He's not running, and he's not alone. The dogs have retreated for the moment. Pearl is *not* happy."

"Will she obey?"

Stephen nodded.

It was Alex who said, "Dogs—any dogs—have always obeyed Stephen. Pearl is probably the least obedient dog I've ever seen in his care."

"Don't say that where she can hear you. Please."

Nenyane's laugh was quiet and not entirely kind.

GERVANNO STEPPED BACK, becoming perfect cerdan: silent, watchful, and unobtrusive. His eyes strayed to the flowers that glowed pale blue; they seemed, if he narrowed his gaze, to be similar to water lilies, although there was no water beneath their leaves; they had no visible stems. Indeed, they seemed to invite closer inspection.

Gervanno had ignored many such invitations in his time; he understood from the bard's words that idle curiosity courted death, here. If it was a death he deserved—and he labored under no illusion—he nonetheless had duties to fulfill. Perhaps, should he fail again, he might seek to satisfy curiosity, for at that time his life would have less than no meaning.

Still, he found the energy among the six Hunters almost infectious. They were not entirely fearless but, shaped by their words, that fear became caution: the caution itself was rooted in the familiarity of the hunt.

Kallandras spared a glance at the six who had slowly drawn together as the road vanished, but no more; his attention was turned toward any landscape that did not include them. The mage remained to one end of the company, but Nenyane was at Stephen's side.

Gervanno's eyes, accustomed to clear night sky, searched for the movement of shadows—movements that could not be attributed to the breeze that passed between the standing trees; he listened for steps that were heavier or more deliberate than those of the dogs. If his life in the South had not encompassed dogs such as these, he had grown accustomed to their sounds, the weight of their steps, the cadence of their barking or growling. They were as much a part of Stephen as Nenyane's sword was of Nenyane.

He therefore turned when he heard the light padding of paws, the movement too leisurely, too light, to be those dogs.

Kallandras noticed, lifting head; the movement of wind shifted, although it was subtle. "Ser Gervanno, in future, if you are willing to accept well-meant advice, remember: things small and gentle in seeming are often the gravest of threats."

The advice caused little confusion; Gervanno knew, long before he caught sight of him, who was responsible for the steps.

"You cannot change what you have offered, even were it offered in ignorance and silence; you were granted a boon by one of the elders of the wilderness, and the debt will haunt you for what remains of your life. But incur no others if it is at all possible." Thus speaking, the bard rose, stepping from ground to mid-air without apparent effort—or weight.

Into the wild growth the road had become, fur silvered by three different moons, came the fox.

CHAPTER TWENTY

Leial stepped in front of Gervanno, planting four paws and lowering head. Had the dog been smaller, Gervanno would have plucked him off the ground. Perhaps, had he been born to the North, born in lands of the Hunters, he might have intervened regardless. But he had been raised in the South, where the first duty was to show perfect respect to the powerful, lest the powerful seek to take umbrage, which would lead to deaths.

Thus had parents been forced to abandon children in the face of their lord's ire. A dog was not a child, to cause such bitter grief, but Gervanno felt an echo of that fear, that immobility. It was dark, in the wilderness. Darkness was the Lady's time. Gervanno prayed in silence that the Lady intervene in some fashion, that she prevent this stray dog, this mongrel that had entered his life, from offending an ancient, wild creature.

Perhaps She listened; perhaps She did not. But Leial did not bark, did not growl; he remained in position to leap, to attack, should that be required. It surprised Gervanno; he had seemed, on first meeting, a cowardly creature, one better suited to running and hiding behind a larger person.

The wind moved, then, gracefully lifting Leial—who did squeak—out of the fox's path.

The fox looked up, exposing the white of its throat. "Do not," he

said, his voice far deeper than his form implied, "seek to interfere with
my business, bearer of wind." Of the dog, the fox did not speak,
although his whiskers twitched.

The bard did not return to the earth, but nodded, Leial firmly in the
folds of the wind at his command. His weapons remained hidden, but
his gaze was narrow, sharp. The bard, who could bespeak the wind,
understood the nature of the fox. "I am not here on your business," he
told the fox, his tone gentle. "But on my own. I travel with Illaraphaniel, and we seek —"

The fox roared. The roar obliterated what remained of the bard's
words, although Gervanno knew, should the bard desire to be heard, he
would be. "Do not interrupt me," the fox said, as the roaring died into
stillness. He once again turned to Gervanno, lifting his chin.

The roar had been heard, he was certain, by the entirety of the
forest's denizens. Gervanno considered their mission, and considered
the fox; he bent knees to offer the fox the conveyance of his arms.

"You should not be here," the fox said, climbing into the cerdan's
arms. "This is no place for you — or have you perhaps wandered down
the wrong road again?"

"Perhaps, but it was intentional."

The fox sneezed. "Mortals have oft been foolish." He turned his
head toward the airborne bard, sniffing. "I dislike the company you
keep. It is not safe for you here."

"I am cerdan," Gervanno replied, voice gentle. "My very occupation
promises lack of safety."

"There is very little in the mortal world that would challenge your
companions. That is not the case in the wilderness, and these lands, in
specific, should be avoided. Come. I will lead you out."

"Are you safe here?"

The fox's brows rose. His tone implied that he was mildly offended.
"There is nowhere I cannot walk should I choose to do so. Not even the
lord of these lands would dream of closing borders against me; I would
take it amiss. And Illaraphaniel, while not as old as I, is afforded similar
respect. But even he cannot imagine that that respect will trickle down
to the rest of you."

Gervanno now had the silent attention of all of the members of
Stephen's party.

"Why are you carrying the fox?" Nenyane demanded, her gaze on
the fox, not the man of whom she asked the question.

"It was thanks to his intervention that I escaped the wilderness in Maubreche," Gervanno replied.

"Why did he help you?"

The fox *tsked* loudly. "Because I *wanted to*, obviously."

"What did he demand of you?"

Gervanno shook his head. "Nothing."

"And yet you carry him as if you're his servant?"

"He is wise enough to offer assistance," the fox said, "but foolish enough to wander into these lands. I am unconcerned about the fate of the rest of you, but I believe I would like this man to survive."

"He is not yours," Nenyane said, stepping forward. The mage placed a hand on her shoulder; given her expression, Gervanno considered it a small miracle that she made no attempt to part the hand from the mage's arm.

"And he is yours? He has offered me his blood."

Nenyane snorted. Gervanno would not have dared. "You cannot call biting him and drawing blood an *offer*."

"Can I not? I required his blood in order to lead him from the wilderness."

"And you informed him that you would be aware of him ever after?"

"I do not believe that would have changed his decision, given circumstances."

"So you didn't."

"He is not a complete fool; I am certain, if I failed to mention a trivial detail, he has become aware of it nonetheless. I made no attempt to hide it. Regardless, he is mortal, as you are not. You will not be troubled, surely, if he departs?"

Gervanno's arms tightened briefly. He then bent knees again, and set the fox down; the fox was not of a mind to go.

"I have undertaken this duty," he told the fox. "I cannot leave until the duty is done, or I am dead."

"This is not the place for you. I could take you back to your own home, if you desired it."

"And what would you ask in return?" Nenyane demanded.

"Hush, child. I have been polite and respectful, but you are trying my patience." The fox meant it; Gervanno wondered what impolite and disrespectful would look like. "You do not want to know as you are unlikely to survive it—and after the fact, that will pain me."

Gervanno agreed, but silently. If the fox's version of respectful was one for which Gervanno's childhood and early training had left him unprepared, his long years of familiarity with the powerful did not desert him. Very patiently he said, "The situation is dire, and I am considered of use."

"It's that girl again, isn't it? The sword master for whom you yearn."

Gervanno was long past the age of blushing; had he not been, he would be red with embarrassment.

"I wish an answer, having taken the trouble to ask the question."

Gervanno exhaled slowly, his eyes on the fox and not the woman of whom the fox so dismissively spoke. He had said these words before — but not directly to Nenyane. "Yes. Nenyane of Maubreche is the best swordsman I have ever encountered."

"Better than Illaraphaniel?"

Caught between the desire to speak truthfully and the desire to skirt the edge of a man of power's ire, Gervanno chose his words with care. "I have not yet seen enough of Illaraphaniel's blade work to fairly answer that question."

"By which you mean *yes*. How interesting. You," he added, speaking to Nenyane, his tone insultingly dismissive. "What do you intend to do here?"

"We intend to find — and stop — the lord of this land from breaking the barriers that keep the hidden world enclosed."

The fox snorted. "The barriers are falling, regardless. Surely even you must be aware of that."

It was the mage who now stepped in. "We are aware of it, yes — and we are aware of the root cause. It is in the interests of the god we do not name that the barriers fall, and quickly; it is therefore in our interests that the opposite be true.

"The lord of these lands consorts with the dead; the dead in mortal lands move at her command."

"You do not honestly expect me to believe that? I would be insulted, if I did not realize you believe your own words."

"None know the dead better than I, Eldest. But perhaps you are one of the few elders who disregard the taint of the dead."

The fox's body began to vibrate in Gervanno's arms; it grew heavier as the silence between the mage's words and the fox's reaction grew. "Put me down," the fox growled.

Gervanno did not immediately obey. "Eldest," he said, "I have seen the demons in the mortal lands; I have fought them — inasmuch as I am capable. Our party was attacked at a mortal inn. I am not Illaraphaniel; I do not have his experience, and I cannot therefore claim greater knowledge. I can only claim my own."

"You are not expected to know the dead," the fox began.

Gervanno took a risk. He continued to speak. "I know what the dead look like unleashed. I have seen the armies that serve the Lord of the Hells. I have met them in battle."

"And you survived. Perhaps you *are* as good with your blade as she thinks. Well," the fox said, curling into Gervanno's arms as if he meant to nap there immediately, "I have, as I said, taken a small interest in you."

"He is not Jarven ATerafin," the mage snapped, voice low with barely contained irritation.

"No, of course not. Gervanno could not survive me."

"I highly doubt Jarven could either."

"The important part is not what *you* think, but what *he* thinks. My cub thinks he can, and he is far more aware of who and what I am than young Gervanno here. But he has his own hunt, and for some reason he feels that I am *interfering* in it. It's almost as if he doesn't trust me." At that, the fox's voice lightened; he broke into laughter that was both affectionate and unkind. "I am therefore at loose ends. I wish to spend some time with Gervanno."

"Perhaps later, Eldest," the mage exhaled slowly. "While I appreciate your many games, they require time, and mortals—as you are well aware—have so little of it."

"Later? Where mortals are concerned, that merely means *never*; one can nap and they are bones and absence. I will therefore condescend to travel with you."

Nenyane's jaw dropped in shock; it snapped shut in barely contained outrage. "Illaraphaniel is not our captain; the decision is not his to make!"

"Very well. Who is your so-called captain, if not Illaraphaniel? The wind-voiced man? The god-born child?"

Lord Ansel, silent until that moment, cleared his throat.

The fox, who looked in Lord Ansel's direction, clearly considered this ridiculous. Ansel understood, but to Gervanno's surprise, took no offense.

"I am. I am Lord Ansel, and the edges of this wilderness are in *my* lands. It is to save the rest of my people that we have come. I welcome your aid if you intend to ally yourself with our cause."

"And if I do not?"

"You've woken half the forest with your roar, no doubt — but forces have not been sent to silence you. I suspect they will know where you are."

"They?"

"The lord of this land."

"If I do not wish to be seen, I am not seen. If I do not wish to be found, I am not found. The lord of this land cannot change the base nature to which I was born. Yes, yes, the little forest creatures are no doubt aware that I am here — and that I am not best pleased. But they would not dare to interfere; if they approached me at their lord's behest, they would die.

"If they approached me with intent to harm, they would die miserably. If I discovered that they acted upon their lord's command, their lord would die."

"Or you would," Nenyane said, unimpressed. "Perhaps you are not aware, but we have evidence that the lord of these lands has captured at least one of the Silences."

At that, the fox stilled. "That is not possible."

"Perhaps you will see it for yourself."

For the first time Gervanno could remember, the fox seemed at a loss for words, and when he did find them — as Gervanno had no doubt that he would — his tone was softer and far more serious. "If what you believe is true, you are in grave danger. Let me take my mortal —"

"He is *not* yours."

"Oh? And you intend to claim him? Have you not already chosen your master?"

"Eldest," Meralonne said, voice now as sharp as Nenyane's. "If you intend to alleviate your obvious boredom by occupying Gervanno di'Sarrado, we will accept that. But we must move." He transferred his gaze to Gervanno, and exhaled at the Southerner's expression. He then turned to Lord Ansel. "We believe we have found our prey's harbor; Stephen has ordered the dogs to wait, but we will lose the opportunity if we tarry further."

Gervanno lifted chin. "Did he flee to the side of his lord?"

The mage shook his head. "The dogs would be dead, and we would be besieged. We are fortunate; we may find the information we require."

GERVANNO WAS NOT A HUNTER, although he had hunted in his life. His preferred hunting weapon was a bow, which he did not have with him. Had he, he would not have been able to use it; it required two arms, and while the fox could—in emergency—be shunted to the crook of one elbow, he could not be set down.

The path of his youth had been straight, if narrow; he had grown into it with the passage of time and the experience gained by acts of war —and their survival. That path had led to the Averdan valleys, where he had lost so many of his comrades; where he had felt like a blade of long grass in a gale—his survival dependent not on his skill with blade and his understanding of tactics, but on luck; on being so irrelevant his existence had been deemed unworthy of notice.

That was how he viewed the death of his comrades: demons, like fallen gods, had simply walked across a field of grass, almost unaware of the blades crushed beneath their feet. Like any such grass, some would survive. Gervanno had survived.

Gervanno had come north with merchants, disgracing himself in the eyes of his family, in an attempt to forget those fields of slaughter, the victory bought so far beyond his meager abilities; his presence had counted for nothing at all.

And here he now was, carrying a talking animal as if it were the cozened, favored pet of the Tyr'agnate himself, chasing a creature of a type that he had never encountered before, and hoping to unseat a lord who vied for control of mortal lands with the aid of those very demons he had fled.

And yet it was those demons who had unmanned him, exposing the worst sort of fear; it was against the demons he hoped to prove himself, or die trying.

His angry grandfather in the distant South of his childhood had said, *It's not making a mistake that destroys you, boy—it's what you do afterward.* He clung to those remembered words.

The mage's attention was now with the Hunters. Lord Ansel returned to them. Nenyane lingered near Gervanno and his burden.

"Do not assume that his lingering curiosity is reliable," she finally said. "Affection from the wild beings is no guarantee of safety."

"It is almost a guarantee of its opposite," the fox replied, amusement in his tone. "But surely if safety was Gervanno's concern, he would not now be following a blade master with his almost endearing desire to prove himself worthy."

She glared at the fox but finally turned to join Stephen. The Hunters were speaking in low tones.

"Will Jarven ATerafin also appear here?" Gervanno asked the fox before he joined them.

"I should hope not, but mortals are oft unpredictable, and it is a mortal he is tasked with hunting. Should that mortal's trail lead here..." The fox shook head. "Then it would lend credence to Illaraphaniel's claim: the lord intrigues with the dead."

"Would that change your position?"

"Hardly. But if it is truth and not conjecture, I will be forced to aid in the disposal of the lord in question. The dead do not rule. Not here."

"Is there a place where the dead rule anything?"

"Hearts and minds, perhaps. But yes. I will not allow you to pass into those lands; you would never emerge."

STEPHEN COULD SENSE Nenyane's worry and frustration, and he let it pass: she was not worried about Stephen. It was novel; he had been the heart of her worry for so long he had thought the two—worry and himself—inseparable.

Had he time, he would have asked her about the fox, but he knew that the questions would have to be carefully couched; the fox was of the wilderness, which she knew instinctively, even remembering nothing of her former life.

Now, however, was not the time. He turned to Ansel to report what his dogs could see.

"You are certain?" Meralonne asked. "The creature we seek has found harbor in a building?"

Stephen nodded.

"What is the architectural style of that building?"

Nenyane rolled eyes.

"It isn't like Breodani buildings. Not even in the classic, modest style." This was clearly not a helpful answer; the mage's eyes narrowed. "It has a roof, but the walls seem to be almost absent between its pillars."

"Wood or stone?"

"The walls?"

"The *pillars*, boy."

"Stone, I think. It's not a large building." He sent the dogs around the sides. "It's not long, and it's not terribly wide. Is the building itself a danger?"

Meralonne shook head. "You are certain?"

Nenyane said, "Yes. Yes, he is."

"Do not send the dogs anywhere near that building. I would tell you to call them back were it not for the need for information. But that is not the dwelling of the lord of these lands. If we are to move, let us move quickly; I highly doubt our prey will remain in place."

MAX AND ALEX split their trance as the Hunters began their run. Gervanno found it difficult to keep pace with them for long; carrying the fox made running more awkward than he would have anticipated, had he been asked. The fox, however, had no intention of being set down; Gervanno tried once more, and got small, pointy teeth in the mound of his palm in response. The fox did not draw blood, but his meaning was clear.

The trees were tall but almost slender nearest what had once been road; they extended for as far as mortal eye could see, silver and grey in moonlight. There was no movement in the undergrowth; even the wind seemed to hold its breath.

When running a hunt, silence was not the first consideration; they therefore moved as if tracking. The trance's gift of preternatural awareness and reflex could not entirely dim the sound of feet against the earth. Kallandras lifted hand, and moonlight was swallowed and held in the single gem on the ring he wore on his thumb. The stillness in the forest air was alleviated by the shallow breath of wind which seemed to blow against their faces, rather than at their back.

"I cannot do more," the bard said, as if apologizing. "Not if we wish to catch our quarry unaware."

"Illaraphaniel offered safety if he chose to flee," Nenyane's voice was the loudest of those present. "Our options are therefore limited."

Meralonne's expression made clear that he, like many of the Northerners, did not consider his offer in any way binding. It was an offer made in the moment; it carried no weight, no relevance, when that moment had passed.

Nenyane's expression made clear that she felt as Gervanno did. Her eyes narrowed; her fists clenched. Gervanno had always believed that she would be a disastrous child in the South. She was a young woman, and her mastery—her absolute, unquestioned mastery—of the blade might not be enough to save her family when she failed to control her tongue, her expression, her stance.

This would have been one of those occasions, and for the first time in a long while, Gervanno felt blessed that he was in the North, and not the lands of his birth. While survival in these strange and foreign lands, where lords conspired with demons, was not guaranteed, Nenyane's life —and the life of her companions—would not be spent on necessary social grace. Stephen's family would not suffer the consequences of Nenyane's open disapproval. Gervanno's own expression was, by custom and instinct, carefully schooled; he was guard, not lord.

He was therefore surprised by two things.

The first, the fox bit the mound of his hand, and this time, his small, sharp teeth drew blood; the second, Nenyane turned to him and said, "What does Ser Gervanno think?"

Her eyes narrowed; had it not been for the sudden tension in jaw and sword arm, they might have been closed. She did not wait for Gervanno's reply—perhaps because she already knew the answer. Instead, she swung her blade around, tip pointing at the fox. "What do you think you are doing?"

As if he'd been struck by lightning, Gervanno felt all of the hair along his arms and neck attempt to stand on end. He knew she made the demand not of Gervanno, but the fox—the fox who had now drawn Gervanno's blood.

The Northern mage was quick to intervene; he stepped between the fox and Nenyane, avoiding the tip of her extended blade.

"Eldest," he said, his voice quiet. Quiet, but not soft.

"I told you, Illaraphaniel. I have an interest in this mortal. I would not intervene had she not attempted to draw him into a pointless argument; her argument is with you, not with my Gervanno."

Nenyane almost roared with frustration.

"He is not yours," the fox continued. "He has walked a long road, and the road has divested him of kin and companionship. He was a stranger to you."

"He is not a stranger now," Nenyane snapped, her expression hidden by the Widan's physical presence. "He's one of the only decent swordsmen I've met in these lands, and we will have need of those in the battles to come. He is *not* your pet; his life is not yours to either command or squander.

"And he cannot use his talent, his gift, while he is serving as your conveyance. I would have you walk—that's what you have feet for."

The fox growled, the sound low.

"She is correct," a new voice—a familiar voice—said. "And as I *am* yours, perhaps you will do me the honor of allowing me to bear your weight in these benighted lands."

Gervanno tensed. Instinct reminded him that Jarven ATerafin was never a man one wanted at one's back, especially when one's sword arm was occupied.

"I see you have chosen to grace Ser Gervanno with your blood."

"It is *his* blood, as you well know. Why are you here?"

"I believe I am the beneficiary of a happy coincidence. Having entered the palace, I have discovered which offices house the former Rymark ATerafin. Imagine my surprise to learn that he was called away on very short notice due to a family emergency."

To Gervanno's surprise, the fox relaxed in the cradle of his arms. "You are therefore continuing your hunt."

"Indeed. And I appear to have interrupted the Breodani hunt that is also occurring in a geographic location so similar to my own."

"And why have you chosen to reveal yourself?"

"I believe our end goals are very similar."

The fox growled again. This time, Jarven bowed to the fox, and held that bow until the fox bid him rise. He did not do so immediately.

"Gervanno is not my cub," the fox said, in a voice better suited to the great, prowling cat Gervanno had first encountered when the Breodanir roads had gone strange. "He is not your rival. He is not your competition. I will be *very* displeased should your machinations inadvertently—or deliberately—cause his death. He is not as you are. He has a brief, brief span of years remaining to him before he falls into decline and dotage."

"He would have to survive to do either."

"Indeed."

"And you came here to ensure that he does?"

The fox said nothing for a long beat. "I was bored," he finally conceded, the growl receding from his tone. "You have been meticulous but ineffective in your own hunt; I did not expect to see it to fruition soon. Perhaps I have grown impatient with age." He lifted head, exposing the underside of his throat—to Gervanno, not Jarven. "And perhaps I have been too demanding. I will allow my cub to bear my weight.

"If you would accept a meager request," the fox continued, while Jarven remained bowed, "I would ask that you consider an alliance with my cub. If he is here, it means his quarry has involved himself with the lord you seek; we are already aware of his interconnections with the Shining Court. It is possible that he is the link—in Bredan's lands— with the lord who would destroy the walls that have become so porous.

"My cub will not interfere in your hunt, and he would not *dare* to ally himself with those who serve or collude with the dead."

Gervanno turned, not to the man Stephen called Meralonne and Nenyane called Illaraphaniel; nor did he turn to Nenyane. His gaze fell squarely on Lord Ansel, the captain of this mission. He could see the effect of youth on the young lord's shoulders; could see the determination and passion of that youth as it was buffeted by the insecurity of being new to command.

Such men, Gervanno had served in his time; fully half grew into the commands they had undertaken.

"Interesting," the fox said. "What happened to the other half?"

Gervanno found the fox's ability to hear his internal—and silent— deliberations uncomfortable. Of what use was the effort to hide all hints of those thoughts when they could be so easily revealed? But he also understood that the fox was the greater lord; he could not ask a boon of the fox.

"Oh, you could, little mortal. You would even survive the asking."

"I would not survive the price," Gervanno replied calmly.

"Perhaps. Perhaps not. Mortals are oft surprising; the only inevitably about them is the death they face. Born to die, they walk towards it. Some struggle mightily against that fate. I would not, if I were you; it generally ends poorly. So, too, does refusal to answer my harmless questions."

"The other half perished before they could grow into their rank."

The fox nodded. Without looking at Jarven, he said to him, "Do not annoy me. Rise. I am certain you will be far better at interacting with these Hunters when you are not staring at the ground." To Gervanno, with an expression that indicated reluctance, he added, "You may deliver me to my cub. We can listen to his reasons for believing that here is where the trail he has followed must lead."

Gervanno, however, failed to follow instructions. His gaze turned once again to Lord Ansel, as if he required that lord's permission.

Lord Ansel nodded. "Yes. An enemy of our enemy would be welcome to join us. He did not require permission to cross the border, as we did; his knowledge may well be of use to us."

Gervanno did not trust Jarven; that distrust was amplified by the smile the man now offered Lord Ansel.

"Very good. I am Jarven ATerafin. I serve as head of the Terafin merchant arm in the Empire. Kallandras and Meralonne APhaniel can vouch for me."

"By vouch," the mage said, "he means we can confirm his claim to be of Terafin, only that."

Jarven's smile was slender. "Indeed."

Alex, however, was frowning. "You are ATerafin?"

"I am." He seemed to expect the name to have weight, to imply power.

"As in House Terafin, one of The Ten?"

"Indeed. I came to Breodanir on House business."

Nenyane snorted. Loudly.

Jarven raised a brow. "While you are not in a position to determine the truth of my words, you might be should we succeed and make our way back to the King's City." He held up a hand; he wore a large ring on one of his fingers. "I will not say that I had no other business in your fair kingdom, as you clearly suspect. But I traveled here on legitimate House business.

"Might I suggest that now is not the time to either defend or justify my credentials?"

The eyes of five Hunters turned to the sixth. Ansel, however, chose to be temperate. He nodded, but the nod was cautious. The mage joined Jarven and the fox he now carried; the bard remained at a polite distance. The breeze that ruffled hair did not touch the fox.

"If we accept your credentials, we must still ask: why are you here, in this forest?"

A long-suffering look of deliberate patience crossed Jarven ATerafin's face. He glanced down at the fox, who seemed both amused and unconcerned.

"Rymark ATerafin once served House Terafin, but he served at the behest of the Shining Court."

The words meant something to the mage.

"The Terafin—the lord who has so graciously condescended to allow me to bear the name of her House—has tasked me with finding Rymark; he did some damage to the House and the city in which the majority of it is situated. If the Shining Court is unfamiliar to you, it is the court over which the Lord of the Hells presides—and it exists now, in the distant Northern Wastes, in mortal lands.

"It is to that lord that Rymark swore service; in that lord's interests that he labors. He is...unwelcome in Averalaan; should he cross the borders of that city's lord, his existence would be noted instantly." There was a tinge of regret in Jarven's voice, which seemed at odd with his words.

"And you believe him to be here?" Ansel's voice remained cool.

"Yes. Here, he might go undetected. He is both powerful and somewhat canny, and we have no reason to suspect that he has disavowed the lord whose service he chose. If The Terafin has chosen to have him apprehended, it is not the primary reason I seek him. My master is the Eldest, and he has set me a task. A trial, if you will, in which I must prove my worth and my competence."

Meralonne spoke before Ansel could. "You are hunting Rymark ATerafin."

"Indeed."

"And you would hunt him at the Eldest's behest if the world was burning around you, without pause to attempt to extinguish the flames."

Jarven's smile was sharp, deep; he nodded at the mage. "I would. Until I have passed the test my master has set me, I remain profoundly poorly armed to fully engage with the creatures we call demons and you refer to as the dead. It is a battle I wish to enter, but I am not so foolish as to enter it unarmed."

When the mage turned his attention to the fox, rather than the man who carried him, the fox said, "It would suit the purposes and desires of *my* Lord; it is not a test created at odds with her. I have lived in many lands, traversed the high and low wilderness; I have spent my time in the tangle, looking for some glimpse of things lost. But in that time, I have seldom met a lord I was willing to call my own."

"She is mortal."

The fox snorted. "She is Jewel. Mortality is irrelevant. While she lives, while she *rules*, I have chosen to serve her—and serve her fully."

Nenyane's jaw was slightly open as she stared at the fox, her brows folding. *Did he just say he served a mortal?*

Yes, if I understood him.

I don't believe it. Her tone implied the world had been upended; that reality had somehow broken. Ironic, considering the situation in which they now found themselves.

"My test was created with the subtle dictates of the lord I serve in mind. Jarven?"

"Rymark ATerafin was serving as an official of middling power within the King's Palace. Alliances or no, he is not demonic in nature; he had no difficulty entering the palace or its offices. I had hoped to find him resident there—and quickly. But as I mentioned, he took a sudden leave of absence. On the road his trail was much easier to pick up than it has been within the King's City.

"It led me to you, but not entirely directly. He is, however, somewhere in these lands."

"You are certain?" the fox demanded.

"I would bet my life on it."

The answer satisfied the fox, who added, "And clearly, you have."

Jarven turned once again to Lord Ansel. "He is my quarry. I have already warned Ser Gervanno that his death must come at my hands; I ask that you respect the test I have been given. If I find him, I wish no intervention in whatever battle results.

"But inasmuch as his forces are here, I will aid you. While our paths converge, I will follow your lead." He then offered Ansel a perfect bow. "And while they converge, I will take your orders, saving only those that conflict with my master's."

Ansel nodded after a long pause that implied some conversation with his huntbrother. "We are here having tracked a collaborator to this area. We hope to gain information about this land's lord."

"Very well. Unless that collaborator is Rymark, I will not interfere."

NENYANE DID NOT TRUST JARVEN, but it was the fox who was her chief concern. *Of course I distrust him. You look at him and you think he is small and harmless. Foxes are not harmless to chickens, penned in coops.*

We're not chickens.

In the fox's eyes? We most certainly are.

Gervanno seems to accept him.

Nenyane snorted. *Gervanno owes him a debt. He accepts the elder's presence as payment for that debt—but he considers the debt to be his life, which means he might* always *accept the fox. He doesn't trust Jarven—which is another point in his favor. If we were anywhere else, I'd consider killing Jarven just to make certain he's not at our backs.*

She meant it, but Stephen was not a stranger to his huntbrother's visceral dislike. He knew that Nenyane would not act on the desire without good cause. If she considered someone an immediate threat, Stephen was given no warning; she reacted instantly.

Her attack on the bard—in the Queen's audience chamber, no less—was a prime example of that. She understood, grudgingly, that that attack had perhaps been too hasty; the bard himself had made no attempt to injure either Stephen or Nenyane.

She put distance between Stephen and Jarven, but that was for Stephen's sake, not her own; she did not otherwise consider Jarven ATerafin a threat.

Stephen returned his attention to his dogs, and the Hunters began to close with their quarry.

THE HUNT DID NOT FINISH at a run. The dogs were not best pleased to be ordered to both watch and wait, but obeyed. Pearl pushed against Stephen, but he had become accustomed to her oppositional streak. As long as she obeyed, he accepted the equivalent of angry ranting. It had always been his way to accept what could not be changed.

Nenyane found Pearl annoying, but his huntbrother had a plethora of things to find annoying at any given moment, and Pearl had therefore moved down the list.

She is who she is, Stephen said, because defiant or no, Pearl had moved herself into the best position to offer Stephen a clear view of their target—or rather, their target's shelter. The building itself seemed composed of pillars, with a small bit of wall between each; Stephen did not expect to find a door, and was not therefore disappointed. He had expected to find an opening of some sort, but that expectation—at least at a distance—was to be disappointed.

"Is it safe to move?" Ansel asked of Stephen.

Stephen nodded. Nothing had emerged from the building. "I can send the dogs toward the building itself. I can't see a way to enter."

Meralonne, brooding, shook his head. "Come. Let us join your animals."

"What do you fear?" Nenyane asked.

"Very little," the mage replied, a thread of annoyance underpinning his tone. "There is a reason we allowed him to walk away; he cannot harm me."

"You're not the only person present," she snapped.

"I am, I assure you, skilled enough that I would not allow harm to befall any of you." He glanced briefly at the fox.

The fox rolled eyes and lofted nose into the air. He then exhaled, and a breeze once again moved through them, a gust of warm air that did not last. "Very well. I understand your interest in the god-born boy, but I consider most of this a pointless fuss. If it is true that the lord of these lands has chosen to join the dead, she will learn that death is her only natural reward."

"If you wish to head directly into her presence, we will make no attempt to detain you." The mage's eyes were silver; Stephen thought they were the color of the fox's fur, illuminated by moonlight.

Ansel opened his mouth.

"The elder is known to act entirely on his own whims," the mage then said, before Ansel could speak. "The lord will not assume he is here at anyone else's behest, and it may distract her, which would serve us well."

Nenyane's silence was loud, at least if one were Stephen. She struggled in that silence, and at last turned to Jarven and the fox. "There is strong evidence that the Silences are caged and bound to her service — at least some of them. They serve the lord of these lands against their will. If you wish to approach her, you must be aware of that fact."

The fox's eyes narrowed as he turned head to Nenyane. Jarven observed her as well, his eyes narrowing.

Nenyane found it annoying that Stephen considered Jarven the greater threat. *He is nothing compared to the creature he carries.*

Stephen made no argument. But he considered the fox a force of nature; nothing he could do could change its whims. Jarven, however, was human, and actions could be taken to diminish any threat he might pose.

He can't threaten me. If he can't threaten me, he can't threaten you. The elder could harm us, but he understands that you are of interest to Illaraphaniel; he will make no attempt to harm you unless he wishes to incur Illaraphaniel's enmity. Illaraphaniel forgets nothing. Unlike me.

The bitterness in the last words remained with Stephen as he turned once again to Ansel. "Let's go."

———————

THE BUILDING that they approached was the building the dogs had seen. No door magically appeared; it seemed to be a rectangular box composed of pillars and walls. Around the pillars, vines of ivory and gold twined; those pillars supported a roof that seemed very gently sloped, if at all; it might have been flat.

The mage grimaced. "This is a safe harbor; only those who are invited may enter."

Kallandras, so silent he might have been forgotten, stepped away from the group to approach the building itself. "Is it necessary that we seek the intruder?" he asked, voice soft, although the words carried clearly. "He has not led us to his lord, which is the information we desired. As the Eldest has chosen, for reasons of his own, to join us, I believe the creature's presence has been rendered irrelevant."

"Oh?" the fox said, ears twitching.

"You will know where the lord is to be found."

"Why are you certain of that? If she wishes to remain hidden, even I would find it difficult."

"Impossible?"

The fox snorted. *"Difficult.* Why do you wish to abandon this path?"

"You cannot hear it, can you?" was the bard's soft reply.

"There is very little of interest to hear. To what do you refer?"

"The name. The soft sounds of lamentation. This building was never meant to be a dwelling; nor, I imagine, a place of shelter, although clearly that is now its use. Oft are things used for purposes their builders did not intend in long-ago history. But I believe it was meant as a memorial, perhaps even a mausoleum."

"What name?" Meralonne asked, arms falling to his sides. Stephen thought he detected a tremor in the mage's hands.

Kallandras shook his head. "Were it meant to be heard, you would hear it."

"You hear it nonetheless."

"That, as you well know, is both my curse and my gift."

Meralonne then joined the bard; or, rather, walked toward him, but did not pause at the almost respectful distance from the memorial the bard kept. He was therefore the first person to reach out and lay his palm against the flat surface of wall. It looked almost like an interior wall, not an exterior one.

Nenyane frowned and walked toward the mage, but the bard raised arm to gently block her passage.

"The dead cause pain and grief to the living when their loss is new."

"The dead cause pain and grief to the living regardless," she replied. "The *Kialli* were lost to the living in ancient times, and yet the blades they wield have never lost their edge. The dead memorialized here are truly dead; there is no echo, no mockery, of their former life that still wanders the vast planes. There is no desire on their part that all of the living they abandoned now join them in their death."

"No. No, there is not. But there are notes of pain and loss that imply the creator of this small shrine would willingly join them if they were allowed. I do not know why he chose to retreat to this place, bleeding as he was."

Without turning, Meralonne said, "I do."

Those two words silenced all who now bore witness. Even the dogs sensed something in the mage's tone that made them silently wary.

The wind moved in the clearing between forest and pillars; it was not the gentle breeze the bard had summoned. The bard grimaced and lifted his face; the wind whipped hair from that face, as if it desired to see him more clearly. He spoke. Or rather, he opened his mouth and his lips moved; Stephen could not hear his words.

But the wind's ferocity dimmed as he silently bespoke it. He then looked down. "Lord Ansel?"

The clearest indication that Ansel was accustomed to command, although young, was the lack of confusion on the Hunter Lord's face. "The mage is more familiar with the wilderness than any of the Breodani. If he believes it wise or necessary, I will defer to his expertise."

Stephen heard the emphasis on the words *wise* and *necessary*. He glanced at Heiden, whose brow was furrowed in concentration, recognizing the phrasing as the huntbrother's, not the Hunter's. But he concurred; Nenyane did not believe there was a gentle force that could stop the mage. Working in concert, their combined efforts stood a chance, but it was not large.

Meralonne APhaniel touched the wall. It remained a wall. He closed his eyes; the dogs remained positioned around the building; Stephen could therefore see the mage's profile through their eyes. He could see the sweep of silver eyelashes, gleaming as if caught in bright light; the moons were high, but they were not the source of the illumination.

"Kallandras, tell me."

"It is not a name that is meant for you," the bard replied.

"No." The voice was low. "But I understand, now, the modest shape of this dwelling and what it means to the one who created it."

"Do you know who created it?" Nenyane asked.

He did not respond to her. "Kallandras."

If Kallandras obeyed the mage, it was done in such a way that no others could hear the word.

The mage, eyes closed, lifted chin; his face was of ivory, as if an Artisan had crafted it perfectly to capture this moment. Nenyane tensed, her shoulders curling toward the ground as if to ward off a blow.

Stephen was by her side in two long strides; this was not the reaction she had had to the statue she had seen in the public galleries meant to impress the impressionable. As if a vortex of dark emotion were a cliff, she stood on the edge of that grief; he could feel it well up beneath her feet. He would not let it sweep her away. Not again.

He placed an arm around her shoulder. "Nenyane."

Nenyane.

She was rigid; she was fighting the undertow of memory in her own way. Had the pain promised to give her the memories, the things lost to her, she would have accepted it, would have dived straight in.

Stephen was uncertain that he would not have tried to stem the tide of grief regardless. But here, she found her way back to him, her way back to a present she both knew and remembered.

The dogs demanded his attention, and he turned; they had remained silent, but they were almost quivering in place.

The walls between pillars had begun to dissolve. It was an odd dissolution; they did not simply vanish, as illusions created by magic did; they crumbled, as if they were made of sand and the sand was returning to its base state. The pillars remained where they had been placed, but they, like the mage, seemed to reflect a light with no visible source.

The hand that had been placed against the wall remained there as the wall vanished beneath it; when it was lowered, the palm was shining silver. Without turning Meralonne said, voice clear, "You who envy eternity, you who desire immortality, fail to understand its curse. Grief and loss are endless; nothing loved is, in the end, unchanged or preserved.

"Death is an end to pain, and unless we fail, it is beyond us."

"There is also joy in life, APhaniel," the bard's voice was soft, measured.

"Joy is not endless. Grief is. Loss is permanent." But the mage bowed head, and the strange luminosity that touched his face and hands began to dim. "One day, I would have you sing of it; no one of my kin ever shall.

"No; memorials and the truest expression of grief must be left in the hands of those who are not, and were never, kin. Almost, I wish to walk away, to wash my hands of this hunt." His head remained bowed. "This memorial is an expression of respect and devotion that is forbidden us, but those who knew the dead best, who loved them longest, cannot fail to be moved."

Nenyane tensed, but did not speak.

What will he do?

What do you think? He's Illaraphaniel. His dead were monstrous.

You don't believe his grief is true?

Of course it's true, she snapped. *But he is Firstborn, and Winter is never far from his heart.*

As if he could hear Nenyane's unspoken words, the mage lifted his face; his hand fell to his side. Through Patches's eyes, Stephen could see the cool, slender smile eradicate all signs of grief from the mage's expression. He faced the memorial. He spoke to whoever resided at its heart.

"Were the situation not dire, perhaps I would be content to offer quiet respect and walk away." His smile deepened. "But I have survived, where my brethren did not, because I have always, and will always, bow to the desires of the White Lady.

"This alliance between your lord and the dead is forbidden, and the consequences for breaking the laws of the living wilderness cannot be evaded."

Look at Gervanno, Nenyane said, which surprised Stephen enough that he immediately obeyed.

Gervanno's expression was neutral; there was nothing about it that implied a strong reaction. But his stance was slightly stiffer, and his hands were momentarily clenched.

He understands.

Clearly, Stephen didn't.

Honor and law are the corridors through which we walk as warriors. Warriors are human; they suffer from the same emotions as those who have elected to follow a different path. But Gervanno understands power, and the flow of power; he understands hierarchy and the respect hierarchy demands if all is not to fall into chaos.

Stephen frowned.

The man you call Meralonne is, was, and will be a power to be reckoned with. In Gervanno's lands, there is not one who could stand against him, should he unleash the totality of his power. But he does not rule. He has never ruled. He serves the White Lady to his dying breath. So, too, the dead he mourns, until their last moment in which they could not face the consequences of her commands — to her, not to themselves. Misguided love. Misguided allegiance. They believed, in the end, that they knew more and better.

She may have loved them, Nenyane continued. *But she is the power that governs the whole of Illaraphaniel's existence — he who was exiled but granted neither sleep or death. He grieves his loss. But he accepts. Those who disobey, those who betray, must perish, love or no. He might weep — as Gervanno might weep in similar circumstance — but the sole sign of respect or gratitude he is allowed to offer will be a clean, a dignified, death.*

Stephen remained uncertain; he could not see what Nenyane saw in Gervanno. Not until Gervanno briefly bowed head, as if to shield his expression.

He might have said something, but at that moment, light engulfed the structure; pillars blazed as if they were pieces of sun, not the stone from which they had been carved.

Meralonne APhaniel stood, arms by his side; it was only his voice that he raised, but he spoke in a language Stephen did not understand.

Nenyane did.

KALLANDRAS HEARD THE SPOKEN WORDS. It was not their meaning that struck him, it was what lay beneath them: a sense of loss and anguish, a sense of betrayal—both received and given—and a sense of rage at life itself, when life could offer such loss and such tragedy.

Entwined with rage was yearning and bitter self-condemnation.

And beneath that: determination. It was that determination upon which the Firstborn prince had rooted what remained of eternity.

Once, once before, Kallandras had heard the cry of this man in a battlefield made of rock and darkness. Once before, he had felt it resonate with his own internal voice, his own bitter determination. They were walking, separated by centuries and history, toward the end of the path they had chosen, and perhaps that walk itself would finally earn them the peace of silence.

Illaraphaniel, to his White Lady.

Kallandras, to his Dark Lady. The bard felt something he would never share as the last of the mage's voice died into echoes and stillness: pity.

Pity for one whose loss was so far in the past no mortal could remember it, but who had walked the road Kallandras had walked from that moment on. He could not imagine eternity on that path, the decades frayed and faded, the burden growing with the passage of time.

"Illaraphaniel," he said, "please. Leave this to us."

Silence, and the slight movement of platinum hair, were the whole of the mage's answer. He spoke. *"Come out. Come out; the First Prince of the White Lady's court commands your presence."*

The bard glanced at his companions, the glance brief but thorough. Only the Maubreche huntbrother appeared to understand the words the mage spoke. To his surprise, she seemed to understand the emotion behind them; the lines of her face, often harsh and almost planar, had fallen into an unfamiliar expression. Sympathy. Empathy.

The bard had been sent to Breodanir by the only other person who might command action from him. *You will meet the Maubreche pair. Stephen is the god-born son of Bredan. Nenyane is not. She will kill you if she believes you pose a threat to her Hunter. She will kill you if you attempt to touch him at all.*

"Illaraphaniel," the fox said.

The mage ignored the interruption. Kallandras noted that the fox seemed unruffled by what would be a sign of disrespect in any other person present.

"You will get nowhere with this approach," the fox continued, as if the mage had heard and acknowledged his words. "I understand some part of your loss, but not all; the White Lady was not, and could not be, my god. She had no hand in my making, and she will have no hand in my unmaking.

"You are a scion born of the White Lady in her youth, before her power was tested. Do not fear for her future; she has finally condescended to wake her daughters. I can hear them in my Lord's forest, where they walk and converse. They are angry, and it is the anger of the Firstborn, of whom you are the sole remaining son of that generation.

"They wait for your return, even now. Your long exile is over—and it is an ending you have desired from the moment it began. And yet you have not returned, you who lived for naught but the White Lady. Is exile now so comfortable to you? Dignity and power are essential, now; bring your self-imposed exile to an end, or so I was bid to inform you."

This gave Meralonne pause; he turned toward the fox, his eyes silver and shining. "Bid? *Bid*? By who?"

The fox's fur rose as he leapt from the cradle of Jarven ATerafin's arms; Jarven seemed to find the entire proceeding amusing given his expression, although it was subtle.

The fox's eyes now glowed a bright gold, and the color of his fur shifted.

"Who dared to use you as a messenger? Were you sent to find me?"

The fox made a noise very similar to a sneeze.

The mage was not impressed.

"I was asked—*asked*—to deliver this message should our paths cross. Our paths have crossed. It was asked by one who will never again witness the glory of eternity; she made a choice dissimilar to your own, and yet, in the end motivated by her love of the White Lady—as were those now lost.

"Were it not for that long-ago choice, the world would continue in Winter, and perhaps because it is now Summer, and your lady the Summer Queen, she has been forgiven. Or perhaps it was because no orders were given, no obedience demanded, in the face of her choice. Shandalliaran, she was once called. My lord is fond of her, and I am therefore inclined to listen to simple requests."

"And what favor did you demand in return?"

The fox chuckled; Kallandras heard the anger in the sound. He tensed; the breeze came to him, gently tugging at his hair. He did not know what had possessed Jarven ATerafin to make a bargain with this elder creature; he wondered if the former Terafin merchant would survive it.

"Shianne was concerned. You spent little time with her when you occupied my lord's forest. She is not what she was, but she has not lost the memories of her youth, her childhood. She is grieving, Illaraphaniel. She is grieving the new loss—and all losses are new to both her and her wakened sisters.

"Even I feel her loss keenly, although it is ancient history to me now."

"The loss of my sleeping brothers is not ancient," the mage replied.

"Ah, no. But she lost Darranatos as well, and it was by her hand— her mortal hand—that he was returned in defeat and ignominy to the hells of his master. The anger of her sisters is ancient, wild; they are only barely contained by their devotion to the White Lady, and the lesson taught by the loss of the three."

"That has nothing to do with this structure and its occupant."

The fox *tsked*. He walked past the mage—walked, in fact, between his legs toward the open space between the pillars. Kallandras whispered a benediction to the wind, but did not move.

"Your sisters are not angry with the White Lady—it is beyond their ability. So, too, is it beyond yours. But you are of her in a way that the denizens of the wilderness are not. While your brothers slept beneath the mortal earth, there was hope.

"When they awakened, the wilderness heard their voices through my Lord's lands. The earth woke. The wind whispered their names. You could hear the sound of held breath, Illaraphaniel; you could hear the trembling of joy.

"It did not last."

Meralonne bowed head. "Stop, Elder. Stop or we will come to blows in this forest, and only one of us will leave it alive."

"Perhaps. Perhaps not. I have said I have an interest in the lord of these lands and her alliance with the dead. But if you expect to enter the heart of the wild lands and encounter no grief, no hint of the passage of those who will never visit again..." the fox shook his head. "Your sisters remain by the White Lady's side—all save Shianne, whose child will face the end of Summer. The last Summer King.

"Think you that your loss is the only loss? That it is the most profound? Such arrogance, Illaraphaniel." The fox was amused. "Hold fast to it. If you have come this far, you will not plead with the wilderness—not now. If you cannot be what you were, you will perish here, and the long hope upon which the White Lady spent so much of herself will end in failure."

"Then we face failure," the mage said. "I cannot be what I was. I cannot return to her side until I have redeemed the failures of those I loved. I cannot face her, cannot speak their names, cannot make any attempt to redeem them in her eyes. Only should we finally succeed will they know a measure of peace."

"They know peace now. They are dead."

Meralonne was silent for one long breath. Before he could speak again, he turned and headed into the forest, past the watching dogs.

NENYANE ALMOST FOLLOWED; Stephen caught her arm. *Don't. It's not safe.*

I know. He knows that he could be a danger—an unintentional danger—to all of you. He will not abandon this mission; he will not forsake the battle, long delayed, in which his brothers failed. He understands that only by winning, in the end, will he redeem them. But redemption in the face of evidence of their loss is bitter—and it is the only thing that he has yearned for since the Sleepers were entombed.

Stephen wanted to ask her how she knew; it was a struggle to hold back. But...she knew. When she spoke this way, she was certain.

Let me follow him.

You might get lost.

I won't. Not if you're here. I will always find my way back to you—I've told you that so many times. Let me follow, she said again. It was a plea.

He understood, then. The grief, built upon memories lost to her, was —in her mind—as profound as Meralonne's. And it was somehow connected. He released her arm.

He was afraid. Perhaps he'd always been afraid. He held Nenyane to the only place she could build memory: here. Now. By his side. But she had always been more than that. He understood, as he forced his feet to remain still, that their life together was, in the end, less than a mortal decade.

And the life she had lived before Evayne had brought her to Maubreche was much, much longer, all of it shattered, as if it were a mirror into which she could no longer look and see herself. Was it just that he had never wanted to know? Had he held her back deliberately, his attempt to soothe her pain tied into her existence as his huntbrother?

He was surprised when Gervanno gently touched his shoulder. The Southerner said nothing, the gesture the only comfort offered—and that, lightly, wordlessly, as if words had no meaning.

The fox cleared his throat very loudly, pulling their attention back to the matter at hand. "I will do what Illaraphaniel did not. Time—for all of you—is ludicrously brief, even in the absence of conflict. Which you are not."

It was Alex—it was almost always to be Alex—who said, "Who, or what, was the guard Meralonne allowed to flee?"

"A memory," the fox replied. "A living memory. One who dedicated himself to hope in the face of grief and loss. He has no hope now, and those without hope are ever a danger, if not to themselves, then to all that surround them. It has been long, in the reckoning of my kind. But once, little mortal, he had wings." The fox shook his head. "Stand back, all of you. No, not you, Jarven."

"This is not the task I was set," Jarven replied, tone so congenial he might have been politely refusing a second glass of wine at a dinner table. "Whatever this creature is to the wilderness and the ancients, he is not Rymark ATerafin."

The fox *tsked* once more. "Do not play word games with me; I have spent much effort on words this eve and I am reminded of why I considered such communication imperfect and exhausting. You are not young by the reckoning of your kind, and you have an ambition better suited to my kin than your own. Experience must have taught you that there are connections—unseen until the right moment—between smaller, traveled paths. Threads of fate, if you will; connections between disparate elements that might never otherwise coincide.

"Or perhaps your time does not grant you the depth of that insight. Very well. It was your task, and I will not further guide you; either you will complete it, or you will perish." He turned, then, to Gervanno di'Sarrado. "Come. You are not a being driven by the need to be heard.

"Listen, instead, Gervanno. Listen, remember. What passes here may be of no use to you in the future—as Jarven assumes it will not be to him—but it might be of value, of weight, to the master you have chosen, even be she incapable of accepting the oath you would offer her."

But Gervanno di'Sarrado shook his head. He offered the fox the respect that Jarven had not, but said: "If you understand that much, you must understand that she left because I was here; I am meant, lesser to her in all ways, to remain by Stephen's side. I am her sword in her absence."

The fox looked over his shoulder. "You make me hate mortality, little mortal. If you could but see yourself as I see you in this moment, if you could understand that what I see is a truth that time will destroy... very well. It was a passing fancy; the bard is here, and he will remember. There is nothing he will hear that he will easily forget."

He then turned back to the pillars. His feet, silver and almost weightless, crossed the barrier that seemed to separate the pillars from the forest itself.

The fox spoke a single word. "Steane."

The wind fell silent, as if silence itself were a stone dropped into the still surface of a pool of water, rippling outward to rob the clearing of even the sounds of breathing.

CHAPTER TWENTY-ONE

The first movement Stephen felt was not of air; the fox's voice seemed to echo in the stillness, but it was not an echo one could hear. It was felt first beneath his feet; the earth seemed to rumble, and the rumble itself felt like attenuated syllables. He knelt, Gervanno above him, to place palm against the forest floor.

Instinct made him call the dogs back, surrendering the vantage they offered.

The earth rumbled. It was not the angry movement that had threatened to destroy the inn and its passing occupants, but it was there. A whisper in the language of earth, not a roar.

The fox spoke the word a second time, and a third.

When no answer followed, the fox did what the earth did not: he roared. The roar seeped into the earth and trembled there; the pillars began to shake in response to the fox's anger. No, Stephen thought, not anger; the fox was merely annoyed.

He wondered, then, what Gervanno saw when he carried the fox; what Jarven felt when he had taken Gervanno's place. Stephen would have avoided the fox had circumstances permitted; he would never have accepted the fox's boon, aware — perhaps because Nenyane had been — that it would be a costly, costly gift.

He rose. To Gervanno he said, "I am not your responsibility, Ser Gervanno."

"No," the Southerner agreed. "You are Nenyane's."

"And you are not Nenyane, to take on that burden." He spoke to Gervanno's back; the swordsman looked out, standing between Stephen and the pillars that trembled in place.

"I am not Nenyane." The words, on the surface, were an acknowledgement of immutable fact; they were not, however, an agreement in any other way.

Stephen exhaled. Pearl, of the eight dogs, lingered closest to the fox, pulling against Stephen's command to return; she looked between the pillars, and he slid behind her eyes. He saw darkness, alleviated only by the subtle illumination of the fox's silvered fur, as if the fox were an aspect of moonlight come to earth.

"If Steane did not appear for Illaraphaniel," the bard said, voice characteristically soft, "I do not believe he will come for anyone."

The fox looked over his shoulder at the bard. "If he continues to be so disrespectful, I may lose my temper."

Jarven ATerafin's shoulders lifted, as did his chin; his eyes gleamed in the dim light. To Stephen's discomfort, he realized that Jarven wanted to see it: the loss of that ancient temper. The fox in full fury.

Stephen moved almost instinctively toward the fox.

"**Stay where you were**," the bard said. Speaking thus, although Stephen was certain no one else heard the words, the bard removed the backpack he carried, and from it, with care, withdrew an instrument. A lute.

"There are many ways to speak," the bard said to the bristling fox. "Not all language translates comfortably or easily to those who are unfamiliar with it."

"Kallandras." Jarven ATerafin made of the name a warning. It was not a warning Stephen would have ignored.

Kallandras was not Stephen. He began to pull soft notes from the strings of the lute, as if Jarven had not spoken.

Jarven, closest to the fox on the ground, turned to the bard. "Kallandras," he said again, and there was a hint of rumble in the word, a hint of the depth of the fox's voice. A warning, yes, or a threat. It was not a normal voice.

Gervanno heard it as well. His hand dropped to the hilt of his sword, but he did not otherwise move.

Alex joined Stephen; Max remained beside Heiden and Ansel. Every Hunter present understood Jarven's intent. They understood some part of Kallandras's as well, but it was to Kallandras that they owed a debt. Ansel was silent, his gaze on Jarven's back. Heiden, however watched the bard.

Stephen watched the fox, aware that the fox could stop Jarven with a word—and a word, given all other options, was preferable.

The notes continued. If Kallandras had heard threat in Jarven's simple use of his name—and given the talent to which he was born, he must have—it was a threat he did not acknowledge. Instead, he opened his mouth to join voice to the notes he pulled from the lute.

Stephen was not certain what he expected of the bard's song; traveling bards had come at least once a year to Maubreche, there to stay and exchange news in return for their songs and stories. He knew, however, that none of those bards were in any way equal to this one: Master Bard of Senniel College.

Had he any doubts at all, the bard's voice would have destroyed them; for a moment, all Stephen could hear was his song. All he *wanted* to hear was his song.

Stephen realized, as he listened, that the voice did not wrap itself around words; that the notes were not modulated by syllables, but rather by tone, by emotion. The song itself, shorn of words, was a structural ode to loss, to grief—to something so deep, and so endless, words were too weak a containment to express it.

He was grateful that Nenyane had followed the mage; were she here, he was almost certain she would be weeping. The memories she had lost had not taken emotion with them. What possible meaning did forgetting have when only the pain remained?

As they had progressed into what Nenyane called the wilderness—or sometimes the high wilderness—Stephen began to surrender his certainty that Maubreche, and her life in Maubreche, was enough to sustain her. He had wanted her to feel at home, to feel that Maubreche was the home that mattered. And while they both grew, it had been. It had been enough for his restless, prickly huntbrother.

But the advent of demons, the encroachment of wilderness, and the presence of Meralonne APhaniel had shattered the thin veneer of home. Nenyane needed her memories back, and the mage had implied she could retrieve them if she was willing to risk a journey into the most dangerous lands the wilderness contained.

They had to take that journey. He accepted it. Nenyane wanted to leave him behind, but he knew her well enough: she wouldn't take that risk. Not when she knew, without doubt, that he would attempt to follow her, regardless.

He would suggest it after they dealt with the danger to Bowgren—if they survived.

Gervanno tensed, his stance shifting as he bent slightly into his knees; the hand on sword hilt tightened, but he did not unsheathe it.

From between the pillars that now shone silver, walked a man. Or perhaps a woman. It wasn't scant light that made it hard to tell; it was the texture of hair—long—and skin. If this was the man who had imitated a Margen guard at the border, no sign of that imitation remained. No, the skin of face, shoulders, and arms were almost grained, as if they were carved from hard wood; the chest could not be seen for the fall of vines and leaves from the crown of the creature's head. The man—or woman—had no feet; ankles seemed to end at ground level, implying feet existed beneath the surface of earth.

The eyes, however, were green. Even at this distance, their color could be clearly seen—and it was a green so bright, so luminous, it might forever define the color in Stephen's memory. From those eyes fell tears, and the tears that traveled down the grained lines of face caused the vines that served as hair to grow, and grow again, as if they sought earth in which to root themselves.

Those eyes did not seem to see the fox, although the fox stood between the pillars; the creature drifted toward the bard, moving as if compelled, and weeping as it approached.

Kallandras did not move; he did not stop his mournful, wordless song. But the bard's eyes were closed; he raised chin, exposing the length of throat, turning his face to the darkened heavens as if to demand answers, to demand reasons why such pain, such loss, must exist. Was this the eventual destination to which all love must walk?

So, too, the emerald-eyed being, as if he knew the song Kallandras sang. Stephen was nonetheless surprised when a second voice joined the bard's—wordless, as the bard's song was wordless, but louder. For a moment the melody stretched between two voices, and each carried grief as its signature.

But the bard gave way, his song becoming harmony to the rising voice of the stranger, wrapped around the melody the second voice had taken, and climbing with it as their voices grew louder, and louder still. The notes of the lute fell away, the accompaniment unnecessary; for a moment the two voices existed in a realm of their own, the intensity of emotion almost too private for an audience.

But the audience was there, regardless. Stephen glanced at the fox, but the fox was utterly silent, watching both bard and whatever this new being was as if their song had invoked similar memories. The fox did not sing, did not open his mouth, but the anger at perceived disrespect slowly vanished.

To Stephen's surprise, the fox moved—swiftly—not to Jarven's side, but to Gervanno's. He butted the Southerner's leg, and his small head clearly had enough weight to cause the swordsman to stumble. Gervanno righted himself and knelt instantly; the fox leapt into his arms, as if he were a frightened cub, not an ancient. Gervanno then rose, the fox cradled carefully in one arm, hand still touching sword hilt.

From this distance, Stephen could see the soft gleam of tears in the fox's facial fur.

Stephen himself did not weep. But he could see that Ansel and Heiden shed tears as they bore witness to this unlooked-for concert.

Only when the last note—loudest to start, softest by end—had quieted did the fox speak. "You who are not moved have been fortunate indeed; you have suffered no great loss, and you do not carry the endless pain of the memory of that grief. Believe me when I say that I hope you never will.

"For beings such as I, it is inevitable that the song resonates; when life is as long as ours, it carries such loss in its folds." To the bard, he added, "I forgive you your interference; it has been long indeed since such a song has been carried on the wild winds. Do not be emboldened by such forgiveness." He turned nose in the direction of the singers, indicating by movement that Gervanno should now convey him toward them.

Gervanno did not hesitate. Stephen noted that Jarven, lips pursed, moved to join them; the fox glanced once at Jarven, and Jarven stopped.

Alex and Max turned to Ansel, a question in their twinned expressions.

Ansel shook his head. He glanced at the pillars from which the creature had come.

Stephen, however, reached for Nenyane. *We have our quarry.*

Nenyane did not respond.

NENYANE UNDERSTOOD the power of the bard-born on a visceral level; she had never considered it a threat. But when the bard began to sing, she could feel the wind respond; the earth beneath her feet rumbled very softly, as if in attempt to lift its ancient, wild voice to meet the bard's. In the distance, she could sense that Stephen was surprised—but he was safe.

This was the first time she had taken the risk of leaving Stephen's safety in another's hands; she strained against worry with every step she took. No, not worry. Fear. She could hear the bard's lament as if it were a dirge sung only for Nenyane. Nenyane and Stephen. She had always feared to lose him—not because she worried that he would somehow be fickle or careless, but because he could die.

Demons could kill him.

Magic could kill him.

The wilderness could devour him.

Standing against those things, those possible deaths, was Nenyane herself. Sentinel, guard, friend. Huntbrother.

And yet, here she was, following in Illaraphaniel's wake. Should Stephen be attacked, he might be injured or dead by the time she could once again reach his side.

Why had she left him? What had she thought to accomplish? Had she thought at all? She drew a deeper breath than running necessitated; she could almost taste the tang of grief in the air, but perhaps that was Illaraphaniel's grief—and her own fear.

When Illaraphaniel came to an abrupt stop, she stopped as well, maintaining a distance that could be broken by the simple lift of an arm. His back faced her; what he saw, she could guess.

"There was no song," he whispered, as aware of her presence as she was of his. "I have oft wondered at the complicated demands of mortal funerals. Mortals have so little time, it seems a waste to me to spend it thus: in mourning and grief, in lack of color, in lack of what scant joy life might offer to the ephemeral.

"But perhaps it is true: mortals live quickly because they must; they feel loss as we feel it, but deeply, and in such a short span it evades our notice unless we are physically present. Grief is a complicated binding," he said. He did not look back, but his hair shifted as he lifted face to the light of three moons.

Ah, no.

Two moons. The third, clouds took, obscuring its brilliance. Illaraphaniel had shrouded its light; she could almost feel the invocation of his ancient power. The third moon was the moon said to be the eye of this land's lord.

There were some things Illaraphaniel would not share. Nenyane would not have taken the risk — but it was not a risk within her capabilities to take.

"My kin have always understood that grief is a weight we must carry; what we do not clearly see is the bridge grief can build between those who understand its weight. You are here," he added, still failing to turn to face her, "because events that brought us, in the end, to this place, bind us; their terrible gravity threatens to drag us into a chasm from which we might never escape.

"Is that not so, Nenyane?"

She did not speak of grief or loss, but felt it now as undertow she must avoid; it would pull her under and carry her away from the life she had built.

"You fear grief." His voice was soft, but almost unbearable. "You fear the loss that presages it. You fear the moment when *forever* becomes *never again*. So, too, did I fear in my youth. But I knew the moment when *never again* was inevitable. Perhaps I have aged in the way mortals age, who have spent so much time amongst them.

"Perhaps that is why mortals do not, and cannot, have forever. Forever is the illusion; forever is the daydream, the fever dream, the nightmare. Could I but live as they live, I might be able to set down this burden."

"Mortals don't remember the way you remember."

"No. It is the second blessing given them by the rivers of time. The second gift."

"They don't consider it a gift. They don't consider age and death a gift, either."

Illaraphaniel nodded, aware, as Nenyane was aware, of the great price paid by those powerful enough — and foolish enough — to desire eternity. "Perhaps, were they to experience loss as we have experienced it, they would." He did not move; he listened to the distant song of the bard, stiffening only once when a second voice joined his.

She was aware of the moment he bowed head; aware of the moment he lifted hands to face. Aware of the moment he let those hands fall as he looked, once again, to the two moons that governed all of the night skies Nenyane had walked beneath since her adoption into Maubreche.

But she was shocked into immobility when he lifted voice as well. Wordless, because the words had been denied Illaraphaniel and all of his kin at the White Lady's command, he joined, his voice holding notes, harmonies, the thread of song escaping his control as grief pulled him under, only to return, stronger than before, as he bore that grief, returning it to the song that had evoked it.

Nenyane could hear and feel the wordless emotion, but could not raise voice to join it. Even a whisper would have been beyond her, so frozen was she in the moment those emotions, given voice, transcribed. It was not the loss itself but, rather, the recognition of what loss meant: not death, but the realization that death was the final wall, beyond which the gestures that made life matter could not pass.

She could not remember.

Her grief had no mooring, no roots—just the certainty that the loss had been so profound she could not encompass it, could not face it, could not hold it. This time, however, she was prepared for it; this time, she did not weep, as she had wept at the foot of a statue in the distant King's City. Nenyane of Maubreche did not weep.

Illaraphaniel did; she heard it in the cadence of the notes he carried, notes so precious to him, so unlooked for, he had no defense against the moment. Or perhaps he had no desire to defend himself against it. Perhaps the expression of grief and a loss so akin to his own allowed him to offer those emotions, emotions forbidden by the White Lady, and therefore denied by her kin, her people.

Her kin, who could not speak the names of the lost, could not offer the companionship of that loss to any—Illaraphaniel most of all.

She understood his pursuit of the lord of this land's collaborator, then. He was angry at the effrontery of that person, furious at that lord's alliance, at a distance, with the dead—those who had surrendered their life, and their life's meaning, to the Lord of the Hells. But he had recognized the creature they had tracked here, even if Nenyane could not, and he understood that all meaning had been sundered from this creature when one of the three princes—she did not know which—had died.

The dead—the demon-kin—might be a mockery of what they had once been in life, but that mockery itself could be both insult and comfort, for the dead remembered the lives they had lived, the lives they had surrendered.

The three who had fallen, the three who had betrayed their lord's sole command, would never appear again, except in dream or night-mare; their names never again to be spoken by the lord to whom they had dedicated the whole of their existence.

She did not feel it as a loss.

Illaraphaniel did. His voice dwindled and silence returned; the song had ended. Nenyane reached out, hesitating when her hand was an inch above his shoulder. She did not remember.

But absent memory, she knew. She knew what the loss meant to him. She had always known it. Her hand touched his shoulder; beneath the layers of cloth, she felt ice, cold. He did not stiffen, and he did not retreat. Instead, his shoulders moved as he righted himself.

When he turned to face her, there was no sign of grief, of tears, of loss. His eyes, silver, were clear as moonlight.

"I would not have guessed that, at the end of the journey, the companion I would retain would be you—you who were not mine. You who cannot remember the moment when all oaths were broken and all bonds shattered."

"Is that why you want me to remember?" she asked, voice low.

"No. You are not what I am, nor what I was." He exhaled. "I am uncertain, now, that the memories will be of value to you."

"But you said—"

"You believe that you were almost destroyed by demons." It was not a question.

She nodded. "I was being pursued by demons when Evayne found me."

"Yes—pursuit. And in your current state, I believe the strongest of the *Kialli* could effectively destroy you. It is their goal. It must be—you are a clear and present danger to the lord they serve. But they do not understand what they are looking for; driven by the echoes of ancient fears and ancient powers, they have searched in vain.

"That time is ending, Nenyane. They will not understand why you were so injured; they will not understand why you were almost destroyed. It is not a destruction they themselves could countenance, they who are forsworn.

"I believed you would have to face that truth to overcome it. But I did not see clearly. Tomorrow, I will not see as clearly as I do in this moment. I am not you; the White Lady binds me. It is not a coercion; she made me all that I am, and it is to her that I owe both life, while it lasts, and loyalty.

"It is the loyalty that she prizes most highly. It is why I alone of my brothers survive. But I failed her. Could I but return to her side, I would never leave it save at her command—and it would grieve me, who have spent more of life as exile than as servant.

"The bitter hope that I might once again be accepted into her court is the hope that has guided me, however threadbare and damaged it has become. But I am not what I was, and she is not what she was; if she will tolerate my return, she will not exult in it, will not find peace in it; our greatest enemy still lives. For his death, for his destruction, she crippled the power to which she was born; she is scarred by that choice. And, until and unless he is destroyed, the choice has no meaning.

"It is all that I now desire: to finish the war that should have ended eons past when I rode to war with my brothers; to ask that she forgive them enough that we might acknowledge their lives once again, that we might speak their names, that we might mourn as a people. If the Lord of the Hells perishes at my hand—or at ours—it is a boon I might ask, and then...only then will I know grace and peace. But it is not so, with you. In my determination to reach that elusive state of grace, I have all but forgotten.

"Your grief, child. Your loss. Perhaps it is best that you cannot easily touch or recall it." He turned toward the clearing in the silence and began to walk, donning the distance, the neutrality, that grief had momentarily broken.

"I believe we two, should we survive the past, will face the future, our fates entwined. And because you are here, Stephen will follow, who is oathbinder. I will not press him; it is the only gift I can offer you."

"But you think oathbinding is necessary."

"Yes. But Nenyane, I thought I could not survive in the absence of the White Lady or my brothers. Yet I remain. I have cursed survival. I have cursed existence. And I have found a scattering of joy in it, regardless. Even the wise cannot clearly see the shape of the future and the way it will break or bind us."

She hesitated, following, her steps heavier as she did. "Illaraphaniel."

He nodded.

"Do you believe my injuries were somehow self-inflicted?"

"I was not present at your birth," he replied. "And even those who were could not discern your strengths — or your weaknesses. Of that enchantment, that binding, that wild making, only one element was undeniable; only one would not waver. I remember the first time I heard your voice."

"Oh?"

"Do not be angered, child, for I will tell you the truth: I pitied you. I could not understand how one such as you had been given voice at all. Better that you not have one, for voice implies consciousness."

She was silent for a long moment. When she spoke, she had distanced herself from his pity. "What will you do with our quarry?"

"If he cooperates, I will not destroy him, for he has given me a gift today that was unlooked for."

"Tears are a gift?"

"Grief, shared grief, is a gift. It has edges, yes, but it is a reminder that my loss was not the only loss, and my grief perhaps not unique. It is thus when one shouts in a dark and empty cavern; it is the returning echoes that make clear that the voice itself was audible."

STEPHEN COULD FEEL Nenyane's approach, but she did not speak. She had pulled as far away as the huntbrother bond allowed, and he had learned with time that when she did so it was better to give her the space and time she needed.

Had she appeared in the clearing in tears, he would have taken the risk of approaching her regardless, but her face, if pale, was clear.

The mage, however, was less so. His eyes were silver light, his hair the color of the bright moon, his skin pale as the dead. The woodland being who had been drawn to Kallandras's wordless song stood rooted in place, as if he might grow there, but he faced the bard, his luminous green eyes reflecting what he saw.

Kallandras met his gaze without fear, without curiosity, as if the last note that had joined them had not yet faded, although it had.

As Meralonne approached, both turned to look at him, and the moment was broken. Or perhaps not, for the mage turned to the creature they had hunted, and offered him a bow. It was not a Southern bow, such as Gervanno offered, but it was not Imperial, either; it was unadorned but somehow perfect, as if respect imbued every small movement.

"I would ask of you a boon," the creature the fox had named Steane said to Meralonne.

"It is not in my power to grant what you seek," the mage replied, the softness of his voice implying regret. "For if you mean to ask of any of my three brothers, I cannot speak their names. It is not lack of desire; it is lack of ability. Thus, the White Lady's anger at their betrayal."

"Can you tell me why? Why did they perish? None could stand against them—against you—when you took to the field."

"We faced the Lady's one true enemy, the god we do not name, in the fullness of his power."

"Yet they lived. And you as well."

Meralonne's smile was bitter. "If this is life, then yes, I survived. And they slumbered long against future need. I...had hoped they would ride again, to atone for their betrayal of the White Lady's commands. But that is not her way. They have returned to her the power she granted them when she first breathed life into them. She is stronger than she has been since the sundering."

"But she is not what they were. She does not sing with their voice or speak their words; she does not remember their ancient history."

"Have care. If you will mourn in a fashion forbidden me, I accept it —but speak no word of ill against the White Lady in my presence."

Leaves and vines rustled as the creature bowed. "Forgive me."

"I will. But understand that I cannot let you simply vanish. Your lord works in concert with the dead and their lord. Their lord has been our greatest enemy, and to vanquish him, to destroy him, the White Lady surrendered much. She will not be at peace until that long-cherished goal is achieved: the enemy, and those who serve him in death, must perish.

"Understand that the lord of the lands you now call home is my enemy. Had my brothers survived, she would receive—and deserve— their fury, their hatred, their contempt."

"Yes."

"So, too, all those who have pledged allegiance to her. I know, now, for whom you built this memorial; he was quick to anger, quick to judge. He would not now forgive you for your choice of lord."

"And if the choice was not mine to make?"

"Do you think that would have stayed his hand?"

Silence, then; breeze through vines and leaves. Stephen could see the profile of the speaker, but could not fully discern expression. The silence extended for long enough Stephen thought it would not be broken by the stranger, but the mage waited.

"No. No, Illaraphaniel, it would not have stayed his hand. But he is gone; I will never weather his contempt or disgust. And could I, I would face it now without qualm, for it would mean he lived. If my life is the price demanded, I would pay it: sight of him, even in his profound fury, would be the last thing my eyes would see.

"It will not come, now. And if the White Lady chooses to ride, if she chooses to bring war to these lands, I might face the full measure of her fury without similar comfort."

"If she knew, she would ride," was the mage's soft reply. "But you may yet see older and wilder scions of the Lady, for she has chosen to wake her sisters, and where the prince you loved has fallen, the princes that will come—older, wilder, closest of kin to the Lady herself—will take his place in this final war.

"And it is war. It is a war without end, until either the Lord of the Hells or the White Lady lies dead. There is no other ending possible."

"She is not what she was."

"No," was the grave reply. "And when we understood the price she would pay should our lands be sundered from mortal lands, he could not pay it. Be the price his death—or worse, his exile, his banishment—he could not force himself to do what she commanded. None of the three could."

"And you could."

"I am here. I did not expect mercy from the White Lady. I failed in the height of Winter. But I serve her still."

"The lords are waking," the creature replied. "It is not only the lord I serve; I can hear other voices, tentative and hesitant, carried by the great winds. I can feel their names spoken as echoes and tremors by the earth in which I have taken root.

"But I do not feel young again. I do not feel joy. If the dead are riven from the lord they once served, so, too am I. I do not know if, upon death, I will wither and perish; I do not know if I will emerge in the tangle, one voice among many who lament. But I know, even in death, I will not see him again: I will feel no hint of his presence; I will hear no song from his lips. He is gone.

"He is gone because he served the White Lady."

"He is gone because he *did not serve*. If, in your anguish, you have chosen to stand against the White Lady, know that he would have burned your forest to ash in the instant he discovered your choice."

"Yes. Yes, Illaraphaniel. But in this terrible twilight, I feel that would be the better fate, for me — an end, at last, to grief and yearning." So saying, he straightened, or at least it appeared so to Stephen. But this straightening had sound, texture, even weight; he lifted both face and arms toward the moonlight, and something in the curve of his lips implied that he would never be touched by sunlight again. Twilight, he had called it.

Meralonne watched, eyes narrowed, as if he could read something in the lines of a face that slowly but certainly lost all semblance of movement, of the motion that implied life. Ah, no. That was wrong. But it was the life of the tree which Steane had resembled — a witness, something rooted in place that had no choice in the soil in which it had been seeded.

"So be it," the mage whispered, the words so soft they should have been inaudible.

"As you, Illaraphaniel, I cannot disobey my lord. Could I, in memory of shared loss, shared grief, I would." Although the stranger's lips had ceased to move, his voice continued, the tone of it shifting into something reedy and whistling. "Had I the choice, I would grow in the lands of *Taressarian* until the end of days. But those lands are also lost to other lords, other wills."

"Once, I might have removed you from this soil, but I kept no lands of my own. My existence was the White Lady; how could I have the responsibility of rulership in the face of my allegiance? When she called, we rode. When she commanded, we warred. When she gifted us with song, we wept, wordless; there were no words that could properly contain our joy.

"But you have made your choice. Even now, I can hear the movement of your roots in the earth beneath my feet; I can hear the way the earth speaks your name, you who it once sheltered. You have gifted me with a song of grief forbidden me.

"But you have allied yourself with our ancient enemy. I will therefore grant you what you seek: an end to endless grief and loss, here, in a place of your choosing."

There were no tears, no further words.

Meralonne lifted hand, and to it came sword, shining so brightly the light could not be reflected from any source Stephen's eyes could perceive.

But if the stranger believed that death was the better ending, he was nonetheless alive; the instinctive desire of the living to persist, to continue, could be felt now beneath Stephen's feet. Beneath all of their feet.

Nenyane seemed to be the only person present not caught in the weft of their mutual grief. She was silent, but she moved, leaping from Meralonne's side to Stephen's, her blade flashing in the light of the mage's as it traced an arc in front of her huntbrother.

Steel bisected wood.

He accepted me for a reason, Illaraphaniel. As did the lord in whose lands I dwell. Branches jutted from what remained of Steane's still body; bark enclosed it, as if it were armor. Nenyane's blades severed the branches that extended—as if they were spears—for Stephen. Had she been slower, he would have been gravely injured.

Or dead.

The thought, fleeting, was dislodged by the same imperative for survival; Stephen moved, falling behind his huntbrother as he drew sword. Gervanno was already in motion; he had been slower than Nenyane, but not by much. The fox leapt from the cradle of his arms to land—loudly and far too heavily for his size—upon the trembling earth.

The wind howled.

The bard rose in its folds—as did the remaining four Hunters. Only Ansel had been deliberately targeted by sharp, spear-like branches, as if all others present were irrelevant, beneath notice. Had they been beneath the bard's notice, Ansel would be dead.

But the bard, bard-born, could hear all the layers in a speaker's voice, unless the speaker understood the nature of the bardic talent.

Kallandras was not surprised. **"Remain here. Do not engage."** Speaking thus to the Hunters he had lifted from the earth, he drew his own weapons; the wind carried the lute whose notes had been the beginning of their song from his hands. The bard's weapons reflected an almost reddish light. They were not demonic weapons, but something about them reminded Stephen of the demons themselves.

Or perhaps it was the expression that transformed the bard's face: it was cold, harsh, focused. So too Meralonne's—as if grief and loss were ephemeral, as if all bridges across which one might walk were meant to be bring them within striking distance of their enemies, and only that.

Keep the dogs back, Nenyane told him, as she joined both bard and mage. "Gervanno — retreat."

Gervanno obeyed; he understood Nenyane's intent almost as well as Stephen. Or perhaps better. He did not sheathe blade; he stepped back from the fray and into the wind's edge. But the wind let him pass.

It was the bard's wind. It obeyed the bard.

THE MAGE'S sword shattered branches; leaves, caught by wind, flew past.

Stephen failed to understand why the bard did not set the rest of the Hunters down until the earth beneath his feet began to shake.

Move back. The earth won't attack you — it's the reason Illaraphaniel hasn't summoned the wind. No one sane summons two elements at once; it's hard enough when another element is present.

As Stephen watched, as he listened, he felt the chill of winter: no regret marred the features of bard or mage. No regret, no compassion, no hesitation. No mercy.

Mercy was death, Nenyane said, for she saw what he saw. *Don't expect it from me either — he would have killed you had I not been present.*

He had never expected mercy from his huntbrother in the face of such an attack. But he had never felt chilled by the lack, either.

Don't touch the earth with anything but your boots. Whatever else you do, do not *bleed on it here.* Before he could ask any questions, she added, *Gervanno's blood won't have the same effect. Only yours, as the son of Bredan.*

But the wind —

Kallandras made no attempt to lift either Stephen or Gervanno into the folds of moving air that carried the Elseth and Bowgren Hunters. Something about Nenyane's hurried tone implied that was deliberate. The dogs came to Stephen at his command; Pearl put up some resistance, but Stephen was fairly certain that was simply a matter of her overweening pride.

The earth continued to rumble beneath their feet; Stephen bent knees, shifting position to ride it out.

Beyond his feet, however, the earth broke, exposing pale, ivory-colored roots that seemed to spread in all directions. He understood the movement of earth, then; Meralonne was somehow forcing those roots away from the small patch of earth Nenyane had told him not to abandon.

Gervanno faced outward as branches continued to fly, his sword blocking and cutting them where they strayed within blade's reach. He kept Stephen behind him as he worked.

Stephen could not see past him except through the eyes of the dogs; his own eyes had a view of Gervanno's broad back. Stephen's sword was unnecessary, even useless; he had been trained by Nenyane since childhood, but realized he was not, and would probably never be, Gervanno's equal. No wonder she liked him.

Ah, no. It was also the Southerner's dogged loyalty, his certainty that his duty was to protect, to defend as he was doing now. Splinters had cut his hands.

But the fight that occurred beyond their little, trembling island was more visible, because so much of it took place in the air. Only Nenyane favored the crumbling earth, leaping from patch to patch, root to root, as if she herself had wings. Her sword cleaved roots as they became exposed, but the man who was a tree uttered no words, no pleas; showed no rage.

She made no attempt to bisect the body of the tree. Perhaps another observer would have assumed the proliferation of near deadly branches prevented that approach. Stephen did not. Kallandras likewise dealt with the branches, parrying even those that were suddenly ejected as projectiles. Stephen felt that the bard was attempting to reach the tree's heart, but he wasn't bound to the bard in the way he was to his hunt-brother.

To the left and right of the mage, they fought; the mage held lightning in his hand, and where his sword connected with wood, the wood blackened and charred as if the blade were lightning in truth, and not in visual echo. It was Meralonne's blade, Meralonne's approach, that brought him closer and closer to the body of his enemy.

Nenyane, half visible when her attacks drove her into the air, and Kallandras both seemed to be fighting in a holding pattern, as if they knew the combat, or the heart of it, belonged entirely to two: Meralonne and tree. He had never seen his huntbrother make that choice, before.

It was Meralonne's sword that pierced the opponent's body; Meralonne's sword that shattered the armor of bark; Meralonne's blade that withdrew, leaving a trail of golden blood in its wake. If branches regrew, the bark encasing trunk did not; the edges of the wound the mage had made smoldered.

Stephen saw this through Nenyane's eyes. He saw the riot of color and the odd fuzziness of form that characterized his huntbrother's vision, but he did not speak to her while she fought. He did not speak when she put up her sword, and barely noticed when the bard sheathed his weapons.

Instead, he watched. He couldn't squint, couldn't narrow his field of vision; had he been watching with his own eyes, he would have. The mage was almost incandescent. He knew that the mage was not human because Nenyane knew it. The truth of that was seared into memory, as well as vision. He watched as the mage lowered blade, retaining his grip on the hilt; watched as he raised that sword, and cut, and cut, and cut. Were it not for the mage's expression—remote, neutral—he might have assumed Meralonne acted in uncontrollable rage; he could not.

Although the mage's movements were attacks—and attacks on a defenseless, living being, at that—Stephen thought he was almost carving the flesh beneath bark, chipping away at it the way sculptors did, to reveal what lay at its heart.

What he had carved, in Nenyane's vision, was something shaped like an egg, but larger; it was of shining gold, a gold the same color as the blood their enemy had shed. Stephen held breath, and couldn't say why, as the mage raised blade in front of the exposed shape.

But he failed to stab it, although that was what Nenyane expected.

Instead, he reached out with his left hand, his exposed palm the color of his blade. He cupped the egg, and he withdrew it—carefully—from what remained of the trunk.

"I do not know what you will remember, if you remember your life at all; you are not as we are, and it is in your nature to spread seedlings into soil that will nurture it. But if you have chosen enmity with the White Lady, you have nonetheless offered me what I wanted, if only briefly. I will take what remains. I will plant you in the soil of a land that you might find familiar. There are those among my kin, now, who can grant you some measure of the peace you once found in the lands of my brother.

"And I will plant you there in his memory."

The seed did not respond.

Nenyane returned to Stephen's eyes; her eyes were darkly circled, implying an exhaustion she seldom felt. She glared at him.

Stephen, however, exhaled slowly. He understood that the tree was dead; he understood the crime it had committed. He knew that were his own heart to be ripped from his dying body, it would not be considered merciful. But he felt that he had misjudged the three who had fought.

Nenyane's expression soured at what she considered sentimental drivel, but she made no argument. In as much as he could, the mage offered his enemy a single grace note, a single gesture of respect.

That's not why, she snapped, truly annoyed.

Then tell me why, he snapped back. The dogs growled, and he forced himself to better contain his annoyance.

You didn't pay attention to the earth, to the roots, to the shape of their spread, did you?

I was told to stay where I was. I couldn't see much.

Liar. You could see what I saw, and I saw it.

Containing his annoyance was difficult. *I am not lying. We both know I don't see the world the way you do. If I saw what you saw, I didn't interpret it the way you did.*

Gervanno examined his blade, and after some consideration, sheathed it. He glanced at Stephen's expression, and then at Nenyane's, and took a small step back, as if the air between them was thick with disagreement in which he had no part to play.

Fine. There was the wilderness equivalent of writing in the shape of those roots; they transcribed a boundary—the boundary of the lands ruled by the lord. It was frayed in three places.

You cut the roots.

Yes. I cut everything that did not conform to that pattern.

Stephen tried to sit on frustration, and only barely succeeded. He had seen what Nenyane had seen—but at the speed she had seen it, he could not detect a pattern to the placement of, the growth of, roots. He doubted he would see it even if he had the time to study it.

Nenyane exhaled slowly. *No. No, you wouldn't. Sorry. The lord is powerful, here. You probably couldn't hear her name.*

I couldn't.

We could. Kallandras, because he's bard-born, Illaraphaniel because he is of the wilderness.

And you?

I don't know. But what they could sense, I could sense. By dying, by fighting, he could expose a truth that he could not otherwise speak, and even then, it was a struggle. The root structure was a map; the earth held it and contained it at

Illaraphaniel's command. He studies it now, for certainty's sake. She sheathed her blade. *We know where we must go. Come. Bring Ansel. I'll try to explain it.*

THE HUNTERS SPENT some time removing splinters and wood chips from their clothing and hair. They did not speak until Stephen approached, and even then, words were sparse. Stephen asked Ansel to accompany Nenyane; when Ansel nodded, the other three silently followed.

The mage was, once again, wearing the cloak of the Order of Knowledge. His sword was absent. His eyes, however, did not lose the luminous silver that marked them so intensely in the battle. Of the tree's heart, there was no sign.

Nenyane said, "Can you see the rounded curve of that root?" It was to Ansel she looked, not Stephen.

Ansel nodded.

"That's the area of overlap between Margen and these lands. There, and there."

"And Bowgren?"

She exhaled. "Come. We'll need to walk around to it."

They followed. It was Alex whose eyes finally rounded in that blend of surprise and discovery. "Could he not have just told you?"

"No. Whatever oath of allegiance he swore bound him to obedience; under the weight of that vow, he had very few choices. It was not an oathbinding," she added, deliberately failing to look at her Hunter. "It was a compulsion. Had he the power to do so, he could have rid himself of compulsion and answered Illaraphaniel's question; he could not. The power to which he was wakened was not that kind of power.

"He could—and was expected to—fight." She fell silent, as if choosing words—which everyone noted, because Nenyane seldom bothered. "The compulsion was powerful enough that he chose to attack Illaraphaniel—something I'm certain he would never have otherwise done. We're intruders in his lord's lands. But obeying that compulsion allowed him to disobey it in a subtle fashion."

"This isn't subtle," Alex said. He knelt carefully so as not to dislodge dirt, and pointed at one small clump of exposed roots. "This is where we are, yes?"

Nenyane frowned. "How are you so certain?"

"The odd tangle of roots here, and here—I think they're the memorial building. They're the pillars; look, they match in number."

"Indeed," the mage said, startling all of the Hunters present, he had moved so silently. "You have a clear eye for one so young."

"Do the smaller roots surrounding the memorial mean anything significant?"

"It's possible. The dead he loved were feared, Alex. Feared but loved in greater measure. It is perhaps because the lord of these lands shared his grief that the memorial was allowed to stand in lands that were never my brother's." He closed his eyes. "Or perhaps the lord hated the scion of the White Lady Steane so revered, but regrets the inability to express that hatred in its truest form." He walked toward the cluster of small roots; his feet did not touch them, but by this point that surprised no one.

"And this—the dead area where the bard and Nenyane seemed to have destroyed most of the roots?" It was a circle, thick around the edges, and in its center, roots that had not been burned, blackened, or cut.

Meralonne looked to Nenyane, who shrugged. It was her most common gesture, but it was stiff and uneasy.

"If it is as I now fear, we cannot traverse it easily."

"Are the lands dead?"

"No. But they are rooted in, blanketed in, silence."

"Then it was true," Nenyane whispered.

"The Silences are here, and it would appear they serve a lord who had no hand in their creation. It will be very, very difficult to traverse the wilderness where they reside. But at the heart of that dead circular area, where the root formation is most dense, I believe we will find the lord."

"She can't keep the entire area blanketed in silence," Nenyane finally said. "It will cause the same difficulties to her that it would any of us. It would cause more difficulty to her followers."

Ansel nodded, but lifted neither head nor voice as he studied the placement, the shape of roots.

"Memorize what you can," the mage said. "Exposed as they have been, these roots will wither; there is nothing, now, to sustain them."

The threat of silence was real, now. Silence had once, in Stephen's mind, been something to aspire to; it implied peace. In a life that encompassed demonic attacks and the voice of a god, the silence itself had been among his most traumatic experiences. He could hear nothing. He could say nothing. His link to dogs and huntbrother had been, functionally, all but broken; he could make no commands. His steps had made no sound. The steps of predators would likewise have passed unheard.

He could see, of course; the silence had not robbed him of vision. But he had had no way of easily contacting his huntbrother, and she, no way of contacting him. Unless he could see her, could see her gestures, he had had no way of knowing her thoughts, her intent.

No more could he command the dogs as he had always instinctively done.

Silence, until the moment he had encountered the Silence, had referred to the noises outside of him. This Silence, however, had reached in, cutting lines of communication so natural he had almost frozen at the sudden lack, uncertain of how to interact with the world itself.

"It doesn't look like a small area."

"It cannot be that large," Meralonne said, as he studied it. "The power necessary to enslave and enforce obedience of this nature should be beyond this land's lord."

Should be.

"Is there any way we can avoid it? Could we maybe fly above it?"

"That would almost certainly lead to injury, possibly death," the mage replied. "The wind *listens*. Where it can be cajoled it will obey, but the attention of the wind is naturally fickle. When it hears nothing, when its summoner suddenly ceases to speak, it will do as it desires.

"Transporting mortals carefully would not be among those desires. She has expended power in an attempt to break the Bowgren-facing border. But if we approach her here, at the seat of her power, the heart of her lands, she will retain that power."

"This is Bowgren's border," Ansel said, voice low.

Meralonne nodded, although Ansel had not looked up. "Yes."

Stephen joined Ansel, who then pointed out the frayed sections of this dimensional map. "The sections of intrusion into Margen are small and discrete. The Bowgren-facing border is…not. Here, and here—the roots that transcribe them are almost nonexistent. They're there, but they won't hold."

Heiden immediately placed a hand on his brother's shoulder. Ansel stiffened; Heiden closed his eyes. What passed between them was wordless, but Stephen had no doubt it was intense.

"We don't want to face the lord at her seat of power if we can avoid it?" It was Heiden who asked, Heiden whose hand was now white-knuckled where it sat on Ansel's left shoulder.

"We do not," the mage replied. "It is an absolute truth in the wilderness, high or low: the lord is most powerful, always, at the heart of their domain. They are not invulnerable, but it is there that their defenses are strongest. But she is aware that we are here; she may not be aware of what it signifies. She will be cautious. She has time. You do not.

"But because so much of our slender hope of survival rests upon the shoulders of mortals, we are all trapped within your scant time."

Ansel exhaled. "You showed us—in the Redoubt—images of the creatures you believe attacked our villages. We lost one village entirely. Is it likely to have been absorbed nearest the border here?"

"It is, but Lord Ansel, the nature of the wilderness is transformative. If you think to walk through these lands and enter a village—one either devoid of life or not—you fail to understand its base nature. Our nature is not yours. It is possible you may find remnants or hints of your village; it is more likely that you will not."

"You are a pessimist, Illaraphaniel," the fox said, speaking for the first time. "It has been little time, and mortal things are stubborn and yield slowly to the call of the wilderness."

Stephen had forgotten him.

Yes. Nenyane's internal voice was sour with disapproval. *He didn't intend to be remembered. He might look like that, but he's an ancient power. The fox, like many elders before him, often led the unwary—or the ignorant—astray.* She paused, and then said, *Gervanno didn't forget.* Her tone revealed worry.

I don't think the fox will harm him.

The elders can harm without any intent whatsoever, she snapped.

"I think the young mortal has an interesting point." As if he could hear every word that Nenyane did not say aloud, the fox once again approached Gervanno. The Southerner knelt immediately, and the fox leapt into his arms. "Much effort was spent on this border, but the border still holds in some fashion. I believe that you might find some remnant of the village that was taken from your lands.

"Were those lands in any other mortal kingdom, I would concur with Illaraphaniel; it is not. The earth in Bredan's blessed country bears the blood of centuries of sacrifice; it is complicated, and I will not explain the whole of it now."

He can't, Nenyane said.

"But those centuries of blood shed at Bredan's command might give this mortal village some wavering permanence. I cannot say the villagers have survived. I am almost certain they have not—but stranger things have happened.

"Think: she has thrown the whole of her power against the barriers here. That they have not fallen is remarkable. If we wish to draw her out, if we wish to force her from her seat, what better place to harry her forces?" He then turned muzzle to Ansel.

Ansel, however, turned to the bard. "Heiden wishes to know if you can hear anything unusual."

Everyone blinked except for Heiden, who instantly reddened.

The bard's eyes narrowed. Heiden's indirect question had clearly disturbed him. "I can. Can you?"

"Not on my own. I can hear what Heiden hears—but I have to concentrate, and it's so faint it almost feels like imagination. Mine," he added, in case anyone should doubt his huntbrother.

"Heiden," Kallandras said, turning to the Bowgren huntbrother, "when I sang my duet, what did you hear? Did you hear as Ansel did?"

Heiden was pale, silent, as if the question had been a threat. It wasn't; Ansel's protective instincts were therefore unruffled. But the Hunter Lord was disturbed.

Meralonne said, "We have decided our course; we cannot tarry. Kallandras."

The bard nodded, but his gaze remained on Heiden's pale face for a long beat.

It was Nenyane who broke it. In her left hand she carried a wooden horse, and in her right, an antique horn. She held them with care, but with concentration, her eyelids closing, her shoulders tensed. Her arms began to shake, as if the weight of each was growing with the passage of time.

Ansel watched her, breath held; Stephen realized that while Ansel desired to reach the fraying Bowgren borders, it was to Nenyane he now looked. Should Nenyane's odd search point in a different direction, it was Nenyane's advice or information he would follow.

Nenyane's hair—unruly, uncut because cutting it had no effect—began to rise in tendrils that reminded Stephen of the mage's hair, and when her eyes snapped open, they were gold. Gold, as the fox's eyes were sometimes gold, and as Nenyane's eyes were not.

She began to walk, her steps short, her arms trembling. Stephen wanted to help, to take on the burdens she carried. His hands remained by his sides. She was walking in a fashion that made it almost impossible to offer aid.

But he could follow, and he did, stepping where she stepped, annoying her with his worry, his fear, the ugly rise of insecurity. Or perhaps not; perhaps she was now so focused she couldn't hear him at all.

I can hear you, she snapped.

It was a comfort.

Ansel joined Stephen, although his steps were less certain; Nenyane was walking across the map made of roots. She stopped at the periphery of the dead zone; the sound of Ansel's breathing banked as he watched.

Stephen understood why. Ansel's visceral, entirely natural desire was to go to the borders; it was the shifting borders of the wilderness that threatened Bowgren. But Ansel understood, as leader, that securing the borders now would not keep Bowgren safe, and the powers that he relied on in the wilderness—Meralonne's, Kallandras's—weren't as interested in Bowgren because it wasn't their home. It wasn't their responsibility.

Nenyane circumnavigated the dead zone; her feet touched it once, twice, and then moved forward again. Stephen held his breath, as if Ansel's hope and anxiety was a contagion. He watched as she moved toward the border made of fraying, breaking roots.

She said a word Stephen had never heard, it was a whisper of sound, but he felt it as if it had been spoken into his ear; it tickled his spine. The horn began to glow; the wooden horse became a pale, shining ivory.

"Here," she said. She turned then, pivoting on the pads of her feet, toward Ansel.

"They're here, Ansel. And both of them are still alive."

CHAPTER TWENTY-TWO

A nsel said, "We will go to the borders."

The mage and the bard exchanged a glance; Kallandras's expression was neutral. Meralonne's was not.

They had, however, ceded leadership of this company to Lord Ansel. At this moment, Stephen was uncertain why, but accepted it. Bowgren was Ansel's, and this was an action undertaken—at least by the six Hunters—for Bowgren's sake.

Did you ever think you'd be risking your life for Ansel? Nenyane asked, as the luminosity she contained in her hands faded. She was amused, if bitterly so.

He's a Hunter. He's Breodani.

Nenyane nodded. *And that's enough for us. But I actually want to help him. I want to help Bowgren. When I first met him, I wanted to punch him in the face every time he opened his mouth.* She handled the toy horse with care, holding it gently, as if it were an extension of a living, breathing person —a person to whom she was attached.

The horn, however, she attached to her belt. "Are you ready?" she asked the group at large.

Meralonne opened his mouth, but closed it, choosing a curt nod instead of words.

"I am," the fox said. "Gervanno?"

Gervanno, fox in arms, nodded. He glanced once to the gathered

dogs, as if to ascertain that Leial was still among them; Leial did not like
the fox, and kept his distance when the fox was too close.

To the fox, he said, "Can you track as Nenyane must track?"

"No. I could, however, lead you to the lord. She will know I am
here; she will not know that she has offended me. Not yet."

"How has she offended you?" Nenyane asked. Gervanno maintained the silence he found most comfortable when he performed the
role of cerdan.

"I wonder," the fox replied. "If it is not *obvious*, I will leave you to
think on it. But you must lead. The map Steane created with the last of
his life will not be of use for much longer; the wilderness is not always
fixed, and its geography not therefore stable or predictable. But if I
understand the unusual sympathetic magic you have cast correctly, it
will remain a certain guide until the owner or owners of those items
perish."

Ansel drew sharp breath, but maintained silence.

"Go," the fox continued. "We will follow."

Stephen frowned.

"What?" the fox asked.

"I think we're missing a person."

The small creature chuckled. "He is impatience personified; the fact
that he survived so long among mortals, given his tendencies, seems
almost miraculous. Jarven is not your problem, and he does not obey
any commands save mine. He has his own mission, his own priorities; it
is better that they do not clash with yours."

STEEL, Stephen ceded to Max, although Max's bond with the dog was
purely emotional. That could be changed, but not now; they didn't have
time. The fox's words hung in the air, an unspoken, impersonal threat.

The rest of the dogs traveled around Stephen and the Hunters; he
sent Pearl ahead with Patches because fighting with her while they
were on the move would be counterproductive. They needed a scout;
Pearl needed to work; lymers worked in pairs. The rest of the dogs he
held back; the wilderness had already shown itself to be, if not immediately deadly, unpredictable.

He was unwilling to risk his dogs until he had a better sense of the
lay of the land.

Nenyane, as usual, was annoyed. The dogs were a vital part of the Breodani hunt, and Stephen was failing in their use. But her annoyance was tempered by a growing sense of urgency. Meralonne did not remain with the Hunters, and chose to scout ahead.

Kallandras remained one step behind Nenyane, which was awkward, because that was the space Stephen would normally have occupied. He knew, however, that Kallandras was more capable at navigating the dangers of the unknown wilderness, and he chose to be pragmatic.

The moons, Stephen noted, did not sink. The color, the texture, of the sky, did not change. But clouds had taken the disturbing third moon, and those clouds did not disperse. Its absence made him feel better.

Given the geography, the Hunters moved quickly. Ansel jogged at the bard's side.

Max and Alex took up the rear. Neither had called the trance for which they were justifiably well-known. Gervanno, fox in arms, jogged beside Stephen. The fox looked ahead, eyes narrowed, as if he was unaware of the mortal who carried him.

It was the fox who called the first halt; Meralonne had not returned.

Everyone—even Pearl—stopped at the fox's command. But Ansel looked to Nenyane for guidance. Nenyane came to an immediate halt, but did not look back.

"Can you not feel it?" the fox asked.

Kallandras nodded, although it wasn't clear that the question had been asked of the bard.

"We must be close to the border, here; the air is still, but the ground well-traveled. She has indeed put some work into the destruction of the walls that separate your two lands. Her servants—and slaves—will be here; they will not expect an attack from behind.

"They may not expect much resistance from the mortal side; they are focused on the barriers themselves—those ancient, god-created constructs made when the world changed. Mortals are the detritus that confirms the success of their attempts.

"But I see that the mortals must have provided some resistance— else the threads Nenyane follows would point toward the land's heart, not its border. Put me down," the fox added, shifting conversational focus without obvious pause for breath.

Gervanno knelt and set the fox gently on the ground; he then rose,

his hand falling to the hilt of sword, his eyes narrowed as if to see past
the trees through which they had traveled.

Stephen glanced back at Ansel. Heiden had place a staying hand
on his Hunter's shoulder, but both of their expressions were grim;
they teetered on the narrow edge between hope and despair, as if hope
itself must inevitably plunge into despair, but must be grasped
regardless.

He expected Ansel to say something to Nenyane, and was surprised
when no words left Ansel's lips; those lips were almost white. He knew
that the items Nenyane held, the threads that she now followed, would
lead them to Brandon and his huntbrother, Aelle. If the two were on the
border, they might have found the village that had vanished in its
entirety from Bowgren's lands.

NIGHT HUNTING WAS something Hunters were taught once they came
of age; none of the Hunters present had more than two years' experience with night hunts. Stephen, impatient with limited vision in the
night forests, had found those lessons frustrating and impractical; hunts
were not called at night. He might have argued against them—he
seldom argued with his father—had it not been for Nenyane.

Nenyane considered those lessons practical. Necessary. If hunting
was an adjunct to governance in Breodanir—and it was—she considered hunting safe.

Night hunting was, in Nenyane's mind, about survival. Its purpose
was not to fulfil the responsibility of supplying the villages with meat. It
reminded Hunters that Hunter and *hunted* were two sides of the same
blade. One could easily start as the former and end as the latter. Some
creatures were nocturnal; it was at night that their power was at its
zenith, and it was at night that they were most likely to change the
balance of the hunt itself.

Regardless, Corwin had been particularly insistent. Although night
hunts were largely silent, there were horn calls that were only used at
night, and at that, sparingly.

All of the Hunters present had gone through that training to a
greater or lesser degree.

"And I thought it was a waste of time," Heiden murmured, as if his
thoughts mirrored Stephen's. His words passed by as he approached

Ansel; at night, Hunters and huntbrothers worked in physically closer pairings.

As was always the case, Alex and Max were different. They were silent, but they approached night hunting as if it were day hunting; they'd always had preternaturally good night vision. Max was impatient by nature, and never more so than when Hunters whined about this element of their training. The two Elseth Hunters were almost better at night than they were in the day—which said a lot, because they had always been excellent, gifted Hunters.

Were it not for the laws governing Hunters, they would never have been summoned to the Redoubt. They wouldn't become the rulers of Elseth. They had a terrifying oldest brother to fulfill that responsibility, and the respect their abilities were due would have been theirs without blemish or question.

It was Max who took the lead, circling Nenyane's path as he observed it; Max who took on the responsibility of the lymers. Steel kept pace with him; as he entered trance, Alex allowed the gap between them to widen. They would switch when Max had pushed the trance to safe limits.

Stephen did not call trance. Neither did Ansel. They were wary of their surroundings, aware that their lack of knowledge—of geography, of fauna—might necessitate the use of the trance to compensate for missteps, and they could not maintain it indefinitely.

Stephen touched his huntbrother's thoughts as they progressed; she moved far more slowly than was her usual habit. He felt the strain of her impatience, and felt how she mastered it. The toy horse was of more import, for just this moment, than her sword or the creatures that might be seeking their scent, their track, just as she sought the Hunters she had never met.

The trees by which they passed, darkened and silvered, could almost pass for normal trees—the forests with which Stephen was familiar—but they were wider and denser here. There appeared to be footpaths, but Nenyane's path seldom intersected them, and she never followed where they appeared to lead.

Alex paused briefly at one such intersection. It was not Nenyane—who was only peripherally aware of her companions—but Kallandras who tapped Alex's shoulder and shook his head. "Unless you are an invited guest, take no paths the wilderness offers."

Nenyane's speed remained steady, constant, but she felt she was no closer to her target than she had been when she started. Stephen, listening, wondered if it was a function of the way the wilderness worked; if geography was somehow stretched and elongating in a bubble that contained them. She didn't snap or disagree; she focused.

But she stopped when she reached an enclosed field, a place of golden, glowing flowers that seemed to stretch out in a circle whose edges disappeared into the softer shades of night sky and twin moons. The gentle light reminded Stephen of the fox, although he couldn't say why.

Nenyane's path led her into the field of flowers.

The mage returned, then; he said nothing as he observed Nenyane's back. As if unaware of the mage, she stepped into the field.

And vanished.

HE COULD HEAR HER. He knew she was now standing in the field, the edges of which they could all see clearly. Max followed, and Max also disappeared from view.

Alex nodded in Stephen's direction.

"It's safe?" Ansel asked the remaining Elseth Hunter; they had slowed, and then come to a stop at the periphery of the field.

"It seems to be. There are a lot of flowers—once you step through the line of flowers, it's all field."

"Can Max come back to you?"

Stephen understood why Ansel hadn't asked him the same question: Nenyane's spell. Ansel did not want it broken in any fashion; he didn't want her to move backward.

"We're testing that now," Alex replied.

"Steel sees what Max sees," Stephen added. "He'll retreat if Max does. I don't want to call him back if Max can't safely exit."

Ansel nodded.

"It is safe to enter," the mage said. "Or rather, it is safe for you to enter. I believe both I and the elder would not be entirely welcome."

Kallandras glanced at the mage.

"Take the risk of entry only if Maxwell can safely retreat. If he can, I suggest that you take advantage of the geography; have Nenyane follow the trail for as long as she can within the field."

"Max says there's no third moon."

"No, there wouldn't be."

"Why?"

"What seems luminescent to your natural vision would be almost blinding to that eye; should the eye remain above that field, it is all the lord would see."

"Is that why the field exists?"

The mage's brows rose, followed swiftly by the corners of his lips; his smile was one of approval. "I will not say you are right, but I am impressed; it is a very perceptive question. Nor can I say you are wrong. But if you are not wrong, there is more at play here. Is Maxwell coming?"

Alex nodded. "He's found the tree line, and he thinks he can see us now. Or rather, he can hear us."

WHEN MAX EMERGED, Steel by his side, Ansel motioned the rest of the Hunters forward. The fox sneezed. "I believe I will wait with Illaraphaniel." He stretched, his whiskers twitching. "Jarven will accompany you."

Gervanno tensed, and glanced at Stephen, who shook his head as the merchant appeared, as if at the fox's call. He understood that the cerdan did not trust the Imperial merchant, but no one trusted Imperial merchants overmuch. Stephen was certain that Jarven would obey the fox over the objections of any others present.

To his surprise, Meralonne said, "If you would prefer not to take the risk of Jarven's companionship, let me add my voice. I think it unwise."

"Oh?" said the fox, who was clearly unaccustomed to being accused of lack of wisdom.

"He bears your scent very strongly, Eldest. If there is enmity between you and the caretaker of this field, it will sour the welcome the young Hunters might otherwise receive."

"They are not my concern."

"No. But Gervanno di'Sarrado is someone for whom you have evinced some fondness, and he is duty bound to the Maubreche Hunters. He will go where they go."

The fox was not pleased by unasked-for advice, but he appeared to consider it. "Very well. We will attempt to circumnavigate this field. If it is a trap, I will send Jarven in."

Gervanno looked to Stephen. As the fox moved away, Leial once again crept toward him, tail wagging, head cocked to one side. "Will you risk the dogs?"

"Yes. Neither Meralonne nor the fox consider this field to be a threat to us." Stephen didn't ask about Leial. If Leial was not a working dog, Stephen nonetheless understood the cerdan's attachment; it was kin to his own.

"Well?" the Southern cerdan said to his dog.

Leial jumped up, both paws on Gervanno's leg. He then turned and sprinted for the edge of the flowers. Where Nenyane and Max had vanished almost instantly, the dog, oddly enough, did not—Stephen could see him running, tail and ears above the flower line.

Gervanno frowned; he could see what Stephen saw. But the frown was one of concern, not suspicion, and if Stephen were being fair, it was hard to be suspicious of dogs. The cerdan waited until Stephen nodded, and then passed through the tree line a step before the Maubreche Hunter.

"SORRY," Alex said, as he stepped on the back of Stephen's foot. Stephen had stopped moving; Gervanno, more aware that the rest of the Hunters would follow, had taken two long strides before freezing in place as Stephen had done.

Nenyane and Max were visible, but their backs faced Stephen; Steel's did not. He had turned toward Stephen, or perhaps toward the rest of his pack, as the dogs followed their Hunter. Stephen had taken a step between two large trees in the dead of a clear night; he had stepped into bright, full day. The two moons were invisible in a sky that shared only clarity with the one under which they'd walked for some time.

The sun was too bright; Stephen squinted against the harsh blanket of a perfectly clear day. Gone was the muted grey and blue of the permanent night; the sky above this field was a blue that deepened as it reached horizon. That horizon stretched out in gold and green for as far as the eye could see. The dogs saw what Stephen saw.

Heiden and Ansel came last, but very close on Alex's heels. They too stopped to draw breath—as if all of them had been subtly holding breath until this moment.

Gervanno was the first to break the silence. "I believe there's a house in the distance."

Nenyane, turning back, said, "There's a house." Her voice was flat.

"Do you recognize it?" Alex asked, given her tone.

"I don't. But something about it feels familiar."

"And you don't like it."

"Not really, no. But it's more like eating peas—I don't like them, but they aren't a threat to my life."

"Yeah, just the lives of whoever tries to make you eat them," Max added.

"Says the person who turns green if he sees a carrot."

Ansel and Heiden exchanged a glance; it was Ansel who smiled first. Yes, Stephen thought. Something in the air, something in the field, felt almost safe.

There's no safety in the wilderness, Nenyane snapped. But she grudgingly added, *This might be as close as you get. But be wary.*

"House?" Heiden asked.

Ansel had already decided, but waited to hear the opinions of the four Hunters he'd traveled with, Nenyane chief among them. They all agreed. Gervanno did not offer an opinion; he didn't appear to have one to offer. He had chosen to serve as guard here, and had fallen into the habitual silence of that role.

Leial, however, was as loud as Stephen had ever heard him. The dog bounced around the flower field as if he were a puppy—an energetic puppy excited to be here.

Gervanno stared at the dog in confusion, but confusion passed into acceptance. "I don't know how," he said, in more heavily accented Weston than was his wont, "but I think Leial has come...home." This was not Gervanno's home; not a place the Southerner would ever choose to live, had he choice. His duty had carried him into the foreign and oft terrifying wilderness. He had not thought—could not have suspected—that this place would be where he would leave his dog.

Gervanno's face usually lacked all but subtle expressions; it was the first time Stephen had seen his reactions so clearly writ there. But the wry smile that crossed his face remained as he moved to follow the dog.

"I knew I never liked that dog," Nenyane murmured, expression far blacker than Gervanno's.

"You named him," Stephen pointed out.

"I suggested a name. Gervanno named him." She shook her head. "You should never name wild things."

"Well...the dog doesn't seem to be part of the wilderness."

"No," she agreed.

"Do you think the dog's owner is here?"

"Probably. Houses in the wilderness don't last long if they're abandoned. And yes, death counts as abandonment."

THE HOUSE WAS modest in size, modest in shape; it seemed composed of wooden logs, and rested flat against the ground. On all sides, flowers grew, but the small outline of dirt between field and house indicated that the house hadn't somehow been dropped atop some portion of field.

The house had one door, and windows — or shutters — on each wall. It was short enough that, while it might be possessed of a basement, the structure was a single storey in height.

Hunter lodges were far larger, far grander, than this dwelling had ever aspired to be.

Nenyane wasn't comfortable. Her natural suspicion, for the moment, followed a path of mild discomfort. She didn't like the house, the field, and, at the moment, the dog she had helped name, but feared none of them. Nor did she cast backward glances to make certain they had not been followed.

The toy horse she held in her hand remained there, but she no longer looked at it, or just beyond it; whatever spell had led her — led all of them — this far had frayed. Still, she did not put the toy away.

"Well?" she said, when they had stopped, staring at a single closed door.

Gervanno shook his head. "Not us," he said. As if it were a command, Leial immediately leapt up on the door, his paws making loud scratching noises, his barking high, fast, and almost whiny.

Sound — possibly voice — came from behind the closed door, which caused Leial to become even more frantic. He almost fell over when the door opened.

Standing in the frame, besieged by an excited dog, stood a man. He was older than Corwin; older, Stephen thought, than Iverssen, and far broader of chest and shoulder than either. His hair was silver-gray, his beard full as it dropped from square jaw in a spill across neck and chest.

His brows were a single silver line, his eyes a deep brown. Nothing about him seemed to belong to the wilderness.

Certainly not his clothing, which had seen heavy use and better days.

"Yes, yes. You've not learned an ounce of patience, have you?" The man knelt; the dog—as excited dogs everywhere—proceeded to practically bathe his face.

Nenyane winced. She'd never liked that particular display of affection from any of the Maubreche dogs, and complained—on the rare occasions it happened—about dog breath. Loudly.

"Well, well, well. It's been a while, hasn't it? And who have you brought with you?" He rose; sun touched his beard and hair, rendering it gold, although his face was creased by wind and age.

Ansel would have answered, being titular leader, but it was to Gervanno di'Sarrado that the man looked. His eyes did not narrow, but it was Gervanno on whom his gaze, and attention, was now focused.

Gervanno offered the man a very correct, very Southern bow. From what Stephen had intuited in observing the Southerner's bows, this was one of complete respect—the type of bow offered to a superior.

"He's certainly more patient and better mannered than you, isn't he?" The man's smile was warm. "I owe a debt to you, stranger. I had begun to think I would never see him again. You are?"

"Ours," Nenyane snapped before Gervanno could answer.

At that, the man's smile faded. "Child," he said, his voice slightly cooler, "I mean you no harm. I have not lied—I owe a debt to the young man."

"The young man," she replied, voice sharper, "knows better than to give his name to strangers he meets in the wilderness. Especially those who do not offer their own name in greeting."

"Ah, an oversight. An oversight on my part. I should have left you at the border."

Gervanno tensed.

"But I have seen people in the colors your companions wear; I offered them shelter for a time, and advice similar to the advice you have offered the man in whose debt I find myself. I will therefore not repent of my welcome."

Ansel tensed for an entirely different reason.

"And I see you have come in search of my previous visitors." The man's smile was broad and gentle, but something about it made Stephen feel like a precocious four-year-old.

There's a reason I find him annoying.

If Ansel was annoyed—and he disliked condescension almost as much as Nenyane—that annoyance was nowhere to be found in his posture or expression. "Are they still here?"

"No. Just as you have your duties, they have theirs. And I—ah, I have mine. I have mine, but I believe, if I am not mistaken, that those duties—that vigil—are finally coming to an end. You come with the god-born child," he added.

At Nenyane's expression, he chuckled. "It is the reason I allowed you to pass. I sensed a disturbance just at the periphery of my lands, but no hostility. Did you come with friends?"

"You sense Illaraphaniel and an elder whose name I will not speak. He has good ears, and can hear his name spoken almost anywhere, his ego is so vast."

"Illaraphaniel?" The man's expression darkened. "You brought him here?"

"He led us here," she countered. "At our *request.*"

"No good comes of association with his kind. Or no good did; I hear the whisper of Summer on the breeze, and the sun is warmer. He will survive; he has survived far, far worse than the lord of the lands that surround us. But in general, his companions fare very poorly."

"It is because we wish to survive that we accepted his aid," Nenyane countered. She tried to speak respectfully; indeed, had she been in Maubreche, their mother would have almost approved of her tone. But this was not Maubreche.

The man, however, had moved on. His eyes narrowed; he was not yet glaring, but his expression had reached the fine divide between concern and suspicion. "Come here, child." He spoke to Gervanno, the oldest member of their group.

Gervanno looked to Stephen for permission, which was technically correct. If the Southerners valued the flow of power, they also valued hierarchy, and he was cerdan to Maubreche. Stephen nodded instantly.

Gervanno approached the man to whom he had offered a bow.

"Give me your hand." Speaking thus, the man held out his own; it was rough, callused, and much larger than Gervanno's.

Gervanno raised his left arm, and placed his palm across the older man's. Gervanno's dog began to bark up a storm. It was a high-

pitched, almost confused bark that couldn't quite descend into a warning: he was concerned for Gervanno, but he trusted the man Stephen
assumed was his owner, and he couldn't quite decide how to express
his worry.

The man frowned; he did not close his palm, but dropped his gaze to
the barking, quivering dog. His eyes narrowed, brows folding before
they widened. He laughed, the laughter long, loud. "Aha! So you've
finally found him. You've found the one!" Eyes crinkled in corners, he
looked to Gervanno. "You've named him. You've given him a name that
he wishes to bear. Leial."

"Apologies if I have offered offense. I was told that the dog was a
stray; he'd run away from his previous owner."

"He is not the only creature to find shelter in my meadow," the man
replied. "But he has been here longest."

"But he's a dog," Nenyane said, surprised.

"Aye, he is that. In Scarran and Lattan, the ways open briefly. He
fled here when he was barely more than a pup, and it is here he has
remained; he is a timid creature, as unlike the dogs that you travel with
as he could be while still remaining part of the same race.

"But he has found what he did not know he sought. Very well, you
who bear the taint of the wild. I would not have chosen you as master —
you are far too burdened with both guilt and obligation, and your life
has been lived upon fields of battle, numerous for your short-lived kind;
you bear the scent of blood.

"But you bear Leial's scent as well, and it is perhaps by your side
that the dog will grow into his full measure."

He was fully grown, but Stephen understood that it was not size to
which the man referred.

"And I have been remiss. I will not offer you further hospitality; I
sense the wild impatience of the man who is your titular leader." The
surprise, the delight, ebbed from the man's face. "It is not you for whom
I have waited, Lord Ansel.

"But even the oldest of the Firstborn cannot see the way the threads
of life and fate, ever growing, ever entangled, will become a tapestry. I
would know," he added. "I have been plagued by the Firstborn — the
eldest of the eldest — almost since my time began.

"She it was who asked me to wait, and I have waited with as much
patience as I can muster. I have almost grown complacent in this calm,
golden meadow, watching, waiting. In my time, I have encountered

your people; only once did I choose to end them, for they sought to kill one of my friends.

"Hunting is part of life, but there are some hunts you should never call, in this land or any other. Those who are wise understand; those who are not perish."

Nenyane was not impressed.

"And you, daughter of all, I see you have indeed chosen as the Oracle foresaw. Yours is a hard path, and the decision you have made will be costly for the young man with the golden eyes. Bredan's son. Neither of you should be here, and yet I was told to wait for you, and I have waited."

"What were you to wait for?" Nenyane demanded.

"Only this meeting," the man replied. "The lands have changed much around me in that time, but these lands *are* mine, and have remained mine. The lord of the lands in which this small meadow is set has changed only once, but the wind is shifting, and even my meadow will not be spared. You do not believe me, I see."

"Does it matter?" She folded her arms.

Nenyane—he's not an enemy yet.

You don't know that. She was annoyed, but she'd always been annoyed at his so-called naïveté, his willingness to trust.

I'd take him over the demons or the lord of the land.

It's because you have that attitude that I worry, she snapped back. *Because he looks like a big, friendly old man, you aren't cautious. Look, there's a reason Illaraphaniel, the fox, and even Jarven chose not to take the risk of crossing into this meadow. There's a reason this meadow still stands independent of the lord that has claimed—and holds—all of the surrounding land.*

And there must be a reason that he mentioned the Oracle and the Firstborn.

Stephen kept frown from his lips. *You think he lied?*

No. Ah. She was afraid he had not.

The large man frowned, turning his attention to Stephen. "You have stepped foot on a dark road, young son of Bredan. I will not pity you overmuch, but I am uncertain that it is a road I could walk. We are endless, we who survive, and suffering is, if we are not cautious, eternal. You do not understand yet. I am not the Eldest; I was not cursed with the burden of the Oracle.

"But I have learned with the passage of bitter years to trust my instincts, and my instinct says you will. You will understand." He rose, then. "In the days before I chose this meadow at the behest of the

Oracle, I played in the wilderness. I coaxed wood from trees, and ore from stone; I coaxed blue crystal from the singing sea when water was still its element. I coaxed fire from the wild fire—that was almost my doom.

"That it was not was due to the intervention of the Oracle. Pay heed to this, Stephen, son of Bredan. Debts to the ancients must be paid. If your life is not considered worthy coin because its duration is so short, payment will be taken regardless. There are those who sought eternity who now seek only death, but death has been denied them, time and again.

"Incur no debts."

"I've already told him that," Nenyane snapped. She wanted to leave, or rather, wanted to grab Stephen by the arm and drag him out.

But she knew that Ansel wouldn't countenance it until he had received whatever word he could about the Margen brothers. Or about his own lost villagers. She also knew that Stephen wouldn't willingly leave until Ansel had his answers—they were answers Stephen needed as well.

"Do not consider anything I gift you today to be a debt on your shoulders; it is a debt I pay to the Oracle, and with it, I gain freedom. Understand? You do not owe me anything."

"What do you want in return?" Nenyane asked, voice dagger-sharp.

The man's eyes flashed, as if momentary lightning had cut across a clear, azure sky. "Were you not listening? I want nothing in return save to be free of the debt I owe the Eldest. Perhaps I will even be in debt to your master, should he accept what I have held for so long. I ask you, with all due respect, not to interrupt me again; I am beginning to find it vexing."

Nenyane fell silent.

"Follow me," the man said, as he turned to go back into his small house. "Ah, no. I wish only for the company of Bredan's son." To Gervanno, he added, "If I understand correctly, you are his guard. Because of the company you keep—or have kept in the past—I would not have you anywhere near my abode were it not for Leial. Leial trusts you. He has chosen you. I understand the customs adopted by guards. I will allow you—and only you—to accompany Stephen." He paused, as if to consider the other possible needs of his guest. "My home is not large, as you can see. I would prefer that you did not bring your dogs, but if you feel it necessary, select two."

Nenyane opened her mouth; she snapped it shut again before words could escape.

"I will not harm your master," the man told her. "He will be safer with me in my abode than he would be even at your side. I am willing to bind myself to that oath."

Her expression tightened.

He could not know the effect his words would have; Stephen's expression remained neutral. It wasn't an act. Something about this man put Nenyane's Hunter at enough ease he felt no pressure, no expectation, from the offer; it had no edge. The man understood Stephen's god-born talent; he could not be expected to know that Stephen would never use it.

Nenyane struggled for composure and won, but it was a close thing. She offered a grudging nod, accepting what couldn't be changed. She was huntbrother; what Stephen knew, what Stephen saw, she would see. She would have warning if there was threat or danger—and she believed the only person who could or would pose that threat would be the old man himself.

But when the door closed behind them, she lost Stephen. Where he had been, there was sudden, suffocating silence. Emptiness.

She drew sword, then.

STEPHEN FROZE the moment the old man closed the door. His eyes narrowed; the interior of the house itself had darkened, as one would expect without immediate exposure to the bright clarity of sunlight. He was accustomed to having to visually adjust when crossing between full daylight and building interior.

He was not accustomed to losing all connection with his hunt-brother.

He was Stephen, not Nenyane; he didn't immediately panic. Nor did he draw sword or point the dogs—Patches and Sanfel—at the building's owner. He could not imagine that Nenyane had suddenly died; it was not that kind of silence. But it reminded Stephen of the Silence to an uncomfortable degree.

There were no weapons on the walls; the interior walls, as the exterior, were comprised of round logs. But no windows adorned these walls, and no art of any kind; a dull-grey apron hung on in the corner farthest from the door. Stephen looked for a light source, but as he suspected, the only source of light in the room was the man himself.

Here, the luminosity of weathered skin and hair, of oddly shining eyes, was more obvious than it had been under direct sunlight. Or perhaps it was stronger. Recalling what both Meralonne and Nenyane had said, Stephen knew that this was the seat of the man's power. This man's sky had no third moon, nor would: he was lord of this land. The lord of the lands through which they had passed to reach him could not destroy him.

Or perhaps she had never tried.

Perhaps they were allies; it was the silence that caused the suspicion to take root. He reached for his dogs; Patches was confused, Sanfel eyed their host suspiciously.

Both dogs could hear him. He made no further tests, re-examining the situation with his admittedly poor knowledge. "We're in a different space." It was a statement, but there was a note of uncertainty in it.

The man nodded. "We are, indeed. My dwelling would be far too large for the paltry lands I have claimed, otherwise."

Leial barked, headbutting Gervanno hard enough that he had to shift stance to stay on his feet. He exhaled slowly. "My apologies," he said—to Stephen. "It appears Leial believes I have questions that I should ask."

Stephen nodded.

"If you could create a second world, a second space, why did you not take larger lands? If you have held these against the lord who rules everything outside of your perimeter, you must have the power to do so."

"And must lords who have the capability require an expansion of their territory? Must power involve conquest?"

Stephen's answer would have been a decisive *no*. The question had not been asked of Stephen, but his guard. If the old man understood the function of guards as he claimed, it would not be to Gervanno he would speak, nor from Gervanno that he would seek answers.

Gervanno's answer, however, was an almost puzzled *Yes*.

The man broke out laughing, his broad chest shaking with amusement. He continued to laugh until tears fell from his luminous eyes; their trail was likewise gold and shining before they were wiped clean by rough sleeve.

"You, boy, you won't understand. Leial's master does. He thinks it odd that I am here at all, when it is not where I should be, or desire to be. And he is *right*." The last word was a crack of thunder in the darkened room; lightning illuminated it, caught by his eyes, traveling along the single syllable as if it were a physical object.

The light dimmed.

"But this is the binding I undertook to repay an ancient debt, and it could only be paid here, in this place, at this moment. I do not understand what she saw for you or your companions; I understood, in some measure, you were hope to her, who had seen so much death and destruction throughout the long ages that hope, if scant, was a most precious coin.

"And perhaps because she had shown me who you might be—for there were so many possibilities it took half of your lifetime to view them all—when I saw the other mortals running lost through the forest, being pursued by those who have newly come to serve the lord of those lands, I intervened.

"They are not you, not of your blood, not your kin, but they were of your kind. And I see that your companion carries items of relevance to them; they quiver with the import those who are mortal might grant things that are not fully alive.

"I did not do this as a kindness to you—I did it, in the end, because of the Oracle, who did not mention those waifs at all. But if you feel gratitude, I will ask of you one favor."

"And that?" Stephen asked, voice soft. Before the man could reply, he added, "They are strangers to me, but precious nonetheless. If it is within my power—my own power—I will do my best to grant you this favor."

Gervanno stiffened.

"I place no geas upon your charge, Ser Gervanno. It is truly a favor I ask. I will not threaten, and I cannot bind as the boy binds. But I would not harm him; I would not see him harmed. It is not yet his time. Without him, in the end, all hope is lost. The lord of the lands beyond my border cannot see it, her frenzy and fury are so great. But should all hope fail, only death will remain in all lands. Even, in the end, my own.

"For if we may stand against each other in our small wars, no one of us can stand long against a god. Even the Firstborn could be swayed by their blood and their desires." The man shook his head. "My favor, boy: fulfill the Oracle's hope. There is one enemy, one great enemy. Survive.

"Face him." He exhaled. "It is too much to ask of a mortal child, even he who bears a god's blood. But mortals have long banded together to survive forces that would devour them should they attempt to stand alone.

"Find your distant kin, if you must. And then, child, go east. Go east, go south, rouse what remains of your ancient peoples."

To Stephen's surprise, he bowed. When he rose, he turned toward a small door—it would have been a cupboard door in any other place, nestled as it was on the wall in the sparse kitchen. "Here." The man opened the door.

Beyond it was not a cupboard. The light of the fields outside of the house was gentler when seen through this door, but the one it opened onto was not one of wildflowers, but of tilled earth, of soil. At the edges of that field, he could see trees—windbreaks, perhaps, but some of those trees bore fruit.

"Yes," the man said. "You are the second person I have allowed into my garden. There are fruits upon the trees there; take them. Take no more than you can carry, and choose carefully; you will not be offered such a choice again."

"Was the other person one of the mortals who reminded you of us?"

The man nodded. "A fey, strange boy; Aelle, he said. I have hopes that he will not so carelessly offer his name to any other, and advised him against such naked trust.

"I offered him a home here, but he would not abandon the boy he called brother. There was no blood between them, no kinship that I could discern, but for all that, he was devoted. He chose those fruits that would be of aid, for the brother had been injured in his flight, and he had almost lost the ability to speak, to hear.

"And the brother, I could not easily house, given his nature. His ties are to the lands he calls Margen. It is not what we call your lands. Aelle carried the fruit he chose to that brother, whose name he did not tell me." At this, the old man offered a wry grin. "But they had the desired effect; the brother recovered.

"He could not speak, and in the end—for reasons of my own—I chose to aid him. But the aid was difficult; your bodies and minds are not meant to withstand Silence. The trees in my gardens do not bear fruit potent enough to combat the effects of the Silences fully, and mortal bodies are very, very fragile. Some part of the blood of the Silences therefore remains within my cabin.

"Take the fruit you can carry, and then you must depart. If I understand things correctly, you must find the two Hunters, and you must find the lost.

"And now, it is almost time for you to depart. Come. I have one last thing to offer you, as I offered it to the two prior guests."

THE MOMENT THE DOOR OPENED, Stephen caught a face full of angry Nenyane. He had chosen to exit first, to the amusement of his host, because angry huntbrother was what he expected. Beyond Nenyane— close enough Stephen suspected that at least one of the two had been foolish enough to attempt to restrain the Maubreche huntbrother— stood Alex and Max, one to the left and one to the right.

The dogs were frenzied with welcome and relief as they pushed past Nenyane's naked blade toward their Hunter.

Sorry, Stephen said. *Our host said something about the blood of the Silences —apparently it was withdrawn from the Margen Hunter in his cabin.*

This did not mollify Nenyane.

"You are too protective," the old man said, speaking to Nenyane, his expression amused. Stephen was grateful, given everything Nenyane had ever said about the wild beings and the respect they demanded. "But see? I have, as I promised, not harmed a hair on your master's head. Indeed, I have burdened him with the end of my debt; he carries the fruits of my garden, against future need.

"They will not wither; they will not rot. They will serve the will of the hands that were allowed to pick them, and perhaps, in time of need, they will provide succor."

As he spoke, Nenyane sheathed sword, her eyes bright and wide. She looked almost chagrined at herself and her previous rage—which was very, very rare.

"As I said: it is the unburdening of debt owed another from which you benefit; you owe me nothing, and I will hold none of you respon- sible for what you have been offered. Will that do?"

She bowed. She bowed very low.

Stephen walked past the twins—with a brief nod to both—and approached Ansel. "They were here," he said. "Aelle and Brandon were here. Brandon was, if I understood what I heard, injured; Aelle was not."

"I did not say that," the old man said. "Aelle was injured, but it was not a mortal injury; his brother's would have been had I not allowed them to stumble into my fields."

"Where are they?" Ansel asked, words too swift, but their tone shy of demand.

"They left, as you must now leave. They came, or so Aelle said, in search of missing mortals—those who fell across the boundary when it was briefly porous."

"Did those mortals come here, too?"

"No. I believe, if you find the two brothers, you will find them. I believe you will find more, besides. It is there you must now travel, you six, for it is there that Oracle foresaw you would go.

"And it is entirely to aid her vision that I have waited, and need wait no more. Come, come, do not dally."

Ansel was almost frozen as he stared at this stranger, his feet surrounded by yellow blossoms beneath a cloudless summer sky. "We have—we have companions who have not been granted your permission to enter."

"Yes. And they will make their own way. Two of those who traverse the wilderness are possibly more intimidating than even I. If you fear for them, you waste effort; they are to *be* feared. I believe at least one will know exactly where you have landed when you reach your destination." He glanced at Gervanno as he spoke.

"Regardless, I will not allow them passage. If you wish to return to them, I will allow it."

Ansel shook his head. He muttered a brief apology, too low for Stephen's ears to fully catch. "Where do you lead us?"

"There is a tree in the field—at the edge of my lands. I lead you there, to its shade and its boughs."

TO CALL it a tree was a disservice, but Stephen could not come up with a more accurate word. He did try. The tree was the largest tree he had ever seen; he could not see its crown from the vantage of ground. The roots of this tree were large; they had broken through the earth in many places, and some were easily half a man's height above that earth. The tree's bark was, at first glimpse, brown as most trees were, but as they drew closer they saw it differently; brown was a blend of many, many colors.

Nenyane reached the edge of the shadows cast by mighty branches and froze there.

"Will you abandon your master?" the old man asked.

"What have you done?" she whispered.

"I told you, I planted a tree. Ah, perhaps I did not say that. But it is what I did."

"This wasn't a tree when you planted it."

"You have good eyes and an unfortunate mouth," the old man replied, a rumble in the words. "It is a tree, now. But as you intuit, it is unusual; the seed from which it sprung was not without power. It has grown roots here, over the passing centuries, and those roots touch many things. Many different lands.

"Touch the tree, and it will create a path that you might walk in safety to reach your destination. But you must touch it at the same time."

"It wants blood," Nenyane said, as if the man had not spoken. Her voice was flat; she was certain.

"Yes, what of it? It is my tree, and if I consider the price of passage paid, it will grant passage." The avuncular warmth had left his voice, his face. Although he retained the same form he had worn for their first meeting, he was taller now, broader; he reminded Stephen of a rabid bear. "Do not question me further, or it is your blood I will offer."

Leial barked. Loudly.

The man's frown shifted. "I am ready to leave, and I am perhaps impatient. I will not harm your chosen master."

The barking continued.

"Very well." He spoke in a growl—almost a literal growl—but some of the anger left his expression.

Before Nenyane could start again, Max climbed up one of the roots and followed it—easily—to the trunk of the tree itself. He then waited for Alex to join him. Neither touched the trunk; they waited as Ansel and Heiden joined them. Max glanced at Steel, who snorted in disgust; the roots were not easily traversed by the hunting dogs.

They began to lift the dogs up to the rounded flat of the root.

The old man almost screeched in frustration. He barked a command; it sounded like elemental weather. The earth rose beneath the feet of the dogs.

"They are yours," he said. "They do not need to place their own paws upon the tree; it would do them no good. They will follow where you walk. Go before I lose all patience and betray the long trust in which I have labored. *Go.*"

Ansel's hand was steady. He placed it against the trunk, palm splayed; it was his left hand, and he was right-handed. In quick succession, all of the Hunters did the same.

All save Nenyane, whose palm hovered above the trunk as if some invisible force refused to let it land.

The trunk did not feel like trunk beneath Stephen's palm. It was disturbingly warm and the visual impression of bark could not be matched by the physical sensation of fur, of flesh. He felt the tree shudder beneath his palm, and would have withdrawn it, but the man had said they had to be in contact with the tree simultaneously; he was not willing to take the risk of withdrawing.

They had been told they must be in contact with the tree at the same time. Stephen's eyes narrowed as he sought his host. The man was far too large to have just vanished, but there was no sign of him.

No sign of him, and no sign of the yellow flowers that had characterized the field, lending it warmth and vibrancy in a land subsumed by moonlight and darkness. What stood in the place they had occupied, reflecting the falling colors of sunset, was a lake. A lake from which roots of trees jutted as the water rose.

The water reflected sky so clearly it was almost a mirror, and the brilliance of those reflected colors was breathtaking. But the wind that rippled the image fragmented it; it was a gust.

"Nenyane," Alex said, voice urgent. "Touch the tree."

"I'm *trying.*"

Never needlessly offend the elders. Stephen reached out with one hand; he grabbed his huntbrother by the wrist and dragged her as close to his chest as he could. "Hold on!" he shouted, as the wind strengthened. "Hold on to me!"

Her brows rose; had she time, she might have been offended. She had no time. She threw her arms around Stephen, cursing liberally into the wind.

You're the one who told me not to offend the wilderness!

Yes. You! I did nothing offensive!

"Gervanno!" Alex shouted.

Gervanno had waited until Stephen caught hold of Nenyane before he placed his own hand upon the tree, a thing of obsidian and light, a thing that mimicked the shape of a tree, and whose shadow, growing longer and longer as the sun went down, looking nothing at all like any tree anyone present had ever laid eyes on.

Night overwhelmed the sky; the water beneath their feet rose. Tree roots sank; as the Hunters were standing on them, they sank as well. But they kept in contact with the tree itself while the water rose.

The wind became colder; the water was warm in comparison. If they managed to make it out of the water, they'd have to work to avoid the chill that would doubtless follow.

LEIAL BARKED.

Gervanno bent and scooped the dog up in one arm; Leial was not a lapdog, but was nowhere near the size of the hunting dogs present—all of whom were utterly silent, their eyes turned not to their master, but to the trunk against which Stephen attempted to brace himself. Their lips were curled, exposing fangs, but they made no warning growl; nor did they tense as if to leap.

Water rose, and rose again; when it was at the level of their knees, it stopped. Reflected in the surface, but rippling and inexact, were two moons. Two moons and a scattering of clouds only at the height of the sky.

The tree shook, the tremor slight at first; the branches moving above their heads could have been shaken by wind. But as seconds passed, it was clear that the tremor came from the trunk to which they attempted to remain attached.

In the distance, Stephen heard the sound of horns, their keening short, low, carried by the wind toward where they stood. He froze; all of the Hunters froze as well. Stephen's brows rose; he smiled and looked to Ansel; Ansel nodded and smiled as well.

Nenyane was first to move, her eyes gleaming as if they were part of the water's surface. She took the horn off her belt—Brandon's horn, given her by a hopeful, desperate younger brother for just this moment.

She lifted that horn, yellow with age, and delicate with history, to her lips.

She had never been *good* at horn calls; she had been adequate at best, and she had never risen to a competency above that. But at this moment, in the folds of wind, standing knee-deep in water, the notes she blew were the clearest of notes she had ever sounded.

They weren't Maubreche calls. They weren't Breodanir calls. They belonged to Margen. Margen and its closest ally, Bowgren.

And coming back across the water, those same calls, with a slightly different beat. Stephen had been taught these calls, but Nenyane knew them. He didn't know if it was the spell that had drawn her toward the two Hunters, or a moment of clarity in which what Stephen had been taught had sunk roots in his huntbrother.

It didn't matter.

Heiden's cheeks reflected moonlight; of the six Hunters and their sole guard, only Heiden wept.

CHAPTER TWENTY-THREE

"Is it safe to let go of the tree?" Alex asked.

The Margen calls came again. This time it was Ansel who lifted horn, and Ansel who replied. He did not lift hand from tree; he looked, as they all looked, to Nenyane for guidance.

"I couldn't even touch the tree," she snapped. "So don't ask me." She hated to be the center of attention, unless she needed attention, in which case she hated to be ignored. "Look at the sky. Look at the tree. We're not where we were anymore—if the horn calls haven't somehow made that clear." She lifted the horn she had received from young Alfric. "The owner of the horn is here, and he's close. In case the noise in the background didn't make that clear."

Ansel didn't even take offense. The look he gave her was one that allowed for no words—not from people like either Ansel or Nenyane. Heiden's tears had started to dry, but Stephen was certain those tears captured a large part of what Ansel would never say aloud.

Ansel leapt free of root first; water rose in a splash. Stephen's dogs joined him instantly, with Stephen's permission; even Steel leapt free of Max, as if the platform of root had been tolerated for as long as it possibly could.

Nenyane leapt clear as well—of both root and Stephen. Stephen was the last to release the tree. But the tree did not release Stephen, not immediately; as he withdrew hand, a vine dropped from above, encircling his wrist.

Thorns pierced his skin as the vine tightened.

Nenyane turned instantly, sword drawn; Gervanno, in water, drew blade seconds later. Both turned. Stephen held his unencumbered hand, palm out; Gervanno came to a stop. Nenyane did not.

Don't cut the tree, he snapped. It was too much to hope she would keep her distance.

It's not a tree, she snapped back. But she slowed as she approached.

Why does everything in the wilderness seem to require blood?

"It is the source of life, child of god. It is the proof of it. It is the name of the nameless, and in your blood I sense the Lord of Covenants."

Stephen nodded. He could not see the speaker. He could see Nenyane swerve and leap to his side, dripping water.

"I have been rooted in lands I will not name, and there is a wildness that has entered me in the long years I have been rooted there; soon, soon, I will be free to move."

"Why have you been rooted? How were you planted at all?"

"I was almost dead, which is of little relevance. All those I sheltered, all those for whom I toiled, were dead. Dead at the hands of my enemy. Once—long ago—these lands were mine. They did not shelter beneath night sky. The dead had not yet surrendered their lives and their beings to one who had no hand in their making; had these lands been mine, they would *never* have dared to set foot here. Not even the smallest, not even those who chose to surrender all memory and identity to be free of their endless sorrow, would have survived.

"But I am no longer the land's lord. I have waited for this moment. I have waited since the day she found me dying and told me I might at last have vengeance; I might at last know some measure of peace."

"She?" Nenyane said, voice a sharp demand.

"It is not you to whom I speak," the tree replied.

Stephen heard the tree's voice clearly; so did Nenyane. But there was no moving mouth to utter words, no face, no eyes; just a trunk of obsidian, whose bark felt like flesh and fur.

"I was promised one chance. One small chance; it was not a guarantee. And so I stood in the gardens of the one who planted me. And waited. And waited. And waited. He was impatient to start, but mindful of his debt. The only debt I owe is vengeance; blood for blood, death for death.

"But I was told that, should I allow myself to be planted, I might yet strike with what small strength remains me. So I ask you now, oath-binder: will you give me what I desire? For you are clearly the person for whom the Elder waited."

"It is our hope and our intent to rescue our kin and end the threat posed by the lord of these lands. If she is your goal, we will naturally do all within our power to give you that opportunity."

"And will you swear oath?"

Nenyane was annoyed.

"I will not. I will not, eldest. The servants—and slaves—of the lord of these lands are numerous and deadly, especially to my kind. We will spend our lives in this struggle—but we may perish at the hands of the servants before the lord ever feels it necessary to come in person."

Don't. Don't reveal any more of our strategies.

"If you mean to aid us at that time, know that we welcome your aid; indeed, we may desperately require it. But we are not so strong, not so powerful, that we can deliberately stay our hand in order to allow you the decisive blow—or indeed any blow at all. I would not stake my life, or the lives of my companions, on such a vow, even were it possible." He offered the tree a deep, but awkward, bow. "But we owe you a debt, and if we can repay it, we will."

The tree rumbled; branches shifted, creaking. "Then go, son of Bredan. Let us meet again. I am not yet unrooted, nor will I be until the end."

Stephen carefully entered the water. Nenyane followed, lips thinned with annoyance. She failed to express it in any other way.

THE MOMENT HEIDEN heard the Margen horns, tears had started. He had almost managed to stem their flow, but Ansel lifted his horn, and Ansel replied in kind. In this dark and terrible land, in this place where geography could shift and change with little warning, those notes spoke of home.

They spoke of the home that Heiden had feared would be lost forever—not to the wilderness, because the wilderness was an enemy on which they could focus—but to despair and rage and fear. Lord

Bowgren had fallen into that abyss when Barrett had died in the Sacred Hunt. He had taken Ansel with him.

Heiden had endured.

Ansel's temper, never perfect, had taken over almost every other aspect of their day. The loss of Amberg, the disappearance of an entire village in the span of a few hours, had cemented the sense that everything was falling, everything was failing. The last straw was the King's demand that Lord Ansel attend remedial lessons in the King's City. Ansel was at least functional, unlike Lord Bowgren; the demesne needed him. It was Ansel who still did the tour of villages; Ansel who hunted.

But Lady Bowgren had acceded to the King's demand. While in theory she had no choice, in practice the pressure the ladies could bring to bear could not be discounted. Had she chosen to reject the demand, she would have reached out to others—even the Queen herself—for support of that rejection.

She had not.

To Ansel that had been a slap in the face of the worst kind. He and Heiden had argued about it, Ansel's mood so irretrievably foul, he had blackened Heiden's eye. It wasn't the first time they'd fought; as younger children, they'd often lost tempers and descended into behavior that had so displeased Lady Bowgren they had once been grounded for a week: no hunts, no lessons, and no time at all in the kennels.

It was Barrett who had attempted to intercede on their behalf then, because Barrett had, as a young man, had his share of altercations with Lord Bowgren; Lady Bowgren would not be moved.

Heiden had never regretted his choice to join Bowgren. He had never regretted his choice to be huntbrother. He thought, if given the choice again—at any time—he would make the same choice. But if Ansel had not died, if Ansel had not met Barrett's fate—and he hadn't— Heiden had almost lost him anyway. Everything Ansel had been seemed to shatter when Lord Bowgren did.

Heiden had been left holding the shards.

Heiden had gathered what he could, but as all such shards, they cut. And cut. Hope, to which he had clung, had become bitter, almost foolish —but he could not abandon it. Had not abandoned it.

And in the streets of the King's City, in the shadows cast by demons, Ansel had lifted his head. Lord Ansel of Bowgren had begun his return.

ONCE STEPHEN and Nenyane rejoined them, they began to move in the direction from which the horns had sounded. Leial, Gervanno set down. They had not yet made visual contact with the Margen Hunters when they were joined by Meralonne APhaniel and Kallandras of Senniel. The fox did not appear to have traveled with them.

Meralonne's glance was brief and almost disinterested; Kallandras's was similar, but he glanced back, in the direction from which they had come, his eyes clear, his expression neutral.

The dogs spread out. Pearl and Patches moved forward as a pair, but without the coupling leads. Because he had his dogs, Stephen was the first person to catch sight of the people they had promised to find, if possible. They caught sight of the dogs.

They were silent but cautious; the light of two moons silvered skin, but the third moon remained under the cover of unnatural clouds.

"They're just ahead," Stephen told Ansel, voice soft.

Ansel nodded. He did not lift horn again, but instead took the lead; Stephen's dogs accompanied him at Stephen's command.

They were therefore present when the Bowgren Hunters met the Margen Hunters; present when tense uncertainty gave way, fully and finally, to certainty. They were almost silent, containing their excitement, the sudden surprise of discovery giving way to hope.

The rest of Ansel's companions caught up, although the mage and the bard hung back.

"We can't talk here," Lord Brandon said. "Come with us."

"Where?"

"You'll like this part," Brandon replied, "and I don't want to spoil the surprise."

"It's not a birthday party," Nenyane snapped, annoyed. She'd been annoyed since they first entered the field of golden flowers, and nothing had dimmed her irritation.

"This is Nenyane of Maubreche," Heiden said quickly. "She is Stephen of Maubreche's huntbrother."

"But she's a girl," Brandon said.

"Nice of you to notice."

Nenyane.

I know. I'm just —

Had she been in Maubreche, she would have stormed out of the manse. She didn't have that option, here. Nor did she have the option of ignoring the reaction of strangers. But she exhaled loudly, and then dropped hand not to sword but to horn. She unhooked it, and reaching into her pouch, retrieved a wooden toy horse.

"My apologies to Lord Brandon and Aelle. I believe these belong to you." So saying, she held out both items, one in each hand.

"Return them when we reach our destination," Ansel said.

Brandon would have agreed, but his eyes fell on Nenyane's hand and remained there. After a long pause, he retrieved the horn that had been his grandfather's gift. Aelle did not move, and Brandon therefore retrieved the wooden horse.

"We're not too far away." But he looked to the tree in silence and stillness, as if offering it a benediction.

THE MARGEN HUNTBROTHER led them to a place so mundane it almost felt to Stephen that they had accidentally found a boundary crossing and had reached Breodanir. It was a village, although it was fenced. The fence would not survive a concerted attack; in Nenyane's opinion, it wouldn't survive a random attack or an accident. She was certain she could topple it by giving it a good kick. But this, too, was normal.

Less normal were the guards at the gate—such as it was.

It's a cattle *gate.*

Yes. It was. It was the kind of gate that could be erected quickly by normal people. The guards were under-armed; one was young and one older than most guards would have been.

It was the older man whose eyes rounded, the older man whose mouth opened, wordless for a long beat. When he found his voice, he uttered two words. "Lord Ansel?"

"Hannes," Ansel said, stepping forward instantly. He turned to his companions and said, "I think this is Amberg. The village that disappeared."

"Aye, or what remains of it," the old man replied, his voice much softer. "Is it really Lord Ansel?"

"It is," Heiden said, joining Ansel, their shoulders almost touching although Heiden had the height disadvantage.

The old man closed eyes and bowed head for a long moment; when he raised it, Stephen's estimate of his age dropped.

"Come in. Come in. Your presence here will give us much needed hope."

"The village elder?"

"Oh, she's here," Hannes replied with a grimace.

Ansel laughed. "She used to terrify me when I was a child."

"She still terrifies me, and I'm a long way from childhood. You met Lord Brandon?"

"Yes. He wanted to surprise me; he should be here soon. Ah, this is Max and this is Alex; they hail from Elseth. These are Stephen and Nenyane, from Maubreche. We met in the King's City."

Hannes grimaced. "That was badly done, sending you off to the King's City now, of all times." As if aware of whom the criticism was leveled at, his expression hardened. "It was. You should have heard the elder—she was enraged."

"She's calmed down?" Heiden asked, a glimmer of humor in his eyes.

"Well, she hasn't killed anyone yet. None of us, that is." The man turned to the four visitors Ansel had introduced. "Meaning no disrespect to Elseth or Maubreche."

"We didn't think it was any smarter, if that helps," Nenyane told him. "But we're here, now. When Ansel traveled to Bowgren, we came with him. We brought a few other people as well. This is Gervanno di'Sarrado; he serves as Stephen's guard. And—I don't know where the other two went."

"How did you find us?" Hannes asked. The question was asked of Ansel.

"It's a bit of long story," Heiden replied. Hannes was clearly familiar with the way Hunters interacted; he didn't appear to notice.

"Ah, apologies, Lord Heiden. Let me get out of your way." He peered into the darkness, eyes narrowed. "And there's Lord Brandon."

"Apologies, Hannes—I was checking on the tree." Brandon approached the gatekeeper. "And we wanted to give Ansel a few minutes."

"You just wanted me to face the elder on my own," Ansel replied, grinning.

These two would be allied Lords in the future—if Ansel accepted the risk and duty of the Sacred Hunt. But they were friends now. The ease, the humor, with which Ansel spoke were new to Stephen. Heiden grinned.

"She's our elder."

"Thank god," Aelle murmured, his expression very similar to Brandon's. The humor remained as he continued. "We were lucky to have her. I don't think there would have been much of Amberg left if she weren't standing at its center. The wilderness is terrifying and deadly, but she's terrifying in an entirely different way."

"She's the most terrifying elder I've ever met," Ansel said. "But if she kept Amberg functioning since its disappearance, we owe her a debt that can't be paid."

"Oh, I'm sure she'll think of something," Brandon chuckled.

Ansel laughed. Had Stephen heard his laughter before? He had not known Ansel for long, but he could not recall hearing it. Could not recall the expression that seemed at home on the face of Ansel's hunt-brother; the lack of fear—either of or for his Hunter.

As if aware of Stephen's thoughts, Heiden smiled at the Maubreche Hunter; he was at ease in a way he, too, had never been for the short time they had known each other.

Ansel, lost in the wilderness, had come home.

HANNES LED the new arrivals toward a home in the center of the village. It was large enough to house a family—or two, in times of emergency, which this clearly was. The village wasn't empty, and word of Lord Ansel's arrival had clearly spread. The streets of the village began to fill in ones and twos as people left their work to see the truth of the rumors with their own eyes.

Hannes's first reaction to sight of Ansel was mirrored and reflected on those faces: Lord Ansel had come. Lord Ansel's presence offered hope. They were lost, yes—but he was a Hunter of Bowgren. It was his responsibility, his duty, to save them. And he had come to fulfill that duty.

Ansel stopped frequently to greet the villagers; he knew enough of them on sight that he could.

The Ansel that Stephen had first met was not this Ansel.

Yes he was, Nenyane said—but not out loud. *You can't separate people from themselves. This is what Heiden remembered. This is what Heiden hoped for—and why he held on. I would have stabbed Ansel and left him to rot.*

It was so easy to judge based on very little knowledge. Stephen therefore judged now, and he almost felt guilt at his first reaction.

Which annoyed Nenyane.

Heiden joined Ansel, and much of the conversation came from Heiden—but Breodani villagers expected that. Only when their questions touched on the reason for Ansel's departure did Hannes interrupt.

"He's got to meet the elder," he said, some exasperation in his tone. "And he'll tire of repeating the same things over and over again. He's a *Hunter*. He's probably talked more in the past hour than he has in the past year."

Heiden laughed; Ansel grimaced. Neither disagreed.

But the group approaching the home to which Hannes led them grew in number. Some, neither Heiden nor Ansel recognized.

"They're Margen's," Brandon said. "The Margen guards that came after us when we attempted to reach Bowgren are here as well. We've been trying to find a way out of these cursed lands, but it hasn't been easy." His expression lost some of the warmth that had characterized his interactions with Ansel. "We've cremated a few of our own. We buried the first two who passed away." He lowered voice. "But the soil here makes all things strange, and the dead didn't remain in their graves. They rose, much changed, as if something had taken their bodies for their own use.

"After that, we didn't bury the dead."

"And we won't, while we're here. But we've kept keepsakes, things that we might bury in their stead when we return to our own lands."

Ansel and Heiden turned instantly at the sound of this new voice; Brandon and Aelle weren't far behind.

"Elder," Ansel said, offering the woman who had spoken a low bow.

"Aye. We've held on, waiting for the lot of you to find us."

THE VILLAGE elder was not an old woman. She was perhaps a decade older than Lady Cynthia of Maubreche. Her hair, dark, had not fully greyed—as if grey hair was just as terrified of the elder as the villagers and the Hunters claimed to be. Her eyes were greyish brown, her jaw square; her skin was dark with sun, even here, where the moons reigned.

Stephen did not find her terrifying. She had that harshness about eyes and mouth that had been worn there by worry and responsibility, but they implied that those responsibilities had been, and would be, met. Something about her reminded him of Lady Maubreche.

He had, of course, traveled the demesne of Maubreche; he had been introduced as a child to the village elders; he had taken part in the hunts that would provide meat over the winter. Maubreche had not faced this loss.

"What have you done to reach us?" the elder demanded, as Ansel rose from his bow. "Lord Brandon informed us that you were sent to the King's City—at the King's command."

"Not by my will."

"Of course not. But I see you've a fair number of companions to add to our village. Our food supplies won't last long as it is."

"We have food, for now. Enough food."

"But not food for the rest of us. We're facing a very harsh winter as it is." The woman grimaced. "But we're grateful for the supplies we did receive when things were normal. I won't offer you food; I can offer you rooms, but they're going to be cramped."

"We've tents," Heiden said quickly. "We thought we'd be traveling overland. We didn't expect to find Amberg." He glanced at Ansel, and then continued. "How many of the villagers came with the village when it moved?"

"All but a handful—some were far enough out that they weren't affected. We lost people to some of the creatures we found here, but we had no intention of hunting until we had a better sense of where we were. We lost half of our fields, but the half that came with us are largely unchanged. But it's night here most of the time, and that's not good for growing.

"We've taken no chances on the plants we don't recognize—but some of the plants we do recognize also made the transition. Water—" She exhaled. "We lost the lake, but there's a pond just outside of the village—a large pond with a tree in its center. The water there is clear; it's clean. If it has long-term effects, we'll suffer them the hard way; we needed water.

"Lords Brandon and Aelle came to us from that tree, or so Lord Aelle claimed. But a day before they arrived, Margen's guards stumbled across Amberg. Some of the villagers of Dunston came with them. We've set them up here, but it's crowded. The guards have helped with the incursions, but we've lost two, and a third might lose his hand.

"How did you find us? Is it a path we can travel?"

"We arrived the way Lord Brandon and Aelle arrived," Heiden replied. "But that way is now closed to us." He exhaled. "The only way back for us is to kill the lord who now rules these lands."

Brandon stiffened. Aelle, however, did not. "Is that even possible? We saw her — at a distance — and almost died. She had no desire to kill us, but her servants..." he shook his head. "Brandon?"

"We became lost in the forest; it turned strange, but the change was subtle — far more than usual. By the time we realized we were no longer in Margen lands, it was too late; there was no way back. Even if the forests aren't our forests, we know how to move in them. We had lost people, and as there seemed to be no way back, we thought of tracking them, perhaps finding them."

Ansel nodded. It was what he would have done in the same situation.

"But it was and is a nighttime forest. Something began to hunt us, to track us." Brandon fell silent. The silence went on, punctuated by shifting expressions; Aelle was speaking with his Hunter in private.

Clearly, Aelle was frustrated. The silence couldn't contain him. He turned to Ansel and Heiden, the two Hunters with whom he was most familiar.

"What Brandon is afraid of saying is that he lost control of his dogs."

Both Ansel and Heiden looked shocked.

Nenyane, however, stepped in. "No. He didn't."

"He could no longer hear them."

"Yes. I won't dispute that. But he didn't lose control of them — they couldn't hear him either. You couldn't hear Brandon, could you?"

Aelle shook his head. "I could feel his reactions, but I had no way of making my own clear."

She turned to Stephen. "The Silences were in play here." Stephen nodded and she turned back to Aelle. "You must have crossed the perimeter of the lord's defenses. I think one of your dogs bit a Silence." She hesitated and then added, "Two of your dogs escaped. They made it to Bowgren."

"Two are here," Brandon said, voice low. "Four are missing."

Nenyane didn't tell him that those dogs would be found again. She didn't believe it.

"If the map we were shown is even partially stable, the outer perimeter is guarded by the Silences; the lord will be found on the interior. But she can't move through the Silences herself without losing the ability to make her commands heard. If she comes in person, we won't have to contend with the Silences."

It was Aelle, watching Nenyane, who spoke first, his gaze narrowed. "You don't think that's likely."

"I think, if I were her, I'd send the servants bound to her will in the company of the Silences. It's risky—they're bound to obey her commands, but no new commands can be issued; she will lose all flexibility in approach. But it's safer, for her."

"She has no reason to fear us," Brandon said, the words bitter.

"She does now. It's not us—not the Breodani—that will be her chief concern. She doesn't care about mortals. No, that's not true; she despises and loathes mortals. It was for their sake that the gods departed; for their sake that the wilderness was caged and walled off."

"Walled off?"

Nenyane exhaled and turned to Alex. "You explain."

"Where are you going?"

"To find the mage and the bard."

"IF THE LORD is that powerful, why would this village remain standing?" It was Max who asked. It was the question all of the Hunters had uppermost in mind. Usually it was Nenyane who asked questions of this nature, but Nenyane had gone in search of Meralonne. Ansel was of Bowgren, and his role had now shifted; he could no longer simply say whatever was on his mind without fear of consequences.

Max was left to pick up the slack.

Brandon and Aelle exchanged a glance, and then sent it in the direction of the village elder, all but forgotten until this moment, at least by the newcomers. "Amberg was standing when we found it. We weren't here when it...arrived." Aelle's words were apologetic.

The elder snorted and rolled eyes. His mother would never have been so informal, but his mother would have held command of this village in the same iron fist. "We think it's the tree. The lake in which you landed is the only source of clean water within easy reach of the village, and lack of rain doesn't cause the waterline to lower. There's something entirely unnatural about that tree, that water. It could be because the entire forest is strange, but I don't think so.

"Lords Brandon and Aelle came to us through the tree; it led them here."

Heiden glanced at Aelle. Aelle nodded; the elder had clearly not heard an explanation of how they had traveled. Probably smartest.

"Amberg — most of Amberg — is here. We lost a few people to panic in the early days, and one or two went exploring and never returned. No one goes exploring now. We made a fence."

"You cut trees here?"

"No." The elder exhaled. "The tree dropped branches. Many branches. No branches have fallen since — but we took it as a sign. The fence is made from those branches — they were large enough to cause severe injury to anyone standing beneath them when they fell. The fence isn't meant to keep monsters out — we know we've no hope of that. But we hope it'll keep the younglings in. When we go to fetch water, we don't go alone; the guards come with us.

"Ah, the guards — the Margen guards — are here as well. They stumbled across Amberg while on some wild goose chase — they were chasing a golden hart or a golden animal of some kind. They lost it by the lake, but we had people on water duty, and they brought the guards in — there were about ten, and we recognized their colors, if nothing else about them. One of the men we lost to exploration was a Margen guard.

"But they've made themself useful. They patrol along the fence line — those who aren't too injured. We know that beyond a certain point, there's no safety. We don't know why — but we'll take it. We don't know your foreign friends, but we'll take 'em too; if they came here by the tree, they're good with us."

Two of those friends had not come here by tree, as she put it.

"Meal times are — well, we'll announce 'em. There's no daylight here, and even the moons don't move much; the darkness has been one of the harder things to get used to." Her hands fell to her hips and she looked up at — and simultaneously down on — the gathered Hunters. "You don't have a plan to get us all home, do you?"

Ansel exhaled. He turned to Stephen.

"We have a plan," Stephen replied, his voice firm, his words slow. Had he been talking only to the village elder, he would have spoken less carefully, but he was aware of the villagers gathered at an almost polite distance; they would hear every word he said.

He knew that fear was the enemy, here. It was fear that the elder kept in check by her brusque, matter-of-fact demands.

But she was like his mother—she understood his hesitance. She even approved of it. She pushed past the Hunters to face the gathered crowd. "Do you think because we've got visitors, you've got a day off? They'll need to be fed. Work needs to be done. Go on, all of you. Now."

They hesitated.

"We've Hunter Lords here. Food won't be as scarce in the future. But we need to show the outsiders Bowgren hospitality, got it?"

Stephen opened his mouth, but Heiden's expression made him snap it shut again.

"Go on, get back to work!"

This time, they moved. He thought they moved with less fear, more hope; Lord Ansel was here. Lord Ansel had found them. Thus, the trust between the villagers and their Hunters.

THE INSIDE of the elder's house was only large compared to the rest of the houses; it was crowded with seven Hunters. Pearl and Steel came in; the rest of Stephen's dogs remained outside. The two that Brandon had managed to preserve followed their master, as well.

There was a large dining table; the elder indicated they should sit. She took the seat at the head of that table, but no one expected otherwise. "Your friend implied you could explain some of what's been happening." She looked straight at Alex, almost pinning him in place.

Alex nodded. "It's short on details because we don't understand the details ourselves."

"Where did this explanation come from?"

"Two sources. The first is the magi from the Order of Knowledge."

"The second?"

"Breodan."

Whether or not this practical woman believed the second claim, she nodded.

Alex then explained the gods, the sundering of the lands, the hidden wilderness and the slow crumbling of the barriers that had kept two worlds separate. He touched upon the god in the Northern Wastes—the god who was implacable enemy to Breodan, and therefore to the Breodani. And he talked last about the stability of Breodanir in comparison with the kingdoms to the west. "I have no proof of the last part; we have no reports from the Western Kingdoms. The Queen would, and Lady Bowgren would be allowed to view those reports if she requested them.

"We're just Hunters. We won't."

The elder nodded. "Never ask a man to do a woman's job. I'll speak with Lady Bowgren when we return."

When.

It was that single word that was the source of all of their tension. The Hunters glanced at each other uneasily; only the Margen two were calm.

"WHAT PLAN DO you have to get us all home?" she asked. It was to Ansel she looked, and of Ansel she demanded an answer, but this made sense to the rest of the Hunters; Ansel was her lord, or her lord's son. He was Bowgren, just as they were.

"We won't get our lands back to anything resembling normal if we don't unseat the lord who rules these ones," Ansel replied. Gone was doubt; in its place was focus. Stephen looked at him, recalling their first meeting. He understood why Ansel had said, publicly, that he would forgo the Sacred Hunt; he would not attend. He knew that this meant abandoning Bowgren; he could not be Lord Bowgren, by law, if he did not attend the Sacred Hunt.

He remained Lord Ansel until the date of the hunt.

The King knew why Ansel had made his declaration. He understood the fear of loss; he had bitter experience with the cost of the lives lost during the Sacred Hunt. Stephen had refused to swear the earliest of the Hunter oaths for the same reason Ansel refused the Sacred Hunt. He was not willing—not then, not now—to allow Nenyane to take the risk.

But watching Ansel as he interacted with the Bowgren villagers, he felt the first pang of something close to regret. Ansel's rage had been almost uncontained in the Redoubt. Here, in Amberg, he had set aside rage, set aside pain; he had duty and responsibility. Stephen had privately believed Ansel would be able to carry neither.

Heiden had believed otherwise, and it was upon Heiden that most of the rage had fallen. The Heiden that stood beside Lord Ansel was quiet; Heiden would always be quiet. But he was confident now. Certain. His role was to be support, and there was something he could now support fully and clearly.

"The Margen lords felt we had no chance against the ruler of these lands."

"Alone, they didn't. But they're not alone now. We're not alone."

"Fine — but that doesn't sound like a plan."

"The tree is rooted here; I think the reason the village has survived is the tree. We don't know how long that will last. Even if it could sustain the village forever, the lands are strange here. We don't know what will grow, what will be safe to eat, what will be edible when we hunt.

"But Amberg stands in part because of that tree. While the tree is rooted, while it persists, we have our best — possibly our only — chance of toppling the lord of these lands. But she has to come here. Brandon's right — we have no chance if we have to take the fight to her."

"Why here?"

"We've been told — and we have no reason not to believe it — that the seat of the lord's power is where they are at their strongest. The further away from the seat they are forced to move, the less certain their power becomes."

"And if we can fight her here, she'll be at her weakest?"

"The lands here are Bowgren lands, transported. The people are Bowgren. Here, if the village is trapped within lands she rules, it's not entirely hers."

"I'd say we're not in Bowgren anymore," the elder said, folding her arms. That was never a good sign.

"No." Ansel exhaled. "But we believe that..." For the first time since he had started to speak, Ansel stumbled. Heiden closed his eyes; they remained silent for a moment, but the moment was shorter than Stephen had expected. "The blood shed during the Sacred Hunt is what has protected Breodanir. It is not perfect protection — demonstrably — but Breodan says the earth of Breodanir remembers. Because of the blood shed."

"Aye. My grandmother used to tell tales after dinner. Tales of our heroes. Tales of our lords. Tales of the lost and the dead and the endless grief of the mothers who nonetheless spent every waking moment governing their lands, only to surrender those duties when their children died.

"I know what happened when the fool king chose to suspend the

Sacred Hunt." The elder bowed head. When she lifted it, her expression was softer. "We all know. We know that the lands, that our crops, depend on the Sacred Hunt. We know about the three years of crop failures, of starvation. And we know, when that fool was deposed by his son, that at least a third of the Hunter Lords summoned to the Hunt that had finally been called perished. Many. Not one.

"We know that Lady Bowgren sees her husband and sons off, certain that someone will die—praying all the while that it won't be one of hers. Hating herself for it. And we know that Barrett died. Barrett was called.

"If blood counts, if sacrifice counts, it's Barrett and Bowgren who've paid the god's price."

She hesitated, studying Ansel's expression. Cracks had formed in the perfect mask of confidence and focus Ansel had donned.

"Yes," the elder said. "Barrett's death served a purpose. He didn't die for nothing; he did the duty that has kept Breodanir safe since the beginning of the kingdom." She held Ansel's gaze.

"I know what his loss has meant to Lord Bowgren. There are stories about lords who failed to survive the loss of their huntbrothers, and we've been uncertain. What will you do, Lord Ansel? Knowing what we face, knowing what the price must be, will you become Lord Bowgren? Will you lead us from this place?"

She might have been speaking of the wilderness; on the surface, she was. It was what the discussion for which she'd sought privacy was about. But Stephen could hear, in her tone, the second question— possibly the larger question.

It was not a question he would have dared ask Ansel, even Ansel as he was now.

"There's something I want to show you. You and Lord Heiden. Come; it's not far." When Ansel hesitated, she said, "I may not get the chance to show you later, if you intend to somehow bring the fight to Amberg."

In the distance, he could feel Nenyane's admiration and amusement —two emotions she would not have felt had the elder attempted that with her.

Have you found the mage and the bard?

Yes. She was annoyed.

The fox is there.

Yes. And the merchant—I wouldn't trust him as far as I could spit him. With my mouth closed.

Stephen nodded, the comfort of the bond a strength he could lean on, could depend on. A comfort lost forever to Lord Bowgren.

Ansel and Heiden followed the elder; she moved to the far wall of the dining room. A sideboard of some age stood there, and beside it—ah. A small shrine. In its center was a painting; Stephen knew without asking who the man captured in the small image was: Barrett. His face was framed in oval wood. Before him lay a bowl; in it were flowers of various types. More than that, he couldn't see from the distance he kept. And he kept that distance: he had not been invited to view what the elder now showed the Bowgren brothers. He was an outsider here. Bowgren's loss was not Maubreche's loss. Their respect was not Maubreche respect.

The silence that enfolded Ansel was awkward. "I will lead us from the wilderness," he said, voice soft.

"Is that all?"

"I think, for the moment, it's enough. If we return, you may ask me your question again." But he lingered for a moment; his hand rose and stopped an inch from the surface of the painting. What he reached for, he could no longer touch. No one could.

"If?" The word was sharp.

"I intend for all of the villagers to return to Bowgren, where they belong. But I am lord here; when the creature we must defeat comes, I will fight." He glanced at Heiden, his eyes narrowing.

Heiden shook his head.

The elder looked to Heiden, but she was silent; she offered no words of encouragement or comfort. No words of command, either.

Ansel waited, but when no further words of advice were offered, he continued. "I want the Margen guards to remain in the village; they're to patrol the perimeter." They weren't technically his to command, but no one doubted that his commands would be followed.

"And Lord Brandon?"

"We're going with Ansel," Brandon said, voice soft. "The ruler of these lands has not only attacked Bowgren; she appears intent on swallowing Margen as well. Bowgren and Margen have long been allies. In this we face the same foe for the same cause: we will protect our people and our demesnes."

Stephen cleared his throat. Everyone looked toward him as he offered an apologetic wince. "My huntbrother is coming with the last of our company. But one of them is very particular about respect—or the respect he believes he is due.

"Foreign nobles?"

"No, sadly. It's a talking golden fox."

The elder stared at him.

"He seems diminutive until he loses his temper. He is deadly; possibly as deadly as the lord we must face. He just doesn't look that way on first appearance."

"A talking fox."

"A talking golden fox. He's ancient."

"Like a golden hart?"

"Please do not ask that question of him, around him, or anywhere he might hear it. His hearing is excellent."

The elder frowned. "Some of the Margen villagers found their way here chasing—but never catching—a golden hart. Do you think they might be connected?"

Stephen shook his head. "No—and it's that type of question to which the fox might take offense."

Will, Nenyane said. *Will definitely take offense.*

"Fine. Let me talk with the villagers before your friends cross the perimeter." She hesitated and then added, "How badly will he react to perceived lack of respect?"

"Very."

She nodded and left; the Hunters remained in her house.

"There are children in the village," Heiden said.

Stephen nodded. "Small talking animals are bound to attract their attention." It was the children for whom he was most worried. "But Nenyane sounded him out, and he has no intention of remaining beyond the village boundaries if the rest of us are here."

In the absence of the village elder, Ansel returned to the table. "Our plan is to draw the lord from her seat of power, to face her here, where her power is weakest."

Stephen nodded. "She won't be weak; weakest in the lands she rules is still very powerful."

"How are we going to attract the lord's attention?"

"I'd say we already have it. But it's not focused, yet. Nenyane thinks Meralonne's presence—and that of the fox—will now be her chief concern if they make clear they have no intention of merely passing through her lands. They'll make that clear.

"When they do, she'll have to respond. She'll have to send something to deal with us—and that something has to fail. If it fails badly enough, I think it likely she'll come in person. But maybe she could just send the Silences."

Brandon tensed. Aelle paled.

"Would they be her first choice?"

"Nenyane says no. They're not equipped to fight—or kill—although they are capable of both when cornered. Their entire purpose is to create silence; to blanket an area so thoroughly their sleeping lord— their former lord—will not be disturbed. They have military uses. Obvious military uses. But Nenyane thinks that goes against their base nature.

"Sending them to the battlefield also strips her of their protection. Nenyane doesn't think she'll send the Silences out first—but she may weaken her defenses by sending them out in tandem with something that *is* capable of mass destruction."

Alex nodded. "Is Nenyane referring to the three-headed beast Meralonne showed us in the Redoubt?"

"She wasn't—and isn't—specific. She thinks it would make the most sense, but the creature in question doesn't work well with others—it's almost certain, if it's sent, it will be the only enemy we have to contend with."

"Why?"

"Because it'll probably injure or kill any others."

"She's certain something will be sent?"

"Yes. Absolutely."

Alex's frown deepened. "In response to something our side does."

Stephen nodded. He rose from the chair he'd occupied. "If we want any say in that something, we should join her. She hasn't entered the village yet; she'll wait for the elder's permission."

NENYANE WAITED by the edge of the small lake, with Kallandras and the fox.

Gervanno had remained outside of the village elder's home, but joined Stephen when he emerged; he followed as the Hunters approached the fence, and exited the village as they did. Stephen had considered having Gervanno work alongside the Margen guards, but Nenyane wasn't keen on that.

The fox caught sight of Gervanno the instant they came into view. He turned toward the Southern cerdan, lifting head in silent command. Gervanno approached the fox, knelt, and offered him an arm; the fox curled up there, as if Gervanno's entire purpose was to serve as a conveyance.

Nenyane was annoyed. It was a stronger annoyance than the usual; she was almost angry. Stephen did not want her to lose her temper here.

I'm not an idiot.

He changed the subject. *Where's Meralonne?*

Nenyane allowed it. *He's talking to the tree.* She spoke without inflection.

Stephen looked to the tree; he could see the glimmer of silver hair across the shallow water.

"You don't need to go," she snapped, correctly divining his intention.

"The tree was willing to speak with me," he replied. "And we owe it a greater debt than I imagined when we first arrived. The tree's branches are Amberg's fence. The fence isn't impressive; given what hunts in the wilderness, it shouldn't have lasted the day. But it has.

"The water here is pure and potable. I'm almost certain it's because of the tree's roots. All of Amberg, and the Margen people who arrived here, owe their continued lives to this tree. I don't understand how the tree maintains its roots, given that it doesn't serve the lord who rules these lands."

"It wasn't rooted—mostly—in these lands."

"It was. It was rooted in both, or we would have had to make the overland trek while the lands changed. There's something here, something to do with the tree." He hesitated, but decided against asking Nenyane the questions that had started to take root in his own thoughts. "The elder who aided us—the elder who was capable of creating his own land within the borders of the hostile wilderness—had something to do with the planting. Perhaps, had his roots not extended through that elder's lands, this tree would not have survived.

"But those lands are no longer claimed, if I understand what the elder said correctly. This tree therefore has a limited lifespan."

And what the tree, or the creature wrapped within it wanted, was a last chance to strike out at the lord of these lands.

Stephen understood that this tree had once been that lord. Whatever remained of it, whatever had been planted, had once ruled and commanded. Perhaps that was why the Bowgren border had managed to hold for so long.

He grimaced as he looked at the water, and shed boots; his had only barely dried from his first encounter with the large pond.

"You're going?" Alex asked.

Stephen nodded.

Nenyane had no desire to bespeak the tree, but even less to allow Stephen to do so without her. She was restless, her hand straying to sword hilt before she remembered where she was. She didn't bother to remove her boots; she leapt from root to root, causing small splashes as she did.

She was standing beside Meralonne before Stephen, and looked back with barely contained impatience.

Stephen made his way to where the mage stood. The mage's hair moved in a breeze that touched nothing else, as it so often did. But his eyes were flashing silver, and his skin faintly luminous in the evening sky.

Stephen placed his hand against the tree's bark. As he did, he marshaled the questions he wished to ask of the magi. And of the tree.

"I am not part of the wilderness," he began. "I am mortal, human. My memory stretches back a decade, although I still remember a few things that happened when I was a young child.

"You have been rooted in these lands for far, far longer than I've been alive. If I understood what the eldest who aided in your planting said, you've been rooted here for far longer than the Kingdom of Breodanir has existed."

The tree was silent.

The wind was not.

"If I understood what you said when you led us here, there was a time when you ruled these lands. They were yours. You were their lord."

The boughs above his head creaked. The tree did not speak.

"We of the Breodani owe you a far greater debt than I had realized. The elder who planted you provided soil in which your roots could safely take root—but he implied that that soil would drift or vanish as he leaves the lands he claimed."

Once again the boughs creaked.

Meralonne was now staring at Stephen; the Maubreche Hunter felt that gaze as an almost physical touch.

"You are rooted in soil that you once ruled."

The creaking grew louder; for a moment Stephen was afraid that the branches would fall on him. Nenyane snorted.

"I don't know if that gives you any advantage at all — I would have considered roots in the lands ruled by a different lord to be fraught."

"She is not aware of his existence," Meralonne said. "She is aware that the Bowgren boundaries are not falling as quickly as she had no doubt hoped — but the barriers she attempts to destroy were placed there by gods. The fact of Breodanir's long compact with the earth has been overlooked; she has assumed that Bredan's absence has opened the field to all those with ambition and power.

"But the compact was made between the earth and the Breodani. She will attribute her difficulties to absent gods. She will not attribute it to fallen lords."

"For how long?" Nenyane demanded.

"For long enough, little huntbrother. Had she time, or at least the willingness to use it, she would know. But her alliance with the dead has shifted the compliant obedience of the earth itself. The wind, when it comes, is angry. Only fire serves willingly, but fire was oft greedy. The water, I think, would no longer obey her, given her allies."

"You think there are *Kialli* here?"

"I think there must be at least one — but perhaps not. If they wish to be of aid to the lord here, they would remain beyond her borders."

"You think the *Kialli* would trust her to do what must be done?"

"No. That is why I think there must be at least one. It is not an alliance made with forethought, but the *Kialli* have information that she might lack. And their goals are similar — they are allies of convenience. She no doubt intends to purge them fully from her lands when she at last attains her goals.

"But that is fair; there is no doubt that they intend the same if she fails to render obedience to the lord they serve. It would have suited our purposes if they had had that argument before the borders became so porous.

"Regardless, the earth is aware of the dead, and it strains against their presence — and the earth does not easily forgive. It never forgets." He looked to Stephen, brows slightly furrowed. "You have very little interaction with the wilderness, high or low—and that will change in the future. But your point is, I think, a good one."

What point? Nenyane asked, unwilling to speak out loud and risk the derision of the mage, which was highly unusual; normally she wouldn't have cared.

"I don't understand ownership of claimed land."

"No. No more do the rest of the Breodani. The earth in the mortal lands is almost quiescent. But even so, the compact between earth and Breodani, blessed by Bredan, is a covenant in the ancient style: blood is exchanged for life. That blood, shed yearly, allows the earth to provide what it would otherwise not provide, and the earth is aware of the lords who rule the demesnes.

"It is a visceral awareness, not a conscious one. It is the reason the lands have not fallen. Were the lord of these lands to be restricted by similar barriers in a different kingdom, she would rule all. It is her misfortune to be here. Or perhaps," he added, voice soft, "there was some design and forethought in the ancient past. I cannot fully say.

"The earth was once wed to the lord who ruled it. But she has betrayed the wilderness by allowing the dead free passage, and the earth is rumbling now as its ancient anger wakes. Understand that rulership in the wilderness is defined by power. If one is powerful enough to defeat the lord, one may become lord in their stead. Not all who are that powerful desire to be rooted and bound to a single patch of land in the wilderness, and some cannot command the earth in the necessary fashion. Some serve other lords, and it is only with their permission that they can become rulers of their own lands; the bindings of service can interfere, otherwise.

"It was thus with my brothers, with the princes of the ancient court." He fell silent.

Stephen was uncertain that the mage would continue, and turned once again to the tree.

"I believe there is damage you might do to the lord and her hold on these lands." Meralonne then looked back across the water to the Hunters. The Bowgren Hunters.

Heiden saw clearly, and turned to Ansel, although he spoke no obvious words. Ansel looked at Stephen, and Stephen nodded. The Maubreche Hunter hoped that he had understood all of the scattered words and experiences that had led them, in the end, to this place, this battlefield. He hoped his ability to bespeak the wild earth was not just because he was god-born, not just because of Bredan's blood—there was an element of Maubreche and of Breodanir within him as the scion of Hunter Lords.

He couldn't be certain.

"It will not work," Meralonne said.

"What won't work?" Nenyane demanded.

"I believe Stephen intends to have Lord Ansel offer his blood to the tree."

Stephen nodded.

"The binding between the earth beneath your kingdom and the Breodani does not require blood; it requires life's blood. Would you have Ansel sacrifice himself here?"

"No. But the earth of Breodanir did not require my life. Just my blood. These are Bowgren lands. Ansel is the next lord."

Meralonne knew why the Hunters had been called to the King's City, but failed to argue against Stephen's claim.

"And Bowgren has paid in life's blood. Theirs was the most recent loss in the Sacred Hunt. Barrett died."

"That is not the way the wilderness works; it is not the way the earth remembers."

"It's not the way it works in the wilderness—but Bowgren is not part of that wilderness. The only connection is the earth and the Sacred Hunt." Stephen continued as Meralonne opened his mouth. "We're mortal. We're not like you. The covenant, such as it was, was created by a god and paid for by the mortals who followed him.

"The lord of these lands assumes she is destroying a barrier created by gods in the distant past, because mortals are irrelevant. They are no part of her consideration, no part of ancient paradigms. And it is true: if those barriers fall completely, our covenant with the earth may well be overwhelmed.

"But it won't be forgotten. It can't be forgotten." He spoke with certainty, because he was, in this moment, utterly certain.

"What do you need of me?" Ansel asked as he drew near. He had not doffed boots, and was now dripping water.

"Bowgren," Stephen replied. "The blood of Bowgren. The blood that has kept your lands—and ours—safe and fertile since the founding of Breodanir."

Ansel grimaced, but nodded. "Your eyes," he said, his voice a whisper meant only for Stephen's ears. Stephen didn't tell him that it was pointless; Nenyane and the mage would hear him even if he spoke so softly that Stephen himself couldn't. "Your eyes are glowing."

Stephen blinked.

He's not lying.

Is it because it's night? Because it's —

Does it matter? If you feel no pain, just ignore it. But she felt his fear rise, and placed a hand firmly on his shoulder. *I mean it. You won't use Bredan's power by accident ever again. This isn't about that.*

What is it about, then? Why — why are my eyes —

It's the oath — not yours. But the covenant itself. You're touching it somehow. You know what was sworn when Bredan led his people here. You understand it enough that you can possibly evoke it.

But this earth isn't ours!

Stephen — Amberg still stands. It's possible — barely possible — that the roots of that tree passed through the lands ruled by two lords; why is it impossible that they passed through to ours? To Bowgren itself?

Is that what had happened? He did not ask her. Instead, he took a deep breath and turned to Ansel. Nenyane was right.

I'm always right.

And annoying.

She grinned. He felt as if it had been a long, long time since he'd seen that expression.

"I think this tree had roots not in two lands, but three — I don't know how, or why — but one of those lands might be ours. Breodanir. Bowgren."

Ansel looked at the obsidian bark. Branches creaked above their head, but the tree did not speak.

"I think…" Stephen inhaled. Exhaled slowly. "I'm sorry — I know this is hard to hear."

Ansel's expression hardened.

"Barrett's death was the most recent death. His life — his life's blood — fulfilled the compact between the earth and the Breodani. Barrett died, and his death renewed and sustained the compact between Hunters and their lands. It's Bowgren's blood; it's Bowgren's sacrifice.

"Because of that sacrifice, I believe the tree protected Amberg inasmuch as it was possible — and I think it was only possible because some of these roots are in Bowgren, a place where such a tree couldn't fully take root.

"And you want me to bleed on the tree."

Stephen hesitated, and then nodded.

"Bowgren owes a debt to this tree," Ansel said, turning toward obsidian bark. He bowed head. He cut his palm without looking at either hand or knife; blood beaded heavily as he raised it and pressed it firmly against the tree's bark.

He was silent for a long beat, and then he bowed head. The Sacred Hunt—the sacrifice it demanded—had almost destroyed his family; it had shattered Lord Bowgren. But he knew, now—they all knew—that that death had served a greater purpose. No, that was unfair. They had always known. But that purpose, that benefit, could be almost forgotten it was so much a part of the daily life of the Breodani.

This was different. The enemy they faced was not starvation, not drought, both of which were deadly. This enemy had will, intent; it broke the world in which they had lived all of their lives.

If Bowgren had any chance of surviving, if Amberg had any chance of returning to Bowgren, it was because Lord Bowgren had joined the Sacred Hunt. He had raised horn, signaling the start of the Hunt; all Hunters were taught those sonorous notes, which were used nowhere else. And Barrett had fulfilled the oath he had sworn to Breodan at the age of eight: he had given his life in return for the life of his Hunter.

It was Barrett. It was Barrett's blood.

Had he been afraid? Had he faced the Hunter's Death in terror? Or had he faced it peacefully? Did some part of his life, his will, his thought remain in the earth of Breodanir? That wasn't the way death worked. It couldn't be. But watching Ansel, Stephen knew that the Bowgren Hunter's thoughts mirrored his own.

Ansel began to speak, his voice low, intent, and slightly unsteady.

"Barrett, if any of you remains in these lands that you loved, lend us the strength your death stole from us. I hated the King. I hated our God. I hated the Sacred Hunt. I think I always will. But I never hated you. And I understand, standing here, why your death was necessary, what it achieved. Bless us, aid us. Help me take our people home."

CHAPTER TWENTY-FOUR

The tree did not answer; it became still. Not even the creaking of branches could be heard. Ansel did not lift head, but he did close his eyes, standing, palm against the tree's trunk, as if by doing so he could fortify the tree.

From across the water, Heiden came to join his brother. Stephen moved to make room for the two Bowgren Hunters to stand side by side. Stephen was not surprised when Heiden cut his palm—more mindfully than Ansel had—and placed that palm against the tree's bark, just as Ansel had done. It was at a height with Ansel's hand, and it was the opposite hand to his Hunter—Ansel's left, Heiden's right—as if one person had raised both hands.

Nenyane caught Stephen by the shoulder, causing him to stumble. "You've done your part here. Come away."

He might have argued, but noted that Meralonne had reached the same conclusion Nenyane had: the mage moved away from the tree toward where his companions awaited him on the bank.

Stephen, feet bare, waded back into the water Amberg relied on, but he moved slowly because he looked constantly over his shoulder at the Bowgren Hunters.

They had entered these dark lands in the early hours of morning. Beneath the night sky, the moons reigned—two that were natural and one that was not. Meralonne had obscured sight of the third moon, but no daylight had returned to the lands. No sun.

What light there was had been pale and silver, beautiful in its fashion.

Light now blossomed from the heart of the tree. It was a warm light, not a blinding one, and it enveloped the two Bowgren Hunters as they stood on its roots, hands against its bark, heads bowed. If they spoke at all, their voices did not carry to Stephen's ears.

But the light grew brighter and brighter until he had to shade his eyes, to squint, to see the silhouettes of the two Bowgren Hunters. Were it not for the quality of that light, and the gentle touch of breeze, he might have panicked. Amberg could not afford to lose them. What little hope the villagers had gained upon Ansel's arrival would be gutted before the battle for Bowgren could truly begin.

He turned to Nenyane, whose hand on his shoulder had become white-knuckled, and froze as he stared at her face. The light shed from the heart of the tree illuminated her eyes—eyes that had not narrowed in the bright light. She did not cry, but her expression was one of sorrow, of empathy; it was funereal in shape, in texture.

"Do not worry overmuch, mortal," the fox said, his voice a low rumble. "Gervanno is likewise fearful—but it is not necessary. Perhaps, in other circumstances, it would be. But here, now, you plan to go to war with forces so ancient you should not dare to raise head, never mind voice, in dissent.

"She will not be pleased; she was always prickly when it came to due respect. Ah, I speak of receiving it, of course. She was not always careful when assessing the necessary flow of that respect." The fox showed teeth; perfect, white, and sharp in the light. "But she bears the scars from the worst of those mistakes, and she did survive.

"Arrogance is natural; it is perhaps the largest advantage you will have in this war."

"You do not consider yourself arrogant?" Nenyane asked, the words more respectful than those she'd been thinking, the sentiment nonetheless the same.

"Of course. But I have seen mortals do surprising things in my time, and the lord I serve is one such mortal. The lord of these lands would not dare to set foot across Jewel's boundaries while Jewel lives. No more that tree."

"You?"

"I am part of those lands, while wilderness persists. But I am not bound to them, else I would not be here." The fox yawned and rubbed his nose on Gervanno's sleeve. Gervanno did not appear to notice; he was watching the light.

"I am uncertain that the tree will have the power it requires to do what it now attempts." The fox yawned again. "But you were right, son of Bredan: the tree's roots were planted in three lands, not two—but the strength of the roots in the third were of necessity insignificant. I did not sense it when I first encountered the tree. Illaraphaniel did not.

"How did you know?"

Stephen almost shrugged. "My apologies, Eldest. It was a guess. It was a guess based on the continued existence of Amberg, a mortal village with no mage-born guardian, no guards, no Hunters to aid in its preservation. If it was possible to root the tree in two lands, it might be possible to root it in a third."

"It should not have been possible—indeed I believe it was possible here only because here is where the scent of Bredan still fills the land. There is a touch of wilderness in the god's covenant—how could there not be? Hmmmm. Very well. You may leave me now; I wish to watch this odd sunrise."

Stephen nodded, but glanced at Gervanno. It was annoying that the fox treated the Southerner as a servant, a personal attendant. He frowned. "Where is Jarven ATerafin?"

The fox, eyes fixed on the tree, nevertheless chuckled. "Now that is an interesting question. He is my cub; he can travel in a fashion that you cannot. There are many, many places he could go or be, but very, very few will help him attain the goal I have set him. Were it not for the unusual events here, I might even follow—just to observe, you understand. If he is easily killed, he will be of little use to my lord, and therefore of little use to me.

"I would not suggest you attempt to find him. It is possible Illaraphaniel could, but that would separate him from your precious village, where he will be needed. Jarven is not your problem, and he is not a reliable ally, as you have no doubt surmised.

"But he will not harm you. He will not directly harm those to whom you owe fealty. If you have decided to save this village and that salvation is possible—and to my mind, it suddenly is—he will not interfere."

"I'm not certain you have that much control over him," Nenyane said, frowning.

The fox chuckled. "Neither is he."

THE VILLAGE elder had prepared rooms where the hunters might camp; they were expected to make do with cramped quarters. Heiden attempted to withdraw so as not to further burden the villagers. She would accept none of it.

"The six of you are tired. If you intend to start this soon, you'll need what sleep you can get." Her expression made clear there was only one possible answer.

Heiden gave it. "Thank you."

JARVEN HAD TRAVELED the wilderness with increasing frequency in the past year. He had learned to listen to the ground beneath his feet, to the wind that passed him by; they whispered names. Sometimes they did not; then, they felt strangely inert. The land did, when there was no lord who presided over it. He had once, against the fox's advice, attempted to assert authority over lordless lands.

It was not a mistake he cared to repeat; not yet. He had not yet developed the power to make such a claim with authority. Ironic, that. Jarven had lived his life with very little respect for authority; he had chosen those to serve when it suited him, and had walked away when it did not. He could ape respect, but it was always superficial.

He knew how to behave in various social contexts. His first foray into such a context had been in the streets of the inner holdings. The only useful social information to come from those lean, difficult years had been a clear understanding of power and fear, and their use. The actual words and mannerisms had been less than useful as he entered the more monied class, but Jarven had always been exceptionally observant. He learned how to behave, the streets of *Averalaan Aramarelas* very different from those of the hundred. He became good at that; at exuding the confidence of wealth and birth, although he lacked the latter. People did not question those who conformed easily to the rules that governed their small corners of society.

He behaved well when he had something to gain from it. In his youth, he had considered the lack of self-respect that naturally resulted from bowing to power far too costly; in his old age, he knew that self-respect was internal, not external, that the gaze and admiration of others did not markedly change him. He was therefore far more willing to conform — largely because he was lazy. He had the choice; he understood the various options and byways. He also understood the effort involved, and chose not to expend that effort.

The meeting with the forest elder had changed his life, upending it. It had not, however, changed Jarven. As if the entirety of the wilderness, the ancient world, and the walking dead, were merely a different social context, he was learning to interact with beings that he would have once considered a delusional fever dream.

He had desired to test the limits of the abilities he had been granted. He felt it necessary to fully understand the paths and byways of the wilderness over which The Terafin ruled, to start. If he did not, on a visceral level, understand his own abilities — and the limits imposed on them — he would not survive.

So he learned. The most useful ability came first: he could walk the forest until he chose to leave it, stepping not onto the loam of that ancient earth but the cobblestones of a far more modern city. It was generally faster to travel the forest route to reach the Merchant Authority, and he could now enter his personal office without first being seen by Lucille. Or anyone but Finch, with whom he shared that personal office.

He learned the hard way, and at some cost, that his newfound health, his newfound strength, was not enough. He had long suspected that, even at the height of his physical prowess in the holdings, he would be considered insignificant by immortals and demons — if they noticed him at all.

Were it not for the intervention of the forest elder, they would not. He had enough money to purchase magical devices and the services of the talent-born; he could at least make himself seen and heard. He could survive. But he could not prosper. He could not assert the authority to which he had grown accustomed.

To do that — to even begin to do that — he required the cooperation, the benison, of the forest elder. Until Rymark ATerafin was dead and his hunt at a close, Jarven would not receive it.

Rymark, a man for whom Jarven had had only a passing smidgen of respect — the respect due an egotistical fool who was nonetheless possessed of some talent — had proved surprisingly evasive. What had started as a matter of course had now evolved into something almost *personal*. How could a man of Rymark's competence be so difficult to end? Perhaps the fox had known. Jarven doubted it. To the fox, mortals were alike; those that commanded respect, such as it was, were the talent-born. The bard. The mage. The Terafin. Jarven had not been born with those talents. He had, he could admit, been born with some small measure of luck, and he had parlayed that into skill, then skill into power, choosing his allies, choosing the lords he served, as if they were each stepping stones. The powerful—the truly powerful—did not serve.

But the fox served Jewel, The Terafin, in a fashion in which Jarven had never served.

The elder's gift, in and of itself, was of interest, of course—who would not choose to be young again, to be physically as strong as one had been in their prime? But it was not just that. Jarven's mortality weighed against him in the war that was even now unfolding. There were opponents. He understood opponents—he practically defined himself by their existence. Without opponents, there was no competition; without losers, there were no victors.

He was not a fool. Even had he not entered into a compact with the fox—if such a pale word could accurately describe his chosen master—he would have trodden the wilderness with care. Talking animals were apparently not rare, although many could be annoying. He treated them with the gestures of respect he had learned as he climbed out of the holdings, through the merchant caravans, to the merchant holdings, where the elite brokered the wealth they transformed into power.

He knew how to bide his time.

But if he had been given the gift of time, he nonetheless could not spend it carelessly. He had entered the game so late, the stakes were almost beyond him. Not, of course, actually beyond him, but it was close.

He had spent much of his later years implying—by behavior—that he was in his dotage. It amused him to watch the minnows in the political pool believe they could suddenly become sharks. Lucille hated it— she felt it harmed his dignity. Finch tolerated it because she understood that it could not be changed.

Perhaps that was untrue. Finch disliked the minnows, because in her youthful world, they *had* been sharks. She was content to watch them commit figurative suicide.

He found that he had no need for that pretense in the wilderness unless he wished to test his combat abilities. Here, no petty honor, no petty social customs, interfered with the rules of power. Those with greater power naturally ruled those with less. Greater power was oft determined by trial, by combat. Often, but not always. The reputation of the powerful preceded them, just as it had in his prior life; had it not, the lands would be in a state of perpetual war.

Jarven understood that respect was earned, not simply granted as if it were of no relevance. He would begin, here.

Here, where the trail that he had followed from *Averalaan* to the edge of the Northern Wastes, and from there to the Kingdom of Breodanir, led. That prey had finally been flushed into the open: the wilderness in which petty things like laws were irrelevant. Jarven had killed before; he had carefully skirted detection in the doing, in all but a handful of cases.

But in all of those cases, the kill itself was never in doubt; the care and deliberation required was in evasion of consequences, of detection. Here, the situation was inverted. Rymark had powerful friends, but legal consequences for his death did not exist. Jarven could kill or he could die, without navigating complex laws. The only law was power. Jarven's power was untested and incomplete; he might fall back on cunning—indeed he almost always did—but there was no certainty.

It was bracing.

Rymark had had powerful friends in Averalaan, but some of those friends were dead, and some had been denied—for as long as The Terafin reigned—a return to that city.

The Twin Kings were the nominal rulers of the Empire; they were the monarchs to whom The Terafin had sworn fealty. But the power was Jewel's. Rymark himself had been forced to flee, a fact Jarven could not regret.

Had Rymark remained within the city, he would now be dead, but possibly not at Jarven's hands. Such death would render the fox's agreement null and void. It had become a cause for concern, given the presence of Meralonne APhaniel. Jarven had known him as a mage—a famously quirky and irascible one.

He was no longer a simple mage. He was, as Jarven had long suspected, a scion of the very wilderness Jarven intended to master. Jarven's largest concern was that the erstwhile mage would interfere; it had not happened yet. But Rymark was here. If Jarven did not kill him first, he might lose the very necessary opportunity.

Perhaps he could negotiate with the mage, although it was doubtful; at the moment, Jarven possessed nothing the mage required. To do that, he needed to finish here.

Adding complication, Kallandras of Senniel College had arrived. Jarven could not help but be aware of the bard's reputation; he had had him investigated in what felt an increasingly distant past. Rumors were seldom proved so true as they were in the case of that bard; indeed, the rumors seemed less remarkable than the bard himself.

Had the demons not attacked, Rymark's position within the petty bureaucracy of the Queen's court might never have come under threat. They had attacked, however, and Rymark had chosen to absent himself from that position almost precisely at the moment Jarven had donned his cloak as the head of the Terafin merchant operations and arrived in Breodanir.

But beyond the confines of the King's Palace, Rymark's trace had become clearer, stronger; there should have been little to prevent Jarven from tracking him. He had not expected that Rymark would also be able to vanish into the wilderness. He was angry with himself for the oversight. Rymark had clearly allied himself with the demons of the so-called Shining Court, and the demons could traverse the wilderness to a greater or lesser degree.

But the wilderness, and most of the lords who called themselves rulers, considered the demons to be walking dead. Treacherous walking dead. He would not, at the time, have predicted that Rymark would flee to the wilderness, given his allies. The lack of prediction annoyed Jarven immensely; nothing was more enraging than his own mistakes. He was not accustomed to making them.

Instead of avoiding the mage and the bard, Jarven had found himself following the same route. Not only to Margen, but to the wilderness itself. Here, the mage and the bard—along with the Hunters —had stationed themselves; here, they intended to wage their unequal war. And here, damn him, was Rymark ATerafin.

Rymark was out of his element; he had always desired status and the acknowledgement of the elite. None of that status would serve him well here; only his talent-born power would, but he had been famously lazy as a student in the Order of Knowledge. He wondered if Rymark had taken to the forbidden arts. Ah, no. He assumed that he had. But demonic summonings were a test of both will and power; he could not imagine that powerful demons were under his control.

But demons were here. Jarven had prepared weaponry crafted and enchanted to dispatch them, but he was not certain they would have the same effect in the wilderness that they did in Averalaan. He exhaled, slowing; impatience could be deadly. Patience had been the most difficult of skills to master, and if he felt young again, he felt impatience far more keenly than he had in decades.

He did not know the wilderness; he understood that he would never know it completely. There was too much of it, and it varied from land to land, as if geography was a waking dream through which one might stumble: here, the edge of a cliff; there, the dangerous humidity of jungle or the white, blank snow and ice of the Northern Wastes.

He had experienced the sudden changes of scenery, of temperature, of weather. The only weather he wished to avoid was raging storm—it obscured tracks, made scent harder to follow. The rest was almost irrelevant; he did not feel cold as he had once experienced it, and heat was similar.

He could move silently and did as a matter of course; he could hear the growling snuffle of a creature who did not care to do the same. He could also hear the snap of branches bent back by someone's passage; could hear, as he stilled, the crack of wood, and following it, the fall of trees. They were distant enough he did not assume they would fall in his direction.

He almost paid for that error. The trees here were thick enough that a falling tree would first hit others, still standing, as it bounced toward the ground. He had not expected that more than one would fall. Had not judged the distance of the collision—he assumed it was collision —correctly.

But he saw the beast who had taken the trees down and stilled his breathing. If he was forced to leap out of the way of falling trees, the trees themselves would make enough noise that he could disguise his presence. It was necessary.

The creature was large—larger than any natural animal Jarven had encountered in person. It had three heads; a lion's head, an eagle's, and something almost human, although the skin was the grey of marble, not flesh. He turned instantly, seeking shelter from the gaze of that third head. He did not wish to be seen, but felt, on an instinctive level, that seeing might be the more dangerous option.

The creature was destroying the parts of forest through which it walked.

And Jarven understood, then, that the reason he had not detected how close the creature had come was the sound.

The noise was muted. In and of itself, this was interesting; Jarven wished to be silent, and as he moved forward, following Rymark's trail, his wish was granted.

One must be careful what one wishes for in the wilderness. The fox's words returned to him as he faced that wish. The advantage to being a lone operative was the lack of underlings; communication could not be intercepted because none was necessary. He had not come with companions in arms of any kind; he wanted this kill for himself, and he would not risk losing it.

Silence was therefore not an issue.

Or so he thought. But as he moved forward, as the sounds of the forest faded and died, he reconsidered. His steps made no sound; the wind made no sound; the movement of branches—and possible wildlife—made no sound. He could see; there was no difficulty with his vision. Vision had always been essential. Over the years, his hearing had degraded to a certain degree; there were notes he could no longer hear when played, whispers that did not reach his ears. With the intervention of the elder, his full hearing had been restored.

He lost it again now, as he moved, and contemplated just how much hearing anchored him to the world through which he moved. The Hunters had discussed "the Silences" as if they were actual entities. If so, there was an entity here that caused this oppressive, unnatural hush. He considered, briefly, attempting to find it to put an end to it.

He discarded the desire. If silence such as this—total, absolute—was caused by a creature that served the lord of this land, their death would be a warning he did not wish to give. He understood that the mage's desire was that lord's death—but that was the mage's problem, not Jarven's.

He focused on what he could see, not hear, as he moved forward, but he did listen; he knew the moment sound of any kind returned that he had reached the edge of the silent boundary. And he considered the use to which such a creature could otherwise be put. A weapon was useful in the right hands. His, of course.

It was interesting the way utter silence seemed to lengthen the distance he now traversed. He understood why the Hunters hoped to draw the lord out—they fought as a team of compatriots, and no word could be easily transmitted between them. Here, the lord would have the ultimate advantage, if she were powerful enough to require very little aid.

She would, no doubt, labor under the same disadvantage the Hunters would. He wondered how the mage would fare, but did not wonder overlong; he could hear the slightest of sounds ahead. He slowed then and moved far more carefully, aware that that sound, muted and indistinct, could belong to a creature that could be upon him with little notice, little warning.

That caution was rewarded. He was uncertain whether it had saved his life, but was certain that it had prevented moderate injury.

The forest was not empty. He had followed the traces of Rymark ATerafin and they had led him here; he could almost see the man who had attempted to win House Terafin's ruling seat through forbidden arts. It had been a futile, pointless attempt. He had known that before he had met the fox—the fox who had come to bespeak Finch ATerafin in the Merchant Authority.

He had known because Haval knew it. Haval, the brightest of his contemporaries, the most deadly, the most skilled. Absent the humor Jarven found relieved monotony, Haval had disappointed Jarven severely: he had walked off the board, walked out of the game of thrones, without a single backward glance.

The whole of his skills, his observations, his power, had been offered to...a clothing business. To *tailoring*. But no, no. He had become Jewel ATerafin's advisor, counsellor; he had become someone to whom the wilderness of Terafin—the wilderness of Jewel —deferred.

No power Rymark could bring to bear could unseat Jewel ATerafin; even before the House Council had voted upon her ascension, that had been true. But what she had done afterward, what she had done when three demi-gods had wakened from their long slumber, had cemented her power. She was absolute. She could be hurt—not physically, of course—but could not be killed. The best Rymark might hope to achieve was to break her.

Breaking her he could have easily done: her den existed entirely within the mortal realm. Destroying them would eventually destroy her. She had the weakness peculiar to most people; the overt attachment to those lesser, those weaker, those less capable of survival.

In the wilderness, following the subtle tracks of Rymark ATerafin, a name returned to him, almost an argument or a denial of the thought.

Hectore of Araven, patriarch of the Araven clan, a man famed for his indulgent love of his grandchildren.

It was an attachment Hectore had never troubled himself to hide. If Jarven had a peer among the merchants over whom he presided, it was Hectore of Araven, but Jarven allowed himself no weaknesses, and Hectore had many. Many, yes—but he was ruthless if a hair on those heads was touched. He had destroyed an entire merchant operation down to the clerks without a hint of mercy; innocent people had certainly died, caught in the determined flames of his endless rage.

Jewel could never have contemplated a revenge so complete, so deadly.

But no one who was not certain they could take down Hectore had ever touched his family again. No attempt had been made. No hint of such an attempt. They had, of course, attempted to kill Hectore; they had attacked his caravans; they had caused almost open war on the trade routes. Those, Hectore had always accepted as the cost of doing business. He might retaliate, but in comparison the retaliation had been measured. Expected.

Jewel could never have been what Hectore had been—not before her ascension. Now? Now the wilderness would destroy, just as Hectore had done. Just as completely, as ruthlessly. She wouldn't have to lift hand; it would be done almost before she had completed a thought, her power was so absolute.

And she feared it.

She feared it so deeply, she had given the governance of House Terafin to Finch, Teller, to the Chosen who had served her first and most completely.

Jarven was not, and would never become, what Jewel ATerafin was. But he could not imagine that such absolute power would discomfort him at all.

He did not have it. He would not waste time envying it; he had not required the blessing of the talent-born to become Jarven ATerafin; he did not require it now. His power was no accident of fate, no whim of birth. It had been in his hands from the beginning. It would be in his hands at the end.

But it would not be fully realized until Rymark was dead.

NENYANE LIFTED HER HEAD FIRST. Before the bard. Before the mage. The wind had not changed; Ansel and Heiden remained by the side of the great tree, heads bowed. He understood what they were asking; understood what they were grieving.

And he understood that perhaps the living always attempted to make peace with the dead by somehow believing death served a greater purpose. How could he not? He was Breodani, son of Hunters, godson of a Hunter who had lost his huntbrother to the Hunter's Death: Bredan.

Lord of Hunters.

Lord of the Covenant.

That death had served a purpose. If there was any chance at all that this mortal world could survive the machinations of a god upon the plane, it had been bought by Stephen of Elseth. The man his mother had loved in her youth. The man for whom she had named her son. The death was a sacrifice that had bought a slender chance. Stephen of Elseth did not regret it, even in death.

Perhaps Barrett of Bowgren was the same. That was the belief that Heiden and Ansel now built and nurtured in this foreign, terrible wilderness. Had he helped them to tell that story? Had he helped them to believe it?

"Stephen," Nenyane snapped. "Now is not the time—get the others."

Stephen glanced at her, and she almost snarled. She leapt toward the tree and toward the Bowgren Hunters, grabbing each by the shoulder and yanking them away from the trunk.

Heiden was shocked; a hint of annoyance had started to settle into his expression.

Ansel's, to Stephen's surprise, held none. He turned his head to face Nenyane and nodded, silent; she released his shoulder. A moment later, she released Heiden's as well, and they sprinted through the water toward the village.

"Illaraphaniel!"

The mage frowned, but did not argue; his name was a demand.

The bard lifted head; shortly thereafter, Gervanno began to move. Stephen was uncertain whether it was the bard's silent voice that had spurred him to motion, or Nenyane herself.

THE FOX GROWLED, his voice a clap of thunder.

Gervanno did not pause. "I will set you down if you command it," he said, his syllables only slightly labored. "But I cannot desert them."

The growling grew. Words were in it, although they were blurred, indistinct.

Gervanno heard them, regardless.

You will die, foolish mortal. You will throw away your life! Come away. Come now. You cannot face what is coming—can you not feel it in the earth? Can you not hear it on the wind?

Gervanno did not point out that the fox had not heard it—Nenyane had. Nenyane had demanded action from all of them—and no one had disobeyed. No one but the fox.

You will die!

"Eldest, we all die. Every one of us. I should have died once. I disgraced myself and that should have been the end of me." He lengthened his stride, the fox growing heavier and heavier in his arms. "This was a gift. I do not deserve it. But if I can die *here*, if I can die with sword in hand, if I can die protecting those I swore to protect...

"It's not enough. It's more than I deserve. But you don't have to die with me."

The fox roared in furious outrage; had Gervanno not been running in Nenyane's wake, he would not have made such a mistake.

"Die? ME? You foolish, ignorant mortal! How DARE YOU?" The fox grew heavier still. If Gervanno was in too much of a hurry to be appropriately respectful, he was not so foolish as to drop the fox. The death he wanted was a true warrior's death. He therefore bore the weight, but he did not slow his steps.

The Hunters—and the dogs—moved swiftly toward the village of Amberg. The gates opened as they approached, although Nenyane didn't bother to wait; she leapt the fence, landing in a forward sprint.

"Brandon! Aelle!"

The mage turned toward Gervanno as the gate rolled open. "You will have to leave the elder, now."

"Illaraphaniel, do not anger me."

"You are already so far gone I hardly think my meager contribution to your foul mood could make it much worse. You know as well as I that this ground is not a ground upon which you can easily stand—it will weaken both the ground and you." He glanced up at Gervanno, but it was brief; his gaze was upon the fox.

Gervanno had been forced to stop as Nenyane and Stephen ran ahead. The villagers were of great import to the Hunters, and he believed what the Northern Widan said: the fox should not enter.

"You know what is coming, Eldest," the Widan continued. "I am surprised that it was neither of us who sensed it—but perhaps that is the work of the Silences. I can hear it now."

"Hah! Are you saying your mortals can stand against it?"

"Not alone. But that is the interesting thing about mortals. Even those who feel adrift and isolated." The look he gave Gervanno was brief but intent. "They do not often stand alone." His smile was slender and cold. "And I am here, Eldest. I will offer our opponent a chance to converse before I end them."

"That is unwise, even for you."

"What wisdom is left us who stand against a god? Now, return to us Gervanno di'Sarrado, or the first such conversation I have will be with you."

"This is not Jewel's forest, fool. This is the lord's, and she is not your friend. This is no place to fight our enemies—not when we have a wilderness of our own."

"Were it Jewel's, Breodanir would not now be in danger. But my power in Jewel's wilderness is not what your power is. Her lands are not my home; I do not serve."

"No," the fox replied, less thunder in his voice. "I had almost forgotten; you have spent so much time in Jewel's lands defending her borders." He was lying, but it was a familiar brand of lie: polite and respectful. "Very well. You may put me down."

Gervanno knelt and gently placed the fox—who had become lighter —on the ground outside of Amberg.

"It is true: this earth is not entirely comfortable to traverse. I would take you with me," he added to Gervanno. "I would not see you extinguished here. You have scant decades ahead of you; I do not understand your desire to cut even those short." His eyes were almost gold as they met Gervanno's gaze, unblinking. "I should have known better. I should have left you in the wilderness when first we met. I should have realized, even then, that this is the decision you would always make."

Gervanno offered the fox the lowest of bows as he rose. "I have been stained by the immobility of terror," he said, voice soft. "Where the choice is mine, I will not surrender to it again."

"The choice, then, was not yours. You faced a death you could not avoid, except by being unnoticed."

Gervanno frowned. He had not spoken of that incident except in generalities that obscured his shame, his guilt. But the fox knew.

"Yes. Yes, I know. I have seen the way fear and guilt shape and break your kind; it is corrosive in a way even grief is not. But perhaps you were created to endure loss, your lives are so short." He exhaled. "You are not mine. Nor could you be, and remain as you are. I will not offer you what I offered my cub—but you have paid the price of my intervention once, and I will be aware of you until the day you die.

"Which is likely to be soon. I find it almost disturbing that I consider your death at all. You are not mine; I cannot command you. But I would be most pleased if you somehow survived. Survive, Gervanno. Survive, and perhaps the day will come when you redeem yourself in your own eyes."

Gervanno nodded.

"And perhaps, as I am now very bored, I will go to see what approaches."

"You already know," Meralonne said, his eyes narrowed, his expression almost neutral. Perhaps to one born in the North, the scant hint of emotion would have remained undetected—but Gervanno's life in the home of his youth had depended on his ability to infer and intuit subtle changes in the faces of the powerful. The fox had surprised the Widan.

As if aware of Gervanno's realization, Meralonne APhaniel turned. "Ser Gervanno, proceed."

Gervanno passed through the open gate.

———

NENYANE RELAXED when Gervanno joined them; they were once again clustered inside the village elder's home. The cerdan offered Nenyane a Southern bow; to Stephen's surprise, she nodded in return, acknowledging it.

Heiden had gone to the small shrine, and remained silent before it; Ansel, however, stood at the head of the table. No one sat, not even the intimidating elder; she stood, eyes narrowed, listening. She offered no advice, no warning; this, to her, was a Hunter matter. She was present because the villagers were hers to govern and protect.

"It's the creature that attacked Clearbrook?"

Nenyane nodded. No one present asked how she knew. Brandon looked like he might, but he glanced at Ansel first and held his tongue.

"How does it turn people to stone?" Alex asked.

"It looks at them," she replied. "And they look at it."

"So those who run in terror don't get turned to stone."

"Running in terror from this creature is the safest option anywhere but here. Here, safety depends on the village itself." She turned to the elder. "It's vital that people stay in their homes and away from windows. If they have basements, they could gather there; it might protect them if the creature chooses to destroy the buildings in an attempt to flush them out.

"If it makes any difference, being turned to stone is the safer option when dealing with this creature."

The elder's brows rose.

"The stone status isn't permanent."

Heiden tensed. "The people who are statues can be saved?"

Nenyane exhaled. "Yes. And no. The creature has the ability to petrify, but it can also reverse the transformation at its own whim."

"Why would it do that?"

"To eat."

Silence. Heiden cleared throat. "Could we save the villagers of Clearbrook? Those who are now statues?"

Nenyane hesitated. "If we kill the creature, the change should reverse itself."

"Is its death necessary?" Stephen asked.

"No—but the boundaries we're attempting to strengthen will prevent it from easily entering Bowgren, and I'm uncertain that the change can be reversed from a distance of this kind. Regardless, we don't expect the villagers to take up arms here. Keep them hidden if at all possible."

"And the guards?"

"The guards can fight if necessary," Nenyane replied, in a tone that made clear she'd rather have them hiding in basements, if those basements existed. "But they'll be affected the same way as the villagers would." She folded arms. "Brandon and Aelle weren't in the King's City with us. They didn't see what Meralonne showed us.

"I told you the two-headed creature he showed us actually had three heads. The third is the dangerous one."

"The other two?"

"They'll just injure or kill. It's the third head that petrifies. But attacking from behind won't be reliable. The roar of the lion's head is loud; it's almost a physical attack. That gives the third head time to turn, and when it does, we lose the people attacking from behind. If we had time, we could train people to ignore the roar—but the first time you hear it, it's impressive. It's meant to catch—and hold—attention.

"In order to fight properly, we're going to need to nullify the third head."

"If I remember, it had a lion's head and an eagle's head."

She nodded.

"What is the third head?"

"It's almost human in appearance. It has, or should have, long hair; the hair is extensible—one form of attack. But the hair serves as a veil, as a way of covering or obscuring the eyes. When the hair is pulled back, it's the eyes that are the danger. It's the gaze you must not meet."

"So we need to remove the head."

"In normal circumstances, yes." She frowned. "But that's easier said than done. Of the three, it's the hardest to injure; Meralonne showed you all what the creature looked like, and it was absent that third head. There's a reason for that. It's the third head that will speak, if speech can be forced; it's the third head that will disappear if speech isn't necessary."

"It can make an entire head disappear?"

"Only that one. Think of that head, that part of the body, as the real creature; it can retract. Which is the wrong word. Removing that head, if possible, will kill the creature—it's the weakness."

"What of the other heads?"

"Those never vanish. Think of them as badly placed limbs. Injuring them won't kill the creature, but may slow it down. Attack those two heads as you would limbs."

"If we manage that?"

"The creature will likely retreat unless under complete compulsion. I think it's pretty clear that the lord of these lands has coercive control over the creature. The how or why is irrelevant. This is the strongest warrior she has in her arsenal. If she's sent it out to attack us, she knows Illaraphaniel—the mage—may be intent on interference.

"In which case, she means to destroy the village. There will be nothing left that requires protection of any kind. We have one advantage, if the map we were shown—a map of roots—remains accurate.

The Silences that serve as defense of this land's lord prevent communication from traveling easily to that lord. She's sent the creature here. If she sends accompanying Silences with it, the creature will hear nothing; there will be no possibility of conversation, and no possibility that she'll receive a report.

"But if it is sent to destroy the village, the villagers, or the Hunters, it will have to rely on scent to track them; that will take much longer. Even the petrification will be less effective, because we won't hear the lion's roar that often precedes it. For that reason, my guess is the Silences will not be in motion."

"When will we know?"

"We assume that the Silences aren't accompanying it; we don't know that they won't be sent. They do not serve willingly; given their nature, I'm surprised they serve at all.

"We have Meralonne APhaniel, and we have Kallandras of Senniel. The bard's power is severely lessened with the advent of the Silences — but she doesn't know that he's here, and even if she did, she'd likely consider him irrelevant. He's mortal."

"That would be a mistake." Ansel's voice was soft, the syllables exact.

Nenyane's smile was sharp. "It will be, yes." She exhaled. "We need to harry the creature; we want to keep it outside of the gates."

"The gates won't hold. The creature could step over the fence without bothering to knock it over."

She nodded. "It could. It might knock the fence over. If it does, the fence has to be repaired as quickly as possible."

"During the combat?"

"During the combat."

Brandon exhaled. "That's what you want our forces to do."

"Yes. I want the Margen guards to watch for stragglers among the villagers — but I want them to repair the fence inasmuch as it's possible during the encounter. We'll hold the beast's attention."

"Why the fence?"

"Because the fence will offer protection against anything the creature might have dragged with it. These lands, this village, are our best chance of surviving. Or winning. Amberg is not the lord's; this small, prescribed area will provide no strength to those who serve her. In all honesty, the best place to make a stand against this creature is within the village itself."

"You don't suggest it," Heiden said, voice soft.

Nenyane shook her head. "We're all Hunters. We have one responsibility, here: it's the villagers. An easier fight would never be worth the risk of the greater losses. We may have no choice," she added. "But while we do, we'll fight outside, just beyond the tree."

Ansel had listened quietly, absorbing Nenyane's words. He was technically the commander here, but he offered no arguments, countermanded none of her suggestions. "How long do we have?"

"Not long. If we're lucky, we have half an hour. If we're unlucky, ten minutes."

The elder moved instantly, her expression a blend of alarm and determination.

"Lord Ansel?" Brandon's voice.

"Follow Nenyane's suggestions. If you have questions and I survive, I promise I'll answer them all. Pass on her commands to your guards. The village will be in their hands."

Stephen turned to Max. "Steel will remain with you. Do you want a second dog?"

Max shook his head. "We don't have time."

Nenyane was the second to leave the elder's home; the first was the elder herself. This time, the Hunters left the villagers and their instruction entirely in the elder's hands. The dogs followed Stephen. They were tense, but not jittery; they focused as their Hunter focused.

He did not call the trance, not yet; he knew that Alex—or Max—would do so first.

Gervanno spoke only when they were once again outside of the elder's home. "Where should I position myself?"

Nenyane's smile was brief, sharp. "This isn't that kind of battle." Lifting her head, she said, "Illaraphaniel, are you ready?"

Stephen couldn't see the mage, but he felt the wind's reply.

THE CREATURE COULD BE FELT—AND heard—long before it could be seen; the crash of falling trees accompanied its movements. Stephen frowned.

What if the creature attacks the tree?

There was only one tree of relevance in this forest. Nenyane nodded. *Where do you think we'll attempt to corner it?*

"If the tree falls," Brandon said, "the village will follow." He spoke with certainty.

Stephen silently agreed.

"If it can knock the trees in the forest over just by walking..." The Margen Hunter didn't finish the thought. "The dogs?"

Stephen shook his head. "Nenyane will scout ahead."

One of the Margen guards opened the gate. Brandon spoke to the guard; Stephen couldn't see the guard's expression, but he could see determination and purpose in the man's posture.

Ansel lifted a hand. "Let's head out."

EVEN BEFORE THEY reached the small lake which encircled the tree, the forest sounded like the heart of a storm. Nenyane's scouting was unnecessary; falling trees made enough directional sound, they knew where the creature was.

Stephen wondered if the destruction of the trees was a sign of carelessness, rage, or planning; if the third head required line of sight to effect its petrification, the trees might be a defense against its power.

It's likely all three, his huntbrother said. *But given the way it's moving, I'd guess rage is the larger motivating factor. That might help us.*

How? He understood that rage and fury often led to mistakes, but he had no sense that this is what Nenyane meant.

They don't want to serve. If they had a choice at all, they would be on our side. It's like Steane. He didn't want to serve either, but the compulsion was too great, the surveillance too prevalent. He attacked because he had no choice; all of his aid to us had to be unseen by his lord.

The lord's eye is inactive here.

It's clouded, it's not inactive—it's another way the lord gathers information. If she cannot see, she is aware that someone with power is obscuring her vision. She can't see us clearly through that third eye; she can still see her servants.

Slaves.

Slaves, then. Understand that in much of the wilderness there is no difference. Do you think the Winter Queen for whom Illaraphaniel yearns does not exert control of her own lands in the same fashion? This is the wilderness. This is how the ancients lived. This is what they want for the rest of us.

Stephen closed his eyes and reached for Nenyane's sight.

Had those eyes been his, he would have winced, would have

squinted. There was light at the heart of the forest—a messy, inchoate, visual blur that failed to fully cohere as she watched. He could see fallen trees as black, long shadows that lay like markers against the ground, but even the ground was difficult to look at for long. Had Nenyane been concerned, that was where her gaze would have been fixed; she was not.

What she saw here, she expected to see.

No, he thought, that wasn't right. What she saw surprised her, but there was no shock. The former lord of these lands, whose remnants were a tree, was exerting what influence he could through roots that extended beyond the lake. He would not have noticed were it not for the huntbrother bond; it was Nenyane's observation, not his own.

Light finally resolved itself into shape as the creature that had seemed so small in the illusion created by Meralonne APhaniel across a distant table in the King's City came into view.

It was the size of a house. A tall house.

The head that he had described to the others as a lion's was nothing so simple, so mundane: gold flowed in a mane that bracketed fur of a similar color, and horns rose from either side of its skull, but it was the lion's eyes that caught and held Stephen's attention, even as its jaws opened to expose its fangs. The eyes were not gold, as the fox's sometimes were, nor silver: they were brown, the whites invisible at this distance; they were a warm color, a living color. This creature belonged in this place; it was one with it, just as the animals in the forests of Maubreche were at home there.

The avian head was similar; the eyes the same deep brown, the beak of gold, the feathers silvered. The eyes of the eagle implied age, wisdom —he did not know why. He stood frozen as he saw what Nenyane saw, his knees almost bending beneath the weight of it, the need to pay respect.

Nenyane wasn't even angry. *Yes*, she said. *I'd forgotten. I'd forgotten this.*

It was different from her rage and her fear, this certainty: she had forgotten, but she knew she would not forget again. Were it not for the fact that this creature was their enemy, she would have treasured what she now saw.

But she slid from that as the third head came into view. Stephen understood then why the third head would prove difficult; unlike the first two. It seemed almost like a phantom, a ghost—it was pale, the whole of face and hair painted in shades of silver and grey. The hair Nenyane had described fell about it like a crown, or perhaps a cloak, and where the two animal heads seemed natural, seemed to belong, the third did not evoke any sense of life. Instead, it was a scion of death, of loss, of sorrow.

That thought did annoy Nenyane. *They're not separate—they're one being, one creature.*

Stephen didn't argue with her certainty. Instead, he turned to Ansel. "She's got it in sight now—and it's the size of a house."

"Single storey or two?"

"Tall single storey, I think. We'll know soon."

"Has she closed with it at all?"

He shook his head. The lion head roared, and the question almost vanished. The roar was, for the moment, the entire aural landscape; even the dogs were frozen. Had the creature been before them, the fight would be over. This is what Nenyane had warned them about.

But the wind blew now, loudly, almost angrily; it struck Stephen with small pebbles, leaves, the debris that was easy prey to the wind's whims. He shook himself—they all did.

Kallandras of Senniel alighted on the far shore of the small lake. He gestured and the Hunters leapt between the submerged roots, crossing the water to join him, to move the fight farther away from the tree itself.

Another roar shook the ground; a third roar stopped them in their tracks. Stephen and Alex had not quite cleared the water.

Kallandras stood for a long moment; his lips moved, but soundlessly —soundlessly for everyone but his chosen audience. He then grimaced. He had not armed himself, but his lute was strapped across his back— an odd choice, given combat.

He removed it, held it in both arms, and began to play.

NOTES FILLED the natural clearing that surrounded Amberg's only source of safe water, the prelude to the bard's voice, the bard's song. In the wilderness, the crashing of distant trees, the roar of a furious beast, became the song's harmony, which Stephen had not expected. He had expected nothing like this: the bard's voice, melodic, was strong, wild.

Perhaps Kallandras's musical strength was grief, for there was grief here, the music, the minor key, the strength and texture of voice wrapped around actual words, none of which Stephen understood. But he understood the grief and loss with which the bard's music imbued those words; they all did.

Ansel and Heiden, whose understanding of loss had been shaped by Barrett of Bowgren, were silent. Stephen could not see their faces, and perhaps that was a mercy. But the roars no longer paralyzed them. They could move, Stephen was certain of it, although they did not; they listened.

Even the dogs felt the weight of the bard's voice, although Pearl immediately stepped forward as if to prove she was above such nonsense.

Stephen closed his eyes as Nenyane reached for him. *Whatever the bard is doing, tell him to continue.* As if he was the bard's master and could command him, which was ridiculous.

But he saw the creature through Nenyane's eyes, and he was surprised to see the third head become far more solid, far more substantial; the song had carried to the creature's ears. To all of them. The lion head's roars softened although it continued as if aware that it had become part of the bard's song, somehow.

But the eagle opened beak, and what emerged was not the angry screech of a great, hunting bird: it was song. It was a deep baritone, and it carried notes, extending them as the harmony intertwined with melody. The sound of the lute did not carry; Stephen heard it because he was standing so close to the bard. He found his footing and made his way to the bank, boots dripping, eyes barely open as he absorbed what Nenyane saw.

It was the third head that came into sharp relief, the transparent appearance of the lingering dead displaced entirely, the grey undertone to its features lost to the growing semblance of flesh. But the hair swayed in a wind that touched nothing else, and the face lifted to sky, to the crown of the trees, as if it could now demand answers from their silent presence.

Stephen was surprised when the third voice joined the song, for the wind responded to that voice; even the skies above seemed to darken with clouds across the perpetual night of the lands. Silver moons vanished, and with it, the visibility they provided; it was not something for which the Hunters were prepared.

Had the song not held them all in its aural folds, apprehension might have blossomed into fear, but it held them.

Nenyane's vision was not impeded by darkness. She had always had excellent night vision, as if darkness was just another color, another filter through which the world was viewed. She could see the creature, and for the first time, Stephen could see it clearly because it was no longer in motion. The forepaws, lion's claws, carved runnels in the earth beneath them, but it no longer lunged at trees; it no longer brought them down.

The eagle sang low; the voice of the third head was higher, stronger.

Just as Kallandras had with Steane, he surrendered melody, stepped into harmony and support as the vocals shifted. In the moonless, clouded darkness, Nenyane could see the luminescent trace of tears grace the almost human face. She could not clearly see its eyes, but the head's gaze was not a danger; what the creature saw in the heart of its own lament was not prey, not quarry.

It occurred to Stephen, watching through Nenyane's eyes, that the lion's roar had contained textures and emotions that none but the bard could hear. But the bard was present, and he had heard what lay beneath the bestial sound; he had used the music he'd mastered and the talent to which he was born to speak, in a fashion, with their enemy.

Stephen heard grief and longing extended over centuries, over a span of time that made Breodanir's history seem so short as to be inconsequential. The creature's loss, its grief, could be a bridge, just as the first tree's song had been a bridge—but it was a bridge that only Kallandras of Senniel could traverse. The Hunters could not. Nor could Nenyane.

Usually she had no desire to do so, no desire to create common fellowship of any kind. He was surprised when he felt her impulse to be heard, to add cadences of personal loss to the small chorus.

But he remembered that if Steane had created a map that they might assess and follow, he had tried to injure—or kill—first.

Yes, Nenyane said. But she did not draw sword. She listened. To his surprise, she closed her eyes.

He would have told her to open them immediately, but a fourth voice joined the three, or perhaps the four; the lion did not sing but its roar was muted and rhythmic. The final voice was similar to it, but that one was the creaking of branches, of bark, the movement of age and weight.

The tree had spoken. It had spoken—in words—to Stephen; Stephen had heard its voice. It had not spoken thus to Ansel or Heiden.

The winds above sheared small branches and new leaves from the tree's boughs; larger branches fell, as they had fallen for the use of the villagers, transported to the wilderness as the lands changed around them.

He wondered if this tree, this remnant of the being who had once been lord of these lands, would find voice again. His sense was that this tree was nearing the end of its life, planted or no, and its one desire was to survive for long enough to strike the creature that had laid it low and deprived it of home.

Perhaps it took power to raise voice at all. Perhaps it took strength that the tree had preserved. For whatever reason, the tree had remained silent except for the creak of shifting branches. Until now.

The tree's raised voice was not a song; it was not a melody or harmony. It did not fold itself into the cadence of the bard's instrument, for the bard had continued to play. No; it was a cry, a single word, in a tone so raw it was painful to hear.

"*Biluude!*"

CHAPTER TWENTY-FIVE

Jarven could feel the tremors in the ground beneath his feet and assumed they were the result of falling trees, but he marked the moment when those tremors became almost rhythmic, a beat rather than a simple act of destruction. He wondered what had changed, but did not spare more thought on it.

He had seen the creature pass by and assumed it had been sent to attack—or destroy—the village. While he did not consider the loss of a village to be strategically good, he was otherwise neutral; he did not know the villagers. Their existence made no difference at all in his life.

There was a possible advantage to his own mission, however: the destruction of the village would provide a focus for his enemies, and he might come upon Rymark while Rymark was intent on fulfilling whatever his duties happened to be in this wilderness. Jarven would not sacrifice an entire village just to distract Rymark and his demonic friends, but if the village was already their target, he might as well seek advantage from events that could not otherwise be changed.

The silence had receded; the earth still moved.

Jarven felt unexpected relief as noise returned more fully. He was far more careful when it did; he understood that the silence itself was a barrier, like the new city walls of Averalaan, beyond which lay the seat of the lord's power.

Rymark had never been the power he had desired to become, but he had always lingered around the edges of that power, his grip too weak to fully take it for himself. What he claimed he was differed greatly from the practical facts, but people were fearful and oft ignorant; some would accept him at his loudly proclaimed word. In his own words, Rymark was a power, a force worthy of respect, fear, and obedience.

Jarven did not expect that to have changed significantly. What he could not fully judge at the moment was how that almost-powerful-enough characteristic would be expressed in Rymark's new context. If he was fair — and it was intellectually useful at the moment to be so — he had no clear metric to evaluate Rymark's hierarchical position. What he knew was that Rymark had chosen to side with the demons. To do their work. The why was far less clear.

What had Rymark seen in the Northern Wastes? He was a man who liked to follow power, who desired to be, always, on the winning side — without a clear plan on how to change the equation. Rymark followed. He could not lead. He could not choose his desired winner, and craft a plan to ensure that outcome.

He assumed power was static.

Had Jarven ever been that ignorant, he would never have left the streets of the holdings. He would never have found a place for himself within House Terafin; he certainly would not have climbed to the pinnacle he had. Had he desired to lead Terafin, he had no doubt he could have become The Terafin. But there were direct responsibilities the ruler of one of The Ten were saddled with, among those more direct access to — and oversight from — the Twin Kings.

Perhaps Rymark had never been self-aware enough to realize what he lacked. He'd assumed he merely lacked the external trappings — that external trappings defined how much power he had. He obeyed others because he lacked those external symbols; he did not command and could not until he himself attained them. His displays of power were therefore reserved for those too menial to have a hope of defending themselves. He was, in Jarven's parlance, a very poor sport. But poor or no, he had, at the moment, a greater understanding of the structures of power that ruled the wild beings than Jarven. Or rather, he had access to knowledge that might lead to that understanding.

Jarven knew things that Rymark did not, and would not. But it was only enough knowledge for Jarven to understand the depth of his own ignorance, which was frankly — even in this wilderness, this place where trees were taller than most of the buildings in Averalaan, where immortal beings in the shapes of beasts spoke with tongues of silver and gold—appalling.

His exploration of the wilderness beyond Jewel's borders had given him some information. The fox's gift had allowed him to gain greater knowledge than he might otherwise have gained; he could survive so much more. But the Shining Court of which he heard rumors and whispers was a grave unknown; how could he fully comprehend the structure of power, the permutations of hierarchy, without a better practical understanding?

Rymark was, therefore, the closest he had yet come. Had he time, he might have attempted to interact with Rymark in a different fashion, to subtly lever that information from the disgraced Terafin councillor. But no. To take that time was to deny himself the power he needed to begin to fully traverse the wilderness in all of its varied forms. The advantage of information was weighed against the need; it was close enough to warrant consideration, but not close enough to change his course of action.

Here, he listened carefully. The wind moved branches, leaves, but this breeze at least did not carry the lord's name in its folds; it moved as breeze moves in the outer world. That was not a guarantee that it did not obey the lord's command. The fox had expected Jarven to know the difference, but his explanation had been extremely lacking.

Seeing Jarven's expression at the time, the fox had added, "the wind is not a good spy. You might think it could be a useful tool, but it is capricious at heart; best to use it for immediate results, rather than to rely on its ability to pay attention to important facts.

"The wind, however, will note when and where the dead walk. The wilderness knows, and those who can summon wind and force the earth to move at their will summon neither in the presence of the dead, unless they wish to destroy the dead. It can be difficult to control the elements in their rage.

"They will, however, rage at each other. It is always best to avoid calling more than one."

Jarven could, at the moment, summon neither.

The demons used fire; Jarven had assumed that the fire was entirely a magical construct. It was only after his compact with the fox—and his endurance of the pain and brief debilitation that agreement had caused—that he could hear the whispers of the fire, the sibilant hiss of something almost sentient. The fire could hear the voice of the dead; the fire would accept their commands. Nothing else.

Jarven wondered if that was why the hells were considered a place where fire reigned.

Assuming that there were demons within the lord's stronghold, he could infer one thing: the lord had enough control of the earth here that the demons could remain relatively unharmed. A mortal like Rymark would be almost irrelevant.

He was uncertain what to expect from the stronghold of a lord of the wilderness, but again, his exploratory forays had taught him much.

In mortal lands, human lords expressed power through wealth, and the obvious signs of that wealth: land, buildings, works of artists of renown.

In the wilderness there were often no such markers. He had once encountered the lord of a wild, uncivilized land, a creature like unto a boar but larger, with fur of silver and eyes of gold; he could not make sense of the creature's animal sounds, but he had felt, in the moment, that he had trespassed, that these lands and that singular creature were one and the same.

He had survived that encounter, and his approach into different lands had been far more careful, far more respectful. But the wilderness was not a one-to-one map of the geography Jarven knew; it was larger by far than the simple outlines of continents could contain. The skies were often amethyst when absent clouds; they were sometimes amber, sometimes blue, and sometimes shades of ash grey. In this land, they were indigo, the color of fallen night; they had not changed yet.

He did not assume that this was a land of perpetual night; he assumed dawn would follow. Eventually.

Each of the wild lands had to be approached as if they were an individual person with whom he had never interacted before. He could make certain base assumptions: people required air to breathe, water to drink, food to consume were they not to perish. Beyond that, age and experience could be inferred—but slowly and with careful observation. People were not a single thing.

Years of honing his skill at observation were an advantage in the wilderness, and Jarven, accustomed to playing a man in his dotage, had no pride to lose in pretending to be an insignificant mortal if it achieved his goals. He did not make that mistake here, and for one reason alone.

The *Kialli* version of sustenance was mortal pain, mortal souls riven from bodies and tormented for the length of three full days. This, too, had been wisdom handed down by the fox, who seemed largely unconcerned with the fate of mortals foolish enough to become demonic fare. The fox was not entirely unconcerned, but the fact of that concern was entirely because he served — truly served — Jewel, the lord of the wilderness in which the elder was rooted.

What she did not allow, he would not allow. No, it was more than that. Jarven played by rules; he obeyed the laws whose breakage would be immediately visible, and whose consequences would be more than a passing inconvenience. His respect for laws was theoretical, but being seen as a law-abiding citizen had distinct advantages. The fox was similar in nature.

But there were things the fox would not allow because of the grief it would cause Jewel. It was an odd combination. Absent Jewel, and the obvious differences in their base state, he and the fox would have been very, very similar people.

But the fox prioritized Jewel's *emotions*. Her feelings. Jarven had made similar choices in the distant past, but it was nonetheless qualitatively different. The fox did so not because he feared the consequences of the loss of Jewel's control — he did not. Whatever occurred should she lose that control would not harm the fox. No, it was her actual feelings, her pain, that he desired to prevent. He made choices in order to spare her from guilt, from the anguish of guilt.

It was the one way in which Jarven considered himself and his chosen master to be very different creatures — the only way. *You do not understand service.*

I do not serve.

Technically this was untrue, but they both understood such service was not a matter of contracts and simple words.

THE FIRST VOICES he heard were muted whispers. The fox's gift had greatly increased the range and acuity of Jarven's hearing; it had done the same for his vision. To his eyes, the night sky and its three moons shed more than enough light. It might have been day had the colors not differed in shade, in hue.

He was not surprised when the trees behind which he had moved and sheltered thinned markedly; he was surprised that they ended

before the shore of a lake. Unlike the tiny lake that existed just outside
the boundaries of Amberg, this lake was larger and deeper; he could
only see its ends because of the trees on the far horizon. The lake itself
was placid, almost undisturbed, but from it rose a large edifice.

There, he thought, with some regret. A palace. A tower. Something
crafted, planned, created from base stone and wood and metal. The lord
of these lands was not animalistic in form or shape, to build such a
structure as the seat of her power.

She was a creature of the wilderness, more akin to Meralonne
APhaniel than the long-ago boar he had first encountered. She clearly
understood the majesty of architecture that defied the normal
constraints placed upon it by gravity, for the palace was, to his eye, an
edifice of stone. It rose; its reflection in still water almost reached the
shoreline.

He wondered how far down it went. Were there basements?
Dungeons? He would likely never know.

He did not immediately approach the trees that existed as thin
extensions of forest; they had a scent that was different, a possible indication of sentience and will. So many of the citizens of the wilderness, in
any land, were planted thus; they could freely roam the lands, but it was
to the trees themselves that their existence was tethered. It was thus in
Jewel's lands, although the *Arborii*, as they were called, could travel—
and take up mortal arms—at their lord's command.

The fox was rooted in Jewel's forest; Jarven had never seen, never
been able to discern, which of the great, ancient trees was the fox's
truest form. Nor had he ever been foolish enough to ask. But his awareness of trees that served as housing for the denizens of the wilderness
had grown; he would not mistake the trees of his prior life with these
ones.

He could hear their voices. He could not understand their speech,
their voices were too quiet—a murmur of sound not unlike the breeze
or the subtle motion of water against short.

But those voices rose in volume, the leaves on thick, high
branches rustling as if in gale. Something had happened. Something
had drawn their attention. He was almost certain that he was not the
cause of their alarm, but retreated, stepping back, drawing silence
and shadow around him slowly and carefully. It was like weaving; or
rather, as he imagined weaving would be had he ever chosen to take
it up.

He stood as trees might stand, as if he were one of them, a simple part of a growing forest.

And he heard a word.

Biluude.

HEIDEN HEARD THE SINGLE WORD; he heard its syllables clearly. But he felt, as it traveled through him in a shock of sound and tremors, that it was not a foreign, unfamiliar word: it was a name. A name that had, until they had stood beneath this very tree, caused nothing but grief and a certainty of the bitterest of losses.

Barrett.

Ansel heard it as Heiden did, and felt it as strongly. But from the shattered remnants of the life they had lived when Barrett had been alive, he heard a terrible, piercing *yearning*. In the days after Barrett's funeral, in the days when Lord Bowgren had descended into drink and fury at things that could not — could never — be changed, Ansel might have uttered that exact cry.

Might have, had not his father's entire existence become just that. Ansel had done what he could as Lord Ansel, but he could not lie to himself: he was not Lord Bowgren. He was not Barrett. He could not do what they did. No one could.

No one did.

Ansel knew now, accepted now, that Barrett would have wept to see what Bowgren had become. What his father had become. He might have even expressed genuine anger and fury of his own.

Instead, he had given his life, and it was his life's blood — his and huntbrothers like him throughout Breodanir's history — that sustained enough of Amberg that the villagers for whom he had hunted and aided in governance still survived. Life, not death. Love, not loss.

Love was not guaranteed to lead to grief in life — but it was far closer for those who hunted, those who ruled, those who were part of Breodanir's nobility. Barrett would have been proud to have been part of the compact that gave Amberg's people any chance of survival, any chance of returning home.

Yes, Heiden said, resolute. He was not Hunter-born. He could not call the Hunter's trance. The endurance with which he ran hunts had been hard-won; he had trained, he had run, he had built stamina through constant, dedicated practice. He had found, in Ansel, a truer brother than he had ever known, ever expected to know.

And he had been *gutted* when Ansel had followed Lord Bowgren's path. He had always known who Ansel was, until that moment. He had always believed—and it was bitterly, bitterly hard by the end—that Ansel would finally emerge from the fury of loss, the fear of it, to become himself again.

And he had.

Heiden knew why Ansel had declared his intention to abandon the Sacred Hunt. He had argued against it in every way he knew how. But he knew he would never have to have that argument again, if they both survived. He would hunt by Ansel's side. He would face the Hunter's Death if Ansel was the chosen quarry.

He would face Barrett's death in that case, as he had promised, when they were children, to do. And he knew, in his heart of hearts, that dying was the easier option. Facing the death of his Hunter, the loss of it, the terrible, terrible emptiness, was far harder than simply dying first.

"The creature stopped." Stephen lifted his voice to be heard. "When the tree spoke, it stopped."

Ansel's eyes narrowed. "What is it doing now?"

"It's moving faster. Much faster. But it's given up on bringing the entire forest down before it reaches us."

"What's Nenyane doing?"

"She's struggling to keep up. But she tells me to tell you that, at the moment, the creature seems to be entirely unaware of her presence; if she wanted, she might be able to bisect a leg or two."

"She hasn't tried?" Heiden asked, before Ansel could.

Stephen nodded. His eyes were closed, which shouldn't have been necessary—but Nenyane was in no way the usual huntbrother.

"She shouldn't. Not yet."

Stephen was silent for a longer beat.

It was Meralonne who answered him, as the bard continued his song, his voice rising as he neared its end. "No. She should not," the mage said again. "Not yet. But you, Stephen—you must now prepare yourself."

"For what?" Ansel demanded, stepping between the mage and Stephen. "We're all prepared for the fight."

"For the small possibility that the creature and the tree who spoke its name so loudly might be somehow saved. I would not be surprised if every sentient being in the lands heard that name—which would not be a problem. They no doubt heard the voice that uttered it, and Lord Ansel, that *will*."

"What do you expect Stephen to do?"

The mage shook his head. "Perhaps nothing," he finally replied, his gaze upon a distant spot Heiden could not see. What he could see was Stephen's growing tension, the line of his shoulders rising, his hands balling slowly into shaking fists.

WHAT STEPHEN DID NOT SAY, what he could not tell them, was that their reaction to the single utterance was lesser in every way to Nenyane's. The word—the name—stopped her in her tracks. She did not recognize it the way she recognized the creature and its abilities; she did not know it, or had not known it, before the reliability of her memories had been riven from her.

In the stillness, her entire being resonated with grief-stricken yearning, the hopeless desire, the way pain informed syllables.

If Heiden and Ansel thought of Barrett—as Stephen knew they must—Nenyane thought of no one. There was no name to contextualize what she felt. The name itself would have been a grace note, a relief. But he had felt this before, when she stood in the Queen's gallery, this terrible, desolate sense of loss, of grief—not the end of the world, but the desire that it end.

She shook herself free of it when the creature cried out, wordless, in shock, all of the heads losing the song, the beat of the more deliberate elaboration of attenuated, distant loss. Nenyane began to move when the creature did. But it was large, and if it had looked cumbersome, if its movements had looked slow, it was not wed to lack of speed as it began to sprint. The trees, it no longer destroyed except incidentally; where there was no clear path, it made one.

The lion exhaled fire, choosing the destructive power of flame instead of the force exerted by bulk and collision; the fire was far faster, and the trees did not burn so much as transform into falling ash. The creature charged in the direction of the tree itself. In the direction of the Hunters, the mage, the bard, and Gervanno.

The fox, good to his word, had vanished. The bard ended his song and set lute aside, drawing two weapons in its place, as if the transition between instruments of song and instruments of death was completely natural and expected. Perhaps, in the wilderness, it was.

Stephen lost sight of the creature as Nenyane raced ahead; he caught sight of the great tree at the heart of the water as she did.

What he saw was not a tree. What she saw in that moment was so different from what his own vision could perceive that he once again forced his eyes to close, losing the overlap of images that would not cohere into a single object. What stood at the lake, legs leading into water, was not a tree; no more was it a man, a person, although it had two legs. Boughs became the frayed and frantic feathers of splayed, pinioned wings. Its edges, the shape of it, were blurred; it seemed to be quivering in place, trapped and held there as it strained for freedom from its cage of roots and water.

Nenyane reached the water ahead of the beast she'd been following; she leapt toward Stephen and he opened his eyes, reality as he understood and perceived it reasserting itself. But he had seen himself through her eyes. He seldom spent time looking in mirrors, and when he did, he was generally inspecting his appearance before he went to dinner, or to meet his mother's friends.

Nenyane saw him almost as he saw himself. Almost. In her vision, he was luminous; a faint, golden light permeated every aspect of his face, his hands. Brightest of all were his eyes, the golden eyes of the god-born, the eyes that had set him apart from his own people because they were the first thing anyone seemed to see.

Which would have been uncomfortable, if his eyes were not closed. He was afraid as she approached, afraid of what she saw, because what she saw was not what he was—not what he thought he was. His eyes did not feel unnatural to Stephen. Until this moment, he had accepted that he was god-born. As the living son of Bredan, he could speak with his father when he chose to do so; he could call the God, and the God would hear his voice.

He knew that other powers had been granted him by the accident of birth parent. He knew that he could bind a person to an unbreakable oath and that breaking that oath was death—a death that Stephen could not prevent, because the oath was inviolable. Once made, it could not be retracted, even should both parties desire to do so.

It was a curse. It was worse than a curse. No child—no young child

—should ever be made to swear an oath that would lead, could lead, to their inevitable death.

The gods didn't *care*. Bredan didn't care. It was the oath that mattered, not the context, not the person who had sworn the oath. Their lives were the bond on which the oath was built—and it took no will, no power, to consecrate. If the oath at the time it was offered was true, was meant, the God accepted it.

He swore, had sworn, he would never, ever consecrate such an oath again. Would never be the vessel by which murder, at a distance, was done. Had the world remained as it had been from the moment of his birth, he would have been determined. Determined and content.

But here, in this wilderness, in this wild, ancient place, he saw his eyes as Nenyane saw them. And he understood that the gods were the very heart of the wilderness: that they had been birthed to it, in it, and they belonged to it so fully they could not—even by abandoning it—be entirely removed.

He was the son of a scion of the wilderness.

The high wilderness, Nenyane said, landing—as if she had literally taken flight—by his side. *I'm sorry.*

The earth had heard his voice when he had offered the living, sentient earth his blood. It was the blood of the Breodani, but he accepted now that it was also Bredan's blood. It served as a potent reminder of Bredan's compact with the wild earth, the slumbering giant upon whose back the whole of Breodanir depended.

Nenyane had sworn no oaths to Stephen. He had not allowed it.

Would not allow it, while she lived.

But he turned—Nenyane turned—her eyes and her sight his while his own eyes once again became tightly shut. She looked to four Hunters: Bowgren and Margen. Alex and Max, as Stephen himself, had not sworn that early oath to anyone, not even to each other. The reasons were different, but the fact was the same.

Between Ansel and Heiden, Stephen could see subtle, golden strands—gossamer, like webbing, the binding so pale were it not night even Nenyane's eyes would not have seen it so clearly. It stretched as they moved, but it never tightened; it never came close to breaking.

Her gaze moved, and with it carried Stephen's—but he knew that he would see the same threads, the same strands, between Brandon and Aelle.

She nodded, although he did not speak. *They can't be broken. They*

*cannot be cut. They look insubstantial to our eyes, but if they could see them
clearly they might be blinded by the truth of it. It is the binding, Stephen. It is*
their oath.

And Nenyane could see it clearly.

She shook her head. *No. I can see it only because of what we are: Hunter,
huntbrother; Bredan's son and Nenyane. Were you not Bredan's son, but Hunter
to my huntbrother, I would see nothing, just as you normally do.*

Something about her words felt off, felt subtly wrong.

Now, watch, she said. *Look. Look at the trapped giant, and see.*

He did as bid, following the direction of her gaze, the intent focus
of it. He could feel the movements of the creature they had assembled
to fight shake the ground beneath their feet, but it had been joined by
the shaking of roots, the trembling of water as those roots twisted and
rose.

Amberg would perish, he thought. If the tree were not here, where
it had been placed so long ago, Amberg would never have survived.

Nenyane concurred, but she felt no fear in this moment — not for the
village, the villagers, or the Bowgren Hunters for whom that village was
revelation and hope.

There are bindings you can see, she told him, as he held breath. *And there
are bindings that* can *be broken. Watch.*

Meralonne did not move. Kallandras did not move. The air did,
pulling hair back and ripping leaves from branches. Stephen did not feel
the voice of earth, and was grateful. Wind touched him, wind pulled
him above that ground; Nenyane paid no mind to it. He could see what
wind touched — or did not touch: the rest of his companions.

There was no oathbinding between the tree and the creature that
could now be seen in the distance — if the only visible evidence of such a
binding were the strands that existed, barely visible, between the two
sets of Hunters.

The creature did not, as Nenyane's previous lectures had indicated,
roar to paralyze those it must defeat; it did not seem to see them at all,
so focused were all three of its mighty heads upon the tree itself.

If the tree had uttered a single word — a name, Stephen now thought
— it followed with no further words, but its branches turned toward the
creature that approached, straining toward it as its roots strained
against the confinement of ground, of earth and water. The momentum
of the creature slowed as it approached the tree; the Hunters scattered
to the left and right because they were directly in its path. It had been

their intent to protect the tree inasmuch as they could, because the tree
was Amberg's survival.

Only Pearl wanted to stand her ground. She resisted Stephen until
he commanded obedience—which he would no doubt pay for later. It
was normal; it was comfortable. It was not what these two creatures
were.

Nenyane did not move. Instead, she held out a hand. *Take it*, she told
him. *Take it, and hold on: I can't do what must be done if you don't.* Her interior
voice trembled. Her hand, as he gripped it, his right to her left, did not.
Her hand was cool, almost hard; when their palms met, she tightened
her grip.

No one could stand and fight like this, not for long. He felt a thread
of giddiness, a thread of something he had never felt in Nenyane's
thoughts before. *Look*, she whispered. The whisper traveled through
him.

He had a blinding headache—the aftereffects of seeing through his
huntbrother's eyes for far too long—but he accepted the pain and
pushed through it.

He could see what she saw. If there were no threads binding the tree
and the creature, there *were* strands—silver and shadow, entwined—that
trailed from the third head of the creature, streaming past its back. He
would have thought them hair, but they extended into the distance from
which it had come.

Yes, Nenyane said. *It's like—and unlike—an oathbinding; it asserts
control continuously. An oath is a choice, a continuous choice; this is unlike that.
Strong bindings allow a master to assert complete control. In theory, you have
complete control over Pearl.* She spoke the dog's name without her usual
disgust. *In practice, the master has control of this creature in the same way.*

Look at Pearl, Stephen said. *Just for a second. Look at my dogs.*

Nenyane did. It was brief—a glimpse, no more—but he could now
see what she meant: there were subtle strands that bound or leashed the
Maubreche dogs, and those strands led to Stephen.

These bindings can be made and they can be broken, Nenyane told him. *But
it is a binding inherent in dogs themselves; they desire the attachment; they grow
into their obedience. You can use it against them at need.*

This is like that?

This is exactly *like that. Come*, she whispered, as the wind lifted them
both. *Come. Let me show you.*

She did not control the wind, but the wind came regardless, lifting her—lifting them both, their hands still joined. As if the tree could see them, as if he could hear them, branches creaked and turned toward the creature, for the creature had, at last, come to a full stop, its attention bound and held by sight of the tree itself, as if the single word the tree had all but screamed continued to echo in its ears.

Why could she see this? Why had she never seen it before? Or had she always seen it? The cost of seeing as she saw had always been high; he couldn't run a proper hunt and slide into and out of her gaze the way he could with his dogs; the way his father could with Arlin.

No, she whispered. *No. I didn't see this, then.*

Then why now?

Because now, she answered, the fear of uncertainty, the self-loathing at lack of clear memory and its deliberate recall, almost obliterated, *now, there is something to cut.*

As she spoke, she drew blade.

"Illaraphaniel!" It was the mage's wind, then. She did not speak anything but the mage's name, but lifted sword, pointing to a spot beyond the creature's back—a safe enough distance from the head whose gaze petrified if one met it with one's own.

Stephen could almost feel the wind pass through him, as if he had lost solidity and could become one with it. But Nenyane's hand was solid in his. He drew no blade, but Nenyane's was glowing, the edge a bright, hard line of gold.

He did not understand what she intended until the moment the wind, presumably obeying the mage, carried them beyond the creature's back, past the flow of wind-swept hair, toward the ashes left in the creature's wake. She raised blade.

Be ready.

Stephen's free hand was empty when his huntbrother swung down, her blade turning at the last moment as she bisected the strands only she could see. No, he thought, that they could both see now.

He reached for the strands as they separated almost in slow motion; her blade rose and fell again, the strike weaker than it might have been had she been standing on the ground. He understood what she wanted, then; he reached for the ends of strands that were still attached to the creature.

Reached for them, expecting they might pass through his palm. He had never experienced his bond with the dogs the same way; had never seen it as a visible attachment, as something that stretched between him and the dogs he loved.

He could not and did not love this deadly, strange creature in the same fashion; he could not think of it as a member of his hunting pack, because it would never be that. He did not fully understand the similarities between it and his dogs, but the strands remained in his hand as he tightened it into a fist. That hand felt empty to all of his senses.

The creature turned its third head, its most human visage, toward Stephen, eyes widening.

Almost without thought, Stephen said, *no*. Then, again, in a stronger and more certain voice, *No*.

It is a binding, Nenyane said. *It is not an oathbinding*.

But —

Yes. There is a reason beyond the oathbinding itself that you are feared, that your death is desirable. And a reason, she added, *that you are necessary. Speak to it*, she added, her own voice becoming far more urgent.

How did one speak to a creature so wild, so ancient, from a vantage of a handful of mortal years? What could be said? What could be asked?

The wind lifted him, lifted them both. Nenyane let go of Stephen's hand.

I am Stephen of Maubreche, he said. *I am Bredan's son*.

To his surprise, the head that turned to face him now was the lion's, the mane gold and shimmering in Nenyane's vision. He opened his own eyes, saw the overlapping images — his, his huntbrother's — and let her vision fade. He could no longer see the strands he'd grasped in his hand, but felt certain they remained there, a subtle, invisible leash.

No, *leash* was the wrong word.

Dogs had always been drawn to Stephen. The Elseth dogs. The King's dogs. He was certain the Margen dogs and the as-yet unmet Bowgren dogs would respond in similar fashion. It wasn't the result of any action Stephen had taken or could choose to take. The Maubreche dogs had — if childhood stories were to be believed — fled their kennels the day after he had been conceived, to rush into the house and toward Lady Cynthia, there to place paw prints all over the front of her dress.

Perhaps it made sense that the head that turned to look directly at him was the lion head, closest to hunting beast. The lion's eyes were gold as they examined Stephen, the light warm and oddly lively.

It was interesting to watch the heads almost collide; the eagle faced forward, and the lion moved swiftly enough, directly enough, that the eagle had to move in order not to be struck by it; its mane, however, covered the eagle's eyes for a moment, and the eagle voiced annoyed displeasure.

The lion head lowered itself, sniffing air; the body trembled in place, indicating that the lion had attempted to reposition its bulk. The eagle was unamused; even the third head glared at the lion.

Stephen understood; he attempted to move closer to the lion head, which was made more difficult by his lack of familiarity with the air upon which he was standing. He did narrow the distance between himself and the creature, the wind carrying him to within reach of the lion head — and its massive jaws.

The dogs were unhappy; they moved of their own accord, positioning themselves far closer to the creature's body than had been originally intended. The rest of the Hunters and their allies stood their ground as the lion opened its mouth, and a tongue far larger than Stephen's arm extended to lick his hand.

Nenyane, help me out here.

Why? You don't need it now. I've done what I could.

He might have argued; arguments were no stranger to their bond. But the third head, the mortal head, turned as well. It made no attempt to lick Stephen, or to touch him at all. The moving strands of hair reminded him of the mage, perhaps because the mage was often caught in a wind that touched little else.

The third head grew in height, or so it seemed, but that was wrong. The neck remained the same length, but beneath it, shoulders emerged from the bulk of the fur-covered body, followed by shoulders and arms. It had two, each longer than Nenyane was tall. Hands emerged last. For the moment, they held no weapons.

Stephen had seen the mage pull weapons from thin air — and sheathe them into it. He had no doubt that the creature could do the same, but took minor comfort from their absence. He waited.

"Oathborn we were, oathbinder. You are mortal, but perhaps your blood will give you some instinctive understanding of what our birth means; perhaps it will not. You travel with the last of the first princes, and he will understand, scion of the great White Lady who once ruled the primeval forests.

"We do not bind ourselves to oaths easily—or at all—while we stand in our creator's shadow. We might swear blood oaths, but they are not the covenants of your parent. My parent still lived when I first agreed to serve the lord of these lands. And I served him well, and willingly. If there was a binding, it was not a binding of fear, not a binding of power, for truly we were evenly matched."

He did not ask how the creature knew.

"For many long years I did serve. In his stead, I traversed the wider wilderness, fashioning tales and songs of the experiences that were no longer to be his while he ruled. Understand that those who desire to rule are bound by what they rule; only if they choose to forsake it do they know freedom.

"I had freedom, in his stead. When war came at last to these lands— as it must when gods walk—I fought by his side. Those days are so far behind me I feel them as a dream: as a time when the world felt new and I had hope. Perhaps hope is for the youthful; I cannot say.

"But I was not by his side when he perished, for we had known peace for some centuries by then, and he was restless. Always restless. But he would not abandon the lands he held, or the creatures who depended upon his rule.

"I do not know how he perished. I know only that he did—but even distant, I heard his cry of grief and rage and I hastened my return. I did not recognize the lands that had been my home, not at first; those elements that were familiar were changed, the shadows across them darker, harsher, as if bright color had fled.

"And it had been Winter for so long Summer was almost a myth, a story. But Summer has returned to the lands, and the lands struggle to throw off Winter's grip. Most lands."

The head turned now toward the tree.

"I was told he had died, betrayed by a trusted servant. I was told he had been buried. Perhaps only one of these was true—but the lord I have served since his death did not speak of this.

"She is not what he was. Our freedom to leave—and return—was of little interest to her; she feared to lose us, always, to other lords, other lands. I wished vengeance, as you must suspect. Even that was to be denied me. She assured me that vengeance was impossible for the traitor had perished in the ensuing battle, and in the absence of lord and traitor, she had taken the lands; she had always been a power. She had preserved his people.

"But it was hollow. In truth, I did not wish to leave again for a long time; leaving the lands had been my worst mistake. Had I been by his side, he would not have fallen. But I was not; I had traveled to find new songs, new stories to bring him, to ease the restlessness of the captivity of rulership."

"And you remained here?"

"I slept when grief abated; I slept long enough that, were I a tree, I would have grown roots so deep I might never know movement again. I dreamed in my sleep; I dreamed of war and death and the Lord of the Dead; I dreamed of the rot of the land, as death encroached and transformed all. I did not care. Even in the worst of those dreams, I did not struggle. Death had claimed the only thing that gave life value." They bowed head, eagle and person; hair framed the human face.

She had not once attempted to petrify Stephen, and he did not believe she would.

Above the creature's heads, the heaviest of the tree's branches creaked ominously.

"When I woke, I was bound. I was bound to her, to her will; I was chained to her, to the lands she ruled. I was angry. I considered it a betrayal. But even the anger was dim and distant; what matter servitude, when existence itself was attenuated pain?

"Only when the dead came did I realize the error I had made. For if I had countenanced loss and a new lord for these lands, not even I could stand still and acquiesce to an alliance with the dead. Thus, my long slumber; thus, the portent dreams offered one who was too numbed by loss to respond well."

"You broke through the barrier that separates our lands."

"Yes, at my lord's insistence, at her command. I found a land of mortals, and only mortals; they were as forest creatures to me. She desired the breaking of boundaries put in place by gods. I did not. But her control was strong; I could not move entirely by my own will.

"Were it not for the dead, I would not have struggled against it. But the dead brought the Silences to these lands." Stillness enveloped her, as if the mention of these creatures was enough to end conversation. But conversation continued. "With the advent of the Silences, some of her control slipped. Not all, but some.

"And with your intrusion, the rest. I cannot hear her. I cannot feel her endless compulsion. I am free. I could, if I desired to do so, flee these tainted lands."

Stephen raised head; she was looking directly at him. This time, he did not attempt to look away. "If you would leave these lands, I have a boon to ask of you, in return for the freedom I have returned."

The creature smiled. Mortal teeth were not so sharp as theirs. "You have not returned freedom to me, not yet, little mortal. Can you not feel what you hold?"

Nenyane moved, then, leaping forward, her feet far more certain in the folds of air than Stephen's. Her blade was in her hand.

Nenyane, don't.

She failed to hear him.

But it was not her sword that drew the creature's eye. Perhaps it was Nenyane's expression; Stephen couldn't see her face, just the line of her shoulders almost in front of his eyes.

Silence fell again. The lion growled at Nenyane.

No, Stephen said, as if the lion were one of his pack. *She is also mine.*

The growl edged into a whine, and from there into silence once again.

"You. It is you. I did not recognize you, you have changed so much. I might never have recognized you at all. Is he your master?"

"He is mine," Nenyane said, an edge in the words. "You will not harm him."

"Even had you not attempted to warn me, I would not, now." To Stephen's surprise, the creature laughed, the sound warm, almost affectionate. "But I understand why you are here. The dead drew you, as they must." Her hair moved, not her hands; tendrils reached up, crossing the divide that separated Nenyane and this third head. Strands touched Nenyane's face, Nenyane's hands, before once again falling away. Nenyane made no move to cut them.

"Bredan's son, come. I give my word—and I will swear a binding oath—that I will not harm you or your companion. I will not threaten you, and if you desire to hold my leash, I will accept its weight—it will be gone before I could feel it as prison or restraint, for the god-born are not granted even the normal span of a mortal life."

Stephen shook his head. "I will not bind you."

"Will you not? But why?"

Nenyane was, predictably, annoyed, but the annoyance was deeper. *You don't understand,* she snapped.

He almost snapped back, but this was not the time, not the place; he was aware that his words could touch the wound that festered.

This is the wilderness, and they are a creature born to and of it. They did not offer on a whim. They offered because that's what they expect. It's the only true oath they can swear to you.

"I know it is the gift of my blood, my birth," Stephen said, the words more measured than they would have been had he not had Nenyane shouting in his ear. "But there are many reasons—some good—to become forsworn, and the oathbinding will not recognize any of them."

She was confused; she made no effort to hide this. "The binding oath is not a cage," she finally said, voice soft, confusion infusing the words. "Perhaps you do not understand its effect?"

Stephen said nothing.

"Or perhaps you only see the cost of its breaking. To one such as I, it still offers freedom. Understand that. The oath does not change my desire, my will; it does not prevent me from making a choice. It will not prevent me from choosing my own death, should that be the only choice I feel I can make. It is the gentlest of bindings. It is my choice to offer an oath from which the binding can be woven; were it not, the binding could not be made.

"And the choice to break it is also mine, should the need arise. It is unlike the binding you have broken in every possible way; it was the gift of Bredan to those who dwell in the wilderness."

"Death isn't a gift."

"And now, you speak as a child. There are many, many ways in which death is exactly that. But I have offered; if you will not accept, you will not. It is a far kinder, far less restrictive bond than the one you have cut and taken for yourself. But regardless, I will not harm you. I will not harm your companion. If you value those who stand beyond us now, I will not harm them, either.

"I am not certain that I could escape an attempt to do so without harm—or death. Illaraphaniel is here. Illaraphaniel is here, as he should be." The almost human head turned toward the mage as she spoke; the expression she sheltered was a soft grief, the echo of loss contained only in distant memory. For a moment, Stephen thought she would raise voice to speak to the mage; the moment passed in silence before she once again turned to Stephen. "You asked a boon for the freedom that you have not entirely granted me; I would hear it now, for I have one to ask as well."

"When you attempted to break the barrier, you entered a mortal village. Fully half of the people who dwelled within it were turned to stone."

"Indeed. It was the kinder choice, given those who serve this land's lord." The smile was sharper, thinner. "And no, I did not do so as an act of kindness."

"I wish you to reverse the petrification. Free them."

"I would have to return to the village to do so."

"Could you?"

"There is no guarantee, unless the lord of your lands allows it."

"You did not require that permission the first time."

"No. I could possibly force my way through the cracks in the barrier that separate us; it is how I reached that mortal village at all. But the barrier holds, and the cracks shift."

Stephen had so hoped the petrification could be revoked at a distance. Nenyane was, predictably, annoyed.

"You might attempt to compel me."

"You don't believe I would succeed."

"Will is not power," the creature replied. "I am far less certain of your failure than you yourself seem to be. I am, however, almost certain you will not make that attempt."

Stephen should have been surprised; he was not. Something about the binding itself clearly went in both directions—just as it did with his dogs. He could command his dogs; could force them to act against their desire. He very seldom did. They obeyed him almost perfectly because that was their desire. To force them to do something that was intrinsically against their nature was, he knew, to break things if the power was not used very sparingly. Even in Pearl's case, he cajoled; it was his tone, his urgency, that pushed the dog in the direction he wished her to take.

This creature was not his, not of his pack, and would never be. But he knew there was similarity in the interaction: if he could compel, the binding itself would bear the cost.

"What boon would you ask of me in return?"

"Allow me to touch this tree."

CHAPTER TWENTY-SIX

Jarven was at a crossroad; he felt it in the sudden hush that descended in the wake of the single spoken word, as if even the wind did not wish to interrupt the voice, the resonant echoes of the syllables it had uttered. His night vision far excelled that of his youth; he could see clearly. Could see the moment the sky itself rippled, becoming, for a heartbeat, the clear sky of a cloudless day, sun at its height.

Night reasserted itself in the moment that followed, the moons once again supreme. He had not seen the sun at all. Instinct made him withdraw further into the forest. It was perhaps not the wisest of choices, for in the wake of returning night, even the moons' light dimmed; the darkness was deeper, blacker. For a moment the stars were absent.

It was not the darkness that alerted Jarven; it was the cold. The forest had not been chilly in his travels, although his tolerance for shifts in temperature, like his night vision, had become far better. He was accustomed to unpredictable changes in climate, in geography that should not have been possible; he could take two steps and find himself in desert, where he had walked in northern forest, or southern jungle. The climate was dependent in all ways on the will of the lords that ruled those lands. Only in lands as yet unclaimed did the seasons revert to summer.

Here, it was no longer summer. It was, he thought, winter, the like of which he had encountered only once before at the edge of the Northern Wastes. It was the only place in which the mortal lands and the hidden wilderness meshed as if they were one and the same.

There, Jarven had heard the name of the ruler of those frozen lands so clearly even he had been impressed into almost apprehensive stillness. It had not lasted. It would not last. Will was the coin the wilderness demanded for autonomy. Will, intent, focus.

He had not found purchase or entry into the heart of the Wastes: the citadel, glimpsed in the distance, in which the Shining Court made its home. There, the winds that howled were almost natural; here, he felt their echo. The cold they carried was death to the man he had once been.

He was not that man. If he succeeded here, he would never be that man again.

He could sense the creatures the fox called the dead; he understood, as he looked up, that this night was theirs, now. But he could no longer sense Rymark; the scent of the dead was so strong, it overwhelmed subtler trails. He found his hands clenching and was annoyed; instinct could not be allowed to override will.

He had thought to traverse the lake, if possible; to find entry into the citadel at the lake's heart. He was accustomed to revision of plans when the circumstances changed — so accustomed, in fact, that planning at all could seem like a waste of his time. But the plans required some knowledge, some ability, and those made turning on the spot far safer.

Safety was illusion. It had always been illusion.

Had it been safety he desired, he could have simply curled up and perished. Did he believe in security? Yes. If he, or those he had chosen to safeguard, were the target, why make it easier for the would-be killers? It was a game.

It was a deadly game, but Jarven did not play games of any kind to *lose*. He did not prize *safety* except as a measure of victory.

This was a game, yes. Not *the* game, not yet — he did not understand the rules well enough to deliberately engage with it. But he understood them far better than he had on the day he had accepted the fox as master. Soon. Soon, he would join the true game.

Let it be soon.

Rymark was a coward at heart, a man who did not take risks with any willingness or acknowledgement that they were, in fact, both choices and chances. Were he Rymark and the sky had darkened thus, the air chilled, he would flee. He might disguise that flight as retreat or possibly the need to relay information to a distant lord, a distant power; he would not stand and fight.

He would leave that, Jarven thought, to the dead. The *Kialli* and the lord who had chosen to ally herself with their power.

There.

A bridge rose up from the water of the lake. He had seen many things in his travels and would not have been surprised had that bridge been a thing of contained water or frozen ice; it was not. He thought it wood, or perhaps steel—but steel was in very short supply in the wilderness. Wood, then—but dark and perfect as it stretched from citadel to shore.

A gate opened; light could be glimpsed from the interior of the palace. That light was broken by the movement of the lord's people. The lord's allies. Long were the shadows each cast. None were familiar.

———

STEPHEN TURNED TO ANSEL. Bowgren's fate was Ansel's burden, Ansel's responsibility; if he granted the favor asked by this creature and it was the wrong choice, what remained of Amberg would never return home. They had gathered and planned to face this creature—and to defeat it—but they had understood that the creature was not the ultimate enemy. If the creature were dead, if they could achieve that, they would catch enough of the lord's attention that that lord herself would come.

As if the creature could hear his thoughts, the human-seeming head said, "She will come. What you have done is a far graver threat to her rule than my death would have been. Had you killed me, she would merely gauge your power from my death. You have not. But should you kill me now, she would not know. She cannot command me. Even were she to arrive in person, she could not—and it is loss of control she fears.

"How many do you believe serve willingly?"

The creature waited. Two heads were turned to the tree and its high branches, its crown. The lion watched Stephen. "Will you allow me to approach the tree?"

He had no answer; it was not his answer to give.

Ansel understood command in an emergency; he knew how to use the tools his nobility had granted him. A flicker of doubt, of uncertainty, crossed his face; he brought his expression under control. He glanced once at Meralonne APhaniel, who had neither moved nor spoken since the creature had come to a halt; the glance was brief. The mage had no intention of intervening.

Nenyane almost did; Stephen held her back. *He must make the decision.*

He doesn't have enough information —

He has enough. He is Lord Ansel. He understands the weight of the title, and it is Bowgren lands under threat, and Bowgren people at risk.

Nenyane took a step toward Ansel—the first away from Stephen since they'd arrived. She stopped before Stephen could speak again, and turned to glare at the bard—who had disarmed himself, but had not otherwise moved.

Ansel stepped toward the creature who waited. He bowed to the human head. "I am Lord Ansel of Bowgren," he said, voice low but steady. "I owe a great debt to this tree. It is to defend it that we gathered here."

"Not to kill me?" A thread of amusement colored the words.

"We have not attacked. Nor will we unless you attempt to harm the tree."

"What debt do you owe?" the creature asked, although the head that spoke did not turn back to Ansel. Hair moved, lengthening as if tensile; it reached for the tree's branches, but fell short.

"It protected what remained of our village. The water over which it presides is pure, and safe to drink. Amberg built a fence with the branches it allowed to fall, and they have been safe within its boundaries."

"I see. The roots here are intricate and deep; the tree has grown in this place for a long time. How did it come to be here?" They asked the question not of Ansel, but the tree itself.

"We believe that the tree was planted here long ago." It was Ansel who answered, his answer far more careful, far more deliberate, than the replies that had come before. He turned to Stephen.

Stephen nodded, and moved to stand beside Ansel, Heiden at his back. "What we understand, we were told by a man who ruled a small field within this domain. When the previous lord was betrayed, that lord did not perish; he was offered a choice, should he desire it, to strike back against his enemy."

"Continue."

"He was planted. There, in lands that were not under the dominion of the new lord, and here, in lands that were once his." He did not mention the third land the tree's roots touched.

"What was the name of the lord who saw to this planting?" the voice had cooled.

"He did not give it."

They glanced at Ansel. "You did not ask."

"Had he desired to share it, he would have offered it."

"And he planted the former lord?"

"So he said. But he also said he owed a great debt to the Firstborn. The Oracle." He swallowed. "She told him we would come to these lands, and that we would require his aid. His aid, and the aid of the tree."

"And you are here. I mean no harm to this tree. I could never harm it; were it in my power I would strengthen it enough that it might stand eternally against its foes." The creature turned once again to Ansel. "Your permission?"

Ansel could not doubt those fervent, softly spoken words. He nodded, and offered the creature a bow.

They did not see it. The whole of their attention—saving only the lion's—was focused on the tree itself. The creature's great feet sank into water, but avoided crushing obvious roots, a difficult dance given the size of those feet and the number of roots that lay between them and the heart of the tree itself. Had wings sprouted from that body, Stephen would not have been surprised; the head of the eagle almost implied their existence.

But no; wind came instead. He was uncertain under whose command; the creature evinced no surprise at its presence. Hair reached out, straining, until it touched the trunk of the tree itself.

The wind crackled; small branches and leaves fell. The whole of the tree seemed to be straining—as strands of hair had done—without success. Stephen almost looked away; there was something so raw about the way these two, tree and three-headed creature, reached for each other; nothing else in the world existed for them in that moment.

———

WHEN FIRE CAME, Jarven was not surprised; fire was the weaponry of the demons.

"You should not be here, cub."

Visceral annoyance hovered beneath Jarven's expression as he gazed down at his foot; there, one paw far heavier than something so small should be, stood the elder.

"Here," Jarven replied, voice soft as he knelt, "is where my quarry is—or was." He knew better than to offer the fox frustration, but it was exceedingly difficult to be respectful. Jarven had never worked well with others. He could command them, and had; but in the field, he worked alone. Had insisted on working alone.

In part, he wished secrecy. He did not wish to reveal his methods or movements to those who might, in future, become his opponents. In larger part, he simply disliked the need to consider and coordinate with others. He had not expected the fox to come.

"You are not yet at your full power."

And whose choice was that? Jarven's smile was austere; he said nothing.

"She comes, now."

"Not yet, Eldest." He did not ask if the fox could see the demons. Of course he could. But to Jarven's eyes, the host that marched across the bridge seemed entirely demonic in nature. They were not few in number. He rose, fox in arms, and observed.

He was annoyed; the annoyance was sharper, harsher, than it had been in decades. Almost, it moved him to act impulsively. He had survived such impulses in his youth, but not easily; he could not afford it here. Age had brought him self-governance, the ability to control his immediate desire.

The dead in the wilderness were not numerous. He knew that greater demons could compel lesser kin; given the numbers here, there was at least one *Kialli* of note. Possibly two. Fire replaced the interior light of the citadel as this force moved, wreathing them in its redder glow.

The fox tensed; he grew weightier in Jarven's arms. "Was your quarry in this place? I do not sense him now."

Nor did Jarven, which was the cause of his growing anger.

"Perhaps I have set you too difficult a task," the fox said, as if he were discussing inclement weather. Jarven knew the tone well, he had used it so often in his previous life.

"Too tedious a task, certainly."

The fox chuckled. "Were the Lord of the Hells to descend upon the wilderness where we stand, not one lord of any land would now come to the aid of this lord. Not one."

"They would have to know, Eldest. Were I lord of this land, I would make certain that not even rumor of such association escaped."

"Perhaps that was her hope, but if so, she is far more foolish than a lord should be and remain ruler."

Jarven thought of the impenetrable Silence, but did not argue. "What do you wish done now?"

"I wish the dead to perish. She has not joined this army."

"No. I do not believe she will."

"Oh?"

"It is a gamble of power. You are correct: should word escape—and it will—the wilderness will turn against her. The earth is quiet, here; she cannot call it, if I have understood your lessons correctly. She cannot call wind or water—not while the demons are too close. They have summoned fire."

"It is arrogance, yes. Fire in the forests will damage her lands."

"She may choose to leave the citadel once there is enough of a gap between her forces and those of her allies; she cannot march with them if she hopes to retain any vestige of respect."

"She has forsaken that," the fox replied, watching the demon-kin, his expression almost bored. Jarven noted the moment it changed.

He had thought the demons had summoned wild fire. He saw, in a moment, that he was wrong. Wings of flame unfurled beneath the twin moons, rising and spreading until they covered much of the visible sky.

"Come away," the fox commanded. "While it is safe to travel, come. She is foolish beyond belief to have accepted this one as ally."

"If we wait, we might gain entry to the citadel once they have passed."

"They will not pass us by," the fox snarled. "I might go unseen by the dead should I choose to remain hidden, but you are cursed with the gift of mortality; that one will see you no matter where you choose to hide."

"I wish to ascertain that my quarry has indeed fled these lands."

"He has," the fox growled. "We will retreat, cub. Now."

TO JARVEN'S SURPRISE, the fox leapt out of his arms and proceeded on foot. Jarven followed.

"Why are you lagging? You are capable of greater speed."

"I am uncertain that you have chosen the right direction if we wish to avoid conflict."

The fox's growl was low, deep.

Jarven met the elder's glare in silence. It was not yet the silence that was, in Jarven's opinion, the lord's best defense. He had no need to ask the fox where he intended to travel; he knew. He considered his own options. He did not wish to be drawn into a conflict between the Hunters and the demons, but did not labor under any illusions; should the fox return to what remained of the mortal village, Jarven would follow.

And it was to that village that the fox turned.

Or perhaps to Gervanno di'Sarrado.

Jarven lacked—had always lacked—comrades, largely by his own choice; he had allies, but allies were always a matter of mutual goals and momentary convenience. He was irritated because, at base, the fox was the same. Had been the same, when they had first met. It was the recognition of a kindred spirit that had drawn the fox to Jarven, and Jarven to the fox, much to Finch's worry.

Jarven had no desire to double back for a Southern cerdan. "May I point out that Illaraphaniel is with the Hunters?"

"You may. I fail to see the relevance. Or perhaps you wish to imply that my presence, my power, is irrelevant?"

Jarven shook his head. "I am merely surprised that you involve yourself in something you have clearly stated is of little concern."

"Do not test my patience. I find I have little of it." The fox stalked away.

Jarven followed.

———

STEPHEN DID NOT UNDERSTAND what the lord of the small, gold field had meant by planting; nor did he understand what the tree itself meant. Mortals were not planted, to his knowledge; if they lay beneath the earth's surface it was because they were dead.

Dead beneath graves and headstones, some stone, some wood. Above their corpses, mourners gathered, many at the day of interment, in ones and twos thereafter; it was where they might grieve in silence and privacy. The dead caused pain, but time lessened it; the dead did not speak.

The tree was not dead, but had been buried in secret in the wild earth. Something still remained of its essence and will, and it reached now for the creature they had meant to face and kill. And that creature reached for him, the lion head at last turning away from Stephen of Maubreche.

"It is not the time," Meralonne said, which surprised Stephen; no other dared to speak, as if the silent yearning between the two beings was a demand for privacy.

Not one of the creature's three heads turned toward the mage, but the human head spoke. "What is the time? I am here, now. I am here, and I will never leave his side again."

The mage nodded. He drew blade; it was a blinding blue that seemed by the harshness of its light to reach for white and hold it in its heart. "It is not of you, or to you, that I speak. It is to the one who called your name; to the one who, betrayed, allowed himself to be buried, to grow roots in many lands while he bided time.

"It is almost time, but not yet; if he uproots himself here, now, he will fail in the only hope that has sustained him."

"You are seldom so artless in the lies you choose," the creature replied, but without heat. "The lord will come, and if he but uproots himself, he will face her as he desired. It is for the lesser mortals, all, that you are concerned. You know as well as I that uprooting is done at risk to the land itself."

"Perhaps. But had he not cared about the land itself, he would never have been betrayed; he would not be here at all. It is by his roots in a land that will drift that he survived at all; by the roots that he laid in other lands that the mortals survived. And it is by the hands of one of those mortals that you yourself have the freedom to choose where you make your final stand.

"You are not the only one to be bound in such a fashion; I wish Bredan's son to travel."

"Where, Illaraphaniel?"

"Where he will. You know what he must face, in the end."

"I know what you must face," they countered, their expression softening not with kindness but attenuated grief. "But it is not your desire that I must discern. If you wish to kill me, you may try—you must know my death will not be guaranteed. I have no desire to prove my power in such a battle."

"You have aged."

"As have you, Illaraphaniel. The time that should never have touched you sits heavily upon your shoulders; it is not the mantle I would have ever guessed you would choose." Her smile was of a piece with her expression: dangerously compassionate.

Stephen did not need to be told that pity was *never* offered those of power in the wilderness; not where it could be witnessed.

"But it is not your choice that is my concern. It is his, and his choice is not yours to make, be you ever so gracious as to offer your advice."

Meralonne's hair began to move in the breeze; he did not put up his sword. The hair of the creature's human head moved in a similar fashion, but she turned once again to the great tree.

It creaked as if it were attempting to move; the creature moved instead, until its human chest was pressed against the obsidian bark. Arms lifted—the arms that had emerged from its body—and wrapped themselves around the trunk, at a greater height than anyone who could not walk the air could achieve.

Biluude sang.

Song had so much power in the wilderness. Even Breodani funeral dirges seemed pale echoes in comparison—but they were the closest comparison Stephen could make. He could not understand the singer's words, but words were almost superfluous; they were barely necessary to anchor emotion.

Kallandras did not sing. But when the mage began to move the bard turned toward him, his eyes clear, his expression oddly neutral. The mage stopped, sword in hand, silver eyes narrowed. Kallandras nodded. His hands remained empty until Nenyane spoke.

"They're coming." Her hands gripped sword instantly, and a few yards away, Gervanno di'Sarrado armed himself in like fashion. "Illaraphaniel."

Meralonne turned then, away from the three-headed creature and the tree they embraced. He shook himself, or seemed to; his robes gave way instantly to bright, clean armor. "It appears that we have visitors. Perhaps all advice will soon be rendered meaningless."

The creature did not answer; the song did not bank.

As voices rose, the light of the twin moons dimmed almost to grey, and into the clearing around the lake came shadow and fire.

WINGS OF FLAME spread beneath the darkened sky, lending it a red cast. The being who had spread those wings carried fire in his hands: a bright red sword and a shield of similar color. Around him, shadows he did not cast, were demons. Stephen did not count them.

Twelve, Nenyane said. *Twelve of any note, and a few imps cowering behind them.*

To Stephen's surprise, it was the imps that drew her attention and her concern.

They're no advantage on the battlefield, but they are demonic in nature, the equivalent of rats that scurry underfoot. They cannot arrive here by their own locomotion — not yet, and if we are victorious in the end, not ever. Yet they are here.

He understood. They did not surge forward; were it not for Nenyane, he might not have seen them at all. His dogs spread out, and he jumped between their eyes, counting again. *They are only six.*

They should be zero.

He understood. His sword was in his hand — he had drawn it almost at the moment Gervanno had drawn his. *Can the Margen guards handle them?*

They could handle one, perhaps. But they don't have the weapons, and their skill with the weapons they do have will make the imps very hard for them to kill.

The imps were here for the villagers.

Nenyane did not tell Stephen that the villagers of Amberg would be able to defend themselves against the imps. It would have been a lie.

Can they breach the fence?

The answer should have been yes. Yes, they could — just as easily as anyone present. The fence might have stopped placid cows were it situated in a field; it would not stop anything else. But the fence itself had protected Amberg from the encroaching, living wilderness. Given the hatred the wilderness felt for the dead, he felt that the fence itself might keep the imps at bay.

He looked across his huntbrother to Heiden. "Demons are coming," he said, voice low. "Nenyane says some of those demons would be considered powerless by their own kind. No demons are powerless against mortals. We believe they are meant to attack the citizens of Amberg while we fight here."

Heiden tensed.

"Nenyane also believes that the fence made of the branches of this tree will prove a defense against those demons—but it's essential that no one in Amberg leave the boundaries of the village transcribed by that fence. No one."

Heiden knew, just as Stephen did, that the only people likely to leave were children.

"Can you deliver word to the village head? From you, it will carry more weight."

"Are you certain there are none already there?"

Stephen nodded, because Nenyane was certain. "Sanfel will go with you."

Heiden's eyes widened in surprise. "You can't afford that if you're here."

"I can. I'll have seven dogs. The King's dogs require more control than mine—Sanfel won't attempt to run back unless I'm mortally injured."

"You have six dogs," Heiden said, obviously referring to Steel, who remained by Max's side. He started to speak, stopped, and glanced at Ansel. He then inhaled. "I'll be back as soon as I can."

Ansel met Stephen's gaze, nodded, and turned to face the coming fire. Stephen's dogs watched the imps, but it was difficult; the flame-winged demon drew the eye, demanding attention.

It always seemed wrong to Stephen that beauty could be so dark, so deadly, so inimical to life, but this demon was beautiful. In size and shape—excepting only the wings—it was of a height with Meralonne, and its hair was the same silver sweep, unbound, unfettered. It did not move in the breeze, if breeze touched it at all.

Even at this distance, the demon's eyes could be clearly seen: they were silver, just as Meralonne's, and they widened briefly when Meralonne APhaniel took to the air, stepping lightly into the wind's folds as the wind grew frantic.

"Illaraphaniel," the demon said, voice soft but strong enough to carry to all present—all save the tree and the creature who had once served it loyally.

"Vallarion."

IT WAS A NAME; Stephen heard it almost as if the mage had two voices. One spoke the name wearily, each syllable tinged with grief and sorrow; the other spoke with the very essence of rage.

Nenyane was silent.

You recognize him.

Kialli, she said. He had heard her speak the word before, but within the huntbrother's bond he felt the world differently. To walk at all as they walked was to walk in pain, to surrender nothing of their past, of the lives that had ended when they had chosen to serve the Lord of the Hells. Memories dimmed with time—but not their memories. He wondered if the *Kialli* regretted the choice they had made.

Yes.

Could they not make a different choice?

Could Barrett? Now, in this moment, could Barrett make a different choice? He can't. He's dead.

Demons did not look dead to Stephen, but they never had; how could something that moved, that spoke, that *felt* so strongly be dead?

Nenyane did not answer; to her, they were dead. *Yes. And if you've grown to understand Ansel at all, you know just how destructive death can be.* Her interior voice softened, then. *Illaraphaniel and his kin are strong, but it is not grief alone that motivates them; it is rage and pain at the worst betrayal in the annals of the White Lady's history.*

She turned, briefly, in the direction of the mage. *Were they not what they are, were they not dead, they would be dead by the hands of the* Arianni. *They chose. You do not understand. She was their creator, their personal god, their everything; her whim was their will. They fought gods, Stephen, when the gods walked. They rode in her host at her command. She was their sun, their moon, their seasons, their reason for war and for peace.*

They could ride as one because they were almost one.

But the demons are those who chose—for reasons none of the Arianni *could truly understand—to betray the White Lady. They chose Allasakar.* Nenyane frowned, then.

He did not ask her how she knew; she did not have the leisure to rail against her ignorance. *It is what the Arianni are: part of the White Lady. She gave them some of her essence, as Firstborn, as Queen, as mother. While they live, that essence is theirs; once they perish, it returns to her. It returns to her, and should she desire it, she can remake, or make anew. Should she so choose, she might annihilate all of the* Arianni, *and the power that gives them life would return to her. She would be far, far stronger than she is now.*

But those who chose to betray her, those who chose the god we do not name, pledged that essence, that essential self, to the enemy. How, I do not know. Why, I can guess. While the gods walked the plane, while the traitors were among the living, it was not known. But that essence was lost the moment they made their choice. Her power was lessened, forever. They would not return to her. But the Kialli have will, power, identity; it is to hold onto those bitter memories that they are what they are.

Stephen looked at his huntbrother in the silence that remained after the two names had been spoken. *Who was he?*

He was one of the princes: when the host was whole, he rode at Illaraphaniel's side. Of those princes, only Illaraphaniel remains among the living. Those who chose the enemy reside in the Hells; it is seldom that they return to these lands which would reject them.

Stephen didn't understand the words the demon had spoken. Kallandras stiffened but said nothing; he had armed himself but did not move, his gaze upon the lesser demons shadowed by wings of fire.

Meralonne broke the hush. The wind howled as he took to the skies, blade drawn; it almost screamed when the winged demon did the same. The lesser demons leapt forward as well, as if the movement of these two were the only signal required.

It was certainly the only one Nenyane needed.

SHE COULD DO what Stephen could not; he had always known it. But it had become clearer and clearer as their stay in the Redoubt—and beyond—extended. She stepped into the folds of Meralonne's wind, and they carried her as if she were a simple extension of the mage, the mage's desire; he could not do the same.

The bard could—and did—but made no move toward the winged demon, instead tracking the progress of those on the ground. Stephen turned his attention the same way; even could he stand on the wind as his huntbrother did, all of his training was ground-based, dog-based.

Max and Alex were also on the move, Ansel between them, Heiden absent from the line as he ran to deliver the message vital to Amberg's continued survival. What was a village, after all, if all of its occupants were dead?

Stephen summoned the trance as well; here, reflexes, speed, vision, hearing, even scent would be necessary.

GERVANNO DI'SARRADO WATCHED as Nenyane of Maubreche launched herself into the sky and failed to land. His observation of the Northern Widan made clear where her feet found purchase, but she had gone to a battlefield that Gervanno, without intervention, could not join. Nor did he regret it.

He stood in the lee of demonic wings, and froze there, the heat they shed not touching him at all. He was, he knew, beneath the creature's notice—as he had been once before, on the merchant roads leading toward the King's City in the Kingdom of Breodanir.

This was not the demon who had destroyed Evaro's caravan—and every living being that comprised it, saving only Gervanno. He knew it; there were no wyverns, no breaths of fire that instantly turned the landscape to ash and dust. But every instinct within him screamed in sudden, immobilizing terror: this creature was far, far more dangerous.

He had not felt this terror in the streets of the King's City; had not felt it in Maubreche. It had destroyed his life on the merchant road, and it attempted to destroy him again; although his hand gripped his sword, he was frozen.

Perhaps he would have remained that way as the demons closed in, shadows moving against a sky made crimson by fire. Crimson gave way to sheets of blue as red sword and blue sword clashed; he looked up involuntarily. There, Nenyane and the Northern Widan attacked the demon who was clearly in command of the rest.

"Gervanno!" He heard Nenyane's cry.

Heard it, absorbed it, understood it. Stephen was on the ground. Gervanno was meant, in this moment, to protect the boy because Nenyane, in the air, could not.

As if his spoken name was a spell, or more accurately, a key, he found both breath and motion again. Beneath his feet, Leial barked. Had he forgotten Leial? Yes. In fear, he had forgotten even the one companion he might be allowed to keep.

Gervanno stepped in, stepped up, as the demons converged. He counted twelve, although they moved so quickly in the darkness they blurred, and he wasn't confident in that count. As one, they converged on Stephen of Elseth. Gervanno had no time to fear; instinct and experience moved him now.

Stephen was accustomed to fighting in pairs. He was accustomed to taking the flank; Nenyane was always the primary combatant, the primary aggressor. Gervanno stepped into the role Nenyane played. His assessment of the Maubreche Hunter's swordwork matched Nenyane's: Stephen was good, but too young to the art, too lacking experience. He was not callow enough to be greedy, to step too far, to respond to the feints that might precede the blow that killed him.

Gervanno was not yet accustomed to the dogs, because in battle, the dogs were weapons in which he had not been trained. They were, in some ways, better than cerdan; there was no chance that miscommunication between commander and soldier would become a deadly inhibitor. They moved, these dogs, leaping, lunging, retreating; none of their steps put them in the line of Stephen's blade, no matter how close they drew.

The demons were not so controlled, not so disciplined as the Hunters. It was easier to feint, to draw them out with the possible promise of Stephen's death, and to cut them down before they could withdraw. Nor did they work in concert and, given their greater number, that would have made them more difficult opponents. They had been—clearly—ordered to kill Stephen, but they did not cooperate, did not *plan*.

Perhaps, had their commander not been occupied, they would have; but he was. Lightning flashed, thunder following it—a ruinous roar of rage, possibly pain. Gervanno did not look up; he could see the color of the sky dance and shift in the background, but it was the foreground that concerned him.

Here, he was not in command of other cerdan. The lives of the Hunters, who had become comrades in arms, were not his responsibility; his orders, shouted or lost to the chaos and noise of the battlefield, would not be responsible for either survival or death. He had one duty, one alone: protect Stephen of Maubreche in the absence of Nenyane. He was not soldier here, but cerdan.

It was the one thing the sword master had asked of him, the one thing she had entrusted him with.

Instincts honed by those early fields took over as he struck, parried, feinted, struck again; he could not move as Nenyane moved, which required that he fight at a greater distance from Stephen than Nenyane would have. She would have run no risk of accidentally injuring Stephen—or any of the other Hunters.

He was surprised when the ground briefly gave way beneath his feet, and surprised when he did not fall or stumble; the air caught him. The air and the bard. He had never doubted the bard's martial skill, and in any other situation, he would have paused to watch the bard fight: there was an artistry, a grace, in all of Kallandras's movements. The fact that they were deadly accentuated that elegance, that economy of perfect movement.

Kallandras was not Nenyane, who was far wilder in her focus, but he was a master in his own right. His voice was not wrapped in song, but the song of the wild, three-headed creature persisted.

Orange light changed the nature of the sky as wings folded and snapped; some of the flame flew out in a circle. Where it landed, it leapt to life, changing visibility: Gervanno could see the demons far more clearly. And he could see the fire that enrobed them; it did not burn their flesh.

It would his comrades: the Hunters, the dogs. The bard grimaced and the wind that had shored Gervanno up became in that instant far more wild, far more frenzied. It didn't so much set Gervanno down as drop him—but it dropped him onto ground that was, for the moment, solid.

NENYANE COULD NOT KILL the *Kialli* on her own. She accepted that; she was not alone. She did not understand why Illaraphaniel, one of the firstborn princes of the ancient court, fought without his shield. It hampered him, and it hampered Nenyane. In the aerial battle, the *Kialli* had the advantage of wings of fire—a second weapon, used to effect.

She therefore attacked from the shield side of the man Stephen called Meralonne; she could not *be* his shield; they were not bound in such a fashion. But she could time her attacks in such a way that the lack of shield was not the deadly vulnerability it would have otherwise been. She could not do so and return to ground; could not stand and fight beside her Hunter.

Had Gervanno not been present, she would have, regardless. She could see what Stephen saw, but dared no more than a brief glance; she knew Gervanno had stepped into the position she would have occupied. She knew that the bard's wind, and the bard himself—whose skills she had been forced to grudgingly acknowledge—were there.

And she knew if Illaraphaniel fell here, it was over. Even with

Kallandras's control of the wild air, she was certain they could not face the *Kialli* and survive. Beneath her feet, she could almost *feel* the song the three-headed creature sang; she had suspicions about its power and intent, and those suspicions were proven correct when the *Kialli* sent quills of flame out in a wide spray. She deflected one such quill, severing it in two with blade's edge; the fire continued to travel. She could almost hear its voice.

The fire did not reach the tree. Nenyane was certain the tree was not the intended target: it would simply become—as trees within the forest were becoming now—collateral, irrelevant damage. But the fire did not touch the tree. Nor did it touch the lake. Had it, the fire would not have been doused; it was elemental, living flame, against which normal water had no defense.

She did not curse when the air became wild; she had expected it. But the desire of air to destroy fire—and the inverse—would benefit the *Kialli* far more than it would Illaraphaniel. She hoped the tree, and the creature that protected it, would not wake the earth; if wakened, the rage of earth would render all attempts to protect Amberg moot.

But Stephen was on the ground; the wind did not yet howl there, although leaves flew past. He was surrounded by the dozen lesser demons the *Kialli* had summoned. No, by half that number. She smiled in spite of herself. Gervanno di'Sarrado was as good as she had suspected he would be.

Illaraphaniel fought in bitter, icy fury—he invoked Winter in all its dire incarnations. He offered no further words, no further courtesies—if such words could be considered courtesies between the living and the dead. But Winter was not what was necessary here. Winter in the wilderness, if she understood the feel of the passing seasons, had given way, at last, to Summer. But Winter remained in these darkened lands. Winter, she thought, was the season from which the lord of these lands drew power.

As did the dead.

She could not bespeak Illaraphaniel—or the tree—the way she could Stephen.

It was to Stephen she therefore spoke.

YOU NEED to reach the three-headed beast. We were wrong. We were wrong—and you need to tell them that.

His words were slower to come; he could not easily disengage from the dogs, from their attacks and their very necessary retreats. But Nenyane would not interrupt him without cause, and the urgency of her tone made clear to him that the outcome of this battle might ride upon her words.

What must I tell them?

The tree—it was rooted in Summer lands. Remember?

He did.

It needs to remind these lands that it's Summer. It needs to somehow merge them enough that the earth, the forest, the land itself is aware that it's Summer.

He had no idea how to communicate that to the tree—and a deep suspicion that approaching the tree itself would be deadly. He understood instinctively that the song the creature sang was not just a song of grief, of hope, of communion; it was a weapon, or a shield. That shield was offered to the great tree; while the creature stood thus, no harm would befall it—until and unless the Hunters and their allies fell.

But if he could not reach the tree or the three-headed creature—if he could not make clear what had to be done—he was aware that his instinctive understanding of what the creature did was in part because of the lion head, the beast head. The creature was not one of his dogs; he could not communicate anything so complex to it.

But he felt he *might* approach with caution.

And that was still not what was required. He stepped back, parrying claws; Gervanno bisected the arm from which those claws had extended. Pearl harried the flank of the demon as it howled, stumbling away; the demons could, and did, feel pain.

Pain is all they are—to cause or suffer.

"Kallandras!" he shouted.

"Stephen."

"Nenyane says we have to tell the tree that its Summer roots have to be strengthened and merged somehow with the roots here—she says this land still thinks it's Winter, and Summer is what we need!" He stepped back, stepped to the side, ducking not claws but flame; the wind's roar and the crackle of living fire drowned out the sound of his words.

Kallandras would hear them anyway. Nor would he have to do what Stephen could not do: traverse the battlefield from lake's edge to where the tree stood to attempt to bespeak the tree. The bard could—and did —fight, but he could speak across the distance as if distance was irrelevant. This gift, this talent to which he'd been born, was the reason bards were trained and sent to fields of war. Breodanir did not have bards, but Breodani had heard their colorful stories, delivered as the bards traveled through the small kingdom.

The bard could speak to any combatant at will, if he understood the need.

The creature heard.

Stephen could feel that awareness in the tension of the lion, the shift in its focus. He could not be certain the tree would or did hear the bard; he did not know to whom the bard had directed words that were inaudible to Stephen, Stephen not being the intended audience. He thought the only thing the tree could hear and see at this moment was the creature itself.

He then let it all go and focused on his dogs, on the demons who were becoming ash, and upon the moving fire. The fire was becoming the bigger concern, the bigger danger. He knew Alex had caught a claw, but had not lost limb; he'd lost some blood. He heard Ansel shout orders, but could not yet see Heiden.

Ah, no, that was wrong. Sanfel could see Heiden and Heiden was racing back to the battlefront, dog at his side. Word must have been conveyed to the elder and the Margen guards, but the imps were not yet on the way. If fire threatened the Hunters, it caused no like injury to demons—even the smallest and weakest of them. It became their armor as they at last moved out from behind the ranks of the demons intent on Stephen's death.

Nothing Stephen could do could harm that fire. But the air could and did, passing through fire in a gale of what Stephen assumed was blessed rage. The demons could not remain armored in that fire, because fire made them targets—and the wind could rip them from the earth and send them flying back into the few trees that remained standing nearby.

The fire grew stronger; normal trees, normal wildflowers, were consumed. But the wind grew stronger as well—which was a disadvantage to everyone on the battlefield, here or in the air. Above, the storm of red and blue dominated the skies; shadows shifted on the ground, both those cast by the living and those by the dead.

Stephen couldn't mark the moment when those shadows changed;

could not mark the moment when the perpetual night they had experienced in these lands began to give way to dawn, to a moment when the colors that comprised sky were brighter and steadier than those of the storm of combat.

But as he fought, as he stepped in—and back—drawing the more frenzied attack of burning demons so that they perished on Gervanno's sword, the sky did change. The twin moons dimmed; the clouds that had obscured the disturbing third moon moved on to a clear sky, a sky approaching daylight. In the growing light of early day, there was no third moon.

Demons could—and did—attack during daylight, as Stephen well knew. But the daylight here did not seem to be the mundane light of day in Maubreche—or anywhere else in Breodanir. It almost seemed that the demons lost physical volume as the dawn continued, and the paling of the sky grew stronger.

There were fewer, regardless. Ansel, Max, and Alex had managed to take down two, and Gervanno, six; there were four left standing. Four, and the imps Nenyane believed had been summoned to kill villagers, rendering Amberg's survival as a geographic location moot.

But even those became dust, for Kallandras, mastering raging wind, was not idle.

Here, the clearing gave way to dawn and the peace left in the wake of death, until only the aerial combat remained. The Hunters, however, did not pause to witness the battle; they tended to injuries. Two of the dogs—Sanfel and Patches—had been wounded. The wounds were not severe; in the minds of the dogs they were trivial, so focused were they on combat.

In the minds of every Hunter present, they were not. Salves were applied to both Alex and dogs; stitches were applied to Alex, but the dogs did not require them. Only when this had been done did the Hunters turn to the sky, where the combat had continued.

"Will she be all right?" Ansel asked.

"She will. I'm not so sure about the mage." It was Alex who replied. "Until and unless she asks for our help, I'm more concerned about the tree. And the village."

Heiden joined them. He was huntbrother, not Hunter; he didn't have the advantage of the Hunter's trance to increase speed and general acuity. He did, however, have the hard-won endurance of years of hunts at the side of his Hunter. He was not winded.

"The elder has the village under control at the moment. She knows what's at stake." He looked back, to the tree and the beast that seemed to embrace it. "I don't understand what's happening."

"None of us do," Stephen said, voice soft. "But the dawn is a good sign."

THE THREE-HEADED creature's song continued, strengthened by dawn, by the change in the wind, by the absence of fire. Stephen listened, as he watched his huntbrother. He was proud of her, had always been proud of her; he had hated the lack of acknowledgement and respect she'd been shown by Hunter Lords who were not his immediate family or his godfather's family.

But he knew his pride was almost selfish, and he kept it to himself here: she was Nenyane, had always been Nenyane. He had not shaped her, had not formed her, had not influenced her. Pride was misplaced, but he felt it nonetheless. He could see what she was doing, could feel the reasons for it, and could accept that there was nothing he could do to help her in this fight.

Meralonne's opponent was powerful, and better armed. Nenyane's defense had always been a good offense, and she was his shield arm, here, her blade parrying what shield might have blocked. She avoided the downward rush of wings, as did the mage—she was aware that wings could be deadly when employed as a weapon.

He heard the roar of a demon; heard the roar of unleashed mage. Nenyane was silent save for the metallic cry of parried blade. The storm above stilled, the sounds fading; the sky reasserted its natural hue, no red or blue lightning momentarily blanketed or overwhelmed its color.

STEPHEN LOOKED UP, although he was also aware of what his dogs saw, what they sensed. The *Kialli* had retreated, but a faint uneasiness remained in his wake, and it grew as the moments passed.

It was not the dogs that offered the first warning. It was Kallandras.

"Tell your huntbrother that I will perform her duties here," the bard said, voice low but urgent. "She must come down."

Stephen frowned. "Why?" It was Nenyane's question.

"Because soon, you will not be able to tell her that yourself. Can you not sense it? The song the creature sings is becoming softer as we listen —and it should not be."

Brandon froze. Aelle turned to the bard, paling.

The bard nodded. "The Silences are on the move. You have time— they have time—but it is scant."

"Will the lord come with them?"

"I do not know. For obvious reasons, I would not call them; they would not be a weapon I would dare to use, given my own abilities. But any lord who cannot bespeak their forces cannot command them; she might give commands to those enslaved, but she surrenders all flexibility on the battlefield if she has no method of altering those commands as the situation warrants."

"She will come," a new voice said. It was the fox, fur gold, eyes an odd color that implied gold or silver. "She will definitely come." He sauntered over to where Gervanno stood, sword in hand, and cleared his throat.

"Eldest," Gervanno said, with obvious respect. "I cannot both carry you and fight. Perhaps Jarven can—but it is not within my humble capabilities."

"Fool," the fox growled. "You cannot fight what comes *at all*. I have taken an interest in you, and I wish to make that clear to the lord of these pathetic lands."

Gervanno closed his eyes. The bard turned to him. "Ser Gervanno, I advise you to accept the grace of the Eldest."

The Southern guard swallowed. "I am a Maubreche guard."

"If Nenyane does not come to ground, there is a grave chance that our attempts to draw the lord of these lands to this field will be our deaths." He looked up. "Tell her," he said, and pushed himself off the ground; the wind enclosed him as he rose to the heights commanded by the mage and the demon.

Nenyane surprised Stephen; she descended, landing with force, weight, and cursing.

He'd better be right about this, she snapped, turning to the Elseth Hunters. "The Silences are coming," she said, blunt as always.

Brandon and Aelle understood what this meant—of course they did. It was one of Brandon's dogs who had escaped these cursed lands, and had almost perished, voiceless.

"We'd better come up with a strategy soon—we won't be able to change it much. The Silences swamp all communication—even those between Hunter and huntbrother. We won't hear the bard, if he tries to offer warning, either."

"How? How can they do this?"

Nenyane shrugged. *How* had never been her concern; she accepted the facts and worked to alleviate the worst of the danger. "They were created by a god," she finally said. "A god who hated to have their sleep disturbed. The Silences were never considered a danger unless one was stupid enough to attempt to wake the god—in which case they could be deadly.

"But they don't attack—or didn't attack—outside of their territory; they were bound to it, made *of* it. I have no idea how they were captured."

"Demons," Stephen said quietly.

"Fine. I have no idea how the demons captured them. The Silences don't have the usual weapons; they don't have the weapons that demons have or can make from their own dead flesh. But they won't need them; most people find utter silence incredibly disturbing. It won't be relevant to the rest of you right now, but Stephen won't be able to command his dogs, either. He can see what they see, but he can't tell them how to interact with it.

"If they come and she's right behind them, we need a plan of some kind."

Alex said, "The demon is still alive."

"Yes. And that's not going to help us any. But it won't necessarily help her, either. There's a reason the demons came separately. You don't understand how fraught an alliance of the kind she made is to the wilderness."

"How?"

"Let's just say she'd better not rely on any help outside of her own borders, and those borders had better be impassible going forward. But that's not our problem right now." She looked out, past the flashes of lightning. And then she looked toward the tree.

The earth beneath their feet began to rumble. Stephen bent into his knees, shifting his weight in response.

"What's happening?" Brandon said, lifting voice to be heard.

"The tree," Nenyane told them. "The tree is uprooting itself." She did not look back. She looked ahead.

CHAPTER TWENTY-SEVEN

"Not yet." From above, the bard spoke, the syllables clear although he had not raised voice to be heard over the rumble of earth, the movement of water. His would, Stephen thought, be the last voice to go silent, such was the nature of his power. "If you once ruled, she is ruler now, and the lands—as you must know—are hers. Where she walks, the land will hear her, even if she raises no voice.

"But here, that is not entirely the case. Intentionally or not, you have held this small area; your roots are spread far enough into the earth that this land does not hear her so clearly. The land in which your roots are planted does not speak her name; nor does the wind in your branches."

Blue lightning accompanied his words, but the sound of clashing metal was short, almost staccato.

The trembling beneath the Hunters' feet stilled.

To Stephen's lasting surprise, it was the mage who spoke—the mage who, even now, wielded light as sword in a constant rhythm of attack and defense. "Your time is close. It is coming. This is where we have chosen to stand, and if you withdraw the great roots that are a consequence of your planting, we will lose what advantage we have. I am not, and will never be, your lord. I cannot command or compel, but I ask it."

The three-headed beast raised two heads toward the skies. "And what will you offer in exchange?" Stephen was surprised; he understood the words, although he had to strain to catch them now, even this close to the creature.

It isn't just Illaraphaniel she's asking.

"I will remain. I will fight the lord of these lands. I will aid your master in repaying his long, bitter debt. Do not ask for more." His words lacked warmth, not heat.

The two lifted heads nodded and turned to the Hunters. "And you? Son of Bredan, what boon will you offer in return for this favor? I have long desired to see my Lord—*my* Lord—stride these lands he once ruled by my side. If I surrender that for this battle, and I lose that chance, what recompense do you offer?"

Nenyane's eyes were as narrow as the mage's.

No one replied.

"Illaraphaniel will likely survive should we take to the battlefield together, abandoning this small patch of land; the only creature on this field that might have killed him is now attempting to retreat; he will be ash and dust. But the mortals will not." This time, she looked to Stephen, as he had known she would.

"What would you have of a mortal?"

In the distance, the sound the Silences had absorbed returned briefly, rising and falling as the Silences asserted their one weapon.

They had little time. The earth beneath Stephen's feet still trembled.

"I would have you make a binding oath of my master's choosing when he asks it of you."

Stephen turned to the head that was speaking and met the eyes of the creature without blinking. "Ask another boon."

"There is nothing else that you might offer. I have agreed, should this battle conclude in a favorable way, to liberate those who were petri-fied at the lord's command; I will not forsake that."

Nenyane said, speaking far more formally than was her wont, "Were it not for his intervention, you would not now be standing thus." She exhaled. "Do you not wonder how it was possible that the lord could breach barriers erected by her betters?"

"The gods are gone."

"Not all of them, to our sorrow. Your master has roots in three lands; the first will fade soon, as it has been abandoned. The second is the battlefield upon which we now stand. And the third is the mortal realm. Should we survive this battle, we will not uproot him in those

mortal lands, so prized by the wilderness. Nor will we forbid his presence, or the presence of his servants, in our lands should the need
arise."

You can't offer that—those aren't our lands!

Stephen turned to Ansel.

Ansel's hands were fists; his lips were compressed so tightly they
were white around the edges. He had always had a temper. Stephen
glanced at Heiden, whose eyes were narrowed with effort. Neither
Bowgren Hunter spoke, but Ansel approached Stephen, his movements
stiff.

"I have heard what you offered," he said. "But I did not hear the
why of it."

Stephen blinked. "You couldn't understand what they said?"

"No." He inhaled, his hands white-knuckled.

"The tree wishes to uproot itself before the lord of these lands
reaches us, the better to join in our battle. The mage has pointed out
how much of a disadvantage that will be; the three-headed beast has
pointed out that it will only be a disadvantage for the mortals. The beast
is therefore asking a concession."

"And you are offering a concession that would have to be granted in
Bowgren territories."

Stephen nodded.

"Let me speak for Bowgren; I am Lord Ansel, and Bowgren is my
land."

The creature turned toward him, although the lion head continued
to stare at Stephen. "Speak, then. My master would hear what you have
to say."

To Stephen's surprise, Ansel knelt.

"Bowgren owes you a debt it will never be able to pay. Because of
you, because of your many roots and the branches you let fall, the
village of Amberg is safe. I do not know what the outcome of the
coming battle will be; I may not be alive at the end of it. But if I am, I
swear to you that you will be welcome in Bowgren for as long as
Bowgren stands. Our people will make offerings in your name; should a
tree such as you grow in my lands, it will be sheltered and honored for
as long as it stands; no axes will be allowed to touch it, nor fire to burn
in its lee.

"The elders of Bowgren will tell the children the tale of Amberg's savior, and those children will tell their children; word of your deeds and your aid will echo down the ages for as long as Bowgren exists. What you ask of us, saving only the lives of those we must protect, we will give." He rose slowly, but he did rise.

"It is the only form of eternal we might offer; those living now will age and die. Our future is in the children that will be born, and the children of those children. Stories will fade and fray, becoming less detailed with the passage of generations, but the truth at the heart of it will remain: when Amberg was attacked, when it was swallowed by your enemy, you preserved it. If they ask why, I have no answer. And perhaps that tale will be embroidered; it is our way to ask why."

The tree creaked; the human face of the creature lifted, pale chin exposing perfect, pale throat. Hair flew back from the face and words were spoken—words that Stephen did not understand.

Ansel, waiting, did not understand them either.

Nenyane was surprised. Surprised by Ansel, and surprised by what she heard, for she could understand the language of the wilderness. Had Stephen chosen to listen, borrowing her hearing, he might have understood it as well; he did not.

Biluude then turned to face Lord Ansel. "He has accepted your offer, Ansel, Lord of Bowgren. And he will answer the question that has no answer, that you might pass it on to those of Amberg, and their descendants. He has long been rooted on the edge of the lands that were once his, listening to the name of the new lord; listening to her commands. He was not subject to them, and he made no attempt to be heard—discovery might defeat the purpose for which he was planted.

"He slept. He woke. He slept. He was alone with anger and despair, and they seeped into the roots that held him fast and preserved him, both. Where once he could hear the voices of this land's earth and its inhabitants, all was silent. No song reached his ears. No offerings. No stories of the lands beyond the lands in which he had chosen to remain for eternity.

"He remembered the ancient promise; remembered the acceptance of a confinement far more extreme than the confinement of rulership. But he slept for longer and longer periods, until he could no longer differentiate from dream and waking reality.

"And in that state, he heard the villagers of Amberg. He heard the voices of young, of old, of ruler and ruled, and he understood that a mortal village had somehow grown around him. The villagers were frightened. They were shocked. And they now lived here, in lands where naught but death—slow and unpleasant—awaited them.

"But as they spoke, as he acclimated himself to the sound of their slight voices, he realized that the lord of this land had not yet found them. That she had not placed them here deliberately; that they were not some part of a rudimentary farm. They would not survive without water—he remembered that—or food, but even had they both, they would not survive those creatures that hunted at the edge of the lord's domain. He could not communicate with them, but he created the small lake in whose center he stands, and he offered branches, that they might build a fence.

"They built. They built and people came for water, as he knew they must; they came for branches, and returned, time and again. And they spoke to him; they offered thanks at the edge of the water; they offered gratitude.

"It was pleasant, to my master, so long forgotten. As he listened, he realized that this mortal village presaged the end of his long, long wait.

"Nor was he wrong, but he was always strikingly intuitive. Do not expect kindness or mercy from those who rule," she added. "But gratitude exists, nonetheless. He woke fully, and the presence of people—even be they mortal and foreign—anchored him.

"Planting is unpredictable. Roots are unpredictable in subtle ways. He aided your people because in some fashion he is rooted in their presence." She bowed head to the tree, and then, to Stephen's surprise, bowed to Ansel.

"Soon, my words will not reach you, and yours will not reach me—or any of your companions. The Silences come."

———

GERVANNO COULD NOT FIGHT well when one of his arms was wrapped around the fox. It was not the first time he had been so hampered on the battlefield; no combat conditions were ever consistently ideal, and he often carried the weight of the injured as he attempted to maintain orderly retreats—not the deadly routs that panic caused.

More, the elder was a greater power; it was unwise to carelessly offend him.

Gervanno shifted position; he had not sheathed his sword.

He was prepared for the silence, and it came, enveloping natural sound—breath, slight movements, the brush of cloth against cloth, of foot against earth, of sword leaving sheath. The darkness of night was being pushed aside by day, by sun; his vision was sharper, clearer, which was good. He had to rely on vision. The cues—the necessary cues—provided by hearing were gone. If demons were summoned and they came from behind, he would likely die here.

But this death, this death he could accept.

This was the death that should have been his.

As if the fox could hear his thoughts, he bit down on Gervanno's hand—not hard enough to draw blood, this time, but hard enough to draw attention. By gesture alone—the deliberate motion of head—the fox made his commands clear: Gervanno was to retreat. Now.

But Stephen and Nenyane did not retreat.

Gervanno could no longer hear the words that passed between them —if any words did. But he understood the gesture: Nenyane reached out with her right hand; Stephen grasped it with his left. The breeze continued to move through leaves and branches; it caught strands of Gervanno's hair, cooling the sweat combat always caused. But there was no sound. The sky flashed blue, a blue that lingered as the sun—a single sun—fully crested horizon.

It had not been long enough, but Gervanno understood now that the anchors of time, its familiar passage, had little purchase in the wilderness. An odd peace settled across his shoulders in this silence—a peace he had not expected to feel in the lee of final battle. He allowed it to settle as the two Maubreche Hunters, and only the two, began to move.

THE WIND SWEPT Stephen from the earth. As both the bard and the mage were now engaged in aerial combat, it was not clear to him under whose command the wind moved, but he felt little fear; as silence robbed him of connection with his dogs, his comrades, he once again felt the lack of sound as stillness. This time he felt no panic; he knew what to expect, knew what he would temporarily lose.

He understood that it was not to his advantage, but it was a silence that enveloped all; the disadvantage did not privilege one side over the other. Had Nenyane not gripped his hand so tightly, it might have been different. She had, and she continued to hold on as they moved.

He wondered if the song that had fallen into the folds of unnatural silence would no longer afford the tree, or the creature entwined around it, protection; he could not ask. Nenyane would not hear him, and even if she did, he wouldn't hear her response.

He could feel the lion's anger, but the anger was not at him; he could feel anger deepen into fury, and realized, as he moved, that the fury had always been present, but buried. What point fury when there was nothing that could be done with it?

The existence of the tree had changed that.

The emotions he felt were the lion's. Those emotions were not banked by silence.

The air carried them forward, but Nenyane did not fly, did not make the attempt; they walked, side by side and step by step, as if air were bedrock. He understood what he must do here, and understood that they exposed themselves to the greater danger of the land's lord as they moved.

He remembered the Silences not as physical presences, but as almost abstract existences; they had not been created for combat, although their power could clearly be used to effect. They did not willingly serve the lord of these lands; if he had understood what he had heard, they did not belong in these lands at all.

And if they did not serve willingly, if they were bound to service in the same fashion the three-headed creature had been bound, he knew what was meant to look for, what he was meant to see. If he could not hear his huntbrother, if she could not hear him, he could nonetheless see through her eyes if he made the effort. He made it, now.

THROUGH NENYANE'S EYES, the sky was not blue; it was an odd shade of purple, as if it were in harmony with the blending colors cast off by the swords of the living and the dead. If Kallandras's weapons caused the same visual lightning, they didn't change the color of the sky. But even if the colors were brighter, harsher, in her eyes, there was something about the way the colors merged that carried unspeakable grief, as if all color on this battlefield belonged to a shroud, a pall, surrounding the silence of the grave.

He was almost grateful Nenyane couldn't hear him; she would have been annoyed.

The thought comforted him as he once again returned to the jarring view her eyes offered; he closed his own to lessen the incoming headache. It helped, but not enough; the Hunter's trance was less physically demanding than this. But as he concentrated, she moved her field of vision, allowing Stephen to be more than a passenger; if they could not speak, she could intuit where he wanted her to look.

Nenyane could see the odd displacement of air, the subtle blur. Stephen doubted he would have seen it with his own eyes; he didn't check. He couldn't ask if this was one of the Silences, but he could see that this odd inflection of air was not singular; there were three such distortions, and they were moving. They did not move quickly.

How far did the silence they impose extend?

Another question he couldn't ask. He shook himself. He had seen the threads of grey and black, entwined and leading into the distance, by which the three-headed creature had been bound. He looked for those now. Looked for things that were not golden, not the oathbinding of his father, his father's blood.

And those did exist.

For one moment he forgot to breathe, those strands were so bright; he could see almost nothing else. The Silences were oathbound. If they were oathbound, he could not break that binding, could not release it. Nothing he had tried so desperately had worked when he had been a child of five years of age and the oathbreaker a child as well.

Nenyane's hand tightened. If she could not hear his thoughts—and she couldn't—she could feel what he felt; she was aware of the sudden chasm that opened without warning beneath him, as it so often did. He tightened his own grip; his knuckles were white. If there was a time and place for this gnawing, endless guilt, it was *not now*.

His eyes—her eyes—adjusted the brilliance of gold, the *rightness* of it. As they did, he saw what he had been searching for: threads of grey and black, entwined. Those strands flowed toward the forest, not the lake—but they did not follow the course of the golden strands. He could see that clearly in the odd light they cast.

It was the grey threads they needed to break.

Nenyane nodded and began to run, dragging Stephen with her; he had to adjust his stride in order not to trip or stumble. But he'd practiced that for half his life; he made the adjustment flawlessly, eyes closed. He opened them once, as they approached the first of the odd distortions; as he'd suspected, he couldn't see either the Silences or the threads through his own eyes.

Through Nenyane's, he could.

She did not let go of his hand; she hadn't the first time, either. He understood from this that the contact was necessary for reasons she didn't yet understand. There was no one he trusted more than his hunt-brother; he was certain that the future into which he walked would not change that, no matter how many people he met and how much he grew to trust them.

She approached the first of the Silences; the air rippled, the distortion expanding. She did not let go of his hand, which was awkward: had she, it would have been far easier not to be clipped by the expanding disturbance.

He stumbled, then, bringing his free hand up to his ear instinctively as all of the sound swallowed by the Silence hit it. He hadn't expected that. Maybe Nenyane had or did, but there was no way she could offer him her usual sharply worded advice.

He moved out of the range of the cacophony, into sudden silence — as if that thunderous chaos of noise had deafened him. Righting himself, he lowered the hand cupped protectively over one ear, because he could see the strand far more clearly now.

Without pause, as Nenyane was still moving, he grabbed it. He felt nothing. He saw it break, saw the strand cross his palm. He tried to throw it away, to let the breeze take it. Nenyane's hand tightened. He gave up; the grey strand weighed nothing, impeded nothing, and she would not slow down.

He was braced for impact with the second of these visual disturbances, but she was careful to leave enough room that Stephen could skirt around its immediate visible edges. She headed toward the connected strand Stephen could break, and continued to move as he gripped. She did not look back, or look to the side; she was focused entirely on the last of the three.

The Silences had no desire to cause harm. They had no desire to be here at all. Their desires had been irrelevant until the moment Stephen caught the third of the three binding threads in his right hand.

He felt the three turn toward him as Nenyane scanned the horizon, searching for disturbances similar in subtlety to these three; she found none. Only then did she stop moving.

Beneath their feet, folds of wind calmed but did not lower the two whose weight they bore to earth; it was on a platform of air that Nenyane turned to the Silences.

You can open your eyes now, she said.

He could hear her. He could hear her clearly. Above, he could hear the clash of blades.

He shook his head. He was studying the golden thread, the golden binding; it seemed to brighten as he watched.

Yes. They will not remain here long; it is perhaps the only chance they have to escape.

They did not immediately speak; they made no attempt to create form for themselves from fallen leaves, branches, petals. Stephen felt their attention, regardless; he wondered if it was due to the threads he had cut—threads he could no longer see.

He was surprised when they raised voices. At first, he assumed the sound he could hear was wind through leaves, through wild grass— which, given the returning clamor of steel against steel in the skies above should have been rendered inaudible.

"What would you have of us, oathbinder?"

Dogs lifted voice, and the song of the creature that had embraced the tree continued, rising, louder than the sounds of battle. It was a different song; it was mournful, but at its heart fury, a bitter hope. He did not understand the words. But if the voices of the Silences were so oddly textured, so slight in seeming, he could hear them above the growing din.

He took a risk to conserve energy, releasing the trance as he faced the Silences.

"I would have you be free," Stephen replied. "But elsewhere. If you have been freed from the commands that drove you here, you are bound by older oaths."

Rustling.

"Would you have nothing from us?"

"I would have you leave these fields. I understand that your lord created you that they might know peace and silence. If that lord still sleeps, return to them. Our kind—my kind—does not weather such silence well, and the lord of these lands is coming."

"Would you have us battle her in your stead?"

Nenyane's answer was an immediate *yes*, a certainty that any help was wanted, necessary.

Stephen's was *no*. *We won't be able to bespeak each other if they fight. None of the Hunters will have the ability to communicate. Not even the bard will be able to relay instructions or advice. The creature that loved the prior lord cannot sing her dirge of protection.*

Our enemy won't be able to do any of that either!

It harms us more. "No. You were not created for war or battle. This field is not your field."

The rustling grew louder; Stephen felt the Silences approach. Nenyane drew sword, and Stephen grimaced. *They don't mean to hurt me.*

I don't care. They're part of the wild. You think they were meant for peace — but there's a reason Brandon's dog almost died. Peace in the wilderness requires power. It requires strength.

Strength isn't only swords and the ability to kill, he snapped. It was perhaps their oldest argument, revisited with changing textures and tone over the years, different but at heart the same.

"*It is, little mortal. We cannot hear her, but we hear you; you are master here. Let us offer you our gratitude; we will, should the need arise and it be within our capabilities, owe you a debt. If it is in our power to pay it, we will pay it.*"

"Can you return to your home?"

"*We can.*"

"Will you be safe, there?"

"*We understand how we were attacked; we understand how we were transported here. We will not be attacked in like fashion again. Illaraphaniel will destroy the creature that found us.*"

"If others can find you —"

"*They are not what he is, not what he was.*" In that rustling, creaking voice, composed of flying leaves, splinters, small pebbles, lay things that could not be said, could not be put into words: the detritus of grief, of loss, of a sorrow that would never end.

"Then go. Go in peace."

Only then did his huntbrother clear her throat. "How will he find you should he seek the boon you have promised?"

"*He is oathborn. He will know. One of us will swear the binding oath.*"

Although Nenyane's face was schooled in hard-won lines of respect, she was all but shrieking on the inside of Stephen's head. She knew what oathbinding had cost him; knew why he would not bind another in such a fashion again.

They're not children!

He did not reply, not to Nenyane. "I will not bind you. You are all already oathbound. It is enough."

They murmured among themselves for a time, the texture and tone of their voices the sound of breeze, of wind, of crackling flame—as if their voices were comprised of every other sound, as if they had no voice of their own with which they could form words. Above their heads the Maubreche Hunters heard a cry of rage and fury, despair and endless pain. It did not echo, did not linger.

Sorrow did, but sorrow was a hush, a silence. A silence.

Not one voice, Nenyane said. *Not one, but two.*

"We will take this with us, young mortal."

He understood, then, why the cry did not linger, did not echo; they had absorbed it. He did not look up; nor did Nenyane—as if the end of the aerial battle of which she'd been such a necessary part was irrelevant. As if Meralonne needed privacy.

Some things should not be witnessed.

"We will, perhaps, see you again. We will not silence you forever should you reach the lands in which our lord dreams in peace, unless you should attempt to wake her from that rest."

Nenyane released his hand.

"We will not forget. But we must leave now, for she is coming."

Stephen offered a brief bow to these three creatures, visible only through his huntbrother's eyes. And then he retreated from Nenyane's vision and opened his own eyes. To his surprise, he could still see their wavering, indistinct forms as they shuffled away from the tree and its necessary lake, walking back along the path that must surely lead to the lord that had enslaved them.

STEPHEN RAN BACK to the Hunters gathered on the bank of the lake.

As if they had been waiting for Stephen's return, the three-headed creature waded out of the water on which Amberg had been so dependent. They stopped before Stephen, the human half-body offering him a bow.

"We will fight on your behalf, and our own," that head said. There was a lilt, an excitement, in the words; they were, given the gravity of the situation, almost joyful. They paused, frowned, and turned, all three sets of eyes settling upon Gervanno. "I see you number a familiar figure among your company now." Ah, no. Not Gervanno. The fox nestled in the crook of the swordsman's arm. "We ask the elder to stand back; this is not his fight."

Stephen blinked.

Gervanno did not. Fox in arm, he bowed. "I cannot speak for the Eldest," he said, "but my duty is the protection of Stephen of Maubreche."

"It is not you to whom I speak. Eldest?"

The fox snorted. "These lands are not my lands; this fight is not my fight. I understand." He exhaled, his voice lowering. "But this mortal is a mortal in whom I have taken an *interest*. If he is ensnared in a battle that is not mine, it will become mine. I can offer you no other assurances."

"We would prefer you leave."

"As would I—but the mortal will not leave his sworn duty, and while he stands, I will remain. My lord has no interest in the supremacy of the dead, although I see that is not your concern."

"Your lord, Eldest?"

"My Lord."

"You...serve?"

"I serve. I serve my Lord in a fashion you did not serve the lord of these lands. But perhaps I serve as you served the prior lord of these lands. My Lord has made no demands, no attempt to compel—but she was once mortal, and she does not understand the imperatives of the wilderness.

"You did not remain by the side of your lord when he chose to commit himself to rule here. No more am I required to do so."

"You do not wander as I did." The reply was chillier.

The fox chuckled. "My Lord's hatred of the dead is bonfire to your candle. Where they walk, we walk, seeking the shadows they cast. It is her hope to unseat the Lord of the Hells."

The eagle's eyes rounded as it screeched in disbelief. The human head said, "He walks, now. He walks upon the mortal plane. How does your lord intend to accomplish this?"

"She is Sen," the fox replied. "The Cities of Man will rise anew, and first among them will be her city. We can see it, in the wilderness, although it is a thing of man—and its glory is brighter, stronger, than the Shining Palace. Where she rules, none of the dead can even walk.

"The dead should never have entered these lands; their taint should never have spread across them." In a lower voice, he added, "It is Summer in the hidden lands. This coming war will be fought across the wilderness in Summer.

"The lord of these lands is now at a disadvantage; can you not feel the change in the earth, in the air? She ruled in Winter, relied on Winter; but Winter is passing."

Stephen hesitated to interrupt, but chose to do so. "She is coming. The Silences said she is coming."

"The Silences spoke? To *you*?"

He nodded.

Silence, chosen not imposed, reigned for one long moment. Breaking that silence came the sound of drums.

In battle, the Breodani used horns, and the Hunters lifted horns to lips as one. Margen had its calls, as did Bowgren, Maubreche, and Elseth, but none of those territory-specific notes were blown here. No, here, in lands in which the gods themselves had once walked, they blew the opening notes of the one hunt that had defined—and scarred—their lives.

They had not discussed it beforehand, and perhaps, had Stephen not started, they would not have followed his lead. But they had followed his lead since they had left the King's City, and they understood the import of this battle—a battle for which they had not been trained, but which they could not avoid.

The forefeet of the three-headed creature rose as they reared, lion head roaring, eagle screeching. The mortal body was silent. Stephen stumbled as the earth responded to the momentum of the creature's size, its weight, returned to earth.

Ansel's commands caused the rest of the Hunters to move, spreading out along the shore of the small lake, weapons in hand. The ground was uneven; the tree's initial attempts to uproot itself had taken its toll.

Stephen looked up as a flash of silver caught his eye. Meralonne and Kallandras stood in the folds of the wild wind; the wind was calm. Fire, its ancient enemy, had been banked, and the earth had not yet awakened.

Of the demon Meralonne had fought, nothing remained but silence and stillness. The mage and the bard looked out, past the lake, past the Hunters; if they noticed the creature or the Hunters at all, they gave no sign.

Into the beat of drums and the echo of horns came the song of birds as the sounds of the forest returned to herald the end of Winter, the beginning of Summer, and the beginning, in a fashion, of an ending.

JARVEN KNEW the moment the hold of the Silences had been broken, but more: he knew the moment Winter began its passage into Summer. The moons faded as the sun rose; the night sky gave way, as night did in mortal lands, to the hues of dawn, the touch of morning sun. He could feel that sun on his exposed skin, could feel the gentle heat that came with it in the forest environs.

These lands had not been blanketed—as the Northern Wastes were —in snow, in ice, but the sense of that snow, that ice, had remained in the air, in the night, in the hardness of earth beneath his feet. All were receding even as he observed. Interesting.

Pay attention to the seasons of the land, the fox had said. *You will sense them now. Seasons in mortal lands shift reliably and superficially, spring and autumn your transitions. It is not so in the wilderness. There are ancient dells in which Summer has never passed; there are crevices and mountains that have pledged their allegiance to Winter, and will hold it in their hearts long after Summer has finally returned.*

But the wilderness acknowledges the Firstborn, and she sacrificed much of her essence to ensure that the seasons would spin and turn. It is Summer, Jarven. It is a Summer that will never come again in the seasons of the world. But perhaps you will not appreciate it, who has seen no other Summer in your brief history, and who might see no other Winter before your end.

Jarven was not a man given to either sentiment or awe; he found neither practical. He might use sentiment against those who truly felt it. But sentiment, as Hectore of Araven had taught him at some cost, was double-edged; it was not simple weakness.

He learned this lesson again from the elder, whose sentiment he could almost touch. The form the fox chose was small, almost quaint in appearance, but Jarven ATerafin could see what the rest of the mortals could not: he was ancient, a wild force possessed of a capricious nature —and temper. And he had chosen to stand beside—or within the arms of—a simple Southern cerdan. A man of sentiment. A man who believed in honor.

Had Gervanno di'Sarrado been a mere youth, it would be excusable

—if not survivable. He was not. He was a man full grown, yet he continued to wrap antiquated honor around himself as if the tattered thing were a mantle from which he could extract strength.

As the sun came into view between the trees behind which Jarven concealed himself, he wondered what the wilderness would make of a man of Gervanno's beliefs and stature. He was not averse to betting; it amused him and whiled away the hours. Or it had while he dwindled, waiting for death—and resenting age as he did. He would have bet against Gervanno di'Sarrado's survival. And yet, the man stood. How much of his survival depended on the elder?

How much depended on his skill?

What, in the end, did the Eldest see in a man Jarven would have considered a skilled fool in his tenure in Terafin? He grimaced. He had considered the Terafin Chosen skilled fools, as well. But Jewel ATerafin had viewed them very differently. She, too, had notions that would have led to Jarven's death in his youth had he pursued them.

She had built a city that relied on them.

He wondered, then, how much of an effect the lord of a land had upon its residents, its living servants. Perhaps he would now find the beginning of an answer, for Jarven understood that answers were not simple; the seeds of answers were planted, and they grew, shifting and changing as they did.

He turned as the earth beneath his feet shook; he moved in perfect silence as he made his way past the lake that he was certain would not survive the advent of the lord. He did not wait to catch sight of her; he would see her soon enough. He had discovered, in his exploratory sojourns in the wilderness, that his prior life—the whole of it—had been no preparation for the physical presence of those who ruled.

He acclimatized slowly and deliberately; if he trusted his instincts, he trusted them because he had, with will, with intent, with consideration and observation, honed them to be implements that would not cause self-destruction.

It was the primary reason he had not pushed himself to fully investigate the Shining Court. Yes, it was closed. Yes, there were barriers that he could not simply bypass. But he had no wish to set eyes upon its god until he was certain that sight of a god would not destroy all measure of self-determination.

THE LORD CAME through the forests. The trees that might have blocked her path bent as if to avoid her shadow, her notice. But no; as Stephen watched, he saw those trees begin to move, to enclose the field at her back, following in her wake as if they were soldiers and she, their commander. The shape of the forest changed as she passed through it; the lay of the land rose behind her.

Stephen knew that she was the lord of this land, but he had not fully comprehended what that meant until this moment. The skies above her back were alive with flying creatures—birds of prey, winged creatures far larger than birds. None flew ahead of her; as the trees did, they formed a living cloak at her back.

The sky was not yet the sky of full day, but night had passed; daylight glinted off her hair, which fell below her knees in strands of moving ebony. Her skin was the white of death; it held no pink, but rather a pale, pale grey that might, in different light, look silver.

None of her many followers were the size of the three-headed beast.

None are as strong, Nenyane told her Hunter. *Understand, however, that size and power should not be considered interchangeable. The beast is not a match for the fox attached to Gervanno.* She was not happy with this, but accepted it—for now. *The forces the lord has assembled are a greater danger than a human army would be, but there are no demons among them.*

You're certain?

She snorted, annoyed, which was enough of an answer; clearly it was something Stephen should know by now. To his eyes, the flying creatures in the skies above looked very much like some of the demons they had seen.

They're not dead, his huntbrother said. To Stephen's eyes, neither were the demons.

"Are we expected to have a plan?" Alex said, voice low.

"Survive," was Nenyane's curt reply.

No one who knew her expected a different reply, but it wasn't of Nenyane the question had been asked.

Stephen glanced at the three-headed beast; they had moved past the Hunters. "Support," he told Alex, indicating the three-headed creature. "They're going to attack the lord; we can attempt to defend them, attempt to pick off attackers as they flank them."

Alex nodded. "We're to leave the flying creatures alone?"

"I don't think Kallandras or Meralonne intend to come down to earth anytime soon—leave the aerial attack to them." He then turned to Ansel. "Does that work for you?"

Ansel had been speaking—quietly—with Brandon and Aelle. He nodded, and then hesitated. "Where will you be?"

Nenyane glanced at the Bowgren Hunter. "You're smarter than you look," she said, grinning briefly. She held out a hand in Stephen's direction. Stephen took it. "We're supporting in an entirely different way."

"Like you did with the Silences."

Nenyane nodded.

"You'll want support if you intend to run past her."

"If you're under attack," she replied, "Stephen won't be able to concentrate on what he has to do here. If he can't, I can't, either."

Ansel shook his head. "They'll go after Stephen. If you're hanging on to his hand as if he were a child, you won't be able to defend him."

She exhaled, clearly annoyed. Significantly, she offered no argument. "If he can do what he did for the Silences, the battlefield will be chaos; the lord's perfect control will crumble."

"Then let the beast attack the lord; let the other two keep the flying creatures from attacking those on the ground. And let us support Stephen. He's Breodani. We're Breodani. This is our fight."

Her hand tightened. She wanted to say no. She meant to say no. But she waited—as she often did—for Stephen. Stephen, who knew Ansel was right. He commanded his dogs—seven—to form up around the other Hunters. Pearl pushed back, but he expected that.

Nenyane knew what his answer was.

"I will follow the Maubreche Hunters," Gervanno said. "I am a Maubreche guard."

"Can you do it alone?"

Gervanno did not reply.

Ansel accepted Gervanno because Nenyane did. If he had been antagonistic to Nenyane in the beginning—and he had, there was no way to dim that truth—it had been an antagonism that contained grudging respect. The battles they had fought to get to this place at this time had burned away everything but respect; it was all that remained.

Respect and the loyalty that came from true comrades in arms.

"We've had the same training you've had," Alex said, when Ansel fell silent. "Brandon and Aelle, too. We don't have our dogs; we aren't fully armed. But we're not helpless. Go. Do what you have to do. You're not lord here—these are Bowgren lands, and Ansel is in command. We aren't your dependents. We're combatants. What happens to us is not, and will never be, on your head."

Nenyane nodded. Stephen bowed head, accepting the truth of Alex's words.

Ready? Nenyane asked.

Her Hunter nodded. As he did, he sank once again into the Hunter's trance, calling on the speed, the mental acuity, the increase in vision, in hearing, that came with the trance. Around him, he could feel the Hunters do the same; their breathing synchronized with his.

The huntbrothers had not been given this gift, but knew how to support, how to work with their Hunters. Without the intervention of the Silences, nothing could shatter the teamwork they had spent a lifetime building—nothing but death.

Ready, Stephen finally replied, tightening his grip.

NENYANE DID NOT TAKE the air as she had before. Stephen understood why; the air around the land's lord moved her hair back, holding it as if it were a skilled, obedient servant. Kallandras and Meralonne commanded the wild wind; there seemed to be no conflict in the bubbles over which they had control.

But to approach their enemy by air was to invite a sudden attack that would leave them tumbling into the heart of her followers. It might be faster than movement on the ground, but the ground, at the moment, was safer.

Stephen watched the battlefield from the vantage of his dogs. He could not afford to close his eyes, as he had the two times he and Nenyane had tried this. Then, there had been no other attackers.

He wasn't certain that he would find what he was looking for, but Nenyane was.

She isn't the type of lord to inspire loyalty; she inspires obedience. Those with any power are likely to be bound to her as the Silences were. It's those we have to free. Illaraphaniel and the fox can stand against her for some time—if the fox chooses to join the battle. Were she in her seat of power, it would be less certain.

Stephen hadn't struggled to break the bindings. He had simply touched them, taken them into the palm of his hand. They were not like the golden chains created by the oaths sworn to Bredan; he was certain that those could not be broken, and had not tried. Nor would he; there was far more in those bindings than simple enslavement.

Or perhaps he was simply afraid. If the oaths could be broken — and his father had said they could not — he might have saved that child. He might have prevented the inevitable death that was a result of broken oaths.

Nenyane almost broke his hand, she crushed it so tightly; the physical pain drew him away from those memories, that terrible guilt.

What the dogs saw, he saw without effort. What Nenyane saw required concentration. She was both angry and worried at his hesitance, but didn't argue; she looked.

He found her vision with a snap that was almost physical. He could still see what he saw, what his dogs saw, but this time — for the first time — they blended in a way that caused far less pain. No, more than that: it felt almost natural. Comfortable. He could feel her hand in his, but there was no pain at the tightness of either her grip or his.

He could see exactly what he needed to see; there was a web of grey extending from the lord, the individual strands a blend of black and white as they led to those she commanded. He did not know if those under her command had willingly submitted or not, but knew that her commands were relayed through those bindings.

Maybe some of her people would follow her in their absence; he was certain some would not. He could reduce her advantage here without killing those who were subservient to her will — as Steane had been, who had struggled in his fashion to give them information before his death.

Stephen moved along the side edge of the battlefield; his dogs made clear that the Hunters were following. They were not reckless in their advance, but neither were they hesitant; where he stepped, they followed.

Gervanno di'Sarrado, however, had taken the position to Nenyane's left — the position that Nenyane herself would have occupied had she not been so awkwardly bound to Stephen's side. His blade was in his hand, and the fox — Stephen cursed inwardly. The fox remained in the crook of his arm. Gervanno was accustomed to wielding sword in one hand or two, where two were necessary; he could not do that now. But one-handed and encumbered, Gervanno was far more than competent.

Of course. I chose him.

He chose you, Stephen countered, as he reached out to touch the closest of the strands of binding. It broke in his hand, as the others had done; he held it, tightening hand into fist as he felt the faintest of impressions, the faintest of emotions, from the being in whom it had been planted.

A tree. It was a tree. *Arborii.* A tree like Steane.

No, mortal, nothing like that one; we are saplings, and weak, in comparison. What are your commands?

He started to tell them to leave, but the words failed him. Instead, he looked back at the great, three-headed beast, and beyond that beast to the tree upon which Amberg's survival had depended.

The trees were not his dogs; he could not see as they saw, could not order them to attack—and retreat—in a matter of instinctive seconds. They did not trust him, did not love him, as his dogs did and would. He could not see what they saw—but he could hear them. He could feel their emotions, their confusion, their despair and surrender.

This binding was not a binding they had ever wanted. It was a choice, but the choice was obedience or death. He could feel it in the strands that had crossed his palm.

How was it different than the huntbrother's oath? Was that oath not a matter of life or death, given where huntbrothers were generally found?

Nenyane was highly annoyed by the passing thought, but as they continued to move—and they had not stopped—she wasted no effort on castigation. She was armed, as was Gervanno, but arguably more encumbered. Stephen, however, was unarmed. He could not wield sword and break bindings he could not even see without Nenyane's vision.

He heard the cry of rage the lord of the lands uttered as he swept the bindings that enforced obedience from a small portion of her forces. Not all who served her were enslaved; not all who had joined a growing army had been given any other choice.

But a significant number had been bound, and Stephen freed every single one he could reach.

———

GERVANNO NOTICED the moment the enemy army began to crumble— he had seen it before. He had even been part of that dissolution of will and intent, choosing retreat where retreat had been mandated by circumstances beyond his control: the size of the opposing army, the composition, unexpected and disastrous changes in weather.

The Hunters of the various demesnes bracketed Stephen and Nenyane, stepping in to take on the enemies just beyond the easy reach of Gervanno's sword. Stephen moved at the edge of the battlefield, attempting to circumnavigate the heart of the lord's forces—but his motion was odd, unpredictable.

There was no cunning here, but there seldom was on the field of battle; desperation and the need to survive became the driving force of most soldiers who were far from the instructions of the command center.

But in Gervanno's experience, there had always been one man on the field to whom new soldiers might look should they panic, and as battles became, at last, war, those who had survived built necessary camaraderie with their compatriots; they grew to understand their measure, their ability, their natural inclinations, and they became a unit. Did they care about each other?

Yes. It was that responsibility that often served as bulwark against panic.

None of the enemy soldiers here were human, but Gervanno could see, clearly, that they were not accustomed to battle, to battlefields of this nature. Individually, they might kill those weaker than themselves should the opportunity arise, but they had not learned to consider the abilities—weaknesses and strengths—of those with whom they stood. Only those who feared the swords of the Hunters stood back, watching, observing, waiting for their moment to strike safely.

Some of those would never strike.

Gervanno was uncertain why Stephen did not draw sword; he accepted it because Nenyane had insisted, and she did not enter combat making foolish choices. Stephen of Maubreche was golden-eyed. In the Dominion, that might well have been his death, for eyes of gold were considered demonic. In the North, they were considered a blessing.

Gervanno had not spent most of his life in the North, but in the Kingdom of Breodanir, he could now see how much of a blessing it was. He did not know what the god-born—for so they were called—could do, did not know how much of the abilities that came with their blood overlapped the skills of the Widan.

But he suspected that none of the Widan could—or would—do what Stephen of Maubreche now did. He could see the left flank falter;

he could see the trees—for almost all were trees—peel away from their positions in the lord's army. And he could hear the rage of that lord.

He had time to shout a warning to the Hunters, but no time to be certain they had heard—and could respond—in time. He was certain Nenyane heard, and that, on this unnatural battlefield, would have to be enough. The lord of the lands was not human, not mortal—but she was clearly possessed of the power of the Widan.

The earth, upon which he had been standing seconds before, broke.

THE LORD DID NOT SEEM to be concerned with the effect of the breaking earth on her own forces—but some of the forces were trees, and they could shift their roots in order to remain standing.

The Hunters were not so gifted. Alex fell, as did Heiden, but neither fell into the crevices the movement of earth had created; Ansel retrieved his huntbrother, and Max caught Alex. Both of the Margen Hunters had moved instantly at Gervanno's shouted warning, remaining on the side of the growing divide that Ansel and Heiden now occupied.

The lord could not attack them directly—the three-headed beast had pinned her in place. The earth did not break beneath the creature's feet, or beneath hers, and the rumbling stopped at the first failed attempt. But that attempt changed the shape of the battlefield. Or so it appeared initially.

Gervanno blinked rapidly when the crevices—wounds in the surface of the earth—began to close. He glanced once at the tree which remained rooted in the earth at the center of the small lake; he could almost see its branches move, as if they were stiff limbs. They pointed to the center of the field—just beyond the lord and the three-headed beast.

Had Gervanno been able to communicate with the tree, he would have asked it to stabilize the earth beneath their feet. He could not. But perhaps the tree, in silence, had offered what guidance it could.

Gervanno turned to snap a new set of orders to the Hunters over whom he had no right of command. "There! The ground there should be safe to stand on!"

Nenyane didn't question. She had been leading Stephen by the hand, pausing only to allow him to break the strands that bound servants to their sole master, and she adjusted course. It was unlikely she'd let him fall, but the gifts granted him by birth did not allow him to fly. The Northern mage had—but he was besieged in air, now, his attention focused on the battlefield that had formed in the sky.

———————————

THEY WHITTLED AWAY at the forces directly behind the lord as they moved toward stable ground, but there were far more enslaved directly behind her than in the flanks.

She, who gained her throne by treachery, trusts no one and nothing that is not subservient to her will.

Stephen caught strands, broke them, felt them warm his palm. He let them go—or thought he let them go—but the sense of their presence clung stubbornly. The spears they had made of their branches dulled; leaves, withered at the edges, adorned the field.

And apples.

For some reason, the apples were the thing that made the deepest impression—they were almost haunting. Fallen apples, of all things, at the heart of a battlefield. Trees that grew fruit, apples that were meant —in times of peace—to bud, blossom, ripen, and to become food for those who tended them.

Apple trees weren't meant for war. If the trees in the wilderness had spirits, will, sentience, they were still apple trees: the sense of the wrongness of their presence was sharp and deep. To Stephen, only children—armed poorly and forced to the fields of war—would cause more distress, feel more wrong.

He couldn't even say why. It made no sense.

But the trees he held, the trees he had freed—apple trees, pear trees, even peach—filled his thoughts, for just one moment, with the warmth of orchards, and the safety of them, their only enemy the insects who, like people, wanted to eat what the trees grew.

He thought of the village of Amberg, thought of the people who the great tree had kept safe in the middle of this hostile wilderness, and thought of the orchard that no longer existed except as an ideal.

And then, almost without deliberation, he said to the trees: *go to the tree in the lake. Gather round it; stand beneath its boughs, take root in the earth there. Be safe.*

They obeyed as if they had no choice—and perhaps they didn't, given what he had broken and taken. To his surprise, they moved quickly, skirting their lord's battle, and heading beyond her. She caught sight of them as they passed her and one blade swept down, cutting a tree in two.

The others, however, moved more swiftly; they did not stop to check on their fallen companion. Perhaps they couldn't. Perhaps that was the power of the bindings he had taken for himself.

Perhaps not. For as they approached the tree that stood in the small lake, he could feel a sudden rustle of surprise, of joy, of homecoming.

CHAPTER TWENTY-EIGHT

Nenyane was surprised; surprise was followed by annoyance. She saw the trees that Stephen had managed to liberate move in a rush—leading some to their deaths—toward a single location. But she heard their voices in a fashion Stephen did not. They were raised in astonishment and in a deep, deep joy, Summer voices exposed to the elements. She thought the trees who had died by the lord who had enslaved them did not regret that death, for they died swiftly, and they died without fear or pain.

It was not the cries of delighted surprise that she heard most clearly; it was the name. The name the trees spoke as they reached the destination toward which Stephen had commanded them.

The lord heard the name. It was not, as it should have been, her name. The land spoke her name, when it spoke at all; the trees spoke her name. Those creatures who inhabited this domain spoke it as well, a shiver of syllables, a rustle of sound.

But not these trees. Not the trees that Stephen thought of as nature's hearth. He was wrong; she did not correct him. Some mistakes were harmless, and some were fortuitous. She did not know what had possessed Stephen to send those trees to the great tree, the remnants of the land's former lord. But she knew, as she heard their shivering cries, that the former lord had been loved.

The lord the Hunters fought had not been, not in this fashion; those trees, could they choose to serve a lord, would never have chosen her.

Nenyane had never understood the desire to be loved. To love? Yes. Perhaps to love as they loved, in their frenzied rush to reach the heart of Amberg's protection. She could not hear the voice of the great tree, as she now thought of him, but it wasn't necessary. They had come home, and if home was a tiny patch of land, built and claimed as it could be by the cautious spreading of ancient roots, it didn't matter.

The lands upon which Amberg were situated were not the lord's lands, although they occupied an area within her borders. They were not quite unclaimed, but the claim was tenuous, fragile; Nenyane had assumed initially that this was due to the nature of the barriers the gods had erected to keep the immortal and the mortal from interacting.

She knew, now, that that was not entirely correct.

She wondered if Ansel understood what she understood; his voice had a measure of power—infinitesimally small in comparison to the lord's—in this small stretch of wilderness. If he survived, she would tell him.

Now, she turned her eyes to the battlefield—to the stretch of almost open ground that the great tree had deemed safe enough for the rest of the mortals to stand on.

GERVANNO'S SWORD was not red with blood, as it would have been had he been on the battlefields of Averda. He had cut down the enemies that had blindly attacked Stephen of Maubreche. Although Nenyane had done her share of damage, her blade was hampered; she did not let go of Stephen's hand. He accepted that this was a necessity, and did not question it. He himself was hampered by the fox he had chosen to carry. He had asked the fox if he might get down, and the fox had growled.

Gervanno's interaction with the sentient elements of the wilderness was avoidance where possible, attack where not. The fox was the exception.

He was aware that the fox could increase—or decrease—his weight at will. It was not the weight that was the difficulty; it was the lack of a left arm. He had fought while injured before, and this was a similar situation, absent the physical pain. He was not all he could be on this field. But the number of enemies was decreasing as Nenyane and Stephen continued to move, and some headed past him in a rush that spoke not of attack but flight. He glanced back only once, when Nenyane stepped in to dispatch an attacker, but the trees and the animals seemed to be streaming toward the lake and the tree at its center, not beyond it.

The village had Margen guards to offer protection, but that protection was limited. Should the forces fighting here fall, the village would not survive.

He was certain they would not fall until the moment the three-headed creature roared.

STEPHEN FROZE at the sound of the lion's roar: it was imbued with pain and rage. Nenyane froze as well. Everything they had done so far had relied upon the three-headed creature; the lord of the lands was pinned down by their attacks, and their small group could afford to venture onto the battlefield because the lord was occupied.

Stephen turned, as Nenyane turned; Gervanno stepped past them both, his blade an arc of steel that reflected sunlight.

We've done what we can, his huntbrother said. She glanced once at the sky, the second field of battle, and then focused on the lord and the injured beast. The ground beneath their feet trembled. *And they've done what they could. The sun is in the sky; the lord is far from her seat of power. If she were wise, she would retreat.*

Her tone made clear this would not happen. She tightened her grip on Stephen's hand briefly, and then let go, turning to face the fox. "We need him, now. Let him go."

The fox glared at Nenyane, eyes flashing.

No, Stephen thought, the fox's eyes weren't flashing; they were glowing, the brightness of silver and gold increasing until they were almost painful to meet.

"I have not claimed him; he is free to make his own choices. For now."

She did not stay to argue; when she moved, Stephen moved with her, falling a step behind to her right; Gervanno moved into position to her left. The rest of the Hunters shifted in place, tightening their formation at Nenyane's back. Horns were raised and winded, as if the sound was necessity.

Stephen sent comfort to the lion, as if the lion were in truth one of his pack; he indicated, wordless, that the lion should fall back, making room for the much smaller, much more agile Nenyane.

The lion resisted as if it were Pearl, but did not fight overlong; at this distance, given the creature's size, Stephen could see the wound that had caused the roar of pain. The lord of these lands had surrendered sword to cause it, and the sword shimmered, a faint, angry gold. Gold, not the red of the demon-kin.

It was not the only sword the lord wielded; the other remained in her hand, and it was crimson and burgundy with the blood of landed blows. The three-headed creature's attacks were fang, beak, claw; the head that seemed most human did not wield blades. Sparks left fingertips as that head rose, arms swept wide as if to embrace death.

Magic, Stephen thought.

Nenyane did not reply. If the three-headed creature was the largest being upon this field, the lord was the most powerful, but her weapons were weapons that Nenyane recognized; her own sword was raised and ready before she leapt. Her leap carried her high above Stephen and Gervanno's heads, and when she came down to earth, she landed lightly, her feet brushing earth before she leapt again.

The lord turned to her, but turned late; Nenyane's sword cut halfway through her free arm—the arm she had extended to pierce the beast who had been her only opponent.

The lord did not roar or cry out in pain; she cried out in rage, instead; the skies above them all darkened as clouds rolled in to cover the sun's light. The earth at her feet rose; stones flew. Nenyane avoided them.

Gervanno avoided most.

The fox growled, the growl wrapped around syllables. Given the language—or the lack of recognizable language—Stephen thought the words meant for the lord. She failed to answer, so focused was she on Nenyane; the style of attack the lord now faced was different, the speed far greater. Nenyane should not have had the reach the larger beast had had, but she was unencumbered by bulk, and appeared to be unencumbered by something as trivial as gravity.

Stephen was not surprised when the air came to her aid; it held her when she landed, buoyed her when she leapt. He glanced up at the sky —or rather, Patches did. The mage and the bard continued their aerial assault, but the winged creatures were far more cautious now, as their numbers had dwindled significantly.

The fox roared.

Thunder replied, and with it, lightning. The lightning was neither natural nor unfocused; it struck the ground that Stephen had occupied before he threw himself out of the way. The rain that followed in its wake was far more of a hazard. Visibility dropped instantly—for Stephen. Not for the lord who now wielded lightning and rain.

The flying creatures were not spared the storm. The lightning, yes; it was aimed at the enemies on the ground, and it was far more precise as a weapon. The Hunters dodged, but it was harder: the rain made the ground soft, and slippery; the sound of falling rain muted sounds and scents necessary for reflexive action. It would not be the first time the Hunters had faced storms—but in almost all such instances, they chose to call the hunt and retreat.

If their enemies were likewise hampered by the storm, the playing field remained even—or as even as it had been, given the disparity in numbers.

"How dare you!"

JARVEN REMAINED AT A DISTANCE. The storm that now raged had a distinct circumference, one that covered only a specific part of the battlefield. It was not quite centered on the lord of these lands, but close, and it encompassed every one of Jarven's erstwhile allies. Even the lightning that flashed at irregular—and frequent—intervals did little to illuminate the occupants of the field.

But when he heard his master's voice, he stilled; even breath was held, the words reverberated so clearly. Almost, he regretted maintaining his distance; he felt something in the words resonate, as if they were a single, perfectly struck bell. Perhaps those who were not connected to the elder in the fashion Jarven was would not hear or feel it as he did. Perhaps those whose natural caution tipped over into fear would be frozen with it until the sound passed.

Jarven felt a growing excitement.

He had learned to walk through any natural weather in the wilderness. This was not natural; he was not certain he could walk to one side of the raging storm and remain unaffected. He had learned that the weather in lordless lands was similar to the weather in the mortal terrains through which he had traveled in his youth; the weather in ruled lands became a natural part of their lord's whims.

He had been taught that respect was due the lords of those ruled lands if one wanted to survive. He knew how to offer the gestures that denoted respect—it was very similar to his political experiences in Averalaan. But the fox was a creature of power who understood that the rules he taught were not necessarily rules that applied to himself.

What had happened? The fox had made clear he intended to sit out this conflict, just as Jarven had chosen to do. To bear witness, largely because it alleviated his ageless boredom, his restlessness, his need to move.

Jarven frowned as the fox roared, bracketing his outrage with far more primality. His excitement, his curiosity banked as cold froze his thoughts.

It was the Southerner. It was Gervanno di'Sarrado.

GERVANNO HAD CONSIDERED the fox an unwieldy, unwelcome burden —a dangerous one for a man whose life depended on his combat ability. But when the storm started, when the lightning struck, he revised that opinion: the fox was a cumbersome, necessary shield. In the South, shields were seldom used, seldom relied on.

Here, he had not had the option, but his sword seemed to serve as a rod for the unnatural lightning that was clearly the lord's weapon. Had it not been for the sudden, torrential rain, he would have felt confident he could avoid it—but the rain fell like a wet, cold curtain as lightning continued to strike. He could no longer see Nenyane, could no longer see Stephen clearly; the other Hunters had likewise vanished from view until and unless he was almost upon them.

He failed to dodge once; once should have been the end.

The lightning, however, hit the fox. Gervanno cursed, turning his attention to the small, furry creature in the crook of his arm. He expected to see blackened fur, and indeed the lightning had affected the fox's fur—but there was no burnt flesh. The fur itself was gold; it stood on end, and it was followed by a cry of rage.

Respect was due the powerful. Respect, obedience to hierarchy. When two Tyrs met across a table, they were careful, cautious in the way they even implied aggression or anger, aware, always, that should the wrong words be used, the wrong gestures offered, the wrong food, the wrong cushions, war would follow. In some cases, that war would be small border skirmishes—which had been much of Gervanno's early life. But the threat of something that moved beyond the borders was always present.

The fox was akin to the Tyrs.

The fact that the elder was not the intended target of the lightning strike mattered little. The fact that, should he desire to be an observer, not a participant, he should never have demanded that Gervanno—an active, necessary participant—carry him, mattered less.

The fox leapt from Gervanno's arm, freeing him from burden and warmth. To Gervanno's surprise, he could see the fox through sheets of water as the fox moved toward the lord of the lands. There was no peace to be offered here. *How dare you* was a flag of war. If the fox felt disrespected, he had chosen to offer disrespect in return.

But the fox did not remain tiny. He had never been a fox; it had been a convenient fiction, one that did not imply innate threat if one were not poultry or timid herbivore. He shed it, as his fur shed water. But he did not become a larger fox, did not take on the shape of a larger animal. It seemed to Gervanno that the fox stepped out of his own skin, gaining height as he took on the shape of a man.

A man very like the Northern mage, but with hair of gold that fell like cloak down his shoulders and back. Gervanno could not see his face, could not see his expression, but he could feel it in the air, almost literally; the water that fell in sheets failed to touch the elder at all, as if moving in every possible direction to avoid provoking further rage.

Gervanno raised voice to warn the Hunters not to touch or impede this new combatant, hoping that the rain did not wash all of the sound away.

JARVEN COULD SEE his master clearly. He had very seldom seen him take this form. When the fox had been forced to fight, he usually adopted the form of a golden bear—a very large one. He had discarded that option, a certain sign of both fury and the respect due the lord's power, her chosen shape.

Jarven had seen turtles rule land; he had seen boars. Neither spoke in a fashion Jarven could understand, but he had treated them with the deference their position demanded. He had seldom encountered a lord such as the one who ruled these lands, but he had taken care to avoid any such interaction, assuming the more human a lord looked, the more subtle the danger they offered.

The turtle had made no attempt to enlarge its holdings, its lands; had not appeared to equate power with the number of servants who did its bidding. Had not, in Jarven's opinion, cared to appear to *be* a power. In Jarven's life, such appearance had been a tool or a weapon, depending on what he hoped to gain from it. The turtle did not, and would not, care. But it did not build civilizations. It did not build places of architectural wonder. It did not create works of art. It simply existed.

Simple existence had no appeal to Jarven, nor would it ever.

The fox had not appeared to be a curator of the marvels that caught and held Jarven's attention — but he had power, and it was a power he could bestow on those he considered worthy. Jarven had little interest in living as the fox lived, but a deep and abiding interest in the power that could be bestowed. He understood, when he accepted — and survived — the grant of those gifts, that he had little to offer the fox in return. The power was a loan, the payment, service.

Jarven would never offer service as Gervanno di'Sarrado did.

But as he watched his master lift spear, as he watched his master's hair fly back and up as if cutting water, he wondered what the elder had created in times so long past they might even be forgotten to such an ancient immortal. He wondered if anything created by a creature who did not rule had stood the test of time.

He stood, witness now as his master continued to unfold, the animal skin discarded as the disguise it had always been.

If summoned, Jarven would fight. That was part of the nature of his agreement with the elder. Power was never granted freely to those who were less powerful. Not by the wise.

But it was not, in the end, Jarven who was summoned. No, it was Gervanno. And summon was not the correct word; Gervanno merely stepped up, stepped in, unwilling to back away unless commanded to retreat.

The fox did not utter that command.

HAD Gervanno not witnessed the fox's transformation, he would have recognized him nonetheless. Something about the man who stood untouched by the lord's storm felt both natural and familiar. The respect, the obedience, Gervanno had long afforded the small, demanding creature had come, viscerally, from the certainty that he was capable of this; that his diminutive form was a simple social nicety, a polite mask, a way of reducing unwanted, unnecessary conflict.

But the ability to wage war—to wage it and win it—had always been within him.

He was not Gervanno's lord; he was not Gervanno's master. But it was a truth long accepted by any lowborn cerdan that the undercurrents of power failed to acknowledge the service that could be demanded of the powerless. There was very little Gervanno could do should a lord he did not serve demand it.

That was simple reality—a reality that did not change until he chose to forsake the lands of his birth and sign on with a merchant caravan. A caravan that did not follow the rules of the South, the rules which had guided and shaped the entirety of his life. There had been freedom in it, an unexpected—and possibly, at the beginning, undesired—freedom. All of the minute social rules that had governed his life were irrelevant to Evaro and Sylvia, and Evaro in theory was master. But Evaro, while of the South and a free man, had never played the same games of territory and political dominance; he was concerned about money.

Money was, in a pragmatic sense, a concern for any of the Dominion's cerdan—but it was a concern never to be aired, never to be spoken of. Men of honor did not quibble about *money*. Evaro had rolled his eyes and washed his hands of the discussion. Sylvia, however, had not. She'd traveled the road under all conditions, and looked more Voyani than not; the sun and wind aged a person, and he could see the weight of those lines in her face, her expression.

But he could see, as well, the interior strength of the woman. And in her turn she could see something in Gervanno that she approved of. He had never asked; she had seldom offered. But she had taught him, on that first day, how to negotiate, how to bargain, and how to walk away.

You will never be paid what you're worth if you cannot even speak the word money.

Was it not in her best interest to pay him a pittance, then?

Resentment is tricky, Gervanno. If you have been fortunate enough not to learn this, I would not have Evaro's caravan be your teacher. Yes, we could pay you a pittance. We could pay you less than young Silvo, whose uncle at least has some sense. You would accept it.

But the road changes people; always has, always will. And the needs of caravans are almost universal. If you agree to serve, you will serve. To those younger, your stories of battlefields will build a cohesive group — and that is what I require.

But he had not served honorably. He had frozen, as terrified as a rabbit in the face of a great bird of prey. He had survived because visceral cowardice had kept him in place, kept him hidden. He had known, then, that nothing he could do would give him any chance of survival. Nothing he could do could save any of the men and women with whom he had traveled the merchant road.

But dying might have saved *him*.

He was reckless, his body moving almost synchronously with thought, movement was so instinctive. He wielded sword in rain and out of it — for the rain did not strike either the lord or the fox — moving to cut or parry, refusing to stand still, because stillness might lead to the terror that had unmanned him, had broken him.

In Nenyane of Maubreche, his greed had become far louder than his shame: she was the shining beacon; she was the sword master from whom he might learn to be perfect.

All else was his failure, but the light of her existence shone in even the darkest of corners: if he learned what she had to teach, if he became more powerful, more perfect, he *could have made a difference.*

Fear was the thread that bound disparate elements of his life together. Fear of loss. Of losing face. Of losing honor. Of losing comrades — so many in the battle of the Averdan valleys. So many when he had retired — fled — those fields, searching for an escape from the responsibility of life and death. No more youths to train — and bury. No more men who believed that he was in any way better than the lords he served.

And yet he had come to the same place, on the foreign roads in the cold North. No, a far worse place. He had not escaped the demons of the Averdan valleys.

He accepted, now, that he never would. Never while he lived.

Nenyane fought the lord. The fox joined her. Gervanno leapt into the gap between them, aware, always, of the arc of Nenyane's blade, the thrust of the fox's deadly spear. Aware of the damage he avoided and the damage he caused.

STEPHEN COULD TRANSMIT information about the lord's movements to Nenyane; he could watch through his dogs. None of it would arrive in time. The rain did not ease up and visibility remained poor, but the thrusts of directed lightning stopped as what had been the fox entered the field. The Hunters could feel his fury as if it were a tangible, physical presence: as if it defined his form, his shape, his size.

But the lord of these lands was impressive in a similar fashion. Nenyane had taken down demons; she had attacked those of power without concern. None of those demons had been the opponents this lord was. Even given the advent of the forest elder as he joined the fray, Nenyane was constantly on the move; the lord matched her speed.

Stephen almost pulled Gervanno away, but Nenyane snapped an urgent *No; you go*.

He stepped back, then. He could signal retreat to Max, but the call to retreat wasn't in his hands; it was in Ansel's.

Nenyane did not approve. He could feel her annoyance; the nicety of proper hierarchy on this particular battlefield was impractical. Stephen accepted what he could not change. He drew horn from belt, placed it to lips, and signaled retreat. He hoped that retreat — to the rest of the Hunters — meant what it meant to Stephen: to the tree. Or rather, to the many trees.

The rain did not fall on the lake. It was the first thing they noticed, as the Hunters made their way to the tree — to breathe, to strategize, and to watch what the rain allowed them to see. Stephen could not see the mage or the bard.

The trees that had moved at the command of the land's lord now moved toward the Hunters, branches creaking. But they moved without animosity. Stephen could feel their welcome.

"Don't attack — they mean no harm!" he said, sharing this with the rest of the Hunters. "And I think Max and Aelle need medical attention."

Alex supported his brother. Brandon — and Heiden — supported Aelle. Ansel had emerged unscathed. No one else had, although the cuts, scrapes, and bruises were not serious enough to be deadly.

To Stephen's surprise, the trees opened a small path to the great tree, indicating that it should be taken. Stephen looked back.

Go, Nenyane told him.

She was his huntbrother. He did not want to leave her behind. But he was willing, given the fox, to let the others retreat to safety.

Ansel caught his arm as he turned back.

"There's one thing I can do that will end this," Stephen replied. "And Nenyane won't pull back."

Ansel looked as if he wanted to argue, but let his hand fall away. Stephen turned back toward the wall of water beyond which his huntbrother fought.

You can't, Nenyane told him. *You can't see what you need to see if I'm not with you.*

He nodded, less certain than she was. Visibility was a problem for all of the denizens of this sodden field; they were all equally hampered. But he was certain that, beyond where the lord now fought, strands similar to the ones he had broken remained, compelling those who would otherwise seek peace to fight. If he could break that binding, the army would all but vanish.

But to do that, he would have to be directly behind her, and close enough that he could reach all the bindings he could see. The farther from her, the greater the separation between the strands.

He did not understand why he had this gift; it was not the curse of oathbinding that had shadowed most of his living memory. He was almost certain that it was not due to Bredan's blood, but some combination of god-born gift and Nenyane. But Nenyane would not be beside him; she would not be holding his hand, or dragging him across the field. He had never seen the strands with his own eyes, and hers were engaged with her own survival.

This would help.

He sent three of his dogs to join Steel and Max; he kept four, although they were of less strategic use. That would change if the rain stopped; he had hope, as the lightning no longer flashed. He stepped into the rain and began to move.

———

NENYANE DID NOT ABANDON the fight on the field—it was impossible to do it safely. The lord did not understand why—or how—she had lost control of her many followers, but she recognized that Nenyane—and the fox who had joined her—were not normal. They were not what the other humans were. She might have been cautious around the mortal who seemed to command the wind, but perhaps not; on a field that included Illaraphaniel and the fox, very little would stand out as a threat.

Nenyane stood out. She always would. If she was not Firstborn, not eldest, not a scion of one of the ancient races, she was powerful in a similar fashion. Or she should have been. The lord did not notice the lack; Nenyane did.

She did not expose it. But she felt the gravity of the lord's presence every time her feet touched soil; she felt the weight of her regard as a physical pressure. Had she been only slightly less aware, she would be severely injured. She could not take a blow, even a glancing blow; if it connected, she would be out of the fight.

Injured, the lord was far easier to evade; she felt annoyed that Gervanno could step in and connect, could wound the lord, even if the wounds were insignificant. Annoyed or not, Nenyane created openings in which he could land a blow. If this was a battle of attrition, Gervanno would flag first, tire first—and die first if exhaustion slowed him.

She didn't want that.

Neither, it seemed, did the fox. If she had been concerned—or irritated—by the relationship between the two, she almost repented: it was because the fox had unmasked himself on this field that they could manage to do any damage at all. But the fox's fury was, like the heavy fall of rain, something *felt*. It exerted at least as much pressure as the lord's.

The fox did not rule in the wilderness. Rulership of the wilderness was not in any way straightforward. But had he desired a land of his own, it would be his. Even this one, soon to be lordless. It was how rulership changed in the wilderness, save only during times of great war: the lord was challenged almost constantly, and the survivor renewed the compact with the land itself.

This was not a fight for rulership. It was a fight for the survival of Amberg, of Bowgren, of Breodanir—of Maubreche, which would, of all demesnes, be last to fall.

And it was a simple, small battle in the larger war—but as all battles and wars, it was fought one soldier at a time, one unit, one army. At the heart of it, at the end of it, Allasakar, the Lord of the Hells. She could almost hear his voice in this living, distant place, and she saw, at last, the touch of that lord's grace in the lord of these lands.

She felt, in that moment, she was a bell that had, like great cathedral bells, been struck.

STEPHEN FELT IT AT A REMOVE, and silence—of a different kind—descended on the field. Rain became snow in an instant, and breath came out in clouds. Summer had come to these lands, and now Summer had been driven so far back that the forest of moving trees no longer looked the same.

Drenched skin gave way to ice and cold; snow blanketed the ground and began to climb in height. But the poor visibility lessened; he could not say why. He did not close his eyes; seeing through Nenyane's would not be of aid. But he looked, hands becoming bunched fists. He wore no gloves, and his mobility would soon succumb to the instant, bitter cold.

Go back to the tree!

No. Not yet. Not yet, because in the white of falling snow, he could *see*. He could see the web that extended from the lord, could see that it was similar and dissimilar from the strands he had broken; much darker, the grey going to black, to midnight.

To night and Winter. The Lord of the Hells.

Around her, mired in ice, creatures blinked in and out, glimpses of their forms and shapes revealed and concealed by snowfall. No Hunters accompanied him; he had his dogs, and the Hunter's trance. He used both, keeping himself in constant motion to generate necessary heat.

He reached for the webs, running, uncertain whether or not he should be able to see them, and uncertain whether or not they would break in Nenyane's absence. This time, however, what was left in his hands was not only the bindings that enslaved; for just one moment, he could feel the lord herself.

And she could feel him.

HE ALMOST LOST AN ARM; he was far enough behind the lord that her sudden turn, blade arcing as snow melted against its flat, spun around. He leapt back; the blade's edge had cut through leather and cloth almost without friction.

She could not break what he held. Her blade passed, unimpeded, through it.

He could attempt to exert his own will upon the lord, and did. If it slowed her at all, he could not see it. What he did, however, was gain the entirety of her attention. It was bad for Stephen, but good for the three who faced her — if he survived. His instincts had always been reliable; they were better than that, now. He could sense where she intended to strike — but even knowing it, he had barely enough time to dodge.

The wind howled in rage at his back; it caught him in its folds, held him a moment.

Nenyane was there to parry — and to strike. He saw through Patches's eyes as he moved, and moved again. The lord was forced to face Nenyane, turning from the being the fox had become.

Only the lord's upward leap prevented the fox from impaling her. However, she had moved without turning to look back at the fox, as if attuned to her enemy's movement. It was Stephen she attacked now, her face a visage of fury. He tried to assert his will, to slow her, to make use of what he'd taken.

In a fashion, he succeeded.

He wanted her stopped. At his back, her unwilling soldiers moved toward her in a knot; the earth trembled beneath their feet. They were not dogs; he could not interact with them as he would with his hunting pack. But they responded to his wordless desire, as if all words were irrelevant; they understood what he wanted.

He understood the nature of the binding. He understood the ways in which it felt natural, and the ways in which it did not. He was accustomed to asserting will; one could hardly train dogs if the dogs did not know who was actually in command. But if it was possible to force a dog to obey a person they did not wish to acknowledge as master, it was futile; one could not hunt with such a divided pack.

Will was necessary, but affection and loyalty were just as valuable, just as important; it was the permission required to properly lead a hunting pack.

This binding did not require permission. It required will, demanded subservience, obedience.

He focused on the lord, and she, on him; she could defend from, and attack, the other three who harried her without losing sight of Stephen.

But she could not command him. Whatever binding she had wrapped around the others required some element of consent Stephen had not, and would never, give. This was not the reason for her rage. The many servants who owed her loyalty and obedience had never offered it willingly; he had reduced the size of her host considerably, while increasing his allies.

She reduced it in other ways. The trees could not move as quickly as Stephen or Nenyane. They did not parry her blows, but obstructed them, losing branches—and life—as they did. Had they been terrified, Stephen might have frozen—but they were possessed of a rage that equaled their lord's.

But trees had not been her only servants, her only soldiers. If the demons had been destroyed—and even the thought fueled rage—she had commanded the forest creatures. Stephen had broken that binding in some of the enslaved. Animals were agile in ways trees were not.

They bled, as his dogs would have bled; died, as his dogs might yet die. And they drew blood from glancing attacks, just as Gervanno had done. Stephen could not aid Meralonne or Kallandras in the same fashion; neither were now his concern. They were like Nenyane in some fashion; allies, but not dependents.

But the animals and the trees that were dying were no match for any of the three; no match for the lord who now turned the landscape into a thing of snow and ice as she gathered, and spent, her power. They fought—and destroyed—each other at her command and Stephen's need, beast against beast.

Summer was not her season. He tried to remember what had been said about Summer, Winter, and the permanence of either in the wilderness.

Beyond the snow and ice, a line marked that Summer. A tree held that line.

He knew where the creatures who were dying in their attempts to slow or stop their former lord needed to go. He knew where their roots had to be laid down. And he knew, as well, that he survived in part because they had not. Beneath the boughs of trees, the cold was less brutal; trunks served as windbreaks.

But if he attempted to retreat to where the trees now gathered, she would follow. If she followed, she would become aware of the great tree to which Amberg owed its survival, and if she destroyed that tree, Winter would descend everywhere.

But even thinking it, even watching chips of bark fly, he knew; he could feel certainty growing as the seconds passed. And he knew that that certainty was rooted not in the great tree itself, but in the trees that had made their way to its side. These trees, these animals, still trapped on the battlefield, needed to join them.

He sent them away in ones and twos, touching the frightened who had not yet given way to rage and fury. Nenyane did not argue against it. She had managed to connect, twice, with the lord; her blade cut away something that looked almost diaphanous, but peeled on contact with blade's edge.

This was a battle of attrition, but absent Nenyane and the freed forest denizens, he would have already lost it.

The fox roared; Stephen could not see him, but no one on this field could fail to hear his voice, so different in texture to the lord's, but just as primal. Ice cracked beneath Stephen's feet, but the ground did not break.

Foolish, stupid mortal—go!

Legs shuddering—his, his dogs'—he obeyed the viscerally felt command.

GERVANNO HAD NEVER FELT a cold this chilling, this deep; he knew he had slowed, knew his movements had gained a shakiness that only warmth would dispel. The cold was slow to take him, but when it did, he understood: he had to retreat, if he wished to survive.

The fox knew as well, although the snow and the ice did not seem to touch him at all. Where the fox—where the man—now stood, there was no snow, no ice. But Gervanno could not cleave, like a bewildered child, to his side; the fox was in constant motion, and he was armed. Close proximity could easily become just as dangerous to Gervanno as the lord and the bitter cold.

But as he lost mobility, he saw Nenyane, blade in motion; he inhaled, exhaled, and continued to move.

Until the fox cried out in frustration, the words reverberating through Gervanno as if they were a blow. He did not understand the role of the fox on this field, but understood the meaning behind the words; Gervanno was retreating before the echoes had died to howling wind.

Around the fox, Summer was raiment. Beyond the fox, Nenyane fought in Winter.

And it was to Summer that Gervanno di'Sarrado went. It was not an act of cowardice; it was not mindless flight. As those loyal to the lord attempted to cut him down, he faced, them, stepping back, and back again—aware of his surroundings and the risk retreat could pose. It would not be the first time he had been forced to call a retreat, and this time, he had only himself to consider.

Or so he thought.

But Stephen of Maubreche came around the fox, as if he, too, had heard the fox's disgusted command, and been moved by it in the same fashion. At Stephen's side came a straggling unit composed of beasts of prey, trees, and odd mounds of shivering fur. Had they not moved in a half circle behind Stephen's back, Gervanno might not have seen the Maubreche Hunter at all.

They did; they formed a protective shield as Stephen made his way to where Gervanno was. The Southerner and the Hunter exchanged a glance, a nod. Stephen was aware of what Gervanno's stance and movement meant. Together, they made their way out of the ice and snow of Winter into the immediate warmth of Summer sky.

Gervanno noted that the range of that warmth, that clarity of sky, had grown, as if rooted in part in the trees that had come to surround the great tree.

The remainder of the Hunters were arrayed at the shore of the lake farthest from Amberg. They had made a space for Stephen, or perhaps those who followed and defended him—a passage that led to the tree at the heart of the small lake. That tree was taller now, the trunk far wider, as if the growing presence of those who had deserted the lord of these lands had strengthened it.

From above, creatures deserted the sky, wings folded in angled dives, aimed at a single point on the ground beneath them. Some did not reach the earth; the wind drove them back, into the waiting blades of Nenyane, the polearm of the fox.

One or two managed to evade wind, mage, and bard, and those Gervanno stepped in to parry or strike, but in truth, the reach of his sword was not equal to the reach of the branches of moving trees, honed and sharpened into spears meant to keep wary enemies at a distance.

All of the aerial attackers had turned, as the lord had turned, to

Stephen of Maubreche. All had attempted to reach him. None had yet succeeded. Gervanno did not understand why Stephen was now the focal point of the lord's attacks, but did not doubt his observations.

Nenyane did not retreat; she slowed the lord. The fox did the same, if *slow* was the correct word; Gervanno was certain, were it not for the fox, the Northern mage would descend. That mage could not control the weather, but the aerial portion of the army had been kept largely at bay. Having dealt with flying demons before, Gervanno considered the mage's role of vital import.

Clearly, so did the mage.

THE LORD'S turn toward the retreating Maubreche Hunter changed the texture of the field itself. The storm that moved with her, the storm that surrounded her without ever touching or slowing her, shrank as she attempted to cut through the fox who stood blocking her path. Other servants came to the right and left of where she now fought, streaming past her almost blindly. They froze the moment their paws or roots touched sunlit ground; the line between ice and summer growth was sharp, extreme. None of the soldiers of that lord could fail to take note of the difference.

But they froze when her voice rose on a single word.

She had seen the tree.

For the first time since she had attempted to kill Stephen in earnest, her attention was divided.

Stephen did not know what shape the former lord had possessed when he had ruled; did not know if he was or could, as the fox could, be almost human in shape. He was certain that that lord had not, had never been, a tree.

But regardless, she recognized him. So, too, did the trees and the creatures that Stephen had managed to liberate from the current lord's compulsion. His hearing was not Nenyane's hearing, but as he stepped fully from snow and ice into sunlight and warmth, he could almost hear the faint whisper of a word. A name. It was not the name of the current lord.

The lands onto which Stephen had stepped were no longer her lands. From the moment the tree had been planted—from the moment she had become the lord of the lands the tree had once ruled—the earth in which the tree was rooted had never been hers. But these small lands had been quiet, hidden, tucked away in a corner distant from the heart of her territory—and the heart of her power. She had not seen them.

Were she in control of the lands into which Amberg had appeared, Amberg would not have survived.

She had assumed that it was the barrier erected by gods before their desertion of the mortal lands that had caused so much difficulty; the structures created by gods were almost, of necessity, greater than those that could be created by the lords of the wilderness. If not, how were those lands to remain contained and separate? Perhaps those ancient walls were part of the difficulty as well.

But she understood the whole of it as she gazed, eyes widening, at the tree.

Stephen did not understand immortals. Did not understand how far in the past their childhood and youths extended. But as the newly free followed and protected his retreat, he understood that some had been alive when the former lord fell—and they lifted their almost silent voices as they spoke his name.

A quaver of sound, as if they did not trust their ability to speak the name, gave way to a roar. No, not a roar. A song.

The lord's voice was louder, angrier; Stephen was grateful that he could not understand the language she spoke; to his ears it sounded akin to the language of the demons. But her roar of syllables could not overwhelm the smaller, quieter voices; her rage, her fury, could not completely diminish the song of joy and greeting that rose from the growing many.

Stephen glanced briefly at the tree through Steel's eyes. Yes, it was larger, taller, wider—but it was still at tree. The former lord, betrayed and dying, had been promised one chance to strike out at his betrayer. He had almost uprooted himself to join the three-headed beast, to ride into battle, to strike that promised blow. He had not; instead, his friend and liege strode into battle alone. The creature still lived, but the wounds they had taken were grievous.

They stood, now, by the side of the tree they still recognized as the lord they had willingly served, but their voices were no longer raised.

But perhaps the tree now understood that a blow against his betrayer could be struck in many ways; it was not always a matter of weapons of war and bloodshed. Rooted here in the lands he had once ruled—and shaped, if Stephen understood the rule of the wilderness—

he had caused far more injury than he might have, had he been a combatant like the fox.

Those who had once been his people came home to him.

Stephen understood that the size of a ruled land could be vast, but it could be as small as a perfect field, an orchard; the wilderness was not geographically fixed in the fashion that countries in his world were.

The former lord had been planted; he had waited an inestimable amount of time for this battle. This moment. Whoever had planted him had fulfilled the conditions by which he had agreed to *be* planted in a way he had not expected, not suspected.

But he had chosen protection and defense against pure attack. Perhaps he was the kind of person who always had. Stephen could not imagine that Nenyane would have made the same choice—not especially for the preservation of mortals who had never been part of his lands.

Bowgren owed the survival of Amberg to this tree and the lord at its heart, and Amberg was now safer than it had ever been: the size of the lands, seen in sunlight and Summer, had spread, foot by foot, in a widening circle as those Stephen had sundered from the lord of the Winter lands stepped into the circumference of the tree's branches, the tree's roots.

The shape of the battlefield changed; the shape of the storm compressed. That storm did not touch the fox, who stood in Summer in spite of the lord's bitter cold, but the grass beneath the fox's feet was not the wild growth on the banks. It was the growth of a different Summer, a personal one, and it had held since the moment he took the field, defying and denying the Winter of the lord.

Still, she hesitated at the boundary, for her storm would not cross it. She lost sight of Stephen for a moment, but he made no attempt to hide; he continued his measured retreat, guarded now by fox, by hunt-brother, by Southerner. The trees that had followed his command rushed past him, war forgotten. Only home mattered now, and they had found it.

"Little mortal," the lord said, surprising Stephen as her gaze remained upon the tree. "Return to me what you have stolen, and I will allow you to live."

The three-headed beast rose, although they made no move to leave the side of the great tree. The human head replied. "He has stolen nothing, but regardless, his fate is not in your hands, now. You have leagued with the dead in an attempt to increase your hunting fields, and the wilderness will not forget.

"Return to your lands, lick your wounds, accept the loss. Perhaps then you might have a chance to redeem yourself."

Respect, Stephen thought, was due the powerful in the wilderness. It had not been offered, nor would it be.

"Loss?" the lord snarled. As the word left her lips, her ears changed shape, rising to the sides of her head in long, silver triangles. Fur of the same color grew out from her hair, spreading across her face, her pale arms. "I did not lose when he *was* the lord of a far more vast land than this puddle!"

"You did not face him. You struck him from behind, in the middle of a battle against invaders. You were aided by necessary war. And we have been aided by your unnecessary war. Come, then. Come if you dare."

CHAPTER TWENTY-NINE

Gervanno watched. He had not moved toward the tree, but stood —for the moment—in gentle Summer, absorbing warmth and heat, sword in hand. He had retreated at the fox's command, although *fox* was not a word that could describe the man whose back he now observed. He could feel the elder's anger; it had been slow to kindle, but it burned now. It was no wonder that the fox—in a field of ice and snow —stood in a Summer of his own making.

It was a summer heat that made deserts.

Nenyane had not retreated with Stephen; Gervanno had no doubt that she had uttered the same command the elder had; and Stephen, as Gervanno, had obeyed. But he moved past Gervanno, and in his wake, the creatures that had served the Winter lord followed. They fanned out along the same shores of the small lake at which the Hunters had taken up position; those Hunters now stood interspersed with new trees and the wild creatures that might, in other lands, have been their prey.

If they were aware of it, no sign was given, although many of the newcomers faced in, toward the tree, and not out, toward the battle-field, as if the tree were the greater miracle.

And he understood: to the newcomers, it was. The fallen had risen. The lord to whom they had pledged service and allegiance willingly once again claimed the lands on which they stood. He did not threaten their lives, their existences—and if standing as they now stood did, they

accepted the risk of death in battle. They had had, if Gervanno understood all that had passed, taken to the battlefield with little choice.

Choice had value. Choice defined a man.

Service was not theoretical. If it ended in death—as it often had, in
Gervanno's youth—it was a clean death, a death one could be proud of,
when one at last stood in the folds of the howling winds. A death he had
avoided because fear had overwhelmed him, frozen him, destroyed his
belief in himself.

He stepped forward into the driving snow, the bitter cold, crossing a
visible dividing line between two lands and understanding, as he did,
that the lands *were*, in a fashion he could not describe, alive.

He moved toward the fox's side, toward Nenyane the sword master,
and even as wind slapped skin and cold slowed movement, he knew he
had come home. This was the home that was left him. But even as he
thought it, he heard the high, whining bark of the dog he had adopted,
for Leial, absent until this moment, pushed past the new line of trees,
jumping up to catch the folds of Gervanno's clothing in his small jaws.
With surprising and unexpected strength, the dog pulled him back into
the warmth of Summer.

"I don't think Leial wants you to leave," Stephen observed, for the
wind's howl, on the green bank, did not drive words beyond audibility.
The Maubreche Hunter also held sword in hand.

His answer was swept away, instead, by the roar of the elder. It was
wordless, visceral, but Gervanno could feel the sentiment that lay at its
heart: outraged rejection. In the midst of a combat that had not ceased,
the Winter lord had attempted to parley. "If we finish the combat," the
cerdan replied to the Hunter, "your lands will be safe."

Stephen nodded, his eyes almost unblinking as he watched his huntbrother. "She will come."

Gervanno blinked.

"Here is where we will fight."

As if the very air could hear his words, the Northern mage
descended.

"She will not take that risk," Gervanno said. "There is no winter
here."

Stephen nodded. "There was no winter when she first took these
lands. No winter when we first crossed her borders."

This was true. "But it was night—night without dawn."

"Kallandras said that night, in the South, was the Lady's time—and the Lady was your only mercy."

Gervanno considered this. "Yes," he finally said. "But it was thus because it was the time of day during which the Lord of the Sun could not bear witness to our actions, our desires, our fears. It was the Lord who stood against the demons; it was the Lord who gave the Radann the Swords of God. Mercy has its time, its place, its necessities—but it is not mercy that could defeat the demonic." He shifted his gaze to the dog who was now slobbering over his clothing in an attempt to maintain its grip. "Enough, Leial. Enough. I will wait."

He did not believe the lord would cross the border if she could not bring her winter, her night, with her. He would not, had he the choice.

"The land has expanded," Stephen said, as if he could hear the doubts. "And it will continue to expand as the tree's roots spread. Her servants, those that have not been bound, will cross that border if she is not constantly vigilant. Even those who are bound; she cannot watch them all every waking minute of her day. I can't watch my dogs that way. I can check on them—but not constantly. I have to sleep." Something rustled above their heads; Gervanno could almost hear whispered words in the movement.

"She doesn't need to sleep," Stephen continued. "But she has far more servants than I have dogs. She will not hold the shape of the lands she has held since she betrayed the lord she professed to serve. She will come because she has far too much to lose, and this is now the peak of her power. She might retreat to the seat of the power she holds—but that power will be whittled away.

"She is not like the lord in the orchard. Power drives her—and its appearance. And now, in front of so many of those who've served her, she has lost power." He smiled. "She's lost face."

Gervanno bowed head, then, and when he lifted it, he also smiled; the smile was bitter.

"Nenyane's never cared about it. She's never cared about the perception of others."

"You do?"

"I've learned—with effort—to care less. But I understand that reputation is based, in part, on perception. And it's a weapon that can be wielded if one builds it. But it's double-edged, like our swords, not yours. Look. The storm is moving."

The fox elder did not retreat.

The winter lord's attacks became faster, more focused; she howled in rage when Nenyane wounded her, but the wound was slight, and even as Stephen watched, it closed. If the lord was not fighting in the seat of her power, she remained powerful. He did not know how a rooted tree was meant to attack, but he understood—as the fox did—that it was the tree itself she must face and destroy.

The lightning that had been the heart of her storm would not strike beyond her lands; she could not destroy him in that fashion. But as the seconds passed, the shield that stood between her and the tree had grown in strength; it was built by the bodies of those who had returned home.

Defense of home had a greater weight for those who chose to stand and fight than simple attack and acquisition had ever had. The defenders had the advantage of superior knowledge of the terrain, but it was more than that. They had the strongest incentive to fight. Why did cerdan cross terreans to fight? What had motivated them, especially in their youth? The specter of those homes being destroyed or burned to ash in the flames of war.

At a distance, it was easier to lose sight of that as war and the injuries and losses taken on the battlefield, or in the medical tents after the battle had been decided, eroded all sense of home, sometimes shattering it forever. How could one return when one was so changed?

The visceral sense of home was not attenuated when one fought at the outskirts of one's own village.

And the Winter lord, like the Summer lord, was defending her home; how she had come by it didn't change the circumstance.

Ah, he thought. Stephen was right. A boy less than half his age understood what Gervanno had not, and would not, put into words; had seen it clearly, instantly.

The Winter lord struck a blow against the fox, and the ground beneath his feet shattered. He did not fall, but he was pushed back— back into the summer of a different lord, a different battlefield. Nenyane had leapt clear, her feet touching ice before she once again took to air. This time, the air held her.

The Northern mage was in range, his eyes silver, his blade blue. His feet did not touch ground, but he stood sentinel far closer to it than Nenyane was.

The Winter lord stepped, briefly, into Summer.

HER HAIR FLEW, dark imbued with a sheen of gold; her eyes narrowed.

"Illaraphaniel," she said, her voice thunder. The air chilled as she attempted to bring the Winter storm with her. But storms in Summer were only a danger in the desert; here, they did not carry the same threat of death. At her back, a blizzard raged. Before her, the sky was clear.

"You know why I am here," the mage replied. "You have chosen to ally yourself with the dead, the servants of the one true enemy. I will not leave this field until you are dead—or I am carried off it as a corpse the dead cannot, by their choice and nature, leave."

"You will be *carrion*."

Even at this distance, Stephen could see Meralonne's smile. It was colder than the winter in which he had fought. The mage turned to Stephen. "The field, son of Bredan, is yours."

It made little sense to Stephen; it made less sense to any of the Hunters, mortal, all, who had gathered and fought.

Call her, Nenyane said. There was no anger in her voice, and very little explanation, for she had never stopped her assault; even now, while the lord raged, she sought openings. She was not immune to the lord's attack; she bled. But when fighting, Nenyane had never acknowledged something as trivial as pain—not if it did not prevent that fight.

Stephen could not see what he held; could not see what he'd broken. He wanted to say that he didn't understand the mechanism by which the lord had been stripped of the soldiers who had deserted her, but that would have been a lie.

How did he feel the lord's rage so clearly? How was he aware of a hesitance that did not touch her expression, her movements, the momentum of her attacks?

He had not felt her so clearly when he had first begun, with the aid of Nenyane's vision, to break the bindings that existed between that lord and those who had been all but enslaved. Had not felt it until he had entered Winter, waving hands in arcs that touched nothing his eyes could see.

But he had felt her then, perhaps as an aggregate of those chains, because the chains traveled between two creatures: the enslaver and the enslaved. Permission had not been required. It was not an oathbinding; Stephen would have recognized that. He would never have attempted to break it, fearing for the lives of those who had sworn that oath.

But it was a binding. His divine father was called the Lord of Covenants, when he was not spoken of by name. Stephen wondered if *covenant* meant *binding*. Binding oaths. Bound service. Choices that were so coercive they could not be considered true choices at all. Gods were not people. They were not human. They were inflexible, absolute. What empathy they felt was narrow and very, very difficult to evoke. In the eyes of his father, these shadowed, fragile bonds were nonetheless bonds, bindings, things that grew out of the interactions of the powerful and the powerless. How they had been formed were of little concern. They existed; they were within the domain of his power.

Breaking those bonds had not destroyed either the master or the servant.

But the essence of that binding remained, as if it were something that existed in its own right: not as social contract or spell, but something solid, tangible, invisible to his eye, but not his touch, nor the dormant abilities of the blood he had carried almost as curse, the burden had been so heavy.

This was some part of that burden, this breaking of bonds, this absorption of what they had been fashioned to be. He accepted it. He had to accept it. If he did not, if he could not, this war would never end: she would retreat to the seat of her power, and she would wait. Plan. Build again. She might not make the attempt to conquer Bowgren in Ansel's lifetime, or in Stephen's; she might be forced to take a century to rebuild.

By that time, any knowledge or experience gained by both Bowgren and Margen would become another bedtime story. Demons would once again cross her borders into Bowgren lands. Into Margen lands.

Into Breodanir, the kingdom created by Breodan.

Breodanir was his home. While he lived, it was that home he would fight for.

You killed a child.

Yes. He had been a child himself. The dead child had been oathbound; she had made a childish promise, and he, in anxiety, had accepted it as a true vow. She had died because she was *five*, and she had broken that promise through no fault of her own. His father could not even *see* the problem with that death. She had sworn an oath; he had consecrated it, and it had taken her life.

As a child, broken by guilt and pain, he had vowed never to use the power of his birthright again.

But that promise, his father had not consecrated. Stephen had assumed it was because his father had no interest in, no desire to, accept such an oath; it worked against his plans.

He thought differently, in this moment composed of Summer, Winter, and battle in a wilderness that was not, and would never be, part of his home. The oath had not been consecrated because it was an oath he had made to himself. It was not a binding. It was not a chain that linked two entities.

Had he sworn the oath to Nenyane, the god would have accepted it or blessed it because he had spoken with intent, with belief, with the whole of his truth at that point in time.

I would never, ever have accepted it.

Don't talk to me while you're fighting!

It's not me who's doing most of the fighting—it's the elder.

Meralonne had not joined the battle; he had not stepped into the raging Winter. Stephen assumed that if he had, he would be like the elder: enshrouded in the light and heat of Summer. Or perhaps he stayed his ground because of that elder; there was a hierarchy among the ancient beings of the wilderness that Stephen thought he would never understand.

What he understood, however, was this: he was connected to the Winter lord by the multiple small bonds forged over literal centuries, and he had the power—if he had the will—to use that connection. To abuse it. To suborn another's will, however briefly, by his own.

Nenyane fell silent; he could feel that silence as a hush, a hope, a fear.

He accepted it. No one knew his inner mind as well as his hunt-brother—and no one ever would. But if he reached, if he stretched, if he opened up the parts of that mind that had been shut down by will and guilt and fear for *so long*…he could do what must be done.

Bonds worked both ways. He felt the anger, the rage, and the power —always unstable, insecure—that lay beneath them. He felt the desire that was birthed in rage, and in the very, very heart of the lord, the guilt at the betrayal that had given her everything she had ever wanted. It was almost searing; he might have been lost to the growing enormity of his awareness had it not been for Nenyane.

She kept him grounded, rooted, in the Stephen she knew and had known since the day she'd been left in Maubreche; she slowed her attacks as she felt the shift in Stephen's intent. He looked across the field to where the Winter lord, enshrouded by wind and snow, fought; he could see her gaze flicker. She could not focus only and entirely on Stephen while the fox attacked, but Nenyane was far more aware of the fox than she had been when the Winter lord had focused those attacks on her Hunter.

The god-born were mortal. Their life expectancy was—as he had been quietly and cautiously informed for most of his life—lower on average than the lives of mortals who did not bear divine blood. The mortal body had never been designed to carry divinity. He had never felt that divinity before. Perhaps it was impossible in the lands of his birth—mortal lands, riven from the wilderness.

But he felt it now; it was stronger than the Hunter's trance, stronger than his pack-bond, and almost stronger than the bindings of love and family that he had built over time with his huntbrother.

What he lacked was the knowledge of how to use that power to its fullest extent. The knowledge he did have was simple, instinctive: he compelled the Winter lord to move toward the border of weather that defined two separate lands.

And she came, fighting the compulsion he laid upon her. Perhaps, had he attempted to create the bond between them on his own, she could have easily ignored him; perhaps she could have shrugged him off. If he carried divinity in his blood, he was nonetheless a creature of the mortal world.

But the bonds that she herself had created were what he had gathered; the bonds she had built over centuries, deepening their weight and the compulsion they laid against those who served her unwillingly, that were in his figurative hands now. Nenyane shifted the focus of her battle, although her sword remained in one hand. But she leapt up and back, retreating for the first time.

It's not a retreat, she snapped. Nenyane had long despised retreating from battle while her enemy remained. *It's an attack.* She reached out for Stephen's hand, and as her cold skin came in contact with his, warmer for the Summer heat in which he now stood, he closed his eyes.

He could see what he'd severed; could see the ends he held. Half

had spread in a thin, fine weave of strands that ended in the lands in
which the tree was rooted. But the other half were a twined rope that
led to the Winter lord. He hadn't broken them, as he'd originally
thought. He'd interrupted them, inserting himself—somehow—into the
flow of their power, a third point, a third influence in a bond that should
not have one.

It was to the larger strand that he looked through Nenyane's eyes.
His ability to see what he held was tied to his huntbrother; his ability to
affect it had not been.

*It's not something I can do. It's not something anyone standing here can do.
It's only you.* Her voice was quiet. *Be careful. I'll be here, but—be careful. She
can't do what you've done either, but if you die, everything breaks.*

Had Nenyane always known that he could do this? Had the
demons? Was *this*, not the swearing of oaths whose breaking caused
death, the reason he was hunted?

Nenyane did not reply. Stephen could grip the rope, as he thought
of the thicker combination of strands, with only one hand, but even that
felt wrong; he couldn't *feel* rope in his hand. He could see it only
because of Nenyane's vision. But when he pulled on it, he could feel
weight and resistance.

He could feel shock and fury, the latter a raging disaster as natural
as earthquakes or bitter, blinding storms—things that must be endured
to survive, things that could not be changed. The Winter lord had no
desire to walk into Summer lands; no desire to subject herself to the will
of a land she did not rule.

He pulled. That was the shape of command, of will: he held the
bonds she had created and lodged within herself, and he pulled. It was
an almost physical sensation: his arms ached—both the one that held
the rope and the one that had tightened around Nenyane's hand, as if
she were an immoveable weight by which he could anchor himself.

The Winter lord moved toward Stephen by inches, fighting her way
through the elder who had stood against her, forcing him to retreat until
the edge of the Summer circle that contained him touched the Summer
of the tree's lands. Only then did the circle with which he'd enshrouded
himself dissipate; it was no longer required.

The elder did not appear to notice Stephen—or any of the other
Hunters present if it came to that. But he had stood and fought, and he
knew where his enemy was heading. If Stephen died here, she could
retreat.

No, he thought; if he died here, she could reassert the authority she had built. These bonds, these chains—they were of her. She was the power that sustained them. He wondered, then, if she would simply break them herself, but understood on a visceral level that she would not.

Stephen would never release his dogs in a similar circumstance—not unless it preserved their lives, not his own.

Yes, Nenyane said.

"Illaraphaniel!" the fox shouted, as both of the lord's feet crossed the border between the lands of the two lords.

"Eldest," the mage replied. In the midst of this battle, he tendered the fox a deep, brief bow.

He moved past the Hunters; they were as relevant to the mage as they had been to the man who had been a fox. Meralonne alighted on the earth between Stephen and the Winter lord—the lord whose ice and snow now melted, ripped away like a thin veil that had been torn and could not be repaired.

GERVANNO WATCHED as the Northern mage rose from that bow, sword in hand, and turned to face the lord whose Winter had been dispelled. He stood to one side of Nenyane, whose hand was now tightly clenched around her Hunter's.

The man that had been fox dwindled in shape and form, becoming fox once again. He made his way to Gervanno's side, and butted the cerdan's leg. Without pause, Gervanno knelt before the fox, this ancient, deadly creature, this power against which even demons must fall when faced, and he offered the arm he had offered every time the fox had made the same demand.

He was shocked to see that the fox was injured; red blood lay against golden fur, and had matted it.

"Yes, yes," the fox murmured, curling up between Gervanno's chest and the crook of his arm. "Perhaps not the wisest of my choices, but you are foolish beyond belief, and I am not yet done with you. You would have thrown your life away in a fight that you made your own for the flimsiest of reasons.

"No, don't speak. You may witness the unfolding of this battle, but do so without words. I will sleep. Do not set me down." He closed his eyes. Without opening them, he added, "It goes without saying that your part in this battle is finished. I will be *extremely* displeased should you attempt to rejoin it. The Maubreche Hunter is not at risk; Illara-phaniel is strong, and he bears an ancient grudge against the dead and those who traffic with them.

"But Stephen—"

"Yes. She is determined to kill the child. She will have to kill Illara-phaniel to reach him. Were she in her own lands, she might have some chance—but only were she to draw the fight to the seat of her power. She cannot. Stephen of Maubreche has the one you call Nenyane, now. To kill Stephen, she will also have to kill that child—and that will be impossible for her."

Gervanno exhaled. As if the fox were a gravely wounded comrade, he retreated to the tree at the center of the lake, where the three-headed creature, still bleeding, stood sentinel.

"Eldest," the three-headed creature said, speaking from the almost human face, although all three looked down at the fox. "You have our gratitude. We are in your debt."

"Yes," the fox said, without opening his eyes.

"Is the mortal who carries you your servant?"

"No. He could not be, and survive; he would go mad."

"Ah." The mortal head bowed, then. "There is an air about the mortal that is unusual. My lord would, I think, approve." The creature than looked down, past the fox to the dog that stayed, so silent he could almost be overlooked, by Gervanno's side. To Gervanno's astonishment, the lion's head barked.

Leial looked up, tail wagging, to meet the eyes of the enormous lion. Gervanno would not have dared. The dog barked as if in reply, and a series of such noises were exchanged. He accepted that they spoke a language he could not understand, could not hear *as* language. The lord of the orchard had understood Leial, but in a fashion that implied he was familiar with a dog he had cared for. This was not the same.

When Leial growled, Gervanno hesitated; he sheathed his sword and dropped a staying hand on the dog's head.

"My apologies, Elder," he said, bowing to the three-headed creature. He could not force the dog to bow—not as he had been forced to bow head as a young boy by his father's side.

"Come, then, human warrior. Watch as we watch. Only my lord will join the fray; I am injured, and I cannot fight well with the injuries I have sustained. If you wish it, you may sit upon my back."

Gervanno shook his head, but slowly, as if after careful consideration of the honor offered. He'd considered it quickly, and the idea of riding this enormous beast as if it were a horse felt so wrong he was almost horrified by it. He was not Northern; he could place a firm mask over horror and keep it locked down.

But the fox ordered him to turn, to place his back to the tree, and he obeyed.

NENYANE HELD STEPHEN'S HAND; it was stronger and more solid than even the sword in her own. In front of where she stood, Stephen by her side, she could see Illaraphaniel.

She had recognized him the first time; had recognized his face, his voice. His words, she had not—not until they encountered demons at his side. Then she heard him speak, heard him truly release the loathing, the fury, the rage that the betrayal of those long dead had caused.

She felt it as a physical sensation—not a blow, but something that struck the whole of her body.

"Illaraphaniel," the Winter lord said, standing now in the Summer that diminished her power. The perpetual night in which they'd traveled had been dispersed. Perhaps it would be replaced by a natural night; in the wilderness, things could not be so easily predicted.

"Do not speak even the echo of my name." Winter was in his voice, as if all of the ice and snow had been absorbed and might escape only thus. First prince of the ancient court, riven from brothers and the White Lady he had served for the entirety of his existence. The Wild Hunt might ride through any land when the Hunt was called, but they did not attack the lords of those many domains.

Or they had not.

But this lord had conspired with the dead; this lord had sought the advantage the power of the dead—and their fell god—would provide to one who lacked the power to break the great work that had been done when the two lands had been separated forever.

Nenyane knew this, but knew it the way she knew how to breathe; she did not remember it the way she remembered her childhood in Maubreche. This was knowledge that was deeper than memory, but worse—it could not be deliberately recalled, and it could never be escaped.

Nenyane frowned as she felt the threads of Stephen's binding worry. She had always hated his worry—had hated anyone's worry about her, even as a child in Maubreche. She had found it insulting, condescending. It had taken a few years before she could understand the source of that worry: not condescension, but affection. Love.

Love had seemed so strange, it was given in so many different ways. She had grown to understand that what was offered to an orphan, a strange, underfed child, was familial love. Lady Maubreche could love many people; it was the expression of love and affection that changed depending on the person to whom it was offered.

Nenyane was not Cynthia. She was not capable of becoming Cynthia, who loved her people, her family, her lands, and the many responsibilities vying for time and attention. Nenyane had watched her, in silence, for the first year when she was not training with Stephen and the dogs who disliked her, the horses who shied away—or worse—when she was forced to handle almost useless Hunter weapons.

She had seen no need to speak with Stephen's family, but understood how important it was to him; what they offered their sons, their sons offered in return. Yes, they argued. Nenyane understood that her presence as huntbrother would cause Stephen difficulty. Corwin had offered to find a different huntbrother—a boy, like Mark. Nenyane hadn't cared.

Stephen had.

He refused. She did not understand why. If Stephen had someone like Mark, it made no difference to her; if someone like Mark, some nameless mortal child, could offer Stephen the support Mark grew to offer Robart, it would strengthen, not weaken, Stephen.

Stephen didn't see it the same way. Not then. Not now. And she had grown to understand why. It was part of the way he could be like Cynthia, his mother—could interact with people of no consequence and no relevance as if they were real. To Stephen, a boy like Mark could never be irrelevant.

To Nenyane, *this* was real. Illaraphaniel was real. The great tree and its liege.

But most real, most solid, was Stephen. She didn't have to be called *huntbrother*. Nothing could change what she was to Stephen; nothing could alter what he was to her. This was the battle for which she'd been born, and he was the companion who would see it out to the end at her side.

She had never told him, as Mark sometimes told Robart when they were in the midst of a heated disagreement, *I don't need you! I can just leave!*

She never said things that weren't true, even in anger. Stephen was her choice. She could not make another, and she could not carry the weight of something as complicated—and mortal—as Maubreche; could not carry the weight that Stephen grew to shoulder as he helped his parents in the running of the demesne.

She could not carry any weight but Stephen's. But she would carry that weight for the entirety of her existence.

She watched Illaraphaniel and felt almost as if she were coming home.

He had been born of the White Lady, and she had been the whole of his existence. Even in exile that was still his truth. Would always be his truth. No momentary distraction could replace it or displace it: he was the White Lady's. Everything he did, everything he had done, everything he had endured—all the many, many losses of which immortal life was comprised—had not shaken his essential nature.

She could not be as certain of her own; she lacked memories. But she knew, standing sentinel as she watched Illaraphaniel close with the lord of the lands that had endangered Ansel's home, that Stephen was the one unshakeable conviction she had. The only one.

She could be swayed by him—was constantly swayed by him—because she did not want him to be unhappy. Unhappiness permeated every activity except this one: combat, proof of worth on a field of battle.

Nenyane had never expected happiness. She had never expected joy. She was incapable of it. Stephen had disagreed—but far more as a child than he now did.

Watching Illaraphaniel fight—in the air, his feet never deigning to touch something as common as earth—brought her intense, almost perfect *joy*. She was silent, wordless; she held Stephen's hand tightly because she knew Illaraphaniel's foe would retreat the moment Stephen did not strain against that retreat. That one was bound and she came, inch by inch, at his silent call, until she had no more time to put effort into resistance, or Stephen's death.

Stephen's death would buy the lord's freedom, but it could no longer guarantee her survival—not here, in lands she did not rule. Not here, in the face of Illaraphaniel, prince of the White Lady's court.

Mortal folly, Illaraphaniel expected. He almost accepted it; mortals had such brief lives. But of a lord in the wilderness? Never.

Never while he lived.

His sword was blue light, color of High Summer, his eyes the winter of the Lady's court; his hair was the color of new snow, his skin the color of eternity, pale as death. If he could not have that death for himself, if he could not have the dissolution that was death to those born of the wild, elemental gods at the dawn of time, he could grant it, could deliver it, over and over again, until the one true enemy was finally vanquished, and he could know, if not peace, absolution.

Nenyane *knew*. Who better to know than she?

THE LORD WAS TALLER than Meralonne, her limbs longer. The fur that had now grown to cover almost all of her visible skin was silver and grey. Blood streaked the pale colors as she fought; not all of it was hers. She could hold—and did—a sword in what had once been hands, but the sword slowly retracted into her arm, spreading and becoming claws. The claws were curved, not straight, but her feet upon the earth were similarly clawed. Even her hair melted away; she was no longer human in seeming.

But she was far swifter than she had been with only two legs for balance, her movements far harder to parry. Her face elongated as she gained the muzzle of a hunting creature—a choice that allowed her to fully use the teeth, long and sharp, in her mouth.

Even her words—if they were words at all—sounded like the snarl and roar of an animal to Stephen's ear. An animal he might never have hunted, given the choice.

There was a nobility in her savagery, and power that almost robbed the young Hunter of breath; he had not seen it until that moment.

She reveals all of her power, Nenyane said, *In her last stand*. She caught a flicker of movement to Stephen's side. He could feel the depth of her sudden frown. *No. Tell Ansel no; Illaraphaniel neither desires nor requires our aid*.

Stephen lifted a hand in Ansel's direction, and Ansel stilled. *Not even yours?*

Especially not mine, his huntbrother replied. Something in her interior voice caught Stephen, causing his eyes to widen as he turned to her. He could see her face in profile; she had not looked away from the battle that unfolded between the mage and the lord. Glistening on her cheeks were tears—she did not sob, but she made no attempt to hide them, no attempt to stop their fall, as if tears themselves were an act of nature, of a wilderness he knew he would never fully understand.

To her right, trees had taken up watch, but as Nenyane, they were silent. They bore witness, and only witness, to Meralonne at war, as if such war was an act of intimacy so profound, they should not be here at all.

I hope you never have cause to understand the depth and breadth of his loss, Nenyane said. *I hope you never hear the bitter song of his grief.*

But he had heard it. He had heard such a grief voiced in his stead.

This is the only way he can express it; all else but this terrible vengeance has been forbidden.

And it was only through this battle, and the war of which such battles were comprised, that he could express some part of what he felt. Stephen knew that grief and rage were not the same, but he had seen Ansel, and he had heard Ansel's bitter words all but condemning Lord Bowgren's steep, sharp decline. Had seen the way grief transformed into impotent fury.

Rage and pain had transformed Lord Bowgren most of all, because in Lord Bowgren were the seeds of guilt: he should have prevented Barrett's death. Barrett should never have died. Lord Bowgren lived— and Bowgren's lands continued to be fertile—at the *expense* of Barrett. Because of Breodan. Because of the god to whom they had sworn their oaths and dedicated their hunting kills.

Because of the people who would never risk their own lives in such a hunt, but who required it to survive.

Rage, yes.

Rage could pass, the shroud of its bitterness lifting to expose a grief that did not and would never come to an end; time might gentle it. Nothing else would. But every element of daily life could be a reminder of the loss of the one person in life who was closer than kin. Closer than blood.

Stephen was slowly pulled into the echoes of grief upon which his huntbrother stood. Her understanding of what this fight meant to Meralonne—the man he called mage, but perhaps would never call mage again—bled into him, transforming his understanding of who, or what, Meralonne APhaniel was.

Nenyane's grief was, for the moment, akin to Meralonne's. Akin to Illaraphaniel's. She knew his grief; knew it as endless, as a wound from which he could never recover. No more could she. It had become what they were.

Stephen understood that this was now the mage's battle; the moment Illaraphaniel had stepped onto the field, the moment he had chosen, finally, to face the lord who had called both winter and night to the land she ruled, it had become his fight, and only his. The bard did not descend from the skies; the fox and the three-headed creature had retreated, as if they had set the stage and the sole performer left must take it and hold it, absent all other interference.

This was the purest way his ancient grief and rage could be expressed, this lifting of sword, this blinding, furious aerial attack. Were it not for the Lord of the Hells, were it not for his divine presence, were it not for his *lies*, there would never have been loss; the White Lady would have remained what she had been, and his brothers would have been princes of that ancient court, even to this day.

And this creature had dared—*dared*—to intrigue with the Lord of the Hells, for whom half his kin had betrayed their creator. The White Lady's entire existence was bent toward revenge, and Illaraphaniel followed the will of his master, even into exile. He did not think of beyond; did not think of rebuilding anything.

He would fight on fields such as this one, there to triumph or perish. He had no fear of the latter; it was the only relief from the burden he had carried for so long. His brothers had failed; they had died by the hands of their creator, there to return their very essence to hers, to rejoin the source of their life. Death was the only way he would ever be in their presence again.

Fear affected the immortal; it would never affect Illaraphaniel again. Survival was simply the detritus of power; it was not something to struggle to achieve, not something to engender desperation or the desire for life.

But he had the pride with which he was born: he would not simply walk onto the claws—or fangs—of an enemy. They either had the skill, the power, the determination to kill him, or they did not.

This lord, powerful in her own right, had contaminated that power; it was not a power drawn from the life of the lands she had claimed. It was a power that relied on death, on the dead—on Illaraphaniel's dead. It was a crime that could never be forgiven. Even in death, the stain would not be removed.

So he fought; to Stephen's eyes, he took two blows, because he had never seen the mage fight with a shield on arm. Blood ran down one arm, unheeded; the blow had been glancing, or at least one that did not bisect his arm.

Those were the only blows the creature who had been lord landed; the mage landed far more, and the wind howled his fury all around where his enemy stood. If she could lift voice to the wind, his was the stronger voice.

She tried, only once, to retreat; she did not waste time or effort on a second attempt. He had her now. Even if Stephen no longer exerted his small, imperfect will upon her, she would not escape the raging embrace of the mage's wind.

They watched.

Behind Stephen's back, the sound of drums began. He did not turn to see what those drums were, or who carried them; their beat was slow, deep, as if the earth itself were awake and keeping time. Above the beat of that rhythm, voices were raised. Stephen did not understand the words lifted in song, but he could feel the way harmonies entwined: the first voice, a bass, was joined in turn by higher voices; he thought the last, fluting syllables might be birdsong, if birds sang in words.

The song traveled, the volume somehow increasing until it was a physical sensation; the ground beneath Stephen's feet trembled almost in time with it. The song grew, and it took a moment for Stephen to understand the how, or the why.

But its volume rose as the lord bled. Illaraphaniel's blows were not glancing, and as his enemy bled, she became in trapped in a red, red window: beads of blood traveling in a moving, twisting curtain; her blood, all.

The mage did not speak; the lord did, the words incomprehensible. She did not beg, which was a mercy for Stephen. Nenyane would not have been disturbed had she attempted to save her life in that fashion. Nor would she have stayed her hand.

The lord was not without power; the fight was not short. But her life, and her life's blood, flowed more freely than her opponent's, and it was she, at last, who collapsed. She lost two limbs before she could no longer attack, but her defenses did not collapse in the same fashion until the moment the mage's sword swept cleanly through her neck.

Her head was caught by wind and sent skittering across a Summer field, where it rolled to rest at the foot of the great tree, following the passage made of trees that had never been closed.

Only then did the mage's feet fully touch the earth; only then did he put up his sword. He was silent as his shoulders slumped; he did not look back to see where the wind had carried the head, but he knew. The wind was his.

From above, the Senniel bard descended. Only the bard dared to approach the mage, and landed beside him. The bard was injured, but the injuries were scrapes and cuts in comparison to the mage's. If the bard spoke at all, he spoke in a bard-born fashion; only the mage would hear the words.

There was a long, silent moment before the mage exhaled; as he did, the armor that had caught and reflected light off little links melted away, to be replaced by robes that had seen better days. The difference was immediate, striking. But all around where they now stood, the forest seemed to expel a sigh, as if finally relaxing.

The mage then fished in his robe's hidden pockets for something— and withdrew a pipe. Only then did he choose to speak in a fashion that Stephen could hear and understand.

"I hope we are never in a situation where this kind of scuffle is necessary again." He spoke to the bard.

The bard shook his head, a wry smile transforming his features. "I fear you will be bitterly disappointed, APhaniel." The smile fell away. "The god we do not name will know."

The pipe froze an inch from the mage's lips.

"I could almost hear his voice in the distance when the winter storm blossomed. He will know." The bard turned toward Stephen, then. "I do not know what you attempted, Master Maubreche. But were you not upon this field, I am uncertain how the battle would have progressed."

"She would have died," the mage said.

Kallandras did not reply. Instead, he turned toward the great tree. His lips moved, but Stephen heard no sound—nor had he desire to hear. He knew to whom the bard now spoke, and he knew why.

But if the bard could speak in perfect silence, the tree could—or did —not. "Yes," the tree replied, its voice composed of the rustle of leaves, the movement of breeze, the creaking of branch. "And no, mortal. I did not understand, in the eons I lay at the heart of the earth growing my roots, that this is how the oath sworn so long ago would be fulfilled. If I was not martial, as my treacherous former servant was, I was too literal. I thought—I expected—that I would, at last, ride out to battle against her; that it would be my hand that struck the killing blow.

"But that was not what I was promised. I was promised that I would have the chance to strike her, at last; to have revenge. Or justice. The two words are so tightly entwined.

"And, now, I stand. I am not a sapling; I know how to spread roots across the land, occupied or no. It was a subtle work, but subtlety was required; it is not required now. Yes. I will return to the lands that were once mine.

"But I will not return as I once was, and the seat of my power will be forever here."

The three-headed beast lifted all of its heads in concern; the one head that seemed human was far paler than it had been before. "Lord, you cannot. Here, at the border, you are most vulnerable to invaders."

"Yes. But it was not invaders, in the end, who sundered me from the rule of my lands." Voice softening as if to gentle the words, he continued. "You were bound to her; you thought me dead. You would not have allowed it, otherwise. But in these lands, these frail, brief lives brought stories beneath my boughs. And the roots that I planted were planted in three lands, but the mortal lands were the slightest, for they were the most difficult to reach.

"I did not do so in order to break the covenant. I did so because until I understood where those roots were planted—and I did not immediately—I knew I required every possible anchor against the lord. It was those roots, in the end, that prevented her from destroying the barriers between our wilderness and their tiny echo of what the lands once were. But the barrier, as you must know, is frayed; it is damaged.

"And we do not have the power or the knowledge to rebuild it."

"And you will stay for the sake of *mortals*?"

"I sheltered the village on a whim. I sheltered and I watched and I listened. I gave them clear water, and in the end, the branches from which they might build a fence. But roots are strange things—and you will not know or understand them as I do.

"You never wished—you who had the power to do so—to rule in the wilderness. You always understood that it was a binding, that it was a pretty cage of responsibility. But you left and returned, left and returned, and you brought me the stories of your journeys; you gave me an echo of your freedom. I honored you for it.

"And I feel compelled to honor the mortals to whom I will be no more than a passing miracle as they age and die. Damage was done—by you, by the lord you unwillingly served—and it must be undone, as we can. You know as well as I, who fought against her, that it was the intervention of these frail and ephemeral mortals that turned the tide."

"Illaraphaniel was here. And the Eldest."

The fox snorted. Gervanno had felt his tension the moment the Northern mage was mentioned; he felt it subside. If he did not like the order of appreciation and respect, he was too exhausted to correct it.

"Yes. But would they have come if not for the mortals?"

The beast fell silent.

"Biluude, peace. I have a request for you, who have suffered so much."

"You want me to return to the mortal village."

"And release those you petrified, yes. It is my gift of gratitude, for the young Hunter, Ansel, was most grieved by the losses suffered."

"And will you keep the mortal village?"

"I fear I will have little choice," the tree replied. "The village is here, now. It is not where it once was, and if I have roots in the lands it once occupied, they are weak and slight. I cannot simply will the village away; the voice of my earth is not the voice of theirs, and the wilderness is the stronger voice."

STEPHEN CLOSED his eyes as silence descended upon the Hunters gathered here: Margen, Bowgren, Elseth, and Maubreche.

It was better than death; there was sunlight, now, and the villagers had not died in the battle. Here, they might continue a life similar to the one they had once led; here, they might learn to speak with the wilderness, to farm in it, to feed themselves.

Stephen knew this was better than destruction for Ansel and Heiden. The knowledge that Amberg still survived had weight and meaning. That it had survived because of the Sacred Hunt and the death and pain that hunt caused every single year was clear to all of the denizens of Hunter's Redoubt—all who had been summoned because they could not countenance the terrible loss of a huntbrother.

Barrett's picture remained in the small shrine in the village elder's home. He was remembered, and would be remembered, while they lived.

The Margen guards had mostly survived; those that had been trapped within this territory had been drawn to Amberg, to join the Bowgren village. Margen and Bowgren had always been close allies; they were welcomed, not least because they had some knowledge in martial arts, and the elder believed that would be necessary.

Word could be carried to Bowgren and Margen—if they could leave.

But if they could leave, there should be no reason why the *people* couldn't follow. The village might be lost, but the citizens could be relocated.

He opened his mouth to speak, but Ansel was ahead of him. Or perhaps Heiden; the words, however, came from Ansel.

"Can we leave these lands?"

"I believe you can, you who traced the narrow path to arrive in them," the tree replied. "There are those who travel with you who could lead you to your lands, or to other mortal lands in proximity to them."

"And the villagers?"

"Of that, Lord Ansel, I am less certain. They did not enter our lands willingly; they were part of the village that was transformed."

Nenyane turned to Ansel. "If the lord does not fight for possession of Amberg, if it's true that some of his many roots are planted in Bowgren, there is a way—I think there's a way—to return Amberg to Bowgren."

Heiden turned toward her instantly. Ansel, however, did not; he was facing the tree, his expression almost unreadable. "Perhaps," he said, a trace of bitterness in the words, "you will be a better lord for Amberg than we have been."

Than Lord Bowgren had been. Stephen could hear it in the words.

Nenyane retreated, then. She knew that Lord Bowgren himself would be required; his presence, his *will*, his ownership of the demesne of Bowgren, would have to be asserted. Unless Ansel wished to kill his father, it was his father whose command was required.

They all knew that Lord Bowgren had been shattered in the wake of Barrett's death. Ansel had made it bitterly, furiously, clear. He knew his father; none of the other Hunters who had been summoned to the Redoubt did. Brandon and Aelle both looked as uneasy as Heiden did.

It was Heiden who stiffened, Heiden whose expression became rigid with anger.

This isn't the place for stupid arguments, Nenyane snapped. But she knew as well as Stephen did that there were some arguments one could not join. Hunter and huntbrother arguments were one of them.

"Fine," Heiden said—aloud. "If your companion is to travel to Clearbrook, and they are willing, I'll travel with them to Bowgren."

"And do *what*?" Ansel shouted, hands in fists. "You know what he's become! You know what he's been like! We couldn't even *get to Amberg* in time because he wouldn't move!"

Brandon stepped halfway between the two; the rest of the forest denizens watched with bemusement.

"He thought the world ended with Barrett," Heiden said. Heiden did not raise voice, but there was steel in the quieter words. "It *didn't*. And if I die, it *won't*. Can you not understand that? Barrett saved these villagers. Barrett's sacrifice. Barrett's death. If not for Barrett—if not for people like *us*—they would be dead. Or worse.

"If you had offered Barrett the choice—his life for the entire village —he would have given his life. He would have wanted this. And Ansel, *so would I*. Your father is caught in what *he* wanted. He's caught in what *he* lost. Fine. I'm not saying it's not terrible. If you died—" He swallowed. "But it's not just about you. Or me. It's about them. It's about Amberg and Clearbrook and the villagers we've met in Bowgren. It's about the children who have yet to be born.

"It's about the future, Ansel. And because we're lords, they're our responsibility. Lord Bowgren's responsibility. Lady Bowgren's. Yours. Mine. You don't get to make all of the decisions for me, any more than I can make them all for you.

"But I am going to Bowgren. I am going to Lady Bowgren and Lord Bowgren, and I will drag Lord Bowgren back to where Amberg stood if I have to club him over the head while his back is turned and throw him over the back of a horse!"

CHAPTER THIRTY

A elle coughed. It took a moment for Stephen to realize that the slender, pale youth was laughing.

If Heiden heard, it didn't show; he continued his tirade. "And you know what? I, Heiden of Bowgren, am going to join the next Sacred Hunt, even if you refuse!" He turned and walked over to the side of the three-headed creature the great tree called Biluude. To the creature, he offered a perfectly mannered bow. "My apologies for squabbling in public. Lady Bowgren would have disapproved."

Biluude's mortal face smiled. "So you intend to follow me while I fulfill my lord's request?"

"I do."

"Your legs are far, far too short to keep up. You will get lost."

Stephen watched with both concern and interest, his gaze traveling between Lord Ansel and Heiden. He had never seen Heiden lose his temper in so obvious a fashion.

Nenyane agreed. *It's safe,* she said. *It's safe now. My guess is that this is what Heiden was like before Barrett's death. Look at Ansel.*

Stephen agreed. Ansel was angry, but he was chagrined; the fear that had controlled him, the rage that loss had caused, had receded. He looked at Heiden from a vantage that Stephen had seldom seen: acceptance.

"Is it wise to split up?" Brandon asked.

Aelle shrugged, glancing up at Biluude. And up. They were tall. "I think we killed all the demons, and the new lord of the lands we're in isn't trying to destroy or hunt us. I don't think anything with any intelligence whatsoever is going to attack Biluude. We can just walk in their shadow."

Heiden considered this for a long moment. He then turned to Aelle. "Is it possible for Brandon to come with me? You need to let your parents know that you both survived and escaped."

"You want me there when you speak with Lord Bowgren."

Heiden nodded without apparent embarrassment. "You're family to Ansel and I, but to Lord Bowgren, you're Margen, and he may manage to control himself in the presence of other Hunter Lords. I'm not sure the huntbrother bond will allow us to communicate between the two lands; you might both want to go. Lady Bowgren has a means of communicating quickly with Lady Margen. She may want to send you home immediately—we can finesse it so she doesn't. Unless you want to return home."

Aelle grinned. "I want to see the end of this, for good or ill. Finesse away."

"What do you mean to tell her?" Ansel asked. It was a question, not a demand.

"That we're not certain the road to Margen is safe yet, and Brandon and Aelle need some time to recover?"

"She'll keep them in the manor."

"Ugh. True."

"We just don't tell her everything that's happened. It would take too long, anyway. The roads won't be safe. We barely made it out."

Ansel considered the words and nodded. "That would do it. And Brandon was injured. Rest might not be that stupid."

Brandon shook his head. "We want to see this through to the end. If you mention significant injuries, I'll be held back, even if everyone else gets to leave."

Heiden turned to Brandon. "You're going to keep this from your guards?"

Aelle looked shocked. "No, of course not—but they're going to want to see the end as well, and while Brandon is here, *he's* Margen. They'll obey him until and unless our mother intervenes. We'd like our mother not to intervene."

"Lady Bowgren will send a message to your mother."

"Is it instant?"

Ansel shook his head.

"Good. That's our only window. We need to get Lord Bowgren to agree—and to move quickly—before my mother replies and asks a lot of questions. If she orders the guard to see us home, it's home we'll be going, not Amberg."

Stephen realized that they all meant to lie; he was almost shocked. This amused Nenyane, but she said nothing.

Max and Alex just watched, but it was clear they were interested in the discussion and its outcome. It was Alex who spoke up, although Max was also smiling. "If you don't mind, one of us will also accompany you. You received your mother's permission to invite friends from the Redoubt, if I recall correctly."

Heiden nodded.

"Well, we're the friends. And if we leave Max, Ansel, and Nenyane here, you can make clear to Lady Bowgren—and Lord Bowgren—that we're relying on them to come to our aid and to save what remains of Amberg."

"So you're the added pressure?"

"If you think it's a bad idea, we don't have to do it," Alex replied. "But it seems to me that Lord Bowgren needs a bit of a prod. Lady Bowgren will understand instantly why it's socially necessary to come to the aid of friends who accompanied her oldest. And if Ansel remains here, the incentive is way, way higher—Ansel is the heir. Ansel is the future of Bowgren."

"I'm not sure that'll make much difference," the heir in question said.

"It will make a difference to Lady Bowgren," was Aelle's quiet reply. Everyone else fell silent again; Ansel's fear, Ansel's despair, cast a pall over what had been good-humored discussion. "It's known. Your father's situation is known. Hunters from the dawn of Breodanir have been shattered by such losses. And most recover."

"Some don't," Ansel replied.

"Yes. Some don't. But if your father can be brought to Amberg, if he can be made to see—as you were made to see—it might be the thing that pulls him back."

"And if it doesn't?"

"That's your fear talking," Aelle replied. "But sometimes the things we fear come to pass. Barrett's death. Lord Bowgren was respected. He was known. He was known as a good man. Give him the chance he won't give himself."

Stephen thought Aelle was the epitome of a huntbrother; he admired Aelle's intervention. He was uncertain that he could have done the same. But Aelle had known Ansel for most of the Bowgren Hunter's life; Stephen, he had met only in disgrace.

Ansel was silent. Not a yes, but not a no. Aelle glanced at Heiden, who nodded. It was Heiden who turned to Stephen. "I would take Nenyane and leave you here, but—and I'm sorry to say it—Nenyane as huntbrother might give Father enough friction to refuse to move. You as Hunter won't. And I think we need one of you with us. Not because of the pressure—for pressure, it would be better if you remain—but because you're both sensitive to changes in the land.

"The lord who ruled these lands is dead. But the changes occurring across Breodanir have happened regardless. Meralonne said that the lands overlapping Bowgren, and the lord who ruled them, were the gravest threat—but even the unpredictable turnings are a threat to our way of life. There's just no malice in it.

"We need to reach Amberg from Bowgren lands. We're not certain that the village will *be* in the same location it was before it vanished." He hesitated, and then said, "If this fails, I think it will be the last nail in the coffin."

"He wouldn't leave for Amberg until it was too late," Ansel added, although this was well-known.

Heiden nodded. "But we have more time, now. More to gain. What do we have to lose?" He exhaled and turned once again to his Hunter. "But there is one thing I want to take with us from the village before we depart." He turned to Biluude. "If you are willing to wait for us to retrieve it."

"We have time," the creature replied. "And your kind does not. We are willing to wait if you feel it will aid you in your endeavor, for we owe you all a debt, and debt does not rest easily upon our shoulders. If you like, we could join you."

Heiden bowed, no doubt to hide the ripple of discomfort the suggestion had caused. "We know your intent," he said, as he rose. "But you will terrify our people, who have had so little interaction with the wilderness."

Biluude's human face smiled. "And there is the matter of half of your mortal village."

Heiden did wince, then. "Yes, there is that."

"Very well. We will go to undo the damage done there. We did not kill the villagers, and those who were petrified, we can release. We had no desire to attack your small, quaint village." A shadow passed over that face.

IN THE END, it was decided that Brandon would remain behind with Ansel, Nenyane, and Max. The plans put forward had coalesced around Alex's suggestion. Brandon's loss to Margen would not be the equal of Ansel's loss to Bowgren, but it would be close; Brandon, absent, would add a lever. This was not the reason Brandon remained in the wilderness, however. Aelle claimed that his Hunter had far too much respect for Lord Bowgren to mislead or lie to the man; Aelle didn't think Brandon could maintain the facade that would be used to pressure Lord Bowgren to once again face his duties. Aelle, however, would accompany Alex, Stephen, and Heiden. All four were the most diplomatic halves of their pairings; all could deal well with Lady Bowgren and none were prone to loss of either tact or temper.

The four would accompany Biluude to Clearbrook first. Ansel wanted to see it, but did not trust himself to remain. He had much to say to his father, and he knew that Heiden and Aelle were both right: there was still too much anger, too much pain, and he knew, now, how those drove both his actions and his words. Lord Bowgren had enough pain and rage for them both.

THE EIGHT WENT to the village en masse; the village elder was waiting for them beyond the fence line. She did not need to know the outcome of the battle itself, for the sunlight made clear to the entire village that something had changed for the better. Some anxiety remained; people did not go to war and return unscathed. Some never returned.

Ansel led; Amberg had been a Bowgren village, and he was a lord of Bowgren.

"The enemy is dead," he said, before the elder could ask.

A cheer went up, for a small crowd had gathered behind the elder; some of the people gathered here were Margen guards. They looked, first, to ascertain that Brandon and Aelle were safe, before turning their attention to Ansel again.

When questions began in a rush of clashing syllables, the elder held up a staying hand. The questions died slowly. In time of emergency, she was obeyed, but the relief—the exuberance—felt by the villagers could not be easily quelled outside an emergency.

When Ansel held up a hand, however, silence did follow as parents caught their children and hushed them. "We have hope," he said, "now that our enemy is dead, of returning Amberg to Bowgren, for Amberg is part of Bowgren, part of our demesne."

A whisper spread across the crowd; hands were clenched, lips tightened. Hope, after all, was painful in a fashion. Necessary, but painful. The shadow of failure followed, always, in its wake.

"I will remain in the village, as will three of my companions."

The elder shook her head, but did not deny him that right; she couldn't. Stephen, watching, thought she intended to try, regardless. Ansel was Bowgren's future, the only son, upon whose shoulders rested the weight of their hopes. Better that he return to Bowgren.

"I will," he told the elder. "I will return when the rest of Amberg returns. But to return, we need Lord Bowgren's aid."

A shadow crossed the elder's face. She looked down at her hands, words pressed behind tight lips. "Will you come to my house?" she finally asked.

Ansel wanted to refuse; that much was clear to Stephen, and likely to all of the Hunters. But Ansel nodded instead. It was in her home that the item Heiden wanted to borrow could be found.

She led, lips still white around the edges, as if words were now solid and attempting to burst free. But when they had gained the relative privacy of her home, she did not speak. Silence grew, her expression adding a weight and texture to it that reminded Ansel of his father's loss. He had seen it. He had faced it. He had suffered from it—they all had. This village, his mother, his demesne, his father's friends.

"You have a huntbrother," the elder finally said, the words she had struggled to contain leaving her—and taking with them some of her height, some of the fire that had burned at the heart of Amberg and, in burning, kept it safe.

Ansel nodded.

"You know, then, what your father lost." She bowed head for a long moment, but lifted it again. "We, who have never made those bonds, have never faced those losses—but we have faced loss, as all people must. We have not faced your losses, and we understand that those losses form the foundation for the lives we live. They are not easy lives; the young sometimes envy the lives of those who have power, who were born into nobility. But Barrett wasn't born into nobility; he was brought into it. He was chosen.

"Do you ever wonder why village children are not chosen?"

Ansel shook his head.

Heiden, however, said, "No."

"No?"

"We can't choose your children. The villages require them; they will grow into the villages, grow into the tanners or the farmers on which all of Bowgren depends." He exhaled. "Perhaps there are villagers who would be willing to surrender their sons to Bowgren." Or to Breodanir. Stephen did not say this. "But will those villagers then believe that their sons now owe them more, as children of their blood?

"We're orphans," he continued, "when we're found. When we're adopted. When we're trained. There are no other family members who might pressure us, who might divert us from the responsibilities we've undertaken. No blood kin to whom we owe a debt of service or duty.

"I didn't understand it at first, myself. The children of Bowgren are not always well-fed when the seasons have been harsh and the harvest is poor. But I grew to understand it. Lady Bowgren made it clear. If Barrett had been from Amberg, what anger, what pain, what fury would devolve onto the heads of Bowgren? What resentment would be fostered in the village by his kin?"

The elder's smile was careworn but genuine. "Yes. You understand, then. I didn't want to be village elder when I was a child. I wanted to leave the village. I wanted to travel to the King's City, there to meet scholars and the learned; I wanted to forge my own path to strength.

"And it may surprise you to know that my grandmother approved, much to my mother's dismay. She allowed me to travel as I desired to travel; to learn, as I desired to learn. I made my way to the King's City, there to meet foreigners and the scholars I had so idolized. I saw the way they lived. I saw the wealth that they'd been born to. I saw the convenience of a life that was not Amberg's.

"For a time, it enchanted me. I felt lesser in all ways, but I wanted to prove my worth." This last was said with a bitter smile. "And I did."

"But...you're the elder." It was Aelle who spoke.

"Indeed. My mother became elder upon my grandmother's death — my mother, who wasn't young at the time she came into her responsibility. My mother could read and write. All of the village elders must be able to do at least that; they correspond with Lady Bowgren, writing monthly reports in times of general peace. It's the elders who make requests of the Bowgren granaries and supplies if the harvest has been bad; the elders who make requests for the provisions provided by Hunters.

"Those in line to be elders have their own training. Perhaps, because of that training, I sought more. I'm a person, and people seek more; it's in our nature. And so I went. But I discovered something disturbing within the King's City, within the wealthy merchant families, and within the foreign dignitaries and visitors.

"They didn't believe in the Sacred Hunt's necessity. They didn't countenance our God." She rose, then, and walked into a small room; they waited until she returned. She carried with her three worn books, their leather covers dark with fingerprints and the passage of time. "There are notations for dates here that aren't entirely standard, but the dates refer to the three years during which the Sacred Hunt was not called.

"They were among the first things I was taught to read; they were considered the most important information the journals contained for one who would eventually govern the village." She set them down on the table in the center of the room, and opened one. "This," she said softly, "was a description of the harvests the first year the Sacred Hunt wasn't called by our King — a King who was heavily influenced by foreign scholars and diplomats. They considered the Hunt barbaric.

"The planting that year was poor; there was little rain. The ground hardened. Lady Bowgren had the granaries and the Hunters had meat, which was smoked and preserved. The village didn't eat well that year, but we didn't starve; there had been lean years before.

"But the elder of the time knew, if the Hunt wasn't called, the next year would be far harsher. And so it transpired. The King would not be moved. His people had not starved. The foreigners were *right*." She said the word with astonishing savagery; Stephen was surprised she didn't spit. She took a while to find her voice again.

"The second year was the worst harvest in our history; the lack of rain threatened everything. The lakes receded and the streams in which we fished and from which we drew water became a trickle. The elder wrote to Lady Bowgren of the time. Lady Bowgren wrote back to say Lord Bowgren was aware of the difficulty, but the lords could not call the Sacred Hunt; it was the duty given by God to the King.

"By the King who could call the Hunt, but could never die in it."

She turned pages, looking ahead; it was clear that these pages had been read, and read again; the book fell open naturally to the part she sought.

"The third year, the Hunt was not called. Then, people starved. Children were the first to go; children and the elderly. The elder of the time was not immune; her daughter took over her duties as village elder, and it was very, very hard. The villagers who had the strength were angry—but despair takes no strength. It was the worst possible time to become the new, untried head.

"She was angry. She was younger than I am. Younger than I was when my mother passed away. All that anger and nowhere to send it. Anger's a weapon, but wield it and it points in two directions unless you're very careful. The external anger was obvious: the lords for whom we had toiled for all of our lives, for all of the history of Amberg, had turned away from their duties. They weren't starving. Their children weren't dying. Their dogs lived in better houses than many of us.

"But the anger she felt that turned inward was different. She'd grown up in Amberg, had been taught in Amberg, had become known to all of her people—and she had quietly nursed resentment against those who were born of noble blood, those who were lucky, those who only had one important duty a year if they were to retain their titles.

"And for the three years they hadn't been called to do that duty, the lands had withered. She hadn't appreciated the Hunt," the elder said softly. "She knew that one man died every year, called to the God and taken by him. She knew the *stories*. That because of that single death, the lands flourished, supporting life. But the truth of it? She had never paid it much mind.

"You know—from your own teachings—that the foolish King was deposed by his son, by the priesthood, by those Hunters who believed in the old ways. And you know as well that when the new King called the Hunt, almost a third of all present perished—destroyed by the wrath of their God.

"We lost a Hunter in Bowgren during that time—a Hunter and his huntbrother, both. We understood, the following year, that it was those deaths—those many, terrible deaths—that once again repaid the God; our harvests were bountiful." The elder bowed head again.

"But I know that the foolish King, killed by his own son, was a weak man in a different way. He knew the pain that Lord Bowgren suffers, even now. He knew it because he had seen its like, once every year, for the whole of his life. He had seen it break strong men, and even those that recovered never became what they had been. Some, he took in as Huntsmen of the Chamber. Some, he was forced to retire.

"He wished to believe there was another way. That our kingdom could flourish without such blood sacrifices, such intense losses. And as did many, he believed what he heard, believed what he desperately wanted to be true.

"It was to prevent the deaths of men like Barrett that he decided to forgo the Sacred Hunt. It was to prevent the shattering of men like Lord Bowgren." She closed the book. "That is not the story that is told of that weak and foolish man. But it is a story that I know, and it is a story that I will tell my heir, that I will write in these journals. We understand the price paid, and we cannot pay it. Ever. Our deaths—our many deaths—did not feed the God. Had they, the Hunt could have ended.

"The year that followed the King's death, the Hunt was called. One man died. And our fields continued to be bountiful. Our rivers flowed past, with fish that we might catch; our lakes were full of clear water. The year after, the Hunt was called. And every year since that time.

"We will forget. People forget when none among the living have been touched by the events that are already history. But I know. Amberg knows. It is because of men like Barrett, year after year, because of men like Lord Bowgren, broken by his loss, that we endure. That we do more than simply endure." She closed the book and rose.

They had not yet asked her for the one item they wished to carry back to Bowgren with them, but they did not need to ask; she went to the shrine and lifted the small painting in both hands. "It is because of them that we might have any chance of returning to the lands and fields of our births."

Heiden took the painting with care.

It was Ansel who asked the question that hovered in all of their minds. "Why did you return to Amberg? If you escaped the confines of village life, if you found your scholars and proved your value to them, why did you return? This was not the life you wanted."

She smiled. "No. No, it wasn't. But it was the life I was born to, and as I spent time with the monied and the powerful, it seemed to me there was an emptiness in them. I did not understand it at first, because at first it seemed like freedom—freedom from the responsibilities of Amberg. But Lord Ansel, they served no one. They felt responsibility for nothing. They were defined solely by their own desires, and when those were quenched, they moved on, like children, seeking but never quite finding.

"It felt, to me, that there was nothing beneath their feet—no solid ground, no roots, no sense—at all—of the importance of service, either given or received. It felt empty, to me. And perhaps that is because my dreams were daydreams, but my roots were here.

"I am grateful that I am not new to the responsibility; I am grateful that I did not become village head only when Amberg was lost to this place. The villagers knew me, and they were afraid, but they listened. They listened, they survived until you found us. So, take this portrait—but return it to us when you are done. Lord Bowgren has far, far finer in his keeping, but none will mean what this one does to us.

"It's not evening, but you must be exhausted. Rest, sleep, and leave when you wake."

1ST OF WITTAN, 429 A.A. DEMESNE OF BOWGREN, KINGDOM OF BREODANIR

BILUUDE DID NOT GALLOP. Given the size of the creature and the images that Meralonne had shown them in Hunter's Redoubt, Stephen half expected to be forced to move out of the way of falling trees. This did not happen.

Kallandras chose to remain in Amberg. When they left it, people had gathered to listen to his lute—and his song—in the village center. His talent, given his position within the famed Senniel College, could not be questioned; his ability to interact with a crowd composed of at least three generations was a comfort.

Meralonne, however, chose to accompany them. As did Gervanno. Gervanno didn't carry the fox, who had chosen to remain by the side of the great tree. He had almost demanded Gervanno do the same, and

Stephen would have been more than happy to allow it, given Gervanno's status as Maubreche guard.

Nenyane, however, would have none of it. She was willing—barely —to remain in Amberg, although that had taken some work. She had never been happy to be apart from Stephen, but she understood Alex's plan. She would accept it only so long as Gervanno guarded Stephen in her stead. She spoke briefly with the Southerner in private, but Stephen knew she was both asking and threatening Gervanno.

Meralonne was impatient to be gone. "*I* will accompany Stephen. There is very, very little that could endanger him in my presence." He seemed vaguely offended that she had turned to Gervanno instead.

Stephen could still feel some of the lion's emotions, although that was fading as they walked: the lion was content. It expected no trouble, and found the probable lack slightly disappointing. But while it had been severely injured in its battle against the former lord, and had been forced to withdraw from combat, very little sign of those injuries remained.

Stephen didn't understand the power of the great tree; perhaps it was something that came with rulership of the land itself. But perhaps this was also true of the demesnes of Breodanir in a much more subtle fashion; were it not, Ansel would have walked with them and approached Bowgren from the Breodanir side.

Heiden went ahead, Aelle by his side, when Biluude informed them that they were perhaps ten minutes from the outskirts of Clearbrook.

"It is best that he goes on ahead," the creature said to Stephen and Alex. They seldom spoke directly to Gervanno, as if his position as guard did not require it. Or as if speaking to the guard, and not the master, was an insult. Gervanno, however, was comfortable with this. Biluude's gaze did not include Meralonne, and Meralonne appeared to have no desire to be included. He treated the three-headed creature with respect, but no more. He deferred—inasmuch as the mage could— to Heiden, because Heiden was of Bowgren, and it was to Bowgren they traveled.

Alex nodded. "They'll be terrified if they see you without explanation or warning. They lost half of their villagers to your last visit."

"They are mortal," Biluude replied, with humor. "They will be terrified, regardless. But fear is not a capable driver in any hands; I will wait until Heiden has done what he can to alleviate the worst of it."

True to their word, they waited. When Heiden returned, he

returned by the side of an iron-haired older woman; she was further along in years than the elder of Amberg, but was clearly cut from the same cloth. She did freeze for a second when Biluude came into view, but started moving immediately, her lips a narrow line.

Her gaze took in Aelle, Stephen, and Alex, pausing briefly on Gervanno before it returned once again to the three-headed beast.

She then offered the three-headed beast a decent bow for a villager. There was no friendliness, and no fear, in her expression when she rose from that bow. "I'll go on ahead. I'd tell my people to stay in their homes, but that wasn't any guarantee of safety last time, so they might as well see what you're doing. You can really bring them back?"

"Yes."

"Good. It'll make more difference than any of the lord's assurances." The woman turned, and then turned back. "Why'd you do it?"

"That is complicated, lady."

She snorted but didn't correct the respectful use of the word.

"I am a soldier. I was under orders I could not disobey. I did my best not to harm the villagers —"

"You *turned them to stone.*"

"Yes. But stone does not bleed, it does not age, and the person can be retrieved. Would you rather I had just killed them?"

"Not if you're telling the truth."

Heiden paled. Had she been a villager, he would have instantly asserted his authority to shut her down; she was the village head. He didn't dare. To be fair to Heiden, Stephen wouldn't have dared, either. Yes, in theory Heiden outranked the old woman, but theory was a far, far cry from practice. Women like these were the village equivalent of the ladies who governed the demesnes; you didn't disrespect them unless it was an absolute emergency, and even then, you'd probably spend a decade groveling afterward.

"Given the manner in which we were introduced, I will overlook your suspicion," Biluude replied. Heiden, standing behind the elder, almost sagged with relief.

Aelle laughed, which did nothing to sweeten the elder's mood.

Biluude then accompanied the elder — and Heiden — to Clearbrook.

Stephen, Aelle, and Alex followed. The Maubreche Hunter glanced up at the treetops for any sign of Meralonne's presence. He could detect none, but the lion was almost preternaturally aware of the mage; the mage was close.

He exhaled and turned his attention to Clearbrook.

They arrived at the outskirts of the village at dawn.

TO SEE the statues in person was not what Stephen had expected. He'd known what had happened here; it had been reported, and the mage had made it clear, in the contained space on the tabletop between his hands. But that couldn't capture what Stephen now saw with his own eyes. There were statues of villagers in the fields on the outer edge of Clearbrook; statues in front of a farmhouse; statues on the dirt road that led to the town's center. The ages of the statue subjects varied, but the statues themselves were far, far more realistic than sculpture would have been. Stephen reached out to touch the upturned face of a young child, arm raised as if in greeting.

He withdrew his hand almost instantly; the stone cheek was warm.

"Yes," the elder said, understanding why he'd jerked his hand away. "It was a shock to us, too. I'll tell you now—when the others can't hear me—that it made things harder in some ways. No one could truly mourn. No one wanted these statues buried; they felt alive to the touch. Hope is necessary for life, but it can be a burden when there's too much fear in it. But it appears they were right, those who clung to hope. Hope's not my business," she added. "But you'd know that, wouldn't you?" She looked up at Biluude. "And here I am, getting in your way. You can start with this child."

The old woman's hands were trembling. That she didn't settle them on her ample hips probably took effort.

Stephen had a sense, watching the three-headed creature, that there was theater in the way they responded to the old woman's request. No, he thought, as the heads of the bird and the lion rose, faces lifted to the skies—it wasn't theater. It was story; their actions here were telling a story to those who might bear witness. Stephen was certain that villagers were—at a safe distance—observing what the creature did.

When the creature had first come here—no, when Meralonne had showed them his illusions—the human head had been absent. It was the heads of lion and eagle that had featured prominently in his lesson.

The lion roared, the bird screeched, the two sounds almost rhythmic. The mortal head was silent, bent as if listening to the sounds of the other two.

The lion then bent to the stone child, and licked the top of its head.

The child shrieked. "Don't *do* that!" he cried, covering his now wet hair.

"The song of the two is a song of comfort," the human head said. "It speaks most clearly to those who are trapped thus; the child knows we are not a threat to him."

As if to prove the truth of those words, the child looked around, blinking. He stopped when he caught sight of the village head.

"I think you were correct, lady," Biluude said, bending to reach for the child. Before anyone could intervene, she pulled the child up on her back. "Will you ride with us? We have much work to do here, but I believe it would comfort those we must heal to know that you are safe with us."

The child, no fool, looked immediately to the village elder for permission. The elder nodded, lips compressed, glare making clear that the child would be in a great deal of trouble if he embarrassed the village in any way.

Heiden was smiling, although his expression was complicated. "It's comfort," the Bowgren Hunter told Stephen. "It's so normal." In a much quieter voice, he added, "When I was a boy, I would have been more terrified of the village head than Biluude."

PERSON BY PERSON, the three-headed beast freed those trapped in a skin of stone, and the trapped, the frozen, followed in their wake until they came to the village center. There, Biluude had petrified those on the outside of the buildings, but some of the statues had been moved inside by the grieving; they were extracted from their homes by the rest of the villagers.

There were tears—gratitude, relief, joy—and the village elder allowed the villagers to set aside their very interrupted work to prepare, instead, for celebration.

It was a celebration that Stephen both desired to see and knew he would not. If Clearbrook had been important to Heiden and Ansel— and it had—there was still work to be done, and it couldn't wait. Had they arrived in the dark of night, they might have woken the elder and done their work, there to rest and join in celebration. Dawn had given way to day, and day to the slow sinking of sun.

They would reach the Bowgren estates by nightfall if they left now.

Heiden wasn't ready to confront Lord Bowgren, but ready or no, it was essential. As Stephen had expected, none of the Hunters present could contact their brothers. They had no sense that their brothers were dead, but the absence was far more uncomfortable in reality than it had been in anticipation.

It wouldn't end unless they returned to the great tree, or they brought Amberg back to Bowgren—and they couldn't do the latter without Lord Bowgren. Stephen understood the meaning behind the Amberg elder's words. Lord Bowgren was blessed with her understanding—but he had responsibilities he had all but abandoned to a son who did not have the power to do what had to be done.

The Hunters might not despise Lord Bowgren, but even if they felt a deep and abiding sympathy for his loss, the work still had to be done. Resentment, fear, grief—they were separate from the work itself, but entwined with it. That was the burden of the Breodanir nobility.

BILUUDE DID NOT ACCOMPANY them to the Bowgren manor; they spent a small while surrounded by villagers drunk with relief or alcohol. What they did beyond that, the Hunters didn't know—but they trusted no further harm would be done to Clearbrook. Heiden's presence at the beast's side made clear to the villagers that Bowgren itself was the architect of their salvation, which restored a tenuous faith in the family itself.

"I wish Ansel could have seen it," Heiden said to Alex.

Alex understood. "Ansel is with Amberg, and Ansel has seen what Amberg has, and has not, become. Also, he left the hard work with you. Speaking with Lady Bowgren comes naturally to you now—but Hunters speak with or to Hunters, and Lord Bowgren, shattered or no, is a Hunter Lord." He glanced at Stephen. "In your case, Nenyane might have been better."

"Lord Bowgren is—was—a traditionalist," Heiden murmured. Nenyane was a girl.

"So are most Hunters, but it doesn't take them long to be comfortable with her. She's like a Hunter, at heart—Stephen is far more like a huntbrother, socially speaking."

"To Nenyane and my father's regret." Stephen smiled to show there was no edge in the words, no hidden mote of bitterness. "But there's a reason it's the Ladies who govern, and the governance is crucial."

"Lord Elseth believes it's crucial as long as he doesn't have to do it," Alex added, grinning. "And it means we get to hold onto Lady Elseth until Ingrid is old enough to take over her duties. Or until William gets married and brings a competent wife into the house. Mother is an *excellent* hunter, but she'd be even worse at governing than my father."

Aelle laughed. He always had laughter at the ready, and he had a lot of questions about Lady Elseth; he knew about the Elseth situation. But of course he would; he paid attention to the discourse of the governing Ladies.

They had walked at speed for several hours and could now see the manor grounds clearly. Stephen was surprised at how much Heiden could speak, given how little he'd spoken in Hunter's Redoubt—but it was hard to feel uncomfortable around Alex.

Only as they approached the manor itself did Heiden withdraw. "Let me do the talking," he told Aelle. Aelle nodded; it was clear neither Alex or Stephen had any desire to rush into a conversation with a ruling Lady Bowgren.

Bowgren's Keeper of the Keys was the first person to meet them. He was an august man with a severe expression and perfect posture even given his age. Heiden was clearly happy to set eyes on the man; the man's expression did not show a similar delight, but Stephen suspected the old man's face might crack if he did.

"Master Heiden. I will call for Lady Bowgren." His version of *call* was to wave a hand to a waiting page, who immediately took off—at a run that brought a frown to the keykeeper's face—up the stairs. Only when he was gone did the keykeeper once again turn to Heiden. He asked no further questions until the page came flying down the stairs again.

"We have *guests*," the keykeeper said; he did not raise voice, but the emphasis on the last syllable almost echoed.

The poor page almost tripped over his own feet as he slowed to a more stately walk. It didn't matter. Above him, walking as gracefully as a noble of her station was expected to walk, came Lady Bowgren. Her complexion was pale, her eyes underlined by dark half-circles. When she caught sight of Heiden, she could not mask her expression. But she did not run to him, and he did not—mindful suddenly of the companions who had become guests—run to her. He waited, hands drawn behind his back, and as she approached, he offered her a perfect bow.

Given that his clothing was dusty, and in one place torn, perfect was necessary. Stephen became aware of the state of his own clothing in her presence; no one had thought to change into something more suited to greeting Lady Bowgren, because everyone's eye was on the road that had yet to be taken to the end of their journey.

But they wouldn't travel there tonight, and everyone present did have one set of suitable clothing—in need, of course, of ironing—in their packs.

Aelle, Stephen, and Alex all offered Lady Bowgren the same bow Heiden had offered her.

"You are welcome here. Aelle, did your brother not accompany you?"

"He is, for the moment, safe, but he did not; he was injured and we felt it best that he recover first."

"Where is he? Lady Margen informed us of the difficulties Margen faced." She said no more.

"He is in Amberg, Lady Bowgren," Aelle replied. "With Lord Ansel and Stephen's huntbrother."

"Amberg?" The word was almost inaudible, but the movement of her lips made it clear.

Heiden smiled, then. "Amberg. We found Amberg, and we found Lord Brandon and Aelle there, along with the surviving Margen guards."

"And our villagers?"

"The village head kept the villagers together; they have suffered some losses, but they have mostly survived."

"Then Amberg is—"

"No. Amberg is in what we now refer to as the wilderness. But there is a tenuous connection in the village to Bowgren, and it is to bring them home that we have come."

"Then go upstairs, bathe, change if you have the means to do so. If you require clothing in a better state, you have it here, and I am certain clothing can be found for your companions."

"Lady." Heiden swallowed. "Mother. In order to save Amberg, we require Lord Bowgren's intervention."

She closed her eyes. It was brief, and when she opened them again, her shoulders were straighter, if stiffer. "Very well. But you require food and a bath. Lord Bowgren *will* join us for dinner."

AELLE WAS CLEARLY familiar with the Bowgren manor and the Bowgren guest rooms. Although a page led them to those rooms, Aelle took over the moment Lady Bowgren and the keykeeper were beyond earshot. The page also relaxed. It was clear that Aelle and Brandon were loved, here.

They were offered baths in the rooms to which they'd been lead and they took them gratefully, Stephen with some guilt for the people left behind who couldn't enjoy this singular luxury. Guilt made him finish quickly. If they were to join Lord and Lady Bowgren for dinner, he had to look as much the part of a representative of Maubreche as he could.

It was Aelle who fetched him; Aelle who led them to the rooms Ansel and Heiden shared. They found Heiden going through closets with focus and some dismay. Aelle stepped in to help; Alex and Stephen stood in place while different shirts and jackets were held up against them. There was very little discussion about how to approach Lord Bowgren. Lady Bowgren intended to bring him to the dinner table—a place he had taken to avoiding in the past months, as Heiden informed them.

Heiden had chosen to bring the portrait of Barrett into the dining hall. The keykeeper had seen that Heiden carried something, and he had gestured for a page to carry it until it was required or called for. But when Heiden had showed him what he carried, the older man belayed that order.

They were seen into the dining room by the keykeeper himself, which was unusual; the keykeeper then took up position by the far wall. He intended, Stephen realized, to *serve*. Or to witness. Then again, the keykeeper had no doubt been part of Bowgren since his youth. Watching the disintegration of Lord Bowgren must have been particularly painful.

Lord Bowgren was, as Lady Bowgren had said he would be, at the table when they entered. He was paler than his wife, his eyes so darkly circled they seemed to have been blackened. But he rose, as Lord, to welcome his guests.

His gaze went to Heiden as if searching for something there. Or perhaps he had noticed that Heiden's bow was absent, and Heiden's hands were behind his back. Heiden took his seat and placed his precious burden beneath it, face down.

To their surprise, it was Lord Bowgren who spoke first. He did not offer the traditional greeting; did not offer the traditional welcome or thanks that preceded most formal meals. He looked directly at Heiden, as if their visitors were chimerical mirages. "Where is Ansel?"

Heiden inhaled. Exhaled. "Ansel," he said quietly, "is trapped in Amberg."

"And you're not?" was the sharp question. If Heiden had hoped that by mentioning the village, he would direct Lord Bowgren's attention, that hope was dashed.

Lady Bowgren did not speak at all; she watched both her son and her husband, assessing them in silence. Aelle watched her, but did not speak.

"Only one of us could leave," Heiden replied, his voice steady, his expression grave.

"And you were the one who chose to return to Bowgren?" There was a hint of incredulity in the question; that and a thin edge of anger. To Stephen's surprise, Heiden's lips trembled in a withheld smile.

"Lord Ansel is a Hunter Lord of Bowgren, and if Amberg is no longer situated in Bowgren, it is still to the Hunter Lords that the village elder—and her surviving people—look for guidance and succor. Lord Ansel chose to remain; he sent me to Bowgren in his stead."

Silence.

Lord Bowgren looked at the table. He then lifted head to look at Lady Bowgren, who said nothing; she moved her gaze to Heiden, forcing Lord Bowgren to do the same. He eventually did. "Will you return to Ansel and lead him back to Bowgren?"

Heiden swallowed. All of his careful planning—or Alex's—vanished as he met the eyes of the man he considered his father. "I can't."

"But you've arrived. You're here."

"I am. Ansel will not abandon Amberg, because there's a slender chance that Amberg itself can be liberated and returned to Bowgren, where it belongs."

Silence again.

"But that return requires an anchor; it requires the presence of the ruler of Bowgren. There is only one person who can do what must be done to return Amberg to Bowgren: Lord Bowgren. You."

Lord Bowgren's anger hardened, cracking the neutral expression guests demanded. "My presence didn't save Amberg."

"No. Not then. But you were late and Ansel wasn't on the other side of the divide, waiting for you." Heiden exhaled. "I'm grateful that you sent us to the King's City; it was there we learned the reason for the loss of Amberg and the devastation in Clearbrook. There that we met Stephen," he indicated the Maubreche Hunter with a nod of the head, "and Alex. We meant to return home." He exhaled. "We learned that there was some small possibility that Amberg still existed—that it had been pulled into enemy territory by ancient magics."

Lord Bowgren's eyes narrowed; his lips were white, they were so compressed. He did not interrupt Heiden.

"We intended to cross the divide between our two lands, to wage war against the lord that had declared war upon Bowgren. We were uncertain that we would easily find a way to reach Amberg.

"But a way had already been built. Lady Margen has been in contact with Lady Bowgren; Lady Bowgren knew that Lord Brandon and Master Aelle had vanished in an attempt to find the Margen guards who had taken a road that had turned. We simply followed the road they had taken. As you can see, we found Aelle. We also found Amberg."

"And you survived."

"We had allies," Heiden replied. "And the lord who would have destroyed Bowgren is now dead. In her place rules a lord who has no interest in conquest of, or hunting of, humans. But Amberg remains trapped in a twilight between Bowgren and that hidden land. If you are willing—if you are able—it is your will and your desire that will bring Amberg back."

Or fail to do so.

"I did not bring it back when I went," Lord Bowgren said, voice stiff. "My presence meant *nothing*." Anger again. Anger and beneath it a pain so visible Stephen had to force himself not to look away, not to flinch. Lord Bowgren's pain was the future he feared. It was the reason he had never allowed Nenyane to swear the huntbrother's oath.

Heiden had always bowed head when Ansel's temper was close to breaking. Lord Bowgren's temper, so similar to Ansel's, did not have the same effect. Heiden did fall silent, but his posture did not imply fear or hesitance; it implied determination.

He bent to retrieve what he had carried from Amberg, but placed it face down on the table—moving his place setting, with food, to one side. Food was not the reason he had come this far.

"I told Ansel that when the Sacred Hunt is called next, I will attend. If he chooses to absent himself, I will nonetheless represent Bowgren at the Hunt—and at all Hunts in future, while I draw breath."

Lord Bowgren's eyes widened before narrowing; he stood so quickly, his chair toppled backward. Throughout, Lady Bowgren's face was a chiseled mask; she watched her son and her husband, and said nothing.

"It is because of the Sacred Hunt that Breodanir has been far less affected by the turnings than the kingdoms to the West. It is because of the Sacred Hunt—because of the *deaths* in the Hunt—that we have any chance of preserving Bowgren; it is because of the Sacred Hunt that Amberg had whatever small ability it possessed to resist being over-whelmed and destroyed.

"And our people *know it*." He lifted the portrait then, and turned it toward the head of the table—toward Lord Bowgren, the man who had been shattered by the loss of his huntbrother, whose anger and resent-ment had almost destroyed Ansel, and had left Bowgren itself with far less of a defense than Maubreche or Elseth.

"This came from Amberg," Heiden continued, when Lord Bowgren did not speak.

Could not speak. He was staring at the portrait, and any control of expression or posture was completely lost. The portrait was not expertly done; it was clearly the work of an amateur. But there was, in the rough work, a hint of smile, a hint of softness around the lips and eyes that implied an enduring, an endless, kindness.

Lord Bowgren could not fail to see it. He lifted an arm, as if to touch the portrait; his arm, of course, could not quite reach it. But he murmured a single word over and over again. Stephen tried not to hear it.

Aelle, however, did not; he let his tears fall. Aelle had known Barrett in life.

To Stephen's shock, Lady Bowgren allowed tears to fall as well, although her expression did not change.

"We rule, Lord Bowgren," Heiden continued, implacable. "We have wealth. We have power. We will not starve when the harvest is bad. We will not freeze when the winter is harsh. We create laws and we govern;

we make decisions for the villages that the villages themselves must abide.

"And this is why. This is *why*. Barrett always knew. Maybe you didn't. Maybe Hunter Lords can't. But Barrett and I came from streets in which survival wasn't guaranteed. When we were given everything—more than everything, because neither of us expected to have a brother so close to us that the rest of the world paled to insignificance—we understood what the risks were."

"You were *children!*" Lord Bowgren shouted, the cords of his neck tightening, his face darkening. "You were children! You *did not know!*"

Heiden shook his head. "Barrett would have made this choice if he had known. If Barrett had been told *risk* of death could save the entire village, he would have done what he did. I know, Lord Bowgren. Because I would do the same. I *will* do the same. We live on the backs of those villagers, and if this is what we can do to protect them in turn, this is what we must do.

"If it weren't for Barrett—for men like Barrett—throughout Breodanir's history, Amberg would be gone. It's still there, and we still have a chance to save our people because Barrett made the choice he made. Because *you* made the choice you made. If you resent the villagers, if you resent Bowgren, if you resent the entire world because Barrett died, you dishonor his choice. You dishonor Barrett, because Barrett would never have wanted this.

"And they know it, Father. This came from Amberg. This came from the village head's home. I promised to return it to her, but I wanted to show you that they know. They honor him. They honor *us*."

The silence was terrible. No one but Heiden could break it; even Lady Bowgren was gripped in its folds.

Heiden was inexorable. "You think, because Barrett died, his whole life meant nothing."

"No, I don't."

"You do. This is where you've been while everyone else—*everyone*—has been struggling. It wasn't his *life* that mattered—only his death. Only your loss. It was his life that matters to me. I know that I'd be shattered if Ansel died. I know I'd feel the loss the way you feel it. And I know, if it happened during the Sacred Hunt, that I'd follow him in death—and I'd be happy.

"So this is the choice you have now: honor his life. Honor his duty. Go to Amberg and save the villagers, Ansel, and Brandon. Or refuse.

Commit to refusal. Follow him in death *now* so that Ansel becomes Lord Bowgren and Ansel can do what must be done."

Sharp breaths were drawn around the table. Lady Bowgren opened her mouth.

Lord Bowgren lifted a hand to forestall all other words. He stared at his son—his adopted son, his huntbrother son—his eyes focused but not narrowed, as if the anger that had imbued them with fire and life had been banked but the heat had not.

"Ansel understands, now, what must be done. If you cannot face that without Barrett, he will do it."

"And he'll become Lord Bowgren when he refuses to join the Sacred Hunt?"

"I will go. I will carry Bowgren's banner. If I go, he will follow, in the end."

"And you're certain of that, are you?"

"Yes. We are Breodani. We are Hunters." Heiden spoke without hesitation. "And this is the duty for which we are honored and for which we risk our lives."

"Barrett," Lord Bowgren said, voice shaky, "would have been proud of you. He would be so proud."

"I've learned that there is no replacement for Barrett," Heiden replied, his voice softening. "I tried. I couldn't be Barrett. But Barrett would have told me it wasn't necessary: I only had to be Heiden. Heiden of Bowgren. Ansel's huntbrother."

"What do you feel I must do?"

Lady Bowgren closed her eyes.

"Leave with us for the site on which Amberg once stood," Heiden replied. For the first time, hesitation marked his words. "I can't tell you what to do from there. But the rulers—the Hunter Lords—can sense shifts in the land itself when the land isn't completely Bowgren's, or so I've been told. If they can sense that land, they can assert their claim; they can strengthen the earth that is Bowgren's.

"We believe if you do this, Amberg will return—and all the people Amberg currently harbors will come with it."

Lord Bowgren was silent, but his gaze rested on the portrait he faced. On Barrett's gentle expression, on the familiar face he would never see in life again. "You found this in the village."

"On the shrine set up in the village head's home."

"And you promised to return it."

Heiden nodded.

"Give it to me, then. Give it here."

Heiden's hands tightened on the frame.

"Give it to me, and I will carry it back to Amberg." Lord Bowgren did not resume the seat he had vacated in anger; he walked around the table to where Heiden was seated, and he gently lifted the frame from the hands of his son. "We will leave in the morning." Looking past the picture, he said to the keykeeper, "Make sure the horses are prepared, and pack the food and the meats we could not deliver to Amberg."

The keykeeper bowed.

Lord Bowgren, carrying the portrait with care, left the dining hall.

EPILOGUE

"Ansel."

Had he not recognized the voice, he would have known who had spoken regardless; Nenyane was the only person present who never used his title. He accepted this, but knew it ruffled more than a few feathers within Amberg. Her presence as huntbrother would have had that effect regardless.

Ansel was aware that he would have—that he *had*—been one such ruffled person, but none of that remained. It couldn't. She had traveled with him, had fought at his side, had saved his life, and likely the lives of the other Hunters. That she hadn't done that with Bowgren in mind changed nothing. She was huntbrother. She was more.

He missed the portrait of Barrett at the shrine, but the shrine was still visited, regardless. Throughout the day, as if Barrett were a minor deity, villagers came to the shrine to offer flowers or prayers. Every time they did, he missed Barrett. Missed him and was proud of him, if he could claim that pride as a right.

He missed Heiden ferociously. Not his presence, but the sense of it, the sound of his huntbrother's voice. The nagging. The correction. The quiet support. He wondered what silence like this for the rest of his life would be like. But he knew. He had seen it.

He hadn't allowed himself to believe in his father. He had tried for months, and it had accomplished nothing but pain, anger, and disappointment.

But the village head spoke with him, a few words here, a few there: she made clear that the villagers believed in Lord Bowgren; that they'd seen what loss could do, and they believed he would find his way back from it.

He might find half of himself. That was all his father would ever have again. Ansel was almost chagrined by the respect and deference the villagers showed him; he'd been an echo of his father, and he'd told his parents that he would soon lose the title he had earned, because he would never take part in the Sacred Hunt again.

He no longer believed that. How could he, and be in Amberg?

But he was grateful that his fury and his pain had led him, in disgrace, to the King's City, because there he had met Stephen, Nenyane, Alex, and Max; there he had met Meralonne, Kallandras, and Gervanno. Were it not for that meeting, he would not be here now, in a village that was, if dislocated geographically, nonetheless whole.

"Hello?" Nenyane snapped.

Ansel shook himself and turned toward the Maubreche huntbrother.

"Biluude wants you to come out."

"To the tree?"

She nodded.

If Ansel missed Heiden, it was nothing compared to Nenyane; she had been snappish and impatient since Stephen had left the village. She could not sit still—or stand still—for more than a minute, and in the end had chosen to leave the village to head towards the great tree.

The tree stood in the center of the lake, but the lake was now a different shape; the water remained clear, but deep. A small island had sprung up beneath the tree, and that island had grown larger as the hours passed. Ansel couldn't be certain that Nenyane even remained on that island.

The bard, however, remained in the village, entertaining the villagers and gently supporting their hope. Daylight helped, for there was day in abundance, and the new lord did not seek to hamper that. The sun both rose and fell in a cadence that felt natural to Amberg.

The rest of the surroundings were not natural, and the food stores were very low; Ansel did not go hunting, because he was missing both

Heiden and his dogs. But that was not the only reason; he knew the villagers would be anxious at his absence for however long it lasted.

He trusted Heiden. He trusted Aelle. Brandon was at least as restless as Ansel himself, but Max spent time with the dogs to curb his own restlessness. The absence of huntbrothers or Hunter — it was hard to determine in Max and Alex's case — was difficult for all of them.

Ansel had imagined what life would be like if Heiden died. It had led him on an echo of his father's path.

It was a path he could no longer follow. No, that was wrong. He *could*. But here, in Amberg, in what Nenyane called the wilderness, he knew he must not. He must not walk it now, when Heiden was still alive. And even should Heiden die, he must not follow it again; it led to neglect and death. Not his, not his father's — although he was uneasily certain that death would be a boon to Lord Bowgren — but the villagers'. The people whom they had been charged and tasked with feeding and protecting.

The people loved Barrett, and would, in time, love Heiden the same way, if they did not yet.

But he had had this experience. He had, in resentment and anger, gone to the King's City, and he had emerged as his best self — slowly, and with many missteps. Heiden had become what he had once been, when Ansel had not been driven by fear and rage. He had almost lost that Heiden — because of his own actions, his own fear — and that was a loss he could not even *see* in the beginning, the fear of the endless loss his father suffered was so strong.

But he had come back from that fear. His father had to come back from the reality.

Yes, he trusted Heiden and Aelle — and Stephen and Alex, although he did not know them half as well. It was his father he was afraid to trust. It was his father who had come so perilously close to failing Bowgren. To failing his own family: Lady Bowgren and his sons.

The villagers of Amberg would never see Lord Bowgren as a failure. That much, the village head had made clear. Lord Bowgren had raised and trained Ansel, after all, and Ansel was here as Bowgren. He had come to Amberg. He, with the allies who had accompanied him, had waged their war against the lord who would see Amberg destroyed. They had won. Amberg stood.

And there was now hope that Amberg could return to the lands it had occupied since Breodanir's inception. But if there was hope, it hung by a thread, and as time passed, that thread thinned under the weight.

"WELL, I see you missed your target again," the fox said. He said it in Jarven's arms, beneath the boughs of the great tree. The fur that had seemed almost matted and dull when the fox had withdrawn from battle now almost glowed with health.

Jarven had watched the battle unfold. Of particular interest—as always—was Meralonne APhaniel, the man the wilderness knew as Illaraphaniel. The mage was accorded a respect that would likely never devolve to Jarven, but Jarven was accustomed to that, given his own beginnings; it was not beginnings that concerned him, except in the way they could become snares or traps for the ignorant and unwary.

But of secondary interest was Nenyane of Maubreche. It was the Maubreche girl who had fought by the mage's side. It was the Maubreche girl who had parried, but who had taken advantage of any opening—openings Jarven was not certain he could have exploited as ruthlessly. Her prowess with a sword could not be questioned by anyone who had observed her in combat.

But she could fight almost as the mage himself fought. She could leap, and as if her weight—and the weight of her blade—was inconsequential, could come to ground at a place and time of her choosing, if she so chose. He was not certain she commanded the wind, as the mage and the bard clearly did.

He was annoyed that the bard's battle had been rendered almost invisible by the cloud cover the dead lord had commanded, but he knew enough of the Senniel bard's reputation that it was not a great intelligence loss: just an annoying one.

"Jarven?"

"Apologies, master. Yes. Rymark was present. He fled before the battle could fully start. He is no longer in the wilderness here."

"A pity," the fox said, in a tone that implied its opposite. "I notice you did not choose to join the battle."

Jarven shrugged. If pressed to offer an excuse, he would, but he disliked being forced to do so, as if he were a simple, wayward child caught with his hand in the cookie jar.

"You do not strike me as a fool," the fox continued. "Had you, I would never have taken you in."

"I would not go into a battle of such significance poorly armed," Jarven replied. He had not intended to speak, and was annoyed that he had. "If you understood me when we first met, that would have been clear. I did not judge my interference necessary; what I bring to the table at the moment is not martial skill."

"Do not lie."

"I am no match for you."

"Of course not."

"But I am no match for the man you call Illaraphaniel; I do not think I would be guaranteed victory against the Maubreche girl. Nor could I be guaranteed victory—or escape—from the three-headed creature who first took the field."

"Neither could Gervanno. He is certainly unlikely to survive should you attempt to kill him—but I am certain you will not."

"No, master. I will not." Not yet. Not unless Gervanno stood between Jarven and what Jarven desired—a thing the elder could give, but withheld.

"You made no attempt to intervene when I was injured."

"I did not believe the injury to be a test. Was it?"

"Everything, as you well know, is a test. I had expected some effort on your part."

"Only one man can fight at your side with any safety. You had two."

"Do you believe they were both your equal?"

"The girl is my superior, at the moment. She should not be; she is. The Southerner is not, by martial measure."

"And yet he fought."

"As you expected, yes. That is the type of man he is. He is a useful, even excellent man to have as a guard or a soldier; he could not be useful in the manner I will be. It is not in him."

"Do you expect that your petty political knowledge will have a use in the wilderness?"

"My petty political knowledge is, and has always been, based on my understanding of the currents—both obvious and subtle—of power, Eldest. Of course I believe it will be useful; the wilderness is far more about naked power than the petty politics in which I previously engaged."

The fox chuckled, approval in the sound. "I am not offended that you remained outside of the realm of conflict. You were unnecessary, in the end."

That pricked Jarven's pride, which annoyed him. Truth seldom irritated him, and the fox's words were a simple truth. His absence had not changed the outcome of the fight.

"But your quarry is gone."

"I cannot sense him."

"No, cub, you cannot. I have considered gifting you a greater portion of my ability to track a scent, but I am uncertain it will be of aid. What you have has been good enough to this point, if time-consuming, and I have guaranteed that you will have time."

"Perhaps, perhaps not," Jarven replied. "This battle—and those that might follow—are fought in the cadence of mortal time. Have you not sensed it? The war might pass me by if I am tardy."

"Then it is in your interests not to be tardy."

"It is in *our* interests, surely? Your lord desires an end—a true end— to this war."

"If I allowed the desires of my Lord to rule me, I would never have adopted you; she would not, and does not, entirely approve. She does not disapprove, but she is uneasily aware that you remain her ally, and you are Finch's mentor. We hear Finch's name," the fox added, voice softening. "While we do, she will not interfere. She does not trust your impulse," he added.

"I would find it insulting."

"Yes. But if she does not trust your impulse, she views the work you have done—the work of which she is aware—as largely beneficial to the Empire. She will not order me to abandon you." Something entered the fox's voice, then. "You understand, of course, that abandoning you simply means you would cease to exist."

Jarven nodded.

"Then let us hope that never comes to pass."

"As you say."

"But because you are being almost agreeable, I will tell you this. Rymark ATerafin did not flee to the North, where it is not yet safe for you to travel—if it will ever be. He fled South. It is in the South that you will once again pick up his trail."

ANSEL AND BRANDON headed to the gate that surrounded Amberg; the three-headed creature waited on the other side. They could have easily stepped over the fence without knocking it down, but had clearly chosen not to do so.

Ansel approached the fence, but the beast shook one of its heads: no.

"I greet you, Lord Ansel of Bowgren. Please make certain that all of the villagers of Amberg—especially the children—are within the boundaries of this fence. If they are not, they will not return to Bowgren when Amberg is once again rooted there."

Ansel stiffened, but kept his breathing even. "Is Amberg to return to Bowgren soon?"

"That is not entirely in my lord's hands, but I believe he will aid as he can. Understand that the barriers that separate our two lands have become very porous; the forests drift into each other. It will be far less dangerous than it once was, for the lord now has slender roots in mortal lands. But those roots are not enough to challenge Bowgren's authority.

"Can you hear it?"

Ansel shook his head. There was no criticism in the question, but he felt his inadequacy as a physical blow. He struggled to absorb it. The presence of the villagers forced a calmness he did not feel: that, and the need to act on the information given. He returned to the village head. "Biluude asks that we make certain every villager of any age is within the fence line."

"Now?"

He nodded.

The village head was as restless with hope—and its attendant, fear —as Ansel himself. But she started her head count, because she could: she knew all the villagers by name and home. Brandon took the Margen guards to help with a similar count, and Max went beyond the fences to make certain anyone collecting water returned.

The work helped.

Ansel wasn't certain his father would be able to do whatever it was he needed to do. He knew—had known since the moment Barrett's body had returned home—that Lord Ansel was not Lord Bowgren. He was accorded respect as the future Lord Bowgren, but he could not fill his father's shoes—and his father had deserted them; had left them empty. Had made clear that one man—the fate of one man—had been the thread that bound Bowgren and its lord together.

Were he Lord Bowgren, he could. But to be Lord Bowgren, he would have to surrender what remained of his father; his father would have to die. Ansel could not, and would not, kill him. Instead, he had clung to hope like a desperate child.

Lady Bowgren had done the same. All of Bowgren had.

"Lord Ansel," Biluude said, for the three-headed creature had not moved, "listen now. Listen carefully."

He tried to dislodge the voice of fear; it was hard. He had lived with it for so long, repeating its various phrases, its various dark futures, its terrible loss, as if fear revealed the only truth. As if all of life was that fear and desolation. As if it would never be anything else again.

And now? Now he had picked up hope with both shaky hands, and he gripped it as tightly as he dared, afraid of it, afraid to let go of it. The villagers trusted far more than he did: in him, and in the end, in Bowgren, as if Bowgren itself were a living entity, a mythic power that was beyond them but to which they turned in times of crisis.

He closed his eyes, standing to one side of the fence. Brandon had returned with the guards and the four villagers who had gone to fetch water. They had been the last of the stragglers; the village head had made ruthlessly certain of that.

He listened.

He listened for the sound of anything. He heard the bard's voice, cheerful, calm as it rose and fell; he had the children gathered round him as he told stories of daring, of heroism, of monsters and gods. He heard the village head when those children became boisterous.

And then, as he listened, he heard silence.

Silence in which a pin dropping might be heard, the silence of surprise.

He opened his eyes, turning toward the center of the village from which all other sounds had arisen. He had not spoken, but he understood the difference between lack of speech and silence.

In the village center, standing, arms by his side, was a very familiar man. A dead man. Ansel's lips moved, soundless, over a name. Barrett. *Barrett.*

His body moved through the shock, the surprise; his breath became deeper, more deliberate. He called the Hunter's trance without thought, without intent. He ran.

He ran until he was three yards away from this familiar man; he stopped then. There was no scent, no sound; the breeze carried none of the signs of life to Ansel, whose heightened senses would have noticed them.

But life or no, Barrett turned. His brows rose as he met Ansel's gaze —a familiar expression of surprise. There was no doubt at all in Ansel's mind that this man was Barrett.

The brows fell, and a worn but affectionate smile replaced surprise. "I should have known," he said, the voice so blessedly familiar that Ansel was almost moved—in public—to tears. He held them back.

The village head folded her arms. The surprise—the shock—that had no doubt transformed Ansel's face did not touch hers at all. As if this weren't the first time she had seen this ghost. He thought about the portrait that had, until Heiden borrowed it, occupied the shrine in the village head's house. It had been a recent portrait, if a rough one.

She had seen Barrett—this Barrett—before the portrait had been painted. That's *why* she was so certain that it was Barrett's death that had preserved Amberg. Not the Sacred Hunt on its own, but Barrett in particular.

Given the gazes of the villagers, it was clear that Barrett was visible to all. There was, however, no fear. No fear of Barrett, who was dead. Who they all knew was dead.

Brandon was stiff; if Amberg had seen Barrett, it was before the arrival of Brandon, Aelle, and the Margen contingent.

"Well, Ansel?"

Ansel, silent, was able to move again.

"I hear your father has been struggling."

Ansel's laugh was wild, bitter.

"And everyone else has struggled as a result."

Ansel nodded.

"You've done good work here. Heiden's not with you?"

"Heiden went to Bowgren."

"Ah. Without you?"

"We thought—" Aware of the villagers who were also listening, Ansel cut the explanation off. "Heiden went to get Lord Bowgren. To bring him to the site on which Amberg should stand." There was more he wanted to say—much more—but again, his awareness of the villagers stemmed the flow of his words. He swallowed them back with effort.

But one question remained, and he asked it. "Why are you here?"

Barrett looked down, as if hesitating to answer the question. It wasn't hesitance. "I am with the earth."

"What?"

"When the Sacred Hunt was called—and for centuries—the Hunter's Death was our God—our God made savage. It was in devouring a huntbrother—ideally—that that savagery was dispelled. But the compact created—complicated and meant to endure—between Breodan and these lands was a compact that involved the ancient earth, the living earth, the sentient earth. Even in our lands, even with the separation between the wild and the mundane, the earth could not be divided in the fashion that our peoples could be—mortal and immortal, mortal and eternal.

"Or so I have been informed." His smile was wry.

"Those who have died in the Hunt in recent years have always been huntbrothers—for that was the compact. But their deaths are not what they were. They are far kinder, far less brutal, and far more entangled with the living earth. I am here because I am part of the earth, bound to it."

"Until *when*?" Ansel asked, voice softer. If the death was an eternal captivity, was it not so much worse than even he had thought? The dead were not supposed to be trapped here. That was not what the priests taught. Not what Ansel himself had believed until this moment.

Barrett knew him well. He grinned and shook his head. "You really are Anton's son." He shook his head. "Did you know that the earth is alive? Sleeping but alive? I discovered it when I died. The earth has a voice, if one knows how to listen—a slow, sonorous movement of sylla-bles. It is a wonder, in the darkness. It makes the darkness warm. I did see the bridge, Ansel. I saw it, but could not see what lay across it. It is the bridge that the dead must cross."

"And you're not dead?" Ansel folded his arms.

Barrett laughed. It was the *I've seen this before in an older man* laugh which had always annoyed Ansel as a child.

"I am dead, as you well know."

"Dead people aren't usually so condescending."

Barrett laughed again. Ansel had missed that laughter; his father had not been a man given to much of it, even when Barrett was alive.

"I am not eternally damned, if that's what you've been thinking. I am in no pain. But the earth's voice was both worried and lonely. I could have crossed that bridge; the earth could not prevent it. The compact is bound not by my spirit, but my life, and my life's blood was shed.

"But the earth was lonely, as I said. I chose to remain, for a time. I was given a choice, Ansel. That is all you need to know." He sighed. "The choice I made is not irrevocable. Should I so choose, I could walk across the bridge now."

"I don't see a bridge."

"I should hope not. But I am here. I knew that Bowgren faced difficulty because all of Breodanir does. But the earth thought Bowgren was a focal point. The difficulty was not natural; it was deliberate."

Nothing about the difficulties Breodanir had faced in the past year seemed in any way natural to Ansel. He did not say this.

"It took me some time to reach Bowgren; the earth's sense of our borders is very delicate, but it exists. I have learned how to speak with the earth, of course — but at the borders, in Amberg, the earth's voice was so faint it could barely be heard. When Amberg vanished, I could — barely — follow. The earth itself could hear me — but it could no longer hear the hum of its covenant clearly.

"I am its reminder, here. I am the hum of that covenant, the boundary of it. I am not strong enough to return Amberg to Bowgren — the ties are too tenuous, too narrow, and the covenants and bindings were made for the living, not the dead.

"But I remind the earth — our earth. Here, there is another, and it is waking; its voice is far louder. It has been hard to bespeak Bowgren's earth in this wilderness. But not impossible.

"Heiden is coming with Anton; I will not have to continue for much longer."

Ansel said nothing.

"Have faith in Anton," Barrett said, correctly divining the direction of Ansel's thoughts.

The village head came to stand beside Ansel; she placed one hand on his shoulder, as if by gesture alone she could carry some of the burden he could not quite shed. "We will," she said to Barrett. "As promised."

———

THE WIND CHANGED. The cool breeze of forest gave way to warmer air, and in the folds of that warmer breeze, Ansel could see small leaves. Familiar leaves.

The earth beneath his feet did not change; it looked the same to his eye, felt the same to the soles of his feet. But there was a difference; Brandon sensed it. Max sensed it.

Nenyane exhaled, shaking her head.

Ansel — Ansel can you hear me?

Oh. *Yes. Are you close? Are you near Amberg?*

Yes.

Is my father with you?

Yes. And, I'm sorry to say, Lady Bowgren. She insisted on traveling with us. Lord Bowgren attempted to say no. It…did not go well. He's aware enough that he only tried once.

Ansel winced. *I suppose you'd be unhappy if I stepped out of the village right now and found my way back later?*

Me? No. Your mother? Very.

Ansel reached out for Barrett, and his hand passed through the Bowgren huntbrother's shoulder. He wanted to keep him here somehow. To keep him here until Lord Bowgren once again set foot in Amberg. He had been so angry with his father, so disappointed, so abandoned — but he wanted this moment for that broken man.

"Oh, don't worry. I'm not going anywhere yet." There was a thread of steel in Barrett's voice. People thought Barrett — like Heiden — was kindness and gentleness defined. Only the Bowgren Hunters knew how deep and solid their anger could be.

"Did you not tell me that I am not to blame my father? That I am to trust him?"

"Indeed."

Heiden was close enough now that he could sense what Ansel could see.

Yes. Barrett — Barrett's ghost — is standing in the middle of Amberg.

Is he an angry ghost?

He wasn't. But…this is definitely unhappy Barrett. What is Father doing?

Heiden's interior voice grew clearer, louder, as the seconds passed. *He's…doing what Stephen tells him to do.*

Really?

I know. You could have knocked me over with a feather. But — whatever it is, it's working. Stephen is telling him how to talk to the earth. I think. I've tried, but the earth doesn't hear me.

No — I think it only hears the lord, and only when the lord is present. This is how Lord Maubreche could drive back the turnings in Maubreche: he knew what the earth should be, and he pushed aside all of the things it shouldn't be. According to Nenyane.

You asked?

A bit. She's been a little restless. He glanced back at the village periphery; she was sitting on the fence, arms folded. But she was still, now. If Ansel could reach Heiden, Nenyane could reach Stephen.

She was such a strange person. She was better with a sword than anyone Ansel had ever seen, and she knew things about the wilderness that only the mage seemed to know. She was never happy, she was always impatient—as if this was not where she should or must be. But she was Stephen's huntbrother. Death would sever that bond. Nothing else.

He knew there were Hunter Lords who questioned her existence, who disapproved of her because she was a girl. He would have been one of them had he never met her, but he would never be one of them again. If he could do nothing else for Stephen and Nenyane, he could do that much.

He owed them so much more.

Brandon laughed out loud, causing all of the Margen guards to look askance at him. When he stopped laughing, he said, "Sorry—Aelle said something funny."

"Share. We could all use the laugh."

"And then Lady Margen would have his head." Brandon shook his. Like Ansel, like Nenyane, and like the silent Max, he was relieved to once again be in communication with his brother.

"Look!" someone said—a young girl or boy, it was hard to tell. "The branches!"

Everyone looked up, even Ansel. Above their heads, the branches of the great tree stretched. But they weren't the branches of that tree; they were familiar. Oak, Ansel thought. There had been no tree in the village center, but the branches reached across the sky anyway.

He turned, then, toward the fence line that contained the village of Amberg. Beyond the gate stood an ancient tree—but it was no longer obsidian-barked. This was a tree that might have grown naturally in Bowgren, although he had never seen its like near Amberg before.

"It's not dangerous," Nenyane said, raising voice to be heard.

She needn't have bothered; no one in the village was afraid. They had never seen oak in the wilderness.

"Oak exists," the fox said. He leapt down from Jarven ATerafin's arms. "But it is true they are no part of the former lord's lands. I believe they will be part of the lands the new lord occupies."

The children were silent, and then a rush of sound followed as they ran toward the fox in delight.

Nenyane dropped between the children and the fox.

"He talked! He's a talking fox!"

"Yes," she replied. "But he's a grouchy talking fox, and he's easily offended. Far worse than the village head."

That stopped them as the fox chuckled. "I will not harm them unless they attempt to harm me, little huntbrother. I wish to be here for the moment; they are returning home, and I wish to witness their reaction."

Nenyane hesitated, and the fox growled. To Ansel's surprise, she offered the fox a stiff, but respectful, bow.

She rose. One of the adults shouted—he was closer to the fence, farther from the talking animal—and waved both arms. His back was to the village center; he faced outward. Out to where the road lay—a real road, a familiar one.

Half the adults turned in the direction of the shout, to see that familiar road—the road that led to other villages, and to Bowgren.

They were home. Amberg was home.

MEN WALKED DOWN THAT ROAD. Nenyane remained where she was. Max started toward the people who approached; he froze.

Looking back, he said, "Ansel—is that your mother?"

Ansel winced. "Yes."

"Well, good luck."

"Wait—where are you going?"

"Hunter Ladies are terrifying and I can never manage to say either nothing or the right thing, so I tend to avoid them if I can."

"Coward."

Ansel turned toward the gate, which the villagers were now opening. He waited, aware of the man by his side—a man who cast no shadow in the bright, clear sun.

He knew the moment Lord Bowgren became aware of that man, for his father froze in place; his wife and his guests continued toward the village, but he did not. Ansel counted perhaps thirty seconds before Lord Bowgren began to move again, but he moved far, far more quickly. He had come with dogs; Stephen's dogs remained with Stephen, but the Bowgren dogs began to run, streaming through the open gate into the heart of Amberg, where the gathered villagers waited.

The villagers were not afraid of the dogs, but they kept their distance, moving as the dogs circled Barrett. The dogs made no attempt to touch him, as if they knew that Barrett was not physically present.

Ansel glanced once at Barrett, and then stepped back; the village head made clear that everyone else was to follow. Barrett's expression had descended into that polite iciness that indicated real anger—all of it focused on the man who now walked toward him, his steps slowing at the last possible moment.

Everyone present knew that it was unwise to get between a Hunter and his huntbrother when they were in conflict.

Lady Bowgren did not join the villagers; nor did she join her husband. She stood back, stood apart, and watched.

Ansel couldn't hear what Barrett said. He couldn't hear what his father said—except once, a cry of fury, rage, pain, and outrage. Barrett had never raised his voice, even in anger; when Barrett was angry, he talked far more quietly, far more slowly.

Whatever his mother saw, she was shaking her head; she was absent anger. Heiden stood beside Lady Bowgren.

She should talk to him.

She will, I think, if he remains—but it's Lord Bowgren who needs to hear what Barrett has to say.

Did you know he was here?

Heiden didn't answer for a long beat. *No. But I hoped, because of the village head.* He cringed as Lord Bowgren's voice climbed once again, but he was almost at peace, now.

Lord Bowgren wasn't angry. Not the way he had been since Barrett's death. This shouting was different; they had heard variants of it for all of their lives. And their lives, until Barrett's death, had been good.

They did not expect tears. Tears, Lord Bowgren had eschewed, favoring rage and utter silence, but he offered them to Barrett now—and it made witnessing the two, Hunter and huntbrother, suddenly embarrassing. There were some things that were meant to be intimate, private.

But they did not embarrass Lady Bowgren. She moved past Heiden and toward the two men, one living, one dead. She slid an arm around her husband's shoulder, as if her back could be a shield that warded off witnesses. Ansel could not hear what she said; could not hear what Barrett said. He was certain that Barrett had words for his mother — words that might remain unsaid, given the responsibility and weight of the duties of Bowgren.

Ansel was not married.

His mother had begun the various negotiations that might result in marriage in the future, but the talks had broken off after the death of Barrett. Ansel had had no interest in marriage. But he wondered, watching these three, how marriage itself would strengthen Bowgren in future. Bowgren needed a Lady.

Bowgren needed a Lord; a man who did not rule in name only.

Lord Bowgren's shoulders straightened, as if he could hear the words Ansel would never say again. That he had said them stung, but he could not regret it — not yet. But he had said the words in rage and pain, just as his father had collapsed because of them, and he knew the cost of those words on others, now. Knew that he had almost followed his father's path, and with far less cause.

Yes, Heiden said. *I trusted you to come back.*

I wouldn't have, if I were you.

No. But we've always been very different people; it was our mutual goals that bound us.

My father won't have that.

He will. He will, now. Heiden hesitated; Ansel was surprised. *I think Barrett is dead, but not gone. If your father needs to speak with him, I think he can do so in Amberg.*

Why only Amberg?

Because Amberg is on the border of the wilderness. And the power of the earth is different. Even if it's part of Bowgren. I don't know this for certain, he added, in a rush.

Ansel grimaced. *I feel very, very sorry for the village head.*

Heiden chuckled. *I might, in future. But Amberg is the heart of Bowgren right now. Both its loss, and its recovery.*

Where are you going? Ansel asked, as Heiden walked past Lord and Lady Bowgren.

He did not answer in words. Instead, he removed the pack he carried from his shoulders and approached the village head, who was watching the reunion at a safe distance.

He offered her a perfect, respectful bow—and given he was now wearing clean traveling clothing, was perfectly shaved, and was very lordly in comparison to Lord Ansel, the bow appeared far more impressive. To Ansel's eyes. The village head accepted it as she had accepted the far more scruffy gestures of respect; to her, they were one and the same.

He very carefully took the painting from his pack, and unwrapped the several layers of cloth in which he had wound it for protection.

She smiled as she accepted the portrait. "It was a long road back," she said, voice soft. "But I don't think he'll lose his way to pain again. Thank you. You are Barrett's successor in Amberg; Lord Ansel will be Lord Bowgren. Amberg will not forget that you found us when we were lost." She offered Heiden a bow almost equal to his own.

THE SUN FELL as Lord Bowgren and Barrett spoke; Lady Bowgren came to speak with the village head as Ansel and Heiden retreated.

Their father, however, did not allow them to retreat very far. He approached them, his face free of the near rictus that had been its most common recent expression. He looked almost chagrined—and the only person who had ever had that effect on Anton of Bowgren was Barrett of Bowgren.

Ansel looked up; he could see that Barrett remained, but he was fading now, transparent as a proper ghost should be.

Lord Bowgren rubbed the back of his neck with one hand, the chagrin deepening. "Barrett wasn't pleased with me."

Ansel said nothing.

"He let me know in no uncertain terms that I had almost catastrophically failed our demesne." Our. "I gave him my word that I would never do so again. He felt insulted," he added, the chagrin dipping into a rueful grin.

Heiden glanced at Ansel. He didn't need to imagine what Barrett felt; he had felt it, and expressed it, himself.

"I'll want your help," Lord Bowgren continued. "I won't ask for your forgiveness. I was not a good father to you after Barrett died. I was not a good lord to Bowgren. But you, Ansel—you were. Heiden says he will attend the Sacred Hunt when it is called."

Ansel swallowed. Nodded.

"And you?"

"I'm not sending him there alone," Ansel replied, voice low because his throat felt almost swollen.

Lord Bowgren nodded, as if this was the only possible answer Ansel could give. "He's told me a few things about these strange turnings; told me about how I might be more aware of them, of what I can do to counter them. To keep Bowgren safe. I'll do that." He exhaled. "Your mother messaged the Queen before we left. She has asked to withdraw you from Hunter's Redoubt because you have recanted your previous position about the Sacred Hunt."

He then looked past his sons, to Brandon, Aelle, Stephen, Nenyane, Alex, Max. "I thought we should clear that with you both first."

Ansel might have fallen over had he not locked his knees.

"The Redoubt brought you allies and friends that you would never have met had you remained in Bowgren with...me."

"I'm not certain," Heiden said, "that any of the others will be returning to the Redoubt. Too much has happened here for that. If it weren't for Stephen, I'm not certain we could have reached Bowgren at all; we wouldn't have survived on the road. And Stephen has somewhere else he has to go."

"The King's commands must be obeyed," Lord Bowgren said, his voice growing stiffer.

"Yes. But the Queen has say over matters involving foreign nations. Stephen is a Hunter, but he will never be Hunter Lord. Neither will Max or Alex. There is nothing the Redoubt can teach them that will change that. But Stephen *is* Breodani to the core. If he leaves Breodanir —and I believe he must—it will be, in the end, because Breodanir's survival requires him to do what must be done.

"And we have made our decision. The Redoubt has nothing to teach us, now—no guidance to offer. We are Bowgren Hunters, and we will remain Bowgren Hunters." He hesitated, then. "Will Barrett remain?"

Lord Bowgren grimaced. "If I need to speak with him, he said I can find him here. I'm not sure he'll be *happy* if I have to go to those lengths again. But...yes. He is dead, but he has refused to cross the bridge. It is here, in the earth of Bowgren, of Breodanir, that he will remain.

"He says he no longer trusts me enough to abandon me entirely." Lord Bowgren's wince was acknowledgement of the fact he had earned at least that much. "I will have to prove him wrong. I told him—ah, I told him I did not want to trap him in death, to bind him to earth, even be it living. It was too selfish.

"He was not displeased, but...did not believe me. Actions speak louder than words, and I seldom used words. He wants proof."

Heiden nodded, as if this were natural; Ansel said nothing.

"If I cannot prove that I can become the Lord Bowgren I was before his death, he will remain. He will abide here until I myself am ready to walk across the bridge; we will cross it together." He exhaled.

"Come, sons. Let us return home; we have much to discuss and much to plan, and I am ready, now."

Acknowledgments

When I was told DAW would not be able to publish the last arc in the long-running West series, I wasn't certain what I could do, except panic. I did too much of that.

I then took a deep breath and researched possible options that oddly allow me to finish the final arc. I really wanted to write these books.

In the end, I decided on Patreon. I'd looked at other writers and their Patreons, and I estimated the amount of support I would or could get, as well as the cost of publishing a book: editing, copyediting, proofreading, covers.

I knew I couldn't offer the more highly social interactions that other writers had had great success with; that would have taken all my time and added a lot of anxiety, which really slows writing down (for me). The only thing I could offer was the writing of the books—which isn't a great spectator sport. I started the Patreon, understanding that some readers *want* more social interaction, and would be unlikely to find my Patreon promising.

And readers came.

I literally would not have been able to publish this book if it weren't for the support given my Patreon by my readers. Thank you all so much.

Aëlynn
Jenni Aird
Alfvaen
Summer Allen
Lisa Araya
Amélie
Shyia Bader

Sumita Banerjee

Penny Beard

Elizabeth W. Bennefeld

Katrine Berg

Evan Bergman

Jennifer Biddle

Kelly Bird

Julie Brady

Amy Browning

India Bunch

Stephen Harrod Buhner

Christopher Burger

Cheryl Byers

M Byrne

Linda Scott Campbell

Sean F. Campbell

A. Carmichael

Antony Claughton

Robbin Coane

Delisa Phillips Cook

Alex Cornett

Deirdre Culhane

Angela Cypret

George Dashner

Sherry P. Davis

Evenstar Deane

Becca Lee Deihl

Jaye Derrick

Michael Eisenberg

Gwen Eisenstein

Emile

Stephen Engel

Tamara English

Kimberly Eridon

Sabrena Evanson

Ruth Feldkamp

Mark Fleming

Patrick Fowler

Angie Gaule
Erin Golden
Eleanor GunShows
David Graham
Carrie A. Hamilton
Linda M. Hansen
Taen Hardy
Taia Hartman
Scott Hartup
Teri Hogan
Andrea Horbinski
Daniel Islam
Sue Ivey
Diana Jacomb-Hood
Liss and Bill Jennings
Jeff Jensen
Jeremiah Jordan
Nerissa Juan
Richard Judson
Kerry aka Trouble
Erik Kort
Hacen La Manna
Philippa Lang
Vanessa LaWare
Lisa Lewis
Larry Lobis
Chris Lomas
Nicole Lucier
Jayme Lundeen
Gerri Lynn
Kat A. Mannix
Taylor Martin
Deana McCarthy
Jann McKenzie
Caroline Mersey
Robert Miller
Karl Mueller
Madelaine Murad

Hugh S. Myers
Samuel Nadasky
Amy Nelson
Ken Newman
Melinda Morris Nichols
Audrey Jindra Olsen
Tim Orr
Phillip Ortman
Stephen Owens
Luci Paulk
Jo-Ann Pieber
Julie B. Perry
Leanne Phillips
Dan Pierson
Leanne Powner
Kathryn Prentice
Terrie Aldridge Redmond
Tchula Ripton
Loreen Rowe
Amanda Schaffer
Fred Shaffer
Melissa Siah
Derek Smith
Chris and Karen Starbuck
Jon Stiles
Karissa Stoker
Elizabeth Strick
Mathew Suffal
Wendy Sahyoun
Susan Sumara
Tatyana Venegas Swanson
Libby Swift
Alisha (Lee) Thompson
Karen Tozzi
An Tran
Sarah Urriste-Switek
Esa Valkama
Laura Vo
Hanneke van Vugt

Bella Wang
Kim Warren
Benjamin Wert
Thomas Wiegand
Brian and Kay Williams

About the Author

Michelle writes as both Michelle Sagara and Michelle West; she is also published as Michelle Sagara West (although the Sundered books were originally published under the name Michelle Sagara).

She lives in Toronto with her long-suffering husband and her two children, and to her regret has no dogs.

Reading is one of her life-long passions, and she is paid for her opinions about what she's read by the venerable *Magazine of Fantasy and Science Fiction*. No matter how many bookshelves she buys, there is Never Enough Shelf Space. Ever.

Although she doesn't have a newsletter, if you subscribe to her blog, you will get everything that's posted there—book news, cover reveals, random answers to questions, etc.

If you would like news about new books as they're published—with no other clutter—sign up for her news-only mailing list.

Either can be found here at her web-site.

She can also be found on bluesky.

Also by Michelle West

The Sacred Hunt

Hunter's Oath

Hunter's Death

The Sacred Hunt (omnibus)

The Sun Sword

The Broken Crown

Uncrowned King

Shining Court

Sea of Sorrows

The Riven Shield

The Sun Sword

House War

The Hidden City

City of Night

House Name

Skirmish

Battle

Oracle

Firstborn

War

Related short stories

Memory of Stone: The Collection (includes all following stories)

Echoes

Huntbrother

The Black Ospreys

The Weapon

Warlord

The Memory of Stone